most likely to

Also by Jennifer Echols

Endless Summer

The One That I Want

The Ex Games

Major Crush

Going Too Far

Forget You

Love Story

Such a Rush

Dirty Little Secret

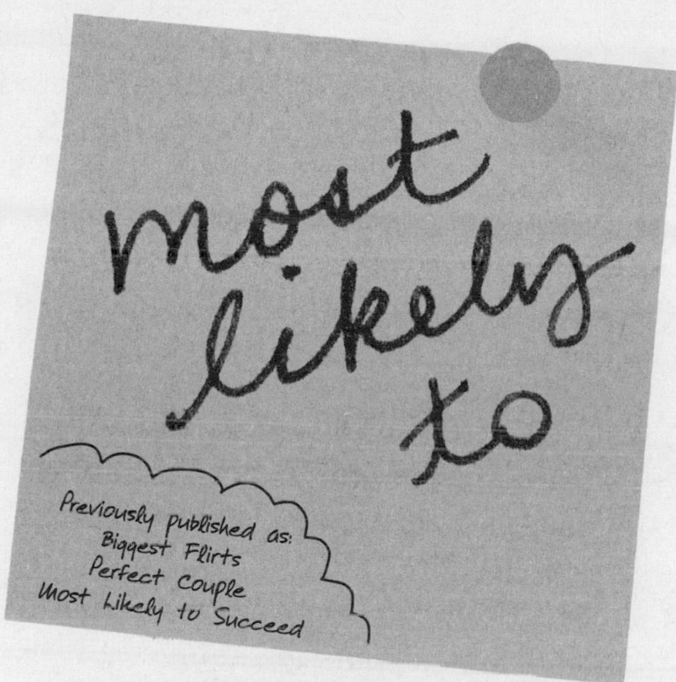

JENNIFER ECHOLS

Simon Pulse

New York London Toronto Sydney New Delhi

This book is a work of fiction. Any references to historical events, real people, or real places are used fictitiously. Other names, characters, places, and events are products of the author's imagination, and any resemblance to actual events or places or persons, living or dead, is entirely coincidental.

SIMON PULSE
An imprint of Simon & Schuster Children's Publishing Division
1230 Avenue of the Americas, New York, New York 10020
This Simon Pulse paperback edition February 2017

For information about special discounts for bulk purchases, please contact Simon & Schuster Special Sales at 1-866-506-1949 or business@simonandschuster.com.
The Simon & Schuster Speakers Bureau can bring authors to your live event. For more information or to book an event contact the Simon & Schuster Speakers Bureau at 1-866-248-3049 or visit our website at www.simonspeakers.com.
Cover designed by Steve Scott
Interior designed by Mike Rosamilia
The text of this book was set in Adobe Caslon Pro.
Manufactured in the United States of America
2 4 6 8 10 9 7 5 3 1
Library of Congress Control Number 2016944533
ISBN 978-1-4814-5721-7
ISBN 978-1-4424-7447-5 (*Biggest Flirts* eBook)
ISBN 978-1-4424-7450-5 (*Perfect Couple* eBook)
ISBN 978-1-4424-7453-6 (*Most Likely to Succeed* eBook)
These titles were previously published individually with the series title The Superlatives.

Biggest Flirts

For my son,
an awesome drummer

One

"YOU MUST BE TIA CRUZ."

I glanced up at the guy who'd sat next to me and said this quietly in my ear, in an accent from elsewhere. We were on the crowded back porch with the lights off, but beyond the porch ceiling, the summer night sky was bright with a full moon and a glow from the neon signs at the tourist-trap beaches a few miles south.

The diffuse light made everybody look better: smoothed out acne, canceled a bad hair day. And I definitely had on my beer goggles. Boys grew more attractive when I was working on my second brew. This guy was the hottest thing I'd seen all summer. He was taller than me by quite a bit—which didn't happen too often—with dark hair long enough to cling to his T-shirt collar, a long straight nose, and lips that quirked sideways in a smile. But I wasn't fooled. In the sober light of day, he probably ranked right up there with the eighty-year-old men who wore Speedos to the beach.

What drew me in despite my misgivings was the diamond stud in his ear. Who knew what he was trying to say with this fashion statement. Unfortunately for me, I was a sucker for a bad boy, and his earring flashed moonlight at me like a homing beacon under a banner that said THIS WAY TO PIRATE.

I told him, "I *might* be Tia." What I meant was, *For you, I am Tia. I'll be anybody you're looking for.* "Who wants to know?"

"Will Matthews. I just moved here." We were sitting too close for a proper handshake, but he bent his arm, elbow close to his side, and held out his hand.

"Really!" I exclaimed as our hands touched. Our small town was stuck in the forgotten northwest corner of Pinellas County, on the very edge of the Tampa Bay metropolitan area. The guidebooks called us a hidden gem because of the artsy downtown, the harbor, and our unspoiled beaches, but the thing about a hidden gem was that it tended to stay hidden. Some tourists came through here. A few newcomers did move here. But most of them were, again, elderly men in banana hammocks. The families who serviced the snowbirds and tourists had lived here forever. My friend Sawyer had shown up only a couple of years before, but even his dad had grown up here. New kids at school were rare. Girls were going to be *all over* this guy: fresh meat.

Will pointed toward the house. "I introduced myself to your friends inside. They told me I would find you by the beer."

"My friends are a riot." My best friends, Harper and Kaye,

didn't drink. That was cool with me. I did drink, which was not cool with them. Over the years, though, Harper's reasoned arguments and Kaye's hysterical pleas had mellowed into concerned monitoring and snarky jokes.

This time their witty line wasn't even correct. I was *not* by the beer. Along with six or seven other people from school, I was sitting on a bench built into the porch railing, and the cooler was underneath me. Technically I was *above* the beer. Drinking on Brody Larson's back porch was standard operating procedure. Most of the houses near downtown were lined up along a grid, backyards touching. When parents unexpectedly came home, interrupting a party, somebody would grab the cooler as we escaped through the palm trees to another daredevil's house to start over. If this was the first thing Will learned about our town, he was my kind of guy. I reached into the cooler, my braids brushing the porch floor. I fished out a can for myself and handed him the beer he'd come for.

"Oh." He took the can and looked at it for a moment. He was expecting, maybe, a better brand of free beer? Then, without opening it, he swiped it across his forehead. "Are you even sweating? Perspiring, I mean."

"Why do you want to know whether I'm perspiring, Mr. Matthews?" I made my voice sound sexy just to get a guffaw out of him.

"Because you look . . ." He glanced down my body, and I enjoyed that very much. ". . . cool," he finished. "It's hot as an ahffen out here."

I popped open my beer. "A what?"

"What," he repeated.

"You said 'ahffen.' What's an ahffen?"

"An ahh . . ." He waited for me to nod at this syllable. "Fen." Suddenly he lost patience with me. Before I could slide away—actually I would have had nowhere to slide, because Brody and his girlfriend Grace were making out right next to me—Will grabbed my wrist and brought my hand to his lips. "Let me sound it out for you. Ahhhffen." I felt his breath moving across my fingertips.

"Oh, an *oven*!" I giggled. "You're kidding, right? It's ten o'clock at night."

He let my hand go, which was not what I'd wanted at *all*. "I've been here one whole day, and I've already gotten my fill of people making fun of the way I talk, thanks." He sounded halfway serious.

"Poor baby! I wasn't making fun of you. I was just trying to figure out what an ahffen was." I elbowed him gently in the ribs.

He still didn't smile. That was okay. I liked brooding pirates. I asked him, "Who made fun of you?"

"Some jerk waiting tables at the grill where my family ate tonight. We can't cook at home yet. Most of the furniture showed up, but apparently the refrigerator got off-loaded in Ohio."

"Uh-oh. Was that all you lost, or did the moving company also misplace your microwave in Wisconsin and your coffee-maker in the Mississippi River?"

"Funny." Now he was grinning at me.

Warm fuzzies crept across my skin. I loved making people laugh. Making a hot guy laugh was my nirvana.

He went on, "I'm sure we'll find out what else we're missing when we need it. Anyway, the waiter at the restaurant seemed cool at first. I think both my little sisters fell in love with him. He told me I should come to this party and meet some people. Then he started in on my Minnesota accent and wouldn't let go." Will pronounced it "Minne*sooo*da," which cried out for imitation. Plenty of people around here talked like that, but they were retirees from Canada. I decided I'd better let it drop.

"Was this grill the Crab Lab downtown?" I pointed in the direction of the town square, which boasted said restaurant where I'd worked until yesterday, the antiques store where I still worked (or tried not to), the salon where my sister Izzy cut hair, and Harper's mom's bed and breakfast. The business district was rounded out by enough retro cafés and kitschy gift shops that visitors were fooled into thinking our town was like something out of a 1950s postcard—until they strolled by the gay burlesque club.

"Yeah," Will said. "We had misgivings about a place called the Crab Lab, like there would be formaldehyde involved. If there was, we couldn't taste it."

"The Crab Lab may sound unappetizing, but it's an unwritten rule that names of stores in a tourist town have to alliterate or rhyme. What else are you going to call a seafood joint? Lobster Mobster? Hey, that's actually pretty good." I doubled over, cracking up at my own joke. "The slogan would be, 'We'll break your legs.' Get it? Because you crack open lobster legs? No, wait, that's crab."

He watched me with a bemused smile, as if waiting for me to pull a prescription bottle out of my purse and announce that I'd missed my meds.

I tried again. "Calamari . . . Cash and Carry? I set myself up badly there. Okay, so Crab Lab is a stupid name. I'm pretty attached to the place, though."

"Do you eat there a lot?"

"You could say that. I just quit serving there. Did this jerk who was making fun of you happen to have white-blond hair?"

"That's him."

"That's Sawyer," I said. "Don't take it personally. He would pick on a newborn baby if he could think of a good enough joke. You'll be seeing lots more of Sawyer when school starts."

"The way my summer's been going, that doesn't surprise me at all." Will stared at the beer can in his hand. He took a breath to say something else.

Just then the marching band drum major, DeMarcus, arrived to a chorus of "Heeeey!" from everybody on the porch. He'd spent the past month with his grandparents in New York. A few of us gave Angelica, the majorette DeMarcus was leading by the hand, a less enthusiastic "Hey." The lukewarm greeting probably wasn't fair. It's just that we remembered what a tattletale she'd been in ninth grade. She'd probably changed, but nobody gave her the benefit of the doubt. As she walked through, some people turned their heads away as if they thought she might jot down their names and report back to their parents.

I stood as DeMarcus spread his arms to hug me. He said, "Harper told me you were back here sitting on the beer. I'm like, 'Are you sure? Tia is *in charge* of something? That's a first.' But I guess since it's beer, it's fitting."

"Those New Yorkers really honed your sense of humor." I sat down to pull out a can for him. Obviously it hadn't occurred to him that, unless a miracle saved me, I was drum captain. Starting tomorrow, the first day of band camp, I would be in charge of one of the largest sections and (in our own opinion) the most important section of the band. I'd spent the whole summer pretending that my doomsday of responsibility wasn't going to happen. I had one night left to live in that fantasy world.

As I handed the beer up to DeMarcus, Angelica asked close to his shoulder, "Do you have to?"

"One," he promised her. "I just spent ten hours in the airport with my mother."

Will chuckled at that. I thought maybe I should introduce him to DeMarcus. But I doubted my edgy pirate wanted to meet my band geek friend. Will made no move to introduce himself.

As DeMarcus opened his beer and took a sip, I noticed old Angelica giving Will the eye. Oh, *no*, girlfriend. I lasered her with an exaggerated glare so scary that she actually startled and stepped backward when she saw me. I bit my lip to keep from laughing.

With a glance at Will, DeMarcus asked me, "Where's Sawyer?"

Damn it! Sawyer and I hung out a lot, but we weren't dating. I didn't want to give Will the impression that I was taken. "Sawyer's working," I told DeMarcus dismissively. "He's coming later."

"I'm sure I'll hear him when he gets here," DeMarcus said. True. Sawyer often brought the boisterous college dropout waiters he'd already gotten drunk with on the back porch of the Crab Lab. Or firecrackers. Or both.

As DeMarcus moved along the bench to say hi to everybody else, with Angelica in tow, Will spoke in my ear. "Sounds like you know Sawyer pretty well. Is he your boyfriend?"

"Um." My relationship with Sawyer was more like the friendship you'd fall into when there was nobody more interesting in prison. Everybody at school knew he wasn't my boyfriend. We tended to stick together at parties because we were the first ones to get there and the last ones to leave. I wasn't sure how to explain this to an outsider without sounding like a drunk floozy . . . because, to be honest, I was something of a drunk floozy. Not that this had bothered me until I pictured myself sharing that information with a handsome stranger.

I said carefully, "We've been out, but we're not together now." Changing the subject so fast that Will and I both risked neck injury, I asked, "What city are you from? Minneapolis?"

"No."

"St. Paul?"

"No, Duluth."

"Never heard of it."

"I know." He raised the unopened beer can to his forehead again. Perspiration was beading at his hairline and dripping toward his ear. I felt sorry for him. Wait until it got hot tomorrow.

"What's Duluth like?" I asked.

"Well, it's on Lake Superior."

"Uh-huh. Minnesota's the Land of a Thousand Lakes, isn't it?" I asked. Little had Mr. Tomlin known when he interrogated us on state trivia in third grade that I would later find it useful for picking up a Minnesotan.

"Ten Thousand Lakes," Will corrected me with a grin.

"Wow, that's a lot of lakes. You must have been completely surrounded. Did you swim to school?"

He shook his head no. "Too cold to swim."

I couldn't imagine this. Too cold to swim? Such a shame. "What did you do up there, then?" I ran my eyes over his muscular arms. Will didn't have the physique of a naturally strong and sinewy boy such as Sawyer, but of an athlete who actively worked out. I guessed, "Do you play football?"

His mouth cocked to one side. He was aware I'd paid him a compliment about his body. "Hockey," he said.

A hockey player! The bad boy of athletes who elbowed his

opponent in the jaw just for spite and spent half the period in the penalty box. I loved it!

But my reverence for him in my mind didn't make it to my mouth. I had to turn it into a joke. "Ha!" I exclaimed. "Good luck with *that* around here. We're not exactly a hockey mecca."

"Tampa Bay has an NHL team," he reminded me.

"Yeah, but nobody *else* here plays. The NHL rinks are probably the only ones in the entire metropolitan area. A high school guy playing hockey in Tampa makes as much sense as the Jamaican bobsled team."

I'd meant it to be funny. But his mouth twitched to one side again, this time like I'd slapped him. Maybe he was considering for the first time that our central Florida high school might not have a varsity hockey team.

I sipped my beer, racking my brain for a way to salvage this conversation, which I'd really been digging. He held his beer in both hands like he was trying to get all the cold out of it without actually drinking it. His eyes roved the corners of the porch, and I wondered whether he was searching for Angelica as a way to escape from me if she and DeMarcus got tired of each other.

Before I could embarrass myself with another gem from my stand-up routine, the porch vibrated with deep whoops of "Sawyer!" The man himself sauntered up the wooden steps to the porch, waving with both hands like the president in his inauguration parade—but only if he'd bought the election.

Nobody in their right mind would elect Sawyer to a position of responsibility. The only office he'd ever snagged was school mascot. He would be loping around the football field this year in a giant bird costume.

What didn't quite make sense about Sawyer De Luca was his platinum hair, darker at the roots and brighter at the sun-bleached tips like a swimmer who never had to come in from the ocean and go to school. The hair didn't go with his Italian name or his dark father and brother. He must have looked like his mom, but she lived in Georgia and nobody had ever met her. A couple of years ago, she sent him to live with his dad, who was getting out of prison, because she couldn't handle Sawyer anymore. At least, that's what Sawyer had told me, and it sounded about right.

After shaking a few hands and embracing DeMarcus, Sawyer sauntered over and stood in front of Will. Not in front of *me*. He didn't acknowledge me at all as he stepped into Will's personal space and said, looking down at him, "You're in my place."

"Oh Jesus, Sawyer!" I exclaimed. Why did he have to pick a fight while I was getting to know the new guy? He must have had a bad night. Working with his prick of an older brother, who ran the bar at the Crab Lab, tended to have that effect on him.

I opened my mouth to reassure Will that Sawyer meant no harm. Or, maybe he did, but I wouldn't let Sawyer get away with it.

Before I could say anything, Will rose. At his full height, he towered over Sawyer. He looked down on Sawyer exactly as Sawyer had looked down on *him* a moment before. He growled, "This is your place? I don't *think* so."

The other boys around us stopped their joking and said in warning voices, "Sawyer." Brody put a hand on Sawyer's chest. Brody really was a football player and could have held Sawyer off Will single-handedly. Sawyer didn't care. He stared up at Will with murder in his eyes.

I stood too. "Come on, Sawyer. You were the one who told Will about this party in the first place."

"I didn't invite him *here*." Sawyer pointed at the bench where Will had been sitting.

I knew how Sawyer felt. When I'd looked forward to hooking up with him at a party, I was disappointed and even angry if he shared his night with another girl instead. But that was our long-standing agreement. We used each other when nobody more intriguing was available. Now wasn't the time to test our pact. I said, "You're some welcome committee."

The joke surprised Sawyer out of his dark mood. He relaxed his shoulders and took a half step backward. Brody and the other guys retreated the way they'd come. I wouldn't have put it past Sawyer to spring at Will now that everyone's guard was down, but he just poked Will—gently, I thought with relief—on the cursive *V* emblazoned on his T-shirt. "What's the *V* stand for? Virgin?"

"The Minnesota Vikings, moron," I said. Then I turned

to Will. "You will quickly come to understand that Sawyer is full of sh—"

Will spoke over my head to Sawyer. "It stands for 'vilification.'"

"What? Vili . . . What does that mean?" Knitting his brow, Sawyer pulled out his phone and thumbed the keyboard. I had a large vocabulary, and his was even bigger, but we'd both found that playing dumb made life easier.

Will edged around me to peer over Sawyer's shoulder at the screen. At the same time, he slid his hand around my waist. I hadn't seen a move that smooth in a while. I liked the way Minnesota guys operated. He told Sawyer, "No, not two *L*'s. One *L*."

Sawyer gave Will another wild-eyed warning. His gaze dropped to Will's hand on my waist, then rose to my serious-as-a-heart-attack face. He told Will, "Okay, SAT. I'll take my vocabulary quiz over here." He retreated to the corner of the porch to talk with a cheerleader.

Relieved, I sat back down on the bench, holding Will's hand on my side so that he had to sit down with me or get his arm jerked out of its socket. He settled closer to me than before. With his free hand, he drummed his fingers on his knee to the beat of the music filtering onto the porch. The rhythm he tapped out was so complex that I wondered whether he'd been a drummer—not for marching band like me, but for some wild rock band that got into fistfights after the hockey game was over.

As we talked, he looked into my eyes as if I was the only girl at the party, and he grinned at all my jokes. Now that my third beer was kicking in, I let go of some of my anxiety about saying exactly the right thing and just had fun. I asked him if he was part of our senior class. He was. It seemed obvious, but he *could* have been a freshman built like a running back. Then I explained who the other people at the party were according to the Senior Superlatives titles they were likely to get—Best Car, Most Athletic, that sort of thing.

My predictions were iffy. Each person could hold only one title, preventing a superstar like my friend Kaye from racking up all the honors and turning the high school yearbook into her biography. She might get Most Popular *or* Most Likely to Succeed. She was head cheerleader, a born leader, and good at everything. Harper, the yearbook photographer, might get Most Artistic *or* Most Original, since she wore funky clothes and retro glasses and always thought outside the box.

"What about you?" Will asked, tugging playfully at one of my braids.

"Ha! Most Likely to Wake Up on Your Lawn."

He laughed. "Is that a real award?"

"No, we don't give awards that would make girls cry. I'll probably get Tallest." That wasn't a real one either.

He cocked his head at me. "Funniest?"

I rolled my eyes. "That's like getting voted Miss Congeniality in a beauty pageant. It's a consolation prize."

A line appeared between his brows. He rubbed his thumb gently across my lips. "Sexiest."

"You obviously haven't surveyed the whole senior class."

"I don't have to."

Staring into his eyes, which crinkled at the corners as he smiled, I knew he was handing me a line. And I *loved* this pirate pickup of his. I let my gaze fall to his lips, willing him to kiss me.

"Hi there, new guy!" Aidan said as he burst out the door. He crossed the porch in two steps and held out his hand for Will to shake. "Aidan O'Neill, student council president."

I made a noise. It went something like "blugh" and was loud enough for Aidan to hear. I knew this because he looked at me with the same expression he gave me when I made fun of his penny loafers. He was Kaye's boyfriend, so I tried to put up with him. But we'd been assigned as partners on a chemistry paper last year, and any semblance of friendship we might have had was ruined when he tried to correct me incorrectly during my part of the presentation. I'd told him to be right or sit down. The only thing that made Aidan madder than someone challenging him was someone challenging him in public.

"Blugh" wasn't a sufficient warning for Will not to talk to him, apparently. Aidan sat down on Will's other side and launched into an overview of our school's wonders that Minnesota probably had never heard of, such as pep rallies and doughnut sales.

"Time for everybody to get lost," Brody called. "My mom will be home from the Rays game in a few minutes."

"Thanks for hosting," I told him.

"Always a pleasure. Looks like this time you may have more pleasure than you can handle, though." He nodded toward the stairs, where Sawyer was waving at me.

Sawyer held up his thumb and pointer together, which meant, *I have weed. Want to toke up?*

I shook my head in a small enough motion that Will didn't notice, I hoped. Translation: *No, I'm taking Will home if I can swing it.*

Sawyer raised one eyebrow and lowered the other, making a mad scientist face. It meant, *You'd rather go home with this guy than get high with me? You have finally lost your marbles.*

I raised both eyebrows: *We have an agreement. We stick together unless something better comes along. This is something better.*

He flared his nostrils—*Well, I never!*—and turned away. He might give me a hard time about it when I saw him next, but Sawyer and I never really got mad at each other, because why would you get mad at yourself?

I turned to rescue Will from Aidan and saw to my horror that Aidan was disappearing back into the house. Will stared right at me with a grim expression, as if he'd witnessed the entire silent conversation between Sawyer and me, understood it, and didn't like it. "Don't let me keep you," he said flatly.

Damn Sawyer! We would laugh about this later if I wasn't so hot for the boy sitting next to me. This was not funny.

Heart thumping, I tried to save my night with Will. There wasn't any time to waste. If word that Brody was closing down the party got inside to Kaye and Harper before I left, they would try to stop me from hooking up with the new guy. They might have sent him back to meet me, but they wouldn't want me leaving with him. They didn't approve of Sawyer, either, but at least they knew him. Will was a wild card. They would find this frightening. I found him perfect.

I slid my hand onto his knee and said, "I'd rather go with you. Could you walk me home?"

And then some.

Two

"FLORIDA ISN'T AGREEING WITH YOU SO FAR?" I asked Will, swinging his hand as we strolled down the sidewalk toward my neighborhood, old houses lining the street, palm trees and live oaks overhead.

"It's too soon to judge," he said. "So far it seems hot and weird."

"Are you sure that's Florida and not me?"

The warm notes of his chuckle sent tingles racing up my arm. "You're not weird. *That's* weird." He nodded toward the crazy monster face carved into the stump by Mrs. Spitzer's house.

"That's not weird either," I said. "That's artistic. Just ask the Chamber of Commerce. We have a large number of creative people in town, but that doesn't make us any stranger than a town in Minneso—"

We both stopped short. An enormous white bird, about a yard tall from feet to beak, stood in the center of the sidewalk in front of us.

Will arched his brows, waiting for me to take back my protest that Florida wasn't weird.

"That is a snowy egret," I said self-righteously. "They are very common. In Minnesota you have moose wandering the streets."

"You're mixing us up with an old fictional TV show about Alaska. Get behind me. I'll protect you." He nobly placed himself between me and the egret as we edged into the street to go around it, then hopped up on the sidewalk again. Will kept looking back at the bird, though, like he thought it would stalk us. "Honestly, more than the weirdness, it's the heat that's getting to me. Right now in Duluth it's probably in the fifties."

I shook my head. "If I lived there, I would lose so many parkas at parties."

"Parkas!" He gave me a quizzical smile. "You don't really have an autumn here, do you?"

"Define 'autumn.'"

"The leaves turn colors."

"No, we don't have that."

"Hmm. It doesn't even get cool?"

"Define 'cool.'"

"Below freezing."

"Jesus Christ, that's *cool*?" I exclaimed. "We would call out the National Guard for that. But it *has* gotten below freezing here before."

"When?"

I waved away the question, because I didn't know the

answer. “There's probably a plaque commemorating the event on the foundation of the Historical Society building. Turn here.” We walked up my street. Even if the power to the street-lights had gone out and the moon and the stars had been blocked by clouds, I would have known when we approached my house from the sound of the crispy magnolia leaves strewn across the sidewalk. Several years' worth.

He nodded ahead of us. “Isn't that the high school behind the fence?”

“In all its glory.” I swept my arm in an arc wide enough that I pitched myself off balance and stumbled over a root that had broken through the sidewalk. Will grabbed my arm before I fell.

The campus didn't look too impressive. I'd had a good time for my first three-fourths of high school, but that was because I had a lot of friends and didn't do a lot of homework, not because the school was some kind of fun factory. It was just a low concrete block labyrinth built to withstand hurricanes, although the gym and auditorium were taller, and our football stadium was visible in the distance. There were lots of palm trees, too, and a parking lot bleached white by the sun.

“That's a convenient location for you,” Will said. “Though I guess you have to go all the way around the fence to get to the front entrance.”

“Yeah, I ride my bike when I have time. Then I can go straight to work after school. But some mornings I'm running late. Well, most mornings. Then I go over the fence.”

"What if you have books and homework to carry?"

"I don't do my homework, so I don't bring my books home."

"Oh." He followed me onto the front porch and waited while I unlocked the door. When I turned back to him, his head was cocked to one side like he was trying to puzzle me out.

I didn't play games with people. Mostly I told the truth. What you saw was what you got. Maybe that confused him.

"Come in?" I asked.

He stared at me a second too long, as if he couldn't quite believe what he was hearing. "Sure."

He didn't *seem* sure, though. The swashbuckling pirate I'd wanted was retreating over the waves, and I didn't know why. He wasn't drunk. In fact, now that I thought about it, had he even opened the beer I'd handed him? Maybe he was tired from his move. I knew if I'd moved to Minnesota after living in Florida for seventeen years, I would have been stumbling around the frozen tundra, crying, *Where am I?*

To reassure him that everything was okay, I took him by the hand and led him into the house. I didn't flick on the light, because that would only have scared him. My dad and I hadn't finished unpacking from the last time we moved. It seemed futile, when the house wasn't big enough to hold our stuff. The space that wasn't taken up with furniture was filled with half-empty boxes. I tugged Will on a path so familiar I didn't need lights, through the den and down a short hall into my room and onto my bed.

He sat down next to me, his weight drawing me toward

him on the mattress. Street lamps cast the only light through the window blind. Stripes of shadow moved up his broad chest and arms, his strong neck, and his sharp chin darkened with stubble. I wondered again if he could possibly look as good in broad daylight as he did in the sexy night.

Will might have been wondering the same thing about me. He pulled my hand toward him and clasped it in both of his, massaging my fingers. He looked me over—my hair, my eyes, my shoulders, my breasts—like he wanted to remember every inch of me. It was oddly touching but also strange. I kept getting mixed messages from him. He seemed to want me as much as I wanted him, but something was holding him back. Maybe he thought I'd be an ugly duck if he saw me walking down the street during the day. Or his reluctance might have had nothing to do with me. I wondered if there was trouble back home in Minnesota.

I reached up to rub my thumb across the line between his brows. "So worried," I whispered. "Relax." I swept my fingers through his hair and gently pinched his earring that I found so fascinating.

I'd hit upon his trigger. He sucked in a little gasp. Then he plunged both hands into my hair and held me steady while he kissed me.

I was surprised at how hot his mouth was. His lips pressed the corner of my mouth at first, then the other corner, then kissed me full on. His tongue teased my lips apart and swept inside.

We made out for a long while. He was a great kisser, gently controlling me. I could have stayed just like that with him for hours. But by this time, most guys would have made another move. When he didn't, I was afraid I'd mistakenly given him the message that I didn't want more. I took him by both shoulders and pulled him down on top of me as I lay back on the bed.

He held himself off me. I thought for a split second he was going to back away. But he was only arranging himself so that our bodies fit together, his mouth on my neck, his hands on my breasts, his erection pressed against me. He settled more of his weight on top of me, and I sighed with satisfaction.

"Wow," he whispered against my lips. "I like Florida better now." He kissed me deeply before moving to my earlobe.

I turned my head so he could reach my ear better. I was rewarded with a gentle explosion of tingles that spread down my neck and made the hair stand up all over my body.

"Do you like that?" he asked, inducing delicious shivers.

"Not really," I said drily.

He chuckled in my ear. This was the hottest thing he'd done yet.

He trailed one hand from my ear down my neck, traced his fingers lightly across my breastbone, and deftly undid the top button of my shirt. "Do you like this?"

"It's okay," I managed between gasps as his fingers continued downward. They blazed a trail of fire across my skin, paused to release another button, and traveled down again.

When he reached the bottom, I panted in anticipation.

He reversed direction and smoothed one side of my shirt back against my shoulder. After fumbling underneath me to unhook my bra, he moved the satin out of the way too. With a light scratch of his stubble across my tender skin, he put his mouth on my breast.

"What?" I murmured.

He laughed against me, each puff of his warm breath sending a fresh chill across my chest. "You don't like this?"

"No, that I'm sure I like."

In agreement, he took me inside his hot mouth. For long minutes I was afraid I might explode with pleasure, holding my breath for each new thoughtful stroke of his tongue. Boys had done this to me before, yet not so slowly or thoroughly. Not like this.

I didn't want him to stop, but I couldn't be greedy. I took his cheek in my palm and brought his lips up to meet mine. Then I moved my hand down between us, under his weight, and into his waistband. I knew he was enjoying it because he forgot to keep kissing me.

"Do you like this?" I asked innocently, as if I didn't know the answer.

Will was holding his breath like I had been before. On a couple of quick exhalations, he grunted, "I haven't decided. Keep doing that . . . until I collect enough data."

This was something I pictured a good-looking, wholesome nerd like DeMarcus saying if Angelica ever had the courage to reach down his pants. But Will said it with the irony of a smart, worldly pirate. I giggled.

Through my laughter, I was careful to continue touching him. I didn't want to make him choose between feeling good and cracking jokes. This perfect boy, sent to sit next to me at a party, was quickly becoming one of my best friends with bennies. If he kept sounding so pleasantly shocked at what I was doing to him, he might even replace Sawyer as my favorite bad boy.

Brightness grew in the room. Headlights shone in from a car turning around in my driveway. The lines of light across Will's face changed and moved. As they caressed his jawline, I was surer than ever that his good looks weren't my imagination.

He was watching me again, and the worry line between his brows was back. "Don't tell me. Your dad's home."

"Oh, no," I assured him. "That's probably my friend Kaye—we talked about her, and I think you met her inside at the party—and her boyfriend Aidan. You know, student council president," I reminded him in a smarmy Aidan imitation. In a normal tone I said, "They stopped by to check that I got home okay before Aidan has to get Kaye back for her curfew."

It must have been a lot later than I'd thought. I didn't have a clock in my room, which was the way I liked it. I didn't want to feel nagged. But I did wonder about the time. It seemed like my night with Will had passed in an instant.

The bright light hung around for an annoyingly long time.

I rolled out from under Will, crawled across the bed, stuck my hand through the slats in the window blind, and waved. The headlights retreated.

When I turned back to Will, he was sitting up on the bed, smiling at me. "You have good friends."

"Yeah. So good I want to kill them sometimes."

He pulled his phone out of his back pocket. "God, it's late. I'd better go. My mom's called me three times."

"That's so sweet!"

"Yeah. She's worried about me in a strange town and all, and I have to be somewhere at eight in the morning."

Something wasn't right here. Will didn't seem like the type of guy who went home so he would be rested for an early morning, or whose mother would check up on him. And even if she did, most boys I knew wouldn't admit this to a girl. But people were different. Maybe even pirates went to bed at a decent hour in Minnesota.

Then he motioned to a spot in front of him on the bed. "Come here, Tia."

I could have made another joke out of it, crawling across the bed to him in a parody of a sex kitten. But he sounded so serious and looked so solemn that I simply slid closer.

He held my gaze as he maneuvered my bra back into place, then reached behind me to rehook it. He had some experience doing this, I gathered. Then he felt for my top button and fastened it, then the next. I'd never had a boy dress me before. As long as he watched me like I was the most beautiful girl he'd ever seen, he could put as many layers of clothing on me as he wanted. He fastened the last button, and his hand slid down to my thigh.

I asked him, "Do you know how to get home from here? Maybe *I* should walk *you*."

He squinted as he grinned. Then his smile faded. Stroking the corner of my mouth with one finger, he whispered, "I'd like that, if you would come inside and we could do this over again." He moved his hand to cup my jaw, coming closer until the tip of his nose rubbed mine. He kissed me again, so slowly, just tasting at first and then more deeply, like we had all the time in the world and he was going to explore each angle, enjoying every second. Finally drawing away, he said, "And then *I* could walk *you* home, and we could do it again."

I wished I *could* spend this night with Will over and over. It had been one of the best nights of my life. Repeating it with no thought to consequences and no concern for what happened next . . . that made it perfect.

After one final stroke of his hand through my hair, he picked up his phone. "What's your number?"

I gave it to him. Since the night did have to end, I wanted him to be able to get in touch with me the next time he got the urge to drink (or not) on someone's back porch and walk me home. It could happen, but only in the next few days. Most guys seemed to love hooking up with me, at least at first, but they paired off with a possessive girl pretty quickly. Afterward they wanted to cheat on their girlfriends with me, and that was something I refused to do. Kaye might not believe it, but even *I* had morals.

Will wouldn't be any different. Alcohol wasn't fooling with my perception anymore. By now I was almost sober, and he was still incredibly handsome as he squinted at his phone in the dark. His soft lips pursed in concentration. His long hair fell forward into his eyes. Looking like he did, and being the new guy at our school, he would have girls hanging off him by lunch on the first day. He wouldn't need me for a hookup anymore. But he'd been heaven while he lasted, and I was glad I'd seen him first.

My phone rang in my pocket, a snippet of a salsa tune, and vibrated too. I pulled it out and glanced at his number with an unfamiliar area code. "That's titillating. Call me anytime."

He laughed, and I sighed with relief. I hadn't realized how nervous I'd gotten when he looked so pensive.

I tensed right back up again when he asked, "Are you busy tomorrow afternoon?"

I countered suspiciously, "What do you mean?"

"I thought I could take you to lunch, and then you could show me around town."

I didn't know what to say. Truthfully, I would be busy tomorrow. But he wasn't asking about just tomorrow. I could tell from his tone that if I wasn't able to go to lunch with him, he would ask for another date. Eventually we would hit on a time that I could fit into my schedule. But I didn't *want* to fit it into my schedule, and I couldn't let him go on thinking that

I did. I might have been a lot of things, but a tease wasn't one of them.

A hookup after a party would have been fine with me. But the idea of a deliberate-sounding date made my stomach twist. All three of my sisters had gotten excited about a date. They'd been smitten quickly. The boys they'd dated became the most important people in their lives overnight. My sisters left high school before graduation to be with those boys. Two out of three boys had already abandoned them.

"Let me guess." Will took my hand and stroked my palm with his thumb, sending a shiver down my arm. "It's such a small town that showing me around would take five minutes, and then what would we do?"

I laughed softly, because his guess was so far off. I pulled my hand away. "No. It just sounds kind of serious."

His brows went down. "Serious? What do you mean? It'll be fun."

"I mean, you're moving too fast."

"Too fast!" He looked around the ceiling. "Weren't you the one who invited me into your bedroom when your parents weren't home?"

So I was a little, shall we say, open with boys. I didn't see how that hurt anything. What bothered me was when boys participated equally, and seemed to enjoy it, then complained about it afterward like I was somehow at fault.

"You know what?" he backtracked. "I'm sorry. I got to Florida yesterday. It's a huge change, and I'm going through some other stuff. Maybe what I said didn't come out right. I didn't mean to creep you out and move in on you. We could just have lunch and that's all. Or just ride around and that's all. Or . . ." Searching my eyes, he ran out of words.

"No," I said, "I mean I don't want a boyfriend. Period."

Not a muscle moved in his face. I couldn't read his expression. He stared at me for a long time, as if he'd never heard of such a thing as a girl who didn't want a boyfriend. He wasn't taking this well.

Finally he nodded very slowly, then looked toward the ceiling again. "What I said *definitely* didn't come out right." He stood up and walked out of the room, headed for the front door. His eyes must have adjusted fully to the darkness, because not once did he scream out in pain as though he'd veered off the path and hit something sharp.

As I trailed after him, I reviewed the night, searching for the point when it had gone wrong. He wasn't the type of guy who just wanted a hookup. How had I missed this? I *was* that type of girl and made a point never to hide it. Why did it surprise him now?

Surely he hadn't been so attracted to me that he'd known I was wrong for him but pursued me anyway. I was okay looking, nothing special. A lot of guys seemed to like my auburn hair, but that usually got canceled out when they saw that I was almost their height. And while some boys enjoyed a flaky girl, others said I was stupid and couldn't stand me. At least I wasn't so flaky that I didn't know I was flaky.

But I felt like the biggest flake in Florida as Will opened the door, letting the warm, humid night mix with the air-conditioning. As he turned to face me, his earring glinted, and I felt myself flush all over again with the longing I'd felt when I first saw him. I *did not* want a boyfriend, but it felt wrong to let Will go.

He looked into my eyes, then gazed at my lips. I thought he would kiss me again. And then—just maybe—we could return this night to the place where we should have left it.

No such luck. Without touching me, he stepped off the stoop and onto what was probably the sidewalk under all those magnolia leaves. "Good night, Tia," he said over his shoulder.

"Are you sure you can get home?" I asked.

"I have GPS." He took out his phone and wagged it in the air. "If I can remember my own address." When he reached the street, he walked backward as he called, "Go inside and lock the door so I'll know you're okay."

"It's my house," I said defiantly.

"I'll worry." He stopped and watched me.

I frowned, but I backed inside and turned the deadbolt. Even Sawyer made me lock the door when he left.

I navigated to my room, lifted a slat in the blind, and watched Will. He turned the corner and disappeared up a dead-end street. I waited.

Sure enough, he came back to the corner, focusing on his phone. Then he gazed up at the sky like a seafarer lost on his Great Lake, looking to the stars for guidance.

He headed down the street toward town.

Three

I WOKE TO THE SOUND OF MY DAD'S TRUCK in the driveway, which meant it was seven a.m. Bright morning light streamed through the window blind. I scowled, remembering what had happened the night before. I didn't understand Will, but I knew enough that I didn't want to. He was so hot, and kissed so well, and that earring! He was the type of guy I could get really attached to if I wasn't careful. And though I might not seem like the most conscientious person most of the time, I was always careful about boys.

Besides, I'd never been one to lament what happened the night before. I had a great day ahead of me.

All summer I'd been looking forward to band camp. I'd spent two and a half months closed up in Bob and Roger's antiques shop. They'd given me a raise last month. They were talking about promoting me to assistant manager, so I'd have to boss around Marvin of the too-small T-shirts printed with cat designs and Edwina of the constant smoke breaks.

I'd have to quit soon if Bob and Roger went through with their threat of giving me more responsibility. Just in case, I'd taken a second job at night, waiting tables at the Crab Lab. That hadn't been ideal either. Sawyer's brother kept coming on to me, which was going to work if he gave me any more beer, and it was getting hard for Sawyer to keep him off me.

Just as something bad was about to happen, I was saved by band. Because there were only four days until school started and two and a half weeks until our first game, we would practice on the football field a *lot*: eight a.m. to noon, then six to ten p.m., splitting the day to avoid the ridiculous heat of a Florida August. There went half my shift at the shop, and going in to the grill wasn't even worth it.

I looked forward to seeing my friends, and beating the hell out of my drum. The only reason I dreaded band this year was that I was drum captain, by virtue of the fact that the three guys and one girl ahead of me last year had graduated. I should have been more careful to place lower during tryouts last spring, but thinking ahead was not my forte. Since then, the other snare drummers had refused to challenge me for drum captain, no matter how nicely I begged them.

So I was saddled with the responsibility of rehearsing all the drums and keeping them in line, which was going to require a constant vigilance of which I wasn't capable. If I didn't convince someone to take over my position, we would make a bad score at a band contest in the fall, I knew it. I didn't mind personal failure so much, but I did *not* want to cause anybody else to crash and burn.

I was holding out for a miracle.

I wandered into the kitchen, where my dad, in grease-stained jeans and a polo shirt with the logo of the boat factory where he worked, stared into the open refrigerator. Good luck finding anything in there. It was packed to the brim, and most of the contents were no longer edible. I was pretty sure the meat drawer contained ham that my sister Violet had bought before she moved out last March.

I kissed my dad on the cheek. "Morning."

"Hey there, *lucita*." He hugged me with one arm while drawing a questionable bag of bagels out of the fridge with his other hand. In Spanish he said, "I thought band camp started today."

"Not until eight," I answered in English. My Spanish was rusty now that my sisters were gone.

"I'm late getting home because we had a safety meeting." He glanced at his watch. "It's eight-oh-five."

"Shit!" I squealed. "I don't have time for a shower! Do I smell?"

He sniffed the top of my head. "On a scale of one to ten? Six point five."

"I'll take it." I didn't ask whether six point five was closer to the stinky or the odorless end of the scale. I dashed for the bathroom, scrubbed my face and brushed my teeth in thirty seconds flat, and grabbed sunscreen and a beach towel. I spent considerably more time in my bedroom looking for my drumsticks and my flip-flops and a big hat and a bag to stuff everything into. I didn't have time to stuff it then. It was just another part of the panicked bundle. I ran back to the kitchen for a sports drink, which was safe to drink because it was sealed, and a pack of Pop-Tarts from the box on the counter. I didn't feel too hungover, but something told me that might change in the heat of ten a.m. if I didn't put something in my stomach. "Love you," I called to my dad, who'd given up on the fridge and disappeared. He was probably in bed already.

Outside on the porch, I locked the door—my keys were still in my pocket from last night—and found my sunglasses in my other pocket. I dashed down the street to the school fence and pitched my drumsticks over, then the sunscreen and my drink and the towel and the bag and the Pop-Tarts. I kicked off my flip-flops, knowing from experience that I couldn't climb the fence with them on, and hiked myself over. I was lucky I had long legs. Kaye refused even to try this stunt. Too-adventurous-for-her-own-good Harper had attempted it and gotten stuck with one leg hooked over. The trick was lifting myself high enough that the rough tops of the boards didn't scrape my thighs. Triumphant, I dropped to the other side and gathered up the stuff I'd thrown over.

The drums were already rehearsing. Their racket carried out of the football stadium, around the school, and across the parking lot. And then I realized that I'd left my flip-flops on the other side of the fence. There was no time to go back.

"Shit shit shit." I took off across the parking lot, loose shells from the pavement cutting into the soles of my feet. I couldn't even go straight to the stadium. I had to stop at the band room first to drag my drum out of storage. By the time I made it to the field, I was twenty minutes late instead of five.

The stadium entrance was at parking-lot level, but the bleachers rose above me and also sank into the ground. As I hurried through the gate, I was high enough in the stands to see that Ms. Nakamoto had put DeMarcus to work pushing flutes into place according to the diagram she'd drawn for the start of the halftime show. Ms. Nakamoto had backed the drums into a corner of the field and appeared to be lecturing them. Maybe I could sneak up behind her and pretend I'd been there the whole time. Maybe I would also be elected the senior class's Most Likely to Succeed. Fat chance.

As I left the stands, hit the grass, and hurried past the majorettes tossing their batons in a bored fashion, Angelica asked, "Isn't that the same thing you were wearing last night?"

Despite that I was *very late*, I stopped. Angelica wasn't normally one to confront people or throw insults—at least not at me. She was more crafty, getting people in trouble behind the scenes. For her to call me out like this, she *definitely* had shared a look with Will last night. Since I'd screwed up everything with Will, he was sure to move on to another girl. It was none of my business, but I didn't want that new girl to be old Angelica.

I told her, "Why, no. Last night I was wearing that new guy."

A couple of majorettes standing close enough to overhear us cackled loudly. My friend Chelsea said, "Girl, you are *crazy.*"

"It's a little early to be dressed to impress," I told her, talking over Angelica's scowling head. Angelica would be sorry she insulted me before nine a.m. I was not a morning person. I turned my back on them and waded through the dewy grass to the drums.

One of whom was Will Matthews.

I didn't recognize him at first in his mirrored aviator shades. He hadn't shaved, so his dark stubble made him look even scruffier than he had last night. But he wore a Minnesota Vikings baseball cap. And he stood tall like a warrior, out of place in our dopey drum line. He'd already taken off his shirt in the oppressive morning heat. His snare drum harness covered most of his chest and hooked over his shoulders, but he held his muscular arms akimbo, with his hands and sticks folded on top of his drum. His earring winked at me from underneath his dark hair.

What was *he* doing *here*?

As I tried to sneak past Ms. Nakamoto into the end of the drum line, a rumble through the drummers told her I was coming. She glanced over her shoulder at me, then down at her watch. "Ms. Cruz!" she called sharply. "You've been challenged, and you were about thirty seconds from forfeiting."

"Yes, ma'am. Sorry," I said with a sigh, trying to sound sad that I would have to give up my drum captain position if someone beat me. Really I was ecstatic. I'd been saved!

And I'd arrived at just the right time. She wasn't making me forfeit. If she had, I would have been dead last in the snare drum line, which could have been a fate worse than being first. Then I would have had to stand between some scared freshman on snare and a timid sophomore on quads. I had a tendency to frighten underclassmen.

With everyone staring at me, including Will, and a couple of juniors, Jimmy and Travis, who were making a point of looking bored to death, I pitched everything I'd been carrying off the top of my drum. Sunscreen, bag, drink, towel, Pop-Tarts. Ms. Nakamoto watched the process like she'd come to count on this sort of thing from me. Then I started the part of the drum cadence that we used for tryouts.

As my too-loud notes echoed around the stadium, I felt that high I loved so much. Playing drum stressed me out a little, because there was no room for mistakes, and mistakes were pretty much my modus operandi. But when I was under pressure, I loved to put things in their proper places, like bubbling in the correct answers on a standardized test. Beating a snare drum was the ultimate pastime if you occasionally enjoyed precision in your otherwise scatterbrained life.

But this time there was a catch. I had to be very careful to make a mistake. Otherwise I'd end up right back where I'd started, as drum captain. And because everyone else had already taken a turn without me here to listen, I didn't know whether to make a bunch of mistakes or just one. In the end I settled for missing the syncopated part that tended to trip people up in the middle. I'd never heard Will play, but something told me my pirate hadn't missed a note.

Sure enough, a moment after I was done, Ms. Nakamoto made a mark on her clipboard, then read off the new order. Will was first on snare, and the new drum captain. I was second.

My hero! I could have relaxed all summer if I'd known that my knight in shining armor would ride out of nowhere—Minnesota, actually, which amounted to the same thing—to save me from my own success, and my certain failure.

There was a lot of confusion as drummers reordered themselves according to Ms. Nakamoto's ruling, purposely knocking each other with their drums as they reshuffled. Then they took off their harnesses and set down the heavy drums. Now that the challenge was over, we were just waiting for Ms. Nakamoto or DeMarcus to pull us into the proper position for the first set. We didn't need to wear our drums for that. Eight snares, four bass drums, three quads, and four pairs of cymbals lay on the grass like the excavated skeleton of a dinosaur. The drummers themselves borrowed space on towels to sit down with the trumpets and trombones near the back of the band, or moved up front and tried to tickle the majorettes.

Normally I would have made the rounds and talked to all my friends whom I hadn't seen during the summer. But I wasn't passing up the perfect opportunity to question the mysterious Mr. Matthews on the percussion skills he'd suddenly acquired. I retrieved my towel from my pile of stuff and spread it out on the grass. "Join me?" I asked him.

"Ssssssure." He eased his big frame down onto half of the towel and leaned back on his elbows, showing off his abs. The guy had a six-pack. Every girl in band—and some of the guys—turned to stare, then faced forward again like they'd just been looking around casually. It wasn't that six-packs were unusual at our school. Athletics were important. But the chiseled chest was less common in band.

Allowing the uncomfortable silence to stretch on, I smoothed sunscreen across my arms, legs, and face. I held the bottle toward him. "Need some?"

"We're in the shade," he said.

True. The high bleachers on the home and away sides provided a lot of shade in the morning and evening, and the ends of the stadium were surrounded by palm trees and live oaks that shaded the grass even more. But because the field sat lower than the surrounding ground, it got no breeze. None. The heat turned the stadium into a hundred-yard pressure cooker and ensured that somebody, sooner or later, was going to die of heat exhaustion. Though the sun wouldn't make us crispy by the end of practice, skin as white as Will's would turn an unhealthy pink. The sun was sneaky and would find its way to him.

"Trust me," I said.

He took the bottle grudgingly and squirted lotion into his palm to spread along one muscular shoulder. "You're saying I look like I'm from Minnesota."

"You look like a hockey player from Minnesota," I clarified.

The flutes stared unabashedly at him as his hands moved over his own body, as if he was putting on a peep show. I asked, "Want me to get your back?"

He watched me sidelong for a moment. At least, I thought he did. His mirrored shades were in the way. All I could see was the shadow of his long lashes.

"Sure," he said again, leaning forward.

I spread sunscreen across his broad back, kneading his shoulders and neck as I went. All the way across the field, the majorettes were looking. Chelsea actually pointed at me. I waved cheekily at her. I wished I could see old Angelica's face from this distance.

I said softly in Will's ear, "You don't seem as surprised to see me here as I am to see you."

Through my own sunglasses, I couldn't tell whether a blush crept across his cheeks. His long silence spoke volumes, though. Finally he said, "I told you last night that your friends had sent me to find you and introduce myself to you."

"Yes, you did," I acknowledged, "but—"

"When I walked into the party, I said I was new and I played percussion in the marching band. They said, 'Oooh, you have to meet Tia Cruz, the drum captain.'"

I liked the way he imitated Harper and Kaye—not in the high faux-girly voice boys used when they didn't think very much of girls. The pitch of his voice stayed the same, but he smoothed over the *oooh* like they'd made me sound delicious, and he'd agreed.

But I was sure he hadn't mentioned anything to me about drums last night. I would remember. I hadn't been *that* drunk. In fact, I'd watched him tapping his fingers to the rhythm of the music and wondered if he was a drummer, but I hadn't put two and two together. "I thought they sent you to me because you wanted to get drunk and hook up."

He shifted to face me on the towel. "They would meet a complete stranger at a party and send him to hook up with their drunk friend?"

He had a point. Kaye and Harper were way more protective of me than that. "I guess not," I admitted. "I was drunk as I was thinking this." I went back over what had happened last night when I looked up from my bench and saw a pirate. His explanation didn't make sense. "No," I insisted. "I thought you wanted a beer. I gave you a beer. You took it."

"I didn't drink it."

I glanced around, suspicious that I had been transported to a parallel universe where high school boys didn't drink the beer they were given. But there was still only one sun, mostly blocked by a tall palm, and I didn't detect extra moons or a visible ring around the planet.

As I thought about it, though, I decided I'd seen his true nature from the beginning—if not when he found me on Brody's back porch, at least by the time he walked me home and acted like a gentleman instead of the scoundrel I was expecting. I'd seen it, but I hadn't wanted to see it.

Yet if he *was* that innocent, what business did he have

coming to a party and deliberately sitting next to the girl over the cooler? I pointed out, "We spent a lot of time together last night. You had plenty of chances to tell me that you're on the drum line, or that we would be seeing each other again soon, as in *this morning*."

He nodded. "You've got me. I didn't intend to hide it from you. Once we started talking, I was having fun with you, and I didn't want anything to ruin it."

That I understood. I'd felt the same way the countless times I'd thought, *This boy is not a real pirate.*

"And I hoped we were heading for something really good. If we'd started dating, which honestly was what I *assumed* was going to happen after last night, the fact that we'd have to spend so much time standing right next to each other would have been *good* news."

"It's still good news," I assured him. "I just don't want a boyfriend."

"I get it," Will said.

Ms. Nakamoto issued instructions through her microphone then, commanding all the drums to move our equipment so DeMarcus could place clarinet players in a curlicue where we'd been sitting. As we lugged our stuff five yards downfield and plopped on the forty-five, I pondered whether Will really did "get it," as he'd said. My reasons for not wanting a boyfriend ran deep. Not even my closest friends completely got what I only half understood about myself.

"Jesus. It's. Hot!" Will took off his cap, poured bottled

water over his head, slicked his fingers through his hair, and put his cap back on.

"You'll get used to it," I assured him, munching a Pop-Tart.

"By the time I get used to it, I'll be gone."

This was true for a lot of the old people who thought they wanted to retire here. They came into the antiques shop to buy knickknacks for the cute cottage where they planned to live out their days. They told me it was a lot hotter in Florida than they'd imagined, and they asked if we were in the midst of an unusually hot spell. I told them no. When they reappeared a few weeks later to sell their knickknacks back to me, they admitted they were packing up and heading back to Cleveland. They weren't as sick of five feet of snow each winter as they'd initially thought.

But a high school senior couldn't do what he chose, obviously, so Will's words sounded bitter. I wondered again whether he was taking my no-boyfriend rule the wrong way: that is, personally.

I teased him, which was my solution to every problem. "If you want to stay cool, getting rid of the Paul Bunyan beard might help."

He rasped one hand across his stubbly cheek. "I can't find my razor."

"Your refrigerator and now your razor?" I poked out my bottom lip in sympathy. "We have razors in Florida, you know. And stores to buy them in. We're not *that* weird."

"I didn't want to be late this morning." He glanced sideways at me. "To beat you in the challenge."

"Ohhhhh!" I sang. "That hurt." It didn't really, but he'd seemed so straight-laced in the bright light of morning that the jab did surprise me. "By the way, how did you memorize the drum cadence so quickly?" I'd arrived too late to hear him, but he must have played the challenge perfectly to pull ahead of me.

"As soon as I knew I was moving here, I wrote ahead and asked Ms. Nakamoto to send me the music," he explained. "I'd already planned to challenge you on the first day. I mean"—he corrected himself when I raised an eyebrow—"I'd planned to challenge the drum captain. I didn't know it was you. Until last night."

Then he leaned over until his breath tickled my ear. By now just about all the boys in the band had pulled off their shirts, and some girls had too if they'd remembered to wear a bikini top or sports bra underneath. But I was very aware of Will's bare chest in particular, and the way he'd set my skin on fire last night, as he whispered, "You let me beat you, didn't you?"

I gazed at him, neither confirming nor denying, and hoped that, behind my sunglasses, my eyes were as unreadable as his. I didn't like to lie, but I wasn't willing to admit this either.

He whispered again, "Don't worry. I won't tell anyone."

Ms. Nakamoto was calling to us again: Everybody up. Back to our places. The drum captain had to provide a beat while the whole band marched through the first formation of halftime. Drummers scrambled toward us from all corners of the field. But Will and I sat watching each other. We understood each other better than either of us was comfortable with.

The moment passed. He stood and pulled me up after him. We marched elbow to elbow through the first thirty-two measures of the song, then stopped to let DeMarcus shift people a few steps up or back according to what Ms. Nakamoto hollered.

"So, this school's mascot is the pelican?" Will asked.

I was relieved that he'd dropped the serious conversation. Or maybe he just didn't care to have one while the third- and fourth-chair snares, Jimmy and Travis, and all the cymbal players could hear us. As long as he wanted to be jocular, I didn't care why.

"You've come to this realization only gradually?" I asked. "How did you interpret the large sign at the entrance to campus that says HOME OF THE PELICANS?"

"I thought it was a *home* for *pelicans*." He gestured to five of them flying in formation overhead, on their way from one inlet to another.

"You did not."

"School mascots are supposed to be fierce," he explained. "Cardinals and ducks and pelicans are poor choices. If you're going to pick a bird, pick one that hunts prey or eats carrion, at least."

"Right. Let me guess. You transferred here from Uptight Northern High School, Home of the Vultures."

"We aren't vultures." With mock self-righteousness, he said, "Our mascot is the Wrath of God."

I snorted with laughter I didn't quite feel. Granted, he'd been in town only two days. But I wished he'd referred to his other team as "they" rather than "we," and in the past tense. He still identified himself as a member of his old school, not this new one. If he had his way, he probably *would* make it back to Minnesota before he got used to the heat. I watched a bead of sweat crawl down the side of his neck.

And I felt a fresh pang of guilt that I was part of the reason he didn't like it here. I certainly hadn't helped matters by taking him home and then brushing him off. But I wasn't about to change my no-boyfriend policy just to make a cute stranger feel more welcome.

I said calmly, "I see. And your marching band was called the Marching Wrath of God?"

"Please tell me this band isn't the Marching Pelicans." He sounded horrified.

"Yes," I said with gusto. We weren't really. We were called the Pride of Pinellas County. "It's weird, but no weirder than lutefisk." Another score, courtesy of lessons on state trivia in Mr. Tomlin's third-grade class.

"Oh!" Will gaped at me in outrage. "No lutefisk jokes. That is *low*."

"Just preparing you for when school starts." Sawyer would be at the top of the list for making lutefisk jokes.

"The Tampa Bay Rays have a good name," Will said contemplatively. "Stingrays kill somebody every once in a while, right?"

"Well, they used to have a manta ray on the logo, but now the Rays are supposed to be sun rays," I informed him. "Like *that's* dangerous."

He took off his hat, wiped his brow with his forearm, and put his hat back on. "Depends on whether you're from Minnesota."

I laughed heartily at this. "I could be wrong. Maybe they're just a bunch of guys named Ray. Plumbers."

"And their logo is an exposed butt crack."

I pointed at him with one drumstick. "Perfect! We should clue Sawyer in. That would make a great look for the team mascot."

Will squinted at me over the top of his sunglasses. "Sawyer?"

"Yeah. He's the school mascot, our dangerous pelican."

"Sawyer, your boyfriend?" He gave me what I imagined was a steely glare through his shades.

I'd made clear last night that I didn't have a boyfriend. And I *thought* I'd made clear—as clear as I could make a relationship when it was admittedly a bit cloudy to begin with—that if I did *acquire* a boyfriend, Sawyer wouldn't be it.

But in Will's voice I'd heard that same bitterness from a few minutes earlier. He pressed his lips tightly together. I was doomed to stand next to this guy for the rest of the year, and he was making sure that I knew at every turn how jealous he felt.

I didn't want a guy *acting* like a boyfriend any more than

I wanted the real thing. But as we watched each other, tingles spread across my chest as if he was kissing my neck.

An electronic beep interrupted us. "Hold on," he said, raising one finger. Obviously he thought it was important that we come right back to this stare-down when he finished his other business. He pulled his phone from his pocket and glanced casually at the screen. As soon as he saw it, though, his jaw dropped. He tapped the phone with his thumb again.

"Fuck!" he shouted in a sharp crack that bounced against the bleachers. He turned toward the goalpost, reared back, and hurled his phone—quite an athletic feat, considering he was still wearing his snare drum.

"Oh, God," I exclaimed, "what's the matter?"

Travis said, "Nice arm," and Jimmy agreed, "Forty, fifty yarder."

Will pointed at them with both drumsticks. Afraid he was going to launch into a tirade and get in trouble with Ms. Nakamoto, I put a hand on his chest to stop him.

Too late. Everyone in the band had turned around to gape at him. The ones who hadn't heard his curse whispered questions to the people standing next to them about what he'd said. And Ms. Nakamoto had definitely heard him.

"Hey!" she hollered, hurrying over from a row of trombones. She must have forgotten Will's name, because if she'd known it, instead of "Hey!" she would have shouted an outraged *Mr. Matthews!* She hustled right up to the front of his snare drum and frowned at him, hands on her hips, whistle swinging on a cord. She was at least a foot shorter than him. "Is that how you talked during band practice where you came from?"

"No." He should have said "No, ma'am," but I didn't think *that* was how people talked in Minnesota either, and he hadn't been here long enough to know better. I hoped she wouldn't hold it against him.

"Do you think that's appropriate language for the drum captain?" she demanded. "Do you think you're a good role model for freshmen when you lose your cool like that? Because I can give the responsibility right back to Ms. Cruz if you can't handle it."

"Let's not be hasty," I spoke up.

"I'm really sorry," Will told her. On top of his drum, he gripped his sticks so tightly that his knuckles turned white. "I got this . . . this . . ."

"Upsetting message on your phone, when phones aren't allowed in band practice?" she prompted him.

Officially we had a rule against phones, but Ms. Nakamoto didn't normally enforce it because a lot of band camp was spent hurrying up and waiting for something to happen. She wouldn't have come down on him like this if he hadn't hollered the *F*-word an hour after becoming drum captain.

But I could save him. Placing one hand on his back, I leaned forward and said quietly to Ms. Nakamoto, "We'll just go for a short walk, okay? Will moved here yesterday all the way from Minnesota. It's a big adjustment, and things aren't going smoothly." I assumed from his reaction to the message that this was the understatement of the century.

Ms. Nakamoto turned her frown on me, then pursed her lips. I couldn't see her eyes behind her sunglasses, but I hoped I'd caught her off guard with my offer of help, which was probably a first for me in three years of high school band.

She muttered something and turned away. Not wasting any time lest she change her mind, I gave Will a little push in the direction of his phone.

"While you're over there, see if you can find some change I dropped at practice last year," Jimmy said.

Will turned to him angrily, his drum knocking against mine. He was beyond caring, obviously, and anything was liable to set him off now. The bad-boy hockey player I'd seen in him hadn't been entirely my imagination.

I whispered to Jimmy, "Shut up. You don't want *me* back in charge, do you?" I put my arm around Will's waist—the way he'd touched me at the party the night before—and steered him downfield.

Four

WHILE MS. NAKAMOTO WENT BACK TO ISSUING orders through her microphone, and the giggles of the clarinets faded behind us, Will and I walked toward the goalpost and ditched our drums. I spotted his phone in the grass and pointed it out to him. He didn't move any closer but instead stared at it in distaste, his nostrils flared like he didn't want to touch it. I plucked it out of the grass for him. It wasn't his phone, though. It was one half of its plastic cover, emblazoned with a logo of a sunset behind evergreen trees and the words MINNESOTA WILD.

A couple of yards farther on, I picked up the other half of his phone cover. It was printed with the slogan MINNESOTA IS THE STATE OF HOCKEY. Sad.

The phone itself glinted in the sunlight—smack on the white goal line. I dusted off some of the lime before holding it out to him.

"You can look," he grumbled.

I didn't want to invade his privacy. But I was dying to know what had happened. And clearly he wanted to tell someone.

I peered at the screen. It was a text from someone named Lance. All it said was "Dude." Attached was a photo of a dark-haired beauty with porcelain skin. She smiled sweetly into the camera, eyes bright. A cute guy with curly blond hair kissed her neck.

"Who's the girl?" I asked, my heart sinking into my stomach.

He verified what I'd been thinking. "My girlfriend. Beverly."

I nodded. "Who's the guy?"

"My best friend."

I looked up at him sadly. "Only two days after you left?"

"The same day I left," he said. "I mean, that picture was from last night, but I already heard they got together the night before that."

"So she didn't waste any time after you broke up?" I asked gently.

"We didn't break up," he snapped. "I'm going to be down here for only a year, and then I'm going back to Minnesota for college."

"Oh," I said. Right. He wouldn't be here long enough to get used to the heat.

"We weren't going to have to do the long-distance thing forever. Less than a year. We were going to see each other at Christmas when I visit my grandparents, and maybe spring break. So we said good-bye two days ago, and I left in my car, right? My parents wanted me to sell it, if anyone would even buy it, because they didn't trust me to drive it down here by myself. But I convinced them." He was talking with his hands now. The car was important. He had this in common, at least, with boys from Florida.

"I was at a gas station in Madison when I checked my texts. I had ten different messages from *everybody* that she was cheating on me *right then* with my best friend at a party." He pointed to the phone in my hands, as though this was all the phone's fault. "I tried to call her, but she didn't answer. I tried to call him. I thought maybe I should drive back and confront . . . somebody. But what good would that have done?" He paused like he wanted me to answer.

"Right," I said. Going back to fix it would have been like trying to repair a house of cards with a window open to the breeze.

He looked toward Ms. Nakamoto as rim taps raced across the field to us. While Will and I were missing, Jimmy was beating the rhythm for the band to march into the next formation.

"I ended up driving around Madison for an hour," Will said. "I knew going back to Minnesota wouldn't do any good. And I needed to get here in time to try out for drum captain today. But the farther I drove from home, the less relevant I was going to be to any of my friends' lives. Then my dad chewed me out for being an hour late to the checkpoint in Indianapolis. He kept asking me where I was all that time. I was watching my entire life go down the drain, thank you."

I set my sunglasses down on my nose so I could look at him in the real light of day. "Therefore, when you came to the party last night, you *were* looking for a good time. A rebound girl. I didn't read you wrong after all."

He folded his arms on his bare chest like he was cold all of a sudden. "I'm sorry, Tia. For the first seventeen years of my life, I did everything right. For the past forty-eight hours, I've done everything wrong."

He hadn't kissed wrong last night. I wanted to tell him that to cheer him up. Then I decided against it because he seemed to be counting *me* as one of the things he'd done wrong.

A lot of boys considered me the wrong kind of girl. I wasn't offended. At least, I thought I wasn't, until this came out of my mouth: "You didn't do the deed with her just before you left, did you?"

"I . . . what?"

"She cheated on you the same night you left. Last night she was at it again. That's why someone sent you this picture, right? Lance can't believe her gall."

"Right," Will said tentatively, afraid of where I was going with this. Good instinct.

"Any guy in his right mind would be outraged at her and think, 'Good riddance.' But you're devastated. You know what would do that to you? Finally having sex with her on your last night together. That's where people go wrong—*not* doing it for a long time, and putting so much emphasis on the act that when it finally occurs, it leaves you an emotional wreck. She probably wanted to do it for months, but you refused because she was a nice girl. She told you she wanted one special night with you, and then she would wait for you until you came back for college. Really it was her way of tricking you into sex and taking advantage of you."

"That's enough," he bit out. He held out his hand for his phone.

Feeling sheepish now, I gave it to him.

He pocketed it and picked up his drum.

I snagged mine by the harness and hurried back toward the drum line. Jimmy thought it was funny to speed up the beat until the band was practically running to their places rather than marching. That was going to annoy Ms. Nakamoto, who was probably nearing the end of her rope already. She would blame Will and threaten to give the drum captain responsibility back to me again. I started running myself, determined to prevent one tragedy today.

Will returned right after I did, taking over the marching rhythm from Jimmy. But the camaraderie between us was gone. He stayed utterly silent for the rest of the hour.

And I felt sorry for him. With only a little glimpse into his life back home, I could tell he was a nice guy. A hockey player and the drum captain, who had friends and a girlfriend. The friends he'd had and the titles he'd held were a big part of who he was. Rip him away from that and he wasn't even a nice guy anymore. Down here he was just an unknown hottie with no tan and a temper.

By the beginning of the third hour, I'd had enough. Will wandered away from me and sat on the grass. I spread my towel out right next to him and sat down. He stubbornly slid away. I picked up my towel again and moved it closer. He looked toward the press box, chin high in the air, but he bit his lip like he was trying not to laugh.

"What I said was way too personal," I whispered in his ear. If he'd been obsessing over our fight as I had been, he would know exactly what I was talking about. "I'm sorry. You said some personal things about me, and I pretended not to care when I really did, and then I jumped down your throat when you came to me for help."

He smiled with one corner of his mouth. "I'm sorry too. We've insulted each other a lot for two people who hardly know each other."

"We've also made out a lot for two people who hardly know each other. It all evens out. But we've got to find a way to make peace. Otherwise it's going to be a long year of standing next to each other. Almost as long as the last thirty minutes."

He gave me a bigger smile. "Agreed. Don't mention lutefisk again, okay?"

"I promise. I will also bathe from now on, or stand downwind of you." I tossed my hat onto the grass and pulled the hair bands off the ends of both braids, which probably looked like old rope on a shipwreck by now. I bent over to shake my hair out, then turned right side up again and started one French braid down my back by feel.

He watched me without speaking. When I finished, he said, "As long as you're tidying up, your shirt's buttoned wrong."

I looked down. Sure enough, one side hung longer than the other. "*You* did that," I accused him.

"What are you saying? That you want me to fix it?"

"If you dare."

He glanced over at Ms. Nakamoto, then at DeMarcus. He unbuttoned my top button and put it through the proper hole, then fixed the next button, periodically looking up to make sure he wasn't about to get expelled for molesting me one button at a time. He never rubbed me "accidentally" or undid more buttons than necessary at once, but the very act of letting him do this in public was enough to make chills race down my arms.

"I think we're sending each other mixed messages," he said.

"I think I've sent you a very clear message," I corrected him, "and you're choosing not to receive it."

His hands paused on the bottom button. "You mean you *do* like what I'm doing right now, but you *don't* want to date me."

"Date *anybody*," I fine-tuned that statement. "See? You *do* get it."

Ms. Nakamoto called through her microphone, "Mr. Matthews, take your hands off Ms. Cruz."

The whole band said with one voice, "Oooooh."

Will put up his hands like a criminal. This time, despite my shades, I could tell he was blushing.

Jimmy called from the next towel over, "At least Ms. Nakamoto knows your name now." Travis gave him a high five.

Will and I sat in companionable silence while the band lost interest in us. Ms. Nakamoto was making the trumpets into a square, which seemed fitting, knowing our trumpets. DeMarcus got into a shouting match with a trombone. A very stupid heron, even bigger than the egret from last night, landed near the tubas, and they followed it around. Out on the road past the stadium, a car cruised by with its windows open, blasting an old salsa tune by Tito Puente. Will absent-mindedly picked up his drumsticks and tapped out the complex rhythm, which he'd probably never heard before, striking the ground and his shoe in turn to create different tones, occasionally flipping a stick into the air and catching it without looking.

I hadn't thrown that challenge after all. He really was a better drummer than me.

"Can I ask you something?" His voice startled me out of the lull of the hot morning.

We were trying to be nice to each other, so I refrained from saying, *You just did.* And I braced for him to probe me about my aversion to dating. He didn't seem to want to let that go.

"There was a girl at the party last night named Angelica." He pointed across the field at her with a drumstick. "I saw her this morning. She's a majorette."

"You're kidding," I said.

"Shut up. I know you're making fun of me. She was with the drum major last night, but some of the cymbals told me they broke up afterward."

Wow. DeMarcus and Angelica had dated since the beginning of the summer. They'd texted each other constantly for the month DeMarcus had been in New York. I knew this because he would occasionally mention it online. And she'd broken up with him the first night he got back? I bet it was because he'd drunk a beer at Brody's party.

I could have told Will, *Better than her breaking up with him on the day he moves across the country, eh?* Instead I said diplomatically, "I hadn't heard that."

"My question is, were they really serious? Because if it was casual, I might ask her out. If they were serious, I wouldn't move in. I don't want people to hate me. Not my first week, anyway."

I had no skin in this game. But I wondered if he was playing me, to get back at me for turning him down last night, and saying what I'd said about his ex-girlfriend this morning. It didn't make sense that he would *really* be interested in both Angelica and me. The gap between the two of us could not be accounted for by the normal boundaries of taste.

So maybe he didn't *really* like *me*.

I told him the truth. I owed him that much, after the trials I'd put him through in the past twelve hours. "As far as I know, it was casual."

“Good,” he said, and then, “Thanks.”

We uttered hardly a word to each other for the rest of the time we sat together. The silence was as awkward as it had been before we made up, but this time it was because Will had designs on Angelica. I wasn’t sure why that would turn him cold to me. For my part, I wasn’t jealous, only disappointed that he had such poor taste in women besides me.

In the last hour of practice, gloriously, we got up, and the whole band played the opening number that we’d been marching through with only a drum tap all morning. I worked out my stress by playing a perfect rhythm, my beat fitting with the quad and bass and cymbal parts like pieces of a puzzle. During the pauses between run-throughs, I showed Will some of the tricks the snares had done at contests in the past, reaching over to play on each other’s drums during some passages, and tossing our sticks in the air, which was only effective visually if the freshmen didn’t drop them. Will taught me some even better tricks he knew from back home. We devised a plan to try some of these ideas in future practices and determine how well the worst players could handle them.

We’d joked around before, but now we were building solid mutual respect. Now we were friends.

Or so I thought. Then Ms. Nakamoto let us go for the morning, and Will didn’t even give me a proper good-bye. “See you at practice tonight,” he called over his shoulder as he made a beeline across the field to catch Angelica. Not wanting to witness their young love, I followed at a slower pace, saying hi to some girls in color guard and playfully threatening to bulldoze right over a mellophone player, snare drum first.

By the time I made it back to the band room to deposit my drum, word among the cymbals was that Will had asked Angelica to lunch. Lunch! I never heard of such a thing. He'd already whisked her off in his famous car. The way the other majorettes out in the parking lot were gossiping about them, Will and Angelica were an item already.

As I headed home, passing the majorettes on my way back to the fence, Chelsea said, "Wait a minute, Tia. I thought *you* were dating the new guy."

Still walking, eyes on the ground so I didn't step on glass in my bare feet, I told her, "That was yesterday." Not that I cared or that Will's date with Angelica was any of my business, because I didn't want a boyfriend. But some days this was hard to remember.

I snagged my flip-flops from where I'd left them on the wrong side of the fence. At home I grabbed a quick shower, which everybody would appreciate, and another pack of Pop-Tarts for lunch, then hopped on my bike to pedal to the antiques shop.

On the last day of school my sophomore year, I'd biked through the historic downtown, thinking that I needed a summer job. There'd been a HELP WANTED sign in the shop window. I'd walked in and applied. A job was a job, or so I'd thought. I never would have set foot in there if I'd known what I was getting into: Bob had cancer. When his treatments didn't agree with him, he needed time off from the shop, and Roger took care of him. I sat through a very stressful half hour while they explained this to me and asked me to work for them. I didn't want to take on that kind of responsibility. My aversion warred inside me against my desire to help them out and my blooming interest in the bizarre junk that cluttered their hideous store.

So I'd accepted the job. And I'd done whatever Bob and Roger asked me to do—a long list of responsibilities that had expanded over the past year and two summers to include inventory, bookkeeping, and payroll. When Bob took a turn for the worse, sometimes I got so stressed out that I cleaned and organized the shop. That just made them love me more, raise my pay, and load more responsibility on my shoulders. It was terrible. I didn't know how to get out of this vicious circle.

Today wasn't so bad. Bob was recovering from his last round of chemo, and he and Roger were both in the back office, so I wasn't technically in charge. I patted the shop dog for a few minutes, then took over manning the front counter from Smokin' Edwina. Almost as soon as I slid onto my stool behind the cash register, Kaye and Harper bopped in with a clanging of the antique Swiss cowbell on the door. I always welcomed a visit from friends, because it might make me look less responsible and more like a frivolous teen to Bob and Roger.

This time, though, I could have done without, because I

knew what my friends were there for. They wanted the scoop on Will. I would rather have done payroll.

They both stopped to pat the shop dog too. Everybody did. But when they straightened in front of the cash register with their arms folded, without so much as a "How you doing?" I amended their mission. They didn't want a scoop. They were there to scold me.

"You left with the new guy last night before we could stop you," Harper said. Admittedly, it didn't seem much like a scolding coming from a soft-spoken artist in retro glasses and a shift minidress straight out of the 1960s.

"You sent the new guy out to meet me," I protested. "If you hadn't done that, I might not have met him at the party at all."

"Was he still at your house when Aidan and I came by?" Kaye demanded. She wore her tank top and gym shorts from cheerleading practice, and her hair stuck out all over in cute twists. No matter how adorable she looked, though, she made a lecture sound like she meant it. "At the time I thought Will couldn't have been at your house. It was so late. But after the rumors I've heard this morning, I'm not so sure."

"What's wrong with him being there late?" I asked. "You and Aidan were still out then."

"We were on a *date*," Kaye said. "Girls are supposed to say yes to a date, then no to manhandling. You're not supposed to say yes to manhandling, then no to a date."

Ah, so that's what this was about. It had already gotten

around that I'd dumped Will at the end of the night. I needed to talk to him about revealing personal information to cymbals.

"First of all," I told Kaye, "*you* are not saying no to manhandling."

She uncrossed her arms and put her fists on her hips, cheerleader style. "That's different. Aidan and I have been dating for *three years*. You were manhandled by someone you knew for an hour."

More like two, by my estimate. "And second, I *want* the manhandling. I don't *want* the dating. That stuff is fake anyway. The guy is taking you on dates just so he can manhandle you later. You're not being honest with each other."

Kaye gaped at me. "Aidan and I have a *relationship* that is built on—"

"You know what?" Harper asked, sliding a hand onto Kaye's shoulder. "This is more confrontational than we talked about, and it's not productive." She flashed me a look through her glasses. We'd tried our best to support Kaye's relationship with Aidan. On paper it looked perfect. They were involved in a lot of the same activities, and they were neck and neck with a few more people for valedictorian. And we loved Kaye. We simply didn't like him.

"Tell us more about Will," Harper said. "He's *so hot*. Everybody stared at him as he walked through the party last night."

"That's because he's new," I lied.

"He seems kind of stuck up," Kaye said.

"Takes one to know one," I said.

"Hey!" Kaye stomped her athletic shoe in protest. The dog looked up at her reprovingly, like she had a lot of nerve, then settled back down.

Harper talked right over Kaye. "I heard he stands next to you in band."

"He does."

"I heard he took drum captain from you," Kaye said. "Did you throw it?"

"How could you accuse me of that?" I asked, looking her straight in the eye. "You and I had that talk recently about me taking personal responsibility. You speak and I listen."

Harper, heeding the signs that Kaye and I were about to lay into each other, switched the subject back to Will. "I heard that he took his shirt off during band, and he was very white and very built."

"He was wearing a drum harness," I said, "so I didn't notice."

Harper and Kaye muttered their disbelief. Because they were talking over each other, I couldn't hear everything they said, but I picked out "sunscreen" and "bullshit."

"But you probably got an eyeful last night," Kaye told me.

"Well, *somebody* got an eyeful of *somebody*," I admitted.

Kaye raised her eyebrows. Harper emitted a cute, embarrassed snort, wringing her hands as if the whole prospect worried her. "Is he like Sawyer?"

Girls at my school were captivated by Sawyer. He was fun

to watch. He was likely to fly off the handle at any moment. And when he chose to be, he was downright sultry. One time he'd talked dirty to me during an assembly in the high school auditorium, just for fun, in a way that made me want to rip my clothes off for him right there in front of Mr. Moxley and the championship tenth-grade robotics team.

But most girls wouldn't hook up with Sawyer, in the same way that they wouldn't hook up with a train wreck. That task was left to me. And Harper and Kaye didn't want *me* hooking up with him either. They'd gotten very upset the first time they'd caught me with him in a compromising position at a party. Kaye told me that if she ever found me with him again, she and Aidan would not be my designated drivers anymore, and I would have to ride home from parties with the trumpets, who listened to a lot of lite jazz.

Kaye and Harper had gotten used to the idea of Sawyer and me after a while, and now, frankly, they were fascinated by our relationship. Harper was more obvious in her enthusiasm. Kaye listened quietly to my Sawyer stories. That told me she was more interested than she wanted to let on, since she was used to asserting herself in student council meetings and was rarely quiet about anything.

"Will is like Sawyer," I said, "but better."

"Better!" Harper exclaimed. "Better how?"

Better in that I felt myself flush every time Will looked at me. Sawyer and I had agreed a long time ago that we were too much alike to have any real chemistry. That didn't stop us from making out when nobody else was available, of course, but it had kept us from trying for anything more than friends with bennies.

The thing was, I didn't *want* more than that out of a relationship with Sawyer. Or even with Will.

"Better . . . taller," I said. Sawyer had only half an inch on me. It wasn't often that I encountered a guy who made me feel downright dainty. I thought of Will looking down at me during band practice, and wondered again what he'd been thinking when I couldn't see his eyes behind his aviators.

"It doesn't matter, though," I said. "Will's out to lunch right now with old Angelica."

"Angelicaaaaaa!" Harper and Kaye moaned in despair. Once, in ninth-grade science class, they'd been passing a note back and forth about Kaye's crush on Aidan. Angelica, instead of passing it along the row like she was supposed to, had turned it in to the teacher, who had read it out loud. That had led to Aidan asking Kaye to homecoming. So the outcome could have been considered a good trade-off if you thought Aidan was a prize, which I didn't.

Or if you had not been completely mortified by the incident, which Kaye had. I could hear it in her voice still as she cried, "How could you let *Angelica* have Will?"

"It wouldn't have worked with Will and me," I told them honestly. "He would get as exasperated with me as you are right now."

They both opened their mouths to say awww, they weren't

exasperated with me (Harper), or they *were* exasperated with me but only because I consistently sold myself short (Kaye). I was saved by the cowbell on the door. After petting the shop dog, a customer asked to see the women's jeweled watches I'd posted to the shop's website. That was going to take a while because we had fourteen, which was why I'd been trying to move them out of inventory. I waved good-bye to Kaye and Harper and led the customer back to the display case, with the dog following.

And I tried to shake the uneasy feeling my friends had left me with. Will and I had shared an unwise night together. Okay. We'd had another argument this morning, yes. But we'd made up, and when things had gotten awkward between us again, that was probably because he was preoccupied with asking Angelica out. Things would be better tonight, and for the next three days of band practice. By the beginning of school on Friday, we would have no problem getting along in the drum line.

I honestly believed this, because I was not the best at foreseeing trouble and planning ahead. I had no idea our friendship was about to go south.

Five

BAND CAMP WENT OKAY AT FIRST. I HAD TEN times more fun with Will than I'd ever had standing between a past year's seniors. They'd taken their shirts off, all right, but they hadn't looked as good as Will did, or laughed like he did at my jokes. And they hadn't had an earring. I'd become a big advocate of the earring.

The thing about Will was, he took being drum captain *very* seriously, and he seemed determined to prove his worth to Ms. Nakamoto after his Monday-morning meltdown. A lot of drum lines I'd talked to, from high schools on the University of South Florida side of town, had student teachers as percussion instructors. Up here in our far corner, we were on our own. And that meant when the drums broke off from the rest of the band, Will ran rehearsal, with Ms. Nakamoto occasionally peeking her head into the palm-tree grove where we'd retreated for shade, making sure we hadn't all killed each other yet.

She would have been right to worry if I'd been in charge. I would have pulled out my braids the first hour I had to deal with these people. But Will was an amazing drum captain. Jimmy and Travis might give him a hard time when Ms. Nakamoto reprimanded him on the field, but they didn't cross him in drum sectionals. Maybe it was because he obviously knew what he was doing and cared that we got the music right. When the bass drums got tangled up in their complicated rhythms, he took the time to figure out exactly which sophomore was tripping them up and why, and he taught that guy a new, less confusing way to count off the measures. He was equally patient with the cymbals and their crashing-at-the-wrong-time issues.

More likely, nobody crossed him because he seemed so serious most of the time, with the worry line between his brows visible behind his shades. And that's what made it all the more delicious when I got a giggle out of him. Sometimes he looked like he wanted to shush me on the field when Ms. Nakamoto or DeMarcus frowned in our direction, but he couldn't shush me if he was too busy laughing.

Best of all, our friendship had stabilized. Will didn't hint about asking me out or being jealous of Sawyer. He was dating Angelica now. And I didn't worry too much about what he was *doing* with Angelica. With night practice lasting until ten, she probably didn't let him so much as come over to watch TV and feel her up, because she needed to be fresh for insulting other girls' outfit choices the next morning. They had only the afternoon to spend together, and how much trouble could anybody get into in the afternoon?

The one thing that bothered me about my week with Will was that we kept touching each other and getting in trouble for it with Ms. Nakamoto. The whole band turned around to stare at us when this happened, including Angelica with her arms crossed. It wasn't like we *meant* to touch each other. We just started talking about TV or music or, God, I don't know. We could make a joke out of anything. And then I pretended to sock him for something he said, and he grabbed me, and we were in trouble again.

Boys with girlfriends had propositioned me before. This made me uncomfortable. I had turned them down. I didn't want to feel like the mistress of a married man. But I wasn't Will's mistress. He wasn't married. This was just being friendly without fooling around. And if he did have some exclusive understanding with Angelica that he was not to touch other girls, that was his problem, not mine.

The only reason I felt uneasy was that I liked him so much. Every time he put his hands on me, I liked him more. This was dangerous.

As problems went, however, it was a happy one to have. I wasn't late to band again, because the minute practice was over I was pretty much dying to see Will again. But toward the end of the week, a couple of things happened to ruin my paradise.

First, at band practice on Thursday, instead of breaking at noon and then meeting up on the football field again at six, we reconvened on the beach at four. Attendance had already seemed pretty good at practice, and you could bet all hundred and eighty of us would be at a party. DeMarcus's dad grilled hamburgers and hot dogs for us. A lot of other parents brought delicious grub. Ms. Nakamoto laid down her whistle, donned a little white one-piece, and frolicked in the surf with her husband and her children like a real person.

As far as sexytimes went, there wasn't much new to see, because most of us had already taken off our clothes during band. But something about Will lying on a towel in the sand with his front to Angelica's back, both of them apparently asleep, got my blood boiling. Sure, for the past three days he'd sat on my towel in band with his shirt off, and I'd taken my shirt off too to show my bikini top underneath. The only differences between that scene and this one were that he was now wearing a bathing suit instead of shorts, she was wearing bikini bottoms instead of shorts, and they were lying like lovers.

Oh—and the girl by his side was Angelica, not me.

I sat with Chelsea on a big rock under palms, taking pics of the great view: the Gulf, the boats sailing in and out of the town's small harbor, and all the boys we claimed not to like *that way*. I didn't take a pic of Will, though. I couldn't believe Will voluntarily lay in the sunshine rather than the shade. His tan wasn't dark enough yet to protect him. And he definitely hadn't gotten used to the heat. Sometimes in band he seemed almost sick with it. He and Angelica must have lain down when that part of the beach was in shade. Now the sun had moved.

As I was steaming about this, I got a text from Sawyer, just a question mark. He was asking if I wanted to hook up after he got off work.

I texted back, "At marching band party, geeking out. Come crash. Great food. I will find you some vegan." I really did want to see him. I wanted Will to see me *with* him even more.

No such luck. Sawyer texted, "KILL ME NOW."

And a second later, when he realized that was a little mean, even for him, "Thx but no thx."

I plopped my phone down on my lap in frustration. I ordered Chelsea, "Go down there and tell old Angelica she has to get Will out of the sun. He doesn't understand that the five o'clock rays will still fry him."

"I'm not getting in the middle of this," Chelsea said.

"In the middle of what?" I asked innocently. But I felt myself blush at the idea that Will and I were in a messy love triangle.

"Besides," Chelsea said, "if that player fries, he deserves it."

"What?" I asked. "Will? Why is he a player?" My heart sank at the thought that he might have dropped Angelica off to go night-night after practice, but he had another girl on the side. This hadn't occurred to me.

Chelsea gasped. "He went home with you after Brody Larson's party, then dumped you for Angelica the next day, and now he's here feeling her up at the beach after he basically felt you up at band practice all morning! Don't you even care?"

I wasn't sure what she meant when she said he'd felt *me* up. True, at every practice, Ms. Nakamoto called through her microphone, "Mr. Matthews, get off Ms. Cruz." In fact, Jimmy had taken to looking at his phone and announcing the elapsed time between her reprimands—"One hour, forty-five minutes"—like we were going for a record. But in one of those instances, Will had been helping me adjust my snare harness. It only *looked* like he was molesting me. On another occasion, he caught me in a headlock, which I really enjoyed, after I mentioned lutefisk to see what he would do. So that was my fault. And several of those times, he was spreading sunscreen on my back at my request. Ms. Nakamoto simply didn't catch me when I was lotioning *him* up.

"He's cute, though," Chelsea said. "I look forward to seeing that around school this year. I'm not helping you, but, yeah, you should go warn him before he gets burned. Hey!" When she called out to DeMarcus, who was passing by, he helped her backward off the rock. They walked toward the open-air pavilion where the food was, abandoning me to carry out my own mission.

I scrambled down to the beach. But as I moseyed toward Will and Angelica, who were oblivious that I was about to disturb their romantic moment, I felt less and less like a friend aiming to avert a medical tragedy and more and more like a scheming bitch. Will was seventeen years old, and he could put on his own sunscreen. He couldn't reach his back, though.

And he didn't seem to have a lick of sense when it came to the Florida sun. I ought to let Angelica take care of him, but obviously she wasn't willing or able.

So I knelt in front of them—I knew I should not be doing this as I did it—and said in a low tone that spoke of my mature health concerns, "Angelica, you can't let Will get burned out here, no matter how much you're enjoying second base." I waited only until she sat up and scowled at me in outrage. Her movements jostled Will's sunglasses down on his nose. He opened one eye and frowned at me.

Mission accomplished. I walked down the beach and got drafted into a volleyball game, baritones versus tubas. They thought I would be good to have on the team because I was tall. By the time they figured out I *wasn't* good at volleyball, it was too late for them to kick me out. I ate until I was stuffed—I realized suddenly that I'd been living on Pop-Tarts for the entire week, now that I wasn't working at the Crab Lab and scarfing free food—and then lounged on the beach with my friends, swam, and got into a splash fight with Jimmy and Travis (which I won).

I had a lot of fun, like always. But the entire time, I was aware of where Will was, and what he was doing with Angelica. My scolding seemed to have shaken them out of sun-worshipper mode, and they secluded themselves on a shady bench. When the sun went down, they joined everyone in the pavilion. DeMarcus's parents had hauled in their huge TV and hooked up their dance-competition video game.

Dorks who didn't mind embarrassing themselves in public (including me) participated in the dance throwdown (which Chelsea won). Will and Angelica sat to one side, near a fan, close and still like a mature couple too lost in each other to have fun with anybody else—another reason never to have a boyfriend. I didn't envy Angelica if dating Will meant acting like they were already in the nursing home.

Yet despite everything else going on, I went over and over that scene in my mind, Will lying behind Angelica on the beach, her body folded into the sheltering curve of his body, his hand on her bare skin, and wondered what that had felt like.

Thank God they stayed until the end of the party. I suspected he took her straight home afterward.

Because Friday was a school day! And that was the second thing that shook me out of my comfort zone with Will. Homeroom was combined with first period, which for me was calculus, through no fault of my own. Years ago the principal and the teachers had conspired to keep me in the college-track classes no matter what I said or how little homework I turned in. At the back of the class sat Will, also not too much of a surprise now that I knew more about him. And just as on the first day of band camp, he looked completely different from the previous night. I walked through the door, headed for the desks, and actually exclaimed to the already half-full classroom, "Your eyes are blue!"

"And your eyes are a lovely shade of shit brown," DeMarcus

told Aidan, not missing a beat in their conversation.

"Shut up," I told them as I passed them in the row.

Will watched me as I approached, waiting for me to explain what was so astonishing about the color of his eyes. I'd never noticed in the five days I'd known him. His Minnesota Vikings baseball hat and aviator shades seemed like a part of him. But when I saw that devastatingly handsome guy with intense blue eyes staring back at me—that's when I realized what I'd been missing.

I slid into the desk behind him, then shrugged helplessly. "I've only seen you from a distance, or wearing your sunglasses, or in the dark."

"In the dark, huh?" asked Brody, across the row from me. "Yeah, that's what I heard happened after my party."

"Do you mind?" I asked him.

But when I turned back to Will, he gave me a small smile like the interruption didn't faze him. He leaned over the desktop between us and squinted at me. I'd thought from the beginning how adorable he was when he squinted. Coupled with the blue eyes, the look made my heart flutter. He said, "Your eyes are so dark, I can't see your pupils. Do you even *have* pupils?"

"Yes, or I wouldn't be able to see," I said, because when I was under pressure, I was nothing but romantic. In my defense, his own comment about my invisible pupils was the kind of pickup line you'd hear at a sci-fi convention. Or possibly he wasn't *trying* to sound romantic, because *he had a girlfriend.*

As if sent to remind us of this fact, Chelsea walked in, calling, "Uh-uh, not during school. Break it up, you two. Keep it classy."

We both straightened the slightest bit—knowing she was right, but not wanting to give in to her teasing, either. And I wasn't done with Will. "Your hair," I said quietly, reaching out to finger the back of it, which was gone. All the bad-ass length of it had been cut short. Yet he retained that look of dangerous energy, possibly because there was no hiding his earring now. He watched me with such an intense expression that I hardly dared touch him. But of course I did, running my fingers up his shorn nape. "Oh my God, you weren't kidding on the field," I said. "You *were* hot!"

"Let me tell you something, Tia," he deadpanned. "I'm *still* hot."

I threw back my head and cackled at that, not really caring who heard me, because now it was close to time for the bell, and the room was crowded and loud.

When I collected myself and grinned at him again, he was grinning at me, too, and doing that cute squint. "I didn't want to cut it. I just hated the thought of band practice today. Mornings and nights were bad enough, but from two to three in the afternoon? It's going to be so hot out there."

"Like an ahffen!" I exclaimed.

Before I could back away, he'd pushed me to the side of my seat and bent me over in the aisle with his arm around my neck—gently but very firmly. He growled in my ear,

"Every time you make fun of the way I talk, you're going in a headlock."

"Do you promise?" Admittedly, catching a girl in a headlock was less something he would do to Angelica or his beautiful, treacherous girlfriend back home, and more something he would do to one of his little sisters. But his arm was around my neck, his breath was in my ear, and I was very aware that this was the most fun I would have the whole school day, until band last period.

"Mr. Matthews, get off Ms. Cruz," DeMarcus called through a rolled-up sheet of paper in an excellent imitation of Ms. Nakamoto.

Will released me. I sat up and flipped my braids back over my shoulders like nothing had happened. "Who cut your hair so fast?" I asked. "Did you let your sisters go at it with Barbie scissors?"

He put both hands on the back of his head in horror. "Does it look that bad?"

"No," I promised him. "I have to stare at you for an hour a day. Two hours, if Ms. Reynolds lets me stay in this desk. When you start falling down on the job, I'll let you know."

He put his hands down. "I was driving to school this morning and stopped in at a shop downtown that opened at seven."

"That was my sister Izzy!" I said with more enthusiasm than I'd felt about her in three or four years.

He pointed at me. "I *thought* . . . well, I did and I didn't. You look a lot alike, but you're completely different."

I nodded. Izzy wasn't funny.

"Are you two close? You've never mentioned her."

"We used to be, a long time ago. I have three older sisters, and all of us were close when they lived at home. They've moved out, though. And I had an argument with Izzy at the beginning of the summer. I stopped in the shop and asked if she needed help taking care of her kids on my nights off from the Crab Lab—"

"Kids?" Will asked. "How old is she?"

"Twenty-two." I glossed over his real question, which was *How old was she the* first *time she got pregnant?* Because the answer was *Younger than me.* "Anyway," I said, "she laughed at me. Admittedly, I'm the last person in the world anybody would want to take care of their kids, but if I offer to help, I don't want to be laughed at."

He frowned. "And then what?"

"And then nothing. I haven't seen her since then."

"Even though you worked just down the street from her all summer?" When I nodded, he said, "Wow, that's some chip on your shoulder."

Yeah, I guessed it was.

The bell rang to start first period. As it clanged, instead of facing the front, he reached across my desk to cover my hand with his. "Have a good senior year, Tia."

"Awww!" I said, a bit mortified that I seemed so pitiful and needed this boost, but also touched that he would think of lifting me up this way, when he was the one who'd moved clear across the country and had to start over. "You too."

As he turned around, Ms. Reynolds was already passing out write-in ballots for the Senior Superlatives elections. Mostly I filled in the names of my friends according to the titles I figured they wanted, until I got to Most Academic. There I jotted my own name on the female side, because I knew I wouldn't get it, and I didn't want old Angelica to have it.

At the last second I felt bad about this. The little egghead deserved (and probably coveted) that title. If the tally was close, my throwaway vote could have denied her dream, all because I was bitter about her boyfriend, whom I myself had turned down. But by the time I made a move to snatch back my ballot, Will had put it on the bottom and passed the stack to the guy in front of him.

His was on top, completely blank. I'd tried to tutor him on who was who in the senior class, but not everybody remembered stuff the first time they heard it like I did. I doubted he knew anybody's full name except mine.

We didn't get another chance to talk during class. As I'd suspected, he was one of those people who actually did calculus during calculus. But I also had AP history and AP English and study hall/lunch with him. Angelica didn't. I hung out with him during those periods so that he had a friend.

In my classes without him, and while traveling the halls, I heard girls talking about how hot he was, and how stuck up. It didn't help that he had a Yankee accent people couldn't quite place, like an elderly snowbird. When I heard them talking behind his back, I tried to help him out by explaining that he was from Minnesota. This elicited moans of "Minne*soooooooo*da!" which did nothing for his popularity.

It also didn't help that he had his eyes on his phone all the time. And since Angelica didn't have her eyes on hers, I figured he wasn't anxiously awaiting her texts. He was probably obsessively checking his friends' photos for more evidence of his ex gallivanting with his so-called best friend. But he'd told me about that disaster in confidence. It wasn't my info to share. And if he hadn't shared it with Angelica, I didn't know what it would do to their relationship when she found out that she was the rebound girl. I didn't like him dating her, but I wasn't going to sabotage it—at least, in a way that he would know about—and make my own relationship with him worse.

I knew about his ex and how lost and lonely he was, because I'd stood next to him in band camp. But he dropped plenty of other hints that he wasn't the prick everyone made him out to be. There was the dancing, for one thing. He might have seemed serious, but he was often dancing. Not flailing like a freshman at a teen club, mind you, but understatedly boogying to his own beat. It was the drummer in him. Anytime music came on—rap spilling out of a car outside the school, or pop blasting over the loudspeakers in the gym for a girls' PE class—he was part of it somehow. It might be his head or his toe or just one pointer finger tapping on his thigh, but he was beating out the music as if it was his own.

There was his shyness, for another thing. When someone

approached and spoke to him—someone besides me—his lips parted, but he stayed silent. A stricken look entered his blue eyes, and it took him five seconds longer than it would have taken most people without a speech impediment to come up with an answer. He wasn't stuck up. He just had a hard time meeting new people. Transferring to a new school must have been his nightmare. I was more sure than ever that, driven by fury at his ex, he'd been bluesing for a hookup when he bravely walked into Brody's party the first night.

Kaye and Harper tried to talk to him in the halls and commented to me later how hard he was to draw out. I felt like I needed to defend him more than ever. But I couldn't, not to them, because they'd think I still liked him despite not wanting a boyfriend, and then they would never leave me alone. The worst thing in the world would be for those two to decide to "help me through it." I couldn't stand to obsess about Will any more than I already did.

It pained me to know that my friends didn't like him. I'd tried and failed to help him fit in. But a sneaky part of me enjoyed knowing things about him that they didn't. I doubted his ex had noticed his fingers drumming on his desk to any little beat. Surely if she had, she would have waited for him to come home to Minnesota next May and never let him go. Angelica might have noticed, but I couldn't picture her appreciating his love for a beat the way I did. Only I understood him, and in some small way, in a tiny warped corner of my mind, that made him mine.

Six

"YOU'VE BEEN LYING TO ME," WILL SAID IN MY ear. A chill shot down my neck in the blazing afternoon.

I straightened and stared at him. We'd both been retrieving our drums from the trunk of his car. His 1970s Mustang gave away, yet again, that this uptight boy had a wild streak. Years of Minnesota winters had rusted the wheel wells like he'd been driving through acid, which was why he'd been able to afford the car, and why his parents had wanted him to leave it behind.

I had mixed feelings about the Mustang. I wished his dad had forbidden him to bring it. Then Angelica wouldn't have shown up in it to night band practice last Monday after their lunch date, waving languidly out the window like a homecoming queen on parade. But I was glad he had this car, because he parked it just outside the stadium. The trunk gave me the perfect place to stash my drum so I didn't have to lug it back and forth to the band room.

Now I tried to read his expression behind his shades. When he accused me of lying, my mind automatically shot to the fact that I liked him way more than I wanted to let on. Rather than melting under his stare into a pool of hysterical shame, however, I reached for my drum again and commented, "Yes, I have. Which lie do you mean, specifically?"

With an impatient huff, he reached into the trunk, too—it was shady in here, our heads were close together, and if it hadn't been a hundred and sixty degrees, it would have been a great place to make out—and he dragged out my drum and held it up for me so I could get my shoulders under the harness. "You've given me the impression, on purpose, that you're some free-spirited surfer girl who doesn't care about school or your future or much of anything at all."

Uh-oh. I had an idea where this was going, and I tried to spin the conversation in a different direction. "We don't have a lot of surfers," I pointed out. "The Gulf is too calm. You'd have to go to the Atlantic side of Florida for that."

"You know what I mean," he said. "You pretend to be an airheaded beach bum. If that were true, your friends should be stoners."

"Well—" I started to point out that Sawyer, though not someone I'd call a stoner because those people had absolutely nothing else to do, had been known to partake. But I wouldn't get Sawyer in trouble, even for the sake of a joke. And how well did I really know Will, anyway? Maybe old Angelica's tattletale ways had rubbed off on him.

As Will dragged his own drum out of the trunk, he was saying, "But your best friends are the photographer for the yearbook and the head cheerleader. Something doesn't compute."

"Oh," I said, relieved that was all he'd meant. I'd never thought about it, but Harper and Kaye and I did make an odd trio. "I'm friends with them because we were in gifted class together starting in elementary school." When he stared blankly at me, I explained, "At your school, maybe they called it enrichment class? Sawyer calls it the loser class." I held my fingers to my forehead in the shape of an L, Sawyer style.

I jumped as Will slammed his trunk. "That's just more fuel on the fire. I heard you're going to be a National Merit Scholar."

"Ha! That's what the guidance counselor *says*, based on my test scores. But I have to get a teacher to vouch for my dedication to academics." I poked him in the ribs with my drumstick as we entered the stream of the band flowing from the school into the stadium. I said more quietly so we wouldn't be overheard, "I took the PSAT last year. Fifteen minutes before I went in, I'd just had this huge fight with Jason Price. I'm sure you haven't met him yet."

"I heard about him." Will pointed one drumstick at me. "Stoner."

"Why, yes," I said, proud of Will for identifying someone in our class by first and last name after all.

"You dated him," Will said.

"Well, not *dated*," I said. "Why are you all over me for having winner friends if you also know I had a loser hookup?"

Will was giving me the look that people gave me whenever I purposely misled them and they lost track of what I was telling them and why. I didn't fool him for long, though. We carefully descended the stadium steps, glancing to the side of our drums so we could see our toes, the air growing hotter as we went. Finally we reached the grass, and he could concentrate on what I was saying rather than on whether he was about to tumble to his death. His brain caught up with my mouth, and he exclaimed in exasperation, "Because if the guidance counselor says you're going to be a National Merit Scholar, you must have made an almost perfect score on the PSAT!"

"Shhh!" I hissed, looking around to see who'd heard. "You'll ruin my reputation. See, I was stressed out about Jason, and when I'm stressed, I like to put things in order."

"But *only* when you're stressed." He must have been thinking of his glimpse inside my dark house.

"Obvs. I find multiple-choice tests soothing."

"That only makes sense if you know all the answers," he grumbled.

"Of course I know all the answers. I mean, I know them if I'm actually trying to figure them out. So, to make a long story short, I made an almost perfect score because the test caught me on a bad day."

"Are you talking about her PSAT score?" Kaye asked,

jogging over. The cheerleaders had practice on the football field last period, at the same time as the band. We used the middle of the field, they stayed on the sidelines, and we tried not to plow through their pyramids. Normally I would have hugged her hello, but she was about to say something to make this convo with Will worse, I could tell.

Sure enough, she volunteered, "Tia's an underachiever. She works very hard at it. One year she made a C in Spanish even though she's bilingual."

Will looked to me for verification.

I shrugged. "Just because I can speak it doesn't mean I can spell it." In Spanish I told Kaye to take her little cheerleader shoes and tumble on over to the sidelines and stay there.

In response, Kaye uttered the only Spanish curse I'd ever taught her, which really was not appropriate for this situation. But she ran across the field toward the other cheerleaders, tossing in a couple of handsprings and a layout as a *so there*. Good riddance. I turned back to Will and grinned like our pleasant small talk had been interrupted but now the children had left us alone again.

"You are incredibly dumb for a smart person," he said.

I laughed. "I've never denied this."

"You're just confirming, over and over, that you've been lying to me."

"I haven't," I insisted. I knew he was only teasing, but something about being called a liar, by Will, when I really hadn't meant to mislead him that first night, ticked me off.

"*You're* the one who's so closed minded that everything has to line up perfectly or it doesn't make sense. Why can't I be an underachiever? This is America. I can be anything I want. Besides, *you're* the one who lied to *me*. When we first met at Brody's party, I thought we were kindred spirits. You gave me the impression that you were a pirate, with your earring."

"Oh." Surprised, he put his hand to his earlobe like he'd forgotten all about his earring.

"I had no idea you turn in your homework," I said. "Traitor."

"You mistook me for something else, and that's the only reason . . ." As we reached our starting spot on the field and faced the home side, his voice trailed off, but his silence told me the rest of what he was thinking. All of it was true. Yes, I'd lured him home last Sunday night only because I thought he was a slacker like me. Yes, he'd ruined everything by being an upstanding Future Pharmacist of America. Yes.

He nodded as if accepting his fate. "So listen, I wanted to ask you something. It's *not* about a date."

I laughed to show him I wasn't uncomfortable that he'd read my mind. And then I kept laughing uncomfortably.

He talked over me. "I'm trying out for Spirit of Atlanta in late November. My parents promised me I could try out for drum corps this year, but that was when we lived in Minnesota and there were three corps right next door in Wisconsin. Now that Atlanta is the closest one, I wondered if you wanted to try out with me."

My heart was beating so hard it hurt. He'd said he wasn't

asking me for a date, but he was issuing me an invitation for something sweet, something kind, something I almost *wanted.*

Drum corps were basically marching bands with superpowers. They took only the best players from high school and college. They toured the country, competing against each other. It sounded like the perfect place for Will to pass the summer between high school and college—especially if most of it was spent bopping around the northern states, where he wouldn't overheat at eight a.m. I could tell from the way he talked so wistfully about it that this was one more thing he'd had to give up when he moved.

"I don't see what my PSAT score has to do with trying out for corps," I said.

Gathering his thoughts, he tapped his stick on my drumhead a few times. "When I met you, I thought you were a random person who randomly was an excellent drummer. Now I know you're an excellent drummer on purpose, the type of person who goes out for corps."

"You're wrong about me," I insisted. "You were right the first time. I'm random. When I succeed, that's the mistake."

"You make a lot of mistakes." He sounded hurt. I hoped we weren't going to have another silent practice like after we argued last Monday.

But he was only waiting for Jimmy, Travis, and the rest of the drummers to arrange themselves in line. When they'd passed, he said quietly, "It would be better to have a friend in corps than to go knowing absolutely nobody, don't you think?

Plus, you have to be there one weekend a month during the school year for practice, and my parents don't want me to make that seven-hour drive twice in one weekend by myself."

I turned to look at him. He wasn't the bad boy he'd seemed at first. Another admission that his mom wanted to keep him safe shouldn't have surprised me. But that just didn't jibe with the tall drummer in front of me, looking so serious with his hair cut short, his expression inscrutable behind his mirrored shades.

"What do you think?" he prompted me. "Would your dad let you spend the night in a car with me?"

He was kidding. This was exactly the kind of joke I ribbed him with constantly.

But I found myself speechless. I was imagining spending the night in Will's car with him. Driving through the night to Atlanta. Talking. Touching. Keeping each other awake behind the wheel.

Then I was thinking about my first night with him. How good he'd made me feel. How I'd decided that one night was enough. How wrong I'd been.

"Tia," he said.

I snapped, "My dad wouldn't notice."

Will's dark brows knitted behind his sunglasses, and that worry line appeared. "You should try out, then."

"I couldn't afford corps." This wasn't exactly true. My dad worked so much, and our house was in such a state of disrepair, that a lot of my friends assumed we must be at the brink of bankruptcy. We weren't. But my dad *was* very tight with our savings. He'd had to support Izzy and Sophia and their kids for a while. Violet hadn't gotten knocked up and abandoned yet, but we figured she would. By now we both expected the worst.

For that matter, I could have paid for corps myself. I'd saved a lot working two jobs. But saying no to Will was a foregone conclusion. I wanted to get involved with him, but I just couldn't do that to myself. I knew what would happen next.

Will had an answer for everything. "It's expensive, but you could apply for a scholarship, or you could get some business in town to sponsor you."

A business like the antiques shop, I thought grimly as I pulled my vibrating phone out of my pocket and glanced at the screen. I used to answer every time Bob and Roger called, because I was afraid Bob had taken a turn for the worse. But lately they'd started calling me about the *shop*, of all things—where the vintage handbags were on the network of shelves, and how to access the catalog of sterling flatware I'd set up in their computer so they *wouldn't have to call me*.

As I slipped my phone back into my pocket, unanswered, Will was saying, "I mean, corps isn't for everyone. Don't let me talk you into it if you're not a fan."

"No, I love corps," I said. "People complain about traveling the whole summer, eating peanut butter sandwiches three meals a day, and sleeping on school gym floors all over the country, but that sounds fun to me. And not too far removed from my current life. I always wanted to try out."

He moved his drumsticks apart, a drummer's version of spreading his hands to shrug. "Why didn't you?"

"I figured I wouldn't make it." A half truth this time. I had a lot of confidence in my ability as a drummer, because I'd listened carefully and compared myself to other players when our band went to games or contests. But I had no confidence in my ability to lead a section or arrive at practice on time. God only knew what I'd be getting myself into in an organization that was actually rigorous.

"You would make it." He looked sidelong at me beneath his shades. "But maybe you don't want to chance getting stuck next to me again."

The highlight of my day, even a fun first day of school like this, was standing next to Will. But I brushed him off. "Maybe *you* don't want to chance getting stuck next to *me* again, and you regret bringing it up."

He shut me down. "Nope. So let's make it official. Will you drive to Atlanta with me for tryouts in November?"

The last thing I wanted was to have a real conversation with Will in which we confronted our issues. But he was watching me with his brows raised behind his shades, which I interpreted as hope in his eyes. Just like Sunday night all over again. I knew he would keep bringing up the idea and I would continue to string him along to avoid either committing to him or disappointing him, unless I went ahead and cut him off. I said, "You think you've got me all figured out, but you're way off the mark. I don't do stuff like that."

"Stuff like what?"

"Stuff requiring effort." As I said this, I turned away from Will. DeMarcus motioned to call the band to order and open practice. It was the drum captain's job to play a short riff that the rest of the drum line echoed, snapping the whole band to attention. I did the job this time, startling Will.

The entire band went completely still, except for Will, who really had gotten caught off guard. He eased his head forward and slowly folded his sticks on top of his drum in our attention position so he wouldn't get in trouble for failing to keep his eyes up front.

The whole standing-at-attention thing was just a little game we played for a few seconds at the beginning of band sometimes. It was a tool Ms. Nakamoto used to make us listen to her if she couldn't convince the trumpets to shut up otherwise. Usually it bored me to death. Today I heard the cars swishing by on the street outside the stadium, the cries of seagulls gliding overhead, a breeze through the palms that definitely didn't make it down to the bottom of the bowl we were standing in, the tiniest tap as Will finally set his sticks down on his drumhead, and his long sigh. Maybe he sighed with relief that he hadn't gotten caught. I was afraid he sighed with frustration that I was playing impossible to get.

Most boys who pursued me stopped trying eventually, frustrated. I would miss Will. I hoped he wouldn't stop trying for a while.

Of course . . . he had already, when he asked out Angelica.

Funny, even though I could see her from where I was standing, way up near the home bleachers in the majorette version of standing at attention with her toe pointed and two batons crossed on her hip, I'd forgotten all about her when Will stood so close.

"At ease," DeMarcus hollered. "At ease" didn't mean "collapse," but that's what happened. The tubas and drums slid their instruments off their shoulders and dumped them on the ground. While Ms. Nakamoto told us through her microphone what we'd be rehearsing for the next hour, Will took off his harness, handed me his hat and shades, then pulled his shirt over his head, just like in every other practice this week.

Much as I wanted to see this, I told him quietly, "You can't take your shirt off."

"Yes, I can," he said through the material. "Watch, it's stretchy."

"No, I mean . . . ," I said to his naked torso.

I stopped and just watched him. This was the hottest thing I'd ever seen at school. His paleness had mellowed into a gentle tan that would protect him from the sun, and his strong build gave him the look of a proud lifeguard. He took his hat and shades back from me. The lenses reflected the palm trees behind me.

"Not during school hours," I managed. "It's against the dress code."

"Suddenly you care about the rules." He cracked a lopsided grin at me, twirling his shirt cheekily in one hand.

"Mr. Matthews," Ms. Nakamoto called through her microphone. "Put your shirt on. We don't allow students to break the dress code when school is in session."

I started to taunt him but thought better of it. He really might be upset that he'd gotten in trouble, and for something so silly.

Just as I was thinking this, he roared back at Ms. Nakamoto across the field, "It's. Three. Thousand. Degrees!"

"Mr. Ma-*tthews*?" Ms. Nakamoto's tone had changed to the one I'd heard her use only on me, last year, when I overslept and made all four buses half an hour late leaving for a contest in Miami.

"He's doing it," I called to placate her. I held out my hands and snapped my fingers for his hat and shades.

He gave heaven a sour look for a second, then obediently passed me his cap and sunglasses again while he pulled on his shirt. Then he took his hat and shades back. From the side, I could see he'd closed his eyes behind the lenses as he inhaled a long, calming breath through his nose.

With Ms. Nakamoto issuing clipped instructions through her microphone, I whispered to Will, "What are you thinking about? Revenge?"

"Snow."

Ms. Nakamoto drilled us for most of practice, so we didn't get to chat. We played and marched through the opening number probably eleven times. In the pauses between, while Ms. Nakamoto stood way up in the stands with DeMarcus and they pointed at the lopsided loops in the formation (not our problem; drums stood in rows), we watched Sawyer working the field in his pelican costume. It was impossible not to watch him.

Sawyer and I were good friends. I knew there was a lot more to him than being the screwed-up son of a felon. But I'd been just as astonished as everybody else when he tried out for school mascot last spring—and made it. He'd told me excitedly about the school paying for him to go to mascot camp a few weeks ago. He'd learned a ton, and he was over the moon the day the school handed him the mascot costume they'd ordered. The new pelican wasn't especially for him, of course. It was just time for a new one. The old pelican had been shedding faux feathers and looked like it had spent time in an inland pond and caught a disease that caused its beak to disintegrate. When the drum line had been bored in the stands at a lackluster football game last fall and feeling snarky, we'd taken to calling it the Pelican't.

This was our first time seeing Sawyer the New Pelican in action, and his hold on everyone's attention had very little to do with the bird's blinding whiteness. He performed an exaggerated version of the cheerleaders' chants and dances while standing right behind Kaye, and he wasn't dissuaded when Kaye frequently spun around and slapped him. His outfit was padded. Eventually he wandered over to bother the majorettes until Ms. Nakamoto called, "Mr. De Luca, remove yourself from the band, and keep your wings to yourself."

The band and the cheerleaders burst into laughter. Sawyer folded his wings and stomped his huge bird-feet back toward the cheerleaders in a huff. Chuckling, I said, "He's going to be good."

"Or dead," Will grumbled. "How does he wear that getup in this heat?" I could see why Will was concerned. Even in his shorts and tee, with his hair as short as Izzy could have cut it without shaving it, sweat dripped down his temple, and his cheeks gleamed with it.

"I told him not to put on the costume in practice during the heat of the day," I said. "He says he wants to get used to it so he doesn't pass out during a game."

"So you're seeing him again?" Will asked. "You didn't tell me that."

His question shocked me. He hadn't mentioned Sawyer, or sounded particularly jealous, since Monday.

No, I wasn't seeing Sawyer. That is, I'd never been *seeing* him in the way Will meant. And something about bantering with Will during practice had made me feel almost like I was seeing *him*, and going out with Sawyer would be cheating.

Of course, if that was true, Will was cheating on me every night with Angelica. And Will had no business thinking I should keep him updated on whether I was *seeing* Sawyer or not.

Logically I knew this. But Will and I were operating on a different plane from everybody around us, it seemed to me. He was in a relationship. He thought I was in a relationship.

We shouldn't have feelings for each other, but we did, and they were more important than anything else—at least when we were together.

"Um," I said as he tapped one stick lightly on the rim of his drum, nervous for my answer. Part of me wanted to tell him I *was* seeing Sawyer, just to give him a taste of what I'd felt like when he'd lain on the beach with his hand on Angelica.

The school bell rang through a speaker on the outside of the school, loud enough for us to hear across the parking lot and down in this hole. It was the signal for the end of the period and the beginning of announcements. The rest of the school sat in classrooms and listened to the principal go over test schedules, game schedules, and threats of *no more artificial sweetener for anyone* if students kept sprinkling Equal on the floor of the lunchroom and yelling "blizzard!" Though the announcements had never struck me as earth shattering, the principal thought they were so important that she typed them up and e-mailed them every afternoon to DeMarcus so he could read them to the band and cheerleaders (and insane school mascot) using Ms. Nakamoto's microphone. I explained this to Will, and we dumped our drums and harnesses onto the grass.

DeMarcus's reserved monotone was great for being the guy in charge of the band, but not so good for reading announcements. Bo-ring. In fact, though we were supposed to be paying attention, I thought we were veering toward dangerous territory where Will would ask me again whether I was seeing Sawyer. I preferred to let the question hang there, unanswered. That way, I wasn't telling a lie, but Will had to wonder about Sawyer and me.

So, to spice up the announcements a bit, I started translating them into Spanish in an even worse monotone than DeMarcus's. After an initial burst of laughter that made the cymbals turn around, Will pressed his lips together while I entertained him with the Telemundo version of soporific crap.

"That's all wrong," he said. "The Spanish I've learned has been super animated. I thought that was part of the language." He took a stab at the next announcement, enunciating it like an overenthusiastic thespian.

"You just mixed up 'swimming pool' with 'fish,' and 'swimmer' with 'matador,'" I informed him. "I'm glad you're not really announcing this, or people would be dressing very strangely for the swim meet tomorrow."

"That's it." He grabbed me and wrapped his arm around my shoulders, threatening the headlock.

"No fair!" I squealed. "The terms of the headlock are *very clear*. I did not mention lutefisk."

"Mr. Matthews, get off Ms. Cruz," Ms. Nakamoto called through the microphone. When Will stood me up straight, she was handing the microphone back to DeMarcus so he could finish the announcements.

Turning around on the towel he was sharing with a trombone, Jimmy tapped his watch and told Will and me, "Fifty-six minutes. Not a personal record, but a damned good time."

In answer, Will held one drumstick out beside him,

flipped it into the air so that it tumbled three or four times, and caught it without looking at it. This was his answer to pretty much everything drummers said to him that he didn't like, and it was effective at awing them into silence.

"How do you do that?" I asked. If he managed to escape back to Minnesota early and left me high and dry as drum captain, I could sure use a trick like that. I'd never awed anyone into silence in my life.

"Like this," he said, showing me his drumstick in his palm. I imitated him. "Now . . ." He raked his thumb under the stick and flipped it into the air. He caught it neatly. I tried it and accidentally launched the stick at his head. He caught that, too.

"Not quite," he laughed. "Look." He took my hand in his, pressed my stick into my palm, and showed me how to scoop the stick out and upward with my thumb. I wanted to learn this trick, really. All the warmth spreading across my cheeks had everything to do with excitement at learning a stunt, and the oppressive heat of the afternoon, and nothing to do with Will standing inches from me, his hands on mine.

"Oooooh," the band moaned loudly enough that I glanced up to see what the commotion was. The entire band, all hundred and eighty of them extending in lines and curlicues across the grass, turned around in one motion to stare at us.

At least, that was my first impression—that they were staring at both Will and me. Maybe DeMarcus had paused in his drone to hand the microphone to Ms. Nakamoto, who'd scolded Will and me for touching again, and we hadn't heard her over our own laughter. But DeMarcus was still reciting the announcements.

I hit on the answer. The band was staring at Will, not me. I still didn't know why, but I wasn't surprised anymore. People stared at Will a *lot*, even when he *was* wearing a shirt. I spent a good portion of my day trying not to do it myself.

No, that didn't seem right either. Girls might gaze longingly at Will as they passed him on the grass, but the whole band wouldn't turn around to say "Oooooh!" unless he'd gotten in trouble.

"What is it? I wasn't listening," I said to Will as a joke, because the fact that I hadn't been listening was pretty obvious.

"I don't know," he said, giving the band a suspicious once-over, "but they're still pointing at us."

At *me*, I thought. I glanced around the drum line to pinpoint someone I could ask, but everybody else had abandoned their drums to sit down with trumpets or clarinets who had towels to spread out. Will and I were the only ones left standing. Nobody was offering an explanation.

"Whatever it is," Will said, "it must be very good, or very bad." He mouthed a question to Angelica way across the field. It was probably my imagination, but I thought she turned away on purpose.

Maybe I would have better luck. I peered in the direction of Kaye and the group of cheerleaders huddled up front. Sure enough, she was waving her arms, trying to catch my attention, mouthing something. I read her lips. "Biggest fart," I said. "I let out the biggest fart? I am sure I did *not*. Only freshman trumpets have contests like that."

"I've got it," Will said. "Biggest Flirt."

"Oh!" I understood now. DeMarcus must be announcing the winners of the Senior Superlatives titles we'd voted on first thing that morning. In fact, he was calling out Most Athletic right now. And while I wasn't listening, I'd been elected Biggest Flirt. "I'm not sure I like this. It has a slut-shaming flavor, like they really wanted to give me Biggest Ho."

"No, Tia." The worry line formed between Will's brows as he explained, "We're *both* Biggest Flirts."

"You?" I laughed. "Why would anybody elect *you* Biggest Flirt?"

"Because of you!" Those bright blue eyes glared at me over his sunglasses.

I'd withstood the Florida heat for an hour with no problem, but suddenly I felt sweat break out on my forehead. Will had been chosen Biggest Flirt because of me? The school thought we were flirting with *each other*?

Well, if I was honest with myself—a twisting pain settled in the pit of my stomach, which was what I got for being honest with myself—I *had* been flirting with Will all week. I just hadn't known anybody had noticed. Except for Chelsea and Brody and DeMarcus. . . . The list got longer as I remembered all the people who'd asked me about Will in the past few days. For some reason I'd had the impression we were invisible here at the back of the field with the whole band turned the other way. Now I knew we'd been in a fishbowl for anyone to see.

Worst of all, Will had been elected Biggest Flirt too. I'd felt like I was only teasing him, but the school thought he'd been flirting back. That gave me a head rush. Will secretly liked me.

Or, he *had*. I could tell by the way he was looking up at the sky that he was angry. Angelica had turned her back on him because she didn't like her boyfriend being named Biggest Flirt with another girl. And that meant my delicious friendship with Will was about to come to a screeching halt.

Seven

STRANGELY, WILL SEEMED LESS CONCERNED about what Angelica would think, and more concerned about what his parents would think. With DeMarcus announcing Senior Superlatives titles in the background, Will told me, "You don't understand what a big deal this is. My parents are going to look through my yearbook next May and see I won Biggest Flirt. If they make friends and start talking to other parents, the rumor may get back to them even sooner."

"So?"

"So, I'm trying to convince them I'm responsible enough to drive up to Atlanta for drum corps in a couple of months, and to go to college in Minnesota like I always planned. They say the extra expense for out-of-state tuition has to be worth their while. In other words, I can't screw up or seem like I'm not serious about school. If I'd stayed in Minnesota, I would have been Most Academic."

"There's no way you would have gotten that here," I said.

"A lot of people are in the running for valedictorian, but Xavier Pilkington sewed up the title of Royal Nerdbait in third grade when he made a working dishwasher out of Legos."

"Right. I understand that. I don't belong here, and everything's already taken. So why couldn't I get no title, rather than Biggest Flirt? If the school puts that stuff on the Internet, my friends at home are going to see it."

"Your friends who cheated on you within two minutes of you leaving?"

He drew back from me and stood up straighter, looking down at me over his shades with astonishment and hurt in his blue eyes.

"Cheap shot," I admitted, "but you have taken on an accusatory tone. You're standing here blaming *me* when we *both* got elected Biggest Flirt. We achieved that honor together. It's like a guy blaming a girl for getting pregnant."

Instantly I was sorry. I'd blurted out my resentment from a fight Izzy had had with her ex a couple of years ago. Will already had a low enough opinion of me. I hadn't meant to make it worse.

His mouth flattened into a grim line. I thought he was going to yell at me.

Instead, he opened his arms and slid them around me, stepping forward until he was giving me a full-body hug. My ear pressed against his damp T-shirt. He was getting me sweaty. I didn't mind. I could hear his heartbeat thumping as the low notes of his voice vibrated in his chest. "I'm not blaming you," he said. "I'm sorry. I didn't mean to make you feel that way."

I allowed myself to stay in his arms, enjoying the way his body made mine feel, for three deep breaths before I started to back away.

"Mr.," Ms. Nakamoto said through the microphone, which she'd taken away from DeMarcus again, "Matthews."

Will put his hands up, a drumstick in each, in the pose he assumed at least once per practice.

Jimmy called from his towel, "Double header!"

Ms. Nakamoto gave the microphone back to DeMarcus, who resumed his slow recitation of the senior titles.

"Are you okay?" I asked Will. His eyes were closed behind his shades.

"It's so hot," he said. "I might vomit."

I glanced toward the sidelines. The lunchroom workers had already taken away the cooler of water they'd set out for us at the beginning of practice. "You don't have any water left?"

He tapped the plastic bottle in his back pocket, which made a hollow sound, and shook his head. A drop of sweat slid from his cheek, over his chin, and down his neck.

"Here," I said, trying not to sound alarmed. I handed him my own half-full bottle from my pocket.

"Thanks." I watched his throat working as he drank all of it in one long draw and tossed the bottle toward his drum on the grass. Then he pulled up the hem of his shirt to wipe his face. Glancing over at me, he said, "I'm okay."

"You worry me."

"I just get kind of dizzy sometimes," he said. "I feel like a dork."

"You *are* a dork," I said, "but not because of that."

He started toward me. I recognized his headlock stance by now.

"Mr. Matthews," I warned him in Ms. Nakamoto's voice.

"Kaye Gordon and Aidan O'Neill." DeMarcus's monotone had continued through the microphone all this time, but he caught my attention only when he mentioned my friend. "Most Likely to Succeed."

That was perfect! Or it would have been, if I'd liked Aidan. At any rate, I could tell *Kaye* was happy about it. She curtseyed, grinned, and gave everyone a two-handed wave like she'd just landed a perfect vault and won the Olympics for the US gymnastics team. I cheered and clapped for her along with everyone else.

One of my hands was jerked down from clapping by something large and fuzzy. I was being attacked by a killer stuffed animal. Glancing behind me, I saw it was Sawyer the Pelican. I stopped fighting him and relaxed my arm before he pulled it out of its socket.

Wrong move. He'd caught Will's arm too. I realized right before it happened that Sawyer was trying to make us hold hands.

I jerked my hand away and cried, "Stop!" because yelling in the middle of announcements was a great idea when I didn't want people staring at me anymore. At the same time, Will jerked *his* hand away, uttering an outraged "Hey!" His face was as red as a sunburn.

"Come on," I said to Sawyer's enormous bird head, which I assumed had an ear hole in it somewhere so he could hear me. "Will's already in trouble with the boss lady."

"Sawyer De Luca," DeMarcus droned.

Distracted from Will and me, thankfully, Sawyer put his weird, furry pelican hands up to his huge beak like he could hardly stand the suspense of what title he'd been given. Most School Spirit, of course. But if that had been his title, a girl would have been named along with him. He must have won an award we didn't give to girls because it would make them cry.

"Most Likely to Go to Jail," DeMarcus called.

"Oh!" I exclaimed. That was low. The title had seemed funny to me when it was a joke. It wasn't amusing anymore when the winner's dad had *actually* gone to jail.

I stopped feeling sorry for Sawyer when he grabbed both my drumsticks. I sighed in frustration and put my hands on my hips. I didn't want to be part of his act. Maybe another day, but not right now, when I felt so mortified that I was partially responsible for mortifying Will. "Give them to me," I told Sawyer.

He shook his huge head. His googly eyes gazed at me, but staring angrily at him did no good because I wasn't sure which part of the head he was actually looking out of.

Will stepped forward to intervene. "Back off, bird."

Good. If Will was defending me, he couldn't be *too* resentful.

Sawyer put one hand over his beak, like he was horrified, and used the other wing—with my drumsticks in that hand—to cover his bird crotch.

"I said *back* off," Will said, laughing, "not *jack* off."

Will was laughing! Now I felt even more relieved—until Sawyer put my drumsticks into his enormous bird beak.

"Oh, Sawyer," I sighed. Almost as if he'd anticipated being named Most Likely to Go to Jail, he'd been stealing things all period and slipping them into his beak—sunscreen, hats, cheerleader pompons so voluminous they didn't quite fit and hung over the edges of his mouth like he'd tried to swallow an octopus. When his victims finally convinced him to give their stuff back, he shoved his wing into his mouth, fished around in there, pulled out the possessions in question, and wiped them on his ample tail like they were covered in bird saliva before handing them back, pretend-wet. I didn't want this to happen to my new Vic Firth sticks. After purchasing them last spring and promptly losing them, I'd found them Tuesday night under my bed and brought them to practice. Will had been impressed. But everyone seemed powerless in the face of Sawyer's act, and I was no exception.

Apparently, Will *was* an exception. He leaped forward and put both hands around Sawyer's padded neck to choke him. This was a pretty funny sight because normally Will was taller than Sawyer, but Sawyer in the costume was taller than everyone. Will growled, "Cough them up, pelican." Sawyer shook his head stubbornly.

Will let him go. "Have you drunk any water since you've been out here? You've got to be dying in that getup."

Sawyer picked up the empty bottle Will had thrown down and tipped it up over his beak.

"That's awesome," I said. "Pantomiming hydration. Seriously, Sawyer, you've got to take your head off for water breaks."

"Harper Davis and Brody Larson," DeMarcus intoned.

DeMarcus had been reading on and on as Will and I argued with the world's largest bird, but at this announcement, Will looked at me in confusion. Sawyer scratched his bird head.

I'd given Will a few possible titles for Harper. And I'd told him Brody might be voted Most Athletic because of his football skills, or Most Likely to Die on a Dare because of the time he jumped from the top of the inflatable water slide on Fifth-Grade Play Day and had to go to the hospital. But Brody and Harper were so different from each other that I couldn't think of a single thing they *both* might have won. I could tell from Will's expression and Sawyer's pantomime that they were thinking this too.

"Perfect Couple That Never Was," DeMarcus said.

"What?" I exclaimed. "How bizarre." It was so strange for Harper to get paired romantically with a guy she probably had nothing in common with and hardly knew—especially when that guy already had a girlfriend, and Harper had a boyfriend.

"Almost as bizarre as the two of us getting voted Biggest Flirts." Will looked over at me, and the big grin he'd been wearing slowly faded.

I don't know what he saw in my face that made him regret his joke. I didn't have a crush on him, exactly. To me, a crush implied that I wished we would get together someday. I didn't wish this for Will and me. The only way we would ever hook up again was if we both got plastered at a party—which happened to me often enough, and likely never happened to Will.

But I did admire him. Long for him. Enjoy teasing him more than I'd ever enjoyed telling another uptight guy dirty jokes. He must have detected this with his Super X-Ray Tall Girl Vision, because his eyes shifted away. He opened his mouth to say something to get us out of this awkward conversation, but he must not have been able to think of anything and closed his mouth again.

Sawyer turned his bird head pointedly to Will, then just as pointedly to me.

"What?" I yelled at Sawyer. It was bad enough that Will was embarrassed to be associated with me. Having a huge bird exaggerate the situation made it worse.

Sawyer had told me before that he never talked in costume, which might have been the weirdest thing about his act, because when he wasn't wearing the bird getup, he never shut up. This time he didn't even pantomime a reaction to me shouting at him. He simply reached into his beak, pulled out my drumsticks, wiped the imaginary spit on his big bird ass, and handed them to me between two fingers like they were so gross that he was reluctant to touch them.

The field was full of noise and movement. DeMarcus must have finished the announcements. Most of the cheerleaders and the band moved toward the stadium exit, with a few trumpets playing runs, like anybody was going to be impressed. Those of us who'd ditched our heavier instruments during the announcements bent to pick them up now, Will and me included.

Normally this would be the time at the end of practice when Will and I would get in one last laugh for the road, some meta-analysis of the sorry excuse for a newscaster that was DeMarcus. But Will was very obviously keeping himself turned away from me as he hooked his snare onto his harness to carry it off the field. It was like we were having a sullen lovers' quarrel without the benefit of making out first.

Across the field, Kaye turned toward me. Anticipating her move, Sawyer had crept up behind her, if that was possible while wearing three-foot-long bird shoes, and stepped into her path. She ran right into his padded belly. "Ooof!" she cried. "Get out of my way, pelican!" Sawyer pumped her hand up and down, congratulating her on being named Most Likely to Succeed. When she didn't protest, he tried to put his wing around her. This time she shoved him away.

She walked toward me with her arms out for a hug. I put my arms out too. We couldn't really embrace because my drum stuck out in front of me like I was fifteen months pregnant, but we leaned around the obstruction and patted each other on the shoulder, then walked toward the stadium exit together.

"Congratulations, princess!" I sang. "I want to go down on record as the first person to ask you for money. I'll give you ten years to become a millionaire before I cash in, but I'm asking you in advance."

"So noted," she said, like we were in one of the club meetings she ran so well. "And congratulations to you!"

Despite myself, my gaze floated ahead of us to Will. Every band practice after the first, Angelica had waited for him, smiling brightly, at the gate separating the field from the stands. Today she frowned at him, hands on her hips.

I had mixed emotions about this. I could actually feel the emotions churning like a couple of different kinds of acid in my gut. If Angelica broke up with Will for being named Biggest Flirt, that would make him available for me again. But I'd already decided I didn't want him. It would be my fault if he lost his girlfriend, and I was afraid he wouldn't forgive me.

Dejected, I asked Kaye, "Congratulations for *what*?" I doubted she'd be happy for me, even in jest, for being elected Biggest Flirt. Not after her lecture at the antiques shop last Monday.

"For *not* getting elected Biggest Party Animal," she explained. "What if a college admissions board saw that when they looked you up online?"

"I beg your pardon," I said. "That's your neurosis, not

mine." I planned to go to college, eventually, when I got around to it, but not one with an admissions board that ran background checks through Homeland Security.

She stomped her petite cheerleader shoe in protest that I wasn't taking this seriously. "What about your dad? Your dad might have grounded you."

This was Kaye's vivid imagination. She was superimposing her own family life on mine. My dad would never find out what I'd been elected. I could have been voted Biggest Ho, or Greenest Teeth, and he wouldn't have noticed. And he couldn't very well ground me even if he wanted to, since he was either asleep or gone whenever I went out. Parents who made their kids stay home had to be home themselves.

"Dodged a bullet there," I said.

"Of course, getting elected Biggest Flirt with Will Matthews when he already has a girlfriend is pretty awkward too."

"Can it, would you?" I knew she was only teasing, but I wasn't in the mood. "You haven't given me helpful advice about boys since the sixth grade."

"Yeah. That was the last time you turned one down."

I glared at her and considered giving her a good whack with my drum, but we were on the stairs.

"I'm kidding!" she exclaimed. "Come on. You've cultivated this reputation yourself. You act like you're upset that you got the title."

"I just didn't think Will and I were attracting that much attention," I confessed. "We're friends, and we horse around, but I wouldn't have thought we would stick out to the whole school after four days of band camp."

"You're hard to miss," she said. "You're both six feet tall."

"We are not." I looked up at Will, who was cresting the stairs with tiny Angelica beside him. I was only five nine, which admittedly was tall for a girl, but not so tall for people in general. Will, on the other hand, had a good four inches on me, maybe more. I corrected myself: "*I* am not."

"The two of you are probably six feet tall on average," Kaye said as we reached the top of the stairs ourselves. Out in the parking lot, Will stood in front of the open trunk of his car, talking to Angelica. He leaned way down. She gave him a peck on the cheek. She flounced smiling across the melted asphalt, toward the band room. Obviously being elected Biggest Flirt hadn't hurt his relationship with Angelica after all.

He pulled off his T-shirt, rubbed it across his muscular chest and arms, and ducked into his trunk again for a dry one. He had a whole pile of them in there.

"Wow," Kaye said reverently.

"Yeah," I agreed.

"And we're heading over there," Kaye noticed, "when he's half-naked, his girlfriend just kissed him, and you and he were chosen Biggest Flirts together? This is messed up."

"He invited me to keep my drum in his trunk," I explained as we reached him. Considering our new title, I thought it might help to remind him that this storage option had been his idea, not mine.

"Oh," Will said, turning around with the fresh T-shirt in his hands. Glancing at Kaye and then back at me, he said, "You can't anymore, because of the flirting thing."

"Wait a minute." I didn't mean to raise my voice, especially not with Kaye standing there. But I felt baited and switched, so I lashed out. "I can understand why we shouldn't flirt anymore because of the title, but not why I can't leave my drum in your car. This is how it ends, after all our time together? What about the mortgage? What about the *kids*?"

His grim mouth slid to one side, like he was frustrated with me and also trying very hard not to laugh. I could hear shouts and slamming doors in the parking lot now that school was dismissed and people were getting in their cars and driving away. His blue eyes swept the area over my head, alert for anyone who might have overheard me and would *tell Angelica oh noes*.

My phone vibrated in my pocket. "Hold on," I told Will, exasperated with absolutely everybody. The shop was on the line, and I figured I'd better answer since I'd ignored their call a few minutes before. "Bob and Roger's Antiques," I said sarcastically. "How may I help you? *From band practice?*"

While Roger complained to me in one ear that Bob couldn't remember where he'd stored any of the Depression glass, I put my hand over the other ear and tried to shut out Will commenting to Kaye, "The shop calls her a *lot*."

"She's their golden child," Kaye explained.

"I don't know," I told Roger, because if I kept helping

him and Bob when they called me, they would me and appreciating my help, which would sur promotion and more responsibility.

Kaye was telling Will, "They have so much shit in that shop, they have no idea where it is or what's even in there. Lucky for them, Tia has a photographic memory."

Though Roger was still talking, I held the receiver away from my mouth while I told Kaye, "I do not." She'd said this before. I wasn't sure whether she was right. I never really put myself in that category or thought about my memory that way. More than being amazed with myself for remembering stuff, I got annoyed with other people for *not* remembering stuff.

She continued to recount the wonders of my brain to Will. Roger kept lamenting to me that Bob's memory was going—what was left of it, that is. Will flexed his thick triceps as he pulled his clean shirt over his head.

And Sawyer wandered over from the boys' locker room, his blond hair soaked from a shower, wearing a crisp yellow polo shirt and madras shorts, a lot like Aidan's preppie style except that Sawyer also wore flip-flops that looked like he'd walked around the world in them. He stuck his hand out to shake Will's. This could not be good. Alarm bells went off in my head. I was trying to get off the phone so I could intercede before something terrible happened, but I was too late.

He told Will, "Congratulations on being elected Biggest Flirt with my girl instead of yours."

Eight

"SAWYER!" I SNAPPED. I DIDN'T CATCH WHAT Will growled at him, but it must have been ugly, because Kaye's eyes widened. I told Roger, "I have got to go. I'll be there in half an hour anyway!" Hanging up on him, I told Sawyer, "Would you stop? All of this is getting blown completely out of proportion. It's just a dumb title. The *definition* of flirting is that it *isn't serious*."

"I'll tell you how it's defined." Sawyer pulled out his phone and typed on it with his thumbs. Kaye gamely looked over his shoulder, as though making things worse between Will and me was the most fun she'd had since her last pedicure. Irked, Will sat on his bumper and felt around in his trunk for his sunglasses without looking at me.

Reading his screen, Sawyer gasped dramatically and slapped his hand over his mouth.

I sighed with relief. The more horrified he acted, the less there was to be horrified about. That's how Sawyer worked.

"What does it say?" I asked drily, to get this over with.

"'Flirt,'" Sawyer read in the clipped tone of a fourth-grade know-it-all. "'To flick or jerk.' *Jerk?*" He opened his eyes wide at Will in mock outrage.

"That's not it," Kaye said. "There's another definition."

Sawyer went back to his screen. "'To make love' . . ." He gaped at Will and then me. "Dirty!"

"What?" It was Will's turn to sound outraged.

". . . 'playfully,'" Sawyer finished. "To make love playfully? According to this, you've been getting it on out on the football field, but it's all been in fun! Thank goodness. Not to worry. I can't imagine why Angelica is so pissed."

With a nervous glance at me, Will grumbled, "Give me that," and grabbed the phone from Sawyer. Peering at the screen, he said, "When they say 'make love,' they don't mean sex. They mean, you know, flirting. Playing around. They're using 'make love' that way because this definition was probably written in 1962, when people still wore hats." He handed the phone back to Sawyer.

"I guess that's what I get for downloading the free app instead of the one for a dollar ninety-nine," Sawyer said.

"You still haven't found the right definition," I said. "You're defining 'flirt' as a verb, 'to flirt,' but in the title Biggest Flirts, it's a noun."

"Always thinking, aren't you, Cruz?" Sawyer tapped his temple with one finger, then looked at his phone again. "'Flirt. Noun. A person who dallies with romantic partners, having no intention to commit.'" He pointed at Will. "That's you!"

Will pointed at me. "That's *you.*"

I pointed at Sawyer with one drumstick. "That's *you.*"

Sawyer pointed at Kaye, who wagged her finger and said, "I don't *think* so."

"Anyway," Sawyer said, pocketing his phone, "you're right, Tia. Angelica shouldn't be upset at *all* that her boyfriend is labeled as someone who's playing her."

"Could you guys let me talk to Tia alone?" Will's words were polite but clipped.

"Yes," Sawyer said, "but don't dally. Ha!"

Kaye rolled her eyes. Bumping fists with me, she put her arm around Sawyer and pointed him across the parking lot.

"Congrats on being Most Likely to Succeed," we heard him say. "Can I borrow some money?"

"Tia asked first," Kaye said. They walked toward Aidan, who sat on his front bumper, glowering at them, like he was annoyed with Kaye or Sawyer or both.

Join the club. I turned back to Will. "Sorry about that. You were saying? Angelica doesn't want my junk in your trunk?"

He gave me the lopsided smile I loved. "Look, from the time I left the field to the time I made it back to my car, four people called me a dog. Everybody thinks I've been flirting with you but dating Angelica."

"You *have* been flirting with me but dating Angelica."

"No." He shook his head emphatically. "I asked her to lunch on Monday. I wanted her to show me around town—you know, like I asked *you* to lunch first—"

I nodded with my eyebrows raised, acting like I was only politely interested, not hanging on every word about what he'd done (or not done) with Angelica.

"—but she didn't seem to know anything about this town, even though she said she's lived here all her life. I brought her back to band practice that evening, and except at other practices, I didn't see her again until the party last night."

"Where you placed your hand on her bare tummy," I reminded him.

He pointed at me. He looked strange doing this without a drumstick in his hand. "I sat down by myself, under a tree, because I had started to feel sick from the heat."

So my instincts *hadn't* been wrong. I wanted to find Chelsea right then and vindicate myself for being concerned about his health last night. "Were you in shade when you first sat down? And then the sun moved?"

"Yes! I'm not stupid."

"Why didn't you go in the water to cool off?" Really, he was going to die here before he made it back to Minnesota.

"It was sunny in the water. So, Angelica sat down with me. We talked for a while, and then I lay down and closed my eyes, just hoping I'd feel better if I rested for a little bit. The next thing I knew, you were waking me up."

"With your hand on her bare tummy," I repeated.

"She must have pulled my arm around her," he said.

I gave him a slow, assessing look, letting him know I was not born yesterday.

"I don't care whether you believe me or not," he said lightly. "*You* won't go out with *me*, remember?"

Tingles spread across my face and chest, and I stepped a little closer to him. He hadn't given up on me in favor of Angelica after all. But something didn't make sense. "No, you hung out with her for the rest of the night."

"Because I've been following *you* around like a puppy all week. It's embarrassing."

"Oh." In my defense, I really had assumed he was dating Angelica. But now I saw what I'd been putting him through. I was his best friend in town, yet I'd made it clear I didn't want to hang out with him any more than necessary. That had to be a blow to the new guy's ego.

"I shouldn't have hung out with her, either," he said, "because she assumed what everybody else assumed, that she and I would go out a second time. She confronted me down on the field just now and told me she wasn't going to date me again if I kept flirting with you. On Monday, when she asked me about you, I said we stand right next to each other throughout band practice, and we're friends. Just friends. I guess that made sense to her then."

I guessed not, judging from the way she'd glared across the field at me. "Right," I said.

"But this label changes everything," he said. "The whole senior class is basically telling her that I'm a liar. Now they'll be watching you and me. It's like being accused of a crime. Even if you're proven innocent, people always suspect you when a wallet goes missing."

I was one hundred percent sure that this analogy had nothing to do with Will's real life. Of *course* this nice boy (in his own mind, at least) would never be accused of stealing a wallet. And of *course* he hadn't meant to flirt with me. He had no feelings for me. It was all a big misunderstanding.

"I finally asked her out on a date," he said. "Tonight. And that means you can't keep your drum in my car anymore."

Suddenly the sun was bothering *me*. I wished he would move over and make room for me in the shade of his trunk. "It kind of sounds like you wouldn't have asked her out again if we hadn't been elected to this stupid title."

"This stupid title is all anybody here knows about me," he said. "I'm the asshole who took Angelica out and flirted with you. Well, now I'm not going to flirt with you, and I'm going to make it up to her."

"What for?" I burst out. "Is this another one of those things you need to prove to your parents so they'll let you out of the nest? You're supposed to be elected Most Academic and have a steady girlfriend?"

"That's enough," he said sharply, just as he had when I'd jabbed at him about his Minnesota ex on Monday.

I felt my face turn beet red. The sun was burning a hole through the back of my neck.

He stood, turned around, and dragged my backpack out of his trunk. "Look," he said more gently, "this is a record for me. I've lost three girls in one week. It's too much." He tried to slip the backpack onto my back for me. I kept my arms stubbornly by my sides. He pried one arm up and then the other, which would have looked *suspiciously like flirting* if anybody in the parking lot had been watching. Then he attempted to hand me my purse. I wouldn't take it. He plopped it onto my drum. The snares rattled. The noise echoed against the wall of the stadium.

"All this is really heavy," I whined. Seriously, the drum weighed twenty pounds. My purse on top of it weighed a lot too. I rarely cleaned it out, and God only knew what was in there. My backpack actually had books in it today. On a whim I'd thought it might be fun to do something unusual this weekend: homework. I poked out my bottom lip, fluttered my eyelashes, and asked Will, "Could you give me a ride over to the band room?"

He just stared at me without laughing this time, without twisting his mouth to keep from laughing. The joke was over. "See you Monday."

Fine. I whirled around—he dodged at the last second so I didn't whack him in the gut with the drum—and I walked through the parking lot, picking spaces to pass through that cars had already pulled out of, because the drum and I were too wide to edge through the path between two parked cars. We would have taken off some paint.

Harper waited for me behind the school, already astride her bike. She could use her granddad's car whenever she wanted, and she drove me to school on the rare occasions when it rained. The rest of the time, she biked. *Voluntarily.*

She said it helped her feel more a part of the community. Harper was kind of a kook.

"Hey!" she called. "You told me you were keeping your stuff in Will's car. Why do you still have your drum?"

"He kicked me out of his trunk. I've got to dump this in the band room, but I'll just be a sec." I dropped my purse and backpack beside my bike in the rack, then walked through the entrance of the school, into a courtyard full of palm trees where people hung out during midmorning break and lunch. This was a bad design on the school's part, because the courtyard was walled in by classrooms with windows that definitely were not soundproof. Teachers let us escape out here, then shushed us constantly. It was like standing next to Will in band.

All the frustration of the last thirty minutes—or the last week, more like it—hit me suddenly. I felt an uncontrollable urge to make some noise. Marching through the courtyard, I tapped out a complicated salsa beat while singing a Marc Anthony tune at the top of my lungs. He was born in New York City and was about as Puerto Rican as I was, but the dude could really write a salsa. And though drumming was second nature to me after years of practice, when I really listened to myself, I was surprised at how good I was and how fast my sticks could strike the drumhead.

I saw movement behind one of the windows. Though school was out, the teachers were still here, planning our demise for Monday. They wanted *quiet*. In the next second someone would slam open a window and tell me to be *quiet*.

Until that happened, I beat my drum as loudly as I could, even threw in some rim taps that would take the skin off an unprotected ear canal. As I backed through the band room door, I saw Harper had stopped her bike a few yards away. She frowned at me with both hands over her ears.

"Sorry," I said. Feeling a little better, I dumped my drum into the storage room and came back outside. "So, what's this I hear about you being the perfect couple with Brody Larson? You're both dating other people, and you hardly know him. You move fast, don't you? Slut."

"Shut it." She removed one of her hands from the side of her head and placed it over my mouth. Then, as I walked through the courtyard to retrieve my own bike, she pedaled beside me. "The artistic side of me says, 'How cool and random for a boy I hardly know, some jock who isn't on the yearbook staff or the newspaper staff or even in the drama club, to be chosen as my perfect boyfriend!' The artistic side of me wants to write a poem about it. Meanwhile, the rational side of me is saying, 'What the fuck?' Also, 'His girlfriend is going to kick my ass.'"

"I'm not rational at all," I pointed out as though this were not obvious, "and I'm saying 'What the fuck?' also. But the difference between you and me is, the second he and Grace broke up—and this is probably going to happen, because Brody never dates anyone for long—I would try to hook up with him just out of curiosity."

"You're forgetting Kennedy," Harper said.

I was *not* forgetting her boyfriend, Kennedy. I simply thought if her choice was between responsible Kennedy and wild Brody, there was no contest. Bring on the hot mess! But that was me, and Harper was Harper. I figured I'd better let the subject drop before I got myself in trouble.

As we emerged from the courtyard again, I gazed across the parking lot, which was almost empty of students' cars now. Of course Will had *not* waited to watch me emerge from the school so he could rush over and apologize. His car was gone. He'd probably picked up old Angelica on his way off campus. I bet she'd slipped her little hand in his before they even passed the HOME OF THE PELICANS sign.

"Worry about your own mismatched boy," Harper said. "Tell me what happened between you and Will. You were elected Biggest Flirts, and that's why he kicked you out of his trunk?"

"Yes! He broke up with me!" As I unlocked my bike from the rack and launched myself down the palm-lined street, I told her all about my argument with Will.

"Let me get this straight," she said. "You want him to like you enough that he doesn't ask anyone else out, even though you've turned him down because you don't want a boyfriend."

"Correct."

"That's just selfish of you."

"I agree."

"You're not a selfish person."

"Apparently Will's my downfall."

"But . . ." Harper pondered this for a couple of blocks before finally asking, "Don't you think it might be worth considering bending your no-boyfriend rule for Will? People at school are talking about you two a *lot*. It's hard to believe this is just a passing hookup."

"A past hookup," I clarified. "I'm sure he wouldn't even take me back now. He wants exactly what he has. Angelica is a tiny blond girl. I'm a gangly *puertorriqueña*." We'd reached a row of shops where we had to get off the sidewalk and stick to a narrow bike lane. I shot ahead of Harper, trying to escape this discussion.

"Tia," Harper called, "that's just weird. If Will has a problem with you being part Puerto Rican, you don't want him anyway."

"I *don't* want him anyway," I threw over my shoulder.

"And you're not gangly. You're tall, which would be an asset on the modeling runway."

"I am not on the modeling runway, however. I am riding a bike through suburban Tampa/St. Petersburg, and my knees are touching my ears." As I pedaled, I bent my head to try to make this happen. I swerved dangerously toward the comic book store we were riding past and straightened just in time to avoid crashing through the window and shocking the nerds.

Harper was laughing her ass off behind me. "I promise you're not gangly. To be considered gangly, you would have to walk funny. In that case, Kaye would have shown up at your house before now to conduct an intervention."

We talked about Kaye then. Harper hadn't seen her after school. I told Harper how happy Kaye had seemed at being elected Most Likely to Succeed along with Aidan—as if either of them needed to be reassured.

Harper asked me how closely I'd listened to the announcements. She said she was taking the Senior Superlatives photographs for the yearbook starting Monday morning, and Will and I should meet her in the courtyard right at the beginning of second period.

News to me. I wondered whether I should call Will to pass along the information. This would violate our new pact to cool it. Angelica would interpret *phone call* as *hot sex* and Will would hate me. No, I would not call him. I could go into the yearbook under the heading Biggest Flirt by myself.

As we approached the antiques store, Harper waved and said brightly, "Ta! See you Monday," as though the coming photo session sounded like good times.

"Ta." I didn't want her to look back and see me watching her mournfully. I locked my bike in the rack and went into the shop.

When we'd first started riding our bikes together, and I'd been headed home instead of to work, I'd always begged Harper to come inside with me—if she would be very, very quiet and not wake my dad—or I would suggest we hang out at her mom's bed and breakfast. She'd explained that I was an extrovert, and extroverts got their energy from being around other people. She was an introvert, and introverts got their energy from being by themselves. She needed to go home, be by herself, and work on her photography project of the moment so that the next time we saw each other, she would have more energy to give me. This scenario made me sound like an alien sucking her brains out through a straw, but it also kind of made sense. It explained why, now that my sisters had moved out and my dad was always at work or asleep, I felt so down at home. But that knowledge wouldn't do anything to fix a long, lonely weekend.

Luckily I was super busy at work, dealing with customers while simultaneously finding things in inventory for Bob and trying to explain to Roger how computers worked. Three hours flew by. Then we closed, and I was out on the sidewalk again, unlocking my bike. I gazed down the street at the salon where Izzy worked. I could forgive her, I supposed, for what she'd said to me months ago about watching her kids. But Izzy could be harsh, and the idea of her saying something else snide was enough to keep me away. Besides, if she'd been at work to cut Will's hair at seven this morning, she was long gone now.

I rode to my house, lifting my bike over the front lawn so I wouldn't crash through the magnolia leaves and wake my dad. The house was deathly quiet, and I hated it. Much as my sisters had annoyed the crap out of me while they lived at home, I would have given anything to ignore Izzy's orders as I walked in the door, and tease Sophia about the fantasy novel she was reading on the sofa, and yell at Violet because I caught her stealing a shirt out of my closet in the room we shared.

It wasn't going to happen. With a deep sigh that nobody heard but me, I nuked a frozen dinner, cleared off a space at the kitchen table, and drew my calculus book out of my backpack. This actually happened. I thought about Will, and what a good student he was, and what a good student old Angelica was, diligently ciphering in anticipation of that bright, shining day in spring when she could take the AP test. Maybe Will would like me better if I wasn't so lame in school.

But I knew I shouldn't do stuff just because Will would like me better for it. That was exactly why I didn't want a boyfriend. There were other reasons to do my calculus homework, such as not flunking. I pulled out my notebook and turned to the page where I'd written down the assignment. This was more difficult than it sounded. Usually I wrote things down on whatever page I opened to rather than starting from the beginning and working through to the end like *some* academically obsessed drum captains. I took a bite of dinner, started the problem . . . and then lost myself in it. I had a hard time starting my homework because I dreaded it, but once I got into it, I forgot what I was doing and didn't mind so much. Until—

HOOOOOOOOOOONK.

I scraped back my chair and ran outside without even looking to see who'd pulled into the driveway. The only important thing was to get the horn stopped before it woke my dad. I rushed blinking into the dusk. When I was halfway across the lawn, I saw Sawyer grinning at me from the cab of his truck.

I sliced my finger across my throat. "My dad's asleep."

Sawyer took his hand off the horn. "Sorry." He wagged his eyebrows at me. "Does that mean I can come in?"

"No." I didn't have to think about that one. Except for Harper, my friends always assured me they could come inside my house and be quiet. They were wrong. They always forgot, somebody laughed really loudly, and my dad woke up.

"You're afraid we'll make some noise?" Sawyer asked.

"I know we will." Bantering with him was easier than explaining that no, I was serious, my dad actually had to work tonight, and this was the last sleep he would get. Sawyer understood a lot about life—way more than he probably should have at seventeen—but he didn't understand factories that ran all night, or trying to support a family on third shift.

"Why'd you give me such a hard time about Biggest Flirt today?" I griped. "And you called me your girl in front of Will. What was that about?"

"You need to stay away from that guy," Sawyer said. "He's a player."

"He's not," I said. "*You* are."

"But you *like* him," Sawyer pointed out. "That makes him dangerous. I don't matter. So come out with me."

"Can't," I said. "Homework."

"*You?*" he asked, astonished. "Are doing your *homework*?"

Normally I wouldn't have been offended by a comment like that, but what Will had said about me making so many mistakes—that must have gotten to me. "It's been known to happen," I said haughtily.

"I'm more fun than homework," Sawyer said.

I was about to point out that cleaning the toilet was also more fun than homework, and I had no intention of doing that, either.

Then an airliner roared over us, bringing the last of the season's tourists. Labor Day was coming up in two weeks, signaling the end of summer—for Yankees, anyway. I cringed at the noise, crossing my fingers that it wouldn't wake my dad.

Yeah. Sawyer was better than homework. He was way better than another night of staying very quiet until my dad finally dragged himself up grumpily, refused to eat what I'd heated for him because he wasn't hungry when he first woke, and left. It was like living by myself except for an outdoor cat we'd once had that passed through the house only to use the litter box.

"Come on," Sawyer said. "My brother's bartending tonight. Come sit on the back porch of the Crab Lab and get wasted with me."

I said, "Just let me lock up."

Nine

ONCE I'D GIVEN IN TO SAWYER FRIDAY NIGHT, IT didn't make sense to turn him down Saturday night or Sunday night. That's why, when Will and I sat on a bench in the school courtyard Monday morning, waiting for Harper to finish photographing Mr. and Ms. Least Likely to Leave the Tampa/St. Petersburg Metropolitan Area, it was like he and I had traded personalities. I was a little hungover, so I wasn't my usual laugh riot. And Will must have had a banner weekend with old Angelica. He was in a great mood, regaling me with all his ideas for the picture being taken in front of us.

"Chain them to the palm trees," he said. "Build a box and pour concrete around their feet."

"Have them get married at seventeen," I suggested. "Find the guy a factory job with lots of overtime and give them so many kids that he keeps the factory job and takes all the overtime he's offered so he can feed everybody."

Will frowned at me. "Who are you talking about?"

"My dad." I pressed my fingertips to my throbbing temple.

"Did something happen? What's wrong?" His brow furrowed, and he took a closer look at me, his gaze lingering on my mouth. Which made me look at *his* mouth. Which made me mad.

"Yes, something happened," I snapped. "You broke up with me Friday. You can't decide to be friends with me again today. Go over there." I pointed to a bench on the opposite end of the courtyard. I'd spoken loudly enough that Harper looked up from her camera and raised her eyebrows. I shook my head at her.

I thought Will would be offended all over again. Maybe I *wanted* him to be offended. It was kind of a letdown that he gamely crossed the courtyard and sat where I pointed. Then he called through his cupped hands, "Do we have to stay in the courtyard? We could take them to the beach and bury them up to their necks in sand."

He grinned at me, but his smile faded as I glared at him. Harper was dismissing Mr. and Ms. Loser. They disappeared back inside the school as Will and I continued to watch each other. I didn't know what he was thinking. *I* was thinking that he was the hottest guy I'd ever known, slouched on the bench with one ankle crossed on the other knee, his arms folded defensively, and his pirate earring winking in the sun. I wished he would go back to the frozen tundra and leave me alone.

He called, "You ruined the curve, didn't you?"

He was talking about the test in our AP calculus class. I

shifted uncomfortably. The concrete was awfully hard all of a sudden. "That is an ugly thing to accuse me of."

Harper looked up from flipping through the images on her camera. "What curve?"

"Tia was the only one who didn't have her calculus homework this morning," Will explained. "Ms. Reynolds chewed her out and said she'd heard about Tia from other teachers and she was *not* going to have a repeat performance of that in *her* class."

"Oh my God!" Harper gaped sympathetically at me.

"Then we had a test on what the homework had covered," Will said. "Ms. Reynolds graded the papers while we were getting a head start on tonight's homework. In the middle of it she announced, 'You can all thank a very surprising person for making one hundred on this test and ruining the curve for you.' She sounded pissed. And at the end of class, when she passed the tests back, Tia shoved hers in her purse before anybody could see it."

Protectively I tucked my purse closer to my hip on the bench.

"Tia, damn it," Harper cried. "Was the curve just for your class or for all of them?" She told Will, "We're used to her ruining the curve in math, but doing it on the second day of school is pretty obnoxious, even for her."

"Aren't you in Angelica's class?" I asked Harper. "Even if I didn't ruin your curve, Angelica will." I was making this up. Math wasn't Angelica's thing. She was more of a prim-and-proper-English kind of girl whom incorrectly corrected people's grammar.

Harper gave me a quizzical look over her glasses, knowing I was only trying to get Will's goat. "Well, hooray. It's your turn for a yearbook photo." She held out a hand toward Will and a hand toward me, her fancy camera hanging around her neck. I wanted to tell her that Sawyer had already tried to get Will and me to hold hands, with lackluster results. Instead, I stopped a few feet away from her outstretched hand and eyed Will.

"Look," Harper said, "I know this title has caused you two some pain, but I have a job to do here. The yearbook is counting on me. I have to take a flirtatious picture of you both. You didn't win Most Awkward." She turned to Will. "Since you're so great at coming up with photo ideas, what's your brainchild for this one?"

He glanced uncomfortably around the courtyard, into the tops of the palm trees, up at the sky, the same deep color as his eyes. "I hadn't thought about it."

"That's what I suspected," Harper said in a tone that made it sound like she had suspected the opposite. Her retro glasses were adorable, but when her art was at stake and she got in this no-nonsense mood, the glasses made her look like a stern 1960s librarian. "I'll give you a hint," she said. "For this photo, you need to flirt."

"What does that mean?" I asked uneasily.

She shrugged. "You're the flirts. You should do what you

were doing to get voted Biggest Flirts in the first place. I never actually witnessed it."

"We were just standing next to each other on the football field," Will said. "That's all."

"Oh, come on, Will. That's not *all* we were doing," I said just to bother him.

It worked. He cut his eyes at me, and his cheeks turned pink. He wasn't smiling.

"Sorry," Harper said, "but you can't just stand next to each other. Not in *my* yearbook photo. We need some action."

It was strange, but my headache was going away now that Will seemed hot and bothered. His discomfort was some sort of elixir for me. I bounced a little and clapped. "What kind of action?"

"He could drag you into the bushes," Harper said. "That's been done in a lot of yearbooks."

"Yes!" I exclaimed. "Drag me into the bushes!"

"I'm not dragging you into the bushes," Will said. "The bushes are prickly."

"So are you." I snapped my fingers. "There's an idea. I'll drag *you* into the bushes."

He folded his arms on his chest and looked down his nose at me. "You will not."

That sounded like a challenge. "Get your camera ready," I told Harper. I slipped both hands around his upper arm, just where it disappeared under the sleeve of his T-shirt.

Then I paused. I'd known all too well that he was built, but

I was surprised at how solid his arm was. I wouldn't be able to move him. But I'd threatened to, and it obviously bugged the shit out of him, so I had to go through with it. I pulled on him and said, "Drag." I gave his arm a couple more cursory jerks. "Drag, drag."

Harper had her camera to her glasses, still clicking away, but she said, "Not enough action. It's less flirtatious and more mournful and hopeless."

I laughed, because it was true. That's exactly how I'd felt about Will all weekend, and it was gratifying that Harper was able to see that through the camera lens. Even Will laughed a little.

In fact, he looked so carefree in that moment, like the Will I'd had fun with in band practice last week, the one I'd lost when we got elected to this stupid title, that I couldn't resist. With one hand still bracing myself against his rock-hard arm, I stood on my tiptoes and moved in to give him a quick kiss on the corner of his mouth, just where his smile turned up. Harper would get the shot, and Will could sigh with relief and go back to his beloved schoolwork. At least until he had to stand beside me again in band.

Just as my lips were about to reach him, he seemed to realize what I was doing and turned his head slightly. Instead of my lips touching the corner of his mouth, his lips met mine.

I was so confused about whether he'd made the move on purpose or not, and so surprised at the zap of electricity racing through me, that I stood paralyzed for a second. Which I shouldn't have done. We weren't even kissing, really. Our lips only pressed together. If I'd stepped away from him and acted embarrassed, we could have laughed off the whole thing like it had been a mistake.

Instead, his lips parted, and so did mine. We were kissing for real. Neither of us had tripped into this one. I wore a sleeveless minidress, so I shouldn't have gotten overheated, but my skin felt like it was on fire.

As quickly as it had begun, it was over. Will unceremoniously took a step back from me.

He turned to Harper and commanded her, "Delete those pictures. You can't let Angelica see them."

A hoot of laughter drifted to us. It didn't sound loud, but it must have made quite a noise inside the building for us to hear it through the closed windows. I glanced around at the windows and saw boys' faces pressed against the glass. They'd been watching us the whole time.

"Great," Will exclaimed. "Now Angelica will find out for sure. Those assholes will run right back and tell her. Angelica may even be *in* that class." He glared at me, then turned and stalked toward the door. Actually, I don't think he stalked. Stalking was uncool and self-righteous, and Will didn't move that way. He sauntered toward the door and threw it open like a rock star.

And I stared after him with my mouth open, desperately grasping for something funny to say to lighten his mood. He would stop, turn on the step, and give me a grudging grin. I would know that, even if I'd messed up things between him and old Angelica, at least he didn't hate me, and we'd be back to normal soon. But without a joke, I was lost.

I turned to Harper. "Think of a joke."

Harper gaped at Will too. Without taking her eyes off him, she said, "I've got nothing. And I don't think a joke would fix this."

The door slammed shut. Will was gone.

"Of course a joke would have fixed it!" I squeaked. "Normally you're hilarious. What kind of friend are you if you can't think up jokes on cue?"

She looked at me somberly through her glasses. "I'm the kind of friend who will support you during what comes next. If you two Biggest Flirts keep claiming you're not going to flirt anymore, you're going to blow each other's lives wide open."

Angelica did indeed find out about her brand-spanking-new boyfriend kissing the girl he'd sworn off. And then everybody else found out from Angelica. During the break after history, I heard her before I saw her in the crowded hall outside my English class, looking small and dead serious as she pointed her finger in Will's face and raised her voice at him. I gave them a wide berth and ducked into class without either of them seeing me, I thought—which didn't change the fact that everybody in the room stared at me as I walked toward the back and plopped down, four rows away from where I'd sat behind Will on Friday.

Will walked in on the bell, mouth set in a grim line, a pink flush crawling up his neck. I wondered if he'd gotten so angry with Angelica that he'd given her the "That's enough!" line I kept getting from him when I pushed him past his breaking point. He didn't look angry, though. He looked mortified. Apparently he got angry at a girl giving him heat only when he didn't deserve it.

Band that afternoon was exactly as awful as I'd suspected. Unlike in the other classes I shared with Will, I couldn't avoid him. I was stuck right next to him for the whole hour. And he didn't say a word to me unless he was barking orders to the section. He'd brought two bottles of water for himself so he wouldn't run out, and he must have spread sunscreen on the back of his neck already. He sat on the grass by himself instead of sharing my towel. It was the first practice we'd had in which Ms. Nakamoto didn't have to tell him to get off me.

As we rehearsed the halftime show over and over, the hour flew by. But the heat was terrible, even to me, and Sawyer's antics in the pelican costume weren't funny. I tried to lose myself in the music and just enjoy it, forgetting Will was there. This was difficult when I was often sliding one stick sideways to play on his drum while Jimmy played on mine. Then we reversed direction, with me playing on Jimmy's drum and Will's stick in my personal space.

I fantasized about switching places with Jimmy, so that I stood between him and Travis. Just moving one person down in the drum line would make all the difference. I wouldn't feel Will beside me constantly, his arm brushing against mine and suddenly pumping my body full of adrenaline. I wouldn't smell the spicy scent of him that dragged me back, against my wishes, to our hopeless night together. With him finally out of my life, I could spend my spare time floating in the waves at the beach rather than trying to party thoughts of him away.

All it would take was one person in the snare drum line to challenge somebody else. Then we'd all have to try out, and I could carefully throw the competition so that I came in third. Problem was, except for Will, our snare drum line wasn't very ambitious. I hadn't convinced them to challenge me after begging them all summer. I wouldn't convince them to challenge Will now.

I could, however, challenge Will myself.

That fantasy turned into an idea. The idea turned into a plan, because I had plenty of peace to think it through without the pesky drum captain teasing and distracting me. By the time DeMarcus started reading the end-of-day announcements, I'd made up my mind. Without a word to Will or Jimmy, I hefted my drum onto my shoulders, marched across the field, and climbed the stadium steps, making a beeline for Ms. Nakamoto. I whispered in her ear.

When DeMarcus finished his monotone of the day, Ms. Nakamoto held out her hand for the microphone. "One last announcement," she said. "Snare drums, report to the band room before school tomorrow. Ms. Cruz is challenging Mr. Matthews for drum captain."

"Oh, man!" was the first cry to come out of the snare drums, followed by some lower-key cursing—likely because they didn't want to come to school early, not because they were worried about keeping their positions in the section. Then came a swell of "oooooh" as the rest of the band realized I must be trying to make Will's life as miserable as possible.

While I had their attention, I used my drumstick to point at him far away across the field, like a tough boxer talking smack at the press conference before a big match: *You, my friend, are dead meat.*

I wasn't sure I'd ever cried at school before. My decision never to have a boyfriend had come early, so nothing much had bothered me even during middle school when everything bothered everybody and girls broke down because a stranger insulted their sandals.

And now, as a senior, I'd been alternating between swallowing tears and outright sobbing for hours, since I'd beat Will and all the other drums in the challenge to become drum captain.

"This is so frustrating," Kaye said. "Why do you get upset when you do well? It makes no sense!"

She and Harper and I stood in the hall outside Mr. Frank's classroom before study hall. Kaye kept Sawyer and other curious boys at bay with the glare of a student council vice president. I ached to talk to Sawyer about what I'd done too. He understood my problem with responsibility a lot better than

Harper and Kaye. But he and they did not get each other at *all*. I couldn't talk to the three of them at the same time.

"I'm not upset for doing well," I grumbled. "I always do well on drums. I'm a good drummer. I just don't want to come in first, because first chair is drum captain and has to be in charge."

"If you didn't want to be drum captain," Harper puzzled, "and Will was drum captain before, why'd you challenge him?"

"Because he's furious with me for breaking him and Angelica up, and I didn't want to stand next to him every day for the rest of marching season. I challenged him and intended to get third."

"Get *third*," Kaye repeated. "Like, you can decide ahead of time what your rank will be."

"Absolutely," I said. "Will should have played perfectly and snagged drum captain again, like he did last week when *he* challenged *me*. Travis is good, but he has trouble with the roll at the beginning of the bridge, so he should have placed second. Jimmy doesn't quite understand the syncopation in the chorus, so he should have placed behind Travis. Actually, he did. The drum line goes downhill from there. All I had to do was throw a couple of minor things and I could have slid in perfectly between Travis and Jimmy at third chair. That way I wouldn't have to slum with the freshmen at the bottom of the section, but I wouldn't have to stand next to Will anymore."

Kaye and Harper shared a look. Harper said, "We know you've thrown challenges before, but I had no idea you were approaching this with the precision of a brain surgeon. Is this how you always try out?"

"Yes."

"So what happened?" Kaye asked flatly. I could tell she was exasperated with me, but she was humoring me. For now.

"I was upset about the whole thing with Will"—I paused to sniffle—"and I forgot to mess up. Now he's even madder at me for taking drum captain away from him. But I didn't want it!"

"That's ridiculous," Kaye said firmly. "You've told us some doozies before. You've been irresponsible and a goofball. But trying to throw a challenge when you love band borders on insane. I can't believe you! You're so smart, Tia. You're so smart that you can pull off looking like an imbecile, just because you don't want to be in charge? You're going to let a guy be in charge so you don't have to take responsibility?"

I had stood there through Kaye's lecture, taking it. I was used to her talking to me like my mom. I didn't mind most of the time, since my mom was gone. It wasn't as if I was getting it twice.

But by the end of Kaye's speech, I was ticked off. She wasn't even through, but I was done listening.

I straightened to my full height, feeling like Godzilla rising out of the Gulf of Mexico to tower over Greater Tampa Bay, and pointed down at her. "You're *vice* president of the student council," I said. "Your boyfriend is *president* of the student council. Is that because you ran for president and he beat you? No, it's because you ran for vice president in the first place. And how did that happen? Either he decided he was going to take the front seat while you took the back, and he informed you of his decision, or *you* decided to take the back seat, so he wouldn't be mad at you."

Kaye's mouth crumpled in a little frown, and her dark eyes blazed. "And how is that worse than what *you're* doing, trying to make sure Will is in charge instead of you?"

"It's worse because *I'm* not giving *you* a damn lecture!"

She stomped off. All I could see was her hair twists bopping down the hall. I had tunnel vision, which happened to me when I got really angry, about once a year.

"Breathe," Harper said.

I'd forgotten she was standing there. Looking around the hall, I saw that I'd attracted everyone's attention, which I was getting really good at lately. Sawyer leaned against the lockers, watching me, waiting to listen to me when I was ready.

Will stood talking with Brody and some other guys from the football team. I was glad Brody had reached out to Will, because otherwise Will probably didn't have a friend in the school. He watched me too, his face stony. When he saw me looking in his direction, he turned away.

I didn't blame him. I'd taken him down in the most public way possible—on purpose, he thought. For the millionth time that morning, I remembered pointing at him with my drumstick yesterday, in front of the whole band. A lot of my problems would be solved if I stopped trying so hard to be funny. I took a long breath. "Do you hate me too?" I asked Harper.

"No. Kaye doesn't hate you either."

"We've never had a fight like that before."

Harper shifted the strap of her camera bag to her other shoulder. "You never told her she was wrong quite so firmly before."

"Do you think I was right, to tell her that?"

Harper raised her eyebrows. "You didn't have to yell in front of everyone. I've never seen you act like this. Will has really thrown you for a loop."

I looked around the hall again. A few people who'd still been staring at me turned away. I didn't want to sit under their gaze all through study hall. I definitely didn't want to spend study hall in the same classroom as Will. "I'm going to clean the band storage room."

"Uh-oh," Harper said. "Like last March?"

"Maybe." I'd gone on a cleaning spree when Violet moved out.

"What are you going to do about Will?" Harper asked.

"I can't *do* anything."

She shook her head. "If you don't try to fix it, it won't get fixed."

"I tried to fix it by challenging him on drum. You see how that turned out."

"I don't mean cook up some cockamamy scheme," she scolded me. "Actually talk to him, face to face, and explain how you feel."

I didn't think that was possible. I wasn't sure how I felt

myself. And even if I had known, the last person I would have wanted to explain it to was Will.

"Later." I held up my hand until she gave me a fist bump. Then I told Mr. Frank I was spending study hall in the band room. Over in Ms. Nakamoto's office, I grinned and sounded perky as I respectfully requested that she loan me a spray bottle of cleaner and a rag.

"Uh-oh," she said, looking up from her desk. "Like last March?"

"Everybody seems to remember that episode as if it was so horrible," I said, dropping the upbeat act after a total of ten seconds. "You got your sousaphones scrubbed, remember?"

"What's happened?" she asked. "Are you upset about the challenge?"

"Yes," I said, actually relieved that she'd guessed.

"Do you want to talk about it?"

"Yes," I repeated with gusto. "I want to undo the challenge and go back to the way we were before, with Will drum captain and me second."

"No." So much for talking about it. She found the cleaner and rag on top of a filing cabinet and handed them to me.

The storage room was tall and narrow, snaking back thirty feet underneath the stage and the auditorium, and lit by a single bulb in the ceiling. The ceiling itself was so high that the janitor had to use a special ladder when the bulb went out, which meant it was sometimes dark in here for days, with everybody falling all over each other trying to locate their instruments and drag them out of their cases. It wasn't much lighter in here even when the bulb worked.

I decided to start with the shady shelf at the back of the room and work my way forward. This involved tugging tubas down and cleaning the dusty wood underneath. Right away I found the trumpet mute that Shelley Stearns had lost and accused the trombone section of stealing last February.

I heard Will's voice out in the hall, creeping into the storage room and echoing weirdly against the concrete block walls. "Wait a minute," he said. "Why do you want to retake a yearbook picture in the storage room? It's dark in there even with the light on."

Suddenly Will came reeling into the room, shoved from behind. Off balance, he couldn't catch himself until he'd already tripped over some trumpet cases and hit the wall.

"Enjoy!" came Harper's voice. The big door slammed.

Will leaped back over the cases and jogged for the door, but the sound of the key turning in the lock outside already echoed through the storage room. He rattled the knob, then pounded the door. "Harper!" he roared. When there was no answer, he called, "Ms. Nakamoto?"

"She's gone to lunch," came Harper's bold little voice through the steel. "I'll come back to let you out at the end of the period. I hope you don't have to pee."

"Damn it, Harper!" Will backed up a pace and rammed the door mightily with one shoulder. It made a terrific noise but didn't budge.

To stop him before he hurt himself, I spoke up. "It's my fault. I left the key in the lock. I should have known she'd try something like this."

He whirled around, squinting in the dim light.

I stepped out from the dark shelves, where he could see me. "She locked us in here together so we'd have to talk about what happened."

His shoulders sagged. "I hate Florida."

Ten

WELL, I HADN'T WANTED TO TALK TO HIM, EITHER, but the idea of five minutes of conversation with him wasn't loathsome enough to make me despise the entire state.

"Tia," he said softly. "Don't look like that."

How did he want me to look? Like a girl who didn't mind being insulted? I tried that, crossing my arms in front of me, which was awkward because I was still holding the filthy rag in one hand and the spray bottle in the other.

He frowned. "What are you doing in here?"

"Cleaning."

"You?"

"You know, just shut up. If I never bathed, you would have smelled me by now. The sun makes that worse. Another reason for you to hate Florida."

He put his hands in his hair, looked perplexed, and then took his hands away again, as if he'd forgotten momentarily that his long hair was gone. "*You've* ruined *my* life, but you're going to make me feel like *I've* done something wrong."

I squinted to keep the tears from slipping out of my eyes. I didn't feel like I was totally to blame for our kiss yesterday, or for us getting elected Biggest Flirts. But I *was* to blame for boasting about knocking him out of drum captain, and then actually doing it. I'd been angry with Will, but I cared about him—way too much—and the last thing I'd wanted was to ruin his life.

I'd never been a girl who cried or otherwise showed my emotions just to get my way. I did occasionally let an emotion slip, but never to manipulate anyone. I'd noticed, though, that my mood swings really worked on Will. He was a sucker for a sad girl. He actually watched my face in band, and if I looked genuinely hurt at a pretend insult he'd thrown at me, he apologized. Now his voice softened. "Hey."

I was too far gone already. Cleaning for a few minutes had helped me put my brain on the right track, but now I was back where I'd spent the whole morning, in tears. "I didn't mean to beat you," I sobbed. "I know you won't believe that now, but you thought last Monday that I'd thrown the challenge. I meant to throw it again. I wanted to get third. I didn't want to stand next to you when you hate me." Stating the case that plainly, I sounded like a kindergartener, but the truth was simple.

He put out one hand, pulled me toward him, and sat me down on a tuba case. With a big sigh, he sat down next to me. The flagpoles behind us, probably twenty of them wrapped in their flags, slid sideways along the wall and draped the silks over us. I had always thought "silks" was a strange thing to call band flags, because clearly they were made of polyester.

"Okay," he said, batting the weird orange cloth off us. "You're not totally to blame for what happened yesterday. You started to kiss me, and I kissed you back. And I agree we were both at fault for getting elected Biggest Flirts. But you *are* ruining my life. You won't go out with me, but you've made sure nobody else will want to go out with me either."

I looked into his eyes. He seemed to be admitting again that he was still attracted to me—which meant asking Angelica or anybody else out was just an exercise.

"Why is it so important to you to date right now?" I asked. "You've been here a week, and you keep saying you're booking it to Minnesota the first chance you get. So the drive to find a girlfriend, any girlfriend, in Florida doesn't make a whole lot of sense." I felt like the lowest of the low as I said this. I really wanted to know, but Harper's words from Friday echoed in my head, pointing out that I was selfish when it came to Will.

His nostrils flared a little, like when I'd tried to hand him his phone on the football field, as though he found the thought of Minnesota distasteful. "I *did* want to go to Minnesota. That was my original plan, and it took me a few days to get used to the idea that it was gone. I don't want to go back. My girlfriend is screwing my best friend now."

I nodded sympathetically, thinking of that beautiful girl getting kissed by that blond boy. "You wish you'd never moved."

"No, not even that," he said. "I wouldn't want to go back to the way things were before I moved, now that I know she's the kind of person who would cheat on me the second I left town. Even if I'd never given her that opportunity, she was *still* that kind of person."

"What?" I asked, puzzling this out. "She was a latent cheater? A cheater waiting to happen?"

"Exactly," he said. "So now, my life here sucks, and I have the knowledge that my life there sucked too. I just didn't know it at the time. My life would suck anywhere. It's completely fucking tragic."

"That's not true," I said, a little alarmed. "You're in a bad spot, Will. Moving is stressful, and you're only one week out. Your girlfriend cheating on you was awful. You feel bad about that. There would be something wrong with you if you didn't."

He gave his head a dismissive shake, telling me I had no idea what he meant. "That's not all." He reached down for a flag and rolled the neat hem between his fingers. "I was supposed to be drum major back home."

"You were?" I could see him as drum major.

"Yes. And student council president."

I could not see him as student council president. He'd never glad-handed a stranger like Aidan did. "You?"

"Yes," Will said bitterly. "Thanks."

"Sorry. I'm so sorry." I put one hand on his knee so he wouldn't pull away from me completely. "It's just that in my experience, that job requires skills you don't seem to possess, such as talking."

He nodded. "Right."

"What do you mean, you were *supposed* to be?" I asked. "You were going to run for these positions in Minnesota this year?"

"No, I'd already been elected."

"Oh my God!" My voice echoed against the concrete walls. "Why did your parents make you move, then? Couldn't they wait another year until you graduated?"

Will sighed. "My dad's office closed down. If he didn't transfer to manage the branch office here, he would have been laid off. So, no."

"Oh."

"And my mom said since I'd done that stuff at my old school, I could do it at my new school. I believed her. Nothing I'd ever been through told me otherwise. It was only when I got here . . ."

"We already had a drum major and a student council president," I finished for him.

"Even if DeMarcus hadn't snagged one office and Aidan the other, I wouldn't have gotten them. I'm not the man my parents thought I was, or *I* thought I was. I'm . . . I think I'm . . ."

I held my breath, my mind spinning at what he might say.

"Shy," he sighed.

I burst into laughter. "Well, you've got that one right."

"It's not funny," he said.

I considered him beside me, looming over me, really, when he was sitting so close, his muscular body making the room seem smaller. He had a big personality, too, one that didn't seem aptly described by the word "shy." "You're introverted," I corrected him.

He shrugged.

"You get your energy from being by yourself," I guessed. This was Harper's description of the strange phenomenon I did not understand. "Having to talk to a bunch of people at once, especially people you don't know, makes you feel drained."

"Exactly!" he exclaimed, surprised that I had any insight. "I guess I never noticed at home. Here, where I have to start over, it's debilitating. I fell asleep as myself one night and woke up the next morning as a loser. This is coming at a really bad time for me. My parents are telling me that I can't follow in my dad's footsteps. If I'm a terrific manager, all that will get me is threatened with a layoff and transferred across the country. I have to be better than my dad. I have to be perfect at everything. So my parents are like, if you can't be drum major, be the next best thing. Be drum captain. I thought I'd done that. And then—"

Before he could say, *A disorganized mess of a girl took that away from me too. IS THERE NO JUSTICE?* I broke in with, "I'm sorry." Again.

"It's not your fault," he said. "You won fair and square. I

was afraid you would. I practiced for hours beforehand, but I still missed a beat when we played the cadence during the challenge, and you didn't. End of story."

I thought about him in his room late last night, lying on his bed with his eyes closed, beating out the cadence on a practice pad propped up on his knees—that's how *I* practiced, anyway, when I practiced—over and over until he thought his head would explode. I hadn't practiced at all, since I hadn't wanted to win. But I had a three-year head start on him, having played this cadence countless times throughout high school. He'd been no match for an experienced drummer so scatterbrained that she forgot herself and won.

"My mom keeps saying if I act the way I acted in Minnesota, I'll have what I had in Minnesota. If I stay the same person, I'll have the same great friends. Well, now it turns out my friends there weren't so great. And no one here cares who I used to be back home. Nobody would believe me anyway."

"I believe you," I piped up.

"You actually know me," he said. "You've been forced to stand next to me. I can't go around the school making people stand next to me for forty hours just so they'll see what I'm made of. People believe the rumors, believe what the Senior Superlatives title says about me, believe what Sawyer tells them."

I snorted. "I doubt anybody in their right mind believes anything Sawyer tells them, ever."

"Well, I'm even less credible than he is, because I'm just the Fucking New Guy. Right?"

I *had* heard Sawyer refer to Will as the Fucking New Guy. I would have to talk to him about that, because, although the consensus in the school was that Sawyer was full of shit, his nicknames for people did catch on. "Sawyer has a chip on his shoulder," I explained. "He hasn't been here very long himself. He used to live with his mom up in Georgia. He only moved here a couple of years ago when his dad got out of jail."

"That sounds about right," Will grumbled.

"Now, wait a minute," I said. "You're judging him the same way that you don't want to be judged."

"Good," Will said. Normally he backtracked when I pointed out that he was being a hypocrite, but I'd noticed he had a tendency to shut down when Sawyer was mentioned. "Anyway, he's not the only one talking smack about me. Back home I was just me, Will. Everybody had known me forever. They knew that I try to stay in shape all year so I don't get killed in hockey, not to show off. I would never take off my shirt unless I thought I was going to pass out from heatstroke, and I would never, ever cheat on my girlfriend. Here I'm a completely different person, and my whole life is changing to match it—all because of this label that I got saddled with."

"Will, it's not that bad," I lied. It was pretty bad.

"Everybody hates me," he said.

"They do not!" Hate was too personal.

He gave me a stern look. "I've overheard you trying to convince your friends that I'm not the stuck-up shit they thought I was."

He certainly had. "I don't see why you care so much," I said. "You have to sit out one year of high school, not doing some of the stuff you thought you were going to do. It'll be over in another nine months. You'll go to college and get on with your life and forget all about us."

"No, that's exactly it. The person I thought I was—that was the fake. I was successful because everybody had known me since we all started kindergarten. But pluck me out of there and set me down in a new school, and I'm completely unrecognizable. I don't have Aidan's charisma or Sawyer's . . . whatever Sawyer has."

"Penchant for catastrophe."

"Yes, that. If the senior class had voted for the Superlatives titles and I'd gotten nothing at all, I would feel better. Nobody had time to notice me. But what do I get voted? Biggest Flirt. With you. Why? Because I want to be around you all the time. You're the only person here who makes me feel like I'm at home."

I waved away his compliment, if indeed that's what it was. "People always tell me I could have a conversation with a rock."

"Exactly. What am I going to do when I start college? Or I start a new job, where my dad thinks I have to be the star performer on day one or else? There's not always going to be someone like you there, following me around, giving me someone to joke with, and talking other people out of hating me."

I resented this. I hadn't thought of myself as *following him around*. And *giving him someone to joke with* sounded like I was his e-reader.

But I wasn't going to get in a fight with him when he was already upset about not getting along with everyone else. I said, "I don't think this is a permanent condition, Will. Yeah, you may have a harder time making friends than you thought. But in the week you've lived in Florida, you've also been angry. You're mad at your parents for moving. You're mad at your dad's company, and now you don't want to work for The Man. You resent everyone here who holds the positions that were yours in Minnesota. All that anger changes what you are, reserved"—I opened my hands—"and turns it into dour." I cupped my hands together in a ball to show Will how he'd closed down. Then I put one hand on his knee again.

"You don't get it," he said. "You're saying everybody is looking at me differently in Florida from how they saw me in Minnesota. I'm saying *I'm* looking at me differently too. I really am not the person I thought I was. When you kissed me for the photo yesterday—"

"Hello, *you* kissed *me*!"

He put his hands up in the air like he did when Ms. Nakamoto scolded him through the microphone. "Whatever happened, that wasn't supposed to happen. I'm not like that. That wasn't me. I really didn't *want* it to be me, because if I cheated on Angelica, I was doing to her exactly what Beverly did to me when I left Minnesota. That was never my intention. I mean, if I'm going to do that to Angelica, I can't really be angry with Beverly, can I? And I would like to be angry at her for a while longer."

"Okay," I said, laughing. I knew he was serious, but I enjoyed hearing him admit to being base and petty every once in a while. It helped to know he wasn't as superhuman as he looked.

"So I'm sorry for the way I acted after the picture yesterday. You didn't know what's going on with me. I came down a lot harder on you than you deserved. And I understand why you challenged me. I drove you to it. I wouldn't want to stand next to me either." He looked down at my hand on his knee. Then he glanced over at the door like he hoped Harper would relent and open it. I wished he would put his hand on mine, some sign that we were cool again, but he seemed only to want to be alone.

"I consider you a friend," I said quietly. "I think we're having such a hard time getting along because, the first night we met, we read each other completely wrong. We went a lot farther than you were expecting, and I was surprised at how you reacted."

He held my gaze and said grimly, "That's not why."

As I watched his eyes, looking dark now rather than blue in his shadowed face, I felt warmth spread across my chest and up my neck. I was more confused and more turned on than I'd been yesterday morning when we kissed, because his words were weightier than his lips on mine. We both understood we had a connection. I'd told him, over and over, that I didn't want a boyfriend. He'd made progress toward getting a different girlfriend. And whatever we said we wanted, we kept ending up close to each other, touching.

That scared the hell out of me. I took my hand off his knee.

He glanced toward the door again, nodding like he accepted what I was telling him: that we would never be together. Not the way he wanted. And he was ready for Harper to come along and let him go.

He'd confessed his feelings to me, and his motivations. I was glad Harper had made us talk. But when he walked out that door, he would still be lost in Florida. The school would still view him as the dog who couldn't stick with one girlfriend—even worse than Sawyer, who at least was up front about his inability to commit. And Will would still be second chair on snare.

"Will you challenge me?" I asked him. "Tell Ms. Nakamoto during band this afternoon, and we'll have another tryout tomorrow."

"No," he said firmly. "You won. I lost. If we went through it again tomorrow and *you* lost, I'd know you threw it. So would everybody else. You've already undercut any authority I might have had with the drums."

"That's not true. You get your authority from being a great drum captain. I don't *want* to be in charge. You'll see in practice this afternoon. If we're so unfortunate that Ms. Nakamoto tells us to have a sectional, Jimmy and Travis will laugh me out of the parking lot."

His brows knitted, deepening the worry line between them. "Can I ask you something personal?"

"More personal than 'Do you like it when I put my mouth on your nipple?'"

A blush shot through his face. He pursed his lips, trying hard not to laugh. I noticed that goose bumps broke out on his skin too—possibly the only time in the last week that he'd felt a chill, unless he'd been taking cold showers. I wondered if he realized he was rubbing his arms with his hands to warm himself as he said, "I'll take that as a yes. The question is, what were you in charge of that you screwed up?"

I shrugged. "Nothing. I've never been in charge of anything."

"Then why are you so scared?"

"I *will* screw it up," I said.

"How do you know?"

"Everybody tells me I will. Everybody says, 'Oh, you'd better not put Tia in charge of anything—watch out.'"

"Who says that?"

"My sisters. Everybody at school. You heard the drum line, and DeMarcus. They were so freaking relieved that *anybody* was drum captain besides me."

Will squinted at me. "Don't you think that's because *you* go around saying, 'You'd better not put me in charge of anything'? It's a self-fulfilling prophecy."

What he was telling me seemed to glimmer in front of me. "No," I said. "You wouldn't think that if you'd known me for more than a week. The people around here have known me forever."

"I just got here," Will said, "and that's exactly why I can see you so clearly."

Suddenly I was the one who was cold. I crossed my arms but tried to disguise the move by putting my chin in one hand.

"Girls look up to you."

"Ha!" I crowed. "That is the saddest thing I've ever heard." I felt my smile dropping away as he watched me silently without laughing along. I asked, "Are you serious?"

"Yes. The girls in the drum line, especially. They watch your every move. They practice the twirls you do with your sticks when you're thinking about something else."

I suspected he was making this up. "I never noticed."

"They wait until you're walking away."

"Well, God help them," I said. "If I can do one positive thing for them between now and when I graduate, it will be to give up drum captain and never be put in charge of anything again."

"That's not a goal," he said. "It's an anti-goal. It's an aggressive stance against any sort of goal, like *that's* going to help you."

I let out a frustrated sigh. He was starting to sound like Kaye. Besides, *I* wasn't the one who needed help. *He* was the one who feared the school would show up at his house with pitchforks and torches. And I could use that to my advantage. "Listen, would you challenge me for drum captain if I did you a favor?"

He grinned at me. "What kind of favor?"

He looked so adorable when he smiled. I *wished* I was suggesting that kind of favor. "I'll explain the situation to Angelica," I said. "I'll tell her the picture yesterday was my fault."

"It wasn't your fault," he murmured. "Not totally. We agreed on that."

"Still, I'll try with her. I'll convince her to give you another chance. You can go out with her again. You and I will keep our hands off each other. Then all your problems will be solved."

His fingers tapped a beat on one knee. "Knock yourself out."

"And you'll challenge me?"

"Yep." He was looking at the bare bulb in the ceiling. He didn't seem very invested in this conversation. I would show him, though. Getting out of drum captain was at stake here.

Then he asked, "If Harper really doesn't come back until the end of the period, we have a few minutes. How should we spend them?" There was absolutely no innuendo in his voice. I knew Will, though. He was flirting with me again, whether he meant to or not.

I handed him the spray bottle.

Eleven

THANKS TO OUR EFFORTS—ACTUALLY MORE Will's efforts, because I lost interest in cleaning once I felt better—the storage room was organized. Or, not *organized* per se, but no longer ready to avalanche its contents on top of anybody. At the beginning of band practice, I was able to extract my drum pretty quickly rather than struggling to free it as usual from a tangle of harnesses and cases and music stands and "silks" and sketchy-looking lost-and-found hoodies. I hurried across the parking lot (yes, while banging out a salsa beat—why not?), where I blew a kiss to Will, who was standing behind the trunk of his car. This was not flirting at *all*. I carefully descended the stadium steps and found Angelica exactly where I thought I would: on the sidelines, practicing baton twirls that she could perform perfectly already, working hard despite the heat because she was so dedicated to her craft, ten minutes before the start of band.

I marched right over. "Hey there, old Angelica. How's it hangin'?"

She lifted her chin and looked down her nose at me. Possibly I deserved this. I wasn't making things any easier by greeting her in the style of drug dealers at a downtown Tampa gas station.

I started again. "Can we talk for just a second?" I even removed my harness and propped my drum nicely against the fence so that my distracting protrusion wouldn't hover between us.

She swallowed before saying, "Sure," almost like she was dreading this convo as much as I was.

"Can you lay down your weapons?"

She bent at the knees to place her batons daintily on the ground, then followed me along the fence to stop a few yards beyond where Chelsea and the other majorettes would gather. When they arrived, they could still inch toward us to overhear, but only if they wanted to be super rude. Which I did not put past them, honestly.

I took a deep breath and belted it out. "I just wanted to say I'm sorry for kissing Will when we were taking yearbook pictures yesterday. It wasn't planned. We were together at Brody's party, when you were still with DeMarcus." I thought it might help my case to remind her that she wasn't the only lady getting around, even if hers was a G-rated version of playing the field.

She grimaced, still sensitive about her breakup with DeMarcus. Good.

"Will and I are friends," I said. "Definitely. But we're nothing—"

I stopped as a large foam beak blocked my view of Angelica. Sawyer stood beside us in his pelican costume, nodding at me as if he was participating in the conversation.

"Sawyer," I snapped, "I swear to God."

Sawyer put his wings up, just like Will put his hands up when he got in trouble. I watched Sawyer sashay along the sideline toward the cheerleaders, exaggerating the wag of his big bird booty, until I was sure he couldn't hear us.

I turned back to Angelica. "Will and I are nothing more than friends," I said. "Except for that one night, we haven't seen each other outside of band and school. And the picture . . . we were discussing what to do in the picture, and then the kiss just sort of happened." I was telling the truth, and yet not. It was an accurate depiction of the events, if not of how I'd felt when they happened. Funny how everything that had gone down between Will and me since that first night had been pretty innocent on the face of it, and underneath, so very guilty.

"Will was upset about the picture," I said, "because he was worried about what you'd think. With good reason, judging from the way you chewed him out yesterday."

She raised her artfully plucked eyebrows at me. Her meaning was clear: *And your point would be* what?

"I promised him I would try to explain it to you," I said. "He's sorry about what happened and how it looked. He knows he embarrassed you. He was embarrassed too.

He's been cheated on himself, and, um." I still doubted he'd told Angelica about Beverly, and I didn't think his treacherous and extremely recent ex back home was a selling point. "He would like to go out with you again."

She faced Will across the field, lowering her chin to look at him through long, thick lashes. I didn't turn around to follow her gaze. I was trying to get these two back together so I could hand off the drum captain position to Will and keep him as a friend. But if I actually saw him gawking at this girl like I imagined he was right now, I wasn't sure my heart could take it.

"You know," she said, still gazing in his direction, "Will is sooooo good looking."

Yeah, I knew.

"And he's pretty nice."

Pretty nice? Try *nicest guy ever*! What was wrong with this chicklet?

She opened her hands and let out a high-pitched sigh. "I don't have to settle for a good looking, pretty nice guy who acts half the time like he prefers another girl."

I nodded, but I was frowning. "Or a guy who will have a beer at a party."

"Or a guy who will have a beer at a party," she confirmed, enunciating her words and opening her eyes wide at me, like she'd already had this argument with DeMarcus and her perspective should have been obvious by now.

I stepped back and looked at Angelica, really examined

her, maybe for the first time ever. She gave the impression of being a gorgeous girl, but she wasn't really, or wouldn't have been without carefully applied makeup and a flattering top hanging at exactly the right length over her shorts. She had taken a lot of shit throughout high school for stuff she'd done in ninth grade, but I'd never heard of her breaking down about it. She just took care of herself, came to school, and plowed through. I'd always viewed her as a stubborn stick-in-the-mud with no personality, but now I was realizing that being a stubborn stick-in-the-mud *was* her personality, and she deserved kudos for being true to herself.

Surprising myself, I told her, "I like you, old Angelica."

She didn't seem moved by this admission. "You like everybody." Then she nodded at something over my shoulder. "We've got to go."

Turning around, I saw that DeMarcus was on his podium. "Oh, shit," I said. He officially started band practice every day by calling us to attention, but we were supposed to keep track of time and find our places on the field before he did that, so people weren't scrambling. As I ran for my drum, I tossed over my shoulder, "Thanks for the talk, Angelica. See you around!" I thought she rolled her eyes at me, but I didn't hang around to see.

I grabbed my harness and tried to fit it over my shoulders while hightailing it across the field to the drum line. Panicked about getting caught on the forty-yard line when DeMarcus called us to attention, but elated about the way Angelica and I had resolved our differences in a nonviolent manner, it occurred to me only gradually that "You like everybody" might have been a dig rather than a compliment.

And it wasn't until I'd almost reached Will that the other shoe dropped. I thought he was in the wrong place next to Travis. Then I remembered I was the drum captain at the end of the line now. And I realized that Angelica had said no to dating Will. My mission to get her back with him had been a complete failure. What if I was stuck as drum captain forever?

Just as I reached my place, DeMarcus must have made the motion to start practice. Will played the riff that the rest of the drum line echoed, snapping the band to attention.

I held my breath. I wasn't in trouble. But I felt like my body, not to mention my brain, was still rushing across the field.

"At ease," DeMarcus called.

As I exhaled and everyone relaxed, Will immediately whispered, "Sorry. I didn't mean to step on your toes, playing your riff like that."

"You didn't!" I exclaimed.

"You did that for me before and saved me from getting in trouble, so I thought I'd return the favor."

"I know!" I sighed, so frustrated in my first few hours of being drum captain that I could hardly stand it. "Look, this is going to be completely insufferable if we're tiptoeing around each other. Let's make a pact that whatever happens for the rest of the year, we will always have each other's backs."

"Deal," he said, sticking out his hand.

My palm touched his. We gripped hands. He slid his fingers down my arm. We touched elbows. "And then like this," I suggested, linking arms with him. It was a badass secret handshake if I did say so myself.

"And now we're flirting," he scolded me.

I wiped my hands on my shirt. "Ew, flirt germs."

I'd hardly gotten this out of my mouth when Will played the riff again. Ms. Nakamoto had finished giving us instructions, which obviously had been very interesting to me, and DeMarcus was calling us to attention to run through the show. This time I realized what was happening in time to echo the riff with the rest of the drums, just like I used to, but damn. This drum captain thing required a lot of concentration and did not agree with me.

It wasn't until we'd played through the entire halftime show, and my ears were ringing with the ending squeals of our trumpets, who really were awesome if you were listening to them rather than looking at them, that Will asked, "What did Angelica say?"

"She said no. But you have to challenge me for drum captain, because at least I tried," I burst out. I'd been worrying about how to say this through three numbers and a drum break. Clearly I'd needed more time to think it through.

"No way," he said. "You promised you would convince her to give me another chance."

"Blugh," I said, shaking out my arms. My shoulders were

sore from wearing the drum harness so long without a break. I looked past Will down the line of drums. I was only one person higher in the line than I'd been yesterday, but from this perspective, the snares seemed to continue forever like they were reflected in two mirrors pointed toward each other.

"Don't give up so soon," he said in the tone of a basketball coach in an inspirational TV movie for preteens. "Tell you what. You and I will go out for a few days, just to make Angelica jealous. That will get her interested in me again."

I snorted, remembering how flatly she'd rejected his offer of reconciliation. "I don't think that's going to work."

He said, "It worked on you."

I felt my face flush red underneath my hat. He must have known how attracted I was to him, but I thought we had an unspoken rule that we wouldn't mention it. My soul seemed as bare to him as my body had been on my bed our first night together.

But he was right, wasn't he? Dating would make Angelica jealous if she felt anywhere as strongly about Will as I did. I'd sworn him off, promising myself our flirtation meant nothing and I didn't want him or anyone as a boyfriend. And one glance at him lying on the beach with his hand on Angelica had transformed me into a scheming freshman.

I jumped as Will played the riff, calling the band to attention again. This time I completely missed echoing him. If I kept this up, Ms. Nakamoto would kick me out of the drum captain position on my own lack of merit. But I had more pride than to leave that way. It was throw a challenge or nothing for me.

I was hopeless.

"Say yes," he whispered, standing stock still at attention and moving only the corner of his mouth as he spoke. "Get Angelica back for me, and I'll challenge you. Think how carefree you'll be as a civilian again."

"Don't talk at attention." I sounded so silly trying to throw my weight around like a drum captain that I almost laughed at myself.

But by the time we'd played through the show a second time and Ms. Nakamoto had sent the band to one end of the field to learn the drill for the pregame show, I'd made up my mind that Will was right. I was lucky there was nothing I could mess up today other than the call to attention. Sometime soon, Ms. Nakamoto was sure to send the drum line to the parking lot to rehearse on our own, and I would spend an hour ordering people around, convincing them to hate me, and generally inviting Armageddon.

"All right," I told Will calmly as we walked toward the goalpost together, though my stomach was turning flips.

"Great," he said just as evenly. Most of his face was hidden by his shades and hat. His cheeks and chin shone with sweat. He betrayed no emotion other than disgust at the heat. "But we're not confiding in anyone that we've engineered this. You can't tell Harper and Kaye. That's going to get back to Angelica. Kaye will hop over here wanting to know how the plan is going before she remembers she's not supposed to say that out loud."

True. Or I would leap to the sidelines, eager to update her on the same thing. Will was observant. I would just tell Kaye and Harper that Will and I were giving dating a trial run, which wasn't too far from the truth. I didn't like discussing bad news anyway. Pretending there *was* no "cockamamy scheme," as Harper had called my thwarted plan to throw the drum challenge, sounded like the perfect way to deal with my problems.

"Can you go out tonight?" he asked. "Might as well get it over with."

"No, I have to work late," I said. "I promised Bob and Roger that I'd train them on the inventory database I set up. I tried writing down the directions, but old people can follow instruction manuals fine until they involve computers, and suddenly their brains explode. I'm going to have to hold their hands and lead them through it."

Will nodded. "Wednesday night? Or are you busy then, too?" He sounded suspicious, like he was afraid I was making up an excuse about tonight and he expected one for tomorrow. I thought we knew each other pretty well, but obviously he didn't understand that I tried not to make excuses. If I hadn't wanted to fake-date him, I would have told him so.

"Tomorrow night," I agreed, "as soon as I get off work."

"Great," he said again, emotionlessly. "What kind of date

would you like to go on? We can do anything you want, as long as we're likely to be seen so the news will get back to Angelica."

I imitated what he'd said our first night together. "I want you to take me to lunch, and then I can show you around town."

He turned so suddenly that his drum knocked into mine—a mistake I made all the time when I was talking to people on the field, but he did not. This time I could hear the hurt in his voice as he said quietly, "I want to do this, and help you out, but not if you're going to take stabs at me."

I put my hand on his back. His shirt was soaked with sweat. I kept my hand there. "Kidding. I didn't mean it ugly. I wanted to go on that date you invited me on last week. I just . . ." The band was loud around us, milling into place in two long lines for the football team to run through on game night, but the silence between Will and me was louder.

"I'll pick you up from the shop when you close," he finally said. "I'll take you to dinner, and you can show me around town." He took my hand off his back and wiped it on his cargo shorts, which were dryer.

"More flirt germs," I commented.

He gave me my hand back hastily and looked around to see if Ms. Nakamoto had noticed him rubbing my palm close to his crotch. Sometimes our flirting was innocent like this: We weren't thinking dirty, and we realized how it looked to other people only after the fact.

Sometimes not.

He put the head of his drumstick on my drum and traced loud circles there, making the snares rattle. It was his way of touching me, I thought, without actually touching me and getting in trouble. As the circles he made got smaller, I started to wonder exactly what was going to happen on our fake date, and whether our facade would include feeling each other up like lusty pirates on shore leave. The heat was finally getting to me.

"One more thing, though," he said, ending his solo on my drum with a loud tap. "I heard you were with Sawyer all last weekend."

I countered, "I heard you and Angelica studied together at the library, and you licked her copy of *Fahrenheit 451*."

"That is a lie," he deadpanned. "The spine doesn't count." He turned to me as if to look into my eyes, which had no effect when we were both wearing shades. "Seriously," he whispered, "even though we're only fake-dating, I don't want you with Sawyer. If you're dating him, we won't do this. If you're just fooling around, I want you to stay away from him. That's my one condition."

I thought through it. Sawyer would be difficult to corral. "Can I flirt with him while I'm dating you, even if it doesn't mean anything? A little tit for tat? No?"

Will lowered his chin so that I could see his blue eyes boring into me over the edge of his sunglasses.

"No!" I concluded. "Okay. Just let me dump my bike in the

back of his truck after school and hitch a ride to work with him so I can explain."

For the rest of practice, Will and I talked but didn't really flirt. Suddenly we were acting reserved around each other, afraid to let ourselves go, like we were telling jokes at a funeral. I wasn't sure what he was thinking, but I for one had a lot of anxiety about our evening together tomorrow. I tried not to get my hopes up. What could happen? It would be, after all, a Wednesday. But when we'd played around in band before, nothing had mattered. Now I felt like we had a lot at stake, and not all of it had to do with the drum challenge and Angelica.

Finally we ran through the pregame show, DeMarcus intoned the announcements, and Ms. Nakamoto dismissed us. As the band walked off the field and Will and I neared the gate, I called out to Kaye, who glowered at me but dropped her pompons to wait for me. I told Will to go ahead while I talked to her. I hoped he understood that I was really asking him to wait to change his shirt until I arrived at his trunk, but I wasn't sure that message got across.

Then I walked right up to Kaye and eased my drum down onto the grass. Facing her with nothing between us, I wasn't sure what to tell her. I'd meant everything I'd said to her in the lunchroom. I thought she was a hypocrite for letting a boy take over her life, then scolding me for doing the same. I just hadn't meant to yell it.

She glared at me a moment more. Then she stuck out her bottom lip and opened her arms.

I walked into her embrace, slid my arms around her, and squeezed. We were going to argue about our issues again, obviously, but not today.

Softness enveloped me like a blanket. Sawyer had put his wings around both of us.

Kaye got the bad end of this deal. She was shorter than me and way shorter than Sawyer in his costume, so her head was down in a hot hole between us. Her voice sounded muffled as she called, "I love you, Tia, but for some mysterious reason, I find your friendship suffocating." Sawyer let us go, but he got very close to patting her on the butt with his wing.

On our way up the stairs, Chelsea asked Kaye and me if we wanted to go to a chick flick that night with her and a couple of other girls from calculus. Kaye said she was going out with Aidan. Remembering that he was waiting for her in the parking lot, she skipped ahead of us on the steps. Then I told Chelsea I couldn't go either, because of work. She asked if it would be better for me if we all went tomorrow night instead. "I would love to," I said, "but it's a school night, and I need to do my homework."

"Do you think I'm a stupid fool?" Chelsea asked. "Don't beat around the bush. Just go ahead and tell me, 'Chelsea, I think you're a stupid fool.'"

"Kidding!" I exclaimed. "Sarcasm! Tonight I have to work, and tomorrow I'm going out with Will."

She gazed up at him climbing the stairs with his drum.

Then she raised one eyebrow at me. "I thought he was dating Angelica."

I grinned brilliantly. "That was yesterday."

"If you were *really* dating Will, of course you and I wouldn't hook up," Sawyer said, eyeing me from across the cab of his truck. He faced forward again as he drove past the HOME OF THE PELICANS sign and turned onto the road by the school. "We're philanderers, but we're not cheaters."

I wasn't sure of the difference. I resisted the urge to ask Sawyer to look up "philanderers" for me using the definition app on his phone, because he was driving. He aced standardized tests, but only the verbal part, never the math, and definitely not the logic.

He was doing a great impression of a logical person, though, backing me into a corner. "If you're only fake-dating Will," he reasoned, "why can't we still hook up?"

"He asked me not to," I said. "I understand where he's coming from. He's trying to make Angelica jealous. If he and I are supposed to be dating, but you and I have something on the side, it won't look like Will and I are serious."

"What if we were careful?" Sawyer said in the voice of a lecherous old man, sliding his hand under the leg of my shorts and up to the top of my thigh.

"I don't think so." Laughing, I tossed his hand away. "You are the opposite of careful."

"This sounds like the opposite of faking," he pointed out.

"Will really cares what you and I are up to. You're genuinely concerned about what he thinks. There's nothing fake about that. Why don't you give in and date him?"

I shrugged to the live oaks passing by the window. "I don't want a boyfriend," I said for the millionth time in my teenage life. "But for once, somebody's come along who's making it hard to keep that promise to myself."

I turned to look at Sawyer, so handsome in an offbeat way. His white-blond hair, even when it was damp from his shower, was a color I'd only seen before on small children, and his preppie clothes looked like something his mom would have picked out for him in elementary school. But his strong hands lay on the wheel, his sinewy forearms tensed as he steered downtown, and something dark behind his eyes reminded me he was more experienced than he should have been at seventeen.

"You've never come across a girl like that?" I asked.

"Nope," he said like he didn't have to think about it.

Suddenly I burst out, "Sawyer, you can tell me if you're gay."

"Gay!" He gaped across the cab at me, then jerked the steering wheel to straighten the truck and avoid hitting the curb. "After what we did Sunday night?"

"Sunday night was good," I admitted sheepishly.

"I thought you enjoyed it," he said as though I hadn't spoken. Turning onto the main drag through town, he grumbled, "You've just got gay on the brain because you work for Bob and Roger."

"No." Well, maybe. "It was just an explanation for why you never commit, even to the point of asking the same girl out twice in a row."

He pulled the truck into a space near the antiques store, killed the engine, and looked over at me. "What's *your* excuse?"

He had me there. Backed against the door of his truck already, I had nowhere to go. I didn't want to talk about this. He knew it. And in his challenge, I heard all the regret I felt myself when I expected to hang with him at a party but he went home with another girl.

Seeming to realize he'd gone too far, he took a deep breath, popped his neck, and settled his shoulders back against the driver's seat. "I like somebody who would never fall for me," he admitted. Then he gave me his sternest glare. "A girl-type person."

"Is it me?" I asked.

He blinked. In that pause, I was afraid the answer was yes, and I was the one who'd gone too far. I wished I could take it back.

"No!" he exploded. "Are you insane?" He started laughing uncontrollably.

I talked over him. "That makes me feel like a million bucks, Sawyer."

Still grinning, he pulled himself together. "Look, Tia, I will just flat-out tell you. I really enjoy getting drunk with you. That's generally the highlight of my week, besides when you give me a hand job."

"I'm so glad." Yeah, I was beginning to regret Sunday night now.

"But you and me, together, we would be the death of each other. I'd be like, 'I know a guy who has some crack. Go with?' And you'd be like, 'Sure!' Somebody has to be the voice of reason in a relationship, Tia, and our voice of reason has had a tracheotomy. If we really dated, in half an hour we'd be face-down in a ditch on the south side of Tampa."

I glared across the truck at him. I wasn't sure whether he was making a reference to my mom doing drugs or not.

The next second, I decided he wasn't, at least not on purpose. He seemed to make the connection only afterward, and he looked sidelong at me with a guilty expression. By way of apology, he said, "I know I can tell you anything. If I wanted to come out, you would be the first person I would tell. I'm not gay. I honestly like this girl."

"Really?" *I honestly like this girl* was no statement of undying love. But I'd never heard Sawyer express even that lukewarm level of affection for anyone in his life, except me.

He nodded sadly. "It's not going to work out. There's nothing I can do. Talking about it won't change that."

"Are you sure?" I coaxed him. Despite all these confessions in the last fifteen minutes, Sawyer and I weren't the kind of friends to discuss our problems with each other at length. We both avoided saying anything serious if we could possibly help it. I was dying of curiosity about who this girl might be, though.

"This is weird," he said, "but I want to keep it private. I'm kind of enjoying, for once in my life, thinking something that doesn't immediately come out my mouth."

That made me laugh. "Let me know how it goes. I've never experienced that myself."

"I know." He extended his hand across the cab. "Come here."

With a glance around to make sure we weren't being watched by innocent tourists on the sidewalk, I scooted closer to him.

He kissed me on the mouth. Easily, languidly, like Sawyer and I had been kissing for the last two years.

He ended by tugging one of my braids, then backing away. Looking deep into my eyes, he said, "Good luck."

Twelve

MY LESSON WITH BOB AND ROGER WENT ON forever. I desperately needed them to learn basic spreadsheet skills so they would stop relying on me, but teaching those two to use a computer for anything more than surfing the Web was like teaching Xavier Pilkington, Most Academic, to play a dance-competition video game. Bob and Roger took a certain amount of pride in not being able to do this, and they wasted my time bragging about how hopeless they were. I got frustrated with them and told them as much, and they folded their arms and told me I was being huffy. I hadn't run a practice as drum captain yet, but this was what it would be like.

The best part of my evening was getting text messages from Will. After we'd politely said good-bye in band and gone our separate ways, I hadn't expected him to check up on me. I definitely hadn't thought he would entertain me with texts like "Sorry you have to work. You should be here. This partay is off da HOOK!" with a photo of his mom scrubbing the ahffen.

I got home so late that my dad had already left for his shift. Then I stayed up later to do some calculus. Ms. Reynolds was totally on my ass about turning in my homework. She had threatened to petition the principal to *make* me join the math team if I didn't clean up my act. I was pretty sure this was unconstitutional.

"Tia," Will whispered in my ear. His warm breath tickled my earlobe.

"Mmmm," I said, enjoying this dream, even if doing my calculus homework on a date with Will *did* cast me in the part of Angelica.

"Time for school."

I sat straight up in bed. Morning light streamed through the window blind. Will jumped backward just in time to avoid my head smashing his.

I scowled at him. "Are you real?" He looked real. He was tall and taking up half my room, in the Vikings T-shirt he'd worn the night we first met.

He sounded apologetic as he said, "Harper told me where the key was. You can't skip. She said you skipped a bunch of days last year, and then, when you got the flu, you had to come to school anyway or you would have flunked. She said whenever you haven't shown up at school by seven fifteen, everybody knows your dad stayed late at work and didn't come home to wake you. You don't wake up when people call your phone, apparently? Or when people bang on the front door."

"Mmph." I collapsed on my bed again. Something stuck me in the back of the neck. I pulled my calculus book out from under me and placed it on my tummy. "Why did she send *you*? She doesn't love me anymore?"

"She and Kaye said it's my turn. I hope you don't mind. I figured it would look like we're into each other if I came to get you." He wagged his eyebrows at me. "You know, for Angelica."

"Oh, we *are* into each other," I assured him. "You are seeing my sexy boudoir and sleeping ensemble. Take it all in, lovah." I flung my arms wide so he had a clear view of my tank top and plaid flannel pants. Then I held out my hand. After he helped me up, I brushed past him, whispering huskily, "Let me grab a shower."

He looked around the room for my nonexistent clock, then pulled his phone from his pocket and glanced at it. "We don't have time."

I winced. "I smell, though. Do I smell?" I leaned down so he had access to the top of my head. "Sorry, I usually ask my dad, but you'll have to fill in."

He sniffed my hair. "Yes, but not unpleasantly."

"Aw, you're such a romantic." I yawned and shuffled toward the door. "Just let me brush my teeth, then."

"You're going to school in pajamas?"

"It won't be the first time. Or the last, probably, because production has picked up at the boat plant, and my dad will be taking a lot more shifts in the next few months." I stopped in the doorway and looked back toward the piles of clothes in my room. "I guess I could put on a bra."

"If you insist." He watched me like he was waiting for me to do this in front of him. Finally he said, "I'll leave you alone to do that."

He was clanking around in the kitchen as I slipped on a bra under my tank top. With weird green lace sewn around the edges of blue satin cups, it looked like something Violet might have bought at a discount store when she was twelve. I didn't know where half my clothes had come from or whether they were actually mine. I used to get in huge trouble for touching my sisters' stuff, but now that they were all gone, whatever they'd left behind had gotten absorbed into my wardrobe. The bra showed under my tank, but I didn't have time to paw through piles for another. While I was at it, I traded my pajama pants for gym shorts. I would have to dash home and change before work. On the other hand, if I showed up for my shift that afternoon looking like I'd just left the gym, maybe Bob and Roger would stop threatening to promote me.

I ducked into the bathroom to pee and wash my face and brush my teeth. When I opened the door, Will was standing there waiting for me with a plastic cup of orange juice in one hand and a Pop-Tart in the other. Toasted! I hadn't had a toasted Pop-Tart in years. "Dude! Where'd you find the Pop-Tarts? I lost them."

"Walk and talk," he said. As I grabbed my backpack and drumsticks and headed for the front door, he told me, "Kaye had some ideas for where they might be."

"Where'd you find the toaster?"

"It wasn't obvious." He held the door open. Locking it behind us and hiding the key, he said, "Kaye told me it was just you and your dad living here."

"It is." We headed up the street to the school fence.

"Why do you have two beds in your room, and someone's stuff that doesn't look like your stuff?" Will asked.

"Oh," I said, laughing at his reference to Violet's purple taste. "My sister moved out last spring when she chased her boyfriend down south of town."

"And you hope she's coming back?"

"I hadn't thought about it," I said. "I mean, do I think her relationship with her boyfriend is dangerously unstable? Yes, but so were my other sisters' relationships, and they haven't moved back home. There's no room for Violet now, really, what with all the stuff in the way. Maybe that's why my dad keeps downsizing." I giggled because that was a funny thought, then stopped giggling because it might have been partly true. "Do I act like I hope she's coming back?"

"Most people who shared a room would take out the extra bed and dresser, or at least spread their own stuff around, when the other person moved out."

"I guess I never felt like I could do anything with Violet's stuff, because it's hers." Of course, Will had a point. Violet had been gone five months. She called me occasionally, but I hadn't seen her at all. If she'd wanted her stuff, she would have come to get it by now.

We'd reached the fence. He threw his flip-flops over first—bright boy—and then vaulted over easily. I tossed my flip-flops over, then handed my stuff to him on the other side. By the time I climbed down, he was peering at my phone.

"You *do* have an alarm on here, like everybody else," he said. "You can make it louder so it will actually wake you up."

"Yeah, I know." I picked up my backpack and followed him across the parking lot, tapping my drumsticks on my hip. "But then it goes off on the weekends when I don't want to get up so early." Specifically, when I had been out late the night before.

"You can set it one way for weekdays and another for weekends," he said. "Look." He held out the phone.

I didn't even glance at it. "Too complicated."

He stopped so suddenly that I nearly ran into him. "Remember yesterday when you were complaining to me about how Bob and Roger won't take very easy steps to help themselves? You were getting really frustrated and wondering why they're such dorks?"

Grimacing, I secured my drumsticks under one arm and took my phone from him. "Point taken. And ambience ruined. I thought we'd had a nice sexy morning together, but you're basically calling me a pudgy old man."

His eyes softened, and he touched my bottom lip with his thumb and forefinger. He murmured, "Does this school have a rule about PDA in the parking lot?"

"I don't know," I whispered. "Let's find out."

He slid his hand down to my chin and held me there while he kissed me. His mouth was hot on mine. My whole body shivered in the humid morning.

"Hey!" somebody shouted from a passing car. "At least stand on a line while you're doing that. You're taking up a space."

Will broke the kiss but pulled me closer protectively. Squinting over my head and looking annoyed, he shot the car the bird.

"That's not going to help your popularity," I warned him.

"This is the Home of the Pelicans," he reminded me. "Shooting the bird is a sign of solidarity. Come on." He slid his arm around my shoulders, and we walked to calculus together, where I took my rightful place in the desk behind his.

In the shop that evening, exactly at closing time, I heard the antique cowbell jangle on the door. I was back in the shelves, cleaning pretty effectively because I was a little stressed out about my "date" with Will. And that was him!

Before I could even make it to the front counter, I heard him exclaim, "What a good dog!" But when I rounded the corner, I didn't see him. I peered over the counter. He was sprawled on the floor (*reserved Will Matthews was sprawled on the floor like a three-year-old*) and tangled up with the shop dog, which probably weighed almost as much as he did. He was scratching the dog behind the ears, but with his arms around the thing, he looked more like he was hugging it. The dog licked Will's cheek, flopped its tongue around in its mouth a few times like it was considering the taste, then lapped at Will's nose. Will laughed. "Good boy. Girl?" He peered up at me. "Whose dog?"

"I have no idea."

He cocked his head at me, perplexed, while the dog licked his temple. "Doesn't it belong to Bob and Roger?"

"No." I hollered toward the back of the long shop. "Bob, whose dog?"

His voice came faintly back. "I think she belongs to somebody on First Street. She's waiting for us when we open in the morning. She likes the air-conditioning."

"Makes sense to me," Will told the dog, who licked his eye. Standing, Will wiped at his eyelid, then brushed some of the dog hair off his T-shirt. "I've always wanted a dog. My mom says no because she doesn't want to clean up the hair, but I'm getting a dog the day I graduate from college."

"Most guys say that about a Porsche, like they could afford one on their starting salary."

Will shook his head. "Dog." He held out his hand to me. "Ready to show me the town?"

"What do you know about this?" It was getting late, and Will had told me he was taking me home. But in the darkness, he stopped the car in front of a white two-story house—a mansion, really, a stalwart survivor of countless hurricanes, built in 1910 in the Georgian style with a tropical twist.

I'd shown him all over our little town in the past few hours. I'd taken him to a seafood joint that was, frankly, way better than the Crab Lab if you were after food rather than free beer on the back porch. I'd taken him on a driving tour of the many beaches besides the one where we'd held the band party. He said he ran long distance on the weekends, so I showed him the trail that extended all the way through town and into the wetlands.

Best of all, we'd run into some basketball players I knew at the seafood joint, a trumpet with her family at the beach, and a sophomore cheerleader on the trail. All of them would alert the media that they'd seen Will and me together. In terms of Will's plan to make Angelica jealous, it was a triple word score.

But I doubted anybody I knew would be walking by on the dark, quiet street where we'd now parked. And this was the first time Will had suggested a stop on the tour.

I stared at the white mansion glowing in the moonlight, trying to puzzle out why Will had brought me here. "What do you mean, what do I know about it?"

"I want to major in architecture in college. My dad says no. He says I have to make sure I'm high up enough in a company that I never get transferred against my will. He wants me to major in business."

"I can't picture you as a business major," I said. "Public Will, the face you show people, yes. Private Will, no. I think you would go a little crazy."

"That's what I think too." He smiled at me in the near darkness. "Do you want to see my super-secret notebook that my parents can never find out about?"

"Sure!" I exclaimed, though I was frightened of what this secret could be. Maybe he was even more of a pirate than I'd imagined. God knew what Private Will had been hiding.

"Here." He reached in front of my knees and opened the glove compartment—not the first place I'd think of for keeping my own super-secret documents, but to each his and her own. He pulled out a spiral-bound artist's pad and placed it in my lap.

I opened the cover. On the first page was a careful drawing of an old building in a row of others, part of a historic downtown district like ours, but three stories instead of two. The drawing wasn't fully executed. Trees and bushes and a big dog on the sidewalk were only quick impressions from a pencil. A stylish wash of light strokes colored them in. But the drawing couldn't truly be called a sketch, either. The lines of the building itself were straight and true, measured and drawn with a ruler.

"Wow," I said reverently.

"I park in front of buildings and draw them," he explained.

I turned the page to reveal an even more detailed drawing of an exquisite old store. "Where is this one?"

"Duluth," he said, looking over my shoulder at the pad. "Most of them are in Duluth." As I turned the page to an elaborate cathedral, he said, "That's in St. Paul. I got grounded for that one, because I didn't tell my parents where

I was going or why. They wouldn't have let me."

I turned the page.

"I'm probably going to get arrested eventually," he said. "Someone will think I'm casing the joint."

I turned another page. There was no end to these gorgeous drawings. Every one of them should have been copied a million times and framed and sold in a tourist shop here in town. They were that pretty.

"I have too much time on my hands, obviously," he said. "I should get a job."

I shook my head. "These are beautiful."

"Thanks." He said this matter-of-factly, proud of his work but confident enough that he didn't need my approval.

"You should major in art, not architecture."

He gave me a thumbs-up. "Great idea. My parents would lose their shit."

"Yeah." I turned the page to a grand house. "I can't even take this in, all the detail. I want to spend a couple of hours with these another day."

He laughed. "Okay."

"I'm not kidding, for once." I turned the page, and there was the house beside us, palm fronds softening the stark logic of the mansion's careful proportions.

"I think it's the coolest house ever," Will explained. "It's so much bigger and so different from everything else in this neighborhood. That's why I wanted to ask you about it. I wondered if it's a city landmark."

"Oh, I'll say!" I laughed. "I used to live there."

He gave me a funny look. "Are you serious?"

"Why would I make up something like that?" I heard my voice rise in anger. I wished it wouldn't, but I couldn't help it when I thought someone was assuming things about my family, and our income, and my dad.

Will's voice rose in turn. "Because I'm the Fucking New Guy, and everybody is giving me incorrect information about the school and the town because that's hilarious and I am a sitting duck."

By "everybody," I assumed he meant Sawyer. I wondered what wild goose chase Sawyer had sent Will on just for spite. And I regretted that our happy talk about Will's cool drawings had unraveled into accusations. I said more quietly, "I really lived here. My dad used to buy run-down houses for cheap so he could fix them while we lived there. Then he sold them at a profit."

"Oh." Will's brows knitted, and he pointed to the FOR SALE sign in the yard. "You weren't able to sell it?"

"We did," I said. "It's been up for sale a couple of times since then. Folks probably buy it thinking they're going to finish fixing it up, and fail miserably, just like we did. I can see why they want it, though. You wouldn't believe the inside. High ceilings. Thick crown molding. An original chandelier in the foyer that makes the light look golden instead of white. And smack in the middle of the house there's an atrium with a fountain, all tiny glass tiles in a mosaic of stylized mermaids. That fountain and the chandelier just *look* 1910."

"That's so cool!" Will exclaimed. "Did the fountain work?"

I almost said yes without thinking. "No. In my mind it works, though. That's funny. I watch all these home improvement TV shows, and couples are always walking through a potential home and saying, 'Ew, we couldn't live here. The walls are blue.' Well, paint them, Sally Jane and Earl! I understand other people can't always see potential like my dad and I can." I paused. "In fact, there are a *lot* of things I can see in my imagination that don't actually happen."

"I know what you mean," Will said. "Me too." His tone told me all I needed to know about what he was thinking.

I grinned across the car at him, so relieved that we were back to normal. But when he didn't make a move on me, I looked toward the mansion again. It drew my eye. I couldn't ignore its white angles glowing in the night. "My dad is brilliant. He has a contractor's license, and he knows how to do everything in a restoration."

Will didn't say anything. As we continued to gaze at the house, I realized why.

I said, "You're thinking my dad is pretty bad at flipping houses, since we didn't finish it. After my mom left, he wanted something more stable. The real estate market was up and down. He had four girls to take care of on one income, and he needed a sure thing. He took a job at the boat factory, thinking he would use that money to supplement his real estate income. Then the factory job offered him extra shifts. He took them. He was never home to fix the house. And then our family shrank, and he realized we'd save money if we moved to a smaller house. That's why we've moved four times in the last seven years. When I leave, he'll probably move into a mailbox. A run-down one."

"Why does your family keep shrinking?" Will asked gently, like he suspected this was a touchy question.

It was. It was so touchy, in fact, that my family had been the subject of many rumors over the years, most of them true. I was surprised Will hadn't heard them all by now.

"I would say you don't have to tell me," he offered, "because obviously you don't want to, but I'd really like to know."

I shifted uncomfortably on the very comfortable black vinyl seat. "Well, I guess it started when I was nine, and my mom was in a car accident."

Out of the corner of my eye, I saw him flinch like he'd been hit. "Oh! Tia, I'm sorry."

"No, she's not dead or anything." I turned to smile at him, reassuring. "At least, we assume. I haven't heard from her in a while. What happened was, she hurt her back, and she got on pain pills, and she couldn't get off. I was so little that I didn't really know what was going on, except that something was wrong, and my sisters wouldn't tell me. Even now when I bring it up, they say they don't want to talk about it. But I gather that she made friends with the people who kept getting the pills for her, and she started a relationship with one of them."

Will took a long, slow breath, giving himself time to think

of some way to respond to that. He exhaled without coming up with an answer. I knew how he felt.

"My parents had Izzy when they were seventeen," I explained, "and Sophia when they were nineteen, and they kept having kids. It's what my mom said she wanted. But I know it was hard on them both. The accident and the pills—it's unfortunate, but I think that opened the door to my mom's downfall. And she walked through it. She started sneaking out to be with the guy she met. She told my dad she was trying to get back something she'd missed out on when they were younger."

"And so you're not going to miss it," Will broke in.

I shrugged. I supposed there was a big contrast between my mom and me, but I'd never given it much thought. "Once when my mom went to see this guy, she forgot about me and left me home by myself. I was ten. I was fine by myself. I should have just stayed cool. But she hadn't told me she was leaving. I couldn't get her on the phone because she'd left it in her bedroom. I panicked and called my dad. He went to find her. And that was the end of their marriage."

I felt Will's hand on my bare leg. Then he mistakenly groped across his art pad and finally found my hand. He asked quietly, "Your dad didn't get her help or anything?"

"They had been talking about it," I said, "but after she left me at home so she could cheat on him, no. Every once in a while, she'll go see one of my sisters and say she's going to clean up, but we've stopped believing it." I looked toward the house again. The front right bedroom on the second floor, the one with the window nearly obscured now by out-of-control palms, had been mine. All my own.

"So!" I turned to Will. "How did my family shrink? That got rid of one of us. Then my oldest sister—that's Izzy—got pregnant when she was—hey! our age. It wasn't exactly a shotgun wedding because my dad has a pistol. Ha ha ha, a little humor there for the boys who want to fake-date me."

"Ha ha," Will said uneasily.

"Izzy moved in with her new husband, and that marriage lasted all of six months. My dad felt more pressure to make money fixing up the house, but also to work more hours, so he could help her out. She was pregnant again by that time. She had to go to court to get her ex to pay child support. And when that finally calmed down, my sister Sophia married her boyfriend because he'd joined the navy and he was about to spend a tour on a submarine. Then she got pregnant. And then he cheated on her."

"On a submarine?" Will interjected.

"No, when he came back to town. And when that calmed down . . . say it."

"Your sister Jane got pregnant?"

"Her name is Violet, and see, that's what she thinks everybody assumes, so she goes out of her way to tell everybody she did *not* get pregnant out of wedlock. Her boyfriend moved south of town for a job. She dropped out of high school to go live with him because she missed him so much. She only had a couple of months left until graduation. That was one of the stupider moves my family members have made, though definitely not the stupidest. And that is how I got rid of my entire family in seven years, except for my dad, and why we have downsized to the point that the next thing smaller is a mailbox."

Will squeezed my hand. "And that's why you say you don't want a boyfriend."

I drew my hand away from his. He was probably right. But knowing where my heebie-jeebies came from didn't make them go away. Suddenly the heat of his skin was burning mine.

"It's not just a sex thing," I said quickly. "You can have a boyfriend without having sex. You can have sex without getting pregs. It's not sex that messes people up. It's love. You can have sex and protect yourself and still keep out of trouble. It's love that starts to tangle everything up, and makes you think that an army private who's been to juvie would make a great dad, and that seventeen is the perfect age to start a family. When my sisters and I used to talk about sex, it wasn't embarrassing as long as we were being honest. It's love that confuses things and makes you unable to explain later why you didn't use a condom. Love and pressure and the feeling that you're everything when you're with this guy, and when he leaves you, you're less than you were before. If you fall in love, you attach yourself to somebody, and you can't do what you want ever again." I examined his drawing of my house. With one finger I traced the outline of my bedroom.

I felt him watching me quietly from his side of the car.

"Sorry," I blurted. "You probably didn't do it with Beverly before you left, after all. You're a virgin, and I've just told you some things you weren't ready to hear."

He didn't say a word.

"Not that there's anything wrong with that," I said to fill the silence. "Some of my best friends are virgins."

Now his silence was making me uncomfortable. Normally I accepted that I was a talker and didn't beat myself up for my big mouth. But right now I felt like I was blathering on and couldn't stop. The only way to fix the blah blah blah was with more blathering, apparently. "You didn't do it with Angelica, did you?" I asked.

At least that got a rise out of him. "No!" he exclaimed. "I've only known her a week!"

That seemed like plenty of time to me, but whatever. "Beverly from Minnesota was your only one, then."

Because of his silence, I assumed that the answer was yes.

"There's your problem," I said. "*You* want to do it with someone you're in love with. Love gets you in trouble. If it were only sex, you could have been getting it on with Angelica by now. But you fell in love with Beverly, and you vowed to make it home to her as soon as you could. Now that she's cheated on you, you're caught between two worlds. You can't move back, and you can't move forward. You're stuck."

"I am," he agreed. "But so are you. You're afraid to make plans because they might get broken. What would having a boyfriend prevent you from doing? Seems to me you don't want to do anything at all."

I glared at him. "You're probably right about getting arrested. We'd better move on before the current owner of this house suspects we're casing the joint and chases us off with a chainsaw."

Will ignored that. Stubbornly he asked, "Why aren't you applying to college or . . . anything? Why won't you even try out for drum corps? You don't talk about any plans after high school, like your life is going to stop. But every one of your close friends is leaving town after graduation."

"Sawyer isn't." As soon as these words left my lips, I regretted them. Will wasn't saying anything that wasn't true, but the truth hurt, and lashing out was my natural response.

"I'll bet he does leave," Will said.

I wondered what he saw in Sawyer that made him think so. There was a lot more to Sawyer than most people knew. He seemed to grow deeper all the time. And since he'd convinced me yesterday that he was interested in someone . . . maybe Will was right. Sawyer would follow a girl elsewhere. I couldn't picture most of our class hanging around town. Not just anybody could get elected Mr. and Ms. Least Likely to Leave the Tampa/St. Petersburg Metropolitan Area.

Will reached over to me. I stiffened, expecting him to take my hand again. Instead, he tugged his art pad out from my hands and tucked it back into the glove compartment where it was safe. He didn't trust me with his work anymore.

He ran his fingers through the shorn back of his hair. "Remember when you told me that Izzy insulted you, and you haven't seen her since?"

I nodded.

"Does Izzy know you're mad at her?" he asked.

"I don't know." I really didn't care. "Why?"

"When you've got a beef with somebody," he said, "you don't act mad. Not right away. You avoid confrontation. It only comes out later, when you make cutting comments. Izzy's lived with you, so she understands that about you. But if you haven't been by her shop, she probably doesn't even know you're angry. She's busy with her job and her kids, but she's wondering why you've gone missing. She thinks you're just busy too."

Letting that hypothesis hang in the air, he started the car.

I was shocked into silence. It made me uncomfortable that he understood so much about me, so quickly. We were already driving through the town's main drag, past the shop where Izzy worked, before I managed to stammer, "I'm—I'm sorry, Will. I'm sorry about unloading all of that on you. I have a chip on my shoulder."

"What you have is not a chip," he said.

As he prepared to turn onto the street leading into my neighborhood, he looked right. His earring glinted under a streetlight. Feeling miserable, I wished I could take back the last half hour of spilling my guts. I tried to balance the evening a little by asking him a personal question, something I'd been curious about since our first night together. "Why did you pierce your ear? Is it a Minnesota thing?"

He huffed out the smallest laugh. "It's a drum line thing."

"Some kind of sick initiation for the Marching Wrath of God? I love it! We should totally do that to the damn freshmen."

"No," he said, "we won the state championship."

"*What?*" I exclaimed. I was impressed with his band, and frustrated all over again about everything our second-rate town was putting him through. Our band made great marks at contests, but we didn't *win*.

"A tattoo would have been better," he said, "but you can't get ink in Minnesota until you turn eighteen."

"You mean, everybody on the drum line got an ear pierced?" I couldn't imagine everybody on *our* drum line doing *anything*, especially not as an organized group.

"Yeah."

"What about the girls?"

"They both had their ears pierced already, but they got another piercing in one ear. Carol—" As the memory came back to him, he cracked up. "They loomed over her with the gun, and she passed out. The first thing she said when she came to was, 'Drum line forever!'" He laughed again, then looked sidelong at me. "I guess you had to be there."

"It sounds like you guys had a lot of fun together."

"We did." He smiled into space and fingered the stud in his ear.

And with a rush, I realized how much he'd lost when he'd

moved here. Not just the position of drum major, the office of student council president, the status of Most Academic, but a group of close friends. Like a second family.

Will put his hand down and glanced at me. "Is wearing a stud uncool in Florida? I thought I might quit wearing it, but then I would have a hole in my ear. Somehow that seems worse."

"I see what you're saying," I told him, because I really did. "And I have never met anyone who took his earlobe so seriously."

He cracked another smile. "I'm a serious guy."

A week and a half ago, I would have agreed with him wholeheartedly. Now I was beginning to wonder. I'd thought Sawyer was growing deeper the longer I knew him, but Will seemed fathomless.

I told him truthfully, "Your earring is the first thing I liked about you."

"For all the wrong reasons." He pulled to a stop in front of my house and looked across the car at me in the dim light. "You were completely wrong about me."

"I'm not sure," I said. "I may be the first person who's been absolutely right."

Thirteen

I FELT SO TERRIBLE ABOUT MY PITY PARTY Wednesday night that I was determined to make it up to Will when we went out Thursday. I'd been wrong when I'd made fun of him for thinking the Tampa area was a hockey mecca. There *was* a rink not far from town. I laced up skates and let him half teach me, half drag me around the oval. But I wished I could have sat there, without being a weirdo, and watched him skate. He made it look easy, even natural. The cold breeze ruffled his short hair as he sped around the rink without me. Best of all, it was cold as Minnesota in the building. While I shivered in a sweater, he grinned in his T-shirt and looked genuinely happy.

Friday we drove a few towns south to a tourist spot full of neon lights and corn dogs for their sunset celebration. The long pier was full of couples embracing each other, acting like they couldn't wait for the day to end and the dark to start their night of romance. More than once I caught Will glancing at girls and guys our age making out. Now that our relationship was fake-official, flirting wasn't as easy as it used to be. An awkwardness still hung between us after I'd gone all TMI Wednesday night.

Saturday was different. I could feel it when I woke up, and I heard it in his voice when he called me to ask about going out that night. We were both sick of these polite dates that ended with him giving me a peck on the cheek at my front door. I made sure that when I opened my front door on Saturday night, he had something to look at.

He gaped at me. Simply looked me up and down with his mouth open.

"You've never seen me quite so clean before." I bent toward him. "Smell me."

He obliged, taking a long whiff of my floral hair. "Great dress." He stared at my legs.

"Thanks."

He lifted my chin with two fingers. "Is that . . . mascara?"

"Yes!" I exclaimed, triumphant.

His eyes roved all over my face, making me feel like our senior class's Best Looking, a title I'd never wanted but that didn't sound too bad when Will was the one bestowing it on me. Finally he said, "Your hair's down."

"It unravels from the braids, sure enough."

"Indulge me for a minute." He tapped his phone, then held it out in front of us. "Selfie. Kiss me right here." He pointed to his cheek.

Taking this picture reminded me a bit too much of Beverly's treacherous selfie with Will's best friend back home. But I wasn't going to deny him this. I pursed my lips—with shiny gloss on them, even—and gave the phone a knowing glance. He snapped the photo.

As we looked down at the image, he slipped his arm around my back with more of that Minnesotan sleight of hand. He said ruefully, "I wanted to post it online to show my friends how cool I am. It's not going to work. You look gorgeous, but I look too exuberant standing beside you, like I can't quite believe it."

I laughed. He did look a little starstruck. Guys didn't get starstruck around me. "I think it's perfect."

Kaye was throwing the night's party in her big, beautiful historic home on a lagoon where the homeowners docked their massive sailboats and had access to the ocean. As we parked at the end of a long line of cars stretching along the grass near her house, I explained to Will that Kaye didn't have parties when her parents weren't home. Her mom actually helped her throw them. Consequently there was no alcohol, but the food was good enough that people came anyway. These gatherings had an innocent, fifties, sock-hop vibe. Frankly, I found them a refreshing change from sitting on the ground and trying to use an empty Coke can as a weed pipe. But guests really bluesing for a drink could always access a box of wine. One had only to determine whose truck bed it was in.

As we hiked up the lawn to her house, holding hands, Will asked the next logical question, knowing me. "Do you want a drink?"

I had a crazy answer: "Not if you're not. It's really hard to communicate with somebody when one of you is drinking and the other isn't."

He gave me a quizzical smile. Now that we were walking near the house, we were getting close to other couples making their way up the yard, so he lowered his voice. "That's an excuse. You don't want to drink every time you go to a party, but by now you have a reputation to uphold. You're glad I'm here, aren't you? You can blame me for all your good behavior."

This boy scared me sometimes, he was so right. I tried to throw him off balance by murmuring, "If I cut down on my drinking, I will still have plenty of bad reputation left. I'll show you later tonight."

He laughed out loud. He looked as pleased and astonished as he had when we took a picture a few minutes before.

"Aw, you're blushing!" I exclaimed, squeezing his hand. "You're cute."

Chelsea and DeMarcus were walking a few yards away—approximately fifteen, in my expert estimation from years of marching up and down a football field. Chelsea called, "I thought it was a robot, but it laughs!"

"It laughs only for me," I called back. I said more quietly to Will, "Seriously, I think that's where we went wrong the first night, why we were misreading each other. I was drunk and you were . . . new."

He winced. "It's terrible being new."

"Is it? Sometimes I fantasize about what it would be like to start over."

"You want to move to Minnesota?" He made it sound like a threat.

"No. I would freeze to death."

Keeping hold of my hand, he backed far enough away to get a good look at my gauzy dress. "You would," he agreed, "because I would want you to keep wearing stuff like that."

"And I think it's beautiful here."

He looked up at the live oaks arching over the house. "It is."

"But I fantasize . . . this is terrible."

He tugged me closer. "You've told me a *lot* of terrible things."

"Er, this is not sexy-terrible but actual-terrible," I said. "I wonder what it would be like to start over without sisters. Not that I want them dead, of course, but if they never existed, and it was just me. I wonder if I would be the same person, or if I would be like Angelica, fighting it out for valedictorian with Aidan and Kaye and DeMarcus and Xavier Pilkington."

Will gave me a dubious look. "You would never be anything like Angelica."

That hurt. After he'd been so nice tonight, though, I was pretty sure he hadn't meant to spray lighter fluid on my feelings and set them on fire. "I know," I said. "I'm sorry."

"I don't mean *that*!" he exclaimed. "It's just . . . Angelica tries really hard, but she's not that bright."

"Really!"

"Yes. Not to be mean. Just my opinion."

Why do you want to date her, then? I wondered. But we didn't all want a rocket scientist, did we? Girls didn't hang out at Xavier's locker. I tried to edit the bitterness out of my voice as I said, "That's my opinion too. I've never heard anyone else say it, but I've known this about Angelica since kindergarten."

He nodded. "She does well in school because she cares and she worries. Like me."

At the bottom of the grand stairs up to the covered front porch, I pulled him to a stop. "You're not like that. Angelica and Aidan care, and they worry, and it's part of their nature. You care and worry too, but it makes you tired." I reached up and rubbed my thumb across the worry line between his brows. "Do you feel tired?"

"Since I've been in Florida, I've been exhausted," he admitted.

I sighed. "Tonight will take care of itself. Angelica will be here. If she's going to get jealous seeing you and me together, we don't have to help that along. Let's forget about our nightly goals and have a good time. Okay?"

The worry line disappeared as he gave me his sexy sideways smile. "What kind of good time do you mean?"

Fifteen minutes later, we were facing off for a

dance-competition video game throwdown. I had thought I would laughingly drag him into the space in front of the huge TV and he would flirtatiously back out again. But as soon as I suggested it, he was ready to go. A crowd gathered around us, bored with my antics but astonished that tight Will Matthews was really going to do this thing.

And then, while the game beeped an electronic countdown to begin and the people around us held their breath, he pointed at me, meaning I was dead meat—just like I'd pointed at him on the football field before the challenge for drum captain.

"Oooooh," the spectators moaned. I felt my face turn bright red. I had to win now.

But at the end of the song, Will had beaten me up and down Kaye's expensively appointed living room. *And* he'd drawn an even bigger crowd. Will Matthews could totally do the Dougie.

"That is not even fair!" I squealed after guys had stopped slapping him on the back and Chelsea had shooed us off the dance floor so she could have a turn. "There's no way I would have challenged you if I'd known you could actually *dance*! I should have made you sign some sort of disclaimer." I poked him in the chest.

He grabbed my hand, grinning. "Never underestimate me."

"I won't!"

"My sisters have that video game. Let's get in line and go again." He tapped me on the chest like I'd poked him. This placed his fingers in the bare V-neck of my dress, just above my cleavage and my heart. "You're mine."

Over the course of the party, he beat the stuffing out of me twice more, then beat Chelsea to become the undisputed champion. The rest of the time, we were mostly standing to one side while somebody else took a turn. His arm circled my waist and my head nestled under his chin in a way that absolutely turned me on, and not just physically. I felt my friends' eyes on us, overheard their whispered conversations about us, and I loved it. I began to understand, just a little bit, why couples latched on to each other and went off into a corner to watch the party instead of participating themselves. There was a certain high, a heady bonding experience, in seeing and being seen.

A bonding experience with Will was the *last* thing I needed when our alliance was only temporary, to drive Angelica to distraction. But I did think the party was good for both of us as individuals. As we moved from circle to circle, entering different conversations, *everyone* told me, "You look great!" I could have taken this to mean, "Normally you look like crap. I am pleasantly surprised that you can hang when the affection of a ridiculously cute guy is on the line!" But there was no point in taking offense about an observation that was true. I *felt* great.

And *everyone* said to Will, "Nice moves!" He colored and laughed when people told him this. He didn't offer his own thoughts on his dancing prowess or join the conversation, but he didn't look like he wanted to crawl away and die, either.

Being crowned our unofficial Best Dancer had given him an identity besides Fucking New Guy or Cheating Dog, and his new title was one he seemed strangely comfortable with. I found myself looking up at him, his earring glinting in the lamplight, and experiencing a wash of pleasure that he was so adorable and, for the time being, mine.

But one thing nagged at me the whole night. When Will was in conversation with some football players about the Tampa Bay Lightning professional hockey team, a subject on which he was the authority and I was clueless to the point of not knowing the nouns from the verbs in this terminology, I took him aside and whispered in his ear. "Look without looking like you're looking. Who is Sawyer staring at so forlornly?"

I held still while Will gazed over my head. Sawyer stood against the wall. He talked to the many people who passed by him, but he wasn't organizing a practical joke or getting plastered on surreptitious boxed wine, like normal. He seemed quiet, for Sawyer—almost thoughtful. And I could have sworn he was staring at one girl in particular.

"Kaye?" Will asked in my ear.

That's what I'd been afraid of. Talk about a girl out of Sawyer's reach.

"Now he's headed for the door," Will reported.

I looked up at Will. "Don't say anything about this, okay? It's sensitive."

"Okay."

"I'm going to talk to him for a sec because I'm worried about him. I am not flirting with him."

"I trust you," Will said.

If he'd genuinely trusted me, he wouldn't have needed to say this.

I couldn't think about that right now. After squeezing his hand one last time, I crossed the crowded living room and slipped out the front door, hoping to catch Sawyer before he disappeared.

From the high porch, I should have been able to glimpse him descending the staircase or walking through the yard toward the street. I didn't see him until I caught a movement out of the corner of my eye. He was sitting by himself on the porch swing, one foot propped on his knee and the other on the floor, propelling himself gently back and forth. I slipped onto the bench next to him.

His arm had relaxed along the back of the seat, but now he pulled it close. "Careful. Your boyfriend will get jealous."

I glanced at the house behind his shoulders. I didn't want anybody inside to overhear us. I was pretty sure the nearest window was the dining room rather than a place where the party was going on. Not taking any chances, I asked very quietly, "It's Kaye, isn't it?"

He gave me that half-crazed look he got when threatened—but this time his raised eyebrows made him look less dangerous and more desperate. "Am I being that obvious?"

"Definitely not," I assured him. "I only saw it because I

was looking for it. Anybody else would be flabbergasted." I gazed at him, his blond hair bright in the dim light. He looked incredibly sad. Now that I saw this, I couldn't believe I hadn't noticed before. "How long?"

"Since I moved here," he murmured.

That was two years ago. By that time, Kaye had already been dating Aidan for a year and was locked into the habits of her life with him.

"It's worse lately," Sawyer said. "I used to think surely she would get tired of him telling her what to do and break up with him. That's when I would make my move. But the closer we get to graduation, the clearer it seems they're not breaking up. Being back at school with her makes it excruciating. The mascot travels with the cheerleaders to every school event, you know. I thought I wanted to be near her, but it turns out I'm just putting myself through hell."

I nodded. "I know what you mean." I remembered marching through the halftime show next to Will on Monday, so close to him physically, but so far away. My stomach turned over. And my heart went out to Sawyer. I couldn't imagine living with that pain for a couple of years.

"I'm blowing this joint," Sawyer said, easing up from the swing so it didn't shift and send me flying. He *could* be courteous, but Kaye would never believe it. "I'm sure I can find a better party."

"I hope you have a good night," I called as he headed for the stairs.

Descending into the darkness, he called back over his shoulder, "I hope you don't fall in love."

Walking back into the party, I tried to shake the uneasy feeling he'd given me. I'd had a great time with Will that night. Just like my very first night with Will, I counted it as one of the best experiences of my life. The key to enjoying myself with Will was making sure I didn't think too hard about it. I wanted that euphoria back again.

Will was exactly where I'd left him, talking hockey with the football team. He was even speaking as I approached. But his eyes cut to me and stayed on me. When I reached him, he encircled me with one arm and whispered, "Angelica watched you follow Sawyer out."

Tingles spread across my face as I whispered back, "Then you and I need to look like we're finally having that good time we talked about."

Fourteen

I TOOK HIS HAND AND TUGGED HIM FARTHER into the living room. I'd thought we could claim a couch in the corner or—if push came to shove—one overstuffed chair. But the night was growing old, and the comfy furniture was occupied by couples getting to know each other better. Will saw this too. He walked through the stately arched doorway of the living room and kept walking until we reached the kitchen table.

I stepped closer to him and spoke in his ear so he could hear me over the video game music and the laughter. "We can't flirt here. All the surfaces are hard."

He turned his head slowly. His eyes were wide and his mouth was twisted to one side to keep from laughing while he pretended to be outraged at me for uttering the word "hard."

"Damn it," I said, "you know what I mean." Surely he did. Settling in for flirting (or more) at a party required plush seating.

"We'll make it work." He pulled out a chair for me from under the table. After I sprawled in it with a dispirited sigh, he sat in the chair next to mine. We might as well have been doing our calculus homework together, the turn-on nobody could deny.

And then he reached around my sides, grabbed the seat of my chair, and dragged me toward him until we were facing each other, knee to knee. "There," he said.

That did seem better for flirting. But all of a sudden, I felt shy around him. I found myself looking toward the cabinets—nothing more interesting there than a state-of-the-art microwave—and then the other way toward the crowd in the living room, where, on the couch, Brody and Grace had not gotten into it sufficiently to draw anybody's attention for real.

Will put two fingers on the side of my chin and pointed my face toward his again. "Hey. You're supposed to be flirting with me."

"Oh, suddenly this is *my* job? *You're* supposed to be flirting with *me*."

"I *did* flirt with you," he insisted. "I touched your chin just now."

"Oooh!" I said, raising my eyebrows and pursing my lips to show him exactly how impressed I was, which was *not*.

"I touched your *chair*," he said.

"If that counts for flirting, I'm going outside to touch the right rear fender of your car. That will count for getting to third base." I started to get up.

"No," he said, grabbing both my thighs just above the knee.

While the shock of his touch shot through me, I eased back down in my chair. He slowly took his hands away, a horrified expression on his face. He started to put his hands up in the air to show me he hadn't meant to touch me quite so high—and then realized this didn't look very flirtatious. He put his hands back on his own thighs.

After another silent thirty seconds of staring at the design on his T-shirt, I said, "I don't know why this is so hard."

Then I realized I'd said the *H*-word again. He gave me the fake-outraged look, which should have broken the ice but didn't. Nothing could. We sank into another excruciating silence. The more our flirting mattered, the worse we were at it.

The song on the video game changed, from an emo classic to a funky groove. Will relaxed as he always did when the beat was good, transforming from an uptight faux-boyfriend to my friend the drummer. His shoulders settled against the back of his chair, and his fingers tapped out the beat on his thigh, his right pointer finger on the snare downbeat and his left finger on the bass drum.

I relaxed too. My unease fell away, and all that was left was the usual desire to be around him, talk to him, joke with him, capture his attention, bask in his glow—coupled with the fun of sitting so close to him, our knees touching.

Slowly I reached across my thighs, across his, and put my fingers on top of his hands. I moved his hands from tapping on his thighs to tapping on mine.

Still drumming his beat, he glanced up at me, flashing those blue eyes, and gave me a sly smile.

I kept coaxing his hands up my thighs, so high that if Angelica had looked in, I might have gotten called a name.

Will was aware of this too, apparently. His lips parted like he couldn't believe I was so forward and he wanted out.

Now I wished I hadn't done it. I'd only been teasing him, frustrated that we were reduced to this awkward silence. I hadn't meant to chase him off and make things worse.

He turned and glanced into the living room. With his eyes still on the front door, he leaned toward me and said, "Angelica just left with Xavier Pilkington."

Inside, I burst into laughter. Of *course* Angelica was finally going to get it on with Xavier Pilkington. They would be rocking his car with their synchronized typing as they spent the end of their Saturday night working on the English paper that wasn't due until two weeks from Tuesday.

But I died a little too. I was afraid of what this meant. Now that she was gone, especially with another guy, there was no reason for Will and me to continue this charade. Our heady night together was over.

"Tia," he said.

I nodded, bowing my head and bringing it closer to his. At least I could feel his breath in my ear one last time before we went our separate ways.

"When we arranged our deal to make Angelica jealous, I didn't say what I really meant, which was, please go out with me. I want to be with you. I don't want it to be fake, and I don't want it to end tonight."

Heart racing, I sat back in my chair. "So, you never really wanted to get Angelica back? That was just a ruse to get me to go out with you?"

He watched me carefully, like he was afraid I would bolt. "No, not exactly. I didn't think it all the way through. But you said you wanted to help me. This was a way you could help me. And in the back of my mind I was probably thinking, *Grab.*" He slid his hand around my waist. *"Opportunity."* He circled my fingers with his. *"Grab."* Holding my hand, he met my gaze and waited for my answer.

I found the courage, but slowly. "Okay."

His fingers massaged mine as he leaned forward and whispered, "You left out a stop when you took me on a tour of town."

"What's that?" I asked, beaming in anticipation of what he would say.

"A place people go to be alone. Do you have one of those?"

"We do." It was Harper's grandfather's strip of beach. He could have sold it for a billion dollars and retired in a mansion, but he chose to continue living in his little bungalow on the same street as Sawyer's house and keep his fishing boat down at the city marina. Harper had given Kaye and me the code to open the gate at this private beach in case we ever needed it.

Now I did. Harper's boyfriend, Kennedy, seemed more interested in talking smack with his artsy guy friends after hours than going parking with her. Aidan and Kaye would stay here at her house until the end of her party. The beach belonged to Will and me tonight.

"Do you have a condom?" I asked.

We were driving in Will's throaty car toward the beach. The question hung so starkly in the air that I almost imagined I could see it centered over the armrest between us, blinking as streetlights and the shadows of palm trees alternated overhead. Asking the question meant clarifying what we were about to do.

After a pause, he said, "Yes. I bought them on my way home from your house that first night."

I hooted laughter. "A little sure of yourself, weren't you?"

He grinned. "No. Just motivated."

"I'm on the pill, too," I said. "Due to my family history, I make sure I'm super safe."

He nodded, then swallowed with difficulty like his mouth was dry. "I want you to know something," he said. "When I got so mad on the first day of practice and threw my phone, and you said my girlfriend had taken advantage of me before I left . . ."

"I was so out of line," I said. "You were right when you said I hold stuff in and pretend I'm not mad, and it comes out later as a backhanded insult. I'm sorry."

He shook his head. "No, I mean, she didn't. Take advantage of me. We didn't do it. The whole time we were dating, she said she wasn't ready. And the night I left, she did it with my best friend. So she *was* ready, just not for me. I guess it doesn't matter. But I didn't want you to think that I was that . . ."

"Experienced?"

"Naïve," he said, "that I wouldn't know what was going on if she tried to trick me into, like, putting out or whatever." He glanced at me. "Or experienced."

I touched his hand on the gearshift, lifted my hand when he had to shift, and settled my hand on his again. "Are you sure you want to?"

"Yes," he said instantly. He wasn't smiling, exactly, but his whole face looked happy, starry eyed and breathless with the idea. Then he started laughing uncontrollably. "Yes!" he chuckled. "Good Lord. But you're not."

"Me!" I exclaimed. Then a rush of warmth flowed through me. It was relief that we wouldn't do this. Not tonight. And something more: a deep appreciation that he knew somehow what I'd been feeling without me having to tell him.

"If it didn't mean anything, you'd be willing," he said. "Now that it means something, you want to go slow."

I gazed at him across the car, his head and shoulders mostly in shadow. The moonlight burnished his short hair, turning it bronze, and kissed his long lashes and long nose, his expressive mouth. This time I knew better than to think he looked handsome only because of the moon. I had been a fool to push this guy away.

"Well," I said, "I don't know about *slow*."

He was laughing again as he pulled up to the gate. After we were through and I'd locked it behind us, he drove underneath the palms. The trees were thick at first, then more sparse, until the grove opened onto the beach. The moonlight streaming toward us across the ocean was as brilliant as the sun.

"Wow," he breathed.

"I told you it was beautiful here."

He cut the engine. Instantly the sound of waves crashing on the beach rushed to fill that space. He turned to me. Now he would hand me one of his delightfully cheesy pickup lines. It *was* beautiful here, he would say, but he didn't mean the beach. He meant me.

He caught me completely off guard when he said instead, "I fell for you that first night we were together. And you can say it's because of what we were doing, or I was rebounding from Beverly, or I was stressed from the move, but I know how I feel. I love you."

We weren't touching anymore. I sat on my side of the car. He sat on his, watching me with a serious expression in his shadowed eyes, the worry line between his brows deeper than ever.

"I love you too," I breathed.

"You have got to be kidding me," he complained. "Now I'll *never* get laid."

I giggled as he tumbled his big frame over into my side of the car and eased the seat back flat. Kissing me deeply, he unbuttoned the front of my dress, then reached around to unhook my bra. Then he bared my breasts and put his mouth on me.

"I like it when you do that."

His lips brushed my skin as he spoke, and his low voice sent chills through me. "Yeah, I remembered you like it when I do that."

A long time and endless explorations later, his warm hand moved into the front of my panties and rubbed me there. He knew what he was doing, and I figured he'd done this plenty of times before. Naïve he was not—not about this. I'd done it before too, but with him, it definitely felt different. Before long, sparkles like points of moonlight on the waves washed down my body. He kissed me deeply as it happened.

Then he placed sweet kisses on the corner of my mouth and chuckled to himself. "I'm the king of the world," he murmured.

In a sexy, satisfied tone that most chicks would use to reaffirm their love, I said, "You are the king of the dorks."

He closed his eyes and rubbed the tip of his nose back and forth against mine. He breathed into my mouth, "I'm the king of you."

"Yes, you are," I said softly, "but not for long." I slid my hand onto him. "Your turn."

Fifteen

THE ALARM ON MY CELL PHONE WOKE ME midmorning on Sunday, and I cursed Will within an inch of his existence. I was justified in doing that now that we were in love. He was the one who'd convinced me to start using an alarm to get myself up in the morning. Now, because I was responsible, the timer had gone awry. After staying up late with him last night, I was up bright and early, rather than sleeping until the last possible second before I had to go in to the antiques shop.

But when I glanced at the screen, I saw it wasn't the alarm. It was Violet calling. That meant she was in trouble.

Five minutes later I was on the phone with Will. "Can I borrow your car?"

"Yes," he yawned. "Why?"

"Don't ask," I said.

"I'm asking."

I let out a sigh that lasted for about seven seconds, one for every year my mom had been gone. "Violet wants to come home. She wants my dad to come get her right this moment before her boyfriend shows up, which means she feels threatened. And I can't wake my dad for this. He has to get a full night's sleep before he goes to work tonight, or it's a safety issue. He used to take off work all the time to get Izzy and Sophia out of trouble, and he racked up so many demerits that they were threatening to fire him. He can't take off work for that shit anymore. I'll go get her myself."

"I'll go with you," Will said.

"No!" I exploded. If I wasn't careful, I was going to wake up my dad with my hysterics. I said more quietly, "This is exactly why I shouldn't have called you, but I thought you would be furious if you found out I called Sawyer."

"Tia!" he barked right back. He must have been afraid his parents would overhear him, too, because he took a deep breath, then lowered his voice. "Sawyer wouldn't let you go alone either. No guy in his right mind would let you borrow his car to do something dangerous by yourself."

"It's not dangerous, exactly," I qualified. "Maybe not. Her boyfriend disappeared with his friends for three days and left her at their apartment with no car. The only reason it might be the slightest bit dangerous is that they have a bad habit of coming back."

"Who is *they*?"

"My sisters' boyfriends and fucked-up husbands," I explained. "And in all the times my dad has rescued my sisters, a gun has never come out, but I wouldn't be surprised. I keep up with the news. This is how people get shot."

"Then why are you going?" Will demanded.

"My dad can't," I said. "So I have to."

"Then so do I," Will said. "I'll be there in five." He hung up.

I cursed him again, not because he'd fallen down on the job this time, but the opposite. I did *not* want him witnessing the Cruz family's annual audition for a reality show. But he was right. I should have known there was no way to borrow a guy's car without the guy attached.

If he was coming with me, though, I was going to use him. After finding something to put on among the piles in my own room, I waded to the laundry room and searched there. When we'd first moved in, I'd been very careful about sorting the clean laundry from the dirty. I knew the clean shirt I wanted was under there somewhere. But we'd had way too much stuff to store in this tiny house, and over the months, the laundry room had become the place to stash things. I excavated the back wall like an archaeological dig. By the time Will knocked softly on the front door, I'd found it.

I pulled him inside the house. "Put this on," I said, handing him one of my dad's sleeveless T-shirts that he used to cut grass in, back when he cut the grass. "It's clean."

Will held it up and eyed the oil stains dubiously.

"Let me rephrase that," I said. "It's been washed. But you know what? You're right. You have a respectable tan now, and you could just take off your shirt when we get over there." I stretched the bottom of his T-shirt up above his waistband to make sure there wasn't a preppie flat front going on, like Aidan would wear. They were cargo shorts, which would do nicely. My eyes moved to his thick arms. Briefly I considered giving him a Sharpie tattoo on his biceps.

"You've got your shades?" I asked. "And a baseball cap you can turn around backward?" When he nodded, I said, "Let's go."

The apartment was worse than I'd pictured. I knew Violet and Ricky had moved three times in the five months they'd been together. They had a nasty habit of not paying their rent. I figured the apartment had gotten worse each time, but I wasn't prepared for this: brick buildings that didn't look so old but hadn't been taken care of at all, tagged with black graffiti—not even colorful, pretty graffiti—underneath a tangle of palm trees and dehydrated-looking water oaks, surrounded by long grass and trash, all practically underneath the interstate.

Will pulled his car into one of the empty spaces, between a rusted-out truck propped up on concrete blocks and a scary-looking van for plumbers or kidnappers. "Wow," he said, gazing at the building. "Really?"

"Yes," I said. "Honk the horn."

"That's rude," he said. "You'll get us shot."

"Not for that," I said. "They're used to it." Teenage high school dropouts had their own code. I was a little horrified that I knew it so well.

He hit the horn, two short beeps.

"No, really lay on it," I said.

Grimacing, he gave the horn a good long honk.

I watched the apartments. Violet opened a door and waved. I waved back so she'd know where we were, because Will's down-and-out 1970s Mustang blended in pretty well with the other vehicles in this lot. Will fit in himself with his aviators on, his hat backward, and his shirt off. I didn't mention this to him.

The next second, Ricky appeared beside her in the doorway. He grabbed her raised arm. She jerked away from him and vanished into the apartment. He shot us the bird before following her.

"Nice," Will said. "Shouldn't we go help her move her stuff? Because it looks like that asshole isn't going to."

"Nah, she won't have much." She hadn't left with much, and I doubted she'd had the money to buy anything while she'd been here. "But here's how you can help." I dug in my purse and handed him the cigarettes and lighter I'd bought when we'd stopped for gas. "Stand against the bumper, light a cigarette, and glare toward the apartment. Flex your guns if you can find an excuse."

He stared at the package in my hand. "I've never smoked."

Sighing impatiently—and then wishing I hadn't, because Will was doing me some very serious favors here—I unwrapped the cellophane and drew out a cigarette for him. "Light the tobacco end, with brown stuff in it. Suck on the filter end. Just inhale the smoke into your mouth, not your lungs, so you don't have a coughing fit."

Taking the cigarette and lighter, Will swore and slid out of the car, slamming the door behind him. He rounded to the front on the side nearest the apartments and leaned back against the hood, as instructed. Though the midday was oppressively hot and sunny and calm, like every August day in Florida that happened to be hurricane free, he cupped his hand around the cigarette while he lit it, as if he were standing in a high wind. Then he exhaled in one steady stream of smoke. He must have seen this on TV. From where I was sitting, I couldn't tell whether he was glaring at the apartment, but he'd followed my other instructions impeccably. He was probably following that one too.

Ricky watched him through the apartment window. If he'd toyed with the idea of convincing or forcing Violet to stay, in the face of my tough boyfriend who'd come to help rescue Violet, now he was thinking twice.

Ricky disappeared from the window. Violet backed out the door. Ricky came after her. I could see him yelling and hear the echo on a two-second delay. But he didn't follow her, just hung on to the doorjamb and hollered as she jogged down the stairs with a garbage bag slung over her shoulder.

"Show's over," I told Will. "Come inside." I was afraid that if he was going to get shot, now would be the time.

He bent toward my window and blew smoke at me. The sight surprised him, and he jumped a little. "Sorry," he said, exhaling more smoke at the same time. He coughed and turned whiter than normal. "What do I do with this?" Discreetly he held up the butt in front of his body, where Ricky wouldn't see what he was asking me.

"Throw it on the ground and step on it to put it out," I said carefully, like I was presenting Smoking 101 on *Sesame Street*.

"That's littering."

I gestured out the window. "They seem to like that here."

He couldn't argue with that. He threw down the cigarette to join the others on the asphalt, ground it out under his shoe, then rounded the car and slipped behind the wheel, reeking of smoke. "I think I might throw up."

"From the heat or the smoke?"

He closed his eyes and leaned back against the seat. "Both."

"Sorry," I said, patting his knee. "You did great."

"How many other sisters do you have, again?"

I watched Violet turn around in the parking lot and scream a parting shot at Ricky before running toward us. "Two," I said absently, "but they've already been through this, so maybe we're done." More likely, we *weren't* done, but Will and I would have moved on from each other by the time history repeated itself.

With a start, I realized that my usual way of thinking about Will was wrong. We were together. He would still be around the next time Violet did something stupid like this.

Or, now that I finally had a boyfriend, maybe it was *my* turn to do something stupid.

Stupid*er*.

I got out of the car and pushed my seat forward so Violet could collapse into the tiny back seat with her garbage bag containing all her worldly possessions—other than the ones littering my own bedroom floor. Will immediately cranked the car and backed out. I think all three of us tensed, watching the rearview mirror, until we made it up the ramp onto the interstate.

Violet let out a long sigh. "Where's Dad?"

"Asleep."

"On the weekend?"

"Yes, he's going in tonight. He's worked the last twenty-eight nights without time off."

"Jesus," Violet said. "Well, thanks for rescuing me, sis." She leaned over the seat to plant a kiss on my cheek. "And you." She kissed Will's cheek.

"Violet is like me but drunk," I explained to Will, "even when she's sober."

"Violet Cruz," she said, sticking one hand very close to Will's face.

Will reached back to shake her hand awkwardly without looking around at her. "Will Matthews."

"You talk funny," she said. "Are you from Russia?"

"Yes," he said.

"Are you a friend of Tia's, or . . ."

"I'm her boyfriend," he said self-righteously.

Violet gasped dramatically. "*You* have a *boyfriend*?" she squealed at me. "You said you would *never* have a boyfriend."

"Yes." My stomach turned upside down. Now I knew how Will felt. I might vomit, but not from the heat.

"Are you pregnant?" she asked me.

I whipped around in my seat. "Sit down and put your seat belt on." Waiting for her to do this, I said, "You look like shit." She really did. She used to put a lot of effort into her clothes and hair and makeup, drinking up anything Izzy could teach her. This morning she wore sweats pushed up to her knees and a tank top. She could have used her blue-and-green bra. She had dark circles under her eyes. At least her dirty hair was done up in a cute topknot like she hadn't completely lost touch with how teenagers dressed when they were trying to look like they didn't care but they actually did.

She smirked at me. "Thanks."

"You look like you dropped out of high school and spent the last five months smoking pot, getting screwed, and watching TV."

"The cable got cut off." She settled back against the seat and let out another long sigh. "Downtown Tampa is really beautiful."

I looked around at the skyscrapers surrounding us as the interstate snaked through town. I supposed it was a pretty city. But then, when we crossed the bay, she said, "This bridge is really beautiful," and when we turned onto the coastal highway, she said, "This town is really beautiful," even though at that point we were passing a used car lot. I thought she was just glad to get away from Ricky.

"Oooh, boiled peanuts!" she exclaimed at a hand-lettered sign in front of a big boiler on the side of the road. "Stop stop stop! I haven't had breakfast."

Neither had I. Will might not have either, but it was all about Violet. He pulled the Mustang into a gas station parking lot and stopped. I climbed out of the car and pushed the seat forward to let Violet out. As she stood, she asked me, "Do you have three dollars?"

"Listen," I told her. When we were little, my sisters had screamed bloody murder at me when I so much as *touched* something of theirs. I wanted them to love me, though, so I let them take anything of mine that they wanted—until I figured out what was going on. I had really gone off on Izzy one day. It had been a week before any of them spoke to me again, much less laughed at my jokes, but they *did not take my stuff anymore.*

"O-*kay*," Violet said, digging in her own pocket for cash and stomping toward the guy ladling peanuts into plastic bags that looked, frankly, used.

I leaned against the car while she finished this important transaction. Will looked at me through the window. "You're not dealing well with this."

"Shut up," I snapped. I knew I should regret that, because Will was helping me out and I was supposed to love him, but all I felt was fed up.

Violet skipped back to the car and ducked inside. As I slammed the door and Will pulled back onto the road, she tried to hand me a peanut still in its shell. "Want one?"

"Violet," I said.

"Jeez!" She exclaimed. "Will Matthews, do y'all eat boiled peanuts in Russia?"

He laughed nervously. "No."

And then, of course, she shelled the peanut and pressed the meat of the nut past his lips, into his mouth.

"Would you stop?" I whined, so annoyed by her manic mood swing. Any other day I might have thought she was halfway cute, but not while Will was there to see.

Will spit the nut into a napkin. "That is horrible! Nuts should not be mushy."

Violet giggled and retreated quietly into the back.

After a pause, Will held his hand out toward her over the seat. "Give me another."

He was so adorable. Handsome, strong, stoic. Vulnerable. Willing to laugh at himself at every turn. A wave of love washed over me, a yearning to touch him and talk to him alone, chased closely by blind panic that this was exactly how Violet had felt at first about Ricky.

"Ahhhhhh!" Violet yelled, teasing Will. "I knew it." She shelled a peanut and put the meats in his palm.

They settled into a companionable silence. The car roared along the road. Alt-rock whispered on the radio. Violet cracked nuts and deposited some in Will's hand whenever he held it out. Only I was fuming in my bucket seat, knowing now that I would have to break up with him as soon as we got home.

Sixteen

HE WAS SO SURPRISED AT MY WORDS THAT HE stepped backward, crunching through the magnolia leaves in the driveway. To give himself time to think, he reached through the open window of his car, snagged his T-shirt, and pulled it on.

He recovered quickly after that, walking forward to tower over me again. "No," he said. "You're upset. It's been a really stressful morning. Just have something to eat, a shower might be nice, go to work. I'll come pick you up after your shift at the shop, and we'll talk about it."

"See?" I spat. "This is how it starts. You convince me of things. You get everything you want, and I forget what I wanted in the first place."

I was serious, and he began to get it. His nostrils flared as he said, "So you're breaking up with me after we've been together for . . ." He pulled out his phone and glanced at it. "Nope, it hasn't been quite twelve hours."

"That's a record for me," I said, "because I've never been with anybody at all."

"*I* don't think this is funny!" He half turned away from me and ran his hands up the back of his neck, where his long hair used to be. "When you said on the first day of band practice that Beverly tricked me . . . no. *You're* the one who did that. You wanted another hookup that didn't mean anything. Maybe you even wanted to see this look on my face again. Do you get off on making me feel like an idiot?"

"Listen," I seethed, then cringed at the volume of my voice. I would wake my dad over this stupid shit. Though my heart was racing, I managed to say calmly and reasonably, "I haven't been the person that you wanted. I've sent you mixed signals. I've also changed my mind. But I've never lied to you. What I've said and done is exactly what I was feeling at the moment, and—"

"*That's enough,*" he barked, putting his hand up to stop me. "I'm going to get in my car and drive away. You can't change your mind after this. Don't flirt with me. Don't cry. Don't stare at me and look jealous when I go out with somebody else. You've jerked me around enough, and now it's over."

"Fine." I shrugged and headed for the house. Behind me I could hear the Mustang backing out of the driveway and roaring down the street. In front of me, my vision collapsed into a tunnel, dark all around and clear only at the center. I opened the front door.

As I stumbled inside, I heard Harper say *Breathe* inside my head. I inhaled a long noseful of stale air, a house full of dust.

I left the front door open.

Violet was in my room—our room—lying on her bed, staring at the ceiling. The manic mood that took over her when she was stressed was fading away now. She and I were opposites in that regard. She was normally more serious and got silly under pressure, whereas I was silly and got serious when everything went to hell, like now.

She looked up at me. "I like what you've done with the place."

"I'm sorry. It's kind of a mess." Just as when Will came over, I was seeing the house through the eyes of someone who didn't wade through it daily.

"Don't be sorry," she said. "You're sweet to come get me in the first place. And the house was a mess when I left."

This was true, but I was pretty sure it was five months' worse now. Before, we'd been kicking things aside to make a path through the den to our bedroom, but I didn't remember that we'd been balancing piles on top of piles like now.

"Anyway," she said, gesturing to her bed, "I won't have trouble finding my stuff, because everything's exactly where I left it."

I took another long breath, shallower now. My body wanted the oxygen. When I was angry, I needed to remember to keep breathing. But now that I'd noticed the stale smell, I didn't want to inhale it. I said slowly, "I . . . am going to call in to work and ask for the afternoon off . . . and clean."

"Really!" she exclaimed as though this was a novel idea,

like hanging festive streamers from the ceiling. She sat up and said, "I'll help you."

We stuffed a towel under the door of my dad's bedroom and set up an electric fan for white noise outside the doorway so we wouldn't wake him with our banging around. With both of us working, it didn't take us long to pick up, sort through, and stash away everything in our tiny bedroom, and vacuum and dust the whole thing. She moved on to the bathroom. I tackled the laundry room. The den was going to take longer. By that time, some of my adrenaline from my fight with Will was draining away, but I wasn't ready to think about him yet. As I folded blankets into boxes and found a place for books on shelves, I listened to Violet talk about Ricky, and what had gone wrong.

"You know, I never liked school, and I wasn't doing too well. The whole thing seemed pointless. The only time I felt great was when I was with Ricky. Then he decided to drop out of school and get a job. I wouldn't see him anymore. He asked me to go with him. And I felt so unexpectedly great thinking about that possibility, like the doors of heaven had opened. I'd thought I was saddled with high school and more school and living here for another few years, but instead of that, I could become an adult *right then*."

I gazed at a history report that I was supposed to turn in last May but had gotten lost under the cushions of the sofa, apparently. I didn't understand what she meant, not really. I didn't see what was so awful about living here, or how a life with Ricky could seem better.

But I did understand how she felt good about herself when she was with Ricky. That's how Will made me feel.

And I understood her view that a different life was within her grasp, a better life, like a magic door opening. I felt that way every time Will wanted us to get more serious. The thing was, Violet thought this was a magic portal. I thought it was a painting of a magic portal, like on the cover of one of Sophia's fantasy novels. If you tried to step into it, you would realize it was only 2-D.

"I don't know what to do now," Violet murmured, wiping off a photo of Dad and Izzy and setting it on a shelf.

"Sure you do," I said with all the fake cheerfulness that went with pathological cleaning. "You'll get a job." I snapped my fingers. "Actually, I have a good fit for you. You always loved helping Dad restore the woodwork and the fountain in the white house, right?"

"Aw, the white house!" She sounded as sad as I was about the loss of our mansion. We'd never talked about it, because moving out of that house had been tangled up with Mom leaving.

"I might be able to hire you at the antiques shop if you wanted," I said.

"I love that place," she said. "How's Bob?"

"Better," I said. Man, hiring Violet for the shop was the best idea I'd had in years. She would get a steady job that paid okay. With her working there too, I could wean Bob and Roger off relying on me to the point of making me feel trapped. I would have been impressed with myself if I hadn't been panicking about Will underneath.

"You get a job there," I told Violet, "live here, and go to school. Look for one of those programs where you study for your GED and take college classes at the same time."

"School!" she said. "I couldn't do that. I was never smart like you."

"Like me!" I snorted.

"Of *course* like you. Are you crazy? We're all proud of you for getting in that special class for smart kids, and for doing so well on the drums."

I almost laughed when she put the gifted class and band together in the same sentence, as if they were related. But I probably sounded just as nonsensical to Izzy when I talked about hair color.

"Dad always said you'd be the first person in the family to go to college," Violet went on.

"Well, of course he would say that now. You and Sophia and Izzy haven't been to college."

"He said that when you were a baby. You picked up on everything so quickly. Mom said Izzy didn't talk until she was three, but she didn't have another baby to compare her with. She said if she'd had you first, she would have put Izzy in an institution."

I laughed. That was the funny yet slightly wrong sort of comment I remembered my mom making. "News to me," I said. "I thought you only kept me around for comic relief. That's all anybody ever seemed to think I was good for."

"Well, sure," Violet said, "back when you were in third grade. But now you're grown up."

That, too, was news to me. My heart started pounding again. It knew what I had done to Will. My brain didn't want to deal with it yet. But as Violet pointed out how old I was, my fear of having a boyfriend seemed immature. It might have worked for me in ninth grade.

Not now.

"This didn't take as long as I thought," Violet said, rescuing the last pair of panties from the sofa and twirling them around on one finger. "If we could get the kitchen counters and the stove cleared off, I could run to the store for groceries."

I inhaled as if the house already smelled like Puerto Rican food instead of dust. "We could make carne guisada," I said.

Her dark eyes flew wide open. "And pasteles? And—"

"Amarillos!" we both said at the same time with all the reverence of two hungry girls who hadn't eaten fried plantains in months. If we made them, maybe Dad still wouldn't eat them. I didn't care anymore. *I* would eat them.

"Divide and conquer," she said. "Kitchen or store?"

"Kitchen." If cleaning would make me feel better about breaking up with Will, I still had a whole town to polish.

After the kitchen was in reasonable order, I went outside. As we'd cleaned, we'd thrown mounds of trash into the yard, which probably frightened the neighbors. I bagged it up and stacked it neatly by the curb. Then I raked the magnolia leaves.

I was pleasantly surprised to see that grass was living underneath. With some rain in September, the yard might start to look like a yard again.

I crossed the street with my rake and looked at our house from a distance, really *looked* at it like a potential buyer would have viewed it if Dad had followed his original plan of flipping it. A previous owner had painted it an unfortunate dark brown, but it had good bones for someone who didn't mind a funky 1950s bungalow with retro lines.

My heart thumped painfully again as I realized I was viewing this house as if I was Will, parked in his Mustang on the street, capturing the proportions with a pencil and a ruler.

"Uh-oh, what's the matter?" Harper said beside me.

I jumped. I'd been so absorbed in my thoughts that I hadn't heard her roll up on the sidewalk. She and Kaye straddled their bikes, watching me with worried eyes.

"We came to ask what was up with you and Will last night," Kaye explained. "But your yard looks beautiful. Obviously something has gone horribly wrong."

That's when I broke down.

"I have a theory," Harper said.

My crying jag was over, but she kept her arm around my shoulders, even though this must have practically dislocated her arm because I was seven inches taller than her. We sat on a handmade bench my dad had brought home and set under the magnolia tree, then lost under the leaves. Cleared of plant rubbish, it was a nice place to sit—or would have been, if the heat hadn't been so oppressive.

Kaye stopped sweeping the sidewalk to circle her finger in the air, telling Harper to cut to the chase. In spite of my despair, I almost laughed at this interaction I'd seen play out between them countless times since third grade.

"Your sisters missed your mother," Harper told me, "and they felt like your family wasn't whole. Starting their own families was their way of getting back what they'd lost. The problem was, they were so young that it didn't work. I mean, I get carried away buying art supplies and run out of lunch money. You"—she poked me—"can't get up in the morning. Could you imagine one of us being the primary caretaker for somebody else?"

"No," I said. Izzy seemed stable now, but I had seriously worried about her children at first. I still worried about Sophia's baby.

"And the boys your sisters hooked up with are even worse," Harper said. "They bailed on their girlfriends and their babies. Seems to me Izzy is doing a pretty good job putting her life back together, though."

"*Now* she is," I acknowledged. Two years ago was a different story.

"You've watched your sisters make mistakes. You're younger, so you may have seen your mother leaving very differently from the way they saw it. You miss your mom, but instead of trying to fix your life by filling her shoes, you avoid further complications by sidestepping responsibility when you can. You have an allergic reaction when you do get put in charge. You stay out of any relationship at all."

"But that's a good thing," I defended myself. "I'm a lot better off than my sisters."

"But what if you don't change?" Kaye asked. "At some point when you're older, you're going to look around and see that everybody is in a relationship while you're alone. And pretty much everybody in your high school classes will have gone off to college."

"*I'm* going to college," I declared. "I'll be a National Merit Scholar."

Kaye raised her eyebrows skeptically. "Not if you don't get your grades up and convince some teacher to vouch for you. I worry that you're going to stay right here because you couldn't be bothered to take the next step."

"At least the house will be clean," I said.

"True," Harper said. "And maybe there will be other boys you can mess around with. But most people want a relationship sooner or later. Even those boys will move on while you stay put. And as for your relationship with Will . . ."

I held my breath, waiting, hoping, praying for Harper to give me some insight into how to fix this.

"I wouldn't have paired you two up in a million years," she said. "But now that I've seen you together, I get why you're so compatible. You're different from each other, but you each understand what makes the other tick. It would be a shame for you to let your knee-jerk reaction rule your life, and let him go."

I shrugged. "Our time together was all a misunderstanding to begin with," I said. "He misread me as girlfriend material. I misread him as a player. By the time we found out we were wrong about each other, it was too late."

Kaye nodded sadly. "You'd already fallen in love with each other."

"Well, I don't know about *him*. That's what he said, yeah. But I . . ." The full meaning of her words hit me. "Yeah, I'd already fallen . . . Oh, God." I put my hands over my face, horrified that I was crying in front of them yet again.

Harper drew me closer on the bench. Kaye called, "Group hug!" and wrapped her arms around both of us. This was a little much in the heat, but I relaxed into their embrace and tried to stop panicking about Will.

Kaye knocked her booty against mine so I'd scoot over to make room on the bench. After I'd crushed Harper sufficiently, Kaye sat down, then stroked a lock of hair out of my eyes with her middle finger. "Teen hygiene tip. If you try to get Will back today, bathe first. Guys love that."

"Yeah, okay," I grumbled.

"I agree with Harper," she said. "After seeing you and Will together, I think you may be meant for each other. It's obvious that he loves you. It would be a shame for your fear to be the only reason you let him go."

We all turned as the front door opened. I hadn't realized

how late it had gotten—time for my dad to wake up. He called across the yard, "*Lucita!* What happened to the top four layers of the stuff in the house?"

Kaye and Harper left when Violet arrived in Dad's truck with enough groceries for a feast. An hour later, she and Dad and I sat down to our first family dinner since we'd moved in, because we had cleared off the table.

"*Lucita,*" he mumbled between bites. "So good."

"Thanks." I wondered why he was into this meal now when he'd never wanted what I'd cooked before. Maybe the table made the difference. Or Violet. Or the fact that the meal was not offered with an air of desperate sacrifice.

"Violet," he said. "Delicious. And—" He put his hand over hers on the table. In Spanish he told her that he was very glad she'd come home. He said he'd always thought she would return eventually. He'd wanted her to figure that out for herself. Love was a complicated thing, but that boy she had picked out would not be his choice for her. Then there was a series of epithets that involved Ricky's private parts.

"I know, Dad." Violet took a bite. "This house doesn't seem like home, though, with Sophia and Izzy missing. I haven't seen Izzy and the kids in months. Maybe I could cook again one day this week, and we could have them over, now that the house isn't a death trap for the children and we've found all the chairs. I could drive up to get Sophia and the baby one weekend." She gazed around the den/dining room/kitchen. "It would be kind of small in here for all of us, though."

"The white house is for sale again," I said casually.

Dad's eyebrows shot up. Suddenly he looked more awake than I'd seen him in years. "Really?" The eager look settled into wistfulness. "I loved that house. I think about it a lot."

"Me too," Violet said.

"Me too," I said.

"I looked forward to tackling that fountain," he said. "Remember, in the atrium, with the mermaids?"

"I'll bet it would be cheaper than it was before," I said. "It's been on the market a few times. Why don't we buy it back?"

He laughed. "I wish. I work too much, *lucita*."

"Yeah, you do," I said. "Why? Izzy is stable now. Sophia is stable-ish."

"Ish," Violet echoed with a laugh.

"Violet will get there," I said.

Violet snorted.

"And you don't have to worry about me," I told him. "I'll get college paid for."

"College!" he exclaimed. "I always said you would be the first one to go to college, but you've been hemming and hawing."

"I decided I'm going," I said.

"When did you decide this?"

"Today. I'm getting online and registering to take the SAT in a minute." I had no doubt I could score high enough on the SAT to get a full ride to college, provided I could get really stressed out with responsibilities before test time. The way things with band and work and Will had been going, that shouldn't be too hard.

"In the meantime, I would help you with the house," I said.

"I would too," Violet chimed in.

"I'll only be here for a year before I leave for college," I said, "but we could get a lot done."

Dad put down his fork and nodded, staring into space. "I was about to sign up for another month of weekends at work. I didn't know how to break it to you, *lucita*, but I was going to miss all your band performances at the ball games. It's funny how you work so much that you don't even have time to think about how much you're working, or what you're working for."

"Yeah," said Violet. "Sometimes when you're in the thick of something, you lose perspective."

I put my fist to my mouth and squeezed a sob back in. Talk about being in the thick of things. I'd been so caught up in my own childish way of dealing with my fears that I'd driven off my favorite pirate, maybe forever. But before that possibility settled into fact, I had to try to get him back.

I stood to take my plate to the sink. On my way, I stopped and kissed my dad on the cheek. "Please consider it. We'd rather have you home."

I'd never been inside Will's house, but he'd pointed it out to me on our tour of town last Wednesday. I rode my bike into his neighborhood, a newer development where the trees were small, the houses all looked the same, and there weren't any unique architectural details for Will to draw. I felt a little sick as I laid my bike carefully on the lawn and walked up to the door. I put out a finger to ring the doorbell and noticed my hand was trembling.

Will's mom was as tall as me, with Will's worry line between her brows. She wore a tank top and shorts. Those clothes would have made sense if she was walking at the beach or working in the yard, but I was surprised she wasn't freezing when she had the air-conditioning in the house set below zero. It seeped out, surrounding me and making me shiver as she said in her own clipped Minnesota accent, "Oh, hello. Will's talked about you a lot. I'm afraid he's asleep right now, though. He said he was feeling sick."

"Sick?" I repeated. "Is he okay?"

His mom nodded. "I think he's just homesick."

I nodded too, because that seemed to be the thing to do. "Homesick."

"There's no cure for that but time," she said sadly. "But thanks for coming by, Tammy. I'll tell him you were here." She backed me out of her house and onto her porch. She shut the door, sealing out my voice, before I could tell her my name wasn't Tammy.

I stood there for a moment in the quiet night, listening to the breeze rattle the palm fronds. It was an evening for staying inside, where it was cool, and wishing you were back in Minnesota, away from me.

I walked down the sidewalk and picked up my bike. What else could I do? Yes, Will and I had argued, and we'd been genuinely mad at each other, with reason. But in the back of my mind, I suppose I'd assumed that we could fix it. We hadn't flirted like we used to since the trouble began—it all started with that stupid title—but I'd thought we would get back there.

And now I knew we wouldn't. I was such a poor replacement for his friends that I made him sick.

I got back on my bike and rode. The Sunday night was bustling with traffic. Folks were driving inland after a day at our beaches, one last weekend before Labor Day. Families had eaten one last meal out on the main drag and were packing into their cars to go home and prepare for work and school. I was riding the wrong way, heading downtown. I steered into the alley and propped my bike against the railing of the Crab Lab.

Employees kept the lights out on the restaurant's back porch so they could do what they wanted without being seen from the alley. I was all the way up the steps before I could make out Sawyer's shape in the darkness. When he saw me, he put down his beer. I walked into his open arms.

"Things didn't work out with Will?" he asked, his breath warm in my ear. "You wouldn't be hugging me otherwise."

I sighed as I collapsed on the bench beside him. "I broke up with him."

"Why?" Sawyer asked.

"Violet finally decided to come home, and we went to get

her, and . . . I don't know. I guess I started comparing Will and Ricky."

"Will is not a shit like Ricky," Sawyer said. "*I* am a shit like Ricky."

This seemed like a new low of self-deprecation, even for Sawyer. I nodded toward his beer. "Starting early, aren't you? How many of those have you had?"

He didn't respond to my question but asked, "What happened then?"

"I cleaned my entire house."

"Oh, poor baby," he cooed. "You *are* upset. I've got something for you." He pulled a joint from his pocket. I watched him light it, closing his eyes against the smoke. He took a long toke and handed it to me.

I held it between my fingers and looked at it. This was what I needed: to forget a problem that couldn't be solved. But my brain was stressed, which put my body in organization mode. It did not want this weed. I needed to take my hit so Sawyer's pot didn't burn down and go to waste, but every atom inside me screamed to hand the joint back.

Sawyer snatched it from me. When I looked at him in surprise, he was staring past me. I turned. Will was on the top step.

"That's exactly what I thought," Will said. He jogged down the stairs again.

"Go." Sawyer nodded at Will, urging me to follow him. "Go, go, go."

I ran after Will, leaping down the last two stairs in my effort to catch him before he reached his car at the end of the alley. Sweating in the hot night, I grabbed his elbow.

He stopped short and whirled to face me. "Don't. I told you that I was done with you. You're just like Beverly. When my mom said you came by, I thought maybe my instincts were wrong, but now I see I was right about you the whole time. I left town for five minutes and she was cheating on me. You and I have one little fight—"

"Little?" I broke in. "I put a lot of effort into that fight."

He raised his voice for some reason. "—and you just move on like nothing happened, and go back to doing drugs and God knows what else with Sawyer De Luca."

"I was *not*," I said emphatically. "I was in the process of politely refusing a joint. Even if I had taken a hit, calling that 'doing drugs' makes it sound like I was shooting up heroin."

"It's the same," he said. "You and Beverly are the same. I don't want you back now that I know what you're like." He stalked to the driver's seat of his car, slammed the door, and roared out of the alley.

I was left standing in a cloud of the Mustang's exhaust, the smell of frying food, and an utterly empty late summer night.

Seventeen

"DON'T YOU LOOK NICE," MS. NAKAMOTO SAID as I sat down in the chair facing her desk. She closed the door on the noise of people dragging their instruments out of the storage room for practice.

I supposed I *did* look nice. I'd set my alarm for school so I had time to iron my dress this morning. I'd fixed my hair and put on makeup. Violet had cooked me a balanced breakfast. I'd gotten my calculus homework finished during class since I wasn't flirting with Will or even sitting near him. I'd taken great notes in history. I'd generally felt like I was about to lose my grip on my sanity.

And didn't Ms. Nakamoto *sound* nice? She'd never spoken so pleasantly to me before, possibly because she was usually yelling at me across a football field to stop screwing around.

"Thank you," I said politely, as though I was pleased with her comment and my brain had been eaten by zombies.

"That usually means something's gone wrong in your life," she said. "Is there a problem you want to tell me about?"

"There is a problem," I affirmed, "but I don't want to tell you about it."

"All right, then," she said, because she was used to this kind of thing from me. "My news probably isn't going to help. I called you in to let you know that Will Matthews has challenged you for drum captain."

"Really!" I crowed. Will was fulfilling his promise. He still cared about me!

Wait a minute. He just wanted his drum captain position back. I amended my previous statement: "Really."

"It's not going to happen," Ms. Nakamoto said. "I told him no."

"But that's the rule," I protested.

"All rules are at my discretion," she said firmly. "We have four contests coming up this season. We're not going to ruin the cohesiveness of the drum line by switching leadership every week."

"I don't want to be drum captain," I whined. "I challenged Will, but it was a mistake."

"Correction: You *meant* to throw it, like every other challenge, but you made a mistake and played a perfect exercise."

I was afraid I would get in worse trouble if I copped to this. But I didn't want to lie to her either, so I sat there blinking.

"You're crafty, I'll admit," Ms. Nakamoto said. "I didn't get wise to you until Señorita Higgenbotham told me you made a C in her class even though you're bilingual. And now there's talk that you've scored high enough to be a National Merit Scholar. A faculty member would have to write you a letter of recommendation, and we're not sure we can do that in good conscience. Why do you sabotage yourself, Tia?"

I uncrossed and recrossed my legs, because that's what respectable women did when they were in a meeting and wearing a dress. I had seen this on TV. "I don't want to be in charge and ruin everything."

"How have you ruined the drum line in the past week? You haven't."

Damn it. "Will would be better."

"I have no reason to think so," she said. "I was happy you were drum captain, and I wasn't looking for anyone to replace you when he showed up. You know when you impressed me?"

"No, I have no idea," I said honestly, refraining from laughing at the thought.

"When Will cursed and threw his phone across the field on the first day of camp. I was going to kick him out of the position right then, but you handled him and you handled *me*. You saved drum captain for him, at least until you challenged him." She stood as if the conversation was over.

"No, wait a minute, nuh-uh," I told her, keeping my seat. "I'm an underachiever. You don't seriously *want* me in charge!"

"Sometimes we put underachievers in positions of responsibility and they rise to the occasion. You are one of those people. You're a sharp young lady and a fine percussionist, Tia. You *are* the drum captain. Why not enjoy it? You only get one senior year in high school." She opened the door for me, letting in the bustle of band, and nodded toward it, since I wasn't budging. "Now I'm running late. Please tell DeMarcus to get practice started without me."

Grumbling under my breath, I trudged across the parking lot to Will's car, where he'd left my drum propped against a tire. I was guessing that I was evicted again. I pulled my harness over my shoulders and carefully descended the stadium stairs.

From this height, the band formation looked beautiful. The circles and curlicues weren't squashed anymore. They were as precise as if Will had drawn them.

He stood in his place in the drums, close to Travis, leaving an empty space for me. And—wonder of wonders—today he was *talking* to Travis. As I watched, he threw back his head and laughed.

He glimpsed me on the stairs. His smile faded. He turned back to Travis.

This was how it was going to be from now on. He must have been furious that he couldn't get his drum captain position back. He'd already been furious with me at school all day. But *furious* on Will was the silent treatment. He simply didn't interact with me. He stayed away from me. The only time he'd acknowledged I existed was in English when a couple of basketball players hit on me. He'd gone out of his way to walk slowly down the row where we were standing, and he'd shouldered each of them in turn, saying "Excuse me" as if he simply wanted to get by. They'd watched him wide eyed and told me they would catch me later. They'd gotten the message.

I should have been angry. Will didn't want me back. Where did he get off elbowing basketball players away from me? Apparently I had a better chance of hooking up with someone new now that I was stressed out and practicing good grooming habits. I had tried to lay out my room and bathroom so that when this stress reaction inevitably faded, I would still be organized enough to look decent in the morning. I'd enjoyed the attention I'd gotten at school all day, along the lines of Ms. Nakamoto's *Don't you look like you've bathed this year!* Too bad the one guy I'd really craved that comment from no longer wanted to take a selfie with me.

When I reached the sidelines, I gave Ms. Nakamoto's message to DeMarcus. He glanced down at his watch, then up the stairs at the stragglers. We had a little time left before practice began. Rather than spend it in a shroud of silent treatment beside Will, I dumped my drum and sat down on a bench, next to Sawyer. I'd never seen him sit down in his costume. He immediately leaned over until his huge pelican head lay in my lap. I stroked his feathers absently.

"Being in love totally sucks when they don't love you back," I said.

He felt for my hand and held it in his feather-covered pelican glove.

Kaye looked over at me from a cheerleader huddle and stuck out her bottom lip in sympathy. She and Harper had taken one look at me when I got to school and had known my talk with Will hadn't gone well.

DeMarcus climbed to the top of his podium. He was about to start practice. I needed to be in the drum section when that happened, ready to play my riff. "Sawyer," I said, "I have to go."

He didn't budge.

"Sawyer," I complained, "not funny. You're going to get me in trouble. You know I'm stressed out, so I actually care about that shit today."

He was incredibly heavy in my lap.

"Now you're worrying me," I said. "You're making me think you've passed out in there. Come on, Sawyer. Joke's over."

DeMarcus made his move and Will played the riff, which the rest of the drum line repeated. The boom of drums echoed around the stadium, followed by silence, just as I pulled Sawyer's pelican head off.

Sawyer's soaked blond head and broad shoulders lay limp across me. He really had passed out.

"Will!" I shrieked.

DeMarcus turned around on his podium. The cheerleaders off to the side of the band rushed over. "No, no, no," I yelled as they gathered around, "Don't crowd us. I need Will."

And then he was there, towering over the girls. "Back up," he told them. They all stared at him with wide, heavily made-up eyes and took two steps back. He shouted to DeMarcus, "Call 911." He told me, "Hold him," and when I put my arms around Sawyer, Will pulled off the rest of his costume. Sawyer wore only a pair of gym shorts. His muscular body flopped like a rag doll. That's when I really got scared.

Will knelt down under Sawyer, then stood so Sawyer's whole body draped over one shoulder. "Come on," he told me. "Get them out of my way."

I jumped up. "Move," I barked to the cheerleaders and majorettes gawking at us. They parted, clearing a path to the gate. I stepped aside to let Will pass, then closed the gate behind me, glaring at the girls and daring them to cross me. I turned and jogged up the stairs behind Will, who was making great time up the incline despite carrying a hundred and fifty pounds.

At the top of the stairs, he grunted, "Help me." I reached up to ease Sawyer onto the ground, in the shade underneath the bleachers. Will nodded toward a hose coiled next to the concession stand. "Turn that on."

I dragged the hose over and let the water gush over Sawyer's legs, then his torso—soaking his gym shorts, which I would have made a joke about any other time—then his arms and his neck, keeping the flow away from his face so I didn't drown him.

"No, get his head." Will turned Sawyer on his side.

I wet Sawyer's hair, then looked to Will for guidance.

"Keep doing it," Will said. "We just need to cool him down." He pressed his thumb over Sawyer's wrist to feel his pulse.

"How do you know this?" I asked, moving the hose down to Sawyer's chest again.

"I googled 'heatstroke' because I've spent the last two weeks thinking I was going to have one." Will glanced up. "You must have known, or you wouldn't have called to me for help."

"I called to you for help because you're you. I knew you would keep your shit together in a crisis."

I sighed with relief as sirens approached. And then Sawyer blinked his eyes open and tried to sit up. "Stay cool, man," Will said softly, pressing one hand on Sawyer's chest. He told me, "One of us should go with him to the hospital."

I wanted desperately to go. More than that, I wanted what was best for Sawyer. "You go, because you'll be more helpful."

"I'll go," Will agreed, "because you have to work after school." He looked up at me. "Kaye and Harper told me you took off work and cleaned your house yesterday. Are you okay?"

I nodded.

Sawyer tried to sit up again, struggling against Will's hand. "What the fuck," he said weakly. "Get the fuck off me."

Will glanced at me. "He'll be okay."

All at once, the parking lot was bursting with sirens, louder and louder until Will and I put our hands over our ears. An ambulance arrived, plus an overkill pumper truck from the fire department, a couple of police cars that had come to see what all the excitement was about, and Ms. Nakamoto, followed by the principal, who was really booking it across the asphalt. I'd never seen an old lady run that fast, especially in heels. I was impressed.

With all those folks crowding around, there wasn't anything left for me to do but turn off and coil up the hose and watch the paramedics argue with Sawyer, who insisted he was fine, and promptly threw up. I shared one last look with Will before the paramedics closed him and Sawyer inside the ambulance. As it retreated across the parking lot, I heaved a long sigh and realized for the first time how tense my shoulders had been.

I wandered back down the stairs to the stadium. The band was running through the halftime show. While I watched, four people tripped over Will's drum, which nobody had the foresight to remove from the middle of the field where he'd dropped it. Before I retrieved my own drum from the bench, I took Kaye aside from the rest of the cheerleaders.

"When class is over," I whispered, "could you hang out around the boys' locker room and ask someone to get Sawyer's stuff for you? I have to work."

Kaye frowned. "You want me to take it to him? His homework can wait until tomorrow."

"No, he needs his wallet with his insurance card," I insisted. "He needs his phone to call people because he won't remember anybody's number off the top of his head, and he needs his keys to get inside his house in case he's actually released from the hospital today."

"What about his dad?"

"His dad is up in Panama City, selling blown-glass

figurines on the pier. They have a bigger Labor Day crowd than we do."

The resistance on her face melted into sympathy. "What about his brother?"

"You can't count on his brother for anything."

I snagged my drum and made my way through the band to my place. As the rest of the period crawled by, I decided it was too bad I couldn't take the SAT on demand. Right this second I would have made a perfect score.

Violet was in a job interview with Bob and Roger in the back office, and I was manning the front counter, when the antique cowbell rang. Will came through the door, his big body blocking so much sun that he made the room turn dark.

"How's Sawyer?" I asked. I hoped he hadn't come by to give me bad news personally.

"He's fine," Will said. "He's dehydrated. He's getting an IV." He touched the back of his hand with two fingers, which I assumed was where the IV went. "A bunch of people from school are there with him now. He wants you to come by after work."

I nodded.

Will looked uncomfortably around the shop, as if he didn't want to meet my gaze, then pointed at the floor. "I'm going to borrow this dog."

"Okay," I said, like that was not weird.

"Come on," he said. Even though his voice hadn't changed

and the dog wasn't looking at him, she jumped up when he spoke to her. They disappeared out the door.

I stared through the window and into the street, which looked like it always did, as though the boy I loved most in the world hadn't just bopped in to steal the shop dog. If it wasn't for the antique bell still swinging on its ribbon and chiming gently, I would have suspected it hadn't happened at all.

I slid down from my stool, emerged from behind the counter, and leaned out the door, peering down the street. Far away, past all the shops, in the tree-shaded park next to the marina, the dog was chasing Will. Will stopped suddenly and reached for the dog, who bent her body just out of his reach and scampered away. Now Will chased the dog. The dog spun to face him. They both crouched in the stance of a dog at the ready, each daring the other to jump first. Will made a grab and the dog dashed away.

I knew Will was still missing a lot of what he'd had back home. But at least he'd taken this first step toward finding what he needed here in town. I watched him and the dog for a while, playing together in the long shadows of the trees.

By the time I made it to the hospital that night, everybody else had cleared out. Sawyer was alone in a room for two patients. The other guy must have died. Sawyer was curled into the fetal position with an IV tube snaking to his hand. He faced away from the door, and his hospital gown fell open to reveal his butt crack, because Sawyer did not care.

"Nice ass," I said from the doorway.

"Thanks," he said without moving.

I walked to the other side of the bed. "Are you hungry at all? I thought you might be, since you lost your lunch. I brought you something." I peeled the aluminum foil off the plate of amarillos, beans, and an empanada. "Violet made it vegan for you."

He sat up, took the plate and fork I handed him, and shoveled in a mouthful. He swallowed and rolled his eyes. "Oh. My. God. They don't do vegan at this hospital. I was starving. This is so good." After a few more bites, he held the plate out to me, offering me some.

"I ate already," I said.

"Good, because I didn't really want to give you any." He ate another mouthful. "Violet should be cooking at the Crab Lab."

"Nah. She'd rather explain to two old men where their antiques are."

He swallowed. "It's been forever since I had Puerto Rican food. I forget y'all are half Puerto Rican."

"Me too," I said. "Can I get you a drink?"

"Yeah, a Sprite. My eleventh Sprite. Down the hall in the fridge."

Wandering back in with the can, I asked him, "When are they letting you out?"

"They would have let me out already, but someone is supposed to watch me. They need somebody to release me to. My dad isn't coming home, and my brother won't get off work until after visiting hours are over. He said he'll come buy me out tomorrow morning."

I flopped down in the chair beside the bed. "Will they release you to me?"

"No. I took the liberty of asking, but when I said your name, the nurse looked all outraged and hollered, 'That girl who—' Well, never mind what she said."

I knew which nurse he was talking about. I'd seen DeMarcus's mom on my way in. DeMarcus had thrown a big Halloween party in seventh grade, and his mom had walked in on me teaching him to French kiss. I guess I didn't have a reputation for being nursing material.

"I can get somebody down here to spring you," I said. "Harper's mom, or—you know who would be perfect? Kaye's mom." She was the president of a bank and looked it. Nobody messed with her.

"I don't want to do that to anybody who isn't you," Sawyer said.

"Aw. Hugs." I stood up and wrapped my arms around him, careful to keep my dress out of the amarillos.

"I'm swearing it all off," he said into my hair. "Alcohol and weed. All mind-altering substances."

I sat back down, shocked. "You are?"

"Yes."

"Working in a bar?"

"Yes."

"Well, you're a vegan working in a restaurant that serves primarily seafood and meat," I said. "If anybody could swear off alcohol working in a bar, it would be you. And I think that would be great. It's not good for you, or me either. But if you're doing it because you had heatstroke . . . I do think being dehydrated the day after drinking didn't help you, but you had heatstroke because you were dressed up in a pelican costume at two p.m. on the hottest day of the year in Florida."

"I know."

"Does it have something to do with your mystery girl?"

"I'm never getting Kaye," he said. "And I wouldn't change my life for her. I've learned that from you. I'm not changing for somebody else, because that person could disappear. The only person to change for is yourself."

I was astounded. I'd thought I had him figured out. It never occurred to me that *he* had *me* figured out in return. And when he took my thoughts and put them in his own words, I sounded halfway noble.

"But like you said," he went on, "alcohol was a contributing factor to my mortifying collapse. I shouldn't be giving in to contributing factors when I already have an asshole brother and a jailbird dad. You know, for the first time in my life, I feel like I'm really good at something. I was a mediocre athlete. I'm an indifferent student. But I'm an excellent pelican. I support the school and I make people laugh."

"You do. You're a great symbol for the school."

"Being an excellent pelican is pretty sad, as career skills

go. It isn't everything. But it's not nothing." He set his clean plate on the bedside table. "What I feel worst about is Minnesota coming around the corner after I'd handed you that joint. I mean, nice guy. I heard he hauled me up the stairs at the stadium."

"He did," I said.

"And he stayed with me here until Harper and Kaye and DeMarcus and everybody showed up. He was as nice as he could be after all the shit I've given him during the past couple of weeks. I ruined everything between you two."

"You didn't," I said sadly. "I did that all by myself."

"Obviously not, or he wouldn't have come looking for you last night."

I stayed with Sawyer, even doing my English homework there while he made fun of me and called me a sellout. When visiting hours were over, DeMarcus's mom kicked me out of the room. But all the while, in the back of my mind, I was formulating a plan for how I could put my stress-induced organizational skills to good use.

The next day, at the beginning of band, I waited until Ms. Nakamoto turned on her microphone and started explaining what we would do that period. Then I set my drum on the grass—Will watched me curiously but didn't ask what I was doing—and I walked through the band and up the stadium steps. Ms. Nakamoto didn't seem to notice Harper walking down the steps in another part of the stadium. She'd gotten out of last period to take pictures and document the coming event for the yearbook.

Ms. Nakamoto kept talking to the band until I stopped right beside her. "Yes, Ms. Cruz?" she asked.

"May I borrow that?" I asked, reaching for the microphone. "Just for a sec."

Surprised, she handed it to me.

I cleared my throat and read from my notes. "We—" My voice boomed around the stadium. The band yelped a protest, and the cheerleaders slapped their hands over their ears. I backed the microphone away from my mouth. "Sorry. We the students present to you, Ms. Nakamoto, the Sawyer De Luca/Will Matthews Heat Relief Proposal. We understand that dress codes are necessary for schools to function in what the faculty thinks is an appropriate manner. However, our school, in allowing students to disrobe partially during summer practices on school grounds, has already acknowledged that its dress code is not always comfortable for its students, or even safe. We would like that exception to be extended to practices outdoors year-round. We would like you, Ms. Nakamoto, to be our advocate in presenting this proposal to Principal Chen. In the interim, while the proposal is being considered, we respectfully request that you stop enforcing the dress code during afternoon practices on the field." I pulled off my shirt.

That was the cue. With a prolonged whoop, all the cheerleaders and the entire band took off their shirts—the girls were wearing bikini tops underneath—and threw the shirts up in the air. The cheerleaders unfurled a long paper banner they'd made like their spirit signs for football games. It said REMEMBER THE FALLEN PELICAN.

When the rainstorm of shirts cleared, Harper still stood on one of the benches along the sidelines, snapping pictures. Besides her, only Will was still fully dressed, because he was left out of Kaye's student council call tree. He looked around at the half-naked band, bewildered.

Ms. Nakamoto glared at my bikini top, then at me. "I told you I wanted you to take on more responsibility, and this is your first foray?"

I put the microphone down where it wouldn't pick up what I said. "Yes ma'am," I told her. "You weren't here when Sawyer fainted yesterday."

She nodded and seemed to search my face for a moment. "Okay," she finally said.

I put the microphone to my lips again. "Mr. Matthews," I said in Ms. Nakamoto's voice, "you may take off your shirt."

The band whooped again, the cheerleaders clapped, and the drums yelled "Take it off!" through cupped hands. Will shrugged off his harness, slowly and sexily pulled off his shirt, balled it up, and hurled it toward the goalpost, just like he'd thrown his phone on the first day of practice.

Ms. Nakamoto was glaring at me again. Hastily I handed her the microphone, dashed down the stairs and across the field, and loaded my drum harness onto my shoulders.

As she resumed her announcements, Will leaned over. "Did you do this for me?"

"I felt really bad about Sunday," I whispered. "I shouldn't have broken up with you that way." I looked into his eyes, as best as I could guess through both our sunglasses. "I shouldn't have broken up with you at all. And I honestly wasn't doing what you thought I was doing with Sawyer. But as you said about putting your hand on Angelica at the beach, you and I aren't together, so it doesn't matter whether you believe me or not. I just wish you did."

He put his drumstick on my drum and circled it slowly. "What if we went back to hooking up, like you wanted at first? We tried it my way, and now we'll do it your way. You can be with other people, and I won't get jealous."

I raised my eyebrows at him.

"Okay, I will," he acknowledged, "but I won't make a stink. I feel like we're meant to be together. We just haven't figured out how. And I would really like to get in trouble for touching you right now."

I crossed my hand over his to place my drumstick on his drum. "What if we tried it your way again? I'll give it more than twelve hours this time."

He grinned. "What are we talking? Eighteen? Twenty-four?"

"Three days," I suggested. "Until the first football game, and then we can decide whether we want to renew our contract."

"Why don't we wait until *after* the first football game to talk about it?" he suggested. "At whatever party we go to. Or at the beach, in my car." Ever so slowly, watching Ms. Nakamoto, he edged toward me. His earring glinted in the light. He turned and kissed the corner of my mouth while I giggled.

Ms. Nakamoto called through the microphone, "Mr. Matthews, get off Ms. Cruz. I'm starting to sound like a broken record."

Down the line of snare drums, Jimmy tapped his watch and said, "Seven minutes."

ACKNOWLEDGMENTS

Heartfelt thanks to my brilliant editor, Annette Pollert; my tireless agent, Laura Bradford; my hilarious critique partner, Victoria Dahl; and the readers who have enjoyed my books, told a friend about them, and made my dream career a reality. I appreciate you.

Perfect Couple

One

FAMOUS PHOTOGRAPHS WALLPAPERED MR. Oakley's journalism classroom. Behind his desk, Martin Luther King Jr. waved to thousands who'd crowded the National Mall to hear his "I Have a Dream" speech, with the Washington Monument towering in the distance. Over by the windows, a lone man stood defiant in front of four Chinese tanks in protest of the Tiananmen Square massacre. On the wall directly above my computer screen, a World War II sailor impulsively kissed a nurse in Times Square on the day Japan surrendered.

Mr. Oakley had told us a picture was worth a thousand words, and these posters were his proof. He was right. Descriptions in my history textbook read like old news, but these photos made me want to stand up for people, like Dr. King did, and protest injustice, like Tank Man did.

And be swept away by romance, like that nurse.

My gaze fell from the poster to my computer display, which was full of my pictures of Brody Larson. A few weeks ago, on the first day of school, our senior class had elected the Superlatives—like Most Academic, Most Courteous, and Least Likely to Leave the Tampa/St. Petersburg Metropolitan Area. Brody and I had been voted Perfect Couple That Never Was. Brody had dated Grace Swearingen the whole summer, and I'd been with the yearbook editor, Kennedy Glass, for a little over a month. Being named part of a perfect couple when Brody and I were dating other people was embarrassing. Disorienting. Anything but perfect.

And *me* being named one half of a perfect couple with *Brody* made as much sense as predicting snow for Labor Day next Monday in our beachside town. He was the popular, impulsive quarterback for our football team. Sure, through twelve years of school, I'd liked him. He was friendly and *so* handsome. He also scared the hell out of me. I couldn't date someone who'd nearly lost his license speeding, was forever in the principal's office for playing pranks, and had a daily drama with one girl or another on a long list of exes. And he would never fall for law-abiding, curfew-obeying, glasses-wearing me.

So I hadn't gone after him as my friend Tia had urged me to. I only found excuses to snap photos of him for the yearbook. For the football section, I'd taken a shot of him at practice in his helmet and pads. Exasperated with his teammates, he'd held up his hands like he needed help from heaven.

For the candid section, I planned to use a picture from my

friend Kaye's party last Saturday. Brody grinned devilishly as he leaned into his truck cab to grab something. I'd cropped out the beer.

For the full-color opening page, I'd taken a close-up of him yesterday in study hall. His brown hair fell long across his forehead. He wore a green T-shirt that made his green eyes seem to glow. Girls all over school would thank me for this when they received their yearbooks next May. In fact, Brody had implied as much when I snapped the picture. He made me promise I wouldn't sell it to "a porn site for ladies," which was why he was smiling.

In short, he was the sailor in the poster: the kind of guy to come home from overseas, celebrate the end of the war in Times Square, and sweep a strange girl off her feet.

I only wished I was that girl.

"Harper, you've been staring at Brody for a quarter of an hour." Kennedy rolled his chair down the row of computers to knock against mine. I spun for a few feet before I caught the desktop and stopped myself.

Busted!

"You're not taking that Perfect Couple vote seriously, are you?" he asked. "I'll bet a lot of people decided to prank you."

"Of course I'm not taking it seriously," I said, and should have left it there. I couldn't. "Why do you think we're so mismatched? Because he's popular and I'm not?"

"No."

"Because he's a local celebrity and I'm not?"

"No, because he broke his leg in sixth grade, trying to jump a palmetto grove in his go-cart."

"I see your point."

"Besides, *we're* the perfect couple."

Right. I smiled. And I waited for him to put his arm around me, backing up his words with a touch. But our relationship had never been very physical. I expected a caress now because that's what I imagined Brody would do in this situation. I was hopeless.

I said brightly, "If I was staring at Brody, I was zoning out." I nodded to the Times Square poster. "I get lost in that image sometimes."

Kennedy squinted at the kiss. "Why? That picture is hackneyed. You can buy it anywhere. It's on coffee mugs and shower curtains. It's as common in the dentist's office as a fake Monet or a print of dogs playing poker."

Yes, because people loved it—for a reason. I didn't voice my opinion, though. I was just relieved I'd distracted Kennedy from my lame obsession with Brody.

When Kennedy had bumped my chair, he'd stopped himself squarely in front of my computer. Now he closed my screen *without asking*. I'd saved my changes to Brody's photos, but what if I hadn't before he closed them? The idea of losing my digital touch-ups made me cringe. I took a deep breath through my nose, calming myself, as he scrolled through the list of his own files, looking for the one he wanted. I was tense for no good reason.

I'd known Kennedy forever from school. We'd talked a little last spring when Mr. Oakley selected him as the new editor for the yearbook and I won the photographer position. Back then, I'd been sort-of dating my friend Noah Allen, which made me technically off limits. Kennedy was a tall guy who looked older than seventeen because of his long, blond ponytail and darker goatee, his T-shirts for punk bands and indie films I'd never heard of, and his pierced eyebrow.

Sawyer De Luca, who'd been elected Most Likely to Go to Jail, had taunted Kennedy mercilessly about the eyebrow piercing. But Sawyer taunted everyone about everything. I'd had enough trouble screwing up the courage to get my ears pierced a few years ago. I admired Kennedy's edgy bravery. I'd thought it put him out of my league.

We hadn't dated until five weeks ago, when we ran into each other at a film festival in downtown Tampa that we'd both attended alone. That's when we realized we were perfect for each other. I honestly still believed that.

I crushed on Brody only because of the Perfect Couple title, like a sixth grader who heard a boy was interested and suddenly became interested herself. Except, as a senior, I was supposed to be above this sort of thing. Plus, Brody *wasn't* interested. Our class *thought* he should be, but Brody wasn't known for doing what he was told.

"Here it is." Kennedy opened his design for one of the Superlatives pages, with BIGGEST FLIRTS printed at the top.

"Oooh, I like it," I said, even though I didn't like it at all.

One of my jobs was to photograph all the Superlatives winners for the yearbook. The Biggest Flirts picture of my friend Tia and her boyfriend, Will, was a great shot. I would include it in my portfolio for admission to college art departments. I'd managed to capture a mixture of playfulness and shock on their faces as they stepped close together for a kiss.

Kennedy had taken away the impact by setting the photo at a thirty-degree angle.

"I have the urge to straighten it," I admitted, tilting my head. This hurt my neck.

"All the design manuals and websites suggest angling some photos for variety," he said. "Not every picture in the yearbook can be straight up and down. Think outside the box."

I nodded thoughtfully, hiding how much his words hurt. I *did* think outside the box, and all my projects were about visual design. I sewed my own dresses, picking funky materials and making sure the bodices fit just right. The trouble I went to blew a lot of people's minds, but sewing hadn't been difficult once I'd mastered the old machine I'd inherited from Grandmom. To go with my outfit of the day, I chose from my three pairs of retro eyeglasses. The frames were worth the investment since I always wore them, ever since I got a prescription in middle school. They made me look less plain. If it hadn't been for my glasses and the way I dressed, everyone would have forgotten I was there.

As it was, my outside-the-box look and the creative photos I'd been taking for the yearbook made me memorable. That's why Kennedy had been drawn to me, just as I'd been intrigued by his eyebrow piercing and his philosophy of cinematography. At least, that's what I'd thought.

I wanted to tell him, *If this design is so great, tilt the photos of the chess club thirty degrees, not my photos of the Superlatives.* Instead I said carefully, "This layout looks a little dated. It reminds me of a yearbook from the nineties, with fake paint splatters across the pages."

"I don't think so." Turning back to the screen, he moved the cursor to *save* and communicated how deeply I'd offended him with a hard click on the mouse.

I kept smiling, but my stomach twisted. Kennedy would give me the silent treatment if I didn't find a way to defuse this fight between now and the end of journalism class. Tonight was the first football game of the season, and I'd be busy snapping shots of our team. I was the only student with a press pass that would get me onto the sidelines. Kennedy would likely be in the stands with my other sort-of ex-boyfriend, Quinn Townsend, and our friends from journalism class. They'd all be telling erudite jokes under their breath that made fun of the football team, the entire game of football, and spectator sports in general. After the game, though, Kennedy and I would both meet our friends at the Crab Lab grill. And he would act like we weren't even together.

"It's just the way the picture is tilted," I ventured. "The rest of it is cool—the background and the font."

In answer, he opened the next page, labeled MOST LIKELY

TO SUCCEED. I hadn't yet taken the photo of my friend Kaye and her boyfriend, Aidan, but Kennedy already had a place for it. He selected the empty space and tilted that, too, telling me, *So there.*

"When are you going to turn in the rest of these photos?" he asked me. "The deadline to send this section to the printer is two weeks from today."

"Yeah," I said doubtfully. "It's been harder than I thought. I mean, taking the pictures isn't hard," I clarified quickly, before he reassigned some of my responsibilities. "It's tricky to get out of class. We've had so many tests. And convincing some of our classmates to show up at a scheduled time is like herding cats."

"Harper!" he exclaimed. "This is important. You have to get organized."

I opened my lips, but nothing came out. I was stunned. I prided myself on my organizational skills. Kennedy should have seen the schedule on my laptop. My arrangements for these photo shoots were difficult but, in the end, impeccable. If the people who were supposed to pose for my pictures didn't meet me, how was that *my* fault? I couldn't drag them out of physics class by the ears.

"I need these shots on a rolling basis so I can design the pages," Kennedy said. "You can't throw them all at me on the last day. If you make us miss the deadline, the class might not get our yearbooks before graduation. Then the yearbooks would be *mailed* to us and we wouldn't get to *sign* them."

My cheeks flamed hot. What had seemed like a fun

project at first had quickly turned into a burden. I'd been trying to schedule these appointments during school, around my classes. At home, I selected the best photos and touched them up on my computer. But I also had other responsibilities. I'd signed on to photograph a 5K race at the town's Labor Day festival next Monday. And of course I had to help Mom. She ran a bed and breakfast. I was required to contribute to the breakfast end of it. I didn't see how I could produce these finished pictures for Kennedy any faster.

"Is everything okay here?" Mr. Oakley had walked up behind Kennedy.

"Of course," Kennedy said. From his position, Mr. Oakley couldn't see Kennedy narrow his eyes, warning me not to complain. Mr. Oakley had said at the beginning of school that he wanted the yearbook to run like a business, meaning we students reported to each other like employees to bosses, rather than crying to him about every minor problem. That meant Kennedy had a lot more power than a yearbook editor at a school where the advisor made the decisions.

For better or for worse.

Mr. Oakley looked straight at me. "Can you work this out yourselves?"

"Yes, sir." My voice was drowned out by the bell ending the period.

As Mr. Oakley moved away and students gathered their books, Kennedy rolled his chair closer to mine and said in my ear, "Don't raise your voice to me."

Raise my voice? *He* was the one who'd raised his voice and caught Mr. Oakley's attention.

The bell went silent.

Kennedy straightened. In his normal tone he said, "Tell Ms. Patel I'll miss most of study hall. I'm going to stay here and get a head start on the other Superlatives pages, now that I know we're in trouble."

"Okay." The argument hadn't ended like I'd wanted, but at least he didn't seem angry anymore.

I retrieved my book bag and smiled when I saw Quinn waiting for me just inside the doorway. His big grin made his dyed-black Goth hair and the metal stud jutting from his bottom lip look less threatening. Most people in school didn't know what I knew: that Quinn was a sweetheart. We wound our way through the crowded halls toward Ms. Patel's classroom.

"I overheard your talk with Kennedy," Quinn said.

"Did you see his designs?" I asked. "I understand why he'd want to angle some photos for variety *if* the pictures themselves were boring. Mine aren't."

"He'll change his mind when he sees the rest of your masterpieces," Quinn assured me. "Speaking of the Superlatives, Noah said Brody's been talking about you."

I suspected where this was going. Noah and I hadn't been as tight this school year, since I'd started dating Kennedy. In fact, if I hadn't checked Noah's calculus homework every day in study hall, we might not have talked at all. But last spring when we'd gone out, he'd told me what great friends he and Brody were. Brody's dad had been their first football coach for the rec league in third grade. They'd played side by side ever since. Now Noah's position on the team was right guard. His responsibility was to protect Brody from getting sacked before he could throw the ball. Friends that close definitely shared their opinions of the girl one of them had been teamed with as Perfect Couple.

Brody must have told Noah it was ridiculous that he and I had been paired. He would never dream of wasting his time with a nerd like me. I should have told Quinn that whatever it was, I didn't want to know. And still I heard myself asking, "What did Brody say about me?"

"Yesterday in football practice," Quinn said, "Brody told the team that you two aren't the Perfect Couple. You're the Perfect Coup*ling*. And then he expressed admiration for your ass."

"Oooh." I was thrilled at the idea of Brody noticing my body and wishing he could have sex with me. But I quickly realized I was supposed to feel insulted. I turned that "Oooh" into a more appropriate "Ewww. He shouldn't kid around like that. Somebody's bound to tell Kennedy."

"Yeah, but . . ." Quinn looked askance at me. "Do you care, after the way Kennedy treated you just now? Why don't you stand up to him?"

"Kennedy has a point," I explained. "He needs my pictures for the Superlatives. If I miss a deadline and make him miss his, it doesn't matter why. An excuse won't fix it. And he doesn't want me to argue with him in class, because it looks bad to Mr. Oakley."

We'd reached Ms. Patel's doorway and stopped outside to finish our talk. Sawyer was in our study hall. Sawyer and private conversations didn't mix.

Quinn put one hand on my shoulder, something Kennedy rarely did. "I've worried long enough about keeping up appearances. I'm done with that today."

I nodded. Quinn was making a big announcement at the end of the period.

"Come with me," he said. "Come into the light. Stop worrying about how things *look*."

I frowned. "We're not in the same situation, Quinn. And how things look—that's everything I care about."

"You'll be sorry." He spun on the heel of his combat boot and disappeared into the classroom.

Perplexed, I turned to frown at the end of the slowly emptying hall. My senior year was supposed to be the time of my life. Two weeks in, all I felt was anxious about my photo assignment. And thrilled that a random hot guy, who would never ask me out, had made a joke about hooking up with me.

Tia leaned against the lockers outside Mr. Frank's room next door. Will propped his forearm above her and leaned down to say something with a grin. She laughed. I was glad they'd gotten together earlier this week. Will had just moved here from Minnesota. After a rocky start, he seemed to be adjusting better. And Tia, a comedian, finally was genuinely happy.

She noticed me watching them and must have read the expression on my face. She stuck out her bottom lip in sympathy.

I shook my head—*nothing was wrong*—and dove into Ms. Patel's room.

"Hey, girlfriend." Brody grinned at me as I walked toward him between two rows of desks. His green eyes were bright, but the shadows underneath were visible despite his deep tan. He'd always had the circles under his eyes. When we were in kindergarten, Mom had wondered aloud whether he was getting enough sleep. In middle school, guys had teased him about being a drug addict. Now the shadows seemed like a part of him, permanent evidence of his rough-and-tumble life—and love life. He held up one fist toward me.

I fist-bumped him. "Hey, boyfriend." The way we'd reacted to our Superlatives title underscored how different we were, and how imperfect a couple we would have made. I never could have admitted this even to Tia or Kaye, but I'd puzzled endlessly over what our classmates saw in us that led them to think we'd be good together.

In contrast, Brody called me his girlfriend and teased me. The "Hey, girlfriend" and the fist bump had been going on for the full two weeks of school. Every time we did it, I was afraid someone would mention it to Kennedy. He would pick a fight with me because I looked like I was flirting behind his back.

Brody didn't seem concerned that someone would mention it to his girlfriend, Grace. The idea of me threatening their relationship was that far-fetched. Although—and this thought had kept me awake some nights—Brody never called me his girlfriend and fist-bumped me when Grace and Kennedy were around. He did it only in moments like this, a period without Grace, with Kennedy missing. Aside from twenty other students and Ms. Patel, we were alone here.

And if Brody had progressed to telling my ex-boyfriend, Noah, what he'd like to do with me when we were *really* alone, he was getting too close for comfort.

After dumping my book bag beside my desk, I asked Brody quietly, "May I talk with you?" I nodded toward the back of the classroom.

His eyebrows rose like he knew he was in trouble—but just for a moment. "Sure." He jumped up with a jerk that made the legs of his desk screech across the floor. Four people in the next row squealed and slapped their hands over their ears.

He followed me to the open space behind the desks, next to the cabinets. In the sunlight streaming through the window, I noticed his slightly swollen bottom lip and a faintly purple bruise on his jaw. He must have been hit in the mouth by another football player—or punched by an irate girl. Leaning against the wall with his arms crossed, he was back to looking as flaked out and heroin-chic as usual. I almost laughed, because he was so handsome and he'd said something so stupid to get himself in hot water—except that the person he'd said it about was me.

"I heard you were talking about me in football," I began.

He gaped at me. I couldn't tell whether he was horrified that I'd found out, or fake-horrified. He didn't say anything, though. He eyed me uneasily.

"What if Grace hears?" I asked.

He gave the smallest shrug as he continued to watch me, like he hadn't considered the possibility and couldn't be bothered to care very much.

Well, here was something *I* cared about. "What if Kennedy hears?"

This time I got the reaction I'd been dying for, though I would never admit it. Brody narrowed his eyes at me, jealous of Kennedy, frustrated that he couldn't have me for himself.

Of course, I could have been interpreting his expression all wrong. But in that moment, the rest of the noisy classroom seemed to fall away. Only Brody and I were left, sharing a vibe, exchanging a message. His green eyes seemed to sear me. He was gazing at me exactly the way I felt about him.

Two

BUT THE NEXT SECOND, I DECIDED I'D BEEN mistaken. He blinked, and the mad jealousy I'd seen in his eyes looked more like sleep deprivation. He shrugged again. The move gave way to a stretch as he raised his arms behind his head and clasped both hands behind his neck.

He wasn't preening for me. Hot athletic guys purposefully showed their bulging triceps to cheerleaders like Grace, not geek bait like me. The message to *me* was, *If Kennedy confronts me, I will squash him like a bug between my thumb and forefinger.*

Frustrated, I whined, "Brody!" just like I had, and every other girl had in kindergarten, when he tickled us and made us giggle during quiet time or dabbed paint on our noses just before our dramatic debut onstage in the class play.

My protest snapped him out of his jock act. He held out his hands, pleading with me. "Harper, I'm sorry. I didn't mean it. You know me. I just blurt shit out sometimes. Or, all the time. The guys on the team asked me about the Superlatives thing. In football, when somebody asks you how you feel, you answer with a sex joke."

"I see," I said. "What you told the guys was a more offensive, more personal version of 'I would totally hit that.'"

Grinning, he pointed at me. "Yes."

I tried an even better imitation of the assholes on the team. "'I would hit that *thang*.'"

He patted me on the head, possibly mussing my careful French twist. "The guys are pretty taken with you. They think the idea of you getting with an idiot like me is hilarious. They'll keep teasing me about you. I'll keep making sex jokes. I'm just warning you."

"Are you going to keep adding that bit about my ass, too?"

He wagged his eyebrows.

"Fine," I said over the bell that started our half-hour study hall. We headed for our desks. To keep up the facade that I thought the idea of us getting together was hilarious too, I made small talk. "Ready for the game tonight?" I hoped he wouldn't give me a detailed answer I couldn't follow and force me to expose my ignorance about football. I'd never been interested in sports. Over the last few days, Mr. Oakley had given me a crash course in what I hadn't absorbed while dating Noah, so I'd know enough about the rules to catch the important plays through a camera lens. Ideally.

But I did want to know how practice had been going for Brody, and how he felt about the pressure he must be under before the game. I'd been part of the crowd at parties at his house a couple of times recently, but we'd never had what I'd call an in-depth conversation. I knew more about his football career from the local newspaper than from him. Seeing the game through his eyes would help me capture a star quarterback's perspective and immortalize it in the yearbook.

Plus, I enjoyed the way he looked at me. I wished he would give me that narrow-eyed stare again, no matter what emotion was behind it. I might have had a boyfriend, he might have had a girlfriend, and the idea of us getting together under any circumstances might have been ridiculous, but I wanted his attention a little longer.

He stretched his arms way over his head again. Sitting this close to him, it was hard to get perspective on how much taller than me he was, but I never forgot. Then he settled himself across his desktop, arms folded, head down, and closed his eyes. "Don't I look ready?" Conversation over.

Ms. Patel eased into her chair at the front of the room and pulled a stack of papers out of her desk drawer. The people who'd been milling around the classroom slid into seats and hauled books out of their backpacks or, like Brody, settled down for a nap. Ms. Patel had said she didn't care what we did in study hall as long as we kept the noise down to a dull roar.

I pretended to check Noah's calculus homework while gathering the courage to ask Brody about our yearbook photo together.

I was on deadline. Taking the easy route would be smartest. I should schedule a meeting in the school courtyard like

I'd arranged for most of the other Superlatives. I could set up a tripod and program a simple picture on a time delay, then dive into the frame with Brody before the shutter opened. But that wouldn't be cute. It wouldn't be original. It wouldn't contribute to the portfolio I needed to get into a college art program next fall.

And it wouldn't put me in proximity to Brody for as long as I wanted.

I raised my eyes from problem number five on Noah's homework and considered the close-shorn back of his head. If Brody and I discussed the photo here, Noah would hear me. I could say one wrong thing and let on that my weird pairing with Brody had developed into a crush, and Noah would make sure the whole locker room knew what was going on. That would *definitely* get back to Kennedy. Noah wasn't one to keep his mouth shut about other people's business. His own business, yes. Mine, no.

Quinn sat in front of Noah. He would overhear the conversation too. He wouldn't spread the gossip like Noah, but when Brody slighted me, Quinn would feel sorry for me, just like he had when Noah broke up with me. That would be worse.

And in front of Brody sat Sawyer. He didn't have it in for me, as far as I knew, but if he overheard my awkward request, he would retell the story in the funniest way possible, which would make my life a living hell. That's just how Sawyer was. He might have been asleep, though. His white-blond head was down on his arms, and he hadn't moved since I'd entered the classroom. As our school's mascot—he dressed up like a six-foot pelican at the games—his first act of bringing about student solidarity had been to pass out from heat exhaustion at a practice on the football field last Monday. He probably was resting for his debut at the game tonight.

And that meant at least *he* would nap through what I said to Brody. As for Noah and Quinn, maybe Quinn had been right: It was time I stopped worrying about how things looked. Once more, I rehearsed what I would say to Brody. *We need to take a yearbook photo for Perfect Couple That Never Was*, and *We need to think of an original way to pose for the photo*, and *What if we met off campus? Like on a date? We'd be a couple—get the joke? Not a real date, of course. We don't want Kennedy and Grace mad at us!* Feeling like I was about to fling myself off a cliff, I took a deep breath and turned to Brody.

He was asleep. In the thirty seconds I'd taken to steel myself, his hunched shoulders had gone slack. His upper body rose and fell with deep, even breaths. I was amazed he could relax amid the buzz of the classroom—but after all, *he* wasn't a geeky girl whose nerves were stretched taut to the point of snapping because the popular quarterback was an arm's length away.

With a defeated sigh, I faced the front and crossed my legs under my desk again.

"Is my homework that bad?" Noah asked, turning his broad body around. "I thought I actually understood this unit, for once."

"No, sorry, I've hardly started." I bent over Noah's work, checking his answers against mine.

My gaze drifted across the aisle to Brody. His handsome face was hidden: the high cheekbones, the expressive mouth. All I could see from this angle was the top of his head, longish light brown hair curtaining over his face, and one strong upper arm straining against the sleeve of his tight athletic shirt. He also wore long athletic shorts and flip-flops, as always. On the coldest day of the year, which admittedly wasn't very cold around here, he *might* add a hoodie. We'd been in various advanced classes together since middle school, but the way he dressed, he looked like he'd taken a wrong turn from the gym. That's how Brody had always been: grinning, a bit of a mess, and a world away from me.

Twenty minutes later, I'd checked Noah's homework. I hoped I had just enough time to finish my questions on the chapter in English so I wouldn't have to take my book home. Ms. Patel interrupted my thoughts. "Class, may I have your attention, please? Quinn and Noah want to make an announcement before lunch."

Sawyer stirred and raised his head from his arms. Brody couldn't even make that much effort. He kept his head down but shifted so he could see around Sawyer. He would be sitting up in a minute, though. Surely he knew what was coming. I put my hand on Noah's back as he stood. He smiled nervously at me before he and Quinn made their way up the row to stand in front of Ms. Patel's desk.

"We. . . ," Noah began, then folded his muscular arms. He was African American, with such dark skin that the fluorescent lights overhead highlighted the indentations of his huge muscles like he was a comic-book superhero. He'd also perfected a threatening scowl he used to intimidate other football players, but he wasn't wearing it now. It was strange to see him look nervous. He glanced over at Quinn.

"Tick-tock," Ms. Patel said. "The bell's going to ring. Better get it out."

Quinn wrung his hands in fingerless black leather gloves, an odd accessory during hot weather in Florida, even for one of *my* friends. Then he ran his hands through his black hair. Finally he burst out, "Noah and I are dating. Each other."

Silence fell over the classroom. It was so quiet that Mr. Frank's voice filtered through the wall from the next room. I wanted to jump up and pound on the wall to stop Mr. Frank, but I felt dizzy. That's when I realized I was holding my breath.

Brody started clapping.

The class burst into applause.

Sighing with relief, I clapped along, harder and harder as the weight of the last year lifted from my shoulders. I'd been so worried about Quinn and then Noah when they came out to me. This positive reception to their official, public coming out was a great sign for their future.

The door opened. Kennedy gave the noisy classroom a bewildered glance. Ms. Patel pointed to an empty desk near the door, indicating that he should park it rather than moving all the way back to sit behind me. As he slung off his backpack and slouched in the desk, Noah mouthed an explanation for the commotion: "We're gay." Kennedy blushed bright red.

Not the reaction I'd expected from Kennedy. He prided himself on being open-minded. I'd thought he'd be mildly supportive, or have no reaction at all.

The applause died down, and Noah cleared his throat. "Some of you may be wondering, 'Why now?' A couple of weeks ago, when we voted on the Senior Superlatives, I wrote in myself and Quinn for Perfect Couple That Never Was. I thought the student council would take it as a joke. Really it was just wishful thinking, I guess. I wasn't even sure Quinn was gay."

Quinn put his gloved hand on Noah's shoulder. "I did the same. Principal Chen called us both into her office and told us that if we had something to say to the school, we could go ahead if we did it in a way that wouldn't disrupt class."

My friend Chelsea raised her hand. "Those were secret ballots, I *thought*. How did Ms. Chen know they were yours?"

"Because she's *creepy*?" Quinn said.

"Careful," Ms. Patel spoke up.

"She's really old," Noah said with a sideways glance at Ms. Patel. "You know how she's always telling us in assemblies that we'd better not try to slip anything past her."

Ms. Patel bit her lip, trying not to laugh.

"Anyway," Quinn said, "we decided to do it here in study hall because we wanted to come out in front of the people who've encouraged us the most." He put his hand over his heart. "For me, that's Harper."

"Awwwww." A chorus of girls' voices echoed how I felt. I'd tried to support Quinn any way I could, but I hadn't expected him to acknowledge me in front of the class.

"And for me," Noah said, "that's Harper and Brody."

"Brody!" Sawyer yelled a raunchy, "Aoow!"

Brody thumped him on the back of the head.

Sawyer turned around and took a swipe at Brody. Brody leaned back in his desk to dodge the blow.

"We also wanted to come out in front of Sawyer," Noah said, "so we'd catch him off guard, before he had the chance to work up any jokes."

"Oooooh," said the class. All eyes were on Sawyer now. It wasn't often that somebody stuck it to Sawyer.

Quinn went on, "And of course, Sawyer is our study hall's student council representative. He can help us address our grievances to the school if anything bad happens."

Sawyer nodded. He must take his position seriously. I'd been as surprised as anyone when he nominated himself for student council representative at the beginning of the year. We'd elected him because nobody else ran. But it was nice to know he would step up for Noah and Quinn if they needed him.

Then he muttered, "I've got nothing. Good material takes time."

"Exactly," Noah and Quinn said together.

Their speech seemed to be winding down. Before anybody else could heckle them, I called, "Cupcakes!"

"Cupcaaaaaakes!" several people cheered.

As I slid out of my desk, Brody cracked a smile at me. "You made coming-out cupcakes?"

"Yeah. Wait till you see them."

"Do you need help?"

"No, thanks." There was only one container. I'd hidden it on the counter at the back of the room, underneath a huge folded poster of the periodic table.

I was halfway there before I realized that I'd just turned down an innocent excuse to interact with Brody. When it came to guys, I was a little slow on the uptake.

Brody was standing beside his desk now, stretching. I grabbed the container and brought it to him. "I mean yes," I said, "I need your help. Could you open these on Ms. Patel's desk?"

"Sure. What are you going to—Oh."

I pulled a camera out of my pocket, the small one I carried when I didn't have my expensive one, so I never missed a shot. "Say cheese," I told him.

"Cupcakes!" He held them up.

It was another killer picture of him, I realized with dismay. Brody was a little too photogenic. I wanted my best work to go into the yearbook, but I couldn't get away with slipping a photo of him onto every page.

I shot a few more candids of the class while I waited for

him to deliver the cupcakes to the front of the room. Then I cornered Quinn and Noah against the whiteboard for the commemorative picture I really wanted. They put their heads close together and held up their cupcakes. I'd used rainbow papers, and each cake was topped with a plastic rainbow and a cutout photo of someone in the class. So Noah's cake had his face on top, and Quinn's had his. After we all three checked the camera display and laughed over that classic shot, I pocketed my camera and reached into the box for the Harper cake.

Brody held his cake, as if he was waiting for me to start eating. "This was why you went around the room yesterday, taking pictures of everybody."

"Yeah." That, and it had been another reason to take a picture of *him*. "I thought if I made cupcakes and put people's faces on them, involving them in the celebration, they'd be less likely to say something ugly once we get to the lunchroom."

"Smart," he said. "Do we have to eat our own cupcake?"

"That was the idea, yeah."

"Because some guy's going to ask if he can eat your cupcake, Harper."

I nearly choked on the icing. After swallowing, I said, "I figured Sawyer might say that. I've done some deep-breathing exercises, and I'm okay with it."

"Sawyer isn't the only person here with a dirty mind." Brody licked his icing. I watched his mouth.

Sawyer walked over. I'd stopped at the bakery that morning and bought him a vegan muffin, since vegan cupcakes were not in my repertoire. He was stuffing the last of it into his mouth. "Quinn," he called, "didn't you date Harper last year?"

"Here it comes." Quinn rolled his eyes. His thick black eyeliner made the whites of his eyes more pronounced.

"And, Noah," Sawyer continued, "didn't *you* date Harper last spring?"

"Fuck you, De Luca," Noah said softly enough that Ms. Patel couldn't hear by the window.

"What does that say about the guy Harper's dating now? What's his name, again, the one with the rad pierced eyebrow?" Sawyer snapped his fingers a couple of times close to Kennedy, who hadn't moved from the desk by the door. "I can't ever remember that guy's name."

"*This* is the joke you came up with?" Brody asked.

"I haven't had time!" Sawyer protested. "And *you*! Be careful about this Perfect Couple That Never Was thing, Larson. Harper obviously has a way with guys."

"Here's what I'm going to do to you in PE," Brody told Sawyer. "Should I say this now, or do you want me to surprise you?"

The bell rang.

Most of the class moved toward the door, their minds already off Quinn and Noah and on lunch. A couple of girls looked over their shoulders, smiling, and said a few encouraging words to Noah and Quinn, who were talking with Ms. Patel. Noah put his hand on Quinn's back. I couldn't hear what Noah said over the noise of everyone changing classes, but I read his lips as he asked, "Are you okay?" Quinn nodded and relaxed his shoulders, tension released.

Happy the announcement had gone well, I started to follow Brody back to my desk to pick up my stuff. Kennedy spoke over the noise. "Harper, I need to talk to you."

Uh-oh. I hoped he wasn't sensitive about what Sawyer had said. Heart racing, I sank down in the desk next to his. While we waited for Ms. Patel and the rest of the class to file into the hall, I did my breathing exercises and tried to center myself.

I managed to calm down quite a bit before Brody passed right in front of me, the last one out the door. My pulse raced again. He looked at me, brows knitted in concern, then at Kennedy, and back at me.

I gave him the smallest shake of my head, which I hoped Kennedy didn't see. My message to Brody was that everything was okay, even though I didn't believe it myself.

After he left, Kennedy got up, shut the door, and leaned against it with his arms folded, scowling at me. After all my efforts to appease him about my Superlatives photos and his yearbook designs, I was *still* headed for a weekend of the silent treatment.

To head him off, I said, "I understand why you're upset."

"I don't think you do," he said. "You dated Quinn, then Noah, and now they're *gay*? What does that say about *me*?"

I wanted to point out that Sawyer had said something similar to Brody, and *Brody* wasn't mad. Maybe Brody was more self-confident.

Maybe Brody wasn't my boyfriend.

"I realize it was a surprise," I said, "but—"

"You're damn right it was a surprise!" Kennedy seethed. "Why didn't you tell me?"

"I don't give away people's secrets," I said. "That's why Quinn and Noah confided in me in the first place."

"Yeah, well, it says a lot about your priorities if you put your two gay friends in front of your boyfriend."

"Kennedy," I said, "I'm not putting them in front of you. This has nothing to do with you."

"Really?" he asked. "You can't turn in your Superlatives photos to me, but you have time to bake cupcakes with pictures for *them*?"

"Um." I didn't have a response to that. The cupcakes had been important to me. I'd baked them with love for my friends' important day. Kennedy made them sound stupid.

"You bring rainbow cupcakes for your last two boyfriends, while your current boyfriend is sitting in the same class," he said. "Don't you see how that looks?"

"Yeah, I get it," I said softly, without really getting it. "I'm sorry."

He shook his head in disgust, focusing his gaze somewhere above my head instead of on me. Abruptly he jerked up his backpack by one strap and opened the door.

Tia was standing in the hall. Knowing her, she'd had her ear to the door. "Kennedy, we need a word with Harper," she said, pushing past him into the room.

"She'll catch up with you in a minute," Kaye added, walking in behind Tia.

"You can have her," Kennedy snarled. He stormed into the hall and slammed the door.

Three

TIA AND KAYE STARED WIDE EYED AT ME. Finally Kaye said, "Brody came to our table in the lunchroom and told us Quinn is *gay*? And Noah is *gay*? And Kennedy is *mad*? Brody asked us to check on you."

Brody had asked my friends to check on me! If I'd been by myself, I would have replayed this in my mind like the best ending to a feel-good movie. As it was, I didn't want Kaye and Tia to know how far gone I was for the unattainable Brody. I said only, "It's been an interesting study hall."

"Cupcakes!" Tia hopped up to sit on Ms. Patel's desk. Crossing her long legs at the ankles, she reached into the container.

"You can have those," I offered, as if I could have stopped her anyway.

She held up the two remaining. "Harper, you made *coming-out cupcakes*?"

"You're adorable," Kaye said.

"I don't *feel* adorable," I grumbled.

"Do you want Kennedy or Shelley Stearns?" Tia asked Kaye. I'd forgotten Shelley had gone to her grandmom's in Miami for the long holiday weekend.

"Shelley," Kaye said.

Tia examined both cupcakes up close. "No, *I* want her," she said. "I don't want to eat Kennedy."

"It's only a cupcake topper," Kaye said.

"Then *you* eat him," Tia said.

Exasperated, Kaye flung out her hand for the cupcake. She examined the topper, murmured, "Cute," licked the icing off the pick, and tossed Kennedy into the trash can. She slid onto the desk beside Tia and elbowed her to make her scoot over. "So, Harper, you knew about Quinn and Noah all along? And you never told anybody, even us! You sneaky mouse."

I moved my own half-eaten cupcake to the far corner of my desk. I'd lost my appetite. "Remember I had a crush on Quinn last year? He wasn't dating anyone that we knew of, and we couldn't understand why he wouldn't ask me out. You both kept telling me to ask him on a date."

They nodded slowly. They didn't look quite as confident as they had when they burst into the room. Obviously they were second-guessing their advice that I pursue Quinn.

"I did," I said. "I told you that part. Here's the part I didn't tell you. He came out to me. He wasn't ready to tell everybody. He was afraid of what his parents would do, judging from how they freaked when he dyed his hair black. But he knew some people at school were talking about him and wondering whether he was gay."

Tia nodded. Kaye said, "I'd heard that."

"Sawyer told me," Tia said.

"How did Sawyer know?" Kaye asked. "Surely Quinn didn't tell *him*."

"Sawyer just knows things," Tia said.

I explained, "Quinn asked me if we could go out a few times as friends but say we were dating, to get people off his back."

"And you said *yes*?" Kaye was livid. "Harper, we had that talk about people taking advantage of you."

"It was fine!" I exclaimed. "I didn't mind."

"And then you did the same thing for Noah?" Tia asked.

"No, Noah asked me on a date himself. Remember how excited I was? I'd wondered why a football player would want to date me. And *then* he came out to me."

"Oh," Tia and Kaye cooed sympathetically at the same time. They were right to feel sorry for me. I'd been devastated when Noah told me the truth. In fact, I'd been so taken with him, and the feel of his huge arm curving around me, that he'd set the stage for my daydreams about another football player.

But this was exactly what I hadn't wanted. The more people felt sorry for me, the smaller I felt.

"And then you got the two of them together," Kaye said. "That's so sweet!"

"No," I said. "They both swore me to secrecy. Ms. Chen outed them to each other by mistake." I told Kaye and Tia the boys' story about the Perfect Couple vote. "I'm just glad they're happy."

"So why's Kennedy mad at you?" Tia asked. "Other than the fact that he's always mad at you lately?"

I winced. It was true, but coming from Tia, the truth was especially blunt.

"Sawyer made a joke about me dating gay guys. He said Kennedy must be gay too. Also Brody, since the school thinks we'd be perfect together."

"Oh my God!" Tia yelled with her mouth full. "Why did Sawyer say that? I'll kill him."

"Nobody cares what Sawyer thinks," Kaye said between nibbles. "Sawyer's a pothead."

"Not anymore," Tia corrected her. "He swore it off. He's turned into a health nut since he passed out on Monday."

Kaye tossed her cupcake paper into the trash and placed her fists on her hips, cheerleader style. "Why are you always defending him?"

"Why are you always so down on him?" Tia turned back to me. "And *that's* all Kennedy's mad about? Sawyer shouldn't have said it, but Kennedy's as used to Sawyer's inappropriate comments as the rest of us. There's no reason for him to be angry unless he was already sensitive about the subject in the first place. *Brody's* not mad."

"No, Brody's not mad," I acknowledged. "Brody and Noah are best friends, plus Brody's so happy-go-lucky. Brody . . ."

Tia and Kaye stared wide-eyed at me again. Any story

including Brody was more delicious than cupcakes. I found myself telling them what Brody had said about me to the football team.

"Oooh, he's into you," Kaye said approvingly. She rubbed her hands together. "Intrigue!"

"Perfect Coupling?" Tia puzzled through Brody's joke. "Like you're a piece of PVC pipe and he's an elbow joint?"

"Yeah, I didn't think it was all that sexy either." Actually, I *did*, but I couldn't admit this. "I confronted him about it, and he said he blurted it out when the team teased him about the Perfect Couple title. Who'd *you* vote for?" I'd been wanting to ask them this for a while.

"I voted for you!" Kaye told me triumphantly.

"And Brody?"

"Oh, God, no! You and Evan Fielding. He looks so cute in his plaid hat, like an old man. You're both so retro."

Wearing an old man's hat was the most interesting thing I'd seen Evan do. He was in my journalism class, and when we brainstormed ideas for the yearbook, he never uttered a peep. I'd been partnered with him a couple of times and ended up doing most of the work myself because I'd expected he would let me down. This was the guy one of my best friends thought was my perfect match?

Kaye read the look on my face. "Only because of his hat," she backtracked.

"Why are you curious?" Tia asked me. "You're dying to know why so many people paired you with Brody, aren't you?"

"Nooooo." I tried to brush it off. "I have a boyfriend. Brody has a girlfriend. Being elected together is a big joke between us."

But joke or not, sometime in the next two weeks, we would have to take our yearbook picture together. And during that short interlude, at least on my end, our relationship would be dead serious.

I wished I could have hung with Kaye and Tia at the football game that night. But Tia stood next to Will in the drum section of the marching band. Kaye was on the sidelines with the other cheerleaders, including Brody's glamorous girlfriend, Grace. I braved the sidelines all by myself to shoot the game.

Though I was a bit unclear on the rules, I'd always enjoyed football games. I loved the band music, the screams of the crowd and the cheerleaders, and the charged atmosphere. And though I feared for my life a couple of times when huge guys in helmets and pads hurtled toward me, the danger seemed worthwhile after I got some great shots of our players.

That is, I got some great shots of *Brody*. In the third quarter, our defense recovered a fumble and returned the ball all the way to the end zone for a touchdown. I missed the entire thing because I was pretending to take pictures of our team watching from the sidelines. Really, I'd zoomed in on Brody, whose helmet was off. He'd pulled his long, wet hair out of his eyes with a band. And he had no idea he was in my lens. He focused on the action on the field and screamed his heart out for his friends on the defensive line.

In the fourth quarter, Sawyer, dressed as the pelican mascot, came marching jauntily toward me. He picked up his knees and big bird feet high with every step, swinging his feathery elbows. I hoped he hadn't caught me gazing wistfully at Brody. I wasn't sure how well he could see out of the enormous bird head he was wearing. If he'd noticed my moony stare, he would make fun of me for it.

He put his wing around me.

I glared up at him.

He turned his huge head to look at me, too. His fuzz-covered beak hit me in the eye.

"Get your wing off me," I said, moving out from under his arm.

He put his hands on his padded bird hips and stomped his foot like he wanted to know why.

"You have a lot of nerve, bird," I said. "Quinn and Noah were so brave today, but you *had* to take a jab at them, and at Kennedy and Brody and *me*. As if people can be turned gay! Now Kennedy is mad at me because of what you said."

Sawyer shrugged.

"I *know* you don't like Kennedy, but he's *my boyfriend*!"

He opened his hands, pleading with me.

"Sure, you didn't mean it. That's the problem. If a joke is funny, you'll go ahead and blurt it out, whether it hurts somebody or not."

He bowed his head, and his shoulders slumped. He was sorry.

"I don't care," I said. "Go away."

He got down on his knees and clasped his hands, begging me.

"No," I said. "You deserve to sweat it for a while." Instantly I felt bad for the way I'd phrased this. He *had* fainted from heat exhaustion four days earlier, and he was probably dying in that getup. The night was at least eighty degrees.

He didn't take offense, apparently. He wrapped both wings around my leg.

I tried to step backward, out of his grasp. He held on tightly. His wings were at my knee, dangerously close to pushing my dress up higher than I'd wanted to hike it in front of five thousand people.

I glanced up at the student section. Kennedy pointed at me and laughed to everyone around him.

Imagining the only thing worse that could happen, I looked over at the team. Sure enough, Brody was watching us too. Suddenly, his friends slugging it out on the defensive line weren't as interesting to him. Shouldn't he be watching the game?

He raised one eyebrow at me.

I protected myself with the only weapon I had. I leaned way back, focused my camera, and snapped a photo of Sawyer's looming bird head, with Brody grinning in the background. The whole episode was so mortifying that I doubted I would find it funny by the end of the school year or when I was in college or by the time I turned thirty, but maybe I could laugh about it before I died.

"Hey!" Kaye came up behind Sawyer and slapped him on the back of his bird head. He spent PE with the cheerleaders. I guessed he and Kaye had been around each other enough, and he'd annoyed her enough, that she knew how to whap him in costume without hurting him. Or maybe she'd wanted it to hurt.

At any rate, he felt it. He let go of me and made a grab for her. She took off down the sidelines, behind the football team. He ran after her. All this happened so fast that I didn't even get a picture.

After we won the game, and the team and coaches and cheerleaders and Sawyer had surged onto the field for a group hug on the fifty-yard line, I watched Brody walk toward the stadium exit with Noah. The newspaper had said this would be a great season for the team and for Brody, but his talk with Noah looked way too serious for two friends who'd just won their first game.

I was thinking so hard about what could be wrong that it took me a few seconds to notice Brody was waving at me. By the time I waved back, he'd given up waggling his fingers and was making big motions with both arms like he was adrift at sea and trying to hail a Coast Guard helicopter. Then he resumed his solemn confab with Noah. I watched them until they'd wearily climbed the stairs and disappeared through the gate.

That was the highlight of my night. Afterward, I met my friends from journalism class at the Crab Lab, but Kennedy was still giving me the silent treatment. He didn't offer me an angry word or even look at me the whole time. He just sat in a two-person booth and had an in-depth discussion about yearbook design with the sports section editor. A couple of times I overheard him pointedly say that placing pictures at an angle was a great way to vary the pages.

He was leaving the next morning to visit his cousins in Orlando and wouldn't be back until Sunday night. I wanted to make up with him so the fight didn't hang over our heads and tarnish the Labor Day weekend. But since he was still ignoring me, I knew he wasn't ready to kiss and make up. I didn't order any food, and I left a few minutes later. I had a lot of stuff to do at home.

I worked most of Saturday and Sunday. My friends were tied up, anyway. Kaye had a family reunion. Tia's dad was about to buy a fixer-upper mansion, and she was helping him get the house they lived in ready to sell.

I wasn't lonely. I actually looked forward to two days almost totally by myself. I planned to process the remaining photos I'd taken for the yearbook but hadn't yet turned in to Kennedy. I would also get my website ready to showcase the pictures I'd take of the 5K on Monday. If I got caught up with this work, maybe I would feel less stressed about corralling my classmates—including Brody—for the rest of the Superlatives photos during the next two weeks.

Both days, I helped Mom serve breakfast. After that, she spent her time working on the B & B—cleaning the guest rooms and bathrooms and the common areas, then painting or replacing boards on the exterior that were rotting in the fierce Florida sun and rain. Most days if I didn't talk to her while she was making breakfast, I didn't talk to her at all.

I also took breaks from my computer to check on Granddad, who lived alone a couple of streets over. I'd been doing this every couple of days since he and Mom had argued a few months ago. Granddad didn't like it whenever Mom said she was willing to take my dad back.

After I made sure Granddad was okay, I walked the other way along the beach road until I reached the private strip of undeveloped sand that Granddad had inherited from his family. When my dad had been around, he used to complain that we'd all be rich if Granddad would give in and sell his beach. Stubbornly, Granddad had never put it up for sale or even built a house on it. He liked to go there by himself and paint the ocean.

I knew how he felt. That's where I'd fallen in love with photography, taking pictures of the palm trees, the sand, the boats on the water. Everybody saw the same thing, but a photographer framed it to focus on one object in particular, telling a certain story.

In fact, I was afraid I was a little too much like Granddad. Someday I would inherit his house on one side of downtown and his strip of beach on the other. Like him, I'd hole up with my art and resent having to interact with other people when I went to the grocery store once a week.

I enjoyed being alone on the beach, but sometimes I wished my friends were there. This weekend, the public beaches were crowded enough that I could hear families laughing through the palms. As I swam out into the warm waves, I could see kids splashing together over on the park side. A teenage girl hugged a guy in the water with her legs looped around his waist. He kissed her ear. They laughed and whispered.

Brody was probably over there too, with Grace.

Never mind. I had work to do.

Monday morning, I got up early, as if it wasn't a holiday, because it wasn't—for me. I chose a fitted blouse tucked into a trim pencil skirt I'd made, and my most professional-looking glasses. I pulled back my hair into a classy bun at my nape. Then I walked from the small house I shared with Mom, which had been converted from a coach house, over to the huge Victorian, her bed and breakfast. Mom was already there, cooking her boarders' one expected meal of the day. It was my job to help serve.

I hated doing this. Since my parents had separated two years before, I'd tried to be supportive of Mom, but the first thing she did to rebuild her life without my dad was to borrow money from Granddad and buy a B & B. She loved people. She thought living on top of a constantly rotating group of strangers was a fun way to spend her days. It was like a sickness. She'd dreamed of running a B & B in the beach town where she grew up. Obviously Granddad's introverted gene had skipped a generation. To me the B & B was a nightmare.

I stood outside the pink clapboard back of the house. Palmettos shaded me from the bright morning sun. My kitten heels ground the seashells in the path. I took a few deep, calming breaths. Then I opened the door into the kitchen.

"Good morning," Mom sang, pulling homemade orange rolls from the oven. She wore a long, flowing beach dress and feather earrings, and she'd put up her dark hair in a deliberate tousle. Her feet were bare. She liked to dress ultra-casual so her guests would feel at home with the beach lifestyle, but I was pretty sure serving orange rolls in bare feet was reason for an inspection by the Health Department.

She turned away from me to snag a bread basket from a shelf, but I heard her say, "You look [unintelligible]."

I didn't ask her to repeat herself. I'd heard all her comments about my fashion sense before.

She kept on me. Handing me a pair of tongs and the basket of rolls to pass out to guests in the dining room, she looked me up and down and said, "I thought you were photographing the 5K this morning."

"I am."

"You don't look comfortable."

Well, I *wasn't* comfortable *right then*, living out somebody else's dreams of owning a business. I didn't say this, because it wouldn't do any good.

"Smile," she said, touching my lips, possibly smearing my perfect red lipstick. Now I would have to check my face before I left the house. Then she tapped her finger between my brows, possibly transferring the lipstick up there, and reminded me, "Nobody likes a pouty B & B." She swung open the door into the dining room, where eight strange adults eagerly awaited me. They would ask me embarrassing, none-of-their-business questions they would never ask if they weren't on vacation, such as, *Do you have a boyfriend?*

Answer: I wasn't sure. Kennedy hadn't so much as texted me since Friday at school.

After the guests were served, Mom sat down to eat with them, putting on her best "colorful local character" act. She was their font of information on the best beaches and restaurants and sights in St. Petersburg and Tampa.

She set a place for me at the table too, but breakfast was the one time I suddenly took great interest in making sure the B & B ran smoothly. I always volunteered to stay in the kitchen and unload the dishwasher or watch the next batch of rolls. I was able to get away with this only because Mom's first rule was never to have an argument where the guests could hear. At the B & B, we were a hotel staff, not a family.

I wasn't trying to sabotage Mom and her business. The truth was, I couldn't stand to sit at the dining room table and talk to a new group of strangers each week as if it was a family meal. I didn't want to answer a million questions about my school and my friends and my boyfriend. It was too much like making get-to-know-you small talk every time Mom brought home some guy she was dating. Inevitably she whispered to me that *this* one was the one.

I supported her dreams. I only wanted her to leave me out of them.

This morning, I hid in the kitchen, periodically dropping a knife in the sink to make actually-busy-in-the-kitchen noises while I noiselessly opened the three-times-weekly local newspaper to the sports page. I expected a triumphant review of Friday night's game. Reading about Brody as a hero would give me the fan-girl fix I'd been bluesing for. Simultaneously it would remind me how out of reach he was.

But the headline was cruelty in six words: LARSON DISAPPOINTS IN PELICANS' FIRST WIN.

The article explained that Brody's signature as a quarterback was his willingness to wait until the last nanosecond to pass the ball. That increased the chances he'd be sacked—tackled, clobbered, hit incredibly hard by the other team, who wanted to take him out of the game so we'd have to rely on our second-string sophomore. Brody didn't care. He braved getting hurt, which gave him more time than quarterbacks normally had to choose a receiver for his long, accurate passes.

At least, that's what had happened in practice, and that's what sports reporters had been so excited about when they hyped the season. But the article went on to say that Brody had lost his mojo. During the game, he'd gotten rid of the ball as fast as he could, like an inexperienced quarterback running scared.

No wonder he and Noah had seemed so down after the game.

I couldn't imagine what had gone wrong.

Strangely, that one negative article about a guy I hardly knew threatened to ruin my whole holiday. That and Kennedy giving me the cold shoulder, and Mom's comment on my outfit. But once I'd passed the second batch of rolls around the table, shouldered the strap of my camera bag, and escaped from the B & B, my mood improved. Just around the corner, the town square had been blocked off to traffic. The sidewalks teemed with laughing people of all ages. They watched down the street for the first finishers of the 5K race.

I ducked under the retaining rope—not over, which would have been awkward in my tight skirt—and walked into the middle of the street, a few yards in front of the finish line. Mom had made me doubt the wisdom of what I was wearing. I guessed her opinion bothered me so much because I was afraid she was right. I was sweating already underneath my waistband and my bra. But dressing this way made me feel as beautiful as Lois Lane and as talented behind my camera as Jimmy Olsen, but with the strength of Superman. I had no identifying badge that said I belonged on the participants' side of the ropes, but nobody challenged me. I looked like I meant business.

Down the street, the crowd noise swelled and moved in

my direction as the first finishers ran closer. I brought up my camera and prepared to focus. My goal was to snap at least one clear picture of every runner. I would use the runners' numbers pinned to their shirts to label the photos for purchase on my website. But that was a tall order: nearly perfect photos of hundreds of people in the space of a few minutes. I took a deep, calming breath.

The crowd noise spiked as the leaders of the race came around the corner and entered the town square. The thirty front-runners were experienced athletes, led by the owner of the running-shoe store who'd sponsored the race and arranged for me to photograph it. I needed a perfect picture of *him*, at least. I focused as well as I could and set the continuous feed to snap a number of frames in quick succession. As soon as the runners had passed, another wave bore down on me. I kept up as best I could, heart hammering in my chest.

And then, *oh*. There, centered in my viewfinder, was Brody.

Four

TINGLES OF EXCITEMENT SPREAD DOWN MY neck and across my chest before I even consciously understood I'd recognized Brody. And I *hadn't* recognized his face. He was still too far away, even through my zoom lens. I recognized his running stride. I'd been looking out the window of English class, watching him run wind sprints for football practice in the parking lot, *way* too often in the past two weeks.

Remembering what I was standing in the road for, I opened the shutter and snapped a picture of him shoving the guy jogging next to him, who laughed and shoved Brody right back. It was Tia's boyfriend, Will, I realized as they came closer. I snapped photos of every runner I could see clearly, then focused on Brody through my viewfinder again.

His sun-streaked brown hair, long enough to fall into his eyes, was held back with the same sort of headband he used on the football field. I watched the defined muscles in his legs move as he sprinted toward me at top speed. He wore red gym shorts and no shirt, showing off his six-pack abs. Strong as he looked, I was surprised at how thin he was compared with his apparent mass when he wore a football uniform and pads. After the newspaper's hype, I'd expected him to be more muscle-bound. Maybe all athletic high school boys looked like this, and they bulked up in college.

The number 300 was printed across his chest in marker—which meant he'd been the last runner to register, because that was the total number I'd been told to expect. But the 3 had smeared into more of an 8 during his shoving match with Will. The two of them galloped toward the finish, gaining speed, cackling as one and then the other got a long arm in front of the other's body.

Suddenly another runner broke from the pack behind them—Noah. His shirt was off too, and his body gleamed in the sunlight as he found an even faster gear and tore past them. Though they were still down the street from me and I was seeing all this through my telephoto lens, I could hear Brody's and Will's moans of dismay at being beaten.

And watching them, something happened to me.

I'd never thought of guys in the same way other girls seemed to. Kaye was devoted to Aidan, but we occasionally caught her following another guy with her eyes. She would let slip a remark about his fine ass that made clear she wasn't about to cheat on her boyfriend but she did appreciate the male physique. Tia offered a constant stream of the same kind of commentary. She was a sexual being and not the least ashamed. I admired her for this, though I didn't tell her. She certainly didn't need any encouragement. In comparison, I didn't consider myself sexual. I wasn't gay, I wasn't bi, I was just disconnected from the entire scene.

So out of it, in fact, that I was gay guys' go-to girl when they weren't ready to come out and wanted to put their friends off their trail a little longer. They figured I wouldn't mind too much because I wasn't that interested in the opposite sex anyway.

Until now. Maybe it was because I'd thought about Brody constantly and planned what I would say to him when I told him we needed to take our Superlatives photo. But I didn't think so. The pure sight of his beautiful body, shining with sunscreen and sweat in the morning sun, running toward me, made me realize I was a part of this scene after all.

A part of the scene that was about to get knocked on its ass. Since the first runners had approached, I'd trusted that my professional attire and large, expensive camera would warn the competitors not to run me down. But Noah galloped past me a little too close for comfort. Brody and Will were barreling straight for me, their shoes slapping the asphalt.

Brody turned away from Will. His eyes drilled straight through my viewfinder, into my eyes. He kept coming. He was about to hit me.

With a squeal, I spun to protect the camera if he elbowed me.

He passed so close, I felt the wind move against my back.

And then I was watching him raise both hands in victory as he crossed the finish line just ahead of Will.

Brody had forgotten me, if he'd even intended to pay me any attention at all.

Grumbling to myself, I turned back to the pack of runners and shot as many of them as I could, thankful I'd taken some of their pictures before I focused on Brody. I wondered if he knew or cared how close he'd come to making me drop my camera. But that was Brody. He was a daredevil who took crazy chances. Nothing bad ever happened to *him*, though. He always landed on his feet.

Except for that time on Fifth-Grade Play Day when he dove off the water slide and had to go to the hospital.

And another time, in second grade, when he wandered away from the group during our class field trip to the children's museum in Tampa, and the teachers found him *inside* a priceless dinosaur skeleton.

In fact, now that I thought about it, I recalled that he'd wrecked his mom's car when he was fourteen . . . and I held on a little more tightly to my camera as the crowd passed me on both sides.

After another thirty runners, I spotted Kaye with two of her fellow cheerleaders, race numbers pinned neatly to their shirts, which matched their shorts. Kaye saw me first and yelled to the other girls. They waved wildly and mugged for the camera as they passed. At least one of them had her mouth open or eyes closed in each frame. The key to getting a great shot of all three of them, so flattering that they would swear forever I was the world's best photographer, was simply to set the camera on continuous feed to shoot frame after frame. If I took enough photos, one of them was bound to be good. Photographing crowds for pay involved more know-how and logic than art.

A few more small groups ran by me, and then Sawyer jogged into view. He might have made it through Friday night's game, but he should *not* have been running a 5K on a hot September morning a week past being hospitalized.

Sure enough, after three miles of running, his wet T-shirt stuck to him, and his normally bright hair was dark, soaked with sweat. His exertion hadn't dampened his spirit, though. As I tried to center him for a good shot, he ran straight toward me with his hand out like a movie star trying to block the paparazzi. I got three brilliant shots of his palm.

"Sawyer, dammit!" I cried as he passed, realizing as the words escaped my lips that this was a common exclamation at our school. Sawyer's middle name might as well have been Dammit.

The groups of runners grew thicker now, and I struggled to keep up, taking at least one clear shot of every face. They still stuck together in packs, though. During a break in the crowd, I looked over my shoulder at the runners who'd finished—but *not* to locate Brody. Only to find Kaye.

The runner I saw instead was Sawyer, standing stock still and staring into space, his face so white he looked green.

Picking up the camera bag at my feet, I strode over and handed it to him. "Get my phone out of the front pocket, would you?" I couldn't watch him because I had to keep clicking away at the runners, but in a minute he was holding the phone in front of me. At least he could still follow instructions. I swept my thumb across the screen, punched in my security code, and handed the phone back to him. "Dial Tia."

When my phone appeared in front of me again, and there was another break in the runners, I spared Sawyer a glance. He was blinking awfully fast. I sandwiched the phone between my chin and my shoulder as I awkwardly peered through the camera and kept clicking.

"Hey there, Annie Leibovitz!" Tia chirped.

"Sawyer might pass out."

"I'll be right there." The line went dead.

I slipped the phone into my pocket. I didn't want to have to explain to the race sponsor, my boss for my first-ever gig as a professional photographer, that I'd missed capturing the last half of the race because my friend was going to faint. But I *would* have abandoned my job if Sawyer looked like he was about to hit the ground.

Before that could happen, Tia rushed over to him. I turned back to the runners. Tia and Sawyer were close enough to me that I could hear their voices above the noise of the crowd and the rock band starting up somewhere behind the finish line.

Tia: "Sawyer, dammit! Are you okay?"

Sawyer: "I will be. In a couple of years."

Tia: "What the fuck did you run this race for? You just got out of the hospital. Are you trying to kill yourself?"

Sawyer: "Not . . . actively."

Tia: "Jesus. Sit down. Sit down right here on the curb. Will!"

She sounded alarmed enough that I glanced over at them again. Will elbowed his way through, holding two bottles of water high above the crowd. Brody followed right behind him.

Tia: "Did you know he was running this?"

Will: "I tried to stop him. Sawyer, dammit, put your head between your knees."

Tia: "Help me take him to the medical tent."

Will: "There's no medical tent. It's a 5K."

Sawyer, muffled: "Fuck everybody."

Brody: "Shut up. Just enjoy the view."

Though I was in the middle of picking out faces from a huge group of slow runners, Brody's voice made me look over my shoulder again. He had his hand on the back of Sawyer's neck, pressing his head toward the pavement. Will was pouring water over Sawyer's hair. Now Kaye and her cheerleader friends circled him. Sawyer was in good hands. I tried to concentrate on the last fifty people crossing the finish line, some of them grimacing with the exertion, others giving me elated smiles and peace signs as they passed.

Finally the race seemed to be over. I watched downstream for a few moments, but the street in front of me was filling with pedestrians as if the police had signaled that no more runners were coming. I heaved a deep sigh, rolled my shoulders, and started scrolling back through the photos to one group in particular. I was curious whether my obsession with the beauty of Brody's body had been a product of my vivid imagination.

It was not. The image was tiny, but I ran my eyes over his shining muscles and his smeared race number, and looked forward to viewing the enlarged version on my computer.

"Whatcha looking at?" Tia asked, peering over my shoulder. "Got a Pulitzer winner? You seem very intent, even for you."

"How's Sawyer?" I asked.

"Oh, fine. Just stupid. Will's walking him home. Don't change the subject. Let me see what's so intriguing in there."

I handed the camera over to her and watched her look at the view screen herself. "I feel like a pervert," I said.

"You should. That is disgusting. Be sure to e-mail me a copy." She handed the camera back to me. "Have you scheduled your Superlatives picture with Brody?"

"I've been trying to find an in," I said. "Seeing him like this makes it harder. We were elected Perfect Couple That Never Was, and I'm thinking . . . in what universe would we be a perfect couple? I'm not built like a gymnast."

I looked down at the view screen and scrolled to the best photo of Brody alone. He was so beautiful, and he looked so happy running and shoving Will out of the frame, that my heart hurt. "Did you vote for Brody and me? You didn't answer me before."

"No," Tia said. "I wrote you in as Most Artistic and Brody as Most Athletic. For Perfect Couple That Never Was, I put a couple of nerds who giggle together at the back of my calculus class."

"So, you paired like with like," I said. "That's how I voted too. And of the guys at school, I think Kennedy is my perfect partner, but we're already dating."

"Yeah, you're such a perfect couple that you're not talking," she said.

"How do you know?" I'd texted her grumpily from the Crab Lab while Kennedy was giving me the silent treatment, but she and I hadn't caught up since. She had no way of knowing we *still* weren't talking.

"He does this to you every week," she said. "Every time you have a date planned."

I thought back over the weeks we'd been going out. Tia was right about the timing. Kennedy couldn't be picking a fight with me just to avoid spending time with me, though. Why would he do that?

The whole idea of him made me uncomfortable, so I changed the subject. "Do you think people elected Brody and me Perfect Couple because we have something in common that other people can see but I can't?"

"No," Tia said as Brody walked over. He must have poured a bottle of water over his own head. He was wetter than he'd been when he'd first rushed past me. His hair was dark and slick, still caught by the headband. He stood so close to me, and his green eyes were so intense, that I looked away shyly. I found myself staring at the dent in his upper arm where his deltoid disappeared underneath his biceps. This was the first time I had ever used eleventh-grade anatomy in real life.

I forced my eyes up his taut pectoralis major, all the way to his face. He seemed to be staring at the barest shadow of baby cleavage in the open neckline of my blouse. Then he saw I was watching him and cracked a guilty grin.

"Later," I heard Tia say, but I was so focused on Brody that it took me a few seconds to realize she was talking to me.

"Later," I responded faintly after she'd already walked away. I was sweating as much as Brody was now. I could feel drops rolling down my cleavage. Holding his gaze had gotten so uncomfortable that I glanced down at my old standby and savior, my mechanical wingman, the camera. "Brody, there's a picture I wanted you to see." I handed the camera to him.

The view screen was paused on the best photo I'd taken of the race: Noah in the foreground, slightly blurry, looking back over his shoulder, while Brody and Will were in sharp focus in the sweet spot of the frame, a third from the top and a third from one side. They'd just realized Noah was beating them, and their outrage was hilarious. Their bare chests weren't bad either. I figured the perfection of the photo was so obvious that even a layperson like Brody would see it. He wouldn't think my admiration for his body was gratuitous. No, that wouldn't be obvious unless he scrolled through my camera and saw all the other photos I'd taken of him.

He peered at the view screen and burst into laughter. I watched his mouth. His bottom lip wasn't swollen anymore, and the bruise on his jaw had faded. When he laughed that hard, the dark circles under his eyes disappeared too. He wasn't some older, intimidating bodybuilder. He was seventeen, like me.

With as deep a calming breath as I could draw without him noticing, I gathered the courage to ask, "Would you mind if I tried to sell this picture to the newspaper?"

He eyed me mischievously and asked, "Are you going to pay me?"

I smiled. "No."

"Are you going to pay me half?"

"No."

He tilted his head, perplexed. "Are you going to pay me a fourth?"

"No." His interrogation had gone on so long that I wondered if he really didn't want me to sell the picture. That was fine. It was his image, after all. I was profiting from his free services as a model. But I'd thought he was so happy-go-lucky that he wouldn't care.

"Harper!" he burst out. "I'm kidding."

"Well, I couldn't tell!" I took the camera back from him, my mind spinning. I wanted to get Will and Noah's permission too. Will was gone and I hadn't seen Noah since the end of the race. I'd never find him now in the milling pedestrians. I could text them both later and then e-mail the photo to the local paper.

All that was easier to work through than one tall guy standing in front of me, too easygoing for me to decipher.

Brody wasn't mortified about our misunderstanding like I was, though. He was still grinning as he said, "I guess you're going to take our photo for the yearbook sometime soon, like you took Will and Tia's."

"Right, like Will and Tia's," I echoed faintly. When I'd shot their picture for Biggest Flirts, they'd shared an unplanned kiss, which had gotten Will in trouble with his sort-of girlfriend Angelica. It had all worked out in the end. Will and Tia were dating now.

I stammered, "Um, I mean . . ." I lost my verbal abilities because I was at eye level with his nipples. This was distracting.

I forced my eyes up to his face. "We have to take the photo," I said. "We need to take it soon, because Kennedy's deadline for the whole section is in a week and a half. He kind of jumped down my throat about it Friday."

Brody raised his eyebrows at the idea of Kennedy scolding me. He'd been trying to flirt with me, and I'd ruined it by bringing up my boyfriend.

Exactly. "Setting up the picture is touchy when we're both dating somebody," I muddled through. "I've been taking photos in the courtyard at school because it's convenient and the light is good, but anyone can look out of the classrooms and see us. I found that out the hard way when I took Tia and Will's Biggest Flirts photo and there was a big fight and a fallout. Also, I don't have an inspiration for how we'd pose. Do you?"

"I was planning to do what you told me."

"Oh, *really*?" I exclaimed, stressing my excitement. This was my only success at flirting for our entire conversation. And when his mouth curled into a sly smile, my heart sped up.

"Here's a thought," I ventured. "I know the football team is practicing a lot, but if we could figure out a time . . ." I sounded like I was trying to get out of our meeting before I even proposed it.

He watched me like he was thinking the same thing.

I made myself continue, ". . . we could go on a date and take a picture of ourselves. It would be ironic, see, that we're the Perfect Couple That Never Was, except we *would* be a couple for the photo. It will be hilarious to, like, the five or six of our friends who would actually give a shit."

He laughed so hard that he took a step back. The space between us was wide enough that a couple of little kids dashed through, chasing each other.

Laughing uneasily along with Brody, I said, "Well, I didn't think it was *that* funny. Maybe seven or eight friends."

He stepped toward me again. "No, it's just funny to hear you say '*shit*.'"

"Oh." Tia had told me this before. I was so prim and proper, apparently, that a curse coming out of my mouth was as charming as a potty-mouthed toddler on a viral video. I felt myself blush as I always did when people said that kind of thing to me, like I wasn't a real person but a wholesome caricature.

Not knowing or caring that he was poking me in the tender parts of my psyche, Brody said, "I like this idea. Would we be going on a real date, or a fake date just for the photo?"

Well, of *course* it would be a fake date, and of *course* he knew this. We were both in other relationships. But the very idea of us going on a real date was so deliciously outrageous that I heard myself saying, "Whatever."

"I'll be at the beach with some friends this afternoon." He nodded toward the curb where Sawyer had sat, as if his friends were standing there, but I didn't see anyone I knew.

A lot of my friends, including Tia and Kaye, would be at the same beach. I was supposed to join them. I'd been thinking I should stay home instead and upload the race photos to my website. A delay was okay—the runners wouldn't expect their pictures to be available instantly—but I needed to get them online a.s.a.p. so I could turn my attention back to the yearbook photos.

Suddenly, Labor Day spent in front of the computer seemed like the world's saddest pastime compared with going to the beach with Brody. Or, not with Brody. The same beach as Brody. A photo of a fake date with Brody, more fun than any real date I'd ever been on with Kennedy. I said, "I'll be there too."

"So, I'll catch up with you there?"

"Okay."

"See you then." He walked toward the curb.

I enjoyed basking in the afterglow of his attention—for about one second. My ecstasy was over the instant I recognized one of the friends he was probably meeting at the beach. I heard her before I saw her. Grace had a piercing, staccato laugh, like a birdcall that sounded quirky on a nature walk and excruciating outside a bedroom window at dawn. Boys had been making fun of her laugh to her face forever—but Grace was so pretty and flirty that they only teased her as a way in.

She stopped laughing to say, "Sorry I missed your race, Brody! You know me. I just rolled out of bed."

The crowd parted. Now I could see her better. Just rolled out of bed, my ass. She stood casually in a teeny bikini top. At least she'd had the decency to pull gym shorts over her bikini bottoms so she didn't give the elderly snowbirds a heart attack. But her hair and makeup didn't go with her beach look. Grace's long blond hair rolled across her shoulders in big, sprayed curls, the kind that took me half an hour with a curling iron and a coat of hairspray. Her locks were held back from her pretty face by her sunglasses, which sat on top of her head. Her eyes were model-smoky with liner and shadow and mascara. She was ready for an island castaway prom.

"Did you win?" she asked Brody.

He chuckled. "No."

She led him away by the hand. And that was that.

I watched him go. I *needed* to watch him *walking away with his girlfriend*, so I could get it through my thick skull that he was taken. Brody and I had exchanged some friendly jokes and agreed to fulfill a school obligation—at a gathering we'd both already planned to attend. He'd seen his girlfriend and forgotten about me. I didn't even get a good-bye, not that I should have expected one. The "Never Was" part of our title was a lot more important than the "Perfect Couple" part.

Then he looked over his shoulder at me. Straight at me—no mistaking it. His green eyes were bright.

My heart stopped.

Still walking after Grace, he gave me a little wave.

I waved back.

He tripped over an uneven brick in the sidewalk but regained his balance before he fell. He disappeared into the crowd.

"That was smooth," Tia said at my shoulder.

Kneeling to pick up my camera bag, I grumbled, "Shut up."

"Does this mean you're going on a real date or a fake date?" she asked. "It wasn't clear from where I was eavesdropping."

I gave her the bag to hold while I snapped the lens off my camera and stuffed the components inside. "I don't know."

"Does this mean Brody's previous plan and your previous plan to go to the beach are actually the date in question, or is there another fake or real date after that?"

Exasperated, I gave her a warning look.

"Sorry," Tia said. "I know. I shouldn't be criticizing your romantic life. Before Will, my dating scene pretty much began and ended with giving Sawyer hand jobs behind the Crab

Lab." Several elderly men walking past turned to stare at her as she said this. She winked at them.

"I'm too polite to bring that up," I said.

"Do you want me to get Will to ask Brody, then report back . . . to . . . you?" Her words slowed as my expression grew darker.

"Thanks but no thanks," I said. "This is already embarrassing enough. No reason to take us back to the fifth grade."

Her mouth twisted sideways in a grimace as she handed the camera bag back to me. Tia clearly wanted to help but didn't know what to say. There *was* nothing to say, because my situation was so hopeless.

"It's okay," I assured her. "I have a boyfriend. This is just a yearbook picture. I'll see you at the beach."

"Later," she said, but she looked uncertain as she wound her way up the street toward the antiques store where she and her sister worked.

Tia was tall. It took a few minutes for me to lose the back of her shining auburn hair on the sidewalk now crowded with shoppers. I should have turned for home, e-mailed Noah and Will for permission to send my shot of them to the newspaper, and started uploading my race photos.

But now that Tia was gone and Brody was gone and I stood alone in the middle of the street, I was aware of the happiness all around me for the first time that day. The rock band had launched into another song. Families stood in line outside the ice cream parlor, even though it was nine a.m., because regular meal times meant nothing and calories didn't count on holidays. Kids giggled as they tumbled out the door of an inflatable bouncy castle. I pulled my camera out of my bag again, attached the telephoto lens, and snapped a few shots of the kids' flip-flops and sandals lined up on the street.

I glanced down at my own kitten heels with their shiny, black-patent pointed toes.

In the midst of all this carefree joy, I looked like a mutant. A mutant on a job interview.

I thought ahead to my meeting with Brody at the beach. He would be shirtless, again, and irresistible, again. I would be wearing my 1950s-style, high-necked, one-piece maillot. If an item of clothing had a French name, it probably wouldn't leave much of an impression on a Florida jock. At least, not the impression I wanted.

Last spring I'd been ecstatic to find a bathing suit made specifically for my retro style. Kaye and Tia had told me it was adorable. But next to Grace, I would look like I was wearing a hazmat suit.

Ten minutes later, I found myself in the dressing room at a surf shop, staring at myself in the mirror, guessing what Brody would think when he saw me in a red bikini.

Five

I MUTTERED TO MYSELF, "I HAVE AN ILLNESS."

"What'd you say, sugar pie?" the lady who owned the store called through the curtain. "Do you need a different size?"

I raked back the curtain to show her the bikini.

"You do not need a different size," she declared. "Maybe an extra bottle of sunscreen to protect all that lovely skin you're showing, but not a different size."

I paid for the bathing suit. The shop lady put it in a pretty bag with color-coordinated tissue paper fluffing out the top. But on my walk home, I felt like I'd stolen it. It was as if everyone at the street festival watched my escape. I was so self-conscious about the bikini in my bag that I stowed it in my room, at the back of my closet, where Mom wouldn't see it. If she asked me about it, I'd never wear it. I would chicken out.

I went to find Mom. She was upstairs in one of the B & B's guest bathrooms, on her hands and knees, scrubbing the grout on the floor underneath the sink. After I located her, I backed out of the bathroom, tiptoed down the stairs, and then stomped back up so she'd know I was coming and wouldn't bang her head against the sink at my sudden appearance. I had found out a lot of things the hard way.

When I entered the bathroom again, she was sitting cross-legged, waiting for me. "Survived the heat in that outfit?"

I skipped right over that one and asked, "Where are the guests?" This phrase was our code to make sure we were alone before we said anything private. Mom had taught me it was more out of courtesy to the guests than to us.

"They're all out enjoying the day," she said.

"Do you still have my prescription for contacts?" Every time I got my eyes checked, I wanted only a glasses prescription. Mom asked the optometrist to give me a prescription for contacts, too, in case I changed my mind.

"You changed your mind!" she exclaimed.

I shook my head. "I just want to try them."

She raised her eyebrows at me. "After five years of me begging you? What happened?"

I would rather have given up on the idea of contacts than tell her about Brody, Grace, Kennedy, Sawyer, Noah, Quinn. . . . I couldn't even reconstruct how the wild ride of the last few days had dumped me off at a place where I never wanted to wear my adorable glasses again, or kitten heels, or a pencil skirt. And even if I could have verbalized my mindset, I didn't want to share it with Mom, who would pass my teen angst around the B & B's dining table tomorrow morning like a basket of orange rolls.

I said, "You don't have to stop working. Just tell me where the prescription is."

She lowered her brows and opened her mouth, ready to put up a fight. But her cell phone was ringing in the hall on her cart of cleaning supplies.

"Get that, would you?" she asked. "If it's your father, tell him I'm unavailable."

Not *that* fight again. I didn't want to get dragged into it. And I didn't want to get dragged into a personal one with *her*, either. I repeated, "Where's my prescription?"

Because she didn't want to take a chance on missing a call from a potential boarder, she quickly told me which office file my prescription was in. After that victory, I dashed into the hall, my heels clattering on the hardwood floor, and scooped up the phone, hoping it *was* my dad. I didn't want to get in the middle of my parents' fight, but I hadn't talked to my dad in a month or seen him in three. I glanced at the screen. Mom had been right. I clicked on the phone and said, "Hi, Dad!"

"Hey there, Harper," he said. "Is your mom around?"

My stomach twisted into a knot. I didn't think about my dad a whole lot because he wasn't home and didn't have much to do with my life anymore. But I wanted him to *want* to talk to me. I said stiffly, "I'm sorry, but she's unavailable."

"Unavailable how?" he asked, suspicious.

I couldn't lie to my dad, but I didn't want to say Mom was

just scrubbing the floor and refusing to talk to him either. I swallowed.

"Harper," he said firmly. "Give the phone to your mother."

Funny how his tone of voice could send my blood pressure through the roof, even over the phone. "Just a minute," I whispered. With my temples suddenly pounding, I walked back into the bathroom, extending the phone toward Mom. "It's Dad."

She started upward and banged her head against the sink.

"Ouch," I said sympathetically.

Dropping her scrub brush and pressing both rubber gloves to her hair, she glared at me with tears in her eyes. Ever so slowly, she reached for the phone. "Hello."

In the pause as my dad spoke to her, I escaped. But her next words followed me, echoing out of the cavernous bathroom, into the wide wooden stairwell, and down the steps: "I told Harper to say that because we're going to court next week. You're supposed to leave me alone until then. *Leave me alone.*"

Inside the house was cool and dark with a faint scent of age and the sound of Mom's angry language. As I shut the heavy door behind me, outside was bright and smelled like flowers. Tree frogs screamed in the trees. I skittered back to our little house and dug through Mom's office files until I found my prescription, wondering how I'd ever thought I could spend the hot holiday at home.

The locally owned drugstores in the old-fashioned downtown around the corner from the B & B couldn't help me today. To get my contact prescription filled on Labor Day, I needed the discount store with the optical shop out on the highway. And that meant I needed Granddad's car.

I knocked on the door of his bungalow, just as I had yesterday and the day before, holding my breath until he answered. He drove to the grocery store once a week, and sometimes he swung by the art supply store to pick up more oil paints. As far as I knew, those were the only times he left the house where he'd lived forever and where Mom had grown up.

Granddad and Mom argued a lot. She told him she wanted to make sure he was happy and safe, and he said she was being a nosy busybody. He told her she needed to get rid of that no-good cheat of a husband once and for all, and she said he was being an overbearing jerk. They were both right. In the middle of these fights, I was the only one checking on him. Sawyer lived next door, and Granddad paid him to cut the grass, but I doubted he thought to conduct a welfare check when Granddad didn't leave the house for days on end. That took a certain level of granddaughterly paranoia.

I'd be the one to bang on Granddad's door someday, grow suspicious when he didn't answer, force open a window, and find him dead—though if he was dead already, I wasn't sure why this idea made me so anxious. It wasn't like finding him dead an hour earlier was going to help.

I knocked harder. "Granddad!" I yelled. "It's Harper." It couldn't be anyone else, since I was his only grandchild.

I sighed with relief when I finally heard footsteps

approaching. Even his footfalls sounded misanthropic, soft and shuffling, like he'd rather wrestle snakes than let his granddaughter into his house.

He turned the lock and opened the door a crack—not even as wide as the chain would allow. At a quick glance, I couldn't see any reason for his secrecy. He looked the same as always, with his salt-and-pepper hair pulled back in a ponytail, and a streak of yellow paint drying in his beard. "I'm fine," he said.

"Would you open the door?" I pleaded. "You didn't let me in the house on Saturday, but at least you opened the door for me. You opened it only a crack on Sunday. This is a smaller crack. I can't tell whether you're less glad to see me or you're trying to disguise the fact that you're getting thinner." He'd already started to close the door completely. Apparently he didn't think I was as funny as I did. Quickly I asked, "May I borrow your car?"

"No." The door shut.

"Granddad!" His footsteps didn't retreat into the house, so I knew he was still listening. "Why not?" And why was I so determined to borrow his car? Why couldn't I drive to the discount store to get contacts another day?

Because I was on a mission to be bikini clad and glasses free when I met Brody at the beach. And I was damned if this was the one day out of the year Granddad decided I couldn't borrow his car.

"I don't have to tell you why not," he said through the

door, which was the adult version of me changing the subject when Mom asked why I wanted contacts.

"You said when I turned sixteen that I could borrow your car whenever I wanted. That was your birthday gift to me. You wrote it on a scrap of paper and wrapped it up in a box." If he didn't remember that, we needed to have a talk about what he *did* remember, and what year it was, and whether he should be allowed to live alone and own a microwave oven.

"That was a fine idea of mine," he said, "when you didn't want to borrow my car."

I demanded, "What are you doing with your car today?"

"I don't have to tell you that, either. I'm sixty-eight years old."

And you're acting like you're two, I thought, but that was Mom's line. Really, he was acting like *me*. I took care never to be as mean as he was, but I wanted to be by myself a lot, and people probably took it as meanness. Tia had asked to hang out with me at my house in the past, and I'd told her no. She was so extroverted that after a few hours with her, I needed to be alone with my art. And I'd ruined some fledgling relationships back in ninth and tenth grade by complaining when guys with boyfriend potential called me and texted me and interrupted my thoughts. They were insulted when I turned my phone off.

Granddad was just dishing out the same antisocial behavior to me, and I couldn't take it.

"All right," I called through the door. "I'll come back to

check on you tomorrow." The way things were progressing, he probably wouldn't even open the door for me then. I would have to wave to him through the window. I turned for the stairs off the porch.

The lock turned. The door opened. He stuck his hand out with his car key dangling from one finger.

"Thank you," I said, sliding the key ring off his pointer before he changed his mind. "I'm going shopping out on the highway and then to the beach. You can call me on my cell if you need the car back."

Instead of answering, he shut the door and locked it.

A few hours later, I parked Granddad's car way back from the beach in the nearly full lot and lugged my bag and cooler out of the trunk. I always brought thermoses of water so my friends didn't have to throw away plastic bottles, which was bad for the environment. The smooth cooler felt strange on my bare tummy. In my teeny bikini, I struggled to haul my load onto the sand, across the beach, and around families and motorcycle gangs and groups of elderly drunken rabble-rousers. Finally I spotted the cluster of towels and umbrellas where my friends had settled.

As I walked, I squinted at the ocean. Compared with my glasses, my new contacts made the sun almost unbearably bright. But I recognized Aidan and Kaye in the waves. Her hair in black twists was easy to pick out. Then I saw the drum major of the marching band, DeMarcus, and his girlfriend,

Chelsea, and the cheerleaders who'd run the race with Kaye that morning. Noah and Quinn and Kennedy sat in the sand with the tide flowing over their feet.

Obviously Kennedy wasn't as worried about being associated with Quinn and Noah as he'd been when he'd sneered at me in Ms. Patel's class on Friday. Maybe Tia was right: He picked a fight with me only when we had a date planned.

Off to themselves in the water, Brody held Grace. I could tell he was supporting her in deep water because she was higher than him. Her sunglasses still balanced on top of her head, and her bouncy curls were dry. In fact, he might have been holding her out of the water specifically to keep her hair dry, which was the dumbest thing I'd ever seen at the beach, and I'd lived here almost my whole life.

"Howdy," I said, plopping down my ice chest and bag near Tia, Will, and the huge dog Will borrowed from the shop where Tia worked. The three of them lay on towels in the shade of an umbrella. Will still had trouble staying in the Florida sun for long.

He and Tia stared at me for a moment. Then he exclaimed, "Oh, Harper! I didn't recognize you without your glasses."

"I didn't recognize you in a bikini," Tia said. "Look at that bod! You could crack pecans with those abs. What gives?"

I spread out my towel next to them and lay down. "I don't know if you heard Sawyer this morning," I said, "but when he was sitting on the curb about to pass out after the race, he said, 'Fuck everybody.' That's pretty much how I feel."

The more I thought about it, the more sense it made. Sawyer had been angry that he couldn't run a race like everybody else. I was sick and tired of trying to make a statement with my look, and sabotaging myself in the process.

As usual, Tia didn't press me for details. "Well, you look super cute in that bright red 'fuck you.'"

"I'm not complaining either," Will said. Tia snagged an ice cube from her cup and placed it in his belly button. He jumped, grabbing his stomach like he'd been shot. Then he dropped the ice in *her* belly button. She shrieked. The dog jumped up. The ice slid off Tia's tummy and onto her towel, where the dog ate it.

"Is Kennedy still maintaining radio silence?" Tia asked me.

"Yeah."

"Wait till he sees you."

"You look hot, Harper," Will said.

Tia told him, "There's 'Thanks for being nice to my friends,' and then there's 'You can stop being nice to my friends now.'" She turned back to me. "Let's go hang with girls. You can walk slowly by Kennedy like your very own Labor Day parade. Brody's going to be pleased by your ass, too." She stood and held out her hand to help me up. The dog lay down in her place.

We shuffled across the beach. The sun was really doing a number on my contacts. I squinted and followed the blur of Tia. It wasn't until we'd reached the water that I realized she'd led me on a roundabout path that veered much nearer Kennedy than necessary.

I didn't look toward the boys, but I recognized Noah's wolf whistle.

Quinn said something under his breath that ended in "Harper."

"What?" Kennedy asked. "Oh."

Now that Quinn had drawn his attention to me, Kennedy must have been watching me pass. But I forgot all about them when I saw Brody coming toward me from the ocean, stepping over the waves—without Grace.

He put out his hand. Tia slapped it as she passed.

He kept holding it out for me. I slapped it. But before I could pass him, his hand enclosed mine. We both stopped calf high in the surf.

"I thought you weren't coming," he said. I couldn't see his eyes behind his sunglasses, which made him somehow sexier. He was so near, and—like that morning—so nearly nude, with almost every inch of his tanned skin showing over tight muscles. I imagined I could smell him over the salt air and sunscreen. Suddenly my entire body was glowing.

Then my brain kicked in. What did he mean by "I thought you weren't coming"? He'd been out in the ocean with Grace because he assumed I wouldn't show up? It didn't matter anyway. We had a date for a picture *only*. I said, "You thought wrong."

"I sure did," he said. "See you in a few." He let my hand go. We walked on.

I hazarded half a glance behind me and caught *him* looking back too, at my butt.

And beyond him, Kennedy sat in the surf with his knees drawn up and his arms around them, watching us. Kennedy was a big guy, but this position made him look like an unsure kid.

Another day, my heart would have gone out to him. He was my geeky soul mate, the boy I belonged with. So what if he wasn't a muscle-bound hunk ready to challenge Brody when he brazenly eyed me? As an independent woman, I didn't need a protector. I wanted a sensitive guy with a great sense of humor and a fresh view of the world.

But today, my heart was cold to Kennedy. For the first time, I felt a pang of distaste when I looked at him. My skin tingled, wanting Brody to touch me again.

I sloshed after Tia until we'd waded shoulder deep where the other girls bobbed in the surf. Grace had joined them. They were all giggling at something one of them had said. Grace's staccato laugh was easy to pick out among the others. But when she saw me coming, she called, "It's Miss Perfect Couple with My Boyfriend."

"Girl, I told you the Superlatives are whack," Kaye said. "There's no telling why the class votes like it does." This was directly opposed to the way Kaye had acted when she was elected Most Likely to Succeed: like it was the most important award of her life. And I was surprised to hear she'd talked Grace down about my title with Brody. Kaye hadn't mentioned this to me. She must have been worried I would worry. She confirmed this by grimacing sympathetically as I swam up.

"Happy Labor Day!" I sang.

Grace glared at me. The other cheerleaders laughed uncomfortably. One of them, Ellen, exclaimed, "Harper! I didn't recognize you without your glasses."

"I got contacts today," I said.

They ooohed and cooed over me and told me how good I looked and how pretty my eyes were, which they'd never noticed before—all except Grace, who stared me down with a look that said, *Oh, you got contacts so you could come to this beach to seduce my boyfriend, eh?* At least, that's how I interpreted it.

At my first chance, when the conversation turned to Chelsea's story about fighting with a stranger over a pimento cheese sandwich at Disney World yesterday, which was the sort of thing that happened to Chelsea, I ducked beneath the surface to wet my hair. That would convince Grace I had no designs on her boyfriend. My hair was long and dark and board straight anyway, whereas she was still sporting her big blond curls. They were wilting a bit, though, now that Brody wasn't holding her out of the surf. Her hairdo was wet around the edges, like a sandcastle nipped by waves.

As soon as I surfaced, I was sorry I'd gone under. My eyes stung. I hadn't opened them in the water, but as I wiped away the drops, I got salt and sunscreen in them. I wiped them again, which made the stinging worse.

"I'm going down the beach," I heard Grace say. "I saw some guys I know who are home for the weekend from Florida State. I'm scoring some beer. Tia, come with."

"No, thanks," Tia said.

"Why not?" Grace insisted. "You're always drunk."

"I am not *always* drunk," Tia said self-righteously. "I am drunk on a case-by-case basis. And not on Labor Day. The beach is crawling with cops."

"Ellen," Grace said, "come with. Cathy?"

The other cheerleader, Cathy, giggled nervously. "Wish us luck!" The three of them waded toward the promised land of beer and college boys.

Kaye called after them, "If you get caught, do *not* admit you're cheerleaders for our high school. We have standards." She said more quietly to the rest of us, "Let's wait five minutes and then go after them. We'll watch from the water and intervene if they get in trouble."

"Or we can just enjoy the show when they do," Tia suggested.

By now I could hardly see through the slits that my stinging eyes had become. "I'll catch up with y'all," I said. "Back to the towels for me. I'm having contact problems." Amid the chorus of "Oh, no!" and "Poor baby!" and "Do you need help?" I explained what had happened. "If I can wipe my eyes and run fresh water over my hands, I think I'll be okay."

I sloshed toward shore. But as I reached dry sand, I was anything but okay. My left eye stung. My right eye was worse. When I opened it, all I could see was blur. The beach was as bright as another planet with no atmosphere to filter the sun. I could hardly see my way back to the island of umbrellas and towels I'd come from. When I finally made it, I tripped over several boys and landed on the dog, who didn't budge.

"Move, dog," I said rudely. She got up, sticking her sandy butt in my face as I opened my cooler for a thermos of water.

Kennedy was telling the other guys about the indie film we'd seen at the Tampa Theater downtown last weekend. They were laughing uncontrollably. Kennedy was brilliant and had great comedic delivery. He would be perfect someday as the vastly intelligent, super dry commentator on a political comedy show. His shtick was as much about what he left out as what he said. At the moment, he was strategically omitting that we'd had an argument in his car on the way to the movie and that he still hadn't been speaking to me by the time he dropped me off at home afterward.

"Right, Harper?" I heard him ask. He wanted me to verify some funny point in the movie—something he hadn't discussed with me one on one, because we'd hardly talked since then.

This was his way of making up. After our fights, he ignored me until he just decided not to anymore. He asked me a question and I responded, and then it was like nothing had happened between us.

This time, instead of answering, I poured freezing water over my hand and wiped at my eye. Now it felt like I'd gotten sand in my eyeball. I tried to shift the offending particle into the corner where my tears would flush it out. That was a mistake. The stinging was intense.

I tried to open my eye. I couldn't. My upper eyelid felt wedged shut by my contact. Was it possible that my contact had drifted that far back? Could it float even farther and get stuck on my optic nerve? *Where was my eleventh-grade anatomy knowledge when I needed it?*

"Guys," I called. Kennedy kept up his blasé movie commentary while I went blind in one eye. Tears streaming down my cheek, I said more loudly, "Guys, do any of you wear contacts? I need help. I think my contact has shifted into the back of my eye socket."

"Harper," Kennedy said, "only you."

I took in a deep breath to calm myself, but I was on the verge of panic. These boys were not going to help me. Kennedy would make fun of me while this piece of flexible plastic sliced its way into my brain and gave me a lobotomy. The girls would help me, but they were too far away to hear me yell over the surf, and I couldn't open one eye, and now I couldn't see out of the good eye because of the tears. I felt like screaming.

Strong hands framed my face. One thumb pulled at my lower eyelid. I was surprised Kennedy had relented and come to my rescue. My hero said, "I wear contacts, and I know all about this, unfortunately. Let me help."

But it wasn't Kennedy's voice. It was Brody.

Six

"OPEN YOUR EYE," BRODY SAID.

"I can't." I was almost sobbing.

"Noah," Brody said, "kneel here in front of her so the glare from the beach isn't in her eyes. Will, pour some water on my hand."

"It's not sterile," Kennedy pointed out from a distance.

"It's a beach," Brody said, sounding irritated. "Nothing is sterile. At least get the sand off."

I heard water hiss in the sand and tried to be patient. So much moisture was coming out of my eyes that the contact should have washed out already, but I could feel it still lodged somewhere it should never have gone.

His hands were on my face again. He pulled at my eye. He was closer to me than he'd ever been, his skin only an inch from mine, but I couldn't enjoy it with all these guys watching us and my eye falling out. "Harper, relax," he said.

Relax? Impossible. I had a boyfriend and a crush on

another guy. I'd given myself a mini-makeover to impress my crush, and now he was trying to help me through my mortifying comeuppance, my punishment for trying to attract him. I felt like a spy who had to stay undercover after she'd been shot.

I sucked in another deep breath, counted to five in my head, and exhaled. I relaxed under Brody's hands.

He opened my eye. The huge blur of his finger came at my eyeball, but I managed not to flinch as he manipulated the contact. And suddenly—*ahhh*. My eye still stung, but I could tell the contact was back in place.

"Thank you so much," I said, cupping one hand over my eye. I kept the other shut too, because that felt better. I couldn't see Brody in front of me, but I felt his warmth there. I said, "It was burrowing into my sinuses and wanted to come out my nose. Is it supposed to do that?"

"No," he said. "You must have rubbed it really hard. Maybe you should take it out."

"I wouldn't have anywhere to put it."

"You're supposed to carry a small bottle of contact solution with you everywhere," he said, "and a contact case, and a spare pair of glasses."

"Do *you* carry all that stuff?" I asked.

"No, I'm a guy. Are your contacts expensive? Maybe you should just throw it away."

"They're expensive," I said, "and I can't see without them, and I have to drive home."

"I could drive you home," he offered.

"Did you get it?" Kennedy called from behind Brody—still several towels away. He hadn't bothered to come any closer to help.

Maybe he wasn't even asking about my contact. The film conversation had continued despite my medical emergency. He could have been asking Quinn if he'd gotten a ticket to next week's indie. At any rate, Brody ignored Kennedy. He asked me quietly, "Did you bring sunglasses?"

"I don't have any," I said sheepishly. "I couldn't wear them before because I've always worn glasses."

"Contacts make the glare worse, so sunglasses are more important. You can have mine." He pulled up my free hand and gave me what I assumed were his sunglasses.

"No, you need them."

"I've got another pair in my truck." I heard him rattling the ice in the chest again. "Lie down."

His voice had a bossy edge. I kind of liked it. I did what he said and lay down on the towel.

He handed me a cold, wet bundle. "Press this to your eye, but not hard. Take a time-out. You'll feel better in a minute. Your eye will re-lubricate or whatever."

"Thank you."

I lay on my tummy in the hot shade, breathing deeply and evenly, willing my eye to feel better. The boys were talking about TV shows now and had obviously forgotten I was there, because they were repeating the kind of jokes boys didn't usually tell when they knew girls were listening. I didn't hear

Brody's voice, but I assumed he'd moved back into the group with the rest of them.

Then a warm, comforting hand settled on my back. My mind spun with who would be so kind to me. Definitely not Kennedy. Possibly Quinn or Noah. They could get away with it because Kennedy would have no reason to be jealous. Probably Brody, and then Kennedy would be jealous. Or *should* be. Maybe Kennedy couldn't see his hand on me.

I tried to enjoy the camaraderie, but I couldn't stand the suspense any longer. I lifted my head and squinted across my body with my good eye.

It was the dog, lying right beside me with her chin on my back. Now that I knew it was her face and not a boy's hand, I recognized the feel of her hair and the trickle of her slobber.

I put my own head back down.

After a few minutes, the guys' voices moved away one by one. I heard them shouting out in the water. Only Kennedy and Quinn were left, making fun of Mr. Oakley, which I kind of resented because I liked Mr. Oakley. When I'd told him I wanted a press pass to photograph the football games, he'd set out to give me a football lesson rather than rolling his eyes like Kennedy had. I felt so distanced from the fun I'd come here to have, wrapped up in my own resentment and pain, that I almost jumped when Kennedy spoke just above me. "Harper, are you okay?"

"I'm better," I said without moving. *I am shocked that you give a shit*, I thought.

"We're going to the snack bar," he said. "Want anything?"

"No, thanks," I said.

Alone under the umbrella, I spent a few more minutes trying to chill. I let the cool cloth soothe my eye. Finally I took it off and blinked. My eye worked, and my contact stayed in place, thanks to Brody. I unbundled the cloth and looked at it. It was a huge T-shirt emblazoned with PELICANS FOOTBALL. Brody's last name was written in marker on the hem.

I placed his sunglasses on my nose and slowly sat up, tumbling the dog off me in the process. I was ready, however reluctantly, to rejoin my safe and small and constantly disappointing world.

Brody sat back on his elbows one towel over, watching me.

"Feel better?" he asked.

"Yes, thanks." I squinted at him, feeling my face slowly flush. I wondered what was keeping him here. Not me.

"I went to my truck to get my other sunglasses," he said, peering at me over the top of them. "When I got back, everybody was gone. Kennedy left you by yourself?"

"Just to go to the snack bar."

Brody glared in the general direction of the snack bar far down the beach as if he disapproved. I would have thought his concern was silly, except that my eye did still burn every time I blinked.

"Do you know where the other girls have been gone so long?" he asked.

"Mmmm," I said, which meant *Yes* and *If I tell you, I will seem like the scheming bitch I am becoming.*

He gave me a knowing look over his shades. "Did Grace go try to get beer from those college guys?" When I didn't answer, his shoulders dropped in frustration.

"Why don't you stop her?" I asked. "Or . . . help her?" Stopping her was what I would have tried to do if I'd been her friend, but helping her was probably more up Brody's alley. He wasn't the class party animal. That would be Sawyer—at least, before Sawyer changed his ways last week, according to Tia. But the gatherings at Brody's house when his mom was out for the night weren't dry.

He smiled at me. "The first rule of breaking rules is that you take some basic precautions not to get caught, right?"

I didn't answer, because I wouldn't know. It *did* sound a lot like Tia's opinion on the subject.

"It's Labor Day," he said, "it's daylight, it's a public beach, and the cops are all over the place. Grace is being stupid. Besides, I think she's getting more than beer from one of those guys."

"Oh." I puzzled through what this meant. He didn't sound upset that she might be cheating on him. But inside, he must burn with jealousy. That's why he'd been paying so much attention to *me*. Grace hadn't been around to see, but he'd hoped it would get back to her.

This didn't explain why he was still here, alone with me.

"Let's see that eye," he said.

Again, I got a little excited at his bossy command. In the last half hour I'd come to think of him as the best candidate to get me to the emergency room if my eyeball popped out. I sat up on my knees. Just as before, our bodies almost touched. He took off his shades, slid the ones I'd borrowed from my face, and placed his pointer finger gently on my lower eyelid. "It's still a little red, but not nearly as bad as it was." He nodded down the beach. "Why don't we go to the pavilion and take the picture for the yearbook? That will get you out of the glare."

"Okay. Let me get my camera out of my car."

"I'll go with you."

I held out my hand. "Sunglasses, please. Definitely. Thank you."

We headed for the parking lot, leaving the dog behind. She made no move to follow us. I supposed she would be okay by herself. Our town didn't have a leash law because the hippie city government thought animals should run free like the wind. Someone needed to relay this to the dog, who rolled over on her back, watching upside down for Will to return.

As Brody and I walked together across the melted asphalt lot, I said, "Sorry, my car's all the way back here."

"We could have gotten in my truck and driven to your car."

"And then driven around the parking lot for the rest of the day after someone stole your space." I laughed.

"That doesn't sound too bad," he said.

Was he implying he'd enjoy driving in circles with me? He kept saying things like this, or I kept interpreting them that way. I had to remind myself the only concrete evidence I had that he liked me was a cold compress he'd constructed from his T-shirt. Lately my brain had turned into a multiple-choice "Does he dig me?" quiz from *Seventeen*.

He snapped me out of it by exclaiming, "A 1990 Dodge Charger! This is you?"

"Yeah," I admitted as we stopped behind the trunk. "Granddad bought it when he was in his midforties. Grandmom had just left him and moved across town with my mom to live with *her* mom. The car was his consolation prize, I guess."

Brody put his hand out to stroke the red metallic paint. He snatched his hand back when the hot surface burned his fingers. "You're driving your granddad's midlife crisis?"

"He lets me *borrow* his midlife crisis." I unlocked the stylish (not) louvered hatchback and pulled out my camera case.

Brody reached up and closed the hatchback for me. "I hear these things are pretty fast. What have you gotten it up to?"

"Thirty."

He gaped at me, horrified. "You've never taken it out on the interstate to see what it can do?"

"Nope."

He grinned and raised his eyebrows. "Do you want me to try it?"

"I heard you were one point away from getting your license revoked because of all your speeding tickets."

"True. See? That's why I need you, Harper."

I looped the strap of my camera bag over my bare shoulder.

As we turned for the pavilion, I said casually, "I've been reading about you in the newspaper."

"Yeah." He smiled wryly. "That's taken some getting used to. You have to keep it in perspective. In a town this small, high school football is entertainment. The only alternatives are the beach and a theater showing two movies. Unless, of course, you drive to Tampa with Kennedy to see the latest indie."

A little sarcasm? His tone wasn't sarcastic, but his message must be. Maybe he liked me after all. But I wouldn't let him change the subject, because I wanted him to explain something to me. "I was curious about this morning's newspaper article. I couldn't believe they were so down on you—and after you won the game!"

His smile faded. Though we were walking leisurely across a parking lot, his whole body took on a guarded look like he was about to get tackled.

"I just wondered whether they were making that up to sell newspapers," I said, "or if there was really something wrong with you at the game."

He watched me silently. Not a muscle moved in his face.

I asked him, "Are you having problems with somebody because Noah came out?"

"No," he said firmly. "Are you?"

I shrugged. "Kennedy was mad about what Sawyer said at the end of class."

Brody nodded. "I felt bad about leaving you alone in

Ms. Patel's room after that. I couldn't tell whether you were upset. You never look like anything bothers you."

"I don't?" I asked, genuinely surprised.

He shook his head but watched me through his shades. As a result, I began to feel very hot and bothered. Heat crept up my neck and along my jawline.

"Now you *do* seem upset," he said. "Kennedy has no right to be mad at you because of something Sawyer said. If he was man enough, he'd take it up with Sawyer."

The idea of this made me uncomfortable. Kennedy was much bigger. Sawyer was more cunning and perhaps a little evil.

We reached the edge of the parking lot and the wooden stairs down to the pavilion. I called over my shoulder, "If it's not Noah, what was bothering you at the game? Or was there anything at all? You won, so the newspaper critiquing *how* you won seems kind of harsh."

He laughed shortly. "I wish the newspaper would hire *you*."

That was a good one. It was all I could do to keep track of which direction the ball was going on the field. I asked, "*Is* there something wrong?"

The pavilion was a large octagon with a vaulted wooden ceiling and thick stucco walls built to withstand tropical storms. Windows cut in all sides gave us a view of the beach. The sound of the ocean echoed inside. Beachgoers tended to use the pavilion as a lunchtime picnic area, or a shelter from the midday sun. In the late afternoon, it was empty.

The shelter was so dark in contrast to the bright day that I had to take off Brody's sunglasses to see. I hung the earpiece on the side string of my bikini bottoms, which I meant to be provocative but probably carried all the sexual overtone of a pair of pliers in a tool belt.

Brody removed his shades too. The shadows overhead descended across his face. The circles under his eyes seemed darker. He blinked and took a long breath. Something *was* wrong.

He set one shoulder against the wall. "Don't tell anybody," he said. "Only Coach knows."

I backed to the stucco beside him. "I'm good at keeping secrets," I promised.

He watched me for a moment and slowly raked his hair out of his eyes. "I got hurt," he said. "That part's not a secret."

"When?" I asked sharply. "It may not be a secret, but *I* didn't hear about it." If I had, I wouldn't have been able to think about anything else. "Are you okay?"

"Don't I look okay?"

"Brody!" I wailed, fed up with his teasing. I didn't want to joke about this.

"Yes, yes, I'm okay," he assured me, waving my concern away. "It happened before school started, in practice. I got dinged."

"Dinged," I repeated. "What's that mean?"

"I got my bell rung."

"Your *bell*," I puzzled. Was that a euphemism for an injury to the jockstrap area? Even Brody would have turned way redder in the face if he was admitting that.

"I got knocked out," he explained.

"Oh!" I gasped. "Brody!"

"It wasn't that bad," he said nonsensically. "It was an accident. The thing is, usually the quarterback doesn't get hit in practice. The whole team is relying on the quarterback during games, so we don't take chances in practice. We just got tripped up this time. We were running a new play. Somebody shoved Noah off balance. He couldn't catch himself, and he elbowed me. *Hard.* I don't know if you've noticed Noah's bony-ass elbows. I fell straight back"—he lifted both forearms and fell back a little to show me—"and landed right on my helmet." He cradled the back of his head in one hand. "At least, that's what they tell me."

"You don't remember?"

"No."

"You had a concussion?" I'd known football was rough, but I couldn't believe I hadn't heard this story before. Why hadn't somebody told me?

Of course, there wasn't a reason for anybody to tell me. Brody and I had had no link with each other until the yearbook elections on the first day of school. And even now . . . a very choice set of circumstances had placed us alone in the beach pavilion.

"Yeah, a concussion. But I recovered quickly, and the doctor was impressed," he said, like he was trying to talk me into something. "The doctor lectured my mom about it, though. A second concussion could be serious. If that happens to me, my mom's pulling me out of football completely. Don't tell anybody, because that's my secret. Only Noah knows." He shrugged. "If my mom nixed my high school career, I could still walk onto a college team, maybe, but my chances of starting would be pretty much over."

"Would you even *want* to play college football if you'd already had two concussions?"

He threw up his hands. I took this to mean that after a second concussion, every possible choice would suck.

I nodded. "The reporter wasn't imagining things. You're being more careful."

"I have to be. When the newspaper said I was so daring and fun to watch, it's not that I had any great talent. I just wasn't scared. And now I am. I don't care about getting hurt, per se, but I don't want my football career to end. It has to end someday, sure, but not *now.*" He looked past me, across the pavilion and out a window to the ocean.

"You're talking like you're about to get a second concussion," I pointed out. "How long have you played football? Since your dad started coaching you in third grade, right?"

He blinked at me, surprised.

"That's what Noah told me," I explained.

"Yeah," Brody said slowly, "third grade."

"You've played football since *third grade* without a head injury. Then you get one as a result of a freak accident. There's no reason for you to be playing like you're about to have another."

"Yeah."

"I mean, I don't want you to get a concussion either. That would make it difficult for us to take our Superlatives photo for the yearbook, and I have a deadline!"

He grinned, which made me smile too.

I said, "But if worrying about a concussion makes you lose your magic, your football career is going to be over soon anyway. Might as well play like you mean it."

He nodded, then thought better of it and shook his head. "I don't know how to unworry about it." He tilted his head to one side, considering me. "A few minutes ago when I was trying to look at your eye and I told you to relax, you did, pretty much instantly. You just took a deep breath and did it."

"I have a lot of practice," I said. "It's a coping mechanism. I'm super high-strung."

"You?" he asked in disbelief. "You're always so calm."

"Me?" I laughed. "No, I'm not. I was able to relax when you told me because I trust you."

He watched me solemnly as he said, "You shouldn't."

Maybe he meant *You shouldn't trust me with your eye* or *You shouldn't trust me with your granddad's car*. But he was so near, I could only interpret his words as innuendo. *You shouldn't trust me when I'm alone with you.*

I gave him a sexy smile. I didn't have a lot of experience with this, but I attempted it anyway. I said, "Between you loving football and Mr. Oakley trying to explain it to me so I can take pictures of the games, you make even *me* want to play."

Brody raised his eyebrows. "That could be arranged." He glanced around the pavilion. "So, will this place work for our yearbook picture?"

I'd been hoping he wouldn't bring that up, because I didn't want our conversation to end. But maybe *he* did.

"Now that I look at it," I said, "no, it won't work. There's not enough light. We can't take the photo on the beach right now either, because it's too bright. All that white sand tends to mess with the camera's light meter."

Brody widened his eyes at me in fake exasperation. At least, I hoped it was fake. "Don't you have a night setting on your camera?"

"Yeah, but that slows down the shutter speed to let more light in, which means I would need my tripod. The shutter's open too long to keep the camera still if someone's holding it. The picture will be blurry. We should try again on the beach at sunset. The light will be perfect then."

"Does that mean you want to go back to the others?"

I asked, "What else would we do?"

He shrugged dismissively. But he held my gaze as he said, "Get to know each other better. We were voted Perfect Couple. I feel like I hardly know you, even though the senior class thinks you're the love of my life."

Seven

BRODY'S WORDS SET MY HEART BEATING rapidly, but I threw back my head and laughed like nothing was wrong. "You've known me since kindergarten."

He shook his head. "Not really. You look completely different today."

"You mean I look like everybody else," I said ruefully.

"No, ma'am," he said firmly, "you do not."

Speechless, I stared at him. His eyes flicked ever so briefly to my bikini top, then back up to my face. My chest and upper arms burned in a delicious way, a feeling I wasn't ready to give up just because I hadn't brought a tripod.

Now that Kennedy had made motions to forgive me, he would miss me. He would look around the beach for me. He would give me the third degree when I eventually returned to our home base on the towels. But I didn't care about that while Brody was gazing at me.

I was alone with him. Neither of us was going anywhere

for a while if we could help it, but I couldn't think of a thing to say to him—which underscored why we were a terrible match in the first place. I wondered if he felt the same way about the title we'd been elected to. I said, "I've been racking my brain about this. Why do you think the class chose us for this?"

"Well, our study hall also chose Sawyer as our representative on the student council, so a good portion of our school is obviously on crack." When he saw my face fall, he said, "The good kind of crack."

"Crack—you know, the nutritional kind."

"Yes."

"Sawyer was the only candidate," I reminded him. "We had no other choice, except to elect nobody. Though come to think of it, maybe that would have been better."

"Look," Brody said, almost impatiently, "here's what I really think about the Superlatives, if you want to know."

"Of course I want to know." He was acting like people usually *didn't* want to know what he thought, which was sad.

He searched my eyes for a moment. Not glancing at my ass or sliding his gaze to my cleavage, but measuring me, as if deciding whether he could trust me on another level.

He said slowly, "I think it's pretty strange for the school to tell students we can't kiss and we're not supposed to hug each other in the halls, then make us vote on two people who should date but don't. I mean, the other titles are bad enough. If you get a good one, like Most Athletic, you feel like you have to live up to it. That's why I'm glad I didn't get something like that."

I wondered if he was telling the whole truth. I bet he would have appreciated getting Most Athletic. It would have caused him a lot less trouble than Perfect Couple That Never Was. I saw his point, though. He was already stressed out about being quarterback. Getting named supreme athlete of the school would have set higher expectations for him and hiked his stress level even more.

He went on, "And what if you got a bad one, like Most Likely to Go to Jail? That's just mean to Sawyer."

"Aw," I said. "It's sweet of you to care. Who did you vote for?"

"I voted for Sawyer, obviously, but it's still mean. I'm predicting the school won't vote on these titles much longer. Somebody's going to sue."

"I don't think so." Most of the titles weren't insulting, and most parents had no idea their kids had received them unless they looked through the yearbook when school was almost over.

"Oh, yes," Brody said, nodding. "The first thing they'll sue about is a couples title like ours. The rule is that it has to be a girl and a guy. Why not a guy and a guy, or two girls?"

His words floored me. This was the sort of philosophical discussion I would have with Quinn or some other free thinker in journalism class or art class. I wouldn't have predicted this devil's advocate position to come from the mouth of the quarterback.

I shrugged my camera bag off my shoulder, set the case on the floor at my feet, and leaned against the pavilion wall again. "How long have you known about Noah?" I figured that's who we were really talking about.

"Forever," Brody said. "I mean, he actually came out to me in middle school. But we'd been good friends since we started football together in third grade, like you said. I wasn't surprised when he came out."

"Did he ever . . ." I wasn't sure how to ask this, or whether I even should, but I was dying to know. "Were you ever the object of his affection?"

"Why do you ask?" Translation: I shouldn't have asked.

Heart palpitating again at the idea that I'd offended Brody, I hurried on, "You've been super accepting of the whole thing."

He laughed long enough that the tension between us disappeared. Then he said, "Well, middle school is just difficult."

"Yeah."

"Back in middle school, Noah and I did have an uncomfortable five-minute conversation," he admitted. "But you know, I distinctly remember having a crush on Tia back then."

"Tia!"

"Yeah. I think all middle school guys—the straight ones, anyway—fantasize about getting in good with the wild girl. But I realized someday a couple of her boyfriends were going to duel each other in the parking lot. I didn't want to be one of them."

That sounded about right—at least, for the Tia I'd known

forever. Tia had turned over a new leaf in the past couple of weeks, since she started dating Will. I asked, "You don't think Will's going to suffer that fate, though, do you?"

"No, opposites attract," he said. "Opposites may repel at first, but in the long run, they're the best thing for each other." He shrugged. "Anyway, I don't think the school should officially pair folks up. People don't naturally operate as permanent couples. You get married and swear that you're one body, operating as one unit. Half the time you unswear it a few years later and swear it again with somebody else. Everybody in my family is divorced. My parents, my grandparents, *everybody*. Christmas day might as well be Halloween, because it's like we're going from house to house, trick-or-treating. People stay individuals as they move through life, in and out of relationships. Being a couple is temporary, like cars in a train. They're detachable so you can switch them around. I'm not saying that's how it *should* be. I'm just saying that's how it *is*."

If Brody had said this to me when we first entered the pavilion, I would have been crushed that he wasn't coming on to me after all. These were not the words of a guy who was interested in a girl and wanted her to be interested in him, too. But we'd been talking for so long, and our conversation had delved so deep, that I no longer thought he was measuring every word against whether it would advance his cause with me. Now he was just telling me the truth.

I said, "My family is like that too."

His mouth twisted. He nodded.

And then, I couldn't let it go, could I? I couldn't just embrace the moment and my newfound, genuine friendship with Brody. I had to bring it back around to my superficial problem, the one that had kept me awake at night for the past two weeks, ever since the Superlatives elections. I asked, "Have you discussed this with Grace?"

He nodded. "I have. I've said all kinds of things to Grace. But did she hear me? I don't know. She has this laugh. Heh! Heh! Heh! Heh!"

I knew the laugh. I hated the laugh.

Brody said, "At first you think it's a cute, nervous laugh. Except that's her response to *everything*. She can't possibly feel the same way about *everything*. Or can she?"

My natural inclination was to smooth over arguments. Kaye had scolded me about this numerous times, and I had smoothed over her scolding. My automatic reaction was hard to turn off, obviously, even when I was smoothing over my crush's problems with his girlfriend. Stupidly I suggested, "Maybe it's you, not what you're saying. You make Grace nervous."

"Why would I make her nervous?" Brody grumbled.

Say it. Say it. Say it. Tell the truth. I felt like I was jumping off a cliff as I said it: "Because you're so attractive. Maybe when you get as close to her as you are to me right now, she forgets what she was talking about." It was a big, brazen mouthful, and after I'd gotten it out, I felt my cheeks turn bright red in the heat. I stared up at the vaulted ceiling as if it was very interesting.

Something touched my neck. I nearly put up a hand to brush away a bug. But the touch was Brody's fingertips smoothing along my skin, back and forth across my collarbone.

I hardly knew how to process that he was touching me. I spent more time listening to my brain than paying attention to my body. I was all mind, and my body was just a vehicle to get me from home to class and back again, like my bike or Granddad's car or the public bus. Sure, I put my look together carefully in the morning, and throughout the day I checked the neatness of my clothes and hair. Other than that, I never gave much thought to my body.

Brody reminded me that I was made of bones and skin and muscle. He was connecting my body back to my brain in a way I'd never experienced. I flattened my hand against the rough stucco wall. My palm turned sweaty. His fingertips felt so good stroking me in—let's face it—a first-date, innocent way.

"Is everything okay, Harper? Now you seem tense again." As Brody said this, he massaged my shoulder with a pressure so strong that it fell just short of hurting. It was intense enough, and good enough, that I wished he would do that to me everywhere.

But after a few strokes of his hand, his fingers followed the strap of my bikini, trailing fire, down to cup my breast. He wasn't technically touching me anymore since my bathing suit top separated his skin from mine. But I could feel the pressure of his hand, and the heat of it. Never mind what I'd thought about the innocence of his touch. Electricity arced from his body to mine.

If he felt the same way I did as he slid his thumb back and forth across my breast, he didn't let on. In the darkness of the pavilion, I couldn't see the green of his eyes, but the shadows underneath were deep. He looked older than me, and serious.

I giggled.

"What's so funny?" he whispered.

"Um, where do I start? Most guys, if they were touching a girl's collarbone and noticed she was acting tense, would take their hands off her before asking after her health, rather than touching her breast." The last word came out as a sigh. I was pretty proud that I'd produced a joke under the circumstances, but inwardly I cringed as I heard myself. I sounded like I wanted him to stop touching me. I didn't.

Incredibly, he was unfazed. "Most guys?" he asked, raising his eyebrows. "You do this enough to have a test group?"

"It's all in the name of science," I said faintly.

"No means no," he said. "They lecture us about this endlessly in PE. Do you want me to stop?"

I shook my head.

"Me neither." He moved toward me. He was about to kiss me.

The nearer he came, the more scrambled my brain got. His lips were so close to my ear that his breath feathered across my cheek.

Suddenly he'd backed away from me. No! I wanted him to kiss me. Hadn't I made that clear?

He nodded toward the nearest arched doorway to the beach. Halfway understanding his message, I jerked my camera bag up by the strap just as Kennedy burst in.

"Harper!" Glancing from me to my camera bag and back to me, he let me hear all the accusation in his voice. "I've been looking everywhere for you."

I smiled. "Sorry. I was right here."

His angry eyes cut to Brody. A breeze from outside caught his wet ponytail and flopped it forward over his shoulder.

Brody didn't do much. He gave Kennedy a subtle look down and back up. I wasn't sure, but I thought this meant, *Come at me, bro, because I can take you.*

Amazingly, I might have been right. Kennedy seemed to get the same message. He didn't engage with Brody. He turned back to me and demanded, "What are you doing?"

I held up my camera bag. "The light's bad, but we were attempting to get our yearbook Superlatives picture out of the way."

"Because her deadline is coming up," Brody chimed in. He said this without a trace of sarcasm. Brody didn't really do sarcasm. But I heard the private joke in his words: Kennedy had been on me to meet this deadline. In a roundabout way, *he* was the one who'd convinced us to stand in a shadowy beach pavilion alone together. *So there.*

Kennedy's burst of anger seemed to have drained away.

We'd managed to talk him down, just as I had in journalism class.

Except this time, he had reason to be jealous. Brody was toying with me.

Kennedy told me quietly, "Come on back."

"I will."

He paused a moment more, seemingly weighing the idea of insisting that I come back with him *now*. But he didn't press it. He walked out of the pavilion.

My feelings were a confused tangle, but Brody and I were casual acquaintances indulging a passing flirtation. I knew how this would play out. We would make a little joke about Kennedy and part ways.

"What did I tell you earlier?" Brody asked. "If you're going to break rules, you need to make sure you can get away with it." He stepped toward me. He glanced out the doorway as if to gauge how clearly someone standing outside could see him. Satisfied, he braced one forearm against the wall above my head, exactly how I'd seen Will standing with Tia in the hall at school on Friday. He slid my camera bag strap off my shoulder and set the bag on the tile floor again. He leaned down.

My body knew what he was doing before my brain did. I was still puzzling through his motives. I'd felt guilty enough about flirting, and letting him touch me inappropriately. This was worse. Actually *kissing*, when I had a boyfriend and he had a girlfriend, was officially cheating. Every bit of this spun through my mind as I closed my eyes and lifted my chin. My lips met his.

His mouth was warm and soft. He kissed me gently, his lips brushing along mine, pressing. When I'd pictured making out with Brody—and I had—he'd come at me forcefully, like an athlete battling to win a game. It surprised me that this tough-guy football player could be so tender.

But admittedly, I didn't have a lot of knowhow for a senior in high school. I'd kissed Kennedy, of course, and Noah, and Quinn when he wanted us to be seen, and a few guys before that when they'd brought me home from a date. I'd never had a long, intense session of experimenting with a boy's mouth, though, the kind I'd seen in movies and read about in books, the kind Tia and Kaye had with their boyfriends every weekend.

Afraid I would mess it up and Brody would figure out how naive I was, I let him take the lead. The tip of his tongue teased my lips apart. He swept inside. For long minutes he held my chin cupped in his hand and kissed me harder, deeper. I kissed him back. Finally he kissed his way across my jawline to the side of my neck. I shivered.

His thumb brushed my nipple again.

That's when everything changed for me. A current of electricity shot from my breast straight down to my crotch and pulsed there. He'd been toying with me before. I'd teased him back. Now he knew I wanted him, and so did I. In that one slight touch, every longing rushed back to me for boys who didn't like me as much as I liked them, every regret that other girls had boyfriends who were into them while mine weren't. Brody supplied me with more heat through the pad of his thumb than I'd experienced in my lifetime.

I set my hands on his hips, which were hard as rocks underneath his bathing suit, and pulled him closer.

"Mm," he said against my neck. The syllable sent tingles down my arms. He lifted his mouth. His breath felt so good in my ear that I could hardly stand it—and that was before he touched the tip of his tongue to my earlobe. I gasped.

He slid his entire hand across my bikini top to cup my breast. Then one finger slid underneath the fabric. I shuddered.

"Okay," he said, backing up again and chuckling uncomfortably. "That's as much as we can get away with here."

I stood there stunned for a moment, trying to make sense of what he'd said, as if it hadn't been in English. He was backing off because Kennedy had already checked on me. Since there was no door, we couldn't lock Kennedy out. If he didn't catch us, someone else would. It was a public beach. Right.

I just hadn't thought ahead to how this tryst with Brody would end. We'd fooled around because the school had made us curious about each other. And now he would go back to Grace, and I would go back to Kennedy.

Only, I didn't want to go back to Kennedy. I wanted to stay here with Brody. He was brilliantly lit now, the sun slanting over the planes of his athletic body. The darkness in the pavilion had lifted. Either my eyes had adjusted or the sun had sunk lower to peek directly into the windows. Or maybe my pupils were dilated, which happened to people who were sexually aroused. My knowledge of eleventh-grade anatomy had returned with a vengeance.

"Are you taking your camera back to your car?" Brody asked.

"Yes," I said, kneeling to pick up my expensive, beloved camera that I had completely forgotten about.

"I'll wait here a minute and walk back on the beach so as not to arouse suspicion." He said this in imitation of a spy movie, but he lacked Kennedy's dry sarcasm. With Brody, I was never sure whether he was kidding.

"Okey-doke," I said like a dork. "See you around." Which was worse. I hurried out to the parking lot, unfolding Brody's shades and slipping them on as I went.

"Hey," Brody called behind me, but I'd had enough. I needed to get over my obsession with him. Spending time with him wouldn't help. The more I knew about him, the more I realized he was *not* the guy of my dreams.

He was better.

And he wasn't mine.

Eight

I CROSSED THE PARKING LOT, LESS STEAMY NOW that the sun had relented. As I walked, I felt strangely taller, with bigger breasts. I returned my camera to the trunk of Granddad's car, then pulled out my second cooler full of water bottles and lugged it toward the beach.

Along the path, I stopped short and set the cooler down when I saw Will. He lay with his knees bent on a concrete bench that wasn't long enough for him. His body was dappled in shade from the palm trees and scraggly vines that liked to grow in sand. Where the sun found a way through the foliage to him, his skin glowed with sweat. The dog lay beside him. Presumably she would have gone for help if she'd smelled death. But Will was so still.

"Are you okay?" I asked, alarmed.

He opened one eye to peer at me over his shades. "Yeah, just hot." He eased up to sitting, his stomach muscles bunching into hard knots. Like Brody, this boy knew his way around a sit-up.

I refrained from commenting, *I'll say*.

He asked, "Does your eye feel better?"

"I'd forgotten about my eye," I said truthfully, "so it must be okay." Actually, now that he mentioned it, it still stung a little when I blinked.

He asked, "How about the rest of you? Kennedy said he found you and Brody taking your Superlatives picture at the pavilion."

"Was he mad?" I asked quickly.

"He didn't sound particularly mad," Will said. "I just wondered, because you were gone a long time. And I know how being voted something like Perfect Couple can mess with your head."

With a sigh, I sat down beside him and handed him a thermos of water from the cooler, my head spinning all the while about what to say. I was so confused. My lips still tingled from kissing Brody, and a fresh chill washed over me every time I thought about what had happened. Will had become good enough friends with Brody that he might be able to give me some insight—if I could phrase the question in a way that didn't expose me as Brody's wannabe girlfriend.

I asked, "Did you know Brody got knocked out in football practice?" Brody had said his mom would make him quit if he got another concussion. That was the secret. The fact that he'd gotten hurt in the first place was public knowledge. But *I* hadn't heard this until he told me, and I felt offended that the public had been keeping me in the dark.

Will was in the process of swallowing half the thermos of water in one long pull. Still drinking, he opened one eye and gave me a small nod. He wiped the wet bottle across his forehead. "Before school started, right?"

"Yes."

"But he was okay."

"I guess. Football players may be used to that kind of thing, but as a non–football player, I'm shocked that people get knocked out, the doctor okays them to play, and they're back at practice the next day. Aren't you?"

"No," Will said, "I play hockey. So, you're worried about Brody?"

"I'm more surprised that the class voted Brody and me Perfect Couple and then nobody thinks to tell me that my phantom boyfriend got knocked unconscious in football practice."

Will's brows knit behind his sunglasses. "That happened at least a week before the election."

"Yeah." I supposed I was just fishing for Will to confirm some connection between Brody and me that wasn't even there. "Who did *you* vote for?"

"Nobody," he said. "The election was the first day of school. I couldn't remember anybody's last name except Tia's. And, of course, Sawyer had made an impression by then too."

Of course. "Well, knowing us a little better now, would you put Brody and me together?"

"The way you look and act at school, no. But I'll say this.

Brody likes pretty girls. Today, you definitely fit into that category. Not that you weren't pretty before, but now, wow. I don't want to get in trouble with my girlfriend, but you look beautiful."

"That's the nicest thing anyone's ever said to me, Will."

"You're not hanging around the right people."

"Okay." I laughed.

"Seriously, you're not. I think you and I are a lot alike. You're good at school. You get used to praise from teachers and your parents about your academics. Sometimes you forget about the rest of your life."

I took a long drink from my own thermos of water. "Yeah."

"Then you get elected Perfect Couple, and you realize that other people see you as something more than a walking, talking brain. Or, something *different*. That's how I felt when I was voted Biggest Flirt. I mean, hello? I was so worried about what my parents would think. I wanted a title that said 'Achievement.'" He spanned his hands in front of us, like framing his title in lights on a movie marquee. "Not . . . I don't know."

I framed my own movie title. "'Social Life.'"

"Yeah. I wasn't known for that at my old school. So I understand if you're kind of . . ." He trailed off, afraid of offending me.

I helped him out. "Obsessed with it."

Clearly that was the word he'd been too polite to use first. "Obsessed," he repeated. "I'll tell you, Brody was thrilled about getting paired with you."

"He was?"

"Yeah. And today . . ." Will gestured to me. His hand stopped in midair, roughly on a parallel with my stomach. I wasn't sure what he meant by this until he said, "Brody was happy to see you. And he was even happier to see you looking like you do today."

"Ah."

"And I know this is none of my business, but he has a girlfriend."

I took another sip of water and said slowly, "I know."

"I don't think Brody takes any of this seriously," Will said. "Not the elections, not dating. You take it *very* seriously, like I do. That was my whole problem at first with Tia."

"I get it."

He drained the rest of his water and handed the thermos back to me.

"Here." I dug another bottle out of the ice for him and pointed toward the pavilion. "Go lie down in there, where it's actually cool. I'll tell Tia where you went."

"Thanks." He stood and turned down the sandy path. The dog jerked to her feet in one motion and followed him.

"No, thank *you*." As I watched Will go, I heard my own nonsensical words. *No, thank* you *for telling me the guy I have a crush on has no real interest in anybody, including me.*

Except that Will had compared Brody and me to Tia and himself.

And he and Tia were now together.

Did I have a chance with Brody?

No, that was ridiculous. To accept that interpretation of what he'd said, I would have to ignore his whole exposition on *Brody already has a girlfriend and it isn't you.*

Frustrated with myself, I stomped back to the towels, kicking up more sand than necessary, and threw myself down next to Tia.

"What's wrong?" she asked with her eyes closed. She didn't even look over to see who'd collapsed next to her. Tia was laid back, and I envied her.

"This is not what's wrong," I said, "but I sent Will to the pavilion because he was melting."

"He claims he's normal and Floridians are made of asbestos. What's wrong with *you*? Does your eye still hurt? Will said you had a real problem with your contact and Brody came to your rescue while Kennedy just sat there."

"My eye is better." Then I said flatly, "And I went to the pavilion and made out a little bit with Brody."

Instantly she rolled over on her side. Her dark eyes were wide. "You don't make out a little bit. The definition of 'making out'— Where's my phone?" She felt underneath her towel. "Without even looking it up, I can tell you that 'making out' means you're hot and heavy. You can't do it halfway."

I told her solemnly, "So I made out with Brody."

"You're turning into me," she breathed, pretending to be horrified.

"No. You've made out with random people, and Sawyer.

But you never had a boyfriend before Will, so you were never cheating. I'm a cheater." Honestly, I didn't care about this as much as I should have.

She shrugged as best she could while lying on one arm. "Brody's a cheater too."

"Yeah," I said, looking down the beach for him. He'd stopped about halfway from the pavilion with his back to me and his hands on his hips. Grace, Cathy, and Ellen walked toward him, presumably victorious after their foray for beer. Ellen staggered a little.

Tia still watched me. "Will told me he was going to warn you about Brody."

"He did, after it was too late." I looked around us to make sure nobody had plopped down near us on the towels. Then I admitted, "Brody felt me up a little."

"Oh, good Lord!" Tia cried.

"Oh, you can't get felt up halfway either?" I asked quickly. "Then Brody felt me up a *lot*. Don't tell Kaye. Grace is sure to ask her what she knows. Kaye can't spill it if she doesn't have the info."

Tia propped herself up on one elbow. "Can I just ask what the *fuck* you think you're doing?"

I gasped. "Are you *judging* me?"

"Of course I'm not judging you!" Tia exclaimed. "I'm just wondering what's gotten into you. The day of the elections, I told you to go after Brody, and you just reminded me you already had Kennedy. Today you're setting up clandestine meetings and letting Brody grope your bosom."

I laughed so hard at her phrasing that I sucked in some sand and spent the next minute spitting it out and wiping it off my tongue. Continuing to giggle didn't help this process.

Finally I sighed and said, "This whole election has shaken me out of my comfort zone. I thought all I wanted was to spend a little time with Kennedy, and take pictures, then sit at home by myself and tweak them on the computer. But if this is supposed to be the most exciting time of my life, I'm wasting mine. The rest of the United States comes to Florida for adventure. I actually *live* here and I don't have any fun at all."

"You started taking pictures *because* it was fun," she pointed out.

"True." Tia and I hadn't worked through any of my problems, but I felt better talking to her. She was so upbeat about everything. My mood had improved. I sat up on my towel, half expecting the beach to hold wondrous surprises for me after all.

Cathy was still walking and Ellen was still staggering in our direction, but Grace had stopped where Brody stood. His head blocked her face from view. I couldn't tell what they were saying or how intense it was. All I saw was that he had one hand on either side of her bikini bottoms. And the pavilion where we'd just spent a very interesting half hour together was in his direct line of sight. That's how much our meeting had meant to him.

"Fuck everybody," I murmured to Tia, "and that's not a quote from Sawyer. Catch you later. I'm going swimming." I jumped up, ran across the sand, and plunged into the water, swimming way out and diving deep. This had been my coping mechanism for countless school gatherings and birthday parties when interacting with others became too much for me. None of that—really nothing about me—had changed just because I'd made out with Brody.

I floated on my back in the warm ocean. Here on the Gulf, the waves weren't high like they were on the Atlantic coast. Occasionally a big one would crash over my face and I'd snort salt water, but mostly the tide rocked me, lifting my head and then my toes like I was a strand of seaweed or a kid's floating toy.

After a while, I turned on my stomach and did the dead man's float—or dead chick's float, in this case—and tried to return to the me I'd been this morning before the race, the one who wanted nothing more than to dot *i*'s and cross *t*'s with nobody bothering her. *That* me wouldn't mind when Brody had his hands on Grace's bikini. *That* me would accept Brody returning to Grace as the natural order of things. *That* me would know his kiss with me had been an impulse, like his four speeding tickets last year, and another ticket for toilet papering the football coach's yard. My stomach hurt.

I felt something flutter against my stomach. This time I wasn't fooled. It was no fish brushing against me. A boy had crept up on me and thought it was funny to pretend to support me as I levitated in the water. I knew it wasn't Brody, who didn't do anything halfway. He would have wrapped his whole arm around my waist and scooped me up. This touch, so light I could barely feel it, was Kennedy.

I surfaced, letting the water stream down my face, careful not to rub my eyes. Kennedy smiled smugly in front of me like he'd *really* surprised me that time! I laughed drolly just to keep the peace.

I wouldn't have felt so indifferent about him last week. One interlude with Brody had ruined my relationship with Kennedy—without Kennedy even finding out!—and I wasn't sure I cared.

"Do you want to leave?" Kennedy asked.

Together? I almost asked in an astonished voice. But I wasn't going to prolong my argument with Kennedy when Brody was all over Grace. I hadn't glanced toward the beach since I entered the water, but I imagined Brody had taken her into the pavilion. That was a euphemism all Brody's love interests could use, the Brody's Fling Club. *Did he take you to the pavilion?*

"This isn't fun," Kennedy said. I'd gotten so lost in my own thoughts again that I'd almost forgotten he was there, complaining. "Funny how one jock turns the entire vibe into a fraternity mixer."

There were two jocks here, counting Noah—three if you counted Will, even though our school didn't have a hockey team. I assumed Kennedy was referring to Brody.

"No, I'm not ready to leave," I said. "The sun hasn't even set."

"We have school tomorrow," Kennedy said. "Are all the Superlatives pictures ready for me?"

"Not yet."

"I need them."

"It's a holiday, and we still have a week and a half until the deadline."

"What's the matter with you?" Kennedy asked. "You're so crabby. Do you have PMS?"

I whirled to face him. The movement of my shoulders made a spiral wave like I was a hurricane. The wave sped toward him and hit him in the mouth as I said, "Listen. Never ask a girl that. It's offensive."

"That answers my question," he said.

A female could never win this argument. I said anyway, "I don't see how you can claim to be such a progressive thinker but make that kind of comment to a woman."

"Sor-*ry*!" he exclaimed.

"You know what?" I asked, my voice rising over the noise of the surf. "You offended me Friday with your meltdown about my friends and my *cupcakes*, for God's sake. Now you've decided I've been punished enough, and you're not mad at me anymore. Well, maybe *I'm* mad at *you*. And I deserve an apology. Not a 'sor-*ry*!' but a real one."

He gaped at me. I stared right back at him. A large wave smacked me in the back of the head and threatened to knock me down. I dug my heels into the sand and held my ground.

Kennedy sighed. "I wasn't saying anything against gays, just that I'm not one. I hear my dad in my head a lot. You haven't met my dad."

I shook my head.

"My dad doesn't approve of my piercing, and he doesn't like my hair." He reached back to grip the ponytail at his nape. "Or enjoy indie films. You should hear what he calls me."

I nodded. I didn't have to meet his dad to identify the type. Plenty of men with this attitude had made their beliefs known during breakfast at the B & B, assuming everyone else agreed with them. Little did they know that gay couples had slept in their beds a few days before.

"At our age," Kennedy went on, "what your dad says should roll off you, right? But for me, it doesn't."

"Me neither," I said. I meant my mom.

"I probably won't get to go to film school," he said. "I might not make it to college at all. My dad doesn't understand why I can't stay here and take over the plumbing business, since the money's good."

In a matter of minutes, Kennedy had transformed in front of me. Knowing what he was dealing with at home clarified why he acted the way he did, and where his anger came from.

But understanding him better didn't help me like him. I should have encouraged him to go to film school no matter what his dad said. At some point, I had stopped caring. I pictured him in ten years, a long-haired plumber claiming he could have gone to film school if he'd wanted, and making bitter comments about blockbuster movies that everyone else loved.

Instead of comforting him about his home life, I surprised

myself by saying this: "You can't give me the silent treatment anymore."

"What?"

"The silent treatment. You get mad at me and stop speaking to me for days. I can't stand it, and I'm not going to put up with it. My mom and dad did that to each other when my dad still lived at home."

Kennedy stared at me across the water, like *he* was now having a revelation about *me*. A wave hit him in the chin, then another. Still he watched me.

Finally he said, "Me! *You* give *me* the silent treatment."

"I certainly do not," I said.

"You never say anything."

"I'm saying something right now. I hear myself speaking."

"You're excruciatingly quiet. Dating you is like being given the silent treatment *all the time*."

Well, maybe he shouldn't date me, then, if it was such torture. Maybe we should break up. These words were on my lips as I glanced toward shore.

Damn my contacts, giving me excellent distance vision. Against my will, I focused on the island of our towels and umbrellas. Grace and Brody were sitting up, facing us, her body tucked between his spread legs. He massaged her shoulders.

Instead of breaking up with Kennedy, I grumbled, "Why don't we ever make out?" If I was trying to prove to him that I was sane and logical and *not* on my period, the question wasn't going to help. At this point, I just wished I could put on a show for Brody akin to the one he was putting on for me.

"What are you talking about?" Kennedy asked. "We *do* make out."

Something told me the way we'd kissed wouldn't meet Tia's standards for "making out," even a little. I asked, "Do you ever want to get down and dirty?" I sounded like an ad for an Internet porn site. I wasn't sure how else to phrase it. A guy like Brody wouldn't have cared how I put it. He would have accepted the invitation without question.

"That just seems cheap," Kennedy said. "It doesn't even sound appealing."

"I'm kidding," I said. "You're right—the whole day's had a fraternity mixer vibe. I guess it's rubbing off on me."

"Do you want to leave?" he repeated.

"I'm not ready to leave," I repeated.

"Let's get out of the water, at least," he said.

Sitting next to him on a towel, listening to him make jokes, wouldn't be any more titillating than standing next to him in the ocean, listening to him make jokes. But there was no way I would refuse his company after what I'd seen Brody do with Grace.

We sloshed toward land. Grace lay on a towel now, with Cathy and Ellen beside her. Brody was tossing a football with Will—"tossing" in this case meant he was bulleting it fifty yards. He wasn't touching Grace anymore, but I'd seen what I'd seen.

As a last-ditch attempt at not resenting Kennedy so much,

I gave him an opening to make me feel good about myself. He didn't even have to make up a compliment. I saved him the trouble. I shouted over the noise of the surf, "Do you like my new bikini?"

"You look like a lifeguard," he said. It was like the time I'd worn a cute, structured blazer to a party and he'd said I looked like a man, and the time I'd worn a gauzy black minidress and he'd said I looked like a wiccan.

After we reached shore, he patted a place for me on his towel—*gee, thanks!*—and we settled side by side, not touching. Sitting next to each other on a towel was his idea of serious physical involvement. What if he made it to film school after all, and we were still dating in college? Would we sit next to each other on a blanket spread out on the quad? Was this how snarky intellectuals got knocked up?

"Ladies and gentlemen." Brody stood at the edge of the towel island, bouncing the football back and forth between his hands without looking at it. The ball was so familiar to him that it might as well have been part of him. "It's time for football. Touch football, so girls can play too."

Grace sat up and raised both hands. "I'm on your team, Brody!" she slurred.

"Drunks can't play football," Brody said. "Seriously, you'll get hurt. But you can cheer."

The drunk cheerleaders high-fived each other in response. Cathy called, "Can we cheer sitting down?"

Disgusted, I closed my eyes and lay back on my towel.

"Brody," I heard Noah call, "if you get hurt, Coach will kill you."

"He won't get hurt," I said to the air. "Just don't fall on him, Noah."

"Ooooooh," everyone around me moaned.

"Ha, good one," Kennedy commented.

Hooray, I'd qualified for the Snark Olympics. I hadn't meant what I'd said to be that funny. I hoped Noah wasn't mad. I opened one eye to look for him.

He was crawling across the towels toward me. When he reached me, he leaned so far over me that I felt a little uncomfortable. Out of the corner of my eye, I saw Kennedy leaning back to get out of Noah's way.

Noah rubbed the tip of my nose with his, just as he'd done when we dated. And weirdly, though I knew he wasn't attracted to me, butterflies fluttered in my stomach the way they had before he came out to me. He growled, "You know I'm going to get you during this game, don't you?"

I giggled. Kennedy scowled beside me. Noah had taken this flirtation too far, and I had let him. If I didn't end this, Kennedy would start giving me the silent treatment again, and I Just. Could. Not. Take it. I turned to Kennedy and asked, "Want to play?"

"Want to drive some bamboo under our fingernails later?" Kennedy asked.

"I'll take that as a no." I told Noah, "I'm not playing." I hoped Brody heard me.

After Noah walked off, Kennedy told me, "Sit up. This should be pretty good. Football oafs, the band's drum major, girls, a dog, the student council president, and a gay Goth in hand-to-hand combat? If only the drunk cheerleaders were allowed in, we'd really have a show."

I did think it would be a show. I also thought it would be infinitely more fun to be part of it rather than watching it, but I wasn't going to play when Brody was the one organizing. Obedient to Kennedy, I sat up and watched the teams gathering and dividing themselves.

Brody jogged out of the crowd. He reached our towel and held out one hand to me. "I thought you wanted to play football."

I stared way up at him. His green eyes sparkled in his tanned face. He beckoned to me like the devil. I wanted *so badly* to play. But I knew taking his hand would be a slap in the face to Kennedy. And there was no sense in goading Kennedy to give me the silent treatment over a football game at the beach, when there was nothing waiting for me as a consolation prize. Brody was just toying with me again.

I opened my mouth to say no. Instead, a yelp escaped from my lips as I was grabbed around the waist from behind. Noah had disrespected the towel island by tracking sand right through it. He hoisted me onto his shoulder.

I told him to put me down, my voice lilting in time with his footsteps across the beach, but I didn't protest too much. I wanted Brody to know I was mad at him for having his hands all over Grace, but I *did* also want to play football. This was the kind of Florida fun I was sick of missing out on. Noah was getting me where I wanted to go, in a way that Kennedy would have no reason to complain about later. As Kennedy sat alone on his towel, I felt incredibly lucky to have a gay ex-boyfriend. Noah set me down gently on my bare feet in the middle of the huddle.

Brody, bent over with one hand on his knee and his other holding the football against his hip, was lecturing the teams. He stopped in midsentence. "Harper. Thanks for joining us finally." He stared at me and I stared back, acknowledging the heat between us.

"As I was saying," he continued, "this is two-hand touch football. No tackling. If somebody gets two hands on you, consider yourself down. How else should we change the rules while ladies are playing?" He paused and squinted into the sun, thinking. "No nudity. If you pull off someone's bathing suit, that's a penalty. Like, a one-yard penalty."

"I don't know," I spoke up. "If you manage to get somebody's bathing suit off, I think you should gain a yard, because that would be pretty difficult and you should get a reward."

"Harper," Brody said over the laughter, "you are my kind of girl. You're on my team, by the way."

Across the huddle, Kaye raised her brows at me.

"Wait a minute," Aidan said. "I missed something. How are we choosing the teams?"

Everyone in the huddle seemed to move a fraction of an

inch backward. Aidan was the student council president, and he liked to govern *everything*.

"The teams should be equally weighted in terms of football experience," Aidan said, "and . . . I don't know. Height?"

"Watch it," Tia said.

"I wasn't talking to you," Aidan said.

"Parliamentary procedure," Kaye spoke up, because she was the student council vice president and had twice as much sense as Aidan. "Who thinks we should re-divide the teams considering football experience, height, and whatever else Aidan deems worthy? This will take roughly six hours. All opposed?"

"Nay," said everyone.

"Aye," Aidan said testily.

"Ready?" Brody asked quickly, before Aidan could make a more detailed argument.

"Break!" all the guys said, clapping their hands and moving away, while most of the girls were left wondering what had happened. Kaye grabbed Aidan and used two fingers to curve the corners of his mouth up into a smile. Silently I wished her luck with that, because Aidan didn't like it when she usurped his authority. I hurried after Brody.

I'd assumed this would be a pretty boring game: Brody scoring for his team, Noah scoring for his, and the rest of us standing around watching. But the two-hands-and-you're-out rule made the competition exciting. Girls really could play. Tia got good at sidestepping Will and slapping two hands on

Brody, sacking him. Other tackles weren't so clear cut. Did your hands have to be flat on the person you were tackling? Did one hand plus one pinkie count? After a couple of scores, we'd had so many arguments about the rules that Will asked Kennedy to referee. Of course he said yes to *this*. The job massaged his ego and met his need to feel superior.

His first ruling came when Brody tossed me the ball and I ran for the goal line. Noah stopped my run by picking me up with one arm around my gut—oof!—and setting me down facing the opposite direction, making the whole game with girls into a joke. I promptly spun and ran, not stopping again until I crossed the line.

"Score!" I hollered. "Noah didn't touch me with two hands."

Noah's side yelled, "Booooo." My side yelled, "Oooooh." Brody dashed across the sand, picked me up, and twirled me around in victory. I wasn't sure how much of this Kennedy saw. Six people already stood in front of him, arguing for their sides. I knew I'd won the point when my team cheered and Noah cried, "Damn it!" with his hands on his head.

"It has to be a two-hand touch!" Kennedy defended his call.

"You're just letting your girlfriend's team win!" Aidan exclaimed.

Kennedy shrugged and said slyly, "Privilege of being a referee." He winked at me.

Clearly he *hadn't* seen Brody twirl me around. I knew my

current limbo between boys wasn't what healthy, wholesome relationships were made of, but at the moment I didn't care. I was mostly naked and testing my body along with lots of other mostly naked friends on a hot evening. Sand stuck to my skin with sweat. I tingled with exertion and the knowledge that two guys desired me. Whatever happened tomorrow, this was the night of my life.

"Pretty sunset," Kaye called.

We all stopped and looked out over the Gulf. Daylight had faded. The change had been so gradual that I hadn't noticed. Now the bottom edge of the orange sun balanced on the rippling surface of the ocean, then disappeared.

As the light grew tawny and soft, Will walked up behind Tia. He wrapped one arm around her. She backed against him until their bodies tucked neatly together as they watched the sunset. He kissed her neck.

I burned with jealousy—not of Tia, but of the sweet relationship she had with Will. In contrast, I was caught between dating Kennedy in name only—he held his ground on the sidelines of our game and hadn't bothered to come any closer to me during this time-out—and making out with Brody, who was more attached to Grace.

At least Brody wasn't enjoying the sunset with *her*, either. After the drunk cheerleaders' boast, I hadn't heard a single "Get fired up!" out of any of them. They lay on the towels and might have been asleep.

Once the sun started sinking below the horizon, it slipped

behind bright pink clouds and into the ocean in a matter of minutes. "That's it for me," Brody announced. "It must be almost eight, and I have homework."

"Homework?" someone shouted. Another guy said, "Traitor!"

Brody held up his hands. "What can I say? I'm the school's scholar-athlete."

"You have, like, a three-point-one," Noah grumbled. "But I have to go too, or my mama will kill me."

Everyone else murmured their good-byes. We reluctantly disassembled the towel island. Gathering my towel and bag and two ice chests, I was surprised when Kennedy came up behind me. "See you in class," he said.

"Okay," I said brightly, as if I looked forward to it.

"And I need more of those Superlatives photos so I can work on the section," he added.

"Gotcha." That meant I would be up past midnight to put together something to show him, after I worked on the race photos. I watched him walk toward the parking lot, laughing with Quinn. I wondered whether the holiday had been worth it.

I'd hugged Tia and Kaye good-bye and had just realized with dismay that I would have to make two trips to lug the ice chests all the way to my car, when I saw Brody sauntering toward me with his towel around his neck. All the men in fashion magazines would be wearing the bulky terry-cloth scarf as haute couture on the runways next season. Brody made a beach towel look that good.

Yes, my holiday had definitely been worth it.

Nine

BRODY GRINNED AT ME. "HOW'S YOUR EYE?"

"Perfect," I lied. It still stung whenever I blinked. Probably I should wear my glasses to school tomorrow. Probably I wouldn't.

I wished Brody and I could pick up where we'd left off in the pavilion, but I wouldn't give him the satisfaction after he'd let Grace hang all over him. And I couldn't help but throw a little barb at him. "You're not driving Grace home, even though she's been drinking? Are you trying to get rid of her?" That would be the meanest joke if she lost a battle with a live oak tonight, but I couldn't imagine he'd really let her get behind the wheel.

"The drunks all rode here with Kaye."

He certainly seemed dismissive of his girlfriend, placing her in the collective of "drunks." He hadn't seemed so dismissive of her when he was holding her hips, or rubbing her shoulders while she sat between his thighs.

Without asking whether I needed help, he picked up one of my ice chests. "You haven't emptied this?" He pulled the plug in the bottom to let the water out.

"No!" When he looked up at me in surprise, I explained, "You're wasting water. If you're going to empty it, at least do that where the plants get watered." I nodded toward a palm grove.

"Anything that needs watering isn't native to the area," he said.

I laughed before I remembered I was supposed to be mad. "Brody Larson," I scolded him, "are you trying to out-environmentally conscious me?"

"No, ma'am." He turned his head and eyed me slyly. "Well, maybe. Come on, let's water your aspens or Rocky Mountain firs or whatever."

We dumped the water on some obviously nonnative flowers, then carried the coolers back to Granddad's car. As Brody shut the hatchback, he asked, "So, what about our yearbook picture?"

"It's too late now," I said solemnly. I meant for the picture. I meant for us, too.

His face fell. "Is it?"

"Yep," I said firmly. Then I sighed and looked up at the twilit clouds, which were rapidly fading into the night. "Seriously, it's too dark. The picture won't turn out. I still need to take it for my deadline, though." At the thought of all the photos looming, dread formed a knot in my stomach.

"That's okay. We'll just have to try again," Brody said happily.

"Yeah." After today, I knew I should take this picture with as little fuss as possible before I fell farther for him, or *went* farther *with* him. But if he suggested a new meeting place, I wasn't going to say no. "We could go back to my original idea of taking it in the school courtyard, just to be done with it. It's going to be hard to get what we want with a lot of other people watching, though."

"You're right about that." He almost sounded like he meant something else. Something more personal. Something very private.

He cleared his throat. "I have football practice every night this week, and when it's over, my mom wants me home. For some reason, she makes me do my homework."

"How odd."

"I still like your fake-date idea, though," he said, "and we have to eat. What if we met at the Crab Lab for dinner tomorrow? We could make that look like a date."

"We *could* make that look like a date," I agreed. And I would look forward to it like a date. I knew this was a bad idea, but today I'd found out how much fun Brody's bad ideas could be.

The next evening, I stepped out of the house wearing high-heeled sandals, shorts, and a pretty, flowing top. I knew I looked stylish. But I *felt* dressed down to the point of ridiculous, like Tia occasionally wearing her pajamas to school, with or without a bra, when she woke up late. I told myself I was uncomfortable only because I was used to wearing the 1960s-style high-necked trapeze dresses I'd made. Showing a normal amount of skin made me feel like I was letting it all hang out.

The last thing I needed was a commentary from Mom. But there was no getting around her. She was replacing the flowers at the base of the sign in the front yard of the B & B.

"Look at you!" she called. "Without the glasses, I hardly recognize my own daughter. Don't you look cute!" She wanted me to tell her that she'd been right about my contacts, and I'd been wrong.

Walking over, all I grumbled was "Thanks."

"Meeting Kennedy for a date?" She eyed the camera bag slung over my shoulder.

"No, I have to take some photos. I'm just grabbing dinner while I'm there."

She sat back on her bare heels and pushed her hair out of her eyes with one dirty garden glove. "I don't like you spending so much time on these photography jobs you're inventing for yourself."

She made my work at the 5K yesterday sound imaginary. It was hopeless to argue with her, though, so I only said, "It's not a job. This is for school."

"But you're going to all that effort at the yearbook to get into a college art program, right?"

"Yes," I said carefully, wondering where she was going with this. The way she phrased it, an art degree was a bad thing.

"I just think you're wasting a lot of time on this," she said, "working your fingers to the bone for nothing. You don't have to go to college. You can run the B & B with me, right here. Stop making work for yourself, and use your time to help me. I need you."

"No, thanks," I said faintly, even though I got the impression she was telling me, not asking me. "I've never wanted to run the B & B. I've always wanted to be an artist."

"You could still be an artist," she said. "You can take pictures in your spare time, just like you do now. Why would you need to go to college for that? Your grandfather never went to college, and look at the beautiful paintings he produces."

"Granddad was an insurance salesman," I reminded her. "He didn't need an art degree because he never tried to make a living as a painter. In fact, I think that's what drives him to paint so much now. He never took a chance and studied what he wanted for all those years, and now he's making up for lost time." I didn't add, *That's probably why he's crazy.*

She shook her head. "Painting gives him an excuse to lock himself in his house and never talk to anyone. But you and I have the perfect life over here. Business is getting better. Our finances would be better if you took on more of the work so I didn't have to hire so much out. And, Harper, the snowbirds would go *crazy* over a mother and daughter running a B & B. They would flock here."

"I have an appointment," I said. "Let's talk about this later." I hurried away as fast as I could in high heels on the soft earth, crossing my fingers this would be one of those weeks my mother was too busy for me.

I clopped down the brick sidewalk into town and swung open the door to the Crab Lab. Inside was dark. At first all I could see were the white lights strung over and around the old crab traps high on the walls. Over the doorway to the kitchen hung an antique diving suit with a picture of the University of Florida Gator mascot taped behind the mask. After my eyes adjusted to the dim light, they skimmed over the other diners and fell on Brody in a booth for two in the back corner. He was watching me.

He stood. His hair was damp from his shower after practice, and long enough that it curled at the ends. Instead of his usual all-purpose gym clothes, he wore khaki shorts and a green striped button-down shirt that made his eyes look even greener. When I reached him, he took me gently by the elbow and said, "You look nice," in my ear. He kissed my temple—which struck me as something adult friends would do when they met in public and were pretending not to have an affair. Something my dad must have done a million times.

We sat down. "Sorry," I said. "Am I late?"

"I'm early," he said quickly, sounding almost nervous. He lowered his eyes as if he was embarrassed. Brody Larson, nervous and embarrassed around a girl: me! Surely I was reading him wrong, but in my fantasy he was affected by my presence, which was adorable.

Then I noticed the long splint on the middle finger of his left hand. A metal brace kept his finger straight, forcing him to shoot the bird perpetually.

"Brody! Did you break your finger?"

"Oh." He looked at it like he hadn't noticed. "Maybe. Probably not. I'm supposed to have it x-rayed tomorrow."

I gaped at him. "Does it hurt?"

He shrugged.

"Well, excuse my concern," I said, laughing. "I tend to overreact. I thought I was going to die from a contact lens gone haywire yesterday."

"You were really in pain, though," he said. "It's hard to think about anything else when you can't open your eye."

"True," I admitted, instantly feeling fifty percent less stupid. Brody did that for me a lot—made me feel less stupid rather than more. It was a strange sensation after weeks and weeks of Kennedy.

"Anyway," Brody said, "the hurt finger isn't on my throwing hand, so who cares?"

"Right!" I said with gusto. "How did practice go—besides possibly breaking a bone, but not a bone you care about?"

He shrugged again, and his mouth twisted sideways in a grimace.

I was afraid I knew what his expression meant. I asked, "Still being too careful when you play?"

"Yes," he said, "but we're also having the other problem you asked about yesterday. Guys on the team are being dicks about Noah."

"Yeah." I couldn't imagine having to put up with teasing or worse from a bunch of ultra-macho guys with something to prove.

"If Noah and I weren't friends," Brody said, "I might be the one being a jerk. I feel like a terrible person."

It took me a moment to decipher what he meant. "I feel like a terrible person" coming from Kennedy would have been sarcastic, but Brody didn't play that game. As I worked through his words, I murmured, "You honestly feel bad for something you *didn't* do?"

"No, I said if Noah and I weren't friends—"

"But you *are* friends," I said. "I mean, this kind of self-flagellation is what *I* do. But in your case, it makes zero sense. You *are* friends with Noah, and you've had his back. When he and I went out last year, he talked about how supportive you've been. *That's* the type of person you are."

Maybe it was just the dim restaurant lighting, but the shadows under Brody's eyes looked darker than ever as he said, "You always make me feel better." He said this seriously, like it was a bad thing.

"That's exactly what you do for people," I said. "You make everybody feel more comfortable."

"No, that's what *you* do," he said.

He was right. I wasn't sure I *did* make people feel more

comfortable, but I tried. Maybe Brody and I were a lot more alike than I'd thought.

"You're an advocate for Noah," I assured him. "You don't have to give a speech about it or scold anybody. All you have to do is stand by him, because guys look to you as an example. You're the center of attention and the anchor of the team. You're so all-American, you might as well have the US flag tattooed on your forehead."

"Really?" he asked so sharply that I automatically responded, "No, of course not."

He eyed me. "You're saying I'm so unpredictable that I'm predictable. A football player who's everybody's friend, and who gets in a little trouble, but has a heart of gold."

I was shocked. That was *exactly* what I meant. And I could tell by his tone that he took it as an insult.

"I was kidding."

"It is what it is," he said. "That's not how I feel, but that's how people see me, and I have no argument with it, really." He spread his hands. The splint on his finger clicked against the tabletop. "Your observations about people are interesting. You don't have to back off just because I question you. I'm not Kennedy. I don't have to win the point every time."

I opened my mouth to respond, but I didn't know what to say. I'd resented Kennedy's power trip yesterday, but I'd thought I was just in a bad mood, crushing on Brody after he brushed me off. I hadn't realized my interaction with Kennedy was obvious enough for someone else to take note.

And I was *very* interested that Brody had noticed.

"Do you think I'm too quiet?" I asked timidly. "Kennedy tells me I hardly say anything, like I'm giving him the silent treatment."

"You speak when you have something to say, unlike Kennedy, who mouths off about movies nonstop until somebody tells him to shut up. Then he sulks and refuses to talk."

He had *that* right. "How do you know?" I asked. "I didn't think you and Kennedy were friends."

"I've had PE with him since kindergarten."

Sawyer appeared beside our booth with a tray. He wore a Crab Lab T-shirt. A white waiter's apron was tied around his waist. His blond hair seemed even brighter than usual in the dimly lit restaurant. He set a diet soda in front of me and a glass of iced tea in front of Brody.

"Thanks," I said. "We missed you at the beach yesterday."

"You could have found me right here." He moved to the next table.

Brody squeezed a lemon wedge into his tea. "Did Sawyer take our drink orders?"

I thought about it. "I guess not. I always get a soda, though." I tasted it. "Diet."

"And I always get tea." Brody tasted his. "Sweet tea. I guess he's cut out the taking-your-order step."

"Does that make him a good waiter or a very bad waiter?"

We both laughed. When we couldn't sustain that anymore, we both looked toward Sawyer as if he would give us something else to say. Especially after I'd shared how self-conscious I was about being quiet, I couldn't run out of words now! I wanted to talk about Kennedy some more, and then again, I didn't.

Suddenly I was aware of how Brody and me sitting together in this dark booth would look to anyone else from school. I reminded myself that we had a perfectly legitimate excuse to be here together.

I dredged up the courage to say, "I wish I'd applied for yearbook editor."

"Really?" Brody asked.

"Yeah . . ." I examined the paper placemat. "Maybe Kennedy would have gotten the position anyway, but I avoided even trying. It would be torture to have to tell people what to do and deal with them if they didn't."

Brody nodded. He knew plenty about that from being quarterback.

"But I didn't apply," I said. "And now Kennedy is in charge of the yearbook. He's in charge of *me*. I thought he had an eye for design, which is what made me like him in the first place. It turns out that he just talks the talk. I cringe every time he sets one of the photos I worked so hard on at some weird angle, or makes it so small that the detail is lost, or so large that the resolution won't support the image."

"I don't know anything about that stuff," Brody said, "but even I can tell you're great at what you do. Everybody is saying you take terrific photos for the Superlatives. You have a reputation for making people look better than they do in real life."

I laughed. "It's called lighting."

"You shouldn't downplay it," he said. "People will keep these yearbooks. When they show them to their kids in twenty years, they may not recall posing for the photos, but they'll see your results. You're framing how they'll remember themselves forever."

You always make me feel better, I thought.

"I guess you're majoring in art in college," he said.

"That was my plan," I said. "My mom told me a few minutes ago that I should drop my photography jobs, forget college, and help her run the B & B."

"No," Brody said in the authoritative tone that was becoming familiar.

"'No' what?" I asked.

"No," he said, "that's all wrong for you. People who cater to tourists around here are outgoing. You like meeting people, but only from behind a camera lens. You don't want to interact with strangers constantly. That would be a nightmare for you."

I laughed at how right he was. "My mom says it would look quaint, just what Yankees are looking for, a mother-daughter B & B."

"Who cares how it looks?"

"She does," I said. "And, hey—speaking of how things look—that shot I snapped of you and Will and Noah at the 5K will be on the front page of the local paper tomorrow."

"Wow!" he exclaimed.

"Yeah! I'm sure it's because you're a local celebrity."

He gave the restaurant a parade wave.

"But I was so much prouder of that picture than I've ever been of some sweet beach scene. I've studied form and color and setting up the perfect static shot, but what really excites me is catching people in action, the way a photo can tell the story of who they are. Maybe I shouldn't go into art after all. I could try photojournalism."

He opened his hands. "That would be great. Why don't you do it?"

I shrugged. "You have to be brave to do that. You can't stand on the sidelines. You wade into the thick of things. Otherwise you won't get the picture. Tia says I have an adventurous spirit without any wiles. I have the instinct to get myself into trouble, but not the courage to stay there or the wherewithal to get out."

"*Tia* said that?"

"Well, not in so many words."

He sat back. "That doesn't sound like something Tia would say to you. It sounds really discouraging."

"Oh, you're right. She just laughs at me for being adventurous, or for *wanting* to be adventurous. But I'm not daring like her."

Sawyer reappeared beside us with an even bigger tray than before. He set my plate in front of me—a green salad with shrimp, avocado, and mango: *yum*—and served Brody a huge fish sandwich with grilled vegetables. There was no "Does everything look okay?" from Sawyer. He tucked his tray under his arm and headed for the kitchen.

"Wait a minute," Brody called after him. "We didn't even order. What if we'd wanted something different from our usual?"

Sawyer marched back to our table and gave Brody a baleful look. "Did you want something different?"

"No," Brody said.

"See?" Sawyer started to move away.

"I did," I said, raising my hand.

Sawyer turned back to me. His eyes were crossed. "The only reason you're *saying* you want something different, Harper, is that I pointed out you always want the same thing." He walked toward the kitchen without giving us another chance to complain.

"That's *not* the only reason I want something different," I murmured in the direction of the kitchen door, which swung shut behind him.

"Very, very bad waiter," Brody muttered, picking up his fork.

We ate in silence for a few minutes. The wait staff was cranky, but the Crab Lab's food was delicious.

Finally Brody said, "You'll have a big adventure next year. You'll major in photojournalism at Harvard or Oxford or somewhere a million miles away."

I shook my head. "Try Florida. I'm on my own to pay for

college. Mom says she doesn't have the money. She already borrowed money from Granddad to buy the B & B."

"Yeah." Brody nodded like he understood. I figured he was on his own too.

"My grades are good," I said. "I'll get an academic scholarship. It won't pay for everything, though, so I've been working on getting my photography business off the ground. That's why I photographed the 5K yesterday. And if I had a killer portfolio to show an art department—or a journalism department—I might get another scholarship from them."

Brody nodded. "You've got it figured out. I wish I did."

"You make good grades too," I reminded him.

"I'm in the college-track classes," he said, "but my grades aren't great. They're okay, but not scholarship level."

"You'll get a football scholarship," I said.

He shrugged.

"What would your major be?" I asked. "Or what would you do instead if you didn't go to college?"

He swallowed a bite and said, "Coast Guard."

Oh. He'd been so positive about my dreams that I didn't want to be negative about his, but I couldn't help the wave of nausea that washed over me. I pictured him in rescue gear, headed across the tarmac at Coast Guard Station St. Petersburg to a helicopter that would lower him over a compromised ship in rough seas.

If that was the life he wanted, I could never be with him.

Ten

BRODY PAUSED WITH HIS FORK HOVERING OVER his plate. "What's the matter?" he asked. "You look sick all of a sudden."

"Nothing." The nausea passed, along with the heat that had rushed to my face. My skin was left cool. A line of sweat had formed at my hairline. I took a deep breath through my nose, exhaled, and forced myself to take another bite of salad. "You know, my dad is in the Coast Guard."

Brody frowned at me. "Really?"

"Yep."

"Is he stationed down at St. Petersburg? How does he run the B & B?"

"It's just Mom," I explained. "My parents have been separated for a couple of years."

"Oh." Brody lifted his chin, puzzling out my words. "Are they getting back together?"

"I hope not. Um . . ." I racked my brain for a way to describe the situation.

"I'm sorry," Brody said. "You don't have to tell me."

"No, it's not a touchy subject, just complicated." I put down my fork. "See, my dad cheated on Mom. Often. She finally kicked him out and filed for divorce. But ending a marriage in Florida isn't that simple. One of two things has to happen." I touched my first finger. "One of you has to be crazy. Actually, both my parents would be good candidates there, but they would have to be proven crazy separately in court."

Brody chuckled like he was familiar with this feeling, then took another bite of his sandwich.

I touched my second finger. "Or, the marriage has to be 'irretrievably broken.' That's the wording. Mom had her day in court. My dad told the judge that the marriage wasn't irretrievably broken. Instead of giving Mom a divorce, the judge sent my parents to marriage counseling. Mom went to the first appointment. My dad didn't show. The judge held my dad in contempt of court."

"Oh, shit," Brody said.

"It gets better," I said with a lot more bitterness than I'd known I felt. "My dad came crawling back to Mom. She comforted him, if you know what I mean. He moved back in. A few weeks later he cheated on her again. She kicked him out and filed for divorce. This has happened, I don't know, maybe four times in the past two years. It's about to happen again, because Mom has another court date next week."

Brody wasn't laughing like he was supposed to. He didn't make a snarky comment about Mom like Kennedy had when I told him this story. Granted, Kennedy's words had hurt my feelings, but I was used to his sarcasm. I couldn't get a handle on Brody's silence. Maybe my description had been too convoluted—too much like my own family life had felt for the past two years—and I needed to clarify.

"My dad wants to cheat on her and keep her too," I explained.

As these words were coming out of my mouth, I realized I was describing Brody when he made out with me, then ran back to Grace. I honestly hadn't made the connection earlier, but now it seemed embarrassingly obvious. And Brody must have been thinking I'd mentioned my dad specifically to make a point.

Brody watched me silently for a moment. He was quiet long enough that I believed he got my ugly unintentional message.

I laughed uncomfortably. "So, I'm the only minor in the state of Florida who actually *wants* her parents to get divorced."

If Brody had taken offense, he let it go. He moved on, because that's what Brody did. "I didn't want my parents to get divorced," he said. "I thought it was the end of the world."

"Yeah," I said gently.

"I don't miss my parents fighting, that's for sure," he said. "I miss my dad, though. I miss him so bad sometimes that it hurts, like, in my chest." He sat up and put one hand on his striped shirt, somewhere between his heart and his throat. Then he took a bite of vegetables, chewed, swallowed.

Without looking up at me, he said, "We used to play a lot of football together."

"I'm sorry," I said.

He shrugged. "At first I thought it was so awful, but I can see how your parents' situation is worse because it's one-sided. At least my parents were both cheating on each other. My mom acts like it's a huge relief to be available again. Maybe your mom needs to date."

"She's in a serious, committed relationship with a bed and breakfast."

"Is that her only job?" Brody asked.

"Yeah, and it's full-time, when you count keeping up with the repairs. Actually, I think we'd be doing okay financially if it weren't for the two-year-long divorce. She might as well be standing on the front porch and tossing cash to the lawyers like Will throws treats to his dog. *The* dog. Whoever's dog it is."

Brody finished the last of his vegetables. He'd wolfed down his entire sandwich and had even vacuumed up any garnishes that might have been on his plate. I'd hardly touched my salad. I'd gotten lost in my own sad story. Vowing to act more sane and less troubled for the rest of dinner, I took another bite.

"My dad doesn't want me to go into any of the armed services because I won't be able to choose where I live," Brody said slowly. "But your dad never got moved. You've lived here forever."

Between bites I said, "We lived in Alaska when I was little."

"You did?" Brody sounded impressed. "No, we were in kindergarten together."

I was surprised Brody remembered me from kindergarten. I remembered *him*. He'd fallen from the top of the monkey bars and split open his chin. (Or he'd jumped. Two versions of the event circulated in the class. Now that I knew him better, I was more inclined to believe he'd jumped.) For the week he was out of school recovering, Chelsea and I had kept vigil for him over a big rock with his blood on it, even though the teacher pointed out that the rock was on the opposite end of the playground from the monkey bars. She assured us the blood was red paint from an art project the year before. That story wasn't as romantic.

I said, "We were in Alaska for a year right before I started kindergarten."

Brody's face lit up. "Did you love it?"

I wished I could tell him I had. "It was cold, and so big I got scared. I think I clung to Mom's skirts the whole time we were there."

Brody nodded. "I want to see it, but if I had to stay there, I'm sure I'd freeze to death." He leaned closer and lowered his voice conspiratorially. "I usually don't admit this, but you're good at keeping secrets, right?"

I grinned as he repeated what I'd said in the pavilion yesterday. He might not take a relationship with me seriously, but at least I knew he'd been listening.

"I've always been terrified of being voted Least Likely to Leave the Tampa/St. Petersburg Metropolitan Area," he said. "The class is passing judgment on the girl and the guy who win that election. But I really like it here."

"Me too," I said.

Brody took a sip of his iced tea, then said, "My dad is a smoke jumper."

"I'd heard that." And it hadn't surprised me at all. Brody Larson's dad went around the country, parachuting out of airplanes to fight forest fires? Knowing Brody, it made sense.

"He's not going to be able to do it much longer. He's pretty old already to make a living that way. His back bothers him. He'll have to retrain for a different job—a boring job. He says I need to find an exciting profession that I can still do when I'm older. I was thinking about law enforcement of one kind or another."

"Perfect!" I exclaimed, and I meant it. "I can see you kicking in doors for fun and profit."

"Yeah." He grinned at the thought. "Well, speaking of high drama and nonstop action, why don't we take this Superlatives photo?"

I set my camera bag on the table. "I guess . . . should I come over there?" The restaurant was behind me, including the windows onto the street, which would glow in the picture and likely ruin the light. Brody's back was to the wall hung with tangled lights and a carved wooden mermaid. Everyone seeing this photo in the yearbook would know exactly where Brody and I had taken it.

"Be my guest," he said, scooting toward the corner. But the seat had room for only one person.

Which was okay with me.

I slid close to him on the bench. My thigh pressed his. "Sorry," I said.

"I'll manage." He freed his arm from where my body was pinning it to his side. He accidentally, maybe, brushed my breast, then laid his arm along the back of the booth.

Around me, sort of.

He smelled like cologne.

My body vibrated with excitement at having him so near. I couldn't take a deep breath to calm myself, because he would notice—and I would likely faint in a cologne-induced swoon. I had to concentrate to keep my hands from shaking as I moved aside the plates, then turned the napkin holder on its side as a platform for the camera. "I may have to do several trial runs to get us centered," I apologized.

"It's not torture, Harper."

"Ha ha, okay." I had never felt so nervous. I set the camera to take five frames in rapid succession on a time delay, then placed it on top of the napkin holder. "Smile when you see the red light, and keep smiling," I told him.

We watched the camera, but my eyes naturally focused on the bright windows beyond it. I wondered if anybody we knew was eating here and watching us. Maybe they'd tell Kennedy that Brody and I had been up to something suspicious. He would break up with me. It would all be for nothing, because

Brody would stay with Grace. But as long as the windows filled my vision, I couldn't see the other restaurant patrons. If I couldn't see them, they weren't there.

Only Brody was in my world right now.

The red light blinked on. The camera flashed five times.

I retrieved the camera and showed Brody the view screen. With our heads close together, we looked down at our heads close together in the photos, too.

I had a dumb moment when I thought I'd opened the wrong file. I hadn't recognized myself with my glasses off and my hair down, cuddling with Brody. He looked perfect with a genuine smile, as usual, but half my head was cut off. I put the camera back to try again.

This time Brody moved his arm down from the back of the booth to my shoulder, with his hand holding my upper arm.

The camera flashed.

We peered at the screen. I was grinning at the camera. Brody was looking at me.

"Oh, God," he said. "I look so lovelorn." He sounded amused, not mortified like I would have been if I'd gotten caught gazing moonily at *him*.

"Or like you're in pain from a possibly, probably not, broken finger."

He laughed. "Or a concussion. Or indigestion. Sure."

Sawyer arrived at our table. He did not have good timing. Brody and I both saw him in the same instant and tried to move away from each other. In such a small booth, there was nowhere to go. Brody removed his hand from my arm.

Sawyer laid our bill on the table very slowly, as if he was trying not to startle us again. "Whatcha doing?" he asked innocently. Sawyer was anything but.

I glanced at Brody. His lips were pressed into a thin line. He gave me a small shake of the head: *Don't tell him.* But I was the world's worst at coming up with lies, and I couldn't think of another way out of this. The truth seemed like the best policy.

"We're taking our Superlatives picture for the yearbook," I admitted. "Want to see?" I slid the camera across the table.

Sawyer peered at the view screen. "Wow," he said. "You're trying to break up with your girlfriend and your boyfriend?"

I was sure my face flushed beet red. I didn't dare look at Brody. I only told Sawyer, "The yearbook won't come out until May."

Sawyer put his tray down on the table and his hands on his hips. "Harper Davis, are you telling me that you're dating a guy you assume you won't still be with in eight months? Why are you with him at all, then? Girl, life is too short."

The truth was, I *did* assume I wouldn't still be with Kennedy in eight months. I'd been cured of any expectation for the future yesterday, when I pictured us sitting together on a college quad. No, thanks. I didn't want to admit this in front of Brody, though, when his long-term relationship with Grace wasn't at issue.

I nodded to the camera and asked Sawyer, "You're saying

Kennedy would be mad if he saw this photo of Brody and me? We're not doing anything wrong."

"Oh, sure," Sawyer said. "You can tell the picture is taken here at the Crab Lab. You've shot all the others in the courtyard at the school. You're making *me* take *mine* in the courtyard tomorrow. The only reason you're taking this one here is so you two have an excuse to see each other alone."

I opened my mouth to defend us, but nothing came out, because there was no defense. I hoped Brody could think of something.

He didn't say anything either. He just slid his hand onto my thigh—not high enough toward my crotch to be dirty, but much more familiar than two people taking an innocent photograph for school. Kind of like patting my hand in reassurance as Sawyer gave me the third degree, except *on my thigh*.

Sawyer couldn't see under the table. "To answer your question, Harper," he said, "I don't give fuck one what Kennedy thinks." He turned to Brody. "I've had the pleasure of spending a lot of time with Grace lately during PE. She's going to shit a brick when she sees this picture." He picked up his tray. "There's no charge." He headed for the kitchen.

We watched him go, speechless.

"I think he meant no charge for the advice," I finally said. "There's no way he's eating the cost of the food." Reluctantly I slid off Brody's seat and returned to mine, taking the camera with me. I pulled a few bills out of my purse.

"I've got it," Brody said, opening his wallet.

"Let's split it," I suggested, "since it's a fake date anyway." I sounded bitter.

Closing my purse, I picked up the camera and glanced again at my favorite of the photos on the view screen, the one with Brody looking truly enraptured with me, or in great pain. "I don't know. Maybe Sawyer's right. Should we try taking this photo again somewhere else?"

"You tell me," Brody said. "You're the one who's so concerned about what Kennedy thinks."

I looked Brody in the eye. He held my gaze. A chill washed over me. Electricity zinged between us just as it had in the pavilion, even though now we weren't touching. It sounded like he was asking me to cheat on Kennedy with him, as if whether he cheated on Grace made no difference to him whatsoever.

But if that's all he wanted, I couldn't play along. I felt such a strong connection with him, way stronger than I'd ever felt with Kennedy. If he didn't feel the same way about me—and he obviously didn't, if he wanted to stay with Grace—we needed to take this relationship back to a friendly flirtation, where it belonged.

"I don't have an idea for another photo right now." I scooted out of the booth and stood.

"If you do," he said, standing too, "let me know."

I was left with the feeling that Brody and I were in a fight. But Brody didn't do the silent treatment. The day after our non-date at the Crab Lab, he chatted with me in all the classes we had together, same as always. In fact, we talked more than I talked with Kennedy. Brody showed me his purple finger without the splint and told me it wasn't broken. Kennedy only bugged me about my deadline.

The only way I could tell there was tension between Brody and me was that in study hall, he offered me a fist-bump but didn't call me his girlfriend, even though Kennedy had stayed behind in journalism class again. Brody said "Hey," not "Hey, girlfriend," and that was it.

I wasn't in study hall very long. As soon as Ms. Patel came in, I asked her to excuse me so I could mark some Superlative photos off my to-do list. I'd called several people who had stood me up for previous photo sessions and told them to meet me in the courtyard—or else. And then, wonder of wonders . . . they showed up! Being stressed out to the point of rudeness might wreak havoc on my nerves, but it was great for locking down these photos.

Halfway through my study hall period, I hurried into Principal Chen's office. After Sawyer's comment last night about all the Superlatives photos being taken in the courtyard except mine with Brody, I'd decided I'd better switch things up for some of the others. We had Ms. Chen's permission to use her office while she was at lunch. I could take an adorable picture of Kaye and Aidan, Most Likely to Succeed, behind Ms. Chen's desk. I'd asked Sawyer to meet me there too. I wasn't sure what we would do for his Most Likely to Go to Jail photo, but surely there was something in Ms. Chen's office he could steal or tag with graffiti. Sawyer would think of something.

When I arrived, Aidan already sat in Ms. Chen's chair. Kaye stood nearby with her arms folded. "Harper," she called sharply when she saw me, "you didn't say *Aidan* should sit behind the desk while *I* stand by, ready to assist him, right? That's not the message *I* got."

"No," I said impatiently. I had only fifteen minutes to snap this photo and Sawyer's, or I would have to reschedule them for tomorrow. And I couldn't do that, because I was photographing other people then. "Look, just—"

They both shifted their gaze over my shoulder. A six-foot pelican sauntered in behind me. Sawyer was dressed in his mascot costume. His backpack was slung over a feathered shoulder, and in one bird hand he held a tattered copy of the book we were reading for Mr. Frank's class, *Crime and Punishment*.

"Sawyer," I complained. "Is that what you're wearing?"

He bobbed his big head.

The purpose of the photos was to capture the Superlatives as people, not hiding in a costume, especially when the costume included a foam bird head. But I was desperate to complete this mission, and I wasn't going to let any of these three go while I had them. I didn't dare send Sawyer to change. And I didn't want him to strip, because underneath he probably had on nothing but underwear. Maybe not even that, knowing him.

I opened the blinds over the windows onto the courtyard.

Sunlight flooded the office and glinted on the four-foot-tall sports trophies too big to be stuffed into cases in the lobby. Then I turned back to Kaye and Aidan. They were arguing again. "I'm the president of the student council," Aidan told Kaye haughtily. "You're the *vice* president."

"We're *both* Most Likely to Succeed," Kaye said. "We're equal."

"Not true," Aidan said. "The class selected us for that title because we're in charge of the student council. And in student council, I'm above you."

"I hope to God that's the *only* place he's above you," came Sawyer's muffled voice from the depths of the foam head.

We all looked at him. I'd thought it was his rule to stay silent while in costume.

I couldn't let this session devolve into a three-way fight. The two-way fight was already bad enough. I told Aidan and Kaye, "Let's take some shots with Aidan behind the desk, then with Kaye behind the desk, then—You know what? Let's kill two birds with one stone—"

"Hey," said Sawyer.

"—and have both of you sit behind the desk at the same time. Kaye, sit in Aidan's lap."

"I don't like Aidan enough right now to sit in his lap," Kaye said. "Anyway, we would just be reinscribing the traditional patriarchal hierarchy of a man being in charge and a woman infantilized in his lap."

"Yeah!" came Sawyer's voice.

"Shut up," she told him.

"Scoot over, Aidan," I said. "Both of you sit on the edge of the chair and share it." I would have given anything to be told to pose like this with Brody. It was sad that Aidan and Kaye were still dating but didn't care anymore about the golden opportunity of sitting together in a chair. "Parliamentary procedure. All in favor?" I asked. "Aye—and my opinion is the only one that counts. I am on deadline with this shit."

"Cussing in the principal's office!" Sawyer managed to make his voice sound horrified even through the padding of his costume.

"I liked you better when you wore glasses and took orders," Aidan told me.

Without adjusting the settings, I brought my camera up from its strap and snapped a quick photo in Aidan's general direction. "There," I said. "I've got a shot of you with your eyes bugged out and your mouth wide open. That's probably all I need." I turned to leave the office.

"You look great without your glasses," Aidan said promptly, "and this newfound assertiveness becomes you." Kaye was laughing.

I waited for them to get into position, then started taking pictures. I was focusing on their faces and snapping photos so fast that I almost didn't notice the light had changed and a sunbeam streamed white through the window. It took me a few frames to realize the light was actually Sawyer's white costume. He'd walked behind Kaye and Aidan. All the shots had a giant pelican in the background.

A picture in the yearbook of Sawyer photobombing Kaye and Aidan would have said volumes about our senior class. But Aidan would resent it. Kaye would be hopping mad. And Kennedy had a sense of humor about his own projects, not mine.

"Sawyer!" I barked. "The white pelican is about to become an endangered species."

He put his hands on his padded hips. "That is insulting," he said, his voice thin behind the foam head. "All our large waterfowl are in danger because we're destroying their wetlands. It's not something to joke about."

No topics were off limits for *him* to joke about. I suspected I'd found, for the first time, Sawyer's sensitive spot. He was an animal rights supporter. Sawyer, *sensitive*!

That was okay. I was sensitive too. Kennedy had called me disorganized last Friday, and I was determined to prove him wrong. I pointed to a chair in front of Ms. Chen's desk, where I assumed Brody sat when he got lectured for playing practical jokes and sentenced to on-campus suspension. I told Sawyer, "Sit down and shut up."

He commanded everyone's attention as he sat, wiggling his bird butt to fit it into the chair's confines. He casually crossed one big webbed bird foot on the opposite knee and opened his copy of *Crime and Punishment*. I wasn't sure which part of the bird head he saw from, but he appeared to be actually reading.

I snapped ten pictures of him. One of these would be perfect.

Eleven

WHEN I FIRST GOT HOME FROM SCHOOL, MOM was wearing paint-stained clothes and carrying a ladder, but then I lost track of her. I closed myself in my bedroom, sat down at my desk, and went right to work on the race photos for my website. I'd made a lot of progress on them the last two nights. I wanted to finish that night and send out an e-mail to the 5K racers saying that their photos were available for purchase.

Then I could get back to processing the Superlatives photos. I'd scheduled my last few photo sessions for tomorrow during school. I could continue fixing the photos over the weekend. I assumed I would meet Kennedy and our friends at the Crab Lab after the game Friday night. He'd also invited me to a jazz concert in the park on Saturday, which sounded suspiciously like we would be the youngest ones there. That happened on a lot of dates with Kennedy. But if Tia was right about Kennedy's pattern of picking a fight with me before our dates, we wouldn't go anyway.

I suspected I knew what the subject of the fight would be too. My photo of Brody, Will, and Noah took up half the front page of the day's local paper. PHOTO BY HARPER DAVIS was printed in the bottom corner. I was so proud. And I was afraid my admiration for Brody shone through in that shot. Even if it didn't, I'd gone out on my own and sold my work to a publication outside school, something Kennedy had never been able to do, despite all his attempts to submit movie reviews and peevish columns about tourists. Either way, he was likely to be pissed with me.

So be it. Frankly, I was getting pretty disillusioned with dating. My boyfriend annoyed the crap out of me, and the guy who made me feel like heaven didn't want to be my boyfriend. Anyway, if Kennedy decided to give me the silent treatment again, that would free up plenty of time for me to perfect the yearbook photos and turn them in to him by Monday. I would get the rest to him on a rolling basis, as he'd requested, so he could complete his (awful) layouts. At the end of the week, he would have them all, and he could put the section to bed by the deadline.

That was my plan.

My dad was shouting. I blinked at my computer screen and glanced at my bedroom window. Night had fallen. My heart sped as fast as it had when he'd reprimanded me on the phone. He was yelling at Mom. He said she wasn't giving them a chance. She was going through with this ridiculous divorce to punish him. No, he would not shut up just because he was disturbing the guests at her Goddamned bed and breakfast.

He'd come over and shouted like this every time my parents got close to finalizing the divorce. Mom said he did it because the best way to hurt her was to make her B & B look bad. He wasn't just shouting at *her*. He was alienating the guests at the B & B, leading them to think the house wasn't safe, and ruining their peaceful vacation. He was trying, in this small way, to destroy her business, which she saw as the one good thing that had come out of their separation.

I did what I always did in this situation. After a few deep breaths so I no longer felt like I was about to faint, I opened my door and walked into our tiny living room. My dad was standing and pointing and shouting at Mom, who sat on the couch with her head turned away, as if he was about to hit her. He wasn't, but that's what it looked like.

I had defused this sort of argument between my parents plenty of times before. Throughout childhood, I'd convinced my dad to stand down by crawling into his lap. Recently when he'd loomed here in the living room and shouted, I'd given him a hug and told him I'd missed him.

This time was harder to stomach. I wasn't sure what the difference was—that I was tired of my own boyfriend dismissing my projects as worthless, or that I knew now how good it felt to start a business independent of everyone—but I had to stop this. He was still yelling at Mom. But I was immune because he never yelled at me. I walked toward him with my arms open for a hug. "Hey, Dad! I—"

He whirled to face me. His eyebrows shot up, and he gave

me a quick look from head to toe. I took people aback now that I'd removed my glasses.

Then he said, "That shit doesn't work on me anymore, young lady. I know exactly what you're doing, and so do you. If you want to act like an adult now, you can do that by staying out of your parents' business. If you want to keep acting like a child, you can *go to your room*!" He was yelling louder than I'd ever heard him, and the finger that had been pointed in Mom's face was now pointed in mine.

I turned, hurried for my room, and closed the door.

The shouting continued.

Panting, I lay down on my bed, pulled the phone and earbuds from my nightstand, and turned on one of my deep-breathing relaxation recordings. *Try to clear your mind*, the lady said. *If you have an intrusive thought, that's fine. Just let it go.* But I couldn't let it go. Now that the initial wave of panic had passed, I couldn't believe I'd done exactly what my dad had told me to do. Just like Granddad, I'd abandoned my mom.

One deep breath. I could call 911. But my dad wasn't breaking any laws, except disturbing the peace. If Mom's guests in the B & B were listening to the commotion, the one thing worse for business than my dad yelling would be for the police to come.

Two deep breaths. I could call some friends to hang out. They could knock on the front door and interlope, making my dad see he was affecting real people when he flew off the handle like this. But Kaye and Tia had been popping in since we were in third grade. They might be so familiar that he wouldn't stop yelling. He might shout at *them*.

Three deep breaths. I took out my earbuds, thumbed through the school's student directory on my phone, and called Brody.

He answered right away. I said breathlessly, "It's Harper. Can you come over?"

"So, you finally got another idea for a Superlatives photo?" My dad's shouting grew louder, and Brody must have heard it through the phone. "What's going on?"

"Nothing."

Brody knew exactly what kind of nothing I meant. "I'll be right there."

I clicked my phone off and lay on my bed, waiting. I wanted to put my earbuds back in and play the relaxation program to block out my dad's voice, but I didn't dare. My dad had already shouted at me, personally. That *never* happened. I listened to make sure my parents' fight didn't escalate. If it did, I would call the police after all. And I listened for Brody ringing the doorbell.

In the meantime, I stared across my tiny bedroom wallpapered with photographs and art I'd cut from magazines. It had seemed cozy in the past, a great place to hide from the world and work on my photos. Now it seemed claustrophobic. I was trapped here, suffocating on what my dad hollered at Mom, and her silence in response.

The doorbell rang.

I opened my bedroom door too quickly. I needed to cool it or my dad would know I'd called Brody to intervene. I waited in the short hallway until I heard Brody's voice. Then I walked into the living room.

"—Larson. I'm here to see Harper," he was telling my dad, who had answered the door as if he lived here. Mom stood behind him, looking lost rather than pissed.

"Brody!" I said in my best impression of pleased astonishment. "Dad, this is my boyfriend, Brody Larson. He's the quarterback on my high school's football team."

"Pleased to meet you, sir," Brody said. He stepped forward and extended his hand, grinning like he wanted to impress, even though he was wearing his usual athletic shirt and gym shorts. A drop of sweat slid down his temple.

The interruption had the desired effect. My dad changed from a monster back into a reasonably friendly guy with a toned, muscular body and a military haircut. "Brody," he said quietly, shaking Brody's hand.

"Not sure you remember my mom," I said.

"Nice to see you, ma'am," Brody said, shaking her hand too.

"Pleasure," she said. I half expected her to widen her eyes at me, wondering why I hadn't told her about my new boyfriend, and what had happened to Kennedy. But my dad had been shouting at her for quite a while. I suspected all she could hear was the ringing in her ears.

Taking Brody's hand and pulling him toward my bedroom,

I made small talk so his appearance would seem casual. "Did you get all your homework done?"

"Not quite," he said. "I still have maybe eight calculus problems left." He stepped into my room and closed the door behind him.

I hugged him.

He wrapped his arms around me and squeezed me gently.

I'd only meant to thank him. But now that I was in his arms, I didn't want to leave. I settled my ear against his chest and listened to his heartbeat: slow, steady.

Finally I let him out of my death grip and stepped back. "Thank you so much," I whispered.

"No problem," he said solemnly.

"I'm sorry about the boyfriend thing," I said. "I was trying to make it seem normal that you'd pop in." Belatedly I was realizing that Kennedy did not pop in. Not once had he crossed my mind when I was considering which friend to call.

"Can you stay for a few minutes?" I meant until my dad left. I swept my hand around the small room, offering him a beanbag chair or my desk chair or . . . the bed seemed a little forward.

"Sure." He kicked off his flip-flops and scooted back on the bed until he sat propped up against my pillows. He seemed comfortable.

I crawled onto the bed and settled beside him. Our arms touched from our shoulders to our elbows. I racked my brain for something to say to the guy I'd fallen for, who was someone else's boyfriend but was pretending to be mine. I glanced at him and was shocked all over again at how green his eyes were.

He watched me intently and opened his mouth to say something. Then he grimaced, shifted on the bed, knocked me with his elbow, and pulled my phone out from under him.

"Sorry," I said. "Remember you asked me how I could just take a deep breath and relax? I was listening to a relaxation program. It's a directed meditation."

"On a recording? I can think of a better way to relax."

"If you can think of a better way, why don't you do it before games, instead of worrying?" Then it hit me. "Oh, you're making a sex joke."

He gaped at me.

"A blow-job joke?" I suggested meekly.

"Harper Davis!" he exclaimed. "Would I make a joke like that while I'm sitting on your bed? I had no idea your mind was so dirty."

"Uh." In my mind I backpedaled through what he'd said, trying to remember what had sent my thoughts in that direction. "Sorry, I—"

"It was a hand-job joke," he said. "I mean, my gosh, a blow-job joke? You have a *boyfriend*."

I burst into laughter—because what he'd said was funny, and because he excited me to the point of giddiness. I swallowed the last remnants of my giggle and said, "You're so different from the guys I usually hang out with. I can't tell when you're kidding."

"I'm always kidding," he said. "And it's always dirty."

"Ha ha, okay," I said.

"Harper!" he said, astonished all over again. "You didn't believe that, did you? I was not making a hand-job joke. It might have been a kissing joke." He was blushing.

I took one of the deep, calming breaths I was famous for. "Sorry. I feel kind of"—I was talking with my hands, but my hands were not forming any shape that was remotely related to what I was trying to say—"deprived sometimes. I haven't done a lot of kissing or . . . anything. And then I talk about it and go overboard, sounding like I'm starving to death."

"You don't," he said firmly, turning on my phone and thumbing through the list of recordings.

"You could download some of these programs and listen to them in the locker room before a game," I suggested. "Or is that not allowed?"

"It's allowed," he said, "but only kickers do superstitious shit like that."

"Well, if you're still feeling anxious, maybe you should start hedging your bets like a kicker." I put my head close to his, peering at the phone, and cued up one of the programs. "Want to try?"

He gave a shrug, meaning he would try anything once. He put the earbuds in. I started the recording.

He laughed. The meditation lady had a British accent. I smiled at him.

He sank down on one forearm on the bed, watching me.

I remembered that the program's first instruction was to lie down. I patted my thigh.

He rolled over with his head in my lap. His hair was a lot softer than I'd imagined. Half the time I saw him, his locks hung in clumps, wet from sweat or a shower or the ocean. His hair was clean and dry now, and baby fine, only a whisper against my skin.

Brody Larson's head was in my lap.

Something told me we were not just friends anymore.

But even as I thought this and felt my face flush hot, Brody seemed oblivious. *Relaxed*, even. He crossed his ankles—the meditation lady was telling him to make sure all parts of his body were comfortable. He rotated his throwing shoulder—the lady said he should work out kinks in any joint that hurt.

I lowered my hand to his shoulder and circled my fingers on his shirt, rubbing gently. This was not part of the relaxation technique, having his not-just-friend-anymore rub his kink. I was probably unrelaxing him.

Maybe I didn't care.

He lifted his opposite hand and put it over mine, as if to tell me he approved.

His breathing deepened. He'd moved on to the part of the program in which he inhaled slowly and visualized his body growing heavy and sinking into the mattress. So I wouldn't distract him, I stopped rubbing his shoulder. He kept his hand on mine.

I gazed down his long body stretched to the end of my

bed in the dim lamplight. When I looked at him from this angle, free to let my eyes roam across the whole of him, he seemed taller, but thinner, as he had when I photographed him at the 5K without his football shoulder pads. His crossed ankles were slender, and his feet were long, not wide, almost elegant.

After listening to a few more of his slow breaths, I started to feel ridiculous that I was still so tense, hovering over him like a buzzard about to swoop down on dead meat. I eased my shoulders back against the pillows, careful not to disturb him, and tried to practice what I'd been preaching, letting myself relax.

Without warning, the door opened. Mom was silhouetted in the bright light from the hallway.

It was like her to walk into my room without knocking. She wasn't trying to catch me doing something wrong—she just thought of herself rather than me. It didn't occur to her that she might startle me. I went out of my way not to startle her, but she didn't do the same.

Now, though, her unannounced entrance felt like an intrusion. I wanted to snatch my hand off Brody's, but that would alarm him and ruin everything. I left my hand where it was and lifted my chin.

Taking just enough steps into the room for her face to appear in the lamplight, Mom mouthed, "Thank you." She knew why I'd called Brody, and she wasn't mad. She was grateful.

I gave her the smallest nod.

She walked her fingers in the air and pointed behind her. She meant my dad had left and she was going over to the B & B for a while. She backed out of the room and closed the door as silently as she'd come in.

Brody moved anyway. We'd disturbed him. But no, he was rolling on his side, as the meditation lady told him. Sitting up was next, and a stretch and a yawn.

Then he pulled out the earbuds and scooted up to sit beside me against the pillows again.

I raised my eyebrows. "Well? Do you feel calmer?"

"I did," he said softly, looking at my lips. "But not now."

Our eyes locked. He moved toward me. We'd shared a moment like this before, with my face on fire and my heart speeding, but it had ended in disappointment. This one would likely end the same way. I waited for Mom to burst back in or for Brody to tell me he'd been kidding.

He reached up to cradle my cheek. His thumb traced my lower lip, sending chills shooting up my arms.

His lips met mine.

He kissed me hard for a second, then opened his mouth. This was a kiss. Quinn and then Noah had faked it pretty well with me in crowded movie theaters when lots of our classmates were around to see. But Kennedy, despite all his sarcasm directed at people who were less worldly than him, had zero idea how to kiss. I kept trying to show him. He obstinately refused to learn.

I didn't need to teach Brody anything. As we kissed, his

hand crept across my waist and circled my hip like he wanted to hold me steady forever. When I took a turn at kissing along his jawline, he lifted his head to give me better access to his neck, then gasped as if he'd never felt so good. This couldn't be true, but he made me feel like I was giving him the sexy experience of a lifetime.

I kept expecting him to touch my breast, which made me nervous with my mom around. But he didn't try—maybe for the same reason. After we'd made out for a good half hour, though, I wanted something more. I slipped my hands underneath his shirt. That's when he slid his hands under my shirt and fingered the hook of my bra.

But in the end, he decided against unhooking it. He broke our kiss and backed a few inches away from me, panting. Between breaths, he grinned at me and said, "You have to know what you can get away with."

"Yeah." I smiled, showing him I understood. But I had something more I needed to say to him, something I was afraid I would regret. "I . . . ," I said, and sighed. I couldn't catch my breath. "Um . . ."

Kennedy would have interrupted by now, asking me if I spoke English. Brody only raised his eyebrows and watched my mouth like I was beautiful.

"I . . . don't want to do this anymore," I said in a rush. "I don't like sneaking around, cheating."

He chuckled. "Yes you do."

He must have been referring to the head rush I got every

time he came anywhere near me. Was I that obvious? I clarified, "It's not right."

"Well, why don't you break up with Kennedy, then?" he asked. "I've been waiting for you to do that."

"Me!" I exclaimed. "Why don't you break up with Grace?"

"I'm not *with* Grace," he said. "I told you, she spent half of Monday with that jerk from Florida State."

"But when she came back," I pointed out, "you sandwiched her between your legs and massaged her shoulders."

He pursed his lips and shook his head. This was the first time since Ms. Patel's homeroom that I'd seen his green eyes look angry. "I did it because *you* were in the ocean with Kennedy—*right* after we made out in the pavilion. Like that meant nothing to you. Like you didn't care."

"Brody!" I said, exasperated. "I stayed out there with Kennedy because the second Grace came back from getting drunk with those college dudes, you had your hand on her ass."

He tilted his head to one side, looking genuinely perplexed. "I had my hand on her ass?"

"Yes!"

"I don't even remember that, Harper. I was probably just holding her up because she was falling-down drunk."

"How can you not remember putting your hand on a girl's ass?" I insisted.

"I dated her on and off all summer. I'm sure I've put my hand on her ass plenty of times. This one instance doesn't stand out."

"I've dated Kennedy for six weeks and he's *never* put his hand on my ass."

"Kennedy is from another planet. That's my only explanation for why he doesn't see you're hot."

I frowned hard. When Mom caught me making that face, she warned me, only half-jokingly, that I'd better lighten up or I'd get wrinkles. I smoothed my brow and relaxed my jaw, then sighed. "You know I don't have a lot of experience with this, Brody. If you're lying to me, I wouldn't get it."

"You think I'd mislead you for fun?"

"For a little thrill, yeah."

He gave me a slow, clear-eyed, disappointed look.

Then he picked up my hand and placed it on his shirt. His heart raced under my fingertips.

"That could be excitement from misleading you," he acknowledged. "Or, just possibly, you turn me on." He held my gaze as he leaned toward me.

I met him more than halfway. I kissed him. He uttered a soft groan and put his hands in my hair. His mouth was soft and warm and sweet. My whole body glowed so brightly that I decided Kaye and Tia had sold this making-out business a little short. It wasn't just the addictive physical sensations, but also something that shifted inside me, in my heart.

He let me go, panting again. He rubbed his rough thumb back and forth across my bottom lip. "My God, Harper."

"I'll break up with Kennedy at school tomorrow," I said hoarsely.

"Do you want me to be there?" Brody asked.

"Oh, no," I said. "Kennedy's never been into me. I doubt he'll mind. He'll probably feel relieved."

"I seriously doubt that." With a final sigh, Brody said, "I'd better go. Calculus calls, and if I'm out too late, my mom will call too."

I scooted off the bed, then held out both hands to help him off—which was a joke. He probably weighed almost twice as much as me. I led him by the hand through the house and out to his truck behind the B & B.

"Now that I think about it," I said, "how'd you know I live in the house out back instead of the big Victorian?"

"I didn't," he said. "I knocked at the B & B first. One of your guests came down in a bathrobe and told me where you live."

"Great," I said. "I'll hear about how cute you are at the guests' breakfast tomorrow."

"Aw, shucks." He laughed. "Speaking of tomorrow, will you come with me to Quarterback Club for dinner? It's a bunch of old people who raise money for the team and invite someone from the community to speak about how violent sports enrich our lives."

"Fun!"

"Yeah. The football players go, and their girlfriends, and the cheerleaders, so Kaye will be there."

"And Grace," I guessed.

"And Grace," he agreed, "but I'm not with Grace."

He didn't add, *I'm with you.* But he didn't have to. It was finally sinking in that I was the star quarterback's girlfriend.

"By the way," he said, opening the door of his truck, "do we still need to take a new Superlatives picture, or was that just a ploy to go out with me?"

"Both," I admitted. "I wanted an excuse to see you again. But we do need to take another picture. The one from the Crab Lab doesn't go with the others I've taken. We don't have to do it tonight, though. We have time."

And when I said this, I believed it was true.

Twelve

THE NEXT MORNING, THE LOCAL TV NEWS WAS tracking a hurricane headed for central Florida. Two rooms of guests in the B & B announced at breakfast that they were leaving. Mom explained that the hurricane wouldn't hit us just because it was moving in our general direction. The storm was still five days away. Anything could happen before it made landfall. It could peter out, or stay strong but veer toward Alabama. If Floridians packed up and left every time a hurricane headed our way, we'd be gone from August to October.

The tourists weren't convinced. The TV news had really done a number on them, pointing out that the Tampa Bay area was way overdue for a direct hit from some kind of Hurrigeddon. They packed their cars and hit the road right after breakfast, determined to make it out of town before everyone else got the same idea and the hurricane escape routes were immobilized with gridlock. Whatever.

The terror was infectious, though. At school, people

were tense, talking about the coming storm and the Yankee transplants in town who'd decided to drive inland for a long weekend, just to play it safe. Maybe the charged atmosphere affected me, too, and that's why I sounded so on edge when I told Kennedy during journalism class that I didn't want to see him anymore. He sensed my weakness, and that's why he said what he said next.

He crossed his arms and demanded, "Is it because of Brody?"

I glanced around the room. Mr. Oakley was out of town. His son played for the Gators, and he and his wife had driven to an away game up in Georgia. We had a sub who babysat for the school a lot. Her agenda was to spend the whole period texting on her phone unless someone actually started shouting, in which case she sent the offenders to Ms. Chen's office.

Therefore, the class was even more disorganized than usual. Instead of working on our projects for the newspaper or the yearbook or journalism independent study, everyone was goofing off like it was study hall—except Kennedy and me, of course. They weren't paying attention to us. The room was so loud with conversations and laughter that nobody could hear us when we talked in a normal tone. I'd thought it was safe to sit with Kennedy and break up with him between assembling the layouts for two Superlatives pages. It never occurred to me that he would care enough to get mad—much less raise his voice.

Quinn and a few other guys eyed us, then turned back to

their own computers. I kept my voice quiet, hoping Kennedy would follow my lead and calm down. "You and I have dated for six weeks," I said, "and we've argued for probably five of them. We got along better when we were just friends, remember? Some couples don't work out."

Kennedy nodded. "Some couples aren't *perfect* like you and Brody. You know he only wants down your pants, right?"

At least somebody does, I thought. "If he did," I said carefully, "it's none of your b—"

"He never would have noticed you if you hadn't started following him around like some rock-star groupie after that stupid vote. And dressing like you wanted it." Kennedy waved at my fitted V-neck T-shirt (no cleavage), chunky necklace, Bermuda shorts, and high-heeled wedges.

What?

"Everybody says you're trying to get Brody by dressing and acting like Grace," Kennedy sneered.

"Oh, really?" I tried to sound scathing, but I didn't feel very scathing. What Kennedy was saying hit too close to home.

Until he said this: "I thought you were a nice girl."

"You thought I was a nice girl," I repeated. "You thought I was a *nice girl*? What the fuck does that mean?" Now everybody from the surrounding computers was staring at us. I lowered my voice. "I can't be a nice girl anymore because I don't wear glasses, or I don't wear high-necked dresses? Or is it because I don't do what you tell me?"

"You know what it means," Kennedy said darkly.

"No, I honestly don't," I said. "But I know it's sexist. Like girls are supposed to be vessels of purity, and I've sprung a leak. Boys, meanwhile, can do whatever they want.

"You know what?" My voice was rising again. I'd stopped caring. "You've never treated me like you genuinely wanted to be with me. You wanted the *appearance* of dating without caring about me or my feelings. I deserve better. I should have broken up with you the first time you gave me the silent treatment."

I got up then, taking my bag and moving toward the back of the room. When I'd brought up the subject, I'd intended to break up with him gently and then listen carefully to his response. But I didn't care what he had to say anymore.

I didn't look forward to sitting at the back of the room for the rest of the period either. Everyone who'd been in earshot of our breakup was still staring at me. But before I'd even sat down, Kennedy was standing close, towering over me.

"I need all of the Superlatives photos tomorrow," he said smugly.

"Tomorrow!" I exclaimed. "My deadline is a *week* from tomorrow."

"No, *my* deadline is a week from tomorrow," he corrected me. "For the whole section. *Your* deadline is whenever I say it is. I've given you as many breaks as I could, but I've told you I need those photos on a rolling basis so I have time to lay out everything. You haven't been turning many in. So I want them all tomorrow."

I looked slowly around the room. All conversations had hushed when Kennedy followed me to the back. Now everyone—not just the people who'd overheard us before, but *everyone*—stared at us like we were a reality show. Only the sub wasn't paying attention. She had her earphones plugged into her phone.

"Kennedy," I whispered hoarsely, "I know you're mad at me, but I can't do that. There's no way. I haven't even taken all the photos yet. And once I did, I'd have to stay up all night to format them."

He shrugged, as if to say, *Serves you right.* "You'd have the section photographed and turned in by now if you hadn't spent the last week creating an after-school job for yourself with that 5K. Maybe we need a different yearbook photographer."

I'd felt myself blushing under everyone's attention before. Now I felt the blood drain out of my face, and my fingers tingled. Photography was what I loved most in the world. I'd busted my ass to get this position. Kennedy couldn't do this to me.

Yes he could. Mr. Oakley had told us to handle our problems like the yearbook was a business and we were employees. That meant Kennedy could fire me.

I gaped at him, wishing away the tears in my eyes. "That makes zero sense! I'm busy, but I'm turning everything in on time. If you'd set my deadline for tomorrow in the first place, instead of a week from tomorrow, I wouldn't have asked for the 5K job."

He smiled. "If you turn all the Superlatives photos in tomorrow during class, I'll consider letting you keep your position."

I wasn't sure whether it was his patronizing tone, or the fact that he'd chosen to make a scene in front of the whole class, or the entire six weeks of him acting like I wasn't good enough for him. But something made me snap. I shouted, "You know what? Don't bother. I quit."

His face fell. His eyes were wide, looking around at the staring class for the first time. "You can't quit! This section is due. Nobody in our class will get a yearbook on time!"

"Oh, I'll make your stupid deadline tomorrow," I said. "The section and the yearbooks won't be late because of me. After that, as long as I can get into journalism independent study and Mr. Oakley promises not to flunk me, I'm quitting. I'm not going to work for a boss like you."

The bell rang. Kennedy and I faced off, with the rest of the class circling us. I wasn't backing down, but the bell seemed to go on forever.

Finally it ended. I grabbed my bag and hurried for the door.

"Harper!" Quinn called, but I made my way to Ms. Patel's room without him. He was the one who'd told me to stop worrying about appearances. And now that I'd stopped—boy, had I stopped. I was already going over and over my public screaming match with Kennedy in my mind, wishing I could take it back.

At least, the part where I quit.

Brody looked more than ready for his daily catnap, arms folded on his desk, chin propped there. He looked so sleepy that the dark circles under his eyes made sense for once. He was watching the door for me, though. When he saw me, he grinned and sat up. "Did you do the deed? Uh-oh, what's wrong?"

"I'll tell you in a minute," I said, unpacking my camera. "We're out of time to take our Superlatives picture. Spend study hall in the courtyard with me."

After the bell rang, we stepped into the empty hallway. As we walked together, I said quietly, "I can't go to Quarterback Club with you tonight. I'm really sorry." I explained that Kennedy had changed my deadline and threatened to fire me.

"Kennedy can't fire you," Brody protested. "Students can't fire each other."

"We can in Mr. Oakley's class."

"But did you complain to Mr. Oakley?"

"He's driving to the Georgia game to see his son play. He won't be back until Monday."

"Oh, right." Brody nodded. I didn't think he'd ever had Mr. Oakley as a teacher, but he must have played on the team with Mr. Oakley's son before he graduated.

"And even when he gets back, I can't complain. He's told us we're supposed to settle our differences ourselves."

"This isn't what he meant," Brody said firmly. Then his face softened, and he touched my elbow. "You should have let me come with you when you broke up with Kennedy. If I'd been there, he wouldn't have gone ballistic on you."

"The next time you offer to strong-arm somebody for me, I will totally let you," I said. "Anyway, Kennedy won't be able to jerk me around like that again, because I told him I'm quitting after I turn in the Superlatives photos."

"Quitting as yearbook photographer?" Brody sounded astonished.

"I mean, it's *high school yearbook photographer*," I defended myself, gesturing with my camera. "I've already made a couple hundred bucks for college from the photo in the paper and my pictures from the 5K finish line. I don't *need* to be yearbook photographer."

Brody nodded. "You'll regret it, though. Didn't you *apply* to be yearbook photographer? You submitted a portfolio, the same way Kennedy had to be chosen for editor, right? You earned that position, just as much as Kennedy earned his."

"Yeah." Unfortunately, I saw his point.

He pushed open the door for me and followed me into the courtyard. "It's not the end of the world, sure, and it's not making you any money, but I'd think about the decision to quit if I were you. It's part of your life. You're throwing away the position because you're mad at Kennedy, which means he's still got control over you. Is that what you want? You're only in high school once."

We were alone in the concrete space dotted with palm trees in planters. I sure hoped the last few Superlatives showed up for their photo sessions, or I was going to miss my new deadline tomorrow. After twelve years of school with Xavier Pilkington, Most Academic, I'd never been so anxious to see him.

"Stand over here, please." I pulled Brody under a palm tree and snapped a few shots of him, then looked around and moved him to a spot where the light was more muted and his green eyes stood out in the photos. He was smiling self-consciously, though, like he was posing for the football program that the student council sold at games. To distract him, I asked, "Are people talking about me behind my back because I got contacts and I'm dressing differently?"

"No," he said. "Well, no more than they talked about you before. You've been a favorite subject of the football team since school started this year. Though, come to think of it, maybe that's my influence."

"That would be very sweet," I said, "except that discussion is about my fine ass."

"Not *just* your fine ass," he corrected me. "You have many quality features. I used to look up from the table in the lunchroom and see you and say, 'Harper looks hot.' Lately I look at you and say, 'Hey, a new hot girl. Oh, wait, it's Harper!'"

"Okay," I said, laughing. I was capturing handsome photos of him laughing too.

"I like surprises." He tilted his head and considered me. "You should wear your glasses sometimes."

"Really?" I could not have been more astonished that he'd said this.

"Yes, really. You look sexy in those glasses. Wear them and surprise me when you're gunning for a little something extra."

"Noted. Okay, you're done." I attached my camera to my tripod and set it to take five photos. Then I took my smaller camera out of my pocket and posed where Brody had been standing. Now I had a picture of me taking a picture.

I scrolled through the view screen, then showed Brody. "Here's what I was thinking of for the yearbook. We'll use this one of me, side by side with this one of you." I flipped back to the best photo of him grinning, on the verge of cracking up. "Before, we weren't a couple. The joke in the picture was going to be that we looked like one. Now we *are* a couple. The joke in the picture is that we're separate."

"I don't get it," he said.

Xavier Pilkington arrived in the courtyard. We gave him a lukewarm welcome, then eyed each other again.

"I know this is your last day to take these," Brody said. "And Lord knows you don't need another guy making trouble for you."

"Thanks for recognizing that."

"I'm just saying, if I had my choice for this picture, we would be together."

I stayed up the entire night perfecting the Superlatives photos. Mom knocked on my door around midnight and told me with a yawn to go to bed. I lied and said that I would. Six hours later, I showered and schlumped over to the B & B to help her with breakfast. By the time I got to school, I was completely brain dead. This must have been what it felt like to be our classmate Jason Price, who came to school stoned.

Lucky for me, the beginning-of-school testing frenzy had died down. I was able to stare into space through my first three classes and avoid Kennedy by sleeping through journalism, since my work there, at least for the yearbook, was done.

I woke, slowly realizing that people were shifting their chairs and talking more loudly in anticipation of the ending bell. As I sat up, blinking, Quinn turned around in his seat, watching me.

"You finally stood up to Kennedy, like I told you," he whispered. "Congratulations!"

"And this is what I have to show for it," I said, yawning.

"Plus Brody," Quinn pointed out.

"Plus I quit the yearbook."

"That's where you went wrong," Quinn said. "I told you to stop worrying about how things looked. You only quit to save face."

Had I? My brain wasn't working well enough for me to remember clearly what I'd been thinking.

"Come on." He put his arm around me and half dragged me to study hall. I muttered a hello to Brody in the desk across the aisle from mine and folded myself onto my desktop, Brody style.

"Are you going to make it?" he asked. I felt him fingering strands of my hair away from my face.

"Mmmm," I said. "And I'll be at the game to watch you play, but I'm afraid I can't go out with you after. Bedtime. Catch up with you Saturday."

He chuckled. "That's fine."

When I woke, the bell was ringing. It wasn't the end of study hall, though. I'd slept right through lunch. Ms. Patel's classroom was dark and empty. A salad, a container of yogurt, and a drink sat waiting for me on Brody's desk.

Thirteen

I RODE WITH TIA AND WILL TO THE GAME THAT night. Brody couldn't take me because football players didn't go home on game days. They stayed at school until the game was over. And after Will heard why I wasn't at lunch, he told Tia not to let me drive myself. He insisted that driving while sleep-deprived was like driving drunk. The way I felt, I believed him.

Much as I longed for bed, I tried to enjoy my last game on the sidelines. Since I'd quit the yearbook, Mr. Oakley would revoke my press pass when he returned on Monday. For now, I snapped the best photos I could and kept my eyes on the game.

In the first quarter, the visiting team ran some trick plays and got down to our ten-yard line. Alarming! Mr. Oakley had taught me that the first team to score had the advantage, because morale was on their side after that. To stop the other team from getting on the scoreboard first, our defense had to prevent them from making a touchdown for three more downs.

But after the next play, I couldn't focus on the excitement. My attention was drawn to Brody *not* acting excited, not even watching.

He sat alone on the bench, feet spread in front of him, arms slack by his sides with his palms up, eyes closed. Underneath his jersey and pads, his chest expanded in long, deep breaths. Another player walked by and socked him on the padded shoulder. He didn't move or even open his eyes.

He was relaxing like I'd taught him. I only hoped this was the answer he'd been searching for.

When the screams of the crowd let him know our defense had held and the visiting team's chances had run out, Brody jumped up. He pulled on his helmet as he ran for the field.

By the end of his first play, I could tell something was different from the last game. Relaxed and in the zone, he managed to complete pass after last-second pass. He waited until he was about to get sacked to toss the ball to our star running back or bullet it to a fullback. With every play, he proved why the local newspaper had fawned over him during the summer.

Brody Larson was back.

And I had helped.

"Harper," called a young woman's voice. I turned around. Brody's sister stood on the other side of the fence, holding one of the chain links. I remembered her vaguely because she'd been a senior when we were sophomores, but I would have known who she was anyway because she looked so much like Brody, with light brown hair and clear green eyes.

She grinned. "I'm Sabrina, Brody's sister."

"I can tell!" While she was still laughing, I asked, "Does he know you're here?"

"Yeah. It was a last-minute thing. I'm driving back to Gainesville tonight. I have to be at work on campus tomorrow morning. I just wanted to see him play."

"So far, so good."

"Yeah! And I wanted to meet you." She put her hand over the fence. I detangled one arm from my camera to shake hands with her. "He's been texting me about you ever since yearbook elections. I can't believe you've started dating. That's so romantic!"

I shrugged and smiled, because I wasn't sure what to say. Honestly, I was flattered that he'd told her about me at all, and floored that he'd been talking about me since the election, weeks before we got together. My hopeful daydreams about him hadn't been one-sided after all.

"When I was a senior," Sabrina said, "a guy and a girl on the track team were our Perfect Couple That Never Was, and they *hated* each other. You can see them in the yearbook turning up their noses at each other. What are the chances that you'll actually get along with the person your senior class picks out for you?"

I grinned at her for a moment, letting her words and the warm fuzzies that came with them wash over me. Then I asked, "Can I get a few shots of you cheering Brody on? He would love to see that."

We didn't have to stage anything. I caught the cutest images of her holding the fence with both hands and screaming at the top of her lungs for her little brother.

Then she returned to the stands. I still snapped photos, but the end of the game had taken on a dreamlike quality. Every time I blinked, I felt like my eyes had been closed for two minutes. And when our team finally won, I didn't realize what had happened at first. I wondered why all the players and cheerleaders had suddenly rushed onto the field. I should have been taking pictures of the melee, but I needed to lie down.

Brody burst out of the crowd, looking huge in his uniform and pads, carrying his helmet. He glanced around at the sidelines and spotted me. Grinning, he dashed straight for me. Recalling how I'd been afraid he would make me drop my camera if he ran into me at the 5K, I removed the strap and packed everything away just before he reached me.

He dropped his helmet on the grass, grabbed me, tilted my body backward, and captured my mouth with his.

I was vaguely aware that some football players and a few kids in the stands were hooting at us. Maybe this kiss looked wildly inappropriate to some people in the crowd. To others, I imagined it looked a lot like a certain sailor grabbing and kissing a certain nurse in Times Square. If two of my friends had kissed like this instead of Brody and me, I would have made sure I got the shot.

But if the purpose of a picture was to capture the memory of a moment, I didn't need one. I would carry this feeling in my heart forever. For once, I honestly didn't care how this looked. I put my hand in his wet hair and kissed him back.

He broke the kiss, then thought better of ending it and kissed me again. He rubbed the tip of his nose against mine and said, "Harper. Thank you."

I giggled. "No, thank *you.*"

He kissed me one more time, then set me on my feet. "See you tomorrow."

"See you then."

I watched him jog back to the players on the field and slowly ascend the stadium steps with Noah. Unlike last game, this time they were laughing.

A few minutes later, I sat in the back of Will's ancient Mustang in the school parking lot, transferring the night's pictures from my camera to my laptop. I was so sleepy I could hardly remember my own password. I'd be gone to dreamland as soon as he and Tia took me home and I caught sight of my fluffy bed. But I wanted to get these pictures uploaded. Then I could e-mail Brody the cutest one of Sabrina, my way of saying *Great job* and *Have a good night* and *Thank you for that kiss, which made my senior year.*

Tia and Will were busy clunking their snare drums into the trunk, then peeling off their band uniforms to reveal their shorts and T-shirts underneath, then tickling each other, it sounded like. I was concentrating on sending an e-mail to

Brody that didn't seem high. Tia and Will's voices suddenly became hushed and concerned. The change hardly registered with me until Tia appeared in the open door.

"Did you see Brody?" she asked.

I didn't understand what she meant. "Did I see Brody? You mean right after the game? Oh, boy, did I. We were *making out*, I tell you, and not just a little."

She tried again. "Did you see Brody leave?"

"Did I see Brody leave?" I hadn't, and I wasn't sure what she was getting at.

"Is there an echo?" Tia asked, exasperated. "Brody just drove off with Grace."

Brody just drove off with Grace. Brody just drove off with Grace. I'd heard Tia, but what she'd said did not compute.

She called to Will, "Did you know Brody was going out with Grace again?"

"No." Will rounded the car to stand with her and peer inside at me. "That's shocking. I don't understand why he would do that."

"You warned me about him," I said quietly.

"Yeah," Will admitted, "but . . ." He stared up at the sky. He couldn't think of a *but*. "Yeah," he repeated.

Tia could think of plenty to say. She was asking me questions about Brody, bad-mouthing him, and grilling Will about how he and Brody could possibly be friends. I didn't really hear her. I was remembering the first time Mom had found out about my dad cheating on her. I was very little. She had told me, "I don't know why that girl thinks he's going to stay with her. If he cheated on me with her, he's just going to cheat on her with the next girl." And he did.

Once a cheater, always a cheater.

Tia clapped her hands, looking irate. Apparently she'd been trying to snap me out of my daze for a while. "Here's what you're going to do. See that truck over there?" She pointed across the rapidly emptying parking lot.

"Sawyer's truck?" I asked.

"Exactly. You're going to march right over there and get in the truck with Sawyer. You're going to drive around town until you find Brody and Grace, and you're going to make out with Sawyer right in front of them."

I squinted at her. "Is that going to help somehow?"

"No," said Will.

"Well, it's sure as fuck going to make *me* feel better," Tia said. "How could he do this to you?"

I was having trouble holding my eyes open, and I felt dead. But somewhere deep down, I was almost as angry as Tia sounded. I'd attracted Brody in the first place by wearing a bikini like Grace. Now, acting like Grace to get revenge on him made a perverted kind of sense. "Okay." I started to tumble out of the car, then paused. "Should I take my laptop and shit or leave it here?"

"Leave everything in Will's car. People are in and out of Sawyer's truck and it can get sticky."

"You don't have to do this, Harper," Will told me. "I vote

no." He said to Tia, "I don't see what this is going to solve."

"We're not *solving* at this point," she said. "There's nothing to *solve*. We're getting even. Maybe you don't have revenge in Minnesota, but this is how we roll in Florida." She turned to me again. "Let's go, girl. *Vámonos.* We'll be right behind you."

I stumbled off the seat and staggered toward Sawyer's truck. The floodlights far above me seemed brighter than they should have been, and the night was blacker. A sudden stiff breeze rattled the fronds of the palm trees scattered around the parking lot, reminding me that a hurricane still barreled toward us.

As I approached the truck, Sawyer, blond hair dark from a shower, looked up from talking with Noah, also freshly showered after the game, and Quinn, dressed completely in black. "What's up?" Sawyer asked me.

"Brody just left in his truck with Grace. They are probably having sex or whatever. Tia says you and I should find them and make out in front of them. Revenge kissing." I laughed like I'd gone insane.

"I think you should go home and go to bed," Quinn said.

"I think you should do the revenge kissing," Noah said.

"Wait a minute," Sawyer said. "If they're having sex, why can't we have sex too? Revenge sex."

"That would make me uncomfortable," I said.

"I guess I'll take what I can get." Sawyer opened the door of his truck for me. It screeched on its hinges. "Hop in."

As Sawyer started the engine, Will cruised up, stopping so that Tia could talk through the passenger-side window to Sawyer. They decided that we would swing by Brody's house and Grace's house near downtown before ending at the harbor. It was a common place for teenagers to park and cops to harass them. Irate old men wrote about the harbor's parking lot in their letters to the newspaper about the downfall of today's youth.

"You look nice," Sawyer said as he crossed the high school campus and pulled onto the road through downtown. "I'm not just telling you that because we're about to revenge-kiss."

"Are people saying I stopped wearing contacts and started dressing like Grace just to get Brody?"

"No," Sawyer said, "and I hear everything. Who told you that?"

"Kennedy."

"Kennedy," Sawyer repeated, low and husky, like Tia cursing in Spanish. "Why do you care what he says? Why don't you just wear what you want?"

"I guess I don't know what I want." I paused. "But everybody dresses the way they do for a reason, right? Even you." I gazed doubtfully at his beat-up flip-flops.

"Not really," he said. "I only have four shirts."

I blinked against the passing streetlights. "And you don't eat anything you want. You're very strict about that."

"I'm a vegan because I don't want to cause the death of an animal," he said. "I mean, I'm not so strict about it that I'm going to insult other people for eating what I don't. I serve what I'm told to serve at work. But I'm not personally going to eat it."

"It's an anticruelty thing?"

He glanced over at me, seeming to consider this for the first time. "Yes."

"You didn't seem concerned with cruelty when you made fun of Kennedy's eyebrow piercing."

Sawyer's glance turned to a glare. "When I first moved to town two years ago, Kennedy ribbed me for one solid hour of PE because my dad had just gotten out of jail. You should have heard all the jail jokes. Oh, he was a fucking laugh riot, right up until I punched him."

I'd known Sawyer got suspended for fighting on his first day of school. I hadn't heard why.

"So fuck Kennedy and his eyebrow," Sawyer finished.

"I'm sorry," I said.

Sawyer heaved an exaggerated sigh. "It's crazy for you to apologize, Harper. You didn't do anything."

"I know. I just don't think Kennedy deserves to be made fun of. Like when you made that joke about him the day Noah and Quinn came out."

"I made the same joke about Brody," Sawyer pointed out, "and he didn't mind."

"Kennedy's dad puts a lot of pressure on him," I said carefully.

Sawyer rolled his eyes. "If you want to know what people are saying about you, they're saying you're hot."

"Really?" I asked skeptically.

"Yes."

"I felt like I needed to wear glasses so my face would have something in it. It just looks kind of blank to me, not pretty."

"We all have issues," Sawyer said, almost kindly.

I nodded.

"But that is the most fucked-up thing I've ever heard. You thought you weren't pretty, so you wore glasses? That's pathological."

"Sawyer!" I protested. "Why are you so mean?"

"I don't know," he said.

He slowed as we cruised past Brody's house. A car was there—probably his mom's. The outside lights were on, waiting to guide Brody safely into the house after his date with Grace.

"You should have gotten Most Original," Sawyer said. "You would have, if you hadn't been elected to that couples thing with Brody." Satisfied that Brody's truck wasn't parked anywhere around his house, Sawyer drove on down the dark, palm-lined street. Will was right behind us. The headlights of his Mustang shone through the back window of the truck cab.

"Who'd you vote for in the couples thing?" I asked Sawyer. "I still haven't found anyone who admits to voting for Brody and me."

"I voted for myself," Sawyer said.

"And who?"

"I can't tell you."

"Sawyer!" I exclaimed. *Sawyer* voted himself Perfect Couple That Never Was with a mystery woman? I was dying to know who.

"It's a secret ballot!" he protested.

I took a different tack. "Are you going to ask her out?"

"No," he said quickly. "It's just a fantasy."

"You never know until you try."

"This I know," he said ominously. He was after a girl he thought he couldn't have. And I was afraid he was right, if I'd guessed correctly which girl he had in mind.

"Is it Kaye?"

I watched blush creep into his cheeks. He asked evenly, "Why would you say that?"

"You wanted to be in the Superlatives photo with her and Aidan, but only in costume. You bug her constantly and taunt her. You act like a seventeen-year-old with a crush, or a twelve-year-old with borderline personality disorder."

He winced, but that was the only indication he heard me, or that I was right about Kaye. The blush slowly drained away, leaving him looking pale.

"I keep secrets," I told him.

"Good." He slowed in front of a house that must have been Grace's. Several cars were parked in the driveway, but not Brody's truck. Sawyer turned the corner and headed for the harbor.

"Brody told me you've started working out with the football team instead of the cheerleaders," I said.

"Yeah," Sawyer said. "Not the plays, of course, just the drills. I want to be able to run a 5K without having to sit down."

"You'd just been in the hospital that week, Sawyer."

"I want to be able to wear a pelican costume without passing out from heat exhaustion."

"It was, like, ninety-five degrees that afternoon, wasn't it?"

"I guess I just want to feel . . . worthy."

"Worthy!" I laughed. "Sawyer, that doesn't make sense. Everybody loves you."

He eyed me skeptically across the cab.

"They do!" I protested. "In a love/hate sort of way."

"Thanks for not making me feel any better."

It surprised me that Sawyer felt bad in the first place.

He pulled his truck into the harbor's parking lot. No streetlights shone here this late at night, which made it perfect for teenagers parked in clusters, blasting music and sitting on tailgates. They squinted into Sawyer's headlights and shielded their eyes. We drove slowly until we saw Brody's truck.

Sawyer parked in front of Brody, about twenty yards away. Sawyer's headlights shone straight into the cab. Brody was behind the wheel. Grace was on the other side of the seat. They weren't touching, as far as I could tell, but who knew what they were doing behind the high dashboard? They blinked like deer.

Sawyer switched off his engine and the headlights. We could still see the dark forms of Brody and Grace. In a few moments, when their eyes adjusted, they would be able to see us, too, and everything we were about to do.

"No tongue," I said quietly.

"No tongue!" Sawyer exclaimed. "That's like saying we're going to have sex with no—"

I was already sliding toward him across the seat as he spoke these words. I slapped my hand over his mouth and gave him a stern look. "Did you just say that to me?"

"No, I did not," he said through my hand.

Cautiously, I took my hand away. And then, before I could think this through any further, we were kissing. The strange, sleep-deprived vibration I'd been feeling all day pushed me against his chest.

He whispered against my lips, "Just a little tongue."

I cracked up. I was so giddy and nervous that I couldn't stop laughing.

"Come on, just a little," he coaxed me. "You'll love it. You'll be saying, 'Sawyer, stud, I am sorry I ever doubted your tongue.'"

"O-*kay*, use it."

As the openmouthed kiss began, I hung on to his shirt with both fists, bracing myself until it was over. Quickly I found myself saying, "Mm," and kissing him back. Tia and other girls Sawyer had been with said he was worth the trouble. Now I knew why. I leaned forward.

We both jumped at a knocking on the driver's-side window. Brody, taller than the truck, glowered at us through the glass.

Sawyer reached toward the door.

"No," I said, putting a hand on Sawyer's arm. I could tell he was about to desert me.

"Sorry," he said. "My man is serious." He cranked the window down and asked Brody, "May I help you?"

"Yes, please," Brody said in the same polite tone with a threat underneath. "I would like to talk to Harper alone for a minute."

"Sure," Sawyer told him, "if I can 'talk' to Grace alone for a minute." He made finger quotes.

"If you can catch her," Brody said.

We all looked toward Brody's truck. It was empty. I could barely see Grace in the darkness, leaning through another truck's window. She opened the door and got inside. The truck roared off.

Brody looked back at us with his brows raised like Grace's departure vindicated him.

Sawyer rubbed my nape and told Brody, "Listen. This here's my girl."

He meant, I thought, that we were friends, and he was looking out for me. I'd never viewed Sawyer as anything more than an entertaining basket case, but he was standing up for me.

"Got it," Brody said.

"Seriously, Larson," Sawyer said. "Even Will thinks this business is shocking."

"O-*kay*," Brody said, ticked off now.

Sawyer turned to me. "Go," he said. "I'll wait here for you."

Fourteen

I GOT OUT AND FOLLOWED BRODY TO HIS TRUCK. He started to open the door for me, but I shook my head. I wasn't going to sit where Grace had just been sitting, like I was her temporary replacement. I leaned against the hood. He leaned beside me.

He swallowed audibly. "I felt bad about leaving with her as soon as I did it."

"Congratulations," I said. "You know what would have been better? If you'd felt bad about it *before* you did it."

He nodded. His nearly dry curls moved against his neck. He said, "I really wasn't trying to get together with her again, because we really were never together in the first place."

Suddenly I was back at school, one week ago, lamenting my boring high school experience. *This* was my foray into the high school party lifestyle? Cross-eyed from lack of sleep, head over heels in lust, and resentful of my gorgeous boyfriend for cheating on me while he claimed he hadn't been cheating?

I stood back, closed my eyes, and put my hands in my hair—something I hadn't done for years, ever since I got on my careful-coif kick. I murmured, "This is some dumb shit."

"Harper," he said. "Are you okay? You're blinking like you can't keep your eyes open."

"I think . . . I've never worn my contacts this long."

"Do you have a case for them, and solution, like I told you?"

"Yes."

"Where?"

"In my purse."

"In Sawyer's truck?"

"No, in Will's car." I gestured vaguely to the Mustang, which had prowled to a position near both trucks so that Will and Tia could watch the show.

Brody hiked across the parking lot to the Mustang. The driver's door opened. I could hear them talking, but not what they were saying. Then came Brody's echoing shout. Everyone sitting on tailgates turned to look: ". . . shocking? What did you say that to her for, Will?" Will's voice was firm. Tia's rose above it: "This is Harper we're talking about, Brody. Harper Davis. You can't do this to Harper."

Brody returned across the asphalt, carrying my purse but not my laptop or camera bag. "Get in the truck, Harper. You're about to fall down."

I shook my head. "Only if I can sit in the driver's seat."

"Fine." He rounded the truck and opened the driver's door for me. It was my first time inside Brody's truck, where Grace and countless other girls had had all sorts of experiences I'd thought I wanted. I sniffed deeply, trying to detect perfume, but all I smelled was cleaner.

He got in the passenger side and closed the door, then offered me my purse. I dug out the contact solution. He held the case for me while I took out the lenses. Then he put everything back in my purse. My dad had made this sort of sweet gesture toward Mom, too, after he'd started a new affair and she'd caught him.

"I see where you're coming from now," I said. "On Wednesday night, you told me you didn't have to break up with Grace in order to go out with me, because you weren't *with* Grace."

"Right," he said warily.

"I assumed that, afterward, you would be *with* me." He opened his mouth, but I kept talking. "I was mistaken. What you meant was, you weren't *with* Grace, and you weren't *with* me either. You're not *with* anybody, and that gives you the freedom to be with everybody."

"Well," he said, clearly not liking where this was going, "not *everybody*."

"Sure, because you're not a slut. You're just a free spirit. You're an individual. Like you explained to me in the pavilion, everybody in your family's divorced. Couples aren't meant to be permanent. You get into a couple—a coup*ling*, like a train car—with one girl and then another."

"Exactly," he said. His shoulders relaxed, and he popped his neck, relieved that I understood where he was coming from.

I nodded. "That is fucking ridiculous, Brody. It's rifuckulous."

His brows knitted. "Are you drunk?"

"No," I yelled, "I am operating on almost zero sleep because my ex-boyfriend moved my deadline because I broke up with him so I could be *with* you!"

He huffed out a sigh. "I know, Harper. It's just that you said you were going home after the game, and Grace and I have been friends for a long time. She asked if I wanted to hang out. We came here and talked about that guy from Florida State, and I told her he's too old for her. I said guys from college trolling for girls from high school are usually up to no good. She got mad. That's when you drove up. She spotted some guys from the University of Miami and left with them. The end."

I wanted to believe him. I sort of *did* believe him, but I felt like I shouldn't. I felt like I was being taken advantage of, and that he'd been taking advantage of me the whole week, and everybody at school knew it but me.

"I shouldn't have done it," he said. "I'm just . . . friends with people. I'm not *with* girls. I figure we can go out, or sometimes make out, and later we can still be friends and *hang* out. It's the girls who don't agree to that plan."

I understood now why there always seemed to be a girl shouting at him in the hallway.

"I knew you were different," he said. "When Grace wanted to hang out, I said okay because that's what I'd normally do, but we hadn't even reached the edge of the school campus before I realized I'd done the wrong thing. I've worked on this—my mom made me go to counseling after my dad left—and I have this checklist in my mind and these things I'm supposed to say to myself, but they take a few minutes to kick in. I have an impulse-control problem."

"You sure as hell do," I grumbled.

"Harper," he pleaded.

"No," I said. "I came here with Sawyer because Tia was mad at you and egging me on. I was trying to make you jealous, but not because I want you back. I don't. When you cheated on Grace with me and said you didn't owe her anything, I should have known you would treat me exactly the same way you'd treated her." I reached for the handle of the door.

He put his hand on my arm—gently, or I would have bashed the shit out of him. When I glared at him, he put up his hand in surrender.

"Harper," he said, "give me another chance. We haven't even been on a real date."

"What does it matter, when you say people aren't meant to be in exclusive couples? I don't want to be with a guy who thinks that way."

He opened his hands. "I thought that because of who I was with. Harper, I don't want this to be about Grace. I want it to be about you, and me. I don't want to lose you. You—" His voice broke. He cleared his throat. "You make me feel smart, and funny, like there's more to me than a good arm."

I drummed my fingers on my bare knee, halfway to a

delirious decision. "You have to understand something. If we date, we're a couple. We're *not* the Perfect Couple That Never Was. We *are* a couple. There's no *never*. And it's *not* okay for you to go out with Grace." Hearing myself, I shook my head. "No, never mind. I shouldn't have to spell that out for you. I'm done." I reached for the door again.

"Hey," he said. Wisely he didn't touch me this time. His voice was quiet. I paused to listen.

"You said we would catch each other tomorrow," he said. "I'd really like to come over then. That can't hurt anything, right? We can talk again when you've had some sleep."

I gazed out the windshield. I couldn't see well enough to discern Sawyer, but I could see his truck, still waiting for me. Sawyer had my back. He'd acted like Brody and I had a claim on each other. Even Tia, in her warped way, had led me here to Brody. Somebody in our school—a lot of people, apparently, though I didn't know who—thought Brody and I were perfect for each other. And because my feelings for him were so strong, I wasn't ready to throw away that possibility just yet.

"You can come over tomorrow," I muttered. "But if you ever pull something like this again, you won't get another chance with me."

He said, "I won't need one. I promise."

My alarm went off at six a.m. I got up, showered, helped Mom serve breakfast, got quietly scolded for dropping a basket of orange rolls in a guest's lap, stomped back to my house, and crawled into bed. The talk at breakfast was that the hurricane had petered out into a tropical storm and was headed farther west into the Gulf, so we wouldn't get a lot of straight-line wind damage or flooding from the tidal surge—only a lot of rain, and possibly tornadoes on Tuesday, when my parents were scheduled to get divorced. I closed my eyes, listened to the light rain from a band of showers far in advance of the storm, and wished I could go back to sleep. I knew it would never happen with my mind spinning about Brody.

At eleven a.m. I woke again, smelling cinnamon. Something was very wrong. Mom seldom cooked for me, and she was never in the house on weekends. She spent all day every day cleaning and repairing the B & B. Taking the precaution of putting on a bra first in case criminals had broken into my house to fix me cinnamon toast, I wandered into the kitchen and saw it was Brody.

"Sorry," he said, looking around from the stove. "Your mom said it was okay. Have a seat." He slid a plate in front of me at the table: the best kind of cinnamon toast, with a buttery, sugary glaze baked to a crisp on top. Eggs. Bacon. Sliced banana. He put another plate with twice as much food down at Mom's place and dug in.

I tasted the toast. Heaven, but I didn't want to admit this. I asked coldly, "Is this a postgame phenomenon, or do you always eat this much for breakfast?"

He said between bites, "I already had breakfast."

"This is lunch, then?"

"No."

We ate in silence for a while. When his plate was clean and mine was still half-full, he said, "Tonight some of us are going to a movie and then the Crab Lab. Will and Tia, and Kaye and Aidan, and Noah and Quinn. Would you go with me?"

I took a bite of bacon.

"You're still mad at me." He sighed. "I don't know what else to do, Harper."

"Maybe there isn't anything else *to* do," I said. "Maybe, as you so eloquently put it last week, the school is on crack. They never should have paired us up."

He cocked his head to one side and considered me. "If you believe that, I'll leave you alone from now on. But I don't think you believe that. I sure don't."

I took a bite of egg. This boy could cook an egg, that was for sure.

"When we go back to school on Monday and everybody hears we've broken up," he said, "fourteen guys are going to ask you out, and probably two or three girls. But I'm thinking you don't have anything else on the horizon for tonight. And I'm better looking than Kennedy. I'm less weird than Quinn, and probably eighty percent less gay than Noah."

I laughed. "When you get all romantic on me, how can I refuse?"

"Good. What are you doing until then?"

I gazed toward the front windows. "Has it stopped raining?"

He nodded.

"I'll walk around town and take photos. The light's great and the colors are bright after a rain. When I had to stay up Thursday night, I thought I'd never want to take another photo again, but I've gotten over it."

"I'll come with," he said.

"No, that's okay."

"I want to," he insisted.

"I'm not just playing around, Brody. I had something specific in mind. Sites online post photos from freelance photographers for people to use in their newsletters and websites. I thought I might try to get in on that gig, but I need a bigger portfolio first."

"I can help you," he said.

"I don't want your help." When his face fell, I said quickly, "It's nothing against *you*. I prefer to work alone."

"How do you know?"

He had me there.

"Ah-ha," he said. "See? You *don't* know. You *think* you prefer to work alone because you've never had a good-looking guy to carry your camera equipment."

"It's a tripod and one small bag," I said. "You just want to grovel to me all afternoon and talk me out of being mad."

He lifted his chin. "I want to spend time with you," he said self-righteously. "And I could help you. I could model for you."

"Now *there's* an idea," I admitted, mind suddenly racing. "I would pay you if I sold any of those shots, of course. But you wouldn't have any control over who bought your picture and what it was used for. Your face could end up as an advertisement for a porn site."

"That could make me *very* popular next year, in college." When I just blinked at him, he hurried on, "No, I'm kidding. You're right. You can't use shots that show my face. My mom makes me keep my online accounts super private, even though my picture has been in all the newspapers. She thinks I'm going to get kidnapped."

"If people tried to kidnap you, wouldn't you just break their heads?"

"My mom still thinks I'm twelve," he said, "but I try not to argue with her. My dad wasn't very nice to her. My stepdad wasn't either. Her new boyfriend is okay so far, but I don't know. I feel bad for her. If I can, I do what she wants."

I was taken aback. I hadn't realized Brody was this mature.

"I mean," he went on, "for a case like this, where she'd find out."

Never mind about the maturity.

"So we can't use my face," he said, "but that doesn't mean you couldn't use the rest of me. Have you seen this?"

Afraid of what he was about to show me, I glanced toward the door, sure Mom would choose that moment to appear. But he only pulled back the sleeve of his T-shirt to show me his biceps.

"That's a great idea," I said. "You can flex your arm with the ocean in the background. I'll type 'The View from Florida' across the photo and have it printed as a postcard to sell in the gift shops around town. Every lady over sixty will want to mail one to her friends back home."

"Only ladies over sixty?"

"Well . . ." Jumping up from the table, I slid the TV remote to him. "Here, you can watch whatever game is on. I'll be ready in a sec."

I dashed back to my room to change clothes and brush my hair, excited about this new project. Afterward, I would need to update my website to read HARPER DAVIS, PORTRAITS, EVENT PHOTOGRAPHY, GRATUITOUS BICEPS.

I was all too familiar with going out with a group of friends and being one half of the Couple That Wasn't Getting Along. I'd spent the last six weeks that way with Kennedy. It was strange to arrive at the movie theater with Brody as half of a brand-new couple who'd spent the entire afternoon together having so much fun that we couldn't stop grinning. Tonight the Couple That Wasn't Getting Along was the one that had been dating for three years, Kaye and Aidan. Kaye made Tia trade places with her so she could sit by me, with Tia and Will between her and Aidan.

"Oooh, I love your hair!" I exclaimed as she sat down.

"Thanks," she said flatly. "Aidan said it looks like I have an afro."

Not the thing to say to Kaye. "An afro would be cute on you, but that's more fashion forward than you usually go."

She glowered at me. I wasn't making her feel better.

"It's not really an afro, the way you have it styled in front. I think of a real 1970s afro as being round all over. Anyway, calling it an afro is not an insult."

"He meant it as an insult," she said.

"If he did, he must have meant you looked retro. He wasn't being racist. Aidan isn't like that." He had many qualities I didn't like, but that wasn't one of them. "I'll bet he was just surprised. You've worn it in twists for a long time."

Her mouth flattened into a line, and flattened again whenever Aidan leaned around Tia and Will, whispering her name to get her attention. She wouldn't turn in his direction.

They were still fighting when we filed around a big table in the center of the room at the Crab Lab.

"Sorry," I heard Tia tell Sawyer in his Crab Lab T-shirt and waiter's apron as we sat down. "I didn't think you'd be working this late tonight, or I would have convinced everybody to go somewhere else."

"I took a longer shift. I have nothing better to do since I quit drinking." He smiled wryly. "It's okay." He moved toward the kitchen.

"What was that about?" I asked Tia across the table.

"He has a little problem with one of us," she said quietly.

"Oh. With Brody or me, because of last night?"

"Gosh, no," she said. "Believe it or not, it's more fucked up than that."

I figured he must dread having to serve Kaye and her

boyfriend. Lucky for Sawyer, Kaye and Aidan were still three seats from each other. Anyway, I'd hardly had time to ponder this before Sawyer marched back with a tray full of drinks balanced precariously high on one hand. He set a soda in front of me and an iced tea in front of Brody.

"Wait," Brody said. "Did we order drinks?"

Ten minutes later, it was the same thing: "Wait. Sawyer. Did we order food?"

"Y'all, save it," Tia warned. "He's in a bad mood."

"When was he ever in a *good* mood?" Kaye asked.

Tia glared at her.

Kaye spread her hands. "If you know he's in a bad mood, don't you need a good mood for comparison? I've never seen it."

"You're picking on him."

"We're not picking on him," Will clarified. "At least, I'm not. *I'm* eating grouper when I wanted shrimp."

Sawyer came back from the kitchen again and bent over the table between Noah and Quinn. "I didn't put in an order yet for you two. Sometimes you want one thing, and sometimes you want another."

A spontaneous snicker burst from two or three people, then instantly hushed. After a moment of silence, Quinn said, "You know what's consistent? You're a complete jerk-off," at the same time Noah stood.

Before I even registered what I was doing, I jumped up and put a hand between Noah and Sawyer. Just as quickly, I was pulled backward. Brody had his arm around my waist, wrestling me back down into my chair. He said in my ear, "Don't."

Sawyer stared defiantly up into Noah's dark eyes, pen to his pad. "Cheeseburger or patty melt?" he asked.

"Cheeseburger," Noah said grudgingly.

Sawyer leaned around him to ask Quinn, "Fried or broiled shrimp?"

"Broiled," Quinn said.

Sawyer made a show of jotting the orders on his pad with a flourish. "Mm-hm," he said as he turned for the kitchen. The way he intoned it made it sound like a "So there."

Noah sank back down into his seat and told Quinn, "I won't miss him when he goes to jail."

Sawyer came back out with another laden tray. Working his way around the table, he set a plate of shrimp and fries in front of Kaye. The food had been arranged in a smiley face. The fries were the mouth, and two cherry tomatoes were the eyes. The shrimp had been spaced in a semicircle across the arc of the head, like Kaye's beautiful new pouf of hair.

"Sawyer, dammit," she said. "What is this supposed to be?"

"It doesn't look quite right, does it? Here." He took one of her shrimp from the picture and tossed it onto Tia's plate.

"We didn't even order," Aidan complained from down the table.

"Kids' grilled cheese?" Sawyer asked. "That's what you always order when you come here with your mommy and daddy, Aidan."

Kaye burst into laughter.

"Kaye," Aidan barked around Tia and Will. When he got her attention, he pointed at her, then firmly pointed to the empty seat beside him.

She set her jaw and shook her head.

He raked back his chair. Everyone in the restaurant turned to stare. He blustered out of the restaurant, hitting the swinging front door so hard that it took several moments to close behind him. Kaye looked sick.

Without missing a beat, Sawyer swept up Aidan's untouched plate and set it in front of Brody, above his usual dish of fish sandwich and vegetables.

"Thanks, buddy," Brody said.

"You're welcome, buddy." Sawyer rounded the table and bent close to Kaye's ear. He said, so quietly I could hardly hear him, "I love your hair like that. You look very pretty."

She blinked in surprise, then stared across the restaurant at him as he headed toward the kitchen. After the kitchen door had already closed behind him, she mouthed the words "Thank you."

Even though I didn't believe Aidan had meant to hurt Kaye's feelings so deeply, I did think he was being insensitive to her. He should have known better after dating her so long. Or cared more. And I wasn't too surprised when Tia leaned over and whispered to me that we should both spend the night at Kaye's house. When Kaye and Tia and I needed each other, boys came second. Whatever adventure Brody and I might have had after dinner, it would need to wait.

Brody drove me home to pack. As we got back on the road again, headed across town to Kaye's house, I asked, "Did it freak you out when Noah and Quinn were holding hands in the movie?"

He was silent for a few seconds. "Was I acting weird?"

"You kept looking over at them."

He laughed uncomfortably. "A little. But Noah is so happy. I mean, if the guys on the team would leave him alone about it, he'd be happy. This town is full of people who are out, but they're not seventeen, you know? It took cojones to do what he and Quinn did. They stood up for themselves. If they can do that, they can get through anything."

As we drove on in silence, I thought about the couples who'd sat at the table. Other than Will and Tia, Quinn and Noah seemed the most stable. Kaye and Aidan were starting to act like Kennedy and me. I could only imagine Kaye must feel lost, especially after spending all of high school together with Aidan.

"Are you mad I'm going over to Kaye's?" I asked Brody.

"No." Pulling to a stop at a traffic light in a quiet intersection, he glanced over at me and smiled. "Disappointed." He accelerated as the light changed. "How about we meet up tomorrow? Would you like to go surfing? Can you surf?"

"Yes. Badly." Surfing was something most of my friends knew how to do. We'd learned when we were too young to know that the small waves on the Gulf Coast weren't worth the trouble. Canadians probably felt this way about swimming in frigid water. But the downgraded hurricane way offshore might produce good waves tomorrow.

I snapped my fingers. "I don't have a surfboard."

"I'll bring Sabrina's for you."

"Will surfing still be safe as the storm gets closer?"

"Define *safe*."

Right. To take advantage of the thrill, we'd have to swim in waters that were far from calm. Kind of like dating Brody. But some thrills were worth the trouble. I'd enjoyed my day with him enough that I was willing to take on the next challenge.

Fifteen

KAYE LAY TUMMY DOWN ON HER BED, HER BARE feet swinging behind her in the air, while Tia slipped on one of my A-line dresses and I pinned the side seam to fit her slender body. There wasn't enough material in the bottom to let the hem out. What had been a minidress on me would be a micromini on Tia. She didn't mind.

I'd brought a few other dresses I would tailor for Kaye. She and Tia kept trying to talk me out of it. "I worked hard on all my clothes," I said, "and I don't want them to go to waste. I'm really attached to some of the dresses, but they do seem kind of stuffy now. I might keep a few for myself and alter them with a shorter hem or a lower neckline. But if I wear them again, do you think people will say I'm not being consistent? They can't figure out anymore whether I'm supposed to be Old Harper or New Harper?" I'd told them what Kennedy had said about me trying to dress like Grace, which still bothered me.

"Consistency is overrated," Tia said over her shoulder as

I pinned her other side. "Some days I look cute, if I do say so myself. Some days I oversleep and don't bathe. I like to keep people guessing."

Straightening, I sniffed her hair and didn't smell anything. Mostly she bathed.

"Brody told me he wants me to wear my glasses sometimes because they're sexy and he likes surprises."

"I would be wearing my glasses, then," Tia said at the same time Kaye said, "Oooh, that sounds like an invitation. So, you guys made up? You seemed really happy tonight."

I nodded, smiling as I thought about our day together, and my new collection of gratuitous biceps photos. "I have fun with him. He's hard for me to get used to, though."

"Because he's talking about football the whole time," Kaye asked, "and you don't understand?"

"No, he doesn't talk much about football. I guess I've always dated guys who constantly make fun of stuff and show off how smart they are. Brody doesn't do that. Sometimes he says things that aren't even sarcastic."

"It sounds to me like you've never dated a guy who wasn't an asshole," Tia said.

"Ha," I said. "Tia, take that off. Switch." Carefully we pulled the dress over her head without dislodging the pins. I would have plenty of free time to sew it for her at home now that I wasn't the yearbook photographer, I thought ruefully. Kaye slipped on the next dress, which only needed to be altered to fit her athletic A-cup.

"I don't know," I said, carefully pinning the bust seam. "I had so much fun with Brody today, but I still have misgivings about what happened last night."

"Why does it have to be perfect?" Tia asked. "Why can't you just enjoy him while he lasts? It's not like you're going to marry him."

Marrying Brody had never entered my mind. But now that Tia had brought it up, the idea didn't sound too bad. I asked, "Do you know you're not going to marry Will?"

"I could marry Will," she acknowledged. "He's endlessly entertaining. Except I'm never getting married."

"Oh," I said in protest at the same time as Kaye voiced my thoughts: "Will is more traditional than you. He'll get married to *somebody*, if not you."

Tia said, "I will cut a bitch," and she sounded upset, like she was actually picturing Will dumping her because she wouldn't commit.

"Calm down," I said. "Who knows? You might change your mind. Anyway, you have years of dating before it's an issue."

"God knows you don't have to hurry things along because you're saving yourselves for each other," Kaye said. "I don't know about Will, but you took care of your end of that a couple of years ago with Sawyer."

"Excuse me, but *you* took care of *your* end a couple of years ago with Aidan," Tia pointed out.

"But I'm *with* Aidan," Kaye said. "You were never *with* Sawyer."

I interjected, "I just had this huge argument with Brody last night about who he was *with*. You two are giving me flashbacks."

Tia talked right over me. She asked Kaye, "What is this obsession you have with Sawyer?"

I figured Kaye would explode, but she didn't. She asked softly, "What do you mean?"

"I mean, lately you're always bringing up what I used to do with Sawyer and being judgmental about it. Do you have a crush on him?"

Now Kaye sounded outraged. "*No!* I'm going to marry Aidan!"

"We know," Tia and I chorused. Kaye had shown us a picture of her wedding dress in a magazine. In tenth grade.

"But that means you'll be with one guy your whole life," Tia said. "Before that happens, maybe you need a little sample of someone else. Like Sawyer."

Kaye muttered, "No, thanks."

"It's good stuff," Tia said. "Right, Harper?"

"We didn't kiss much, but it wasn't bad," I said appreciatively. "I mean, yeah, I enjoyed my sample."

"I'll bet," Kaye said, with surprisingly little scorn in her voice. She cleared her throat. "Anyway, Harper, the one thing I worry about with you and Brody is that he's so much more experienced than you. You hardly dated before this year. You never even had a date for homecoming."

"True," I said, not quite able to edit the glee from my voice. This year I *would* have a date for homecoming. My date would be the star football player. He would give me the traditional corsage, which would be too bulky for me to wear while I was photographing the game, so I would pin it to my camera bag. After he won the game, we would go together to the homecoming dance, and it would be the best night of my life.

So far.

"He doesn't make me feel inexperienced when I'm with him," I said. "It's not like I've *tried* to stay alone and innocent all this time. I've just been searching for the wrong kind of guy. I *thought* I wanted a funny, artistic guy. A successful guy."

I'd meant to describe Kennedy. But when Tia furrowed her brow, perplexed, and Kaye sat back, I realized they seemed to think I was talking about Will and Aidan.

I shook my head and went on, "It took the senior class electing us Perfect Couple to show me what I really wanted, and that's Brody. An athlete with a sense of humor I don't quite understand, who plays dumb sometimes but who's book smart and sensitive when he tries, with impulse-control issues that get him in trouble."

"Yeah!" Tia cheered. "I told you the day of the elections that he would be better for you than Kennedy."

Kaye shook her head. "Just be careful that it's the good kind of trouble."

Brody parked his truck at the edge of Granddad's private beach. Several hundred yards away, on the public section of the beach, we could see the yellow flag flying. That meant medium risk in the high surf. We waded into the ocean with our surfboards under our arms.

Hours later, completely exhausted and tingling from exertion, I floated on my board and watched a lifeguard haul down the yellow flag and hoist a red one. Two red flags would have meant the surf had gotten so rough that the beach was closed to swimmers. One red flag meant the lifeguard eyed us resentfully and only *wished* we would get out of the water so she didn't have to save our asses later.

"Do you think we should go to shore?" I asked Brody, who was floating on his board beside me. The sunset was beautiful and violent behind him, with strange clouds stirred up by the approaching storm. The bright pink light smoothed the ugly purple bruise on his side, courtesy of Friday night's game.

"Brody?" I called over the noise of the tide.

"I heard you," he said. "I'm thinking. I have trouble giving a shit about my own safety. I'm trying to consider this as a normal person would, for the sake of *your* safety."

"That's sweet of you."

He laughed. "You're welcome. Yeah—"

His voice was drowned out by an approaching roar. Before I could turn, a huge wave crashed over my head, forcing me under the water. The surfboard squirted out of my arms, and the tie tugged my ankle. I did a flip and grabbed for the board before it escaped out to sea, dragging me with it.

I surfaced spluttering. Brody was laughing and trying to shake the water out of his ears. "You okay?"

"Fine."

"As I was saying," he said, "yeah, I think we should go to shore."

An hour later, we were still lying on towels on Granddad's deserted beach, kissing in the darkness. Though he'd been exploring my breasts with his hands and then his mouth, I'd wanted to keep on my bathing suit top for a while, in case someone strolling on the beach wandered by. But when Brody fitted himself between my legs and lay on top of me, with only his bathing suit and my bikini bottoms between us, I forgot my modesty. He slowly circled each of my breasts with his tongue.

He held himself above me in mid push-up, his forearms trembling. He said softly, barely audible above the wind in the palms above us, "I have a condom."

I swallowed. "Okay."

"Do you want to?"

My whole body said yes, rising along the length of him, desiring him. And he felt it. He sucked in a small gasp.

"I want to," I breathed. "But I'm not on anything, and I would be terrified of getting pregnant, even with a condom."

He smiled with his mouth only. His eyes were worried.

"But I'll get on something," I said, "and then I want to."

He nodded. "Okay." He lowered himself over me and kissed my lips once more, deliciously, slowly. Then he rolled off me. "Sit up. Let me tie you."

I found my bathing suit beside me and clutched it to my

chest as he tied two bows in the back, his fingers sliding intimately across my skin. We both lay down on the sand again. His feet captured one of mine and massaged scratchy sand between my toes.

All the while, he was inhaling deeply like he couldn't quite catch his breath. "Wow," he murmured, "I feel like I've just run wind sprints in practice." His voice shook.

Down by our sides, I felt for his hand, grasped it, and squeezed.

He took one last long breath and seemed to relax. I couldn't hear him breathing anymore over the surf. The waves rolled in and slipped out. The planet was breathing. Overhead, the front edge of the tropical storm sped through the sky, dark purple clouds glowing on a periwinkle background.

"Are you thinking about how you'd compose a photo of this?" he asked.

"Not exactly. I was thinking I could never take this picture. It would be a huge disappointment, because the lens wouldn't quite capture the intense color of this sky."

"You're so artistic," he said. "It seems like you could just paint the world the way you wanted it, and then you wouldn't have to worry about catching it just right."

"The world is beautiful exactly like it is," I said. "You just have to know how to frame it, and bring it into focus."

I watched the clouds race overhead. Everything in my life seemed more in focus at that moment. My body still tingled where he'd touched me. I felt close to him. His transgressions of Friday night seemed a million miles away. I was beginning to understand how Mom could forgive my dad so many times, if this was how they kissed and made up.

"Do you think everything we feel for each other is physical?" I asked. "Like, we've done some things together and that makes our brains think we should be together?"

"You're dividing the mental and the physical," Brody said, "the head and the heart. I don't buy that division."

"What do you mean, you don't buy it?"

"I mean, sure, you see it in poems and songs, but it's a metaphor. It isn't real. Your brain is part of your body. It's one whole system that has to work together, or not. Nobody knows that better than me."

Right. He was still afraid of getting another concussion—as he should be, honestly. My relaxation programs had helped, but he was still working on staying in the game.

"What you're really asking me is whether what we have together fits into a box you've made." He held his fingers around an imaginary box in the dark in front of him. The box was small. And I was surprised, once again, that he understood what I was thinking a lot better than I understood it myself.

"I'm all for standards," he said. "But it seems to me that you built that box a long time ago, and it hasn't been working for you lately. Maybe it never did."

He turned to me and put one big, sandy hand up to cup my chin. "Here's what I know, Harper. I've never felt more comfortable than I do right now, right here, with you. If this was taken away from me, I would fight to get it back. I'm pretty easy to please, wouldn't you say? I'm more of a go-with-the-flow guy than a fighter. But I'm determined to keep football in my life. And I'll do the same to keep you in it too. Of course, now I've compared you to football, which is insulting, sorry." He took his hand off my chin, reclining on the beach again with the muscle control of many hours spent in the school's weight room, and closed his eyes.

"That's a huge compliment, coming from you," I said.

He opened one eye. "Right."

"I'm serious. You have a box too. You've wondered, 'Will any woman ever be as important to me as football? There is not such a woman. Despair!' Then you found me. I'm proud to sit in that box. Next to the box containing a football."

He rolled to face me. The smile had left his face. He wasn't kidding anymore. He said, "It's not just a game. I mean, it is, but it means more than that to me."

"I know." Admittedly, I didn't understand one hundred percent. But he seemed to love playing football like I loved taking pictures. At some point, an activity became a part of you.

"It could be a career for me," he said, "if not as a player, maybe as a coach."

"You would make an awesome coach," I said.

"But even if the game doesn't pan out for me," he said, "I've been good at it. I've worked hard for it. There aren't a lot of things in my life that I can say that about." He rolled on his back again and reached for my hand. We watched the clouds spin by above us.

After a long silence, filled with the roar of the excitable ocean, I said, "I want to talk about sex again."

He turned his head and gazed at me. "You only want to talk about it?"

"For now. Do you think we should wait for some special event, like graduation?"

"No," he said immediately.

"Prom?"

"No."

"Homecoming?"

He chuckled. "You're asking me if we *should* wait. My opinion is, no. But we *will*, if you want to." He pulled me closer. "I'll always be the one who wants to spend the summer after graduation touring Europe even though we don't have any money, who wants to cut class and go to the beach for the day, who drags you to Vegas the second we turn twenty-one. I'll say, 'Come on, it'll be fun.' You just have to tell me when to stop."

I laid my head on his chest, listening to his heartbeat. He wrapped his arm around me. Whatever my future was with Brody, it did sound like an awful lot of fun.

On Monday in journalism class, Mr. Oakley called me up to his desk. I hadn't planned to tattle on Kennedy. Quinn had done that for me.

Mr. Oakley asked me to tell him my side of the story, but Kennedy hardly let me get a word in edgewise. He followed me to Mr. Oakley's desk, stood right beside me, and denied everything I said. Mr. Oakley did not look happy. At first I thought he was furious with me. Then he barked at Kennedy to sit down—and Mr. Oakley was not a barker. He tried to convince me to stay on as yearbook photographer. I told him *I couldn't work like this* and resisted the urge to throw my hands in the air like a diva. He said we should table the discussion until he'd spoken to Kennedy, and he took Kennedy out into the hall.

Half an hour later, at lunch, Kaye told me, "I know some gossip about you! We're having some minor problems in student council, so I've been spending a lot of quality time in the teachers' workroom. I've overheard things."

"I'll bite," Tia said. We all moved closer together, knowing teachers' workroom gossip was the juiciest kind of gossip. "What are the minor problems in student council?"

Kaye's eyes cut to me, then to Tia. "Top-secret issues that probably will amount to nothing. Anyway," she said, splaying her fingers like this was going to be delicious, "Mr. Oakley was bitching nonstop about Kennedy. He wants to fire him as yearbook editor for moving up your deadline, Harper. He said you were reluctant to accuse Kennedy yourself, but several students told him Kennedy fired you just because you broke up with him."

"Really!" I exclaimed. "Mr. Oakley didn't say anything like that to me."

"He can't," Kaye said. "He doesn't think he can fire Kennedy, because the code of student conduct isn't clear enough. Principal Chen is afraid Kennedy's parents could sue the school. Mr. Oakley is mad. As. Hell. He keeps saying it's a fucking travesty that Kennedy gets away with murder and makes the yearbook's ace photographer feel like she has to quit."

"Did Mr. Oakley actually say 'fucking travesty'?" Tia asked.

"Listen," Kaye said, "I have learned some language in the teachers' workroom that would curl your hair. You should have heard them after Sawyer passed out from heat exhaustion. The principal and the cheerleading coach and the football coach all blamed each other. I cowered in the corner, waiting for them to shiv each other."

I felt like a million dollars for the rest of the school day. I had liked Mr. Oakley before, but it was great to be called an ace photographer. He appreciated me and was trying to come to my aid. Maybe Brody had been right and my decision to quit had been too rash. I would talk to Mr. Oakley about it again tomorrow. Paid or not, yearbook photographer was an important position I'd worked hard for, and I wasn't ready to give it up.

My good mood lasted until about five o'clock, when, as I was in the middle of altering one of my dresses for Kaye, she called my cell and asked me to come back to school. She had student council business to discuss with me and Brody as soon as he got out of football practice. She wouldn't tell me what the business was over the phone, but there was no way I could have missed this. I was afraid this was the reason Kaye had been spending so much quality time in the teachers' workroom: the minor problem, the top-secret issue that probably would amount to nothing. I hopped on my bike and pedaled back to school.

When I arrived, the football team was out of the showers and heading to their cars. Kaye, in her workout clothes and cheerleader shoes, sat on the tailgate of Brody's truck, talking to him. As I watched, Sawyer approached them. I couldn't hear what Kaye yelled at him from that distance, but I could tell she was shooing him. She pointed toward his truck. He retreated and sat on his own tailgate, waiting.

I leaned my bike against a palm tree. Kaye slid off Brody's tailgate and patted the place where she'd been. I hopped up next to Brody, looking in his eyes for some hint of what was about to come. He shook his head no. She hadn't told him yet.

"Sooooo," Kaye said. She'd started a million club meetings since we'd been in school together. She volunteered to give speeches in front of the class. I'd never seen her look this uncomfortable.

"Spill it," Brody said.

She pressed ahead. "The student council made a mistake. In ninth grade and tenth grade and eleventh grade, I was in charge of counting the votes for the Senior Superlatives. This year the student council advisor—you know, Ms. Yates—wouldn't let me because I'm a senior myself and it wouldn't have looked good for me to count the votes for my close friends and for myself. She gave the job to some younger students. I should have found a way to do it, though. I *knew* they would mess it up."

Brody put his arm around my shoulders. "What happened?" His voice was loud.

"Most of the categories include a girl and a boy who don't necessarily have anything to do with each other. Like, Tia was the girl who got the most votes for Biggest Flirt, and Will was the guy. I was the girl who got the most votes for Most Likely to Succeed, and Aidan was the guy. That's how the student council tallied the votes for Perfect Couple That Never Was, too. But they shouldn't have. Because it's a *couple*."

She turned to me. "You won the girl's side of the vote because some people were pairing you with one boy, and some people paired you with another." She turned to Brody. "You won the guy's side because so many people paired you with two different girls. You and one of those girls should have come in second. Harper, you and another guy actually came in third. Two totally *different* people were paired together the most and should have won. But nobody paired Brody Larson and Harper Davis with each other."

Sixteen

BRODY AND I LOOKED AT EACH OTHER. HE MUST have seen something very dark in my expression, because he removed his arm from my shoulders.

"I didn't want to tell you." Kaye sounded almost pleading. "I explained to Ms. Yates that the two of you started dating because of the title. She said it was even more important that we tell you, then. It wasn't fair for you to base your relationship on false information. I see what she's saying about rules and honesty and what have you, but sometimes I think this school forgets we're human beings, just because we're not adults yet. They act like our relationships with each other aren't real.

"But!" She spread her hands and looked toward the sky for strength. "That's as far as their crusade for the truth extends. Ms. Yates insisted I tell you this, but we're supposed to keep the mistake a secret. Otherwise there will be a chain reaction. Since each person can win only one title, they're all intertwined. If Harper wasn't part of Perfect Couple, she should have won Most Artistic, because she got the most votes for that. The girl who we thought won that gets booted to Most Original, and so forth. Brody should have won Most Athletic. The advisor doesn't want any of this to get out. It would take time to photograph the Superlatives again and the yearbooks would be late." She grinned wanly at me. "You're welcome."

"Well." I swallowed against the nausea. "Who'd the senior class pair me with as Perfect Couple, then?"

Kaye eyed Brody before she turned back to me and said, "Xavier Pilkington."

I took a deep breath and let out the longest sigh of resignation. The school had paired me with Mr. Most Academic. He might wind up the valedictorian. He might not. Kaye and some other folks were giving him a run for his money. But when the class had elected him Most Academic, what they were really calling him was Biggest Nerd. Most Repressed.

Just like me.

"And Evan Fielding," she added.

The old man's hat.

"Who'd they pair Brody with?" I asked. It was going to hurt. But if I didn't ask, the curiosity would eat me alive.

Kaye glanced at Brody again, like she was asking permission, before she swallowed and said, "Cathy."

Grace's best friend and fellow cheerleader and beer-searcher-outer. Sure, that made sense.

"And Tia," Kaye said.

Of course. The free spirit. The sexy chick who didn't give

a damn what anybody thought. My complete opposite. The girl Brody had a crush on in middle school.

I'd thought the senior class had gone insane when they put Brody and me together. Now that I knew they'd put Brody with Tia, I understood how smart the members of our class were, and how they'd seen through Brody's exterior to his deepest desires. We were never meant to be together. My admiration for him was real. I'd been talking myself into thinking we were compatible. But my week as his girlfriend had been a sham.

I turned to him. "I'm really sorry."

He frowned at me. "About what?"

About the fact that he was going to make this as hard as possible, but it had to be done. I soldiered on. "About last night. I should have known it was too good to be true."

"Oh, now, wait—" Kaye tried to interject.

"You sound like you're breaking up with me." Brody's voice was rising.

Yep, he was going to make this difficult, all right. I said, "I am."

"You are?" Kaye asked, sounding genuinely surprised.

I widened my eyes at her. Breaking up with Brody was hard enough without Kaye acting like I wasn't doing the right thing. I was sorry she felt guilty about the mistake. It truly wasn't her fault. But she must have guessed the news would break up Brody and me.

In a rush, Brody stood. The sudden shift of his weight

bounced the truck and jolted me as he said, "I should have known."

"Known what?" I slung back at him. Sure, we'd been ridiculously mismatched from the beginning. I *had* sensed this, and he had too. But he didn't have to yell at me about it, as if I was beneath him because I wasn't more like him.

He glanced angrily at Kaye, then held out his hand to me. "Come here."

Reluctantly I let him lead me away from his truck, into the empty center of the parking lot. Pretty much all the football players had headed home, leaving only the vehicles of a few coaches, Kaye, Sawyer, and Brody. He looked at the fast-moving clouds in the overcast sky. Then he said, "You've felt like you were being daring to go out with me. I'm not safe like the guys you usually date."

He heaved a pained sigh. "But that wasn't it at all, was it? Going out with me was the *safest* thing you could do, because our class picked me for you. At least, you *thought* they did." He was very close to me now. "The second you find out I wasn't preapproved after all, I'm not worth the trouble!"

My heart was hammering, and I couldn't catch my breath. His words rang true. He was absolutely right.

Sawyer walked up beside us. "Larson. Can you take a step back?"

Brody faced him. "This is none of your business, De Luca. I'm not threatening her."

"You've got eight inches on her. It looks bad."

Brody blinked at me, as if he saw me for the first time. He stepped backward and put both hands up. "You're right," he said. "I'm sorry."

"It's okay," I breathed.

He laughed. "If we can apologize, this is nothing like my parents fighting."

"Mine, either."

Sawyer eyed me, then glanced back at Brody. "Don't make me come over here again." He sauntered toward Kaye, who still sat on Brody's tailgate.

"Anyway," Brody told me, "I don't know what else there is to say. Nice knowing you?" He followed Sawyer.

"What is that supposed to mean?" I called after him, irate for the first time.

He turned around and kept walking backward. "You broke up with me."

"Yeah, but . . ." I crossed the space between us. "You know, it was just a shock. I've been going crazy trying to figure out why we would be paired together. When I found out we weren't, that made so much sense that my gut reaction was we *shouldn't* be together. But . . ."

He shook his head.

"What?" I asked.

"It's not going to work," he said. "You'll always be on the verge of breaking up with me. You'll assume it won't work between us, and therefore it really won't, all because the senior class hasn't given you permission. We don't *look* right together, so we must be wrong for each other." He started backing up again. "I don't want to second-guess everything between us because you're too afraid to take a chance."

He walked swiftly toward his truck, pausing only to mutter something to Kaye and Sawyer. They slid off Brody's tailgate, and Sawyer slammed it shut. Brody cranked the engine and took off across the parking lot.

There were no screaming tires and burning rubber. That would have made me feel better. I would have known he was angry, and therefore he cared. This calm acceptance meant he was really done with me. He wouldn't ask me to reconsider. He wouldn't make me jealous to try to get me back. Our entire relationship had been a mistake.

Kaye waited for me, leaning against her car next to Sawyer, tears streaming down her face. I could see them glinting in the sun even at this distance. I knew she felt awful, even though it wasn't her fault. I walked over.

"Kaye won't tell me what the problem is," Sawyer said. "It's some huge secret."

"It is," I said.

"Then I don't understand why *you* won't tell me," he said. "I am the *best* at spreading rumors. I could unburden you and let the whole school know in a matter of hours, and you wouldn't have to worry about people finding out anymore. You would feel so much better."

"Sawyer," Kaye bit out. "Damn. *It!*" Her last syllable echoed sharply against the school.

Kaye and Sawyer had picked at each other constantly since he moved to town two years ago. She often seemed exasperated with him, but she was rarely genuinely angry.

And I had never seen *him* fed up with *her*. He shouted back, "O-*kay*!" and stomped to his truck.

Watching him go, I leaned against Kaye's car in his place.

"I am so, so sorry," she said through her tears.

"It's all right, Kaye, really. It's better that we know. Brody's right. We never would have worked out."

"But you were having so much fun together," she protested. "You said you were happy. I could *see* you were happy. Your faces lit up at each other."

I shrugged. "It was only physical, I guess. I can always find another football player."

Kaye gave a big sniff. "You can tell yourself that. The problem with denial is, it's a bitch when it comes to a screeching halt. After that happens in a few hours, give me a call. I'm here for you."

I nodded. My heart was racing, but I felt strangely numb.

"You're good at keeping secrets," Kaye said.

"Yes, I am."

"Guess who the senior class *really* voted Perfect Couple That Never Was?"

I could tell from the look on her face. "You and Sawyer."

"And he hates me," she said. "I wish I'd never heard of these stupid titles."

"He doesn't hate you," I said. I would keep his secret.

Besides, if I told Kaye that Sawyer had a crush on her, that would lead nowhere. Even if she wasn't with Aidan, there was no way she and Sawyer could get along as a couple. But I couldn't let her go on thinking he hated her when the opposite was true.

I could definitely agree with her on one thing: "These Superlatives titles are the worst idea ever." But I wouldn't say I wished I'd never heard of them. If it hadn't been for my title with Brody, I would never have shared last night on the beach with him. And though we'd probably been right to let each other go, I would cherish the feeling of understanding him so deeply, and the memory of his body on mine.

When I got back to the B & B, I found Mom sitting halfway up the grand staircase, oiling the newel posts. I asked her, "Where are the guests?"

"They're all out. What's up?"

I'd been doing deep-breathing exercises all the way home on my bike, so I was able to say calmly, "I would like to get on the pill."

It was dark in the stairwell, with only a little evening light filtering through the second-story stained-glass window. Even so, I could see every drop of blood drain from Mom's face. "Harper. Have you had unprotected sex?"

"No, Mom. I haven't had sex."

"Thank God!" She flopped backward on the staircase with her arms sprawled out and her hair in her eyes, like she'd fainted. After this dramatic show, I waited for her to sit up again, but she stayed there. I patted her hand.

"Never scare me like that again," she murmured.

"That's the point. Brody and I broke up, but—"

"Oh, honey!" She sat up then, flipping her hair back over her shoulders. "I'm so sorry. You weren't dating him very long. What happened?"

"I broke up with him. And then I tried to take it back, and he broke up with *me*. Now I regret it."

"Why don't you try to make up?"

"He's really mad, Mom. *Really* mad. I don't blame him. The thing is . . . last night we fooled around. We didn't have sex, but we wanted to. It scared me. I think it scared me so badly that I pushed him away. I—" I stumbled over the rest of what I'd meant to say. Hearing myself verbalize the problem was what opened the floodgates, and all of a sudden I was bawling in Mom's arms.

Mom led me back to the house and actually cooked me dinner for once. We sat at the table and talked for an hour about Brody, and the Superlatives, and what all of it had meant to me. I explained that being named to the title with him had made me realize that my world was smaller than it needed to be, because I was mostly doing what other people wanted or expected, instead of exploring all my possibilities.

"The pill is just another part of it," I said with a loud sniffle. "I'm not sure I'll be able to get Brody back. Even if I did, I'm not saying we'd do it. For a while, at least. But I'm about to turn eighteen. I'll be at college soon. I think it's time I took care of myself. I'm tired of being afraid."

Mom nodded. "Those are all good reasons. We can definitely get you on the pill. And I know what you mean about being scared. It's a big decision. You should feel confident that you're protected." She eyed me. "But, Harper."

Uh-oh. "What?"

"If you're ever about to have sex and you're not a little bit nervous in a good way, you're not doing something right."

"That's wholesome, Mom. Thanks." I rubbed my eyes. I'd had to take my contacts out after the first fifteen minutes of bawling. "I *am* going to college, you know."

She shrugged and started to get up from the table. "You don't have to decide right now."

"No, Mom." I grabbed her hand and held it until she slowly sat back down. "I don't know why you want me to skip college and help you run the B & B. Maybe you see your relationship with Dad finally ending, and you're afraid to be completely on your own. There's no reason for you to feel that way. You're a successful businesswoman. You don't need me."

She smiled wanly. "Maybe I just *want* you."

"But I don't want *this*," I said. "I don't even want to help with breakfast anymore. I could really use more time in my day to expand my photography business, and that will help me pay for college. Plus, if you hire real employees, you could choose someone who's better company for your guests."

"Oh, honey!" she exclaimed. "You're lovely company."

"You're saying that because you're my mother. And as your daughter, there's another thing I'd like to do, too, if you'll let me."

She took a deep breath before she asked, "What's that?"

"I'd like to testify in court tomorrow and swear to the judge that you and dad don't need to go to counseling. Your marriage is irretrievably broken. Again."

She watched me for a long moment. "Wouldn't that make you sad?"

"No. I would be happy to help you both move on."

"I'll call my lawyer, then. Thank you, Harper." She reached across the table to stroke my hair out of my eyes. "Hey, do you have that pocket camera on you?"

"Yeah." I pulled it out and handed it to her.

She pointed it at me and snapped a picture before I could hide.

"Ugh," I said, putting my hands over my face.

"Uh-huh." She peered at the view screen, admiring the shot she'd taken. Satisfied, she handed the camera back to me. "Be sure to print that picture so you don't lose it as technology changes over the years. I promise you this: When you're my age, you'll look at it and think, 'I was gorgeous, with or without glasses, no matter what I wore or how I did my hair. Why did I waste my time worrying about how I looked?'"

I snorted. "God, Mom, that's something old people say."

"Listen to me," she said, patting the table for emphasis. "We old people are not making this shit up."

A few minutes later, I rang Granddad's doorbell and heard him walk to the door. He didn't open it.

"Granddad," I said.

"Who is it?" he barked.

"Three guesses."

"I'm busy." He took a few steps away.

"Granddad," I called through the door, "did you kill someone?"

"When?"

"Recently," I said. "Are you hiding a body in your house?"

"No."

"Let me in to see for myself."

"No."

"You know what? You're leading me to believe something is very wrong in there. If you don't open this door right now, I'm calling the police."

"Go ahead!"

I thought for a moment. "I'm calling Mom."

The door opened just the width of the security chain.

"All the way," I prompted him.

His face appeared in the opening. He glowered at me for a moment, then opened the door wide.

Before he could protest, I ducked under his arm and dashed for the back room he used as a studio. "Harper!" I heard him shout, but I'd already run though the studio doorway and seen what he didn't want me to see. I screamed.

"Eeek!" the naked lady squeaked.

"I am so sorry," I told her as I retreated into the hallway with my hand covering my eyes.

"It's okay, darlin'," she called. In a moment, she came through the doorway in a luxurious silk wrap. Her red hair was piled on top of her head, and she wore a lot of tasteful makeup. She was between Granddad's age and Mom's, I guessed, and her body was still beautiful. I could vouch for this, as I'd seen every inch of it. What hadn't been showing when I burst in on her was depicted in Granddad's paintings crowding the walls.

I extended my hand. "I'm Harper, the granddaughter."

She shook my hand. "I'm Chantel, the nude."

"Ha ha!" I said. "I beg your pardon. I was afraid Granddad was running an opium den or fight club or something back here. He's been so secretive."

"He's the strong, silent type." Chantel winked at me.

After backing out of that one, I returned to the front door, where Granddad was still scowling. "Granddad," I told him, "you're an artist. And you're a man."

"A *grown* man," he added.

"Well said. And you're within your rights to have Chantel pose nude in your studio. The only thing weird about this is that *you are being so freaking weird about it*!"

"I'm sixty-eight years old!" he shouted. "I'll do what I damn well please!"

I sighed, frustrated. Granddad was right—he'd been weird for a long time. The likelihood was slim that he would change because I complained. But it was nice to know that if I turned out to be an old curmudgeon just like him, maybe I would keep a few happy secrets.

"I actually came to make sure you're watching the weather," I said. "The hurricane's been downgraded to a tropical storm, but we're supposed to get rain and maybe tornadoes tomorrow."

"You think I don't have a smart phone?"

I heard my voice rising, despite myself. "I have never laid eyes on your smart phone. *You never let me in your house.*" I took a deep breath to calm down. "Also, may I borrow your car? I'll bring it back tomorrow after school."

"No," he said. "Same reason I didn't want you to borrow it on Labor Day. Chantel and I may want to get ice cream later."

I put my hands in my hair and pressed my lips together to keep from bursting into laughter, a yelling fit, or both. Granddad was being petty. But I was so relieved to find out it was because he was in love.

I cleared my throat. "May I please walk over and borrow your car before school tomorrow? I'll bring it back as soon as class is over. Mom and Dad have a divorce hearing. Mom needs to be at the courthouse a lot longer than I do because of meetings with her lawyer. I don't want to miss a whole day of school. I'm just testifying that their marriage is irretrievably broken."

Granddad grinned—the first time I'd seen him smile in a long, long while. "In that case," he said, "I'll deliver the car to your house."

The next day at noon, I sat on a polished bench in the marble-lined foyer of the courthouse in Clearwater, holding Mom's hand and waiting for the divorce hearing. Her lawyer was there. My dad's lawyer sat across from us, but my dad hadn't shown. Mom whispered that maybe he wouldn't, and the proceedings could go on without him interrupting them this time.

Thunder rolled outside.

Ten minutes before we were scheduled to appear in court, the front doors of the courthouse opened, and my heart sank.

But it wasn't my dad. It was Granddad and Chantel under an enormous umbrella. Outside on the street, their taxi pulled away.

I looked over at Mom. Her mouth was wide open. I wasn't sure what surprised her more: that Granddad had come to support her, or that he was guiding a glamorous lady friend by the elbow.

Granddad folded the umbrella and propped it up by the entrance, then brought Chantel over. Mom was all smiles as they moved away from the bench to make introductions and talk quietly.

I wanted to give Mom time alone with them. And I was too nervous to make small talk. I watched the clock and crossed my fingers.

Five minutes before we were scheduled to appear, the front doors of the courthouse opened again, and my heart sank all the way to the floor. My dad walked in, wearing his Coast Guard dress uniform, dripping from the downpour. He looked like a handsome, upstanding family man. I knew better.

He glanced around the foyer. His eyes skimmed across his lawyer and Mom's, lingered on Mom and Granddad, and landed on me. "Harper," he said curtly, like an order. He pointed to his feet.

Without even looking at Mom, I jumped up out of habit. It was only when I'd already hurried halfway across the room to him that I realized I was acting like his dog. But he was my dad, and I still had to do what he said—for a few more months.

He stared down at me sternly, trying to scare me. It was working. I considered crossing my eyes at him, because the tension was ridiculous.

He seethed, "If you testify against me in this court today, you are dead to me. Do you understand? I will pay child support until you turn eighteen because the law requires it, but after that, you don't exist."

Suddenly I realized how cold it was in the courthouse. I crossed my arms to warm myself and told my dad, "You've been dead to me since last Wednesday, when you shouted at me. I'm glad we've got that straight." I turned on my heel and walked back toward the bench.

Mom and Granddad looked over their shoulders at me.

I stopped in the middle of the foyer. This is exactly what I'd done yesterday: dumped Brody and regretted it instantly. Taking charge of my life was one thing. It was another thing entirely to throw important parts of it away.

I walked right back to my dad and put my hands on my hips. His jaw was working back forth, and he was blinking back tears.

I said gently, "I didn't mean that. You'll never be dead to me, no matter what. You're my dad."

No matter how I acted, I was still furious for what he'd said to me just then, and how he'd treated Mom for years. But I thought of him taking me to Granddad's beach when I was tiny, before we left for Alaska, and twirling me around in the warm waves.

I stood on my tiptoes and kissed Dad on the cheek.

Seventeen

ONLY A FEW MINUTES LATER, I WALKED OUT OF the courtroom as the daughter of soon-to-be-divorced parents, thank God. I hadn't even needed to testify after all. Dad hadn't contested the divorce this time or asked the judge to send my parents to counseling. Mom hugged me afterward and whispered that I deserved the credit. The way I felt, I expected a bright blue sky and a rainbow when I swung open the courthouse door.

Instead, the tropical storm had arrived. The rain was coming down so hard that an inch of water stood on the sidewalk. I opened my umbrella and waded back to Granddad's car.

Inside, I turned my phone on and checked my messages. I had a text from Brody, sent just a few minutes ago: *Where are you?* I hadn't told him or anyone in study hall that I would be absent.

He cared about me, in spite of everything. I felt myself flush, which meant I was very far gone.

I texted him back, *Parents divorcing, hooray! Driving back from courthouse.* I threw my phone into my purse and my purse into the back seat so I wouldn't be tempted to look at my phone again. Lately I'd been trying to embrace my daredevil side, but I wasn't dumb.

As I drove from Clearwater back home, I kept thinking I heard my phone beep with more texts. I suspected they were from Brody, and I was dying to know what they said. But I couldn't even be sure I'd heard the beeping. The rain was torrential, pounding on the car like a hundred high-pressure fire hoses. When I drove faster than thirty miles an hour, it was hard to keep the car on the road.

By the time I finally pulled into the school parking lot, the rain had stopped. I suspected the calm was only temporary, though. The air was thick with steam and the smells of rain and hot asphalt. The sky was light gray and swirling strangely.

Leaving all my stuff in my car except my camera and tripod, I hurried across the parking lot packed with cars but empty of people, into the football stadium. So quickly that my legs ached, I ran up the stairs to the highest point and looked over the guardrail.

Beyond the school campus stretched a residential section of town. Roofs peeked above the lush canopy of palm trees and live oaks. Then there was a thin strip of white beach, and the ocean: an endless stretch of angry gray waves.

A waterspout—a tornado over the water rather than the

land—snaked down from black clouds to dip its toe in the water elegantly, like a dancer. It glowed white against the sky.

I was glad I had lots of practice setting up my tripod, attaching the camera, and adjusting the settings. In seconds I was snapping photos, then switching the settings and snapping again, so I was sure to get at least one perfect photo out of hundreds.

Several minutes passed before it occurred to me that if there was one tornado, there might be more. We didn't have tornado sirens in Pinellas County, so I wouldn't know until it hit me, unless I saw it coming. But as I looked behind me at the landward side of town, I didn't see another twister. All I noticed was Brody standing way down at the stadium entrance.

"Lightning!" He pointed at the blinking southern sky.

I glanced back at my waterspout and snapped one more rapid-fire set of shots as it twisted up into the sky and disappeared. Then I swept up my tripod without pausing to detach the camera and hauled ass down the stairs.

"There's a tornado warning," he said, following me with his hand on my back as we hurried toward the school. "The rotation is close enough that everybody's crouched in the halls with their heads down, but I was afraid you wouldn't be able to get in because the doors are locked. Ms. Patel said I could come look . . . for . . . What are you doing?"

I sat down in Granddad's car. "Get in so we're not struck by lightning." I opened my laptop and plugged in my camera.

"You're getting online?" he asked, astonished.

"I photographed the tornado, and I'm about to sell the picture to the Tampa newspaper."

"Harper," he said as I typed. "Harper, remember when I told you that you should take risks only when you can get away with them? If that picture is published, the school will figure out you were on top of the stadium during a tornado. You might get suspended. Save it for your portfolio, maybe—"

"I hadn't checked in yet, so the school wasn't in charge of me." I finished composing my e-mail to the Tampa newspaper editor and attached the photo.

"You're not just trying to prove how daring you are to get me back, are you?"

"Hold on for a minute." The photo loaded, and I hit send. "What were you saying?"

"Nothing," he said, eyeing me across the car.

"I would love to date you again," I burst, riding the adrenaline high I hadn't even registered until now. "We had so much fun, and I don't want to throw that away. The school is on crack for *not* pairing us together."

He grabbed me in a hug across the seat. I settled my head against his shoulder. He squeezed me gently and ran his fingertips through my hair.

Then he released me and sat up. "Yes, ma'am," he said, grinning. "Now let's go back, before we get in trouble."

We dashed across the parking lot. Inside the school, students lined the walls three people deep. As we were about to sit down too, the bell rang to cancel the warning. Everyone got up as one body and stretched.

"While we have a minute," I said, putting one hand on Brody's chest, "I've been thinking. Maybe if I told Mr. Oakley I would sign back on as yearbook photographer, he would make a few concessions. The Superlatives section isn't due to the publisher until Friday. I could ask to redesign Kennedy's ugly Superlatives pages and replace our Perfect Couple photo."

"Do you have an idea for it?"

I pulled my camera off the tripod, adjusted the settings, and handed it to Brody. "You take a selfie because your arm is longer. The camera's set to take five in a row, so just grin through it." We put our heads close together. "One, two—"

I smiled, and the camera flashed. By now we were getting pushed from all directions by the traffic in the hall. We moved over to the lockers and peered at the view screen. Both of us laughed. Brody looked happy and satisfied. I looked excited. Behind us, the hallway was filled with people, some photobombing us with their tongues sticking out, some ignoring us and absorbed in their own lives.

"I like this concept," I said. "See? The whole school is behind us."

"I like your glasses," he said. "You look sexy as hell. Come here." He looped the camera strap over my shoulder and wrapped his arms around me.

"This is against school rules," I said. "Talk about being in danger of getting caught—"

"I don't care," he whispered in my ear. "I was worried about you in the storm. I'm just glad you're safe." He squeezed me once more and let me go.

At the football game the following Friday night, the photographer for the local newspaper approached me on the sidelines with his hand out for me to shake. I was thrilled. I knew exactly who he was. I'd seen him snapping pictures of the games for years. I'd wanted to *be* him for years.

He asked, "You're Harper Davis, right?"

"That's right."

He introduced himself, then said, "Great shot of the waterspout in the Tampa paper."

"Thanks. That was just luck. And a tripod."

He shook his head. "You're a photographer. You make your own luck. Even now, look at you. Your eyes haven't left the game. You're scouting for a photo."

I smiled, because it was true. As we'd talked, I'd kept watching the field, determined not to miss a key play.

"You're still in high school?" he asked. "That's impressive work. I expect you'll go places."

We chatted for a few more minutes about my camera and his camera, and the best shots he'd taken of Tropical Storm Debby a few years ago. As I conversed with him, my eyes stole over to Brody, laughing with a local policeman who stood guard every game at the gate onto the field.

I wondered if Brody and I might be back here in five years

or ten years or more, me photographing the game while he kept it safe. This wasn't necessarily *the* future, but it was *a* future. And a nice one to dream about. One I never would have considered if it hadn't been for a botched yearbook election mistakenly telling us who we were, and helping us find out the truth for ourselves.

The photographer moved off in search of a better angle as the other team punted and Brody ran for the center of the field, tugging his helmet on as he went.

And then, on the first play, he got sacked. I had a telephoto view, because I was shooting pictures of him when it happened.

I dropped my camera. The weight of it jerked the strap around my neck as I slapped my hands over my mouth in horror.

Five thousand people in the stadium hushed at one time. Every coach ran onto the grass. The entire football team and the visiting team took a knee. The paramedics from an ambulance parked beyond the end zone wheeled a stretcher onto the field.

I was sure he was paralyzed until Noah, huge in his helmet and pads, jogged toward me. He put both hands on my shoulders. "Brody's okay," he panted.

"Brody's okay?" I shrieked.

"I mean, he will be. He didn't hit his head. Coach ordered a stretcher as a precaution because of Brody's concussion in the summer. This time he only got the wind knocked out of him."

"Thank you," I sighed.

"I couldn't let you freak out over here," he said.

"Thank you, Noah." I wrapped both arms around his wet jersey.

"And I didn't even fall on him this time." Noah put a gloved hand in my hair. "I've got to go." He disentangled himself from me and ran back onto the field with the rest of the offensive line plus the second-string quarterback. Ten men surrounded the stretcher rolling off the field toward the ambulance. The stadium gave Brody a standing ovation.

Blinking back tears, I walked over to the ambulance and stood a few yards away, out of the commotion. Paramedics busied themselves around Brody. Coaches climbed in and out of the truck. Brody's mom appeared from the stands, the tracks of her tears visible through her makeup. I recognized her from a million elementary school parties, and from pictures of her in her own house at parties Brody had thrown when she wasn't home.

I waited, heart racing.

One by one, the coaches went back to the team on the sidelines. But I didn't believe Noah was right, and Brody was okay, until his mom jumped down from the ambulance, smiling and wiping her eyes. She walked around the fence to climb into the stands again.

I heaved one huge sigh of relief, then walked over.

"No pictures," said a paramedic sitting on the bumper of the ambulance, watching the game. He eyed my camera.

"I'm his girlfriend."

"Oh." He moved aside for me.

I climbed into the back of the ambulance, my heart beating harder and faster. No matter what Noah had said, it was terrifying to see Brody lying on a stretcher that wasn't quite big enough for his body, surrounded by sinister equipment. His helmet and jersey and shoulder pads lay heaped in a corner. He wore an athletic shirt with high-tech pads sewn into the sides. With his arms crossed on his chest, he looked slender and young and vulnerable. His long, wet hair had escaped from his headband and stuck to his forehead. His eyes were closed.

I took his hand and squeezed it.

He squeezed back, opening one eye to look at me. He closed his eyes again. "I'm okay. I couldn't breathe for a minute."

"Is that all?"

He laughed shortly. "Did you see the guy who got me? He must have weighed five hundred pounds."

The guy hadn't been that big, but football players probably looked a lot bigger to Brody when they were about to sack him. I decided to delete that series of pictures.

"I was just lying here"—he took a deep breath and exhaled slowly—"doing the relaxation exercise you taught me. I think I'm ready to go back."

"Are you sure?" I asked. The alarm from seeing him flat on the field, not moving, was too fresh.

"The paramedics already cleared me," he said. "I didn't hit my head."

"If you did," I said, "would you know?"

"Maybe not," he admitted.

I let go of his hand and held up seven fingers.

"Seven," he said.

"Who's your best friend?"

"Noah."

"How long have you played football together?"

"Since third grade." He answered every question with no hesitation. His brain was working fine.

"What are you doing after the game?" I asked.

"I'm going to the Crab Lab. With you. We haven't talked about what we'll do after that, but I was planning to get you to your granddad's beach again and show you what a perfect couple we are."

"Oh, really," I said archly. "Are you looking forward to that?"

He crooked his finger at me. I leaned closer. He whispered, "This is going to be our best night yet." His mouth caught mine in a sexy kiss.

Then he sat up slowly. "Goddamn, I'm going to hurt tomorrow. But right now, I feel great. Let's go play some football!"

I fished his pads out of the corner of the ambulance. "You're crazy, you know that? You definitely hit your head."

After we got him suited up, he jumped down from the ambulance. With a last salute to me, he jogged along the sidelines to rejoin his team and finish his adventure.

I brought up my camera and snapped a picture.

ACKNOWLEDGMENTS

Heartfelt thanks to my editor and favorite cheerleader, Annette Pollert. Every author of YA romance should be lucky enough to have an editor who draws little hearts on the manuscript.

To my brilliant agent, Laura Bradford. I would not be here without you.

And to my long-suffering critique partner, the best friend I could wish for, Victoria Dahl.

Most Likely to Succeed

For readers of
Biggest Flirts *and* Perfect Couple
who told me you couldn't wait for
Kaye and Sawyer's book. I appreciate you.

One

I LEFT CALCULUS A MINUTE BEFORE THE BELL SO I'd be the first to arrive at the student council meeting. Our advisor, Ms. Yates, would sit at the back of the classroom, observing, and I wanted her vacated desk at the front of the room. At our last meeting, Aidan had taken her desk in a show of presidential authority. But as vice president, I was the one who needed room for paperwork. A better boyfriend than Aidan would have let me sit at the desk.

A better girlfriend than me would have let *him* have it.

And that pretty much summed up our three years of dating.

The bell rang just as I reached the room. I stood outside the door, waiting for Ms. Yates to make her coffee run to the teachers' lounge and for her freshman science class to flood past me. A few of them glanced at me, their eyes widening as if I were a celebrity. I remembered this feeling from when I was an underclassman, looking up to my brother and his friends. It was strange to be on the receiving end.

As the last of the ninth graders escaped down the hall, I stepped into the room, which should have been empty.

Instead, Sawyer De Luca sat behind Ms. Yates's desk. He must have left his last class *two* minutes before the bell to beat me here.

Sensing my presence, he turned in the chair, flashing deep blue eyes at me, the color of the September sky out the window behind him. When Sawyer's hair was combed—which I'd seen happen once or twice in the couple of years I'd known him—it looked platinum blond. Today, as usual, it was a mess, with the nearly white, sun-streaked layers sticking up on top, and the dark blond layers peeking out underneath. He had on his favorite shirt, which he wore at least two times a week, the madras short-sleeved button-down with blue stripes that made his eyes stand out even more. His khaki shorts were rumpled. I couldn't see his feet beneath the desk, but I knew he wore his beat-up flip-flops. In short, if you'd never met Sawyer before, you'd assume he was a hot but harmless teenage beach bum.

I knew better.

I closed the door behind me so nobody would witness the argument we were about to have. I wanted that desk. I suspected he understood this, which was why he'd sat there. But long experience with Sawyer told me flouncing in and complaining wouldn't do me any good. That's what he expected me to do.

So I walked in with a bigger grin on my face than I'd ever given Sawyer. "Hi!"

He smiled serenely back at me. "Hello, Kaye. You look beautiful in yellow."

His sweet remark shot me through the heart. My friend Harper had just altered this dress to fit me. I didn't need her beautifully homemade hand-me-downs, but I was glad to take them—especially this sixties A-line throwback as vivid as the Florida sunshine. After a rocky couple of weeks for romance with Aidan, I'd dressed carefully this morning, craving praise from him. *He* hadn't said a word.

Leave it to Sawyer to catch me off guard. He'd done the same thing last Saturday night. After two years of teasing and taunting me, out of the blue he'd told me he loved my new hairstyle. I always had a ready response for his insults, but these compliments threw me off.

"Thanks," I managed, setting my books down on the edge of the desk, along with my tablet and my loose-leaf binder for student council projects. Then I said brightly, "So, Mr. Parliamentarian, what's *modus operandi* for letting the vice president have the desk? I need to spread out."

"*I* need to spread out." He patted the stack of library books in front of him: an ancient tome that explained procedure for meetings, called *Robert's Rules of Order*, plus a couple of modern discussions of how the rules worked. For once Sawyer had done his homework.

"Taking the parliamentarian job seriously, are we?" This

was my fourth year in student council. We'd always elected a parliamentarian without fully understanding what the title meant. Ms. Yates said the parliamentarian was the rule police, but we'd never needed policing with a charismatic president at the helm and Ms. Yates lurking in the back. Nobody ran for parliamentarian during officer elections in the spring. Ms. Yates waited until school started in the fall, then pointed out that "student council parliamentarian" would look great on college applications. One study hall representative volunteered, got approved, and never lifted a finger during meetings.

Until now. "I have to be able to see everything and look stuff up quickly." Sawyer swept his hand across his books and a legal pad inscribed with tiny cryptic notes. "Last meeting, Aidan didn't follow parliamentary procedure at *all*. But I'll share the desk with you." He stood and headed for the back of the room, where a cart was stacked with extra folding chairs for the meeting.

Normally I would have told him not to bother retrieving a chair for me. His suggestion that we share a desk was the best way to make me drop the subject and sit down elsewhere. He knew I wouldn't want Aidan to think we were flirting.

But this week wasn't normal. Aidan had hurt my feelings last Saturday by dissing my hair. We'd made up by Sunday—at least, I'd told him I forgave him—but I wasn't quite over the insult. The idea of him walking into the room and seeing Sawyer and me at Ms. Yates's desk together was incredibly appealing.

Sawyer held the folding chair high above his head as he made his way toward me. He unfolded the chair behind the desk. I started to sit down in it.

"No, that's for me. I meant for you to have the comfy chair." He rolled Ms. Yates's chair over, waited for me to sit, and pushed me a few inches toward the desk, like my dad seating my mother in a restaurant. He plopped down in the folding chair. "Will you marry me?"

Now *this* was something I'd expected him to ask. In fact, it was the first thing he'd ever said to me when he moved to town two years ago. Back then I'd uttered an outraged "No!" He'd wanted to know why—he wasn't good enough for me? Who did I think I was, a bank president's daughter?

After a while, though, I'd gotten wise to Sawyer's game. Every girl in school knew he wasn't exclusive and meant nothing by his flirtations. That didn't stop any of us from having a soft spot for this hard-living boy. And it didn't stop me from feeling special every time he paid me attention.

Something had changed this school year when he started practicing with us cheerleaders in his pelican costume as school mascot. He stood right behind me on the football field, imitating my every step, even after I whirled around and slapped him on his foam beak. When we danced the Wobble, he moved the wrong way on purpose, running into me. With no warning he often rushed up, lifted me high, and gave me full-body, full-feathered hugs. Because he was in costume, everybody, including Aidan, knew it was a joke.

Only I took it seriously. I enjoyed it too much and wished he'd do the same things to me with the costume off.

My crush on him was hopeless. He was toying with me, like he toyed with everyone. Plus, I was committed to Aidan. Lately this was hard to remember.

"Yes, of course I'll marry you," I told Sawyer, making sure I sounded sarcastic.

The door opened, letting in the noise from the hall. "Hey," Will said, lilting that one syllable in his Minnesota accent. Lucky for him, derision about the way he talked had waned over the first five weeks of school. He'd started dating my friend Tia, who gave people the stink eye when they badmouthed him. And he'd made friends with Sawyer—a smart move on Will's part. Sawyer could be a strong ally or a powerful enemy.

Sawyer waited for a couple more classroom representatives to follow Will toward the back of the room. Then he turned to me again. "Would you go to the prom with me?"

"Yes." This was the game. He asked me a series of questions, starting with the outlandish ones. I said yes to those. Eventually he asked me something that wasn't as crazy, forcing me to give him the obvious answer: I had a boyfriend.

Here it came. "Will you sit with me in the van to the game tonight?"

A spark of excitement shot through me. A few weeks ago, Sawyer had passed out from the heat on the football field in his heavy mascot costume. Ever since, he'd ditched the suit during cheerleading practice and worked out with the football team instead, claiming he needed to get in better shape to withstand entire games dressed up as a pelican.

I missed him at cheerleading. I'd assumed he would ride with the football players to our first away game, but I wished he would ride in the cheerleader van. Now my wish was coming true.

Careful not to sound too eager, I said, "I didn't know you were riding with us. You've been more football player than cheerleader lately."

"I'm a pelican without a country," he said. "Some unfortunate things may have gotten superglued to other things in the locker room after football practice yesterday. The guys went to the coach and said they don't want me to ride on the bus with them because they're scared of what I'll do. The coach *agreed.* Can you believe that? I'm not even innocent until proven guilty."

"*Are* you guilty?" Knowing Sawyer, I didn't blame the team for accusing him.

"Yes," he admitted, "but they didn't know that for sure." He settled his elbow on the desk and his chin in his hand, watching me. "You, on the other hand, understand I never mean any harm. You'll sit with me in the van, right?"

I wanted to. My face burned with desire—desire for a *seat*, of all things. Next to a boy who was nothing but trouble.

And I knew my line. "We can't sit together, Sawyer. Aidan wouldn't like it."

Sawyer's usual response would be to imitate me in a sneering voice: *Aidan wouldn't like it!*

Instead, he grabbed Ms. Yates's chair and rolled me closer to him. Keeping his hands very near my bare knees, he looked straight into my eyes and asked softly, "Why do you stay with Aidan when he bosses you around? You don't let anyone else do that."

Tia and my friend Harper grilled me at every opportunity about why I stayed with Aidan, too, but they didn't bring up the subject while representatives for the entire school could hear. My eyes flicked over to the student council members, who were filling the desks and noisily dragging extra chairs off the cart, and Ms. Yates, who was making her way toward the back of the room with her coffee. Aidan himself would be here any second.

I told Sawyer quietly but firmly, "*You* would boss me around just as much as Aidan does. What's the difference?"

"That's not true." Sawyer moved even closer. I watched his lips as he said, "I wouldn't ask for much. What I wanted, you would give me willingly."

Time stopped. The bustle around us went silent. The classroom disappeared. All that was left was Sawyer's mouth forming words that weren't *necessarily* dirty, yet promised a dark night alone in the cab of his truck. My face flushed hot, my breasts tightened underneath my cute yellow bodice, and electricity shot straight to my crotch.

The many nights I'd pulled Tia away from Sawyer at

parties over the past two years, she'd drunkenly explained that he had a way of talking her panties off. I'd heard this from other girls too. And he'd flirted with me millions of times, making me feel special, but never quite *this* special. Now I understood what Tia and those other girls had meant.

Abruptly, I sat up and rolled my chair back.

He straightened more slowly, smirking. He knew exactly what effect he'd had on me.

Bewildered, I breathed, "How did you do that?"

"It's a gift."

His cavalier tone ticked me off, and I regained my own voice. "That's what I would worry about. During study hall, you give me the 'gift'"—I made finger quotes—"but you've moved on to the next girl by lunch. No thanks."

His face fell. "No, I—"

Aidan sashayed in, greeting the crowd as he came, already starting the meeting.

Sawyer lowered his voice but kept whispering to me as if nothing else were going on and Aidan weren't there. He said, "I wouldn't do that to you. I wouldn't cheat on you, ever."

Aidan turned around in front of the desk and gave us an outraged look for talking while he was making a speech. Sawyer didn't see it, but I did. I faced forward and opened my student council binder, cheeks still burning.

Sawyer had complimented me, part of a strange new trend.

He'd dropped the playful teasing and blatantly come on to me, a brand-new pleasure.

And he'd gotten upset at my tart response, like he actually cared.

I leaned ever so slightly toward him to give the electricity an easier time jumping the arc from my shoulder to his. His face was tinged pink, unusual for Sawyer, who was difficult to embarrass. I was dying to know whether he felt the buzz too.

Apparently not. I jumped in my chair, startled, as he banged the gavel on the block that Ms. Yates had placed on her desk for Aidan. "Point of order, Mr. President," Sawyer said. "Have you officially started the meeting? You haven't asked the secretary to read the minutes."

"We don't have time," Aidan said. Dismissing Sawyer, he turned back to the forty representatives crowding the room. He hadn't argued with us about who got Ms. Yates's desk, after all. He didn't need to. Instead of presiding over the council from here, he simply reasserted his authority by running the meeting while standing up. Sawyer and I looked like his secretarial pool.

"We have a lot to cover," Aidan explained to the reps, and I got lost in following him with my eyes and listening to him, fascinated as ever. About this time of year in ninth grade, he'd captured my attention. Previously he'd been just another dork I'd known since kindergarten. I'd preferred older guys, even if they didn't prefer *me*.

But that year, Aidan had come back from summer break taller than before, and more self-assured than any other boy I knew. That's why I'd fallen for him. Confidence was sexy.

That's also why, until recently, I'd felt a rush of familiarity and belonging and pride whenever I glimpsed him across a room.

After years with him, however, I was finally coming to understand he wasn't as sure of himself as he wanted people to believe. He was so quick to anger. He couldn't take being challenged. But as I watched him work the room like a pro, with the freshman reps timidly returning his broad smile, I remembered exactly what I'd seen in him back then.

Sawyer looked bored already.

"We're entering the busiest season for the council," Aidan was saying, "and we desperately need volunteers to make these projects happen. Our vice president, Ms. Gordon, will now report on the homecoming court elections coming up a week from Monday, and the float for the court in the homecoming parade."

"And the dance," I called.

"There's not going to be a homecoming dance," he told me over his shoulder. "I'll explain later. Go ahead and fill them in about the homecoming court—"

Several reps gasped, "What?" while others murmured, "What did he say?" I spoke for everyone by uttering an outraged "What do you mean, there's not going to be a dance?"

"Ms. Yates"—he nodded to where she sat in the back of the room, and she nodded in turn—"informed me before the meeting that the school is closing the gym for repairs. The storm last week damaged the roof. It's not safe for occupancy. That's bad news for us, but of course it's even worse news for the basketball teams. The school needs time to repair the gym before their season starts."

Will raised his hand.

Ignoring Will, Aidan kept talking. "All of us need to get out there in the halls and reassure the basketball teams and their fans that our school is behind them."

I frowned at the back of Aidan's head. He used this bait-and-switch method all the time, getting out of a sticky argument by distracting people (including me) with a different argument altogether. Basketball season was six weeks away. The homecoming dance didn't have to die so easily. But hosting the event would be harder now, and Aidan didn't want to bother.

I did.

"Help," I pleaded with Sawyer under my breath.

Aidan had already moved on, introducing my talk about the election committee.

Out in the crowd Will called, "Excuse me." An interruption like this hadn't happened in any council meeting I'd attended, ever. "Wait a minute. My class wants the dance."

I couldn't see Aidan's face from this angle, but he drew his shoulders back and stood up straighter. He was about to give Will a snarky put-down.

Sawyer watched me, blond brows knitted. He didn't understand what I wanted.

"Complain about something in the book again," I whispered, nodding at *Robert's Rules of Order*. "Ms. Yates hasn't stopped Aidan from railroading the meeting. She obviously doesn't want the dance either, but they can't fight the book."

Everyone jumped as Sawyer banged the gavel. "The council recognizes Mr. Matthews, senior from Mr. Frank's class. Stand up, sir."

We'd never had reps rise to speak before. I was pretty sure the rules of order didn't say anything about this. But it was a good move on Sawyer's part. At Will's full height he had a few inches on Aidan, and when he crossed his muscular arms on his chest, his body practically shouted that nobody better try to budge him.

Before Aidan could protest, Will said in his strangely rounded accent, "I haven't lived here long, but I get the impression that the homecoming dance is a huge deal at this school. Everyone in Mr. Frank's class has been talking about it and looking forward to it. We can't simply cancel at the first sign of trouble."

"We just did," Aidan snapped. "Now sit down while I'm talking."

Sawyer banged the gavel. I should have gotten used to it by now, but I jumped in my seat again.

Aidan visibly flinched. He turned on Sawyer and snatched the gavel away. Holding it up, he seethed, "Don't do that again, De Luca. You're not in charge here. I'm the president."

"Then act like it," I said.

Aidan turned his angry gaze on me. I stared right back at

him, determined not to chicken out. Will and Sawyer and I were right about this. Aidan was wrong.

As I watched, Aidan's expression changed from fury to something different: disappointment. I'd betrayed him. We'd had a long talk last week about why we couldn't get along lately. He understood I disagreed with him sometimes, but he wanted us to settle our differences in private, presenting a united front to the school as the president and his vice president.

Now I'd broken his rule. No matter what the council decided, he wouldn't forgive me for defying him in public.

And I didn't care. Keeping the peace wasn't worth letting him act like a dictator.

"We don't have *time* to debate this in a half-hour meeting," he repeated. "There's nothing to debate. The decision has been made. The school already canceled the dance because we don't have a location for it."

"We'll move it," I said.

"It's only two weeks away," he said.

I shrugged. "You put me in charge of the dance committee. It's our job to give it a shot."

Aidan's voice rose. He'd forgotten we'd agreed not to argue in public. "You're only pitching a fit about this because you're still mad about—"

"Give me that," Sawyer interrupted, holding out his hand for the gavel.

"No," Aidan said, moving the gavel above his head.

"Mr. President," Sawyer said in a lower, reasonable tone,

like talking to a hysterical child, "you're not allowed to debate the issue."

"Of course I am. I'm the president!"

"Exactly. *Robert's Rules of Order* states that your responsibilities are to run the meeting and give everyone the opportunity to speak. If you want to express your opinion, you need to vacate the chair."

"I'm not *in* the chair," Aidan snapped. "*You're* in the chair."

"I mean," Sawyer said, rolling his eyes, "you need to step down as president while we discuss this matter, and let Kaye preside over the meeting."

"I'm not stepping down."

"Then you need to shut up."

"Sawyer," Ms. Yates said sharply. I couldn't see her behind Will, who was still standing, but her thin voice cut like a knife through the grumbling and shushing in the classroom. "You're being disruptive."

"On the contrary, Ms. Yates," Sawyer called back, "the president is being disruptive, trying to bend the entire council to his will. Ms. Patel's study hall elected me to represent them. The student council approved me as parliamentarian. It's my duty to make sure we follow the procedure set down in the council bylaws. Otherwise, a student could sue the school for a violation of rights and due process."

The room fell silent, waiting for Ms. Yates's response. Horrible visions flashed through my mind of what would happen next. Ms. Yates might complain to Ms. Chen that

Sawyer was disrespectful. They could remove him from student council or, worse, from his position as school mascot. All because he'd helped me when I asked.

Underneath the desk, I put my hand on his knee.

"Sawyer," Ms. Yates finally said, "you may continue, but don't tell anybody else to shut up."

"So noted." Sawyer pretended to scribble this reminder to himself. Actually he drew a smiley face in *Robert's Rules of Order*. "Aidan, if you're really running the meeting, let Will bring up the idea of saving the dance, then put it to a vote."

Aidan glared at Sawyer. Suddenly he whacked the gavel so hard on the block on Ms. Yates's desk that even Sawyer jumped.

Sawyer didn't take that kind of challenge sitting down. I gripped his knee harder, signaling him to stay in his seat. If he could swallow this last insult from Aidan, he and I had won.

Two

THE REMAINING TWENTY MINUTES OF THE meeting seemed to take forever. But Aidan followed procedure—at least I figured he did, because Sawyer didn't speak up again. By the time the bell rang to send us to lunch, the council had agreed that as head of the dance committee, I would now be in charge of relocating the event instead of canceling it.

On top of leading the committee in charge of homecoming court elections.

And leading the committee in charge of the parade float. I didn't understand why Aidan opposed the council taking on more projects when he simply passed all the work to me.

As everyone crowded Ms. Yates's door, Sawyer stood and stretched. Then he leaned over and said in my ear, "We make a good team. Maybe you and I got off on the wrong foot."

"For two years?" I asked.

He opened his mouth to respond but stopped. Aidan

brushed past the desk on his way out the door. He didn't say a word to me.

Will was the last rep remaining in the empty room. He paused in front of the desk. "Thanks, you guys, for taking my side."

"Thanks for taking ours," I said, standing up and gathering my stuff, which was tangled with Sawyer's stuff. One side of my open binder had gotten caught beneath his books.

"For me, this wasn't just about the dance," Will said. "People have been talking about it, and Tia told me what fun it was last year. Of course . . ." He glanced sidelong at Sawyer.

I knew what that look meant. Sawyer and Tia used to fool around periodically, up until she and Will started dating a few weeks ago. The homecoming dance last year had been no different. Too late, Will realized what he'd brought up.

"It *was* fun," I interjected before Sawyer could make a snide comment that everyone would regret. "Come on." I ushered them both toward the door.

"I was student council president back in Duluth." Will followed us into the hall and closed Ms. Yates's door behind us. Down at the end of the freshman corridor, a teacher frowned at us. Will lowered his voice as he said, "That is, I was *supposed* to be president this year, before my family moved. I know what the president is supposed to do, and Aidan's not *doon* it. Sometimes you have to stand up and tell somebody, 'You're not *doon* it right.'"

I thought Sawyer would make fun of Will's Norse *doon*. He might have stopped insulting Will behind his back, but he wouldn't be able to resist a comment to his face. Yet he didn't say a word about Will's accent.

Instead, Sawyer grumbled, "If the storm had destroyed the gym completely, the business community would rally around us, give us money, and solve the problem for us. They'd get lots of publicity for hosting our homecoming dance. Nobody's going to help us just because our roof leaks."

"Leaking isn't good PR," Will agreed. "I signed up for the dance committee and I want to help, but I'm the worst person to think of ideas for where else to hold an event. I still don't know this town very well."

"Doesn't the Crab Lab also own the event space down the block?" I asked Sawyer. "One of my mother's assistants had her wedding reception there. Could you sweet-talk the owner into letting us use it for cheap? Better yet, for free?"

"It's booked that night," he said.

"That's two weeks from now," I pointed out. "You've memorized the schedule for the event space down the block?"

"A fortieth class reunion is meeting there after the homecoming game," he said. "The owner asked me to wait tables. I said no because of the dance. I have an excellent memory for turning down money."

Sawyer waited tables a lot. While a good portion of our class was at the beach, he often went missing because he was working. Even though he'd helped me in the meeting, I was a little surprised the dance was important enough to him personally that he would take the night off.

And, irrationally, I was jealous. As we stopped in the hall and waited for Will to swing open the door of the lunchroom, I asked Sawyer, "Who are you taking to homecoming?"

He gaped at me. "You!" he exclaimed, like this was the most obvious answer in the world and I had a lot of nerve to joke about it. He stomped into the lunchroom.

Will was left holding the door open for me and blinking at us. He didn't understand the strange social customs of Florida.

"It would help if you could brainstorm over the weekend," I told Will, pretending my episode with Sawyer hadn't happened. "Ask around at lunch and on the band bus tonight. See if you can scare up ideas. Maybe we'll think of something by the next meeting."

"Sounds good," he called after me as I headed across the lunchroom to the teacher section.

Aidan, Ms. Yates, and I had eaten at one end of a faculty table after the last council meeting, discussing projects like the dance. Possibly the one thing worse than spending lunch with Aidan while he was mad at me was spending lunch with Aidan and Ms. Yates, who, judging from the expression on her face, hadn't liked how the meeting had gone down. But I was the vice president, so I straightened my shoulders and walked over.

They were deep in conversation. Trying not to interrupt them, I looped the strap of my book bag over the back of the chair beside Aidan. They both looked up anyway. I said,

"Sorry. I didn't know we were meeting, or I would have gotten here sooner. I'll just grab a salad and be right with y—"

Ms. Yates interrupted me. "This is a private talk."

"Oh" was all I could think of to say. My face tingled with embarrassment as I slipped my bag off the chair and beat a retreat across the lunchroom to the safety of Tia, Harper, and the rest of my friends. By the time I finally sat down with my salad, they were spitting out and shooting down ideas for where to have the dance—led by Will, who repeated how angry he was at Aidan for what he'd been *doon* in the meeting.

I listened and waited for them to come up with something brilliant. For once I stayed silent. I still smarted from Ms. Yates telling me I didn't belong at the adult table anymore. And I wondered whether I deserved it. Lately I got so *furious* at Aidan, but I was probably going through an immature phase, like cold feet before a wedding. We'd known almost since we started dating that we were destined for each other. All summer we'd been planning to apply to Columbia University together. Whenever Aidan annoyed me, I needed to take a deep breath before I spoke—as my mother reminded me each time I mouthed off to her—and make sure the problem was really with him, not me.

And I knew in my heart that the problem was mine. Since the school year started, I'd been creeping toward a crush on Sawyer like peering cautiously down from a great height. The Superlatives mix-up had put me over the edge.

On the first day of school, the student council had run Superlatives elections for the senior class. We *thought*

Harper and our school's star quarterback, Brody, had been voted Perfect Couple That Never Was. If I'd been in charge of the elections, as in years past, that mistake wouldn't have been made. Even though I was still the chair of the elections committee, Ms. Yates wouldn't let me count the votes. Since I was a senior this year, I had a conflict of interest.

But without me to watch over them, the wayward juniors had screwed up the whole election. They said I'd been chosen Most Likely to Succeed with Aidan. That sounded right. He was president. I was vice president.

Here's what didn't make sense: In reality I'd been elected Perfect Couple That Never Was with Sawyer.

When I realized the juniors' mistake, Ms. Yates had made me tell Brody and Harper they didn't really win the title, since they'd started dating because of it. But I wasn't allowed to divulge the truth to anyone else. Each person in the class could get a maximum of one Superlatives position, so the single error had created a snowball effect. Almost every title was incorrect. And since Harper had already taken the pictures and sent them to the yearbook printer, Ms. Yates wanted to leave well enough alone. Not even Sawyer was in on this secret.

Definitely not Aidan.

I was thankful Harper and Brody had been able to work through their problems and keep dating after I told them the truth. They were adorable together, even if part of what made them fun was the fact that they were so obviously mismatched.

Now I was cycling through the same feelings Harper had when she believed she'd been paired with Brody. She'd seen Brody with new eyes and longed for a relationship with him because she'd mistakenly thought someone else had told her it could work. The only difference was, this time there was no mistake. I was *not* Most Likely to Succeed along with Aidan.

The senior class said Sawyer and I should be together.

I'd started to think so too.

Which was dumb, because the election was just a stupid vote for yearbook pictures. Aidan and I would attend Columbia together, take a while to establish our banking careers in New York, and then get married. After three years of knowing that was my plan, letting a class election change my mind didn't say much about my decision-making skills.

Neither did obsessing about Sawyer. On the far end of my table, he attacked his huge salad with the appetite of a seventeen-year-old, half-starved vegan. When he looked up and saw me staring, he tapped his watch, then splayed his hand, wiggling all five fingers. He meant he would meet me at the cheerleading van at five o'clock this afternoon, and we would ride to the game together, exactly as I'd promised (not).

I couldn't wait.

I didn't see Aidan again. Usually he waited in his car for me after cheerleading practice let out at the end of school. Today when I crossed the parking lot, his car was already gone. Angry as I was with him, his conspicuous absence left me feeling empty. I stepped into the heat of my own car and headed home.

As I drove, I decided I should have expected Aidan wouldn't check in with me after school. The first couple of years we'd dated, he'd met me at every chance, even if we had only a few minutes together—before school, between classes. But lately he waited for me less and less. And on the rare occasions when he offered me a ride to school, I told him I'd rather take my car in case I decided to go somewhere afterward. I didn't have specific plans, but riding with him would take some of my power away.

We never stood each other up, though, so I knew I would see him after the game, like we'd said. Normally we might "watch TV" at my house, since my parents were good about leaving us alone. But late tonight they were driving to the airport to pick up my brother, Barrett, who was coming home from college for the weekend. They were likely to return at the wrong time, tromping through the middle of my make-out session with Aidan. So instead, I was spending the night with Harper, and en route, Aidan was taking me to her granddad's strip of beach to "watch the ocean" for half an hour before dropping me off at her house.

Thinking about Aidan, I pulled my car to a halt at a stop sign. Enormous water oaks, dripping Spanish moss, extended their arms overhead. The houses along this section of the main road through town were ugly 1970s split-levels facing a parallel street, as if turning their backs on the history of the place. Aidan lived in the house to my right. The yard was a neat, flat expanse of grass, unbroken by a single tree except the ancient oaks lining the edge. Every time I'd passed his house since he got his license in tenth grade, I'd glanced at his driveway to see if his car was home.

This time it wasn't.

But I would be in that car with him tonight, driving in the other direction down this road, toward the beach. On three occasions at the beach before, we'd gone all the way. Each time I'd fantasized about the next time, dreaming of how it would be better. He would suddenly become a caring lover. He would make sure I enjoyed it as much as he did. We wouldn't get into a snarky argument afterward about whether I really deserved an A two points higher than his on our last English paper.

I wasn't fantasizing about that now. With sudden clarity I saw our half hour together tonight. We would fool around. I would feel like a failure, not heady with love like girls were supposed to feel after they went so far with their committed boyfriends of three years.

A wave of nausea broke over me, and I knew why.

I put my forehead against the steering wheel. "Damn it, Sawyer," I whispered. It was hard to cast Aidan as my hero after finding out the senior class had chosen Sawyer as my perfect guy. And especially after he'd whispered to me in the student council meeting. The setting hadn't been sexy, yet he'd set my body on fire. I could only imagine what he would talk me into if he ever got me alone.

The car behind me honked.

I drove on.

As I pulled in to my driveway, I saw Aidan was there ahead of me. In fact, he'd taken my parking space. I continued around to the extra pad near the front door, like a guest. After I stopped, I checked my phone to see if he'd sent me a message. Nothing.

Wary, I climbed the steps to the wide front porch and opened the door. The scent of fresh-baked peanut butter cookies wafted out—my mother's specialty and Barrett's favorite. I walked through the marble foyer and the formal living room, into the kitchen.

Aidan sat at the kitchen bar with a plate of the cookies and a glass of milk. "Hello," he called with no enthusiasm.

"Hi there," I said with an equal lack of emotion. I rounded the bar to the kitchen side and stopped in front of him. "What'cha doing?"

He nodded toward the door to my mother's office. "I've asked you a couple of times to check on your mom's recommendation letter for me. You keep forgetting. But you told me she was taking this afternoon off since Barrett's coming home, and I figured I could catch her. Sometimes when you want something done right, you have to do it yourself."

I heard the accusation in his voice. He was angry with me about the student council meeting. I didn't understand what I hadn't done right, though. *He* was the one who'd gotten parliamentary procedure wrong.

I didn't pursue it. I was more interested in what he was really doing here. "The deadline for early admission to Columbia is a month and a half away," I pointed out.

"I didn't want to wait until the last minute. I'm way more responsible than that."

Again, I knew he was accusing me of something. I just wasn't sure what. Saving the homecoming dance made me *more* responsible than him, not less.

I slid my book bag onto the counter to remind him this was my house.

It worked. He sat back on the stool and seemed to really look at me for the first time. "It's just that I don't have a ticket to Columbia without this letter." His tone had changed. Usually he spoke with the bravado of a politician, even when we were alone. But occasionally he dropped the act and let me see the boy underneath.

"I know," I said quietly, my automatic reaction to Aidan's half apologies.

"Your ticket to Columbia is living right here in the house with you," he said. "It makes me nervous that I don't have a letter in hand."

I nodded. That I could understand. When I had an English paper due, I didn't even leave it in my locker in case that part of the school caught on fire. I carted the paper around with me until I handed it in. Academic paranoia was one of the many things that had bonded Aidan and me over the years.

And now that I'd half-accepted his half apology, his

attitude was back. He popped a last bite of cookie into his mouth and wiped his fingers on a napkin. "Want to go upstairs to your room?"

The last thing I wanted right now was to make out with him. His apology hadn't been *that* convincing.

He raised his eyebrows, confident I'd say yes, only impatient for my answer. His calm assurance was exactly what I'd fallen so hard for in ninth grade. Now it grated on my nerves.

But I figured I was only shell shocked from the council meeting, and Ms. Yates's dismissal of me in the lunchroom, and the false closeness I felt with Sawyer. I would get over my negative feelings about Aidan soon enough. I didn't want to make things worse between us by telling him the truth.

So I gave him a very good excuse for not taking him upstairs to my bedroom. I looked pointedly at my mother's office door, then back at him. "Are you crazy?"

"She's busy."

"My dad's probably upstairs."

"He'll leave us alone. Your parents love me." He leaned over the counter and whispered, "I have a condom."

My jaw dropped. He wanted to have *sex*? Making out in the middle of our argument might have had some healing properties. Having sex sounded downright repugnant. After all, we'd only done it three times total, on special nights, when we were getting along.

And why take the big risk with my parents home? Now, suddenly? Weird.

"No thanks." I slid a cookie from one of the cooling racks beside the oven and took a bite.

"Why not?" he asked. "You've always jumped at the chance before."

Forcing myself to match his calm, I chewed and swallowed, even though the cookie had gone dry in my mouth. Only then did I say, "*Jumped* at the chance? I don't *think* so."

He glared at me. "It's Sawyer, isn't it?"

My heart pounded. I would have denied it, except that I was such an awful liar.

Instead, I used Aidan's own bait-and-switch tactic, easing out of trouble. With another glance at my mother's door to make sure it was still closed, I lowered my voice and said, "You think I'm cheating on you with Sawyer, and that's the only reason he and I happened to agree with each other in the student council meeting today? No. We agreed because we and the rest of the student council were right, and you were wrong."

Aidan shook his head. "You'd be too scared to cheat on me with Sawyer. But you're taken in by his act. You're as dumb as every other girl at our school."

The door to my mother's office burst open. She wore her business suit from her morning at work. She probably hadn't taken it off while baking cookies because she planned to wear it to pick up Barrett at the airport. As she phrased it, she might be off duty sometimes, but she was always president of the bank.

And she wore a big smile, because Barrett was coming home. Or Aidan was here. Or both.

She turned to me. "Hi, sweetie." She air-kissed my forehead so her perfect plum lipstick wouldn't rub off. Then she glanced at the cookie in my hand. "For shame. Those are for Barrett." No matter that she'd served Aidan the same cookies herself.

She turned back to Aidan. "I think you'll be happy with this, and so will Columbia." She slid an envelope printed with her Columbia alumni club logo in front of him.

Aidan swiped the letter off the counter so fast that it never stopped moving. He raked back his barstool and stood. "Thank you, Mrs. Gordon."

I cringed. My mother hadn't changed her name to Gordon when she married my dad. She was still Sylvia Beale, BA, MBA, President and CEO. I'd heard her chew out people who insisted on calling her Mrs. Gordon as if women had no choice in naming themselves. But Aidan called her Mrs. Gordon, no matter how many times I warned him.

And she always gave him a pass. Her grin didn't falter as he walked toward the back door.

At the last second he remembered me. "See you after the game, Kaye," he threw over his shoulder.

"Yep, see ya," I said, already turning to toss the rest of my cookie in the trash. I'd lost my appetite. I heard the door close behind him.

When I straightened, my mother was watching me with

her hands on her hips. "What's wrong between you two?" she demanded.

I sighed, and kept sighing, like I'd been holding my breath since study hall. "The gym roof got damaged by the storm. Aidan decided to cancel the homecoming dance instead of relocating it, without consulting the rest of the student council. I wanted to move it. So did everybody else. We nearly had a mutiny in the meeting. The upshot is, I have to figure out how to fix the dance now, and he's furious with me for speaking up."

"I would be too," my mother said. "You led a *mutiny*?"

"He wasn't following parliamentary procedure." I felt sheepish for the first time.

My mother closed her eyes and shook her head. "Parliamentary procedure! It's high school, Katherine. It's a high school dance. Your job is to get *out* of high school, holding your student council office in front of you like a key that opens the door to Columbia. Nobody cares what you actually *do* as vice president."

"I care," I protested. "The parliamentarian cares."

She narrowed her eyes. "Who's the parliamentarian?"

"Sawyer," I mumbled.

"The blond boy who works as a waiter at the Crab Lab?" my mother asked. "The one whose father went to prison?"

Now I really regretted piping up at the dinner table on the first day of tenth grade and gleefully dishing to my mother about the school's new bad boy who'd already managed to get suspended. I shifted gears. "Will cares—Tia's boyfriend. Practically everybody at the meeting was on my side."

"What about Ms. Yates?"

"She sided with Aidan because she doesn't want to get off her butt."

"It's hard to hide attitude," my mother said. "Yours won't earn you much of a teacher recommendation, which was supposedly the reason you ran for vice president in the first place." She crossed the kitchen, took down a plastic container, and started transferring the cookies from the cooling racks so I couldn't eat any more. "You may care about the dance today. The real test is, who will care in twenty years, or five years, or even a year from now whether you held this one dance in high school? The answer is, nobody."

A year from now I would be a college freshman in New York. That *did* make a Florida high school homecoming dance sound insignificant. Trouble was, I couldn't picture what I'd be doing on a Friday afternoon in mid-September on the campus of Columbia. But I could picture the dark dance I was supposed to have two weeks from tonight in the high school gym, with a boy's hand creeping down my hip. And in my mind, my dance partner wasn't Aidan anymore.

My mother was still talking. "You need to be smarter about picking your battles. This dance isn't worth the trouble. When we agreed you should increase your extracurriculars for college admissions, I never intended for you to get involved in a time-consuming activity that would distract you from your studies. Cheerleading is bad enough. If, on top of that, you're taking on the responsibility of moving an entire dance, I can only imagine what's going to happen to your AP English grade, and there goes valedictorian. Don't you have a paper to write on *Crime and Punishment* this weekend?"

These last words I heard as an echo down the hall. I'd left the kitchen while her back was turned. I tiptoed up the stairs and through the master bedroom to the smaller front porch on the second story, which we referred to as Dad's "office." Most days he wrote his books and articles here, where he could see his dock through the palm trees, and his sailboat, and the lagoon that served as his escape route to the Gulf of Mexico.

"Hey, my Kaye," he said without looking up from his laptop. He sat in his cushioned lounge chair, sunglasses on, iced tea beside him. Barefoot, he wore board shorts and a holey Columbia T-shirt that he might have owned since college. He would still be wearing this when my parents left for the airport tonight. My mother would look him up and down with distaste and tell him to change. In response, he would put on flip-flops.

"Hi," I huffed, plopping into the other chair.

He examined me over the top of his sunglasses. "Why so glum?"

I told him in a rush how Aidan had canceled the dance and my mother had told me I should have shut up and let Aidan run over me.

As soon as I said "Mom," Dad started making a noise—*rrrrrrrrrrrrrnnnnnnt*—like I was a big loser on a game show. "You know I don't like that kind of talk between my ladies," he said.

"You asked," I said bitterly.

He stuck out his bottom lip in sympathy. "Come on now. Your mom just wants to make sure you don't bite off more than you can chew."

"Oh, ha!" I sneered. "Funny you should say that. She won't let me eat Barrett's cookies, either."

He rubbed his temple like I was giving him a very familiar headache. "Kaye. Your mom sees her baby only once every few months. She couldn't sleep last night because she was so excited to see him today. She misses him desperately. And she'll miss you desperately too. When you go off to Columbia and come home again, she'll bake *you* cookies and get mad at *me* for eating them. Promise."

I doubted it.

"And as for Aidan," Dad went on, "I know you're spending tonight over at Harper's, but you're making some time for Aidan in there somewhere, huh?" He gave me a cocky grin.

"Yeah," I grumbled.

"The two of you are a little high strung, we could say. You might have let Most Likely to Succeed go to your heads a bit. You need some space for a few hours. But when you see him again tonight, I'll bet you both feel completely different about each other."

I didn't know then how right he was.

Three

AN HOUR AND A HALF LATER, I DROVE SLOWLY across the school parking lot, pretending I was concerned about traffic safety, but actually looking hard for Sawyer's dented old pickup truck among the cars near the boys' locker room and the school buses. He wasn't here yet.

Unless he'd ridden with someone else. I'd heard rumors about him being with other girls—usually fooling around with them at parties, not dating them—but honestly, I didn't know much about his love life. If he was dating someone else, Tia would know, but she might not tell *me*, because I acted like I didn't care.

And I didn't. That's what I told myself as I accelerated toward my ride, the cheerleader van. But as I parked, I was still gazing across the vast lot. I watched under the HOME OF THE PELICANS sign for Sawyer's beater truck to appear.

"Loser," I said to myself as I got out of the car. After I stepped up into the van, a quick glance around told me

1) Sawyer wasn't on it, and 2) Grace and Cathy were early, which was bizarre. They hadn't used their extra time to bring our cooler and twenty pompons out of the girls' locker room, though. Rather than disturb them, force them to look up from their cell phones, and listen to their excuses for why they were physically fit to cheer tonight but not to carry pompons sixty feet, I started making trips myself.

And watching for Sawyer's truck as I walked.

By my fourth trek, some juniors had arrived to help me. They were a lot more responsible than the other senior cheerleaders I'd been saddled with. When we had the van loaded, I chose an empty seat toward the back. Ellen tried to sit with me. I got along fine with Ellen, Cathy, and Grace most of the time. That was the head cheerleader's job, and the student council vice president's job: to make friends with everyone. But if I was Snow White, their dwarf names were Shut Up, Hapless, and Drunken. I really could not deal with Ellen's conversation halfway to Orlando.

I told her I was saving the seat for Harper, which was true. She was the yearbook photographer. She'd planned to snap shots on the marching band's freshman bus during the drive to the game, since the yearbook didn't have enough freshman shots, and on the cheerleader van during the drive back. I didn't mention to Ellen that Harper wouldn't be occupying the seat until later. If Ellen sat with me now and complained to me about how her remedial math class was so haaaaaaard, that wouldn't leave the space open for Sawyer.

I stashed my bag beneath the seat, settled against the window, and scanned the parking lot again for a certain undesirable pickup. *There* he was, finally, making a beeline for us, driving right over curbs like he was in a Humvee. That might explain why his truck sounded the way it did. He parked beside my car, got out, and looked up at the van.

I looked away.

A few seconds later the van door rolled open. My stomach fluttered with butterflies. I would not look. I couldn't let him know how I was beginning to feel about him. He teased me constantly, which must be why our class had voted that we should get together. But his teasing came with a side of mean, as surely as the fries he served with shrimp at the Crab Lab. He might turn on me if he knew he had the upper hand.

I wished I could switch my fantasies off.

"Hello, ladies." He stood in the open doorway, waving with two hands like he'd been crowned homecoming king and was surveying his royal subjects during the parade.

Girls cheered him: "Sawyeeeeeerrrrr!" We were cheerleaders, after all. But some of us were more interested in Sawyer than others. The ones who had a taste for danger.

And then there was me.

He locked eyes with me right away. His eyes were clear and blue and made my heart race.

He moved toward me, then past me, into the back of the van with a huge canvas bag—probably containing his bulky pelican costume. Well, fine. If he wanted to ignore me for once, I could ignore him, too. Or pretend to.

That ended when Grace squealed, "Sawyer, damn it!" because he'd tickled her as he passed or bumped her with his bag. Her voice cut through me, my usual reaction to girls squealing when Sawyer bothered them. It hurt to be reminded one more time that Sawyer flirted with me *exactly* like he flirted with every other girl at school. I meant nothing to him, and if I ever thought we had the kind of electric connection I'd felt during the meeting today, that was my mistake.

At the same time, I felt the completely illogical temptation to *do something* to pull his attention back to me, before it was too late.

And then, having dumped his bag on top of the pompons—I heard the swish of the plastic strands—he came back up the aisle and collapsed in the seat beside me.

I felt like I'd won the lottery. Seeing Sawyer from across a football field or a classroom or the van made my heart race. Having him right next to me gave me a sensation like I'd stuck my finger in a light socket. But I needed to calm down. The school convoy would stay parked another fifteen minutes, waiting for stragglers. Maybe he was paying me a brief visit before settling with a girl he liked better for the trip.

"Give me some more room here. I'm hanging in the aisle." He bumped me to make me scoot toward the window. "What's the matter?"

"You, being rude."

"No, what's *really* the matter?" He gave me his special expression, an intense stare with one eyebrow raised like an evil genius, which cracked me up if I wasn't careful. "Is Aidan still mad at you?"

"Yes." I didn't want to discuss Aidan with Sawyer, though. "And my mother's mad at me for expending too much energy on extracurriculars, when she's the one who wanted me to join more stuff in the first place."

He kept giving me the nutty look. "That is *so weird*."

"What is?"

"Parents who give a shit what their kids are up to."

I felt guilty, suddenly, for complaining about my problems. According to rumor and the more reliable account I'd heard from Tia, Sawyer had *actual* problems at home. His mom up in Georgia had kicked him out two years ago, and he'd come to live with his dad, who'd just been let out of prison. His older brother ran the bar at the Crab Lab and had gotten Sawyer a job as a waiter, but there was no love lost between them. Tia had said their fights in the Crab Lab kitchen were legendary.

In short, Sawyer had been taking care of himself for a while. And he'd schooled me for complaining.

The next second, though, he relaxed and moved closer with his elbow on his knee and his chin in his hand. The late afternoon sunlight streamed through the window and into his eyes, making him squint, but he didn't back away. "Seriously, why is your mom on you about that?"

I shrugged. "My brother is coming home from college for the weekend."

"Already?" Sawyer asked. "Didn't their school year just start?"

"He was there all summer," I explained. "Currently he's flunking out of Brown."

"*Barrett?* Is *flunking*? He was the valedictorian here."

"Well, I guess technically he's not *flunking*," I admitted. "He's getting Bs and Cs. To hear my mother tell it, that's flunking. She made him repeat those classes over the summer and bring his GPA up."

"I see." Sawyer's tone made it clear he didn't see at all.

"She was already disappointed that he didn't get into Harvard and had to settle for Brown. His high school GPA was perfect and his test scores were phenomenal, but he didn't have the extracurriculars to look well rounded. That's when she got on me about adding some. But I tried out for cheerleader, and she told me that's not what she had in mind. She's like, 'What career will that help you with, professional cheerleader?' And I was already on student council, but she pushed me to run for office. Now that I'm in charge, she's like, 'Why are you expending effort on something other than school?' It's frustrating."

"I can tell," he said. "Maybe you should concentrate on another kind of extracurricular activity." He put his arm around me, with his hand in my hair.

Here we went again. He came after me because something

about me screamed *target* to him. I knew he was only making fun of me, like he made fun of everybody, and I should stay away from him.

Especially since I had a boyfriend.

My deep, dark secret was this: Lately when Sawyer touched me, my palms got sweaty. And I liked it. My make-out sessions with Aidan weren't as frequent or intense as they'd been when we first started dating three years ago, but we *did* still have them. And of course, there were the few times we'd gone all the way. But nothing we'd done affected me like Sawyer getting a laugh at my expense.

So I would put up with Sawyer exactly to the point that my ironic patience might start to seem suspicious to onlookers, and they figured out I had a crush on him.

Or, worse: *He* did.

Sawyer stroking my hair definitely was something I wouldn't tolerate if I didn't like him. I tried to dodge away from his hand, which hurt because he'd already wound a curl around his finger.

"Ow!" Collecting myself, I informed him drily, as if he wasn't holding me captive by a thread, "I don't like it when people touch my hair."

He raised his brows. "That's a completely different statement from 'Stop touching my hair, Sawyer.'"

It certainly was. And now that he'd pointed this out, I was afraid he *did* suspect the truth. Overdoing my reaction now, protesting too much, would just draw attention to the fact that my crush on him was getting more serious. I gave him my best withering look—I was good at these, if I did say so myself—and grumbled, "I'm sensitive about my hair, Sawyer. I just had a huge fight with Aidan about this." In fact, that's where my recent trouble with Aidan had started.

I'd never straightened my hair, but I hadn't been bold enough to let it pouf twice the size of my head, either. I'd worn it tamed in twists or braids until two weeks ago. Natural hair had been gaining popularity—not so much around small-town Florida, but in the parts of America that mattered, like New York and California and TV. I wanted to try it.

I'd finally found the courage to spend a long Saturday unbinding my hair and nudging my curls to life. My mother had been supportive and helpful at first, working with the twists I couldn't see in back. Halfway through she'd started complaining that she made enough money to pay someone else to do this.

When we had finished, I liked the way it looked. I couldn't wait to show Aidan when we went out that night. He'd told me it looked like an Afro. Logically I knew I shouldn't have taken this as an insult, but he'd *meant* it as an insult. I was wearing my hair the way it grew on its own, more or less, and he told me it was ugly. Or dated. Or at least not what he wanted or expected in girlfriend hair.

"Judging from the part of your fight that I overheard at the Crab Lab," Sawyer said, "I think you came down too hard on Aidan about that." I couldn't see what he was doing, but it felt like he was looping a bit of my hair around and around his finger, then carefully pulling his finger out, curling iron–style, seeing if my hair would stay that way. It would.

"*You?*" I exclaimed. "Are taking up for *Aidan*?" Sawyer made fun of everybody indiscriminately, but later you'd see him having a halfway normal conversation with most people. Not with Aidan. He definitely had it in for Aidan. Probably because Aidan's life was so put together, and Sawyer's wasn't.

"I'm definitely not taking up for him," Sawyer said, tugging at a curl, eyes on my hair rather than my face. "It would be fine by me if you hated him now, but you'd hate him for the wrong reasons. At the Crab Lab, it seemed like you were dancing around the edge of calling him a racist. I don't think that's what he meant. None of the girls at school are doing their hair like yours. It makes a statement. Aidan doesn't want his girlfriend to make a statement."

Sawyer was just running his mouth, saying anything he could think of to get a rise out of me. This time it was working.

"That's not true," I said. "Aidan *wanted* me to run for vice president of the student council. I make statements in that job constantly."

"Correction: Aidan doesn't want his girlfriend to make a statement he hasn't preapproved. You can't make a move in student council without him okaying it. If you did, he'd force you to undo it. He'd make you backtrack even if your idea was good, just for spite. That was really clear in the meeting today." Sawyer paused. His eyes flicked to mine. "I can tell from the look on your face he's done that to you plenty of times before."

I glared at him, neither confirming nor denying. The problem with Sawyer was that he moved through the halls of the school with a scorched-earth policy, insulting everyone in his path, but he actually was perceptive about what made people tick. Including me. That's why his insults were so effective. He understood what buttons to push.

His lips were very near my cheek as he said, "Here's my theory. You've been angry with Aidan for a long time. You knew how he'd react to your hair. That's exactly why you did it."

Sawyer had gotten a rise out of me before. But this time he'd taken antagonizing me to a whole new level. I felt my face burning, and it seemed like the space between us was hot with energy. He'd correctly guessed something incredibly personal about me that I'd only half acknowledged myself.

And he acted like he'd only dropped another insult, or made a comment about our team's chances at the game tonight. "God, your hair is *so cool*," he said. "None of the curls are the same diameter. It's like the track of nuclear particles during fission. It's a shame you waited so long to wear it this way."

"It's hard to maintain," I said weakly. "It gets dry. It gets squashed when I sleep. Boys mess with my curl pattern. You act like natural hair is this strange, exotic thrill. It's patronizing."

Finally (regrettably) he pulled his hand away and looked at me. "Would I patronize you?"

"No, but you also would never be nice to me, even if you were faking."

"That is correct." He bent his head toward me. The lighter top layers of his hair fell forward, revealing the darker blond underneath. "Go ahead, touch my hair. It's this strange, exotic thrill. Get your revenge."

Any second he would decide he'd proven his point and sit up. I could be patient. But while I waited, my eyes fell on his nape, where his thick hair became light and fine. I couldn't help wondering what it felt like.

He repeated, "Touch it," which I now realized was going to attract some unwanted attention from the other girls in the van if they couldn't see what we were really doing. He groped in my lap for my hand. This was dangerous. My cheerleading skirt rode up so high when I sat down that my boy shorts underneath almost showed. His palm brushed across the top of one of my thighs, then the other. He found my hand and placed it on the back of his neck.

My fingers sank into his hair. I needed to pull them out. But as I did, they stroked his hair. It felt different from my own wiry hair or the coarse strands of Aidan's. Sawyer's was like warm water against my skin.

Over the sounds of girls laughing and the van's air conditioner blasting, I heard a muffled beeping. The ringtone wasn't mine.

"Excuse me, won't you, darling?" Sawyer said in a British accent like a debonair spy. He pulled his phone out of his pocket, touched the screen, only glanced at it, and put the phone back.

"You don't answer your phone?" I asked.

"I don't answer *her*."

I felt a pang that he was having a quarrel with another girl.

Then he eased the tension, moving his head into my personal space and shaking it so that his hair fell into his eyes. "You can touch it some more. You know you want to."

I fingered a white-blond lock curving around his ear. "You have such a baby face. Do you even shave?"

He gave me a sideways glare.

"The guys on the football team make fun of you," I ventured. Tentatively I traced my fingertip down the hard line of his jaw. He *did* have stubble, just golden and nearly invisible in the sunlight glinting across his face.

"Right," he said, "I don't need to shave. Let me show you." He grabbed me, one hand cradling the back of my head and the other bracing my shoulder so I couldn't duck away. He rubbed his chin across my neck.

"Ow, ow, ow, rug burn." Normally I would have squealed, but I didn't want him to let me go.

He stopped, eye to eye with me. Our faces had never been so close. This time I knew he felt the electricity buzzing between us as strongly as I did. His lips parted. His breath stroked across my cheek.

We couldn't stay like this. The cheerleaders carried on around us like what we were doing was normal. It wouldn't be long, though, before these gossip-hungry girls took notice.

He was thinking the same thing. Holding my gaze, he whispered, "If you were so mad at Aidan, why'd you run back to him?"

My friends had asked me this so often in the past few months, my answer came automatically. "I was looking at the long term. We're applying for early admission to Columbia." I wanted to get off the subject of Aidan as quickly as possible, though. "Are you applying anywhere?"

"No," he said.

"What are you going to do, live in a box underneath the interstate?"

Sawyer raised his head and backed away. There was no expression in his blue eyes. Sawyer *always* had an expression, easy to read. He poked fun at me. He laughed at me. He enjoyed the fact that he made me uncomfortable. That's why I ribbed him right back. But this time his face was blank.

Without warning, he stood and moved up the aisle.

"Where are you going?" I called. The other cheerleaders turned to me in question. Too late I realized I sounded like I wanted him to stay.

He stopped in the open doorway and threw over his shoulder at me, "Back to my box." He jogged down the steps.

I watched for him out the window. In a moment he crossed behind the van and headed for one of the football team's buses. He disappeared up the steps. A few seconds later he came reeling down to the pavement again like they'd thrown him.

He walked over to one of the four band buses next. The door was closed. He knocked. The door folded inward. I recognized Tia's long auburn hair as she reached down and held out her hand to him. He let her pull him up the stairs.

The door shut.

I stared at that bus until the cheerleading coach, Ms. Howard, finally guided our van into motion, leading the school caravan across central Florida. Maybe Sawyer had planned to ride with the band all along, and he'd only been visiting me. Yet he'd dumped his pelican costume into the back like he planned to stay. I couldn't help thinking I'd actually offended him with my comment about the box. But that wasn't possible, when Sawyer acted like he didn't have any real feelings.

At least, not for me.

Four

I SPENT MOST OF THE DRIVE WITH MY FOREHEAD pressed to the window, staring at the orange groves flashing by beside the interstate, mulling over the homecoming dance. I was *trying* to brainstorm for an alternate place to hold it, but I kept getting sidetracked by my anger at my mother, and Ms. Yates, and Aidan, and a mass of confused feelings about Sawyer. Anger at him, too, for storming off without explanation, guilt that I'd really hurt him somehow, lust as I remembered his hand in my hair.

As soon as the van pulled to a halt in the opposing school's parking lot, Sawyer climbed back up the stairs. He hardly glanced at me as he moved down the aisle. I peered nonchalantly over my shoulder, as if I were just curious about the view out the back windows. He was sitting beside the pompons on the bench, stripped down to his gym shorts, pulling the bird suit up to his knees.

Sawyer had never had an ounce of fat on him, as far as

I could tell. But the last time I'd seen him with his shirt off, after the Labor Day race, he'd looked drawn and sinewy, like he could kick anybody's ass more through sheer force of will than bodily strength. In the two and a half weeks since then, he'd been working out with the football team, and I could tell. He'd gained muscle. Most guys going down that path would have gained confidence, too. Sawyer didn't need any.

Grace grinned at him from the nearest seat. "Want me to zip you up?"

"Yeah," Sawyer said with none of the teasing tone he usually took with Grace. After putting his arms into the feathered suit and flexing his bird gloves, he stood. Grace rose beside him and put her hands at the base of his spine, her fingertips probably brushing across his bare back. She moved the zipper all the way up to his neck. I wondered if he shivered at her touch.

Next she bent, flashing everybody her full butt in her boy shorts underneath her cheerleader skirt, and fumbled with his costume bag. She came up holding the huge pelican head. "Here, Sawyer," she said, "I'm giving you head."

Cathy and Ellen squealed with laughter. Sawyer, who normally would have shot her a sly grin and said something even dirtier in response, only turned bright red and looked straight at me.

Suddenly I realized I'd been staring at him the whole time, and he'd noticed.

"Aw, he's blushing!" Cathy exclaimed.

"Sawyer, blushing?" Ellen echoed. "Grace and Sawyer, sitting in a tree."

Ugh. I faced the front and dove under the seat for my bag.

A huge white shape filled my peripheral vision. The pelican stood beside me in the aisle, holding out his gloved hand. He carried my pompons in the crook of his other wing. I took his hand, and he pulled me up like a feathered gentleman.

The rush I'd felt when he singled me out and paid me romantic attention—bird suit or not—was doubled when he escorted me into the stadium, already loud with crowd noise and brightly lit even though the sun wouldn't set for another hour. My mother might tell me being head cheerleader was the *opposite* of Most Likely to Succeed, but cheering at football games was the most fun I'd had in high school so far.

Thirty minutes later our team kicked off. The stadium was crazy with excitement. The opposing team had beat us last year, but this season Brody had led us to wins in our first three games. If he and the team could pull off a difficult victory tonight, our chances were good of making it all the way to the playoffs. Knowing this, our fans packed the smaller guest side of the stadium and overflowed into the home side. All the football parents and marching band parents were here, and every cheerleader's parents except mine.

Most of the students from our school were here too. Aidan had driven to the game with a couple of other guys: our friend Quinn, whose boyfriend, Noah, was on the football team, and Kennedy Glass, the yearbook editor, who was self-important enough to think someone cared whether he attended the game or not. Come to think of it, Aidan had driven here for the same reason. He didn't understand football, but he felt it was his duty to show up since he was student council president. That's the way he'd explained the trip to me, anyway. He hadn't said anything about wanting to support me personally or see me cheer.

So I didn't scour the stands to spot him and wave. I just cheered. My fellow cheerleaders might annoy me with their weekend drinking and nonstop whining, but they were terrific athletes. We made pyramids—I was lightest, so I was on top—and I knew I wouldn't fall, because they would hold me. We led the crowd in chants, and the students were great about playing along. We hadn't come in third in the state cheer championships last winter for nothing.

For short stints I turned around with my hands on my hips and my back to the crowd, watching for Brody's big plays. Dad loved football. I'd spent many weekends curled up on the couch with him while he explained the rules to me. Now, even from field level, I could watch our formations and warn the other cheerleaders that we needed to get ready to make some noise.

In short, I felt like a successful head cheerleader—way more of a success than I was as student council vice president. If only my mother thought this counted.

But my favorite parts of the night were the dances we'd choreographed. Whenever the opposing team had the ball and it looked like our team would slog through the next several plays without much movement, I pointed at Tia, who was drum captain, up in the sea of band uniforms in the stands. She consulted with Will about what jam to play next, then gave me a hand signal to tell me which one. I passed this along to the cheerleaders. The next thing we knew, we were dancing to a groove. I felt high. Little kids held on to the chain link fence separating the crowd from the field, shaking their bottoms, dreaming about being cheerleaders themselves one day.

And for the whole game, Sawyer acted like he always did with me on the field. He could flirt all he wanted and Aidan would never say a thing as long as Sawyer was in costume, because it was a big joke. He danced right behind me and missed the turns, bumping into me on purpose. Several times I slapped him away when he tried to look up my skirt (which wouldn't have mattered anyway with my boy shorts underneath, but it was the principle of the thing). During halftime he always disappeared to take his suit off in the locker room and pour cold water over his head, but this time he returned a few minutes early. He sat beside me on the players' bench, slipped his feathered arm around my waist, and watched the end of the opposing marching band's show.

Sawyer might be angry with me in real life, but the pelican always loved me.

After the game, exhilarated from our big win, I dumped my pompons in the van and snatched Sawyer's bag for his costume. I wanted an excuse to wait outside the locker room for him. I needed to know whether he was still mad, or the drive back would kill me.

I stood to one side as the football players filed out of the locker room. Brody gave me a high five. Noah shook his freshly shampooed head very close to me, spraying me with water. Then Sawyer emerged in his gym shorts only, carrying the huge foam bird head in one hand, with the rest of the costume draped over his other arm like something dead.

"I brought your bag," I called.

His eyebrows shot up in surprise, but he walked over. "Hold this." He handed me his costume and his head, trading for the bag. He fished a Pelicans T-shirt out of the bag and dove into it, biceps flexing as he pulled it over his head. I was sorry to see his bare chest go. Strangely silent, he took the costume from me and stuffed it into the bag.

I ventured, "You could come back to the cheerleader van for the ride home. I'm sitting with Harper, but we could all three move to the back." As if we were all close friends, and this was the most normal suggestion in the world.

He slung the strap of the bag over his shoulder and eyed me. "That's okay. I'll ride with the team."

"No, you won't," a football player called as he passed.

"The fuck you will," another voice agreed.

Sawyer's eyes never left my face. He said more quietly, "I'll ride with the band. Thanks, though."

"All right." I stood there uncertainly. He shifted his bag from one shoulder to the other, looking past me at the football players and marching band members milling around the parking lot, not quite ready to board the buses for another long drive. Finally I burst out, "We need to talk."

"Or, *you* need to talk," he said, "obviously."

I crossed my arms. "That's exactly what we need to talk about: this attitude of yours."

"Oh, my *attitude*," he said bitterly.

"You're in the costume and you're nice to me. You . . ." I glanced at the football players limping by and lowered my voice. "You come on to me."

"You like that, do you?" he sneered. "When I'm dressed up like a giant bird? That is completely illegal in the state of Florida."

I held my hands out flat. He was proving my point for me. "Then you get out of the suit, and you're an asshole, like now. I don't want to do this dance with you anymore. If this is how you feel about me, stay away from me and keep your hands off me, suit or no suit." I turned my back on him and stomped toward the van.

As I went, my head was swimming with what had just happened. I wasn't even sure where my sudden anger had come from. It was just *so frustrating* for Sawyer to embrace me like I was his favorite—and the instant I tried to show him I felt the same way, he lashed out at me. I wasn't going to do it anymore.

And I wasn't going to stop and peer back at him, either, because that would show him how much I cared—*again*. Five steps later, I couldn't help it. I looked over my shoulder.

He stood where I'd left him, gazing down at his shoes like he was trying to figure out one of Ms. Reynolds's calculus equations.

And now I was caught between *Good, I've hurt him* and *Oh, no, I've hurt him.*

Disgusted with myself, I trudged up the steps of the van, only to see that some strange girl had taken the seat next to mine. It took me a split second to recognize Harper.

She was like a hand-knitted scarf. Breaking up with Kennedy and dating Brody over the past month had unraveled her, but she was made of gorgeous yarn. Now she was knitting herself back together in a new pattern. This meant I did a double take sometimes when I saw her, because she wasn't always wearing her signature glasses with a retro dress. Without them, she was a pretty, dark-haired girl I'd never met.

Tonight her long hair was pulled into a high ponytail. She wore a simple tank top and a few crazy necklaces with olive cargo pants. She looked as beautiful as ever, only with a lot of the effort taken out—as if she was finally more concerned with her photography projects and her sweet boyfriend than her own self-image. I envied her.

The first thing out of her mouth was "Where's Sawyer?" She stood up to let me into the seat.

Flopping down next to her, I grumbled, "On the band bus, I guess. Why?"

"Brody told me the football team kicked him off their bus, and Sawyer said he was going to hitch a ride with the cheerleaders. That's the main reason I wanted to ride back with y'all. I thought I could get some candids for the yearbook before we leave, while the lights are still on. Sawyer is a walking, talking photo op."

"He was going to ride with us to the game," I said, "but he rode on the senior band bus."

She gave me a skeptical look. "But he was all over you during the game."

"That's because he loves me with his costume on, and he hates me when he takes it off."

"I don't think he hates you when he takes his costume off," she said.

I shrugged through the first part of her sentence and talked through the rest. "I don't care anymore." As the van's engine rumbled to life and the overhead lights blinked out, I turned to the window and watched the distance grow between us and all our school buses. I had no idea which one Sawyer was on, or whether he was staring out his own window as our van pulled away into the dark.

I turned back to Harper. "How are things with Brody?"

She eyed me. In her pause, I realized I'd jumped from complaining about my relationship with Sawyer to asking her about her relationship with her boyfriend. Basically, I'd admitted I liked Sawyer way more than I should.

If Harper read my mind, though, she kept it to herself, as usual. She said enthusiastically, "Things are *good* with Brody."

"Have you . . ." I winked at her.

She looked around us—with good reason. Half the girls on this van had dated Brody in the past. Satisfied that they were involved in their own confabs, she said quietly, "Not yet. I did get on the pill, like I told you, but I still don't think I'm ready."

"That's okay," I assured her. Harper had never dated anyone for long. Suddenly becoming the steady girlfriend of one of the most popular guys in school must have been a shock to the system.

"But we've . . ." She bit her lip and looked guilty.

"You've *what*?" I insisted.

"Done stuff I can't tell you about on the cheerleader van." She raised her eyebrows knowingly.

"Sounds serious."

"I guess we're pretty serious. But *serious* makes it sound like we're under pressure, when we're the opposite. My dates with other guys have been ex-cru-ci-a-ting. So awkward. Now"—she shrugged—"I'm just making out with my cool new friend. And really enjoying it."

"Have you thought about what you're doing after graduation?" I asked. "Will you try to stay together?"

"We're both applying in state, mostly. Oh!" She gripped my arm. "A scout from the University of Florida came to the game tonight to see Brody and Noah play."

"That's fantastic!" Brody was the best quarterback our school had scored in years. Noah was the right guard who kept him from getting sacked—or tried to. The opposing team tonight had been tough. Despite Noah's efforts, Brody had landed on his ass a couple of times. "What did the scout think?"

"He told Coach he's impressed. What if Brody got to play for the Gators? And I'm sending Florida my portfolio. They have a killer journalism department. Maybe I'll get a scholarship out of it." She held up her hands. "It might not work out, but we're trying to go with whatever happens. It's not a definite plan, like you and Aidan applying to Columbia together."

"Right." After all my pining after Sawyer tonight, I still needed to make up with Aidan. The thought made me a little ill.

"I hear you and Aidan had a problem in the student council meeting today," she said. "Good thing you're sleeping over with me. We'll talk through what happened. Or help you forget about him, whichever."

"Yeah." I did look forward to spending the night at Harper's tiny cottage where she lived with her mom, behind their huge Victorian bed-and-breakfast. Harper and Tia and I didn't have much time left together. We'd be going to different colleges next August. And if Tia and Will both got into drum corps like they wanted, we wouldn't see much of her past June.

But tonight I would get to hear about Tia's night in marching band with Will, her polar opposite. I would hear more about the mysterious experiments Harper and Brody had been performing on each other. If I couldn't pry the details out of Harper, Tia would. And they would ask about Aidan and me, kissing and making up and then exploding again in the student council drama . . . but they would be reserved with their questions. I could tell their enthusiasm about my relationship with Aidan had waned over the years. Kind of like Aidan's own enthusiasm, and mine.

That was normal when two people had been dating for all of high school. Aidan and I had something good together and, moreover, long term and stable. Hardly anybody else in our school could say that. It didn't make sense for us to break up just because we'd been dating forever and there might be someone better around the corner—like Sawyer, of all people. That kind of search would drive a person crazy.

Harper leaned toward me to whisper, "There will be a surprise waiting for you when you come over."

"Oooh, what is it?" I couldn't imagine. Her parents' divorce was finally going forward, which she said was good. But her mom had a hard time keeping the B and B afloat. There was definitely not any redecorating going on.

Harper looked around the van again before she said, "Sawyer."

I felt the blood rush to my face and goose bumps break out on my arms in the air-conditioned van. "What do you mean, Sawyer?"

"You know," Harper said, "he and his dad have been living in a rental house on the same street as my granddad."

"No, I didn't know." It made sense that Sawyer lived near our little downtown, which enabled him to get drunk outside the Crab Lab, then walk to our friends' parties and then home without getting behind the wheel and killing anyone. But I'd never given a lot of thought to where home was for him. He just appeared.

"He had a big fight with his dad a few nights ago," she said, "and he left. He stayed with my granddad at first. They know each other because Sawyer cuts my granddad's grass. Anyway—"

"How could Sawyer *leave*?" I'd had some huge fights with my mother before, but it had never crossed my mind to sleep at someone else's house because of it.

"He and his dad don't get along, apparently, and this was the last straw. Unfortunately for Sawyer, my granddad has finally rejoined society and gotten a girlfriend. I told you about Chantel. My granddad says Sawyer is cramping his style. Granddad talked to my mom about it, because they're actually speaking again. It just so happens that my mom has been looking for someone to help with breakfast at the B and B, since I refuse to do it anymore."

"I'm so proud of you for standing up for yourself." Harper was introverted. Serving breakfast and associating with her mom's guests at the B and B—different ones every week—had been a special kind of torture for her, like a cat in a room full of toddlers.

"Me too. But I've felt awful that it left my mom in the lurch. Along comes Sawyer, who's willing to work just a couple of hours a day as long as it doesn't interfere with his evenings waiting tables at the Crab Lab. And he needs a place to stay."

"Sawyer is serving breakfast at your B and B?" I asked incredulously.

Harper nodded. "He does a great job, much better than I ever did. After he's fed everybody, he actually sits down and talks to them if he has time before school, whereas I made up any excuse to hide in the kitchen. He can be very charming to the elderly and people he doesn't know. You'd be shocked."

"Wait a minute." The full meaning of what she was saying finally hit me. "Sawyer is *living* at your B and B?"

She laughed nervously. "Actually, no. We don't have an empty room. It's too soon after Labor Day. But one of the rooms will be empty Monday, and he'll move over there. Mom says he can stay through hurricane season, until business picks up again around Christmas. Right now he's staying at our house."

I gaped at her. "The house where you *live*?" Harper's place was a two-bedroom. When she and Tia and I had sleepovers there, one of us had to take the couch in the living room.

"Yeah."

She'd told me all of this so calmly that I sensed I was protesting too much again. I asked logically and rationally, "Doesn't that weird you out?"

"Not really. He basically comes in, grumbles, and wanders away again. He's a lot like my granddad."

"But your whole reason for telling your mom you didn't want to help at the B and B anymore was that you're not a people person," I reminded her. "You need your personal space. You invite friends over occasionally, sure, but people hanging out too long drives you nuts."

"I don't have to entertain him," Harper explained. "He doesn't say much. It's like he's not there." She looked past me out the dark window, searching for a reason that would make better sense to me. Finally she settled on "I feel safer while he's over."

"Safer from whom? Your dad? I thought the divorce was finally going through. You think he'll come back?"

"Probably not," she said vaguely. "I just don't mind Sawyer being there."

"Doesn't Brody mind?" Brody didn't strike me as the jealous type. He was way too confident for that. But bad boy Sawyer living with Brody's girlfriend? That was different.

"Sawyer called Brody to tell him," she said. "And anyway, it's only for a few more nights. Next week he'll move over to the B and B, and it'll be like we're neighbors, that's all. We were neighbors before."

"Now you'll be neighbors who eat breakfast together every morning," I pointed out.

"Yeah, I've thought about that, but Sawyer put it best. He said a lot of people in the same class at school might feel uncomfortable moving in together, so to speak, but he and I have gotten all that out of the way and have nothing left to feel uncomfortable about, because he's already slipped me the tongue." She laughed.

She stopped laughing when she saw the way I was looking at her. "I told you about that," she reminded me. "Two weeks ago, when I thought Brody was getting back together with Grace. Sawyer was doing me a favor."

"He sure was." Brody and Harper's relationship had worked out now, but they'd had a rocky start, complete with Harper and Sawyer trying to make Brody jealous—and succeeding. When I'd heard about this, I'd burned with jealousy myself. Sawyer never offered himself up when Aidan and I had trouble—which, lately, was all the time.

"Why didn't you tell me before now that Sawyer moved in?" I complained. These were big changes in Harper's home life, and they'd been going on for half a week. I couldn't imagine why I'd been left out of the best friends call tree.

"Because." Harper lowered her voice and bent toward me again for privacy from the cheerleading van, a.k.a. the school's rumor mill. "Ever since you figured out that you and Sawyer were really the ones elected Perfect Couple That Never Was, you've acted strange about him."

Before I could protest—*Strange, how?*—she went on. "I didn't want this to be a big deal. It's *not* a big deal. He'll just be there when you come over. Of course Tia won't care, since the two of them are such good friends. I figured you wouldn't mind either, now that you know why he's there. And I wouldn't want to give him the impression he's not welcome, when he doesn't have anywhere else to go."

Harper wasn't one to throw her weight around or scold,

but I was almost sure she was giving me a warning look.

The next second I grabbed her shoulder to keep her from tumbling into the aisle as the van hit the on-ramp for the interstate too fast and we lurched around the curve. My stomach spun with the van. I'd just realized Harper's warning not to kick Sawyer when he was down had come too late.

As the van straightened and Harper was no longer in danger of sailing across it, I took my hands off her and slapped them over my mouth. I opened them to tell her, "Sawyer got mad at me and went to ride on the band bus because I told him he didn't have any plans after graduation and he'd be living in a box under the interstate."

Harper gaped at me. "Kaye!" When even *she* acted outraged, I knew I was in trouble. "Why did you say that?"

"I didn't know he was *actually* homeless! It seemed like a clever reaction to . . . He was . . ." I tried to remember exactly what he'd been doing to me when I insulted him. My most distinct impression was of him running his fingers through my hair, whispering in my ear, and making chills rush down my arms. That's what I'd pushed him away for.

"He teases you and bugs you," Harper said gently. "But he's a real person."

"I know that," I said, careful not to snap at Harper, who never deserved it.

It was a night of firsts. As soon as we arrived at school, I would have to tell Sawyer I was sorry.

* * *

The senior band bus beat us back. Watching out my window as we pulled to a stop, I saw Sawyer open the door of his truck and heft the bag with his costume into the passenger side. I was afraid I wouldn't be able to apologize at Harper's house later with Harper and especially Tia there—at least, not the way I wanted.

"See ya soon." I jumped over Harper into the aisle with my bag and pompons in tow, raced down the steps, and galloped over to Sawyer's truck just as he was glancing over his shoulder to back out. When he saw me, he gave me that cold, emotionless look again, but he cranked down the window.

"Can I have a minute?" I asked.

He bit his lip and gazed at me like he wasn't at all sure I deserved a whole minute. Finally he turned off the engine and raised his eyebrows at me.

"I had no idea you'd moved out until Harper told me in the van," I said in a rush. "When I mentioned the box, I wasn't trying to insult you."

He watched me silently for a moment. "You *were* trying to insult me. Just not about *that*. You were insulting me for not being good enough to get into Columbia."

"Saw-yer!" A shrill majorette, decked out in skimpy sequins, pushed past me to lean through his window. This was a freshman who didn't view the head cheerleader and student council vice president with the proper awe. She was young enough to be rude. "I didn't drop my baton even *once* during halftime. You can't make fun of me anymore!"

"Oh, I can always make fun of you," he assured her.

To put as much of herself as possible through his window, she stood on her tiptoes in her knee-high majorette boots, with her sequined ass in the air. I stood there staring at it, feeling like a bellboy lugging my bag and pompons around. Without ceremony I walked one parking place over, unlocked my trunk, and dumped my stuff inside. I didn't want to interrupt Sawyer when he was busy coming on to his new girlfriend for this particular half hour.

"Kaye," Aidan said beside me.

I whirled around. "Hey!" I was halfway between guilt that he'd almost caught me talking to Sawyer, and satisfaction that Sawyer could peek in his rearview mirror and see me talking to *Aidan*. Maybe *Sawyer* could find out what jealousy felt like, for once. I hadn't been so glad to see Aidan in months.

"Do you want to follow me back to my house so I can drop off my car?" I asked. "Or we could go to the beach now. I brought my bag for Harper's, and I'm sure my car would be safe here overnight." As I heard my own words, I pictured making out at the beach with Aidan, as we'd planned.

And I didn't want to.

He shocked me by saying, "I don't think we should go."

"Okay," I said a little too cheerfully. "Why not?"

"I talked to Ms. Yates."

I nodded. "Again? At the game?" Maybe they'd realized they'd been wrong to protest saving the homecoming dance.

No such luck. "I mean, I talked to her in the lunchroom today," he said. "She told me about the screwup with the Superlatives elections."

"Oh." I felt fresh sweat break out along my hairline. Ms. Yates must have decided Aidan, as student council president, needed to know about the Superlatives problem after all. I wished I'd told him first. I *should* have told him, even if he'd had to keep it a secret from Ms. Yates that he knew.

And now that I'd spent the whole game cuddling with Sawyer, I felt like I'd been caught.

"Being elected Perfect Couple with Sawyer doesn't mean anything," I said quickly. "I'm sure it was just a joke. Sawyer probably organized people to vote for him and me, just to make me mad." I did think this was possible—though if it was true, that was *some* joke, and Sawyer had done more than try to make me mad. He'd tried to get my attention.

"That doesn't matter," Aidan said. "The idea of him going after you is so ridiculous anyway. I mean, it's *Sawyer*." He wrinkled his nose as he said Sawyer's name. "I'm more offended that you lied to me about being elected Most Likely to Succeed with me. But that doesn't matter either. What matters is that you screwed up the election."

His words hit me like a slap in the face. "*I* didn't screw up the election," I protested. "I had nothing to do with it. Ms. Yates wouldn't let me work on the election staff because I'm part of the senior class. That's exactly *why* the election got screwed up, if you ask me."

"But you were still in charge," Aidan said. "You were supposed to tell the staff what to do, and somehow they didn't get the message. When that happens in business, someone at the top resigns so confidence in the organization can be restored."

"You're resigning?" I was astonished. Aidan was way too proud of his position to let go so easily.

"No," he said. "Not me."

"Me?" I squealed. "You're asking me to resign?"

"Yes."

This made no sense. I was counting on entering "student council vice president" on my college applications, and Aidan knew it.

"I don't understand this," I said. "Maybe you're taking this too far because I'm your girlfriend, and you don't want to be seen as soft on me. But, Aidan, there's something to be said for that sometimes. We're *not* in a corporation. We're in high school, and I *am* your girlfriend. You seem to be forgetting that a lot lately."

"Then maybe you shouldn't be my girlfriend." At the shocked look on my face, he blinked and said, "We need to take a break and find out."

I'd been wrapped up in what he was saying to me, trying to maneuver out of his anger. But as he uttered these words, suddenly I became aware again of a good portion of the student body moving all around us. Football players streamed out of the team buses, lugging bags of equipment into the locker room. Members of the marching band wearing bright tank tops and their uniform pants, or plaid shorts and their military-style uniform coats, honked obnoxiously on their instruments as they walked to the band room. Sawyer's majorette followed them, swinging her sequined butt.

But Sawyer hadn't left yet. He might be able to hear what Aidan and I were saying. He could certainly see Aidan scowling down at me like an outraged teacher.

I asked carefully, "You want us to take a break because you're mad about the election? It was a mistake, Aidan."

"Not just because of that. I've been thinking about this for a while. We've been partners for a long time. I'm not convinced we're such a good match, in our personal lives or in student council."

Oh, now I understood. I managed to mumble, "So, when I fucked up the Superlatives election, that was the last straw."

He winced at my curse word, but he said firmly, "Yes."

"Which you found out about from Ms. Yates at lunch."

"Right," he said more uncertainly.

"That's why you came to my house this afternoon." My voice was rising, and Aidan was glancing around to see who was listening, but I didn't care anymore. "You'd already decided you would tell me tonight that you wanted to 'take a break'"—I made finger quotes—"but you wanted to get your recommendation letter for Columbia from my mother first. And you wanted to screw me one last time!"

He reached out for me. I never knew what he intended to do—hug me, hit me. Most likely he meant to slap a hand over my mouth to silence me. But he looked so angry that adrenaline rushed through my veins. Necessary or not, I jumped backward, out of his reach.

He crossed his arms and glowered at me. Nothing made him madder than *me* getting angry with *him*. "This is exactly why you need to resign. Using that language and talking about your sex life in the school parking lot!"

"*My* sex life!" I exclaimed. "Weren't you there?"

He looked up at the dark blue sky, gathering self-control. Then he said, "Don't try to argue your way out of this. I'm not changing my mind."

"*Your* mind?" I asked. "Since when does a student council president get to decide that other elected officials should resign?"

"That's what's best for the school," he said.

"I'm not resigning." Even if I wanted to, I couldn't. What would my mother say?

"We'll see, after I talk to Ms. Yates again," Aidan sneered.

"And after I talk to the parliamentarian," I shot back. "There are rules for trying to make your girlfriend resign just because you've broken up with her."

"Oh." Aidan rolled his eyes and shot me the bird.

Speechless for the first time, I stared at him, trying to get my head around the fact that my longtime boyfriend, the one I'd thought I would marry, had broken up with me and was now shooting me the bird. If *that's* how mature he wanted this breakup to be, I wished I had my mother's entire container of homemade cookies to throw at him one by one.

Finally I said, "Thanks for confirming that I've wasted the last three years with you."

He stalked away. A few band members who'd stopped to witness our fight were watching me and talking behind their hands.

I wondered if Sawyer was listening. I wouldn't give him the satisfaction of turning to look.

No, I took the only possible course of action in this situation. Blinking back tears, I went off in search of Harper and Tia.

Five

WAY ACROSS THE PARKING LOT, WILL STOOD beside one of the band buses. He wore his uniform pants but had already ditched his coat. He pulled his T-shirt off over his head, wadded the cotton into a ball, and reached upward with it.

Tia stuck her head out of the bus window and laughed with him, then accepted the T-shirt and lobbed another out the window at him. At the last second before the shirt fell to the pavement, he snagged it from midair with one of his drumsticks. He shook it out and pulled it over his head. Then he reached up to the window again.

Tia put her hand out the window. They held hands for a few moments while she smiled down at him and told him something. I was still half a football field away from them and couldn't hear anything they said, but I knew they were stalling, milking another minute of excitement out of seeing each other before he walked away to make sure all the instruments safely traveled the distance from the truck to the band room. He and Tia would be separated for only fifteen minutes. They were ridiculous, acting like they wouldn't see each other for a month.

That's how Aidan and I had felt about each other when we were fourteen.

Now Aidan had told me he wasn't sure I was good enough for him because I hadn't upheld his high standards of running an election correctly—even though I hadn't been allowed in the room when the votes were counted.

It had finally happened. My mother had told me a million times that because I was a woman, I had to work twice as hard as a man for the same amount of respect. And I was black, so I had to work four times as hard. To get twice as much respect, I had to work eight times as hard, and that's what she expected of me.

But she'd been wrong. I worked as hard as I could, eight times harder than most people, probably fifty times harder than Tia, who didn't work at all, and Tia was still acing the tests and ruining the curve in calculus. My mother might want me to have twice the respect of other people, but she gave me none. She demanded perfection. I wasn't perfect. I would have to work sixteen times as hard, and I just couldn't do it anymore.

My tears blinded me. I didn't notice Will had come across the parking lot to meet me until he filled my blurry field of vision. "Kaye," he said, "what's wrong?"

"Math," I sobbed.

"Um . . . Come over here." He grabbed my hand and tugged me toward the band instrument truck. "Watch out," he warned, settling his other hand at my waist and guiding me through the half-dressed band members kneeling over black cases laid out across the asphalt. He slid onto the back bumper of the truck and sat me down beside him.

"Now," he said, "what's wrong besides math?"

"I hate it here," I grumbled to the silhouettes of the palm trees that dotted the parking lot.

"Really?" he asked. "I love it here. I just wish it wasn't so hot."

I sniffled. "It's Florida, Will."

"They keep telling me that." He eyed me. "Tia will be out in a sec. She's looking for some stuff she lost on the band bus."

"Uh-oh," I managed to say calmly, my voice gravelly. "What'd she lose this time?"

"Her phone, one of her drumsticks, one of her shoes, and her bra."

"Her *bra*?" I repeated. "You might have had something to do with her losing her bra."

"She said it was uncomfortable on the long drive. I was helping."

A shadow fell over us as the lights overhead were blocked. We both looked up to see Sawyer standing in front of us, his gloved hands on his padded hips. The white pelican suit glowed like it was some mutant creature born of a nuclear accident in a B movie.

"Why are you in costume again?" Will asked.

Sawyer reached out and swatted Will to one side.

Will slid off the bumper and nearly fell. "Hey!" he yelled.

Sawyer settled next to me, then scooted back into the truck to give his padded butt more room. He put his arm around my waist where Will's had been. With his other hand he turned my chin so I had to look at him. His white-gloved thumb erased the tracks of tears on one of my cheekbones, then the other.

I didn't want to admit how touched I was by this gesture. "You're getting mascara on your glove," I said.

He held his glove up in front of his foam head, appearing to look at it. He wiped it on my bare knee.

Out in the field of instrument cases, Will and Tia were talking. He must have told her I was upset. She ran toward me, hurdling rows of cases as she came. "What's the matter?" she called when she was still surrounded by discarded drums.

"Aidan told me he wanted to take a break," I said shakily. Sawyer squeezed my shoulder.

Tia reached us and stomped her foot. "What the fuck for? Was it because of the shit in student council today?"

I sighed. "That probably had something to do with it, but he's mad at me for other stuff too. I don't meet his standards. He wants me to resign as vice president."

"Wait until I find him," Tia said. "I'll take every one of his standards and shove them up his— *What?*" Exasperated, she turned to Will, who was poking her in the side.

"That's not helpful right now," he said.

"It's helpful to *me*!" she exclaimed.

"Come on." He started to pull out the ramp attached to the underside of the truck where we were sitting, but Sawyer's costume overflowed into its path. "Tia and I have to get into the truck. Scoot over, bird," Will said, kicking Sawyer's cushioned butt.

Sawyer rose, pulling me up with him. But he didn't let me go. The soft padding and feathers of his costume enveloped me. Rather than fighting him, I let him hug me.

Will and Tia tromped up the ramp and maneuvered a huge xylophone on rollers onto it. Steadying the lower end, Will walked carefully backward. "Oh, wait," Tia called, "I don't have it. Oh, ack!" The xylophone slid down the last foot of the ramp, knocking Will in the gut. "Are you okay?" she called.

"We didn't really need that lower octave, anyway," he groaned.

Sawyer put his hands over my ears.

Taking the hint, I inhaled deeply and shut my eyes, letting myself melt into his softness. I could still hear Will and Tia flirting as they coaxed instruments down the ramp and other band members laughing as they passed. But their voices were muffled and smoothed over, just as Sawyer's downy but firm hug was soothing.

For those few seconds in Sawyer's arms, I tried to live in the moment and remember what I loved about high school: my friends, our sports events, and our fun gatherings like the homecoming dance, which I was more determined than ever to save. It wasn't until rare interludes like this, when I felt the weight lifted from my shoulders for a short time, that I realized how much pressure I was under, and how that anxiety turned my whole world dark.

Through my closed eyelids I sensed a flash. Blinking, I pulled away from Sawyer just as Harper snapped a picture of us with her fancy camera.

"I'm so sorry," she said. "You two hugging with Kaye in her cheerleader outfit and Sawyer in his pelican costume struck me as a symbolic photo for our school. It's also one of the weirdest things I've ever seen." She turned to me. "I hear Aidan wants a *break*?" She held her camera out of the way with one hand while she embraced me with the other.

"Tia told you already?" I asked into Harper's shoulder. Tia wasn't good at keeping news on the down-low.

"Tia isn't happy with Aidan," Harper said as she let me go.

And then—granted, the lights in the parking lot were bright, the shadows strange, and I was feeling out of sorts after my cry—but I could have sworn Harper gave Sawyer a knowing look, like they were hiding something from me.

Which was ridiculous. I spent way more time with Sawyer while he was in costume than Harper did, and I still didn't know which part of his bird head he saw from.

She stuck out her bottom lip at me in sympathy. "Are you okay to drive?"

"Oh, sure. I'll see you in a few." I turned to Sawyer. "Did

you put your costume back on just so you could hug me, even though you're still mad at me? Because that's kind of sweet, and kind of twisted."

He shrugged.

"Well, go take it off. I know you're hot."

He nodded, nearly poking me in the eye with his foam beak, and curled his arm to show me his bird biceps.

I actually managed a laugh. "Yes, *that* kind of hot. You are one sexy waterfowl."

He swaggered toward his truck, lifting his huge feet high and wagging his feathery bottom.

Suddenly the instrument truck, the cheerleader van, and all the buses around me were moving, like curtains rising and sets changing behind an actress onstage. Everyone in the parking lot drove away at one time, making the windblown palm trees seem stark and lonely. Only Sawyer remained, out of his costume again and unable to get over his anger at me, yet waiting for me behind the wheel of his truck.

I got in my car, and he followed me to Harper's.

It was impossible to stay depressed in Harper's tiny house with the five of us pushing past each other and laughing about it: me, sweet Harper, hilarious Tia, Harper's hippie mom, and of course Sawyer. Just as Harper had said, he didn't draw a lot of attention to himself or make much noise. It was almost like he was trying to blend in so Harper's mom wouldn't kick him out. He kept his clothes in a backpack stuffed under a side table.

I knew this because he drew some out right after we arrived, then disappeared to take a shower.

Harper's mom made us cookies from store-bought frozen dough. They didn't taste nearly as good as my mother's homemade, but I appreciated them more because they were made specifically for me. I was stuffing the fourth in my mouth when Sawyer stepped out of the bathroom in a cloud of steam, wearing his Pelicans T-shirt and threadbare sweatpants that hung low around his waist.

He looked like a different person with his blond hair wet and dark. But the defiant lift of his chin was the same as always when he saw me holding my bundle of pajamas. He motioned with his head toward the bathroom door.

I jumped up, eager to ditch my sweaty cheerleading duds. As I passed him, our bare arms brushed. I asked, "Did you use all the hot water?"

He said quietly, "I wouldn't do that to you."

I locked myself in the bathroom and set my clothes on the counter. Even though I'd had no idea when I packed my overnight bag that Sawyer would be here, luckily I'd brought a cute tank and pajama pants, sexy without being indecent. I wasn't worried about how I would look to him. It was the feel of his breath in my ear as he'd passed me that still sent shivers up and down my arms—and now the idea that I was stepping into the shower where he'd just been. (Naked.)

Harper might think this sleepover was innocent. She was wrong.

I hurried through showering and brushing my teeth so I didn't miss anything. When I exited the bathroom, the living room was empty. Harper's mom's door was closed like she'd gone to sleep. Laughter pealed from the opposite direction. I padded down the hall and found Harper in her room, which was wallpapered with photos and art and fashion shoots she'd torn from magazines. She shared her desk chair with Tia as they scrolled through Harper's yearbook photos on her computer. Sawyer lay on his stomach crossways on Harper's bed with his chin propped on his hands, looking over their shoulders. I stopped in the doorway. He turned around to glance at me and patted the bed beside him.

Any other night we'd found ourselves thrown together like this, I would have flounced across the room to drag Harper's beanbag chair closer to the computer. I *never* would have accepted Sawyer's invitation to lie next to him. But Aidan and I were on a break. I was a free woman who could do what I wanted.

And though I wasn't at all sure where I stood with Sawyer, we'd definitely moved into new territory for us. What I *wanted* was to lie down beside him.

"Oh my God, is that Xavier Pilkington?" I exclaimed, keeping my eyes focused on Xavier's photo filling the computer screen as I crawled onto the bed beside Sawyer. There was a moment when I had to decide whether to settle a few inches from Sawyer or lie right alongside him with our arms and hips and legs touching. I chose to touch him. If he was still so angry with me that he found me distasteful, this would serve him right. Cooties.

"Doesn't Xavier look great?" Harper asked, grinning at me over her shoulder. She did a double take when she saw how close Sawyer and I were lying, but she smiled right through it and turned back to the computer.

"Like a 1940s movie star," Tia agreed, "especially with the grease in his hair. How do you make people look so good, Harper? If you really want to expand your business to wedding photos, you should post what Xavier normally looks like as the 'before,' and this picture as the 'after.'"

"Two-part secret to good pictures." Harper held up one finger. "Lighting." She held up a second finger. "Lots of frames. Let me pull up the rest of my shots for Most Academic, and you'll see why." She opened another folder and expanded a photo of blond Angelica, primly perfect as usual, next to Xavier, who looked like Harper had caught him mid-sneeze.

"Ah, there's our Romeo," I said.

Sawyer laughed. For someone with a great—even if snarky—sense of humor, he didn't laugh a lot. The sound warmed me up.

"Speaking of Angelica," Tia said, turning to me.

"Don't tell her," Harper muttered.

"She needs to know!" Tia defended herself. "Kaye, I swear to God, not ten minutes after Aidan told you he wanted to take a break, I saw him talking to the majorettes and, specifically, hitting on old Angelica."

"You don't know that he was hitting on soned. "She's dating Xavier."

"Oh, and you think Aidan couldn't stea Pilkington?" Tia challenged her. "Xavier's mom still cuts crusts off his sandwiches."

"I'm not saying he *couldn't*," Harper clarified. "I'm saying I saw Aidan having that conversation with Angelica too, but that didn't automatically signal he was making a move in *my* mind."

"You're right," Tia said. "Most likely they were discussing the Higgs boson and the standard model of particle physics. It only *looked* like he was hitting on her."

Tia was what my mother referred to as "highly excitable." She had a reputation for stirring up trouble. Aidan might have been passing pertinent information along to Angelica about the student council's upcoming doughnut sale or something. He wasn't the type to hit on girls. But what did I know? He'd never had the chance before. Maybe he would become our school's playboy now that he'd decided our relationship was temporarily over.

And his choice of Angelica struck me. In the student council's incorrect tally of the Superlatives votes, Angelica had won Most Academic along with Xavier. In the newer, correct tally Ms. Yates had *claimed* we weren't letting out of the bag, Angelica had won Most Likely to Succeed with Aidan. Maybe he wanted to date the girl whom the school had paired him with. He obviously had no use for *me* now that he knew I hadn't really won the title. And now that he had my mother's recommendation letter.

I said, "I guess we won't be on a break after all, then. We've broken up permanently, because there's no way I can out-nerd that girl."

"You got that right," Harper said at the same time Tia said, *"Es la verdad."*

As I uttered this realization, I honestly expected Sawyer to smooth his fingertips across my back. Maybe I would poke him in the ribs in retaliation. Maybe not. But he'd embraced me in a full-bird hug when Aidan handed down his initial decree. Seemed like my letting Aidan go deserved at least *some* touch from Sawyer. He didn't move, though. He kept staring at the computer screen.

"Now *that's* a handsome bloke," he said. The photo was of him in the pelican costume—actually, it could have been *anyone* in the pelican costume, but I assumed it was Sawyer—looking very studious and contrite as he sat in Principal Chen's office with his legs crossed at the knees, reading *Crime and Punishment*. Perfect.

Suddenly I felt a flash of panic that I hadn't started my Dostoyevsky paper, which was due to Mr. Frank on Monday. My mother had reminded me this afternoon that the title of valedictorian probably hinged on everyone's AP English grade because Mr. Frank was a stickler. But getting up from Harper's bed to make a few outline notes when I was trying desperately to flirt with the class criminal was something Angelica would do, *not* something I would do.

Not anymore.

I called, "Are you really using that picture for Most Likely to Go to Jail?"

"Yes," Harper said. "Kennedy complained. He said I hadn't really taken Sawyer's photo for his title in the yearbook if his face wasn't showing. But we were on deadline. Kennedy had to let it through. And we're not using this next one for Most Likely to Succeed, but we're putting it in one of the front collages." She clicked to a picture of Aidan and me grinning behind Ms. Chen's desk—we'd fought over who would sit in the chair that day too, and finally pushed it out of the way—with Sawyer behind us, only one huge cartoon eye of the pelican popping up over Aidan's shoulder. Sawyer had photobombed us on purpose.

"That's classic," Tia cackled.

"You were in the *way*," I said quietly, actually poking Sawyer in the ribs this time. I turned toward him.

When he faced me, we were already so close that I could feel his breath across my lips. His deep blue eyes were serious.

And then he turned forward again without touching me or flirting back at all, like I was some freshman majorette he found more annoying than sexy.

I took the hint. We stayed on Harper's bed for another half hour as she led us through an overview of the senior class. I laughed with Harper and Tia. Sawyer laughed with Harper and Tia. Sawyer and I didn't laugh together.

"Enough," Harper finally said. "Even *I* get tired of photography after eighteen hours." She turned off the computer and led the way out of her bedroom, through the narrow hall to the living room.

We filed behind her. I was the last one out, behind Sawyer. It wasn't often that I was this close to him when we were standing up and he wasn't dressed as a pelican. I was eye level with his shoulder blades. I got a great view of the white-blond, baby-fine hairs at his nape. And I was disappointed he didn't take this opportunity to turn around and grab me playfully. Maybe it was all in my head, but I got the impression he was dissing me by doing nothing.

When we emerged from the hallway, Tia was rummaging through the kitchen, insisting she was hungry again, and Harper was trying to help her find the right junk food. Sawyer put a hand on the armrest of a wing chair and the other on the armrest of the sofa and hopped over both, then plopped onto one end of the sofa, as if he did this four times a day and that was his *place*. My first instinct was to join him on the sofa. The night had been squeaky clean so far, and it would stay that way if we weren't sitting next to each other.

But I wouldn't give him the satisfaction of chasing him around. I chose the wing chair and didn't look at him.

Tia was the one who claimed the other end of the sofa, collapsing her entire five-foot-nine frame onto it while clutching a bag of chips. She looked and sounded like a tree falling in the forest. Harper took the other side chair and clicked the remote so the TV turned on to our usual viewing, a bridal gown reality show.

Actually, I didn't know whether this show was *their* usual viewing. Maybe they only watched it with me whenever we had a sleepover, because it was *my* usual viewing. I'd been planning my wedding to Aidan ever since we started dating. Perhaps a little before. Harper would have a Florida wedding, barefoot on the beach. Tia, if she changed her mind and got married someday, would probably elope. But my wedding would be in New York where I would live and work, and the gown would be the centerpiece. In an old city that embodied intellect and effort and the collective culture of the entire world, my dress would stand out, a white work of art against the somber gray stonework of a church, or a monument, or a bank, wherever Aidan and I decided to hold the ceremony.

This had been my dream for years, more consistent than my fantasy that our next sex together would finally blow my mind. I had recited the slowly evolving details of my dream wedding to Tia and Harper. Suddenly the entire scenario seemed hopelessly naive, an invention of sixth grade instead of ninth.

Now I was in twelfth, and I was hoping against hope that Harper and Tia wouldn't bring up my obsession in front of Sawyer.

"There's . . . ," Harper began as a bride swept across the screen in a classic gown with a slim silhouette. She was about to say the dress was perfect for me. It was exactly the kind of gown I would have called dibs on the other hundred times we'd watched this show.

Behind the retro glasses she'd settled across her nose when she took out her contacts, her eyes flicked to Sawyer. ". . . a dress that should not be accessorized with pink cowboy boots," she finished as the bride pulled up the hem and showed off her special brand of quirky.

"That's a Kaye dress," Tia said, typically missing our hints at subtlety and restraint. "If you wore that with pink cowboy boots, your mama would shit twice."

Luckily, the next dress was exquisitely sewn with hundreds of delicate fabric flowers, a Harper dress. Following that was a cleavage-baring number with sheer panels down to the navel in front and the butt crack in back—definitely a dress for Tia, who couldn't tell sexy from raunchy. The conversation moved far enough from the topic of *me* that I worked up the courage to steal a glance at Sawyer.

He was asleep. His elbow was draped over the armrest, cradling his chin. His eyes were closed, his blond eyelashes casting long shadows down his cheeks.

"Hey," Tia said, shoving his shoulder. Without opening his eyes, he let out a groan.

"Come on," Tia said, pulling his arm until he stretched out across the sofa with his head on her thigh. He never opened his eyes, and the whole process was so seamless that it looked like he'd slept in her lap a million times. Maybe he had. The two of them had been off and on forever. They made my attempts at flirting with him look like something out of kindergarten.

In deference to him, she turned off the lamp on the table

next to her. The only light remaining came from the TV hung over the fireplace, and a faint glow from the streetlights outside through the gauzy curtains on the big front window. Now Sawyer and Tia looked like a boyfriend and girlfriend getting cozy.

Watching them with a ball of resentment burning in my stomach, I realized I didn't have a chance with Sawyer, even if I wanted one. We both pretended I was too good for him. But realistically, why would *he* want a stick-in-the-mud like me? Life-of-the-party girls like Tia were more his speed. Staring at them owning the sofa together, with Tia's hand lying on his chest, was a great way to finally drive that fact home to my beleaguered, lovelorn brain.

That's when Tia piped up. "So, Kaye, tell us more about this break you're taking with Aidan."

Six

"NO!" I WHISPERED HOARSELY AND A LITTLE desperately, nodding toward Sawyer in Tia's lap.

"He's asleep," Tia said in her normal tone.

"If he is, you're going to wake him up." I was still whispering.

"Nothing wakes him up," Harper offered. "He sleeps like a log."

"So it's okay to discuss my personal business in front of him? I don't *think* so. Any second he's going to jump up and startle us. 'Ha-ha, I've been listening to you the whole time.'"

Tia shook her head. "He's always worked such long hours at the Crab Lab, and now the mascot job takes a lot out of him. It's harder than you'd think, so physical, bouncing around in the heat with that heavy costume on."

"I *know*," I said haughtily, offended that Tia would imply she understood more about Sawyer's mascot job than I did. *I* was the one who stood next to him at games.

"Anyway," Harper spoke up, "I don't think he'd tell anybody your personal business."

"I think he would," I said flatly.

"What exactly is your problem with him?" Tia asked, sounding miffed. "You act like he's a criminal."

"He did get voted Most Likely to Go to Jail," I reminded her.

In the dusky room I saw Harper raise her eyebrows at me. She and I knew he hadn't actually won this title, since he'd won Perfect Couple with me. The real winner of Most Likely to Go to Jail was our school pothead, Jason Price.

"Sawyer and I are pretty good friends," Tia said, which was the understatement of the century, "and I can tell he's dead serious about cleaning up his act. He's always been black and white, all or nothing. When he went vegan last spring, that was it. He never looked back. So if he's saying no alcohol and pot now, I can guarantee he hasn't fallen off the wagon. You haven't seen anything to think he has, have you?"

The fact that she asked this question made me think she wasn't quite as sure about Sawyer as she claimed. "I haven't," I admitted. "But, Tia, you talk like he's been clean for years. He passed out at school only *three weeks* ago. And I just . . ."

"You just what?" Tia insisted.

Her usually bright face drew into frown lines. She shifted, moving her arm down Sawyer's body as if protecting him. He didn't move, didn't even stir or flutter his eyelids, as far as I could tell in the near dark. I couldn't see Harper's eyes because her glasses reflected the bridal gowns on TV, but she sat up cross-legged in her chair, attentive to my answer.

Without anyone coming out and saying it, I knew we weren't really talking about Sawyer's reform. They wanted to know why I didn't go after him, now that Aidan was—temporarily, at least—out of the picture.

"Sawyer's never been serious with girls," I said. "But he's been *with* a *lot* of them. He's got this whole secret underlife. Cheerleaders tell stories about him fooling around with girls I never even knew he'd gone out with."

"Why are they doing that?" Tia asked. "They're assholes."

"But what if the stories are true?"

"So? He's not in a steady relationship with anybody. He's not cheating. Why does fooling around with a lot of girls detract from his moral character?" Now she was talking about herself. We were back to the argument we'd had a million times, in which I expressed concern that she wasn't being very picky about whom she slept with, and she told me to stuff it.

I shouldn't have done it, but I took the bait. "When's the last time *you* had sex with him?" I asked. "It probably hasn't been a month."

"Do we want to go here?" Harper asked. "I do not want to go here."

Tia's mouth set in a hard line. "Define sex," she said.

Damn Tia. Now I was thinking about all the ways Tia and Sawyer might have played around with each other in the past few years. They'd probably done things that I'd never tried in three years with Aidan, and that Aidan would have said were too dirty anyway.

"There's no fighting during girls' sleepover night," Harper declared.

"Seriously," Tia kept on anyway, "because there's different kinds of sex."

"Now you're baiting her," Harper scolded Tia. "Just tell her what she wants to know."

Tia scowled at me, then opened her free hand. "Okay. The last time I did *anything* with him was about a month ago, before Will and I got together."

"Well, after you and Will had been *together*," I corrected her, "but before you actually went on a date." I happened to have heard about some of the things she'd been seen doing with Sawyer one weekend *after* she'd already made out with Will.

Tia grimaced and rubbed her brow like I was giving her a headache. "The past is past. I don't see why this matters."

I couldn't believe I was doing it, but I laid my biggest fear down flat on the table for them to peer at. "Because if Sawyer slept around before, he'll do it again."

"People change, Kaye," Tia said solemnly. "I've changed."

I frowned at her. "You're not wearing a bra."

She looked guilty, then pulled out the neck of her T-shirt and peered inside. "I couldn't find it on the band bus. Nine times out of ten, I've changed. I definitely would not run back to Sawyer or to *anybody* when I've made a promise to Will. Will is too fucking awesome."

Sawyer finally stirred—whether because she'd said his name again or she'd said the *F*-word with such gusto, I didn't know. He rolled onto his side, shifting his head on her thigh. Now that he might be awake-ish, I was even more alarmed at what she said next: "As long as you're on a break with Aidan anyway, why not experiment, so you won't spend your entire life since you were fourteen with one guy? I'm sure Sawyer would be glad for you to use him."

I cut my hand back and forth violently across my throat, hoping the horrified look on my face told her how serious I was about her shutting up. Even Harper shook her head.

Ignoring Harper, Tia gave me her best *Who, me?* face and put her hands up like she couldn't imagine what she'd done wrong.

I already felt vulnerable because Aidan had broken up with me and Sawyer seemed to have rejected me. If Sawyer was playing possum and heard this discussion, I would die of embarrassment. Desperate to keep her from saying anything else, I found a notepad printed with the B and B logo, plucked a pen out of the side-table drawer, and wrote her an angry note. "Sawyer wld not b 'glad 4 me 2 use him,' WTF. And if I did, Aidan wld never go out w me again." I tore it off the pad—silently—and reached across the coffee table with it. Harper half stood to grab it, then delivered it to Tia. Harper read it over her shoulder.

Tia snapped her fingers, meaning she wanted my pen. I winced at the noise but handed the pen to Harper, who delivered it. Tia scribbled an answer below my note. This took so long, and I was so afraid of what she'd say, that I had half a mind to look over her shoulder while she was still writing. I was afraid this might rouse Sawyer—with my panicked breathing or the sound of my heart palpitations. Finally she gave the paper to Harper, who read it with a perplexed expression, then handed it to me.

"Aidan wld b more likely 2 go out w u again bc he wld see ur not waiting around 4 him & his Higgs boson BULLshit. In the meantime u cld experiment w Sawyer. Tell me u don't want 2 & ur lying like a dog." Under this she'd drawn a dog stick figure with its tongue hanging out, lying on what appeared to be several yards of shag.

"Shhh," Harper said, even though nobody had said anything for several minutes. I listened, though. Underneath the drone of TV brides, I recognized Will's voice and Brody's laugh on the other side of the front door.

"We'd better go out there before they ring the doorbell and wake up my mom," Harper said more quietly than we'd been speaking before, as if my written exchange with Tia had caused a pall to descend over the night.

"They won't," Tia said as loudly as ever. "Brody wouldn't risk her wrath. They're plotting something."

"Then we'd better go out there before they execute their plot and get me in enormous trouble," Harper said.

"I'm curious what they'll do," Tia said. "Wait."

We waited. The only lights were still the flickering color

from the TV and the soft glow from the streetlights through the window curtains. The only sound was the whisper of televised voices. Then Will's voice again, hushed, and Brody's.

Suddenly the fireplace seemed to explode, making me squeal and Tia jump. Sawyer grunted and rolled all the way over on Tia's thigh with his back to the room.

Harper peered into the fireplace. She rummaged in the ash and brought out a tennis ball.

"Brilliant," Tia said. "You're right, Harper, we have to stop the rogue teens before they cause more harm." She half rose. Sawyer threw both arms over his head to block out sound and light.

"Kaye, come over here right now." Tia said it with such authority, and I was so surprised at this, that I obeyed, edging between the sofa and the coffee table. She rolled out from under Sawyer and held his upper body suspended until I sat down where she'd been. She laid Sawyer's head in my lap.

And then . . . I'm not sure what I'd expected to happen next, but it wasn't this: Tia and Harper left the room as fast as they could go, closing the front door carefully behind them.

Warmth washed over me, followed by a case of the shivers. I couldn't believe, after all the teasing I'd suffered at Sawyer's hands for the past two years, he was in my lap. The night had suddenly come way closer to a wild fantasy I'd only half acknowledged: that we would end up together.

But he *was* asleep. I was convinced now that I felt his deep, even breaths against my hand. An Oscar-winning actor couldn't fake it this well. And when Tia had ordered me over, it almost seemed she was calling on me to protect his rest, not to wake him or flirt with him or make Aidan jealous.

In front of the house, somewhere just beyond the door, Harper talked in a low voice. "I'm surprised you're still up. You got hit pretty hard in the third quarter."

"Yeah," Brody responded. "I don't feel that kind of thing until the next day. You have about eight hours left to use me."

"Oh, *really*. Use you how?" Harper's tone was knowing and provocative—like Tia's was all the time. I'd never heard Harper speak this way before. I recalled what she'd hinted to me in the van about Brody and her exploring each other.

I'd lost my virginity with Aidan not long after Tia had lost hers with Sawyer. Harper hadn't had sex even now. But suddenly I felt like the naive one, because Harper and Brody were in love, and my time with Aidan hadn't meant what I thought.

Their voices faded as they wisely walked away from the house, where Harper's mother wouldn't overhear. I was left with only the TV wedding preparations and Sawyer's warmth in my lap.

He rolled farther forward and slipped his hand between my legs, propping himself in that position, like my thigh was a pillow. I suspected at first he was awake after all—but he never snickered, and if he'd meant to take liberties with me, his hand would have been six inches higher.

I put my hand in his hair, lightly so as not to rouse him, and fingered those baby-fine strands all over again, while I watched all my past goals play out on television like the most mindless reality show.

I lay stretched out on the sofa, with an actual pillow underneath my head, and covered in Harper's psychedelic first attempt at quilting. The TV was off and the room was black, but I knew where I was because of the big window on one side of the chimney, glowing faintly. My arm hung down, touching something warm—and when I peered in that direction, it took me a few moments to recognize Sawyer on the floor right next to the sofa, with his back against it, in a sleeping bag that Harper had owned since at least third grade. My hand was on his shoulder.

Harper and Tia must have bedded us down when they came back inside. They sure hadn't woken me up when they moved me. But they must have woken Sawyer, or he would have landed pretty hard on the floor. And after he'd given me his place on the sofa, he'd stayed as close to me as possible.

I took a satisfied breath, for once wholeheartedly enjoying the tingles in my fingers and the feeling of doing something slightly wrong, and went back to sleep.

The window was pink with sunrise. A tinny alarm sounded quietly.

"It's mine," Sawyer whispered, fumbling with his watch. "Lie back down."

I was bone tired and sore from my night of cheering. I

never complained because I would sound silly compared with football players like Brody getting sacked, and because my mother might use my whining as an excuse to suggest I quit. This morning Sawyer's order to sleep more was almost as delicious as my light touch on him had been the night before. Gratefully I collapsed on the sofa again and curled into a ball, warming myself in the chilly air conditioning.

Covers rustled. A cozy weight fell across me as he draped the sleeping bag over my quilt.

"Thanks," I muttered, snuggling lower.

A shadow descended over me. I felt his lips brush my forehead.

I listened as he crossed the room, opened the front door, locked it from the inside, and quietly shut it behind him.

"Breakfast!" Harper's mom sang. "If you don't get it while Sawyer's cooking it, you don't get it." Before I even saw her, she'd walked out the front door, headed for the B and B.

I sat straight up into bright morning sunlight with a horrible realization, which must have been growing in my subconscious while I slept: I'd lost my back-and-forth note with Tia.

I jumped up and shook out the quilt, then the sleeping bag, then my pillow, then Sawyer's pillow, which he'd tossed into a chair. No note. I looked under the furniture and behind the sofa. Next I scanned the tables. My note could have gotten stuffed into any one of these art books.

"Morning!" Harper said brightly, coming around the

corner and blinking behind her glasses. Tia stumbled after her. Tia was not a morning person.

"Do y'all know what happened to that note we were passing around last night?" I asked, trying my best not to sound hysterical.

"No," Harper said, turning upside down to peer under the furniture herself. Her glasses fell off with a clatter. "Maybe it got thrown away."

"Didn't I have it last?" I asked Tia, who stared back at me like she was still in REM sleep and someone had glued her eyelids open.

"Never mind," I told Harper. "But if you find it, burn it."

"Okay." Harper laughed like it wasn't a big deal. We all washed up and changed into clothes that wouldn't scare the guests at the B and B. But my mind was racing. Harper was probably right. I could tell by looking around that she'd cleaned up the mess of Tia's midnight snacks. Her mom might have been through too, tidying up while I was still asleep. One of them had thrown the note away like trash.

Or Sawyer had found it.

And the last thing he'd done before leaving was to kiss me. If he'd read our note about me having a fling with him, the kiss was his way of saying yes.

Over in the B and B, we sat down to a full breakfast with Harper's mom and her eight guests at the biggest dining room table I'd ever seen, all dark scrolls like the rest of the towering Victorian. That is, Harper and Tia and I sat down. Sawyer kept getting up to check food in the kitchen or pass around a fresh basket of orange rolls.

He used his best waiter persona. He was polite and conversational to the elderly people at the table, offering them ideas for tourist attractions and the best roads to get them there. He was mature like a maître d' in a three-piece suit at a fine hotel, except that he was still wearing his Pelicans T-shirt and sweatpants. I actually *had* seen him in gentlemanly waiter mode before, when Barrett and I ate at the Crab Lab with my parents.

Several of the guests went off to start their day. Harper's mom was deep in conversation with the last two couples. Harper nodded toward the kitchen door, meaning it was safe to make our escape. We took our dishes with us so Sawyer wouldn't have to bus them. He was methodically working through a huge pile of plates, dumping food in the garbage, rinsing the dishes, and setting them in the dishwasher or dropping them to soak in an industrial-size sink. He was doing the work of probably six people at the Crab Lab.

He looked up when we walked in. "Sorry I flaked out on y'all last night," he said.

"What's the last thing you remember hearing?" Tia asked playfully. She winked at me.

Oh God.

Sawyer said without missing a beat, "The girl who had her heart set on a strapless dress, but her mama said she looked like a harlot." If he'd really been awake when we started talking about Aidan—and him—he hid it well.

Harper grabbed the first pan out of the drying rack and toweled it off. "You don't have to do that," Sawyer told her. She ignored him, talking to Tia about our walk to the beach in a few minutes. She turned to him only to ask if he could go with us.

"Thanks," Sawyer said with a quick glance at me, "but I'm working a double shift at the Crab Lab. I need to make up the hours I'm missing on Friday nights."

My heart went out to him. I would spend the morning relaxing by the ocean and trying to recharge for more school on Monday. He would be working and apparently needed the cash rather desperately. It didn't seem right that we both had gotten to play hard at the game last night, but he had to pay for that now, and I didn't.

"I'll dry," I told Harper, "and you put away, since you know where everything goes." She wasn't really paying me any attention, but she moved when I pushed her and dragged the dish towel out of her hands. I took her place. Now I stood beside Sawyer.

"So, you're going to stay at Harper's house until a room opens up here?" I asked him.

"Yeah," he said absently, concentrating on scrubbing something sticky out of the bottom of a pan.

"What are you going to do when you can't have the room here anymore? Harper said that will happen in December." I hoped I sounded like a concerned friend, not the girl in the van last night who'd made the comment about the box. I felt like I'd aged a year since then.

Tia chose this moment to wake up and pay attention. "I want him to move in with us at my house," she interrupted. "We should have the whole main floor done by December, so we'll have plenty of room. I just have to . . ." She glanced at Sawyer. "It's complicated."

"Complicated how?" I asked.

Sawyer looked up from the sink and gave me a warning glance. He didn't want to talk about it.

But Tia didn't understand warning looks, and there was pretty much nothing on the planet she wouldn't talk about. "I have to convince everybody," she said. "The main problem is Will. He says"—she broke into an incredibly bad imitation of a Minnesota accent—"'I trust you, and I trust Sawyer, but I don't trust you and Sawyer. He's quit drinking, and you've cut down, but what if you both fall off the wagon and something happens?'"

Sawyer glanced over his shoulder at her and wagged his eyebrows.

She laughed. "Will worries about these things. I'm like, 'But I am totally devoted to your body, and your accent is so sexy.'"

I should have been glad her family might give Sawyer a place to live. I *was* glad. But my jealousy wouldn't let go. I knew how Will felt.

"The main problem is my sister," Tia went on.

"Which sister?" Harper asked.

"Violet. You know, she's moved back in, and she doesn't

want a guy moving in too, because she's sworn off guys for the next five minutes. But the main problem is my other sister."

"Which other sister?" Harper asked.

"Izzy," Tia said.

"Do you realize there are three main problems?" I spoke up, trying not to sound as irritated as I felt.

Tia looked at me. "What?"

"You've said 'The main problem is . . .' three times."

"Yeah," she said. "That's what I'm trying to get across here. It's an uphill battle. So the main problem is Izzy."

"She doesn't even live with you anymore," Harper pointed out.

"That's what *I* say," Tia said, "but she's working on my dad. She's like, 'I got pregnant at seventeen. Tia's going to college. Trust me, you need to protect her from boys. The last thing you want to do is invite one to stay in your house.' Of course, this whole conversation is going on in Spanish, which I'm not as fluent in as they are, and the word for 'pregnant' sounds like 'embarrassed,' so I misunderstood what she was saying at first. I'm all like, 'I don't need to be protected, and I'm not embarrassed to have a boyfriend! Why should I be embarrassed just because *you* got pregnant?' The discussion kind of devolved from that point. I'll spare you the details."

Sawyer didn't speak through any of this. He left the sink to pull yet another fresh batch of orange rolls from the oven. Passing behind Tia with the basket, headed toward the dining room, he tugged on one of her braids. She responded by patting his shoulder.

"Let's get going," Harper said. "I love the beach in the morning."

I didn't have an excuse to hang around the kitchen until Sawyer came back. We left for Harper's cottage without me exchanging another word with him, or a glance, or gaining any more insight into whether he'd really found our note, or what the kiss was for.

At Harper's granddad's private strip of beach, just across the road and a block down from her house, I grilled her and Tia on ideas for where we could hold the homecoming dance. Tia predictably opted out because she didn't like being told to think too hard. Harper, who was good at thinking outside the box because that's where she lived pretty much all the time, couldn't come up with a single idea when I really needed her.

Finally I gave up and played in the water with them, floated in the ocean, and soaked up vitamin D on the beach to try to feel better about my life spinning out of control. I took deeper breaths, telling myself to *relax or die*, when I thought about going home to lunch with my mother.

I'd gotten a pass for the morning because Barrett and Dad were out on the sailboat. But my mother was making a big lunch with all Barrett's favorites—this was a little strange to me, because she cooked so seldom lately that I doubted she knew what *my* favorites even were—and I was required to be there.

* * *

Sure enough, the family lunch was everything I'd feared it would be, and more. My mother riddled Barrett with questions about college, ending each one in a barb about why he didn't make better grades. Barrett said as little as possible. Dad gently encouraged my mother to back off.

At some point my mother noticed I was there and asked, without much enthusiasm, "How was your game last night?"

"Pretty bad," I said. "Aidan broke up with me." I took another bite of salad.

My mother's jaw dropped. "I warned you about your mutiny. I hope it was worth it."

"Sylvia, wrong thing to say," Dad scolded her in an even tone, which was the only tone Dad had. But I was already pushing back my chair.

"No, ma'am," my mother called sharply. "You are not excused."

I stomped out of the dining room, down the hallway, and halfway up the stairs. At that point I realized the stomping was childish. I wasn't going to sit there at the table while my mother insulted me, but I wasn't going to give her the satisfaction of seeing me throw a tantrum, either. She would use that as ammunition later when I asked permission to do something.

I walked more softly up the rest of the stairs and into my room, not even slamming my door. In my bathroom I spit my mouthful of salad into the toilet and flushed.

Then I sat down in my reading chair, crossed my legs,

and waited for my mother to send Dad up to talk to me. In the meantime I struggled not to cry. I couldn't look like I'd been crying when they made me come back downstairs, and I couldn't let them hear me sobbing.

But I wanted to. I struggled for every breath as I squeezed my eyes shut and thought about how unfair my life had become. This was not what high school was supposed to be like. I felt like an elephant was sitting on my chest, exactly as I had when I'd run the Labor Day 5K keeping pace with Cathy, who had longer legs than mine.

By the time Dad predictably knocked on my door and let himself in half an hour later, I was more or less calmly looking out at the neighbors' gardener cutting their grass behind our house. My parents' bedroom and Barrett's had the views of the lagoon out the front.

I nearly bawled and threw myself into Dad's arms when I saw him, but that's what I'd done when I was little and had an argument with my mother. So I sat quietly while he told me to make my mother happy, just this once, and come downstairs to spend time with my brother in the short space we had left together as a family.

Obediently I sat with Dad on the sofa in the family room, watching college football, which is probably what I would have done even if I hadn't been ordered to, since it gave me time with Dad. I just did it with less shouting at the TV than usual.

My mother was in her office, catching up on the work she'd missed when she left the bank early on Friday.

Barrett was up in his room, on his laptop. So much for spending family time together.

Luckily, we had another happy memory scheduled, one that would trap us all at the table together again. For dinner Barrett wanted his favorite meal, shrimp and fries at the Crab Lab.

The Crab Lab was one of the bigger restaurants downtown, with lots of waiters. Even though Sawyer was working tonight, there was no reason to think he would wait on *us*. We'd been there as a family plenty of times, and he'd never served us before. In fact, I hoped he wouldn't, after what my mother had said about him yesterday.

But I did hope I would catch a glimpse of him. Share a joke with him. I could casually repeat the joke later when I texted him to ask whether, according to parliamentary procedures, Aidan could really oust me as student council vice president. In three years I'd never tried to get close to any guy except Aidan, and I wasn't sure how it was done. I promised myself I would try with Sawyer. At least that gave me something to look forward to on this horrible weekend.

I should have been more careful what I wished for.

Seven

"GOOD EVENING, MS. BEALE," SAWYER SAID IN a tone even brighter than the pleasing-the-elderly speeches I'd heard from him at breakfast that morning. "Hello, Mr. Gordon. I'm Sawyer, and I'll be your server this evening. Barrett." He looked down into my eyes. "Kaye. You look beautiful in blue." He set a basket of bread closest to me.

He wore his usual battered flip-flops, khaki shorts, and a Crab Lab T-shirt, with a white waiter's apron tied around his waist. His variegated blond hair looked halfway styled tonight. I approved. Even my mother had to be impressed by a neatly dressed, hardworking teen, exactly what she'd been growing up in downtown Tampa.

I should have known better when she didn't smile at being called Ms. Beale—even though, as Aidan had proven, it was quite a feat for my classmates to remember her name. Sawyer had been to my house for big parties a few times. He must have seen both surnames on our mailbox. So had everybody else, but Sawyer had *remembered.*

My mother didn't seem to care, though. When Sawyer asked for our drink orders, she just mumbled something to Dad, who opened the wine list. "What do you suggest?" he asked Sawyer.

Sawyer walked behind Dad, and they consulted the list together. Sawyer asked whether Dad was looking for a red or white, then rattled off characteristics of Riesling and sauvignon blanc brands using terminology I'd heard only on foodie TV shows. Sawyer was good at this.

"How do you know that?" my mother broke in. "Are you parroting what the restaurant has taught you about these wines, or do you know this from personal experience at age seventeen?"

I could have defended him by explaining that his brother was the bar manager, but somehow I didn't think that would impress my mother.

Sawyer straightened and appeared unsure for the first time. He said, "I don't have a good answer for that."

Dad chuckled. "*That* is a *great* answer."

I raised my hand. "Are y'all ready to order dinner? *I'm* ready to order." I poked Barrett. "Shrimp and fries, right?" The faster we could get out of here, the better. If my mother kept on like this, Sawyer would never want to look at me again.

As soon as he'd taken our orders and moved to a different

table, my mother pegged me with a stern gaze. "Is he the one who wants you to chase after the homecoming dance, even though the school canceled it?"

"A *lot* of people do," I said defensively. I pulled a slice of bread out of the basket, passed the basket to Dad, and popped some bread into my mouth. If everyone at the table had immediately started eating the Crab Lab's delicious bread, my mother would never have asked this:

"But *you* don't still want the dance, do you? Haven't you abandoned that idea now that Aidan's broken up with you? Who would you go with?"

I was tempted to blurt out Sawyer's name through a mouthful of bread, muffling the truth. I might have gotten away with it if my mother was just making conversation. But my mother never *just* made conversation. There was always a strategy, and this time she was reminding me I should have held on more tightly to Aidan, my great catch.

Besides, I got in trouble when I talked with my mouth full. "Not Florida manners," my mother would remind me. "Ivy League manners."

I chewed carefully, swallowed, and made the whole situation a million times worse by forcing my mother to wait and drawing attention to my answer. Finally I said, "I might ask Sawyer."

My mother choked midsip and put her water glass down with a *bang*, which I was pretty sure was *not* Ivy League manners. She asked sharply, "This one?" pointing with her thumb over her shoulder in the general direction of the Crab Lab's kitchen, where Sawyer had disappeared, thankfully.

"Yes," I said.

"The pelican," she said.

"Yes." I straightened in my chair, determined not to let her make me feel like shit. Or, *more* like shit.

"The one whose father robbed a bank."

"How did a pelican rob a bank?" Dad asked.

I looked over at Barrett. He'd never been very supportive in situations like this. He was good for a sympathetic eye roll, not much else. For once I could have used a comment from him, or a joke, or a subject change to distract my seething mother and befuddled dad, who was only going to make my mother angrier if he didn't stop playing dumb.

Ignoring Dad, I told my mother in a reasonable tone, "Sawyer's dad robbed a bank fifteen years ago."

"And he's out already?" my mother asked. "If he'd tried to rob *my* bank, he would be in there for life."

"He must have gotten time off for good behavior," Dad said helpfully.

"I've never understood that," my mother said. "How can anyone *not* behave well there? It's *prison*."

I took another bite of bread, since they obviously didn't need me for this conversation.

"You're not going out with that boy," my mother told me.

Again, I chewed carefully, swallowed, dabbed daintily at my lips, and returned my napkin to my lap. "Yes, I am," I said.

"You're grounded," my mother said. "Go ahead and ruin your grades trying to find a way to hold the dance, but you're not going."

I set my bread down. "I'm in charge of the parade, the homecoming court election, *and* the dance," I reminded her. "I was counting on impressing Principal Chen, whose glowing recommendation would get me into Columbia. But by all means, ground me because you don't like that I *might* ask out someone whose *father* did something wrong when I was two years old and already paid his debt to society. Because of that, I will shirk all my responsibilities and give up my Ivy League dreams."

"Sylvia," Dad said to my mother.

"I will probably move in with Sawyer after graduation," I continued, my voice getting shriller. "Maybe after a few years, I will have saved up enough money for cosmetology school."

"You lower your voice," my mother seethed.

"Why should I," I challenged her, "when I'm already grounded?"

"You're not grounded," Dad said patiently. He told my mother, "Kaye's not really going to a dance that doesn't exist with a boyfriend she doesn't have." He suggested to Barrett, "Tell us more about your classes this semester. When do you get to particle physics?"

I turned to Barrett as if I was interested in his sophomore-level physics classes too. As if *anyone* was. Dad could carry on pleasant conversation when nobody else wanted to. He'd honed his talents over a period of years in this family. The whole dinner was giving me a headache, though. I was clenching my teeth so hard I'd made my jaw hurt. I realized this and opened my mouth to relax my face, forming a hideous expression, I'm sure, just as Sawyer came around the corner balancing a tray with a wine bottle and an ice bucket.

He wasn't even looking at me, though. He set up a stand for the tray, placed the bucket on the table, then picked up the wine in a white towel. He stood there until Dad finished what he was saying to Barrett. Dad finally glanced around at Sawyer. Then my mother glanced over her shoulder at him too. Sawyer's nervous gaze flashed between them.

"What are you waiting for?" my mother asked.

"Normally I would show the label to Mr. Gordon," Sawyer said, "since he ordered the wine. But I was waiting for some indication from you, because it seems like you might ask why I assume I should show the bottle to the man of the party."

Dad and Barrett burst into laughter. Diners at the surrounding tables looked over.

My mother saw people looking too, and bent forward over the table. "Why are you laughing? I wouldn't do that."

"You *have* done that," Dad and Barrett said at the same time. Dad added, "At that restaurant on our trip to Miami, for starters."

Sawyer kept looking from one of them to the other, with the demeanor of an accused murderer waiting to hear his verdict in court. He still didn't glance at me, which was just as well. He knew he'd gotten himself in trouble, but he had *no idea* how angry he'd just made my mother.

Or how, if we ever *did* have any chance of going out together, he'd just killed that possibility.

When Dad was finally through chuckling, he wiggled his finger, inviting Sawyer to show him the bottle. My mother scowled as Sawyer maneuvered through an impressive display of ceremonial wine pouring. First he cut the foil over the top of the bottle with a large pocketknife he produced from his waiter's apron. I wondered if he brought this thing to school every day, too, and whether that was legal. Next he brought out a corkscrew. Remembering all the comedies I'd seen in which people got hit in the eye when someone popped the cork on champagne, I gripped the edge of my seat, expecting disaster—but Sawyer opened the wine like it was nothing.

He offered the cork to Dad—who shook his head as if that wasn't necessary—placed the cork by Dad's plate, then poured a splash of wine into Dad's glass, turning the bottle carefully so it didn't drip, I supposed. Dad sipped from his glass and nodded. Sawyer filled my mother's glass half-full, then Dad's, and with one practiced movement shoved the bottle into the ice bucket, keeping the white towel wrapped around the top.

My parents always ordered wine with dinner at restaurants. I must have seen this dance performed a hundred times, but I'd never appreciated the choreography, or the performer. Funny how a crush changed everything.

Sawyer stepped back. "Is there anything else I can do for you right now?"

"You have done a *lot* already," my mother said.

This time Sawyer focused on me, his blue eyes huge, before escaping to check on the next table.

My mother shook her head at me. She didn't say a word, but her message was clear: *You are dating Sawyer De Luca over my dead body.*

At the same time Dad was asking, "What did you prove, Sylvia, attacking that child? It's not a fair fight. Let it go." He turned to Barrett. "Next time you're home, I'm hoeing the potatoes and catching the shrimp myself."

"You're making a joke out of it," my mother said, "but your daughter *just* declared she is going *out* with him."

"That's not what she declared." Dad asked me, "Is that what you declared?"

I turned away from both of them to speak to Barrett, for once. "Please, tell us more about particle physics."

That got my parents asking Barrett questions again, at least. I stayed silent and worried about what Sawyer was thinking, and whether he hated me, as he strode from table to table to the kitchen and back to another table. I saw now why he slept so soundly.

After about twenty minutes, he brought out another tray and set up a stand. He placed redfish in front of my mother, trout in front of Dad, shrimp and fries in front of Barrett (damn Barrett and his shrimp and fries for causing all this), and the same in front of me. A couple of weeks ago when a bunch of us from school had eaten here, Sawyer had arranged my shrimp around the edge of my plate like the curls of my new hairstyle. This time the shrimp were piled humorlessly with a garnish of parsley. Judging from this, our prospects were ruined.

After he'd served us all, he drew the wine bottle out of the ice bucket, wiped it carefully with the towel, and poured my mother another glass. She looked up at him and asked, "Isn't it illegal for you to serve alcohol before you're twenty-one?"

He did that turning thing with the bottle again so it wouldn't drip as he brought it away from my mother's glass. Then he said, "The legal age to serve alcohol in Florida is eighteen, not twenty-one." He stepped behind my father and poured the rest of the wine into his glass. "But yes, I'm breaking the law. I'll be sure to tell the police chief at table six when I bring him his third Michelob." His polite waiter voice was gone. His usual snide Sawyer voice had returned.

My mother was glaring at him.

He didn't see her, though. He set the empty bottle on his tray and removed the ice bucket from the table. By that time he seemed to realize all on his own what he'd done. His lips parted. He looked at me.

Suddenly he straightened and turned very pale underneath his tan. "I'm sorry," he said to my mother. "That was uncalled for."

The table was silent. My mother's eyes had never left him, and her expression hadn't changed.

"I'm really sorry," he told Dad. "I apologize."

"It's okay, Sawyer," I heard myself telling him.

He lifted the laden tray high over his head, folded the stand, and hurried across the restaurant. He disappeared through the folding door into the kitchen.

"What did you say that for?" I hissed at my mother.

For the first time in a long time, my mother seemed taken aback. "It's illegal for him to serve us alcohol," she repeated.

"If you're so outraged, why did you let Dad order alcohol from him?"

Dad didn't jump in to defend her. He raised his eyebrows at her like he thought it was a good question.

"I didn't know it was illegal," my mother said.

"Obviously you had some idea, or you wouldn't have tried to catch him doing something wrong and embarrass him." I threw my napkin down on my plate and stood. "I am done eating with you people."

"Not again," Dad said.

"Can I have yours?" Barrett asked.

"Young lady . . . ," my mother started.

I followed Sawyer's path, winding among the tables. I had a hard time doing this without bumping anyone, and I wasn't even carrying a heavy tray and a stand like he had been. At the door to the kitchen, I hesitated, looking around to see if any of the restaurant staff was watching. As I glanced into the bar, a smaller room on one side of the restaurant, my eyes met Sawyer's dark-haired brother's.

He held my gaze, like he wasn't surprised to see me. He made no move to stop me.

I swept into the kitchen, moving fast. If anybody wanted to throw me out, they'd have to catch me first.

That was the last thing on these guys' minds, though. I'd imagined six people worked in the Crab Lab kitchen. There must have been twelve, all hustling. The equipment was new, but the walls were the original exposed brick like most of the buildings that made up downtown. The ceiling was embossed tin. Oil, steam, and Spanish floated in the air. If any cooks called to me, I didn't understand what they said. I made a beeline straight through to the back door standing open, which I assumed led to the Crab Lab's porch for employee breaks. Sawyer and Tia had experienced more escapades there than I'd really wanted to hear about.

Outside was a different world. The night, though warm, was ten degrees cooler than the kitchen, and full of the smells of cooking, not just from the Crab Lab but also from the barbecue restaurant on one side and the Indian restaurant on the other. Industrial-strength air conditioners shouted from all the buildings up and down the alley. But the Crab Lab's porch was an oasis, sheltered with an awning, furnished with picnic tables and ashtrays overflowing with cigarette butts. The railing was spun with twinkling white lights.

Sawyer stood at the edge of the wooden stairs down, arms

crossed, staring at the ancient brick-paved alley. When he heard my footsteps, he turned around. "Kaye!" he exclaimed, sounding startled. "I am so sorry."

I kept coming and walked right into him, wrapping my arms around him.

He didn't move, holding his arms stiffly at his sides.

"Hug me back," I said into his shoulder. "You have to do that sometimes. We can't always run to your truck to find the pelican outfit when we need to hug."

I meant we were both in emotional turmoil. We needed a hug to calm what was going on in our heads. But as he obediently slid his hands around my waist and nestled his face in my neck with his mouth at my ear, he took a step closer. His hard thigh was between my thighs. His body heated mine through his T-shirt and my thin dress.

His arms tightened around me. I tightened mine around him. We'd never hugged before—not when one of us wasn't dressed as a pelican, anyway. I regretted this now, because my body felt so good against his. His breath was soft in my ear. All the best parts of me started to tingle.

Without warning, he released me and took a step back. "Sit down," he said, sinking to a bench himself and patting the space beside him.

I sat very close with my knee touching his. "Will I get you in trouble for being back here?"

"Nobody gets in trouble for anything that happens on this porch. That's one reason I used to drink so much."

"Ah." That must also be the reason he and Tia had felt each other up nightly when she worked here last summer. I hadn't understood then why she put herself in that position with him over and over. I could definitely see the appeal now.

But that wasn't what I'd come here for, and I knew we didn't have much time to talk before he had to get back to work. I said, "About my mother—"

"There's no excuse for me saying that," he burst out.

"No!" I exclaimed. "*She* shouldn't have said that to *you*."

"She should be able to say anything she wants to me. Usually customers can. I don't react."

I found this hard to believe, knowing Sawyer. "Do you save it all up and release it at school?"

"Yes," he said. "But I wasn't expecting you tonight. I saw you come in, and I haven't been able to think straight since."

He was looking into my eyes and admitting that he liked me. My gaze drifted to the blond stubble on his cheeks, and then to his lips, which looked soft.

Reminding myself how little time we had, I slid my hand onto his. "My mother's powerful at her bank. According to everything I've heard, she's kind and fair to her employees. But you know the saying. A man in that position gets called the boss. A woman in that position gets called a bitch. I've been called a bitch at school just because I took charge or expressed my opinion, so I know how she feels."

Sawyer swallowed and nodded.

"And maybe she saves it all up and releases it at home," I

mused. "You had no way of knowing this, but when you mentioned that she might want to see the wine label instead of my dad, you definitely hit a sore spot."

"And then your dad and your brother laughed," Sawyer said. "I know. I never meant for that to happen. I've just had female customers react that way before. I've learned to stand back and read people so I can head off anybody getting angry or embarrassed. I thought I'd gotten good at it. I *have*. I know I have." He glanced sidelong at me. "You're jamming my radar."

"Sorry," I said softly.

Pulling his hand out from under mine, he stood, paced to the porch railing, and turned to face me. "What is she going to do to me? I blurted that dumb shit about the police chief, and suddenly I saw my life flash before my eyes. She could turn me in. I could lose my job. I won't be able to get another job serving alcohol at this age, and that's where I make most of my money in tips. My brother could lose his job for convincing the owner to hire me. Hold on." He pulled his phone out of his back pocket. It hummed and vibrated in his hand. "Oh, holy fuck," he said to the screen, "really? Now?" He pocketed it again without answering it.

"What's the matter?" I asked, alarmed. "Who is it?"

"My mother." Sawyer had a way of conveying loathing in his voice, but I'd never heard him sound quite so disgusted.

"In Georgia?" I checked.

"Yes."

"You don't answer her?"

"No."

I realized something. "Did she call you last night in the van?"

He looked at the porch ceiling, remembering. "Yes."

"Does she call you a lot?"

"Yes."

"When's the last time you talked to her?"

"Two years ago, when I left Valdosta." When I gaped at him, he said, "She only wants money."

I was having a very hard time understanding Sawyer's world. "What if she's calling about something else?" I reasoned.

"She'd call my brother. I know, you're thinking, 'You should send your mom money if she needs it,' but I'm just done with her. I mean, I voluntarily came to live with my father as soon as he got out of prison. That's how bad it was with my mother."

I frowned at him. "Wait. I thought you moved in with your father because your mother couldn't handle you anymore."

He huffed an exasperated sigh. "Who told you that?"

"Several people. Tia."

He squinted at me. "I may have said that to Tia before I really knew her. My first day in town, it got around school that my dad had been to jail. Assholes were picking on me. I hit first so nobody would hit me. That seemed to work, so I started cultivating a tough-guy rep. See how great it works? Arrrrrrg," he moaned with his head in his hands. "Fuck everybody."

I'd heard him say *that* before too, but he hadn't sounded this lost.

He looked up at me. "Everyone but you."

"Aw," I said. "That's sweet, I guess." I got up and walked over to him. He was staring at the floor again. I put my hand under his chin and lifted his head until he looked at me. "My mother's not going to turn you in, Sawyer. That was never her intention. Being critical is her way of making small talk." I was realizing this for the first time as I said it.

He removed my hand from his face and held it loosely between us, looking doubtfully at me.

"She grew up poor," I said.

Sawyer gave a short nod. He needed no further explanation.

But I wanted to give him one, to show him I wasn't completely ignorant of what this meant. "When Barrett and I were younger and she got mad at us for not working hard enough in school or refusing to eat enough dinner, she packed us in the car and drove us across town to gawk at where she grew up." Actually, *I* was the one she always got mad at, but she often made Barrett go too, in case my bad attitude had rubbed off on him.

Sawyer gave me the mad scientist face I loved, raising one eyebrow and lowering the other. "That's heavy."

"I thought so too," I said. "You got off easy." I detangled my hand from his and rubbed his arm, trying to rub some of his usual life back into him. "*I* was impressed with your waiter skills. I had no idea you were so highly trained. You never pull out all these stops when I come here without my parents."

"I'm not going to do all that shit for you guys," he muttered. "You're my friends, and I'm in a hurry to get back to another table, and y'all aren't going to tip me anyway."

"Of course we tip you!" I said, thinking back to the last time Sawyer had waited on me when I'd paid for my food myself. It was the last time I'd been here, two weeks ago exactly, and I could have sworn I'd tipped him fifteen percent.

"Not when Aidan pays, you don't."

My hand stopped on his arm as I gaped at him. *"Really?"* I was horrified. I'd had no idea Aidan was that rude to anyone but me. And Sawyer needed the money, now more than ever.

He looked away. Even in the dim blinking lights, I could tell he was blushing.

I took both his hands in mine. "You know, your parents have a legal responsibility to take care of you until you turn eighteen."

"Yeah, well, I'm about to turn eighteen."

"You don't turn eighteen until March fifteenth, Sawyer."

He raised his eyebrows. "Why do you know when my birthday is?"

"I just do." I didn't let on that I'd surprised myself with this knowledge too. I knew generally when most of my friends' birthdays were, as in, what month. I'd memorized specific days for Tia, Harper, Aidan, and Sawyer.

"That's a long time for you to go without a real place to live," I said. "Did your dad kick you out, or did you just leave?"

"I left," he said darkly.

"Why?"

"I don't want to talk about it," he said so vehemently that, nosey as I was, I didn't dare try to turn over that rock again.

Instead I said, "You should talk to someone. One of the counselors at school."

"No! Guys don't do that."

"Not the weird counselor with the muttonchop sideburns," I said quickly. "The nice one, Ms. Malone. Go in and tell her whatever you don't want to tell me. You obviously need to tell *somebody*. You're this big ball of stress." I reached up and rubbed his shoulders, kneading the soft notches next to his shoulder blades. Sure enough, the muscles there were tight with his anxiety. Even tighter than mine. "Promise me you'll go Monday."

He let out an appreciative sigh and let his head fall forward so that some strands of his hair got caught in mine. He groaned, "No."

Leaving my hands on his shoulders, I stopped rubbing. "Promise me, and there's more where this came from."

"Okay," he said instantly.

I made a few more hard circles with my fingers, then let him go. "I have something to ask you. I know we've been out here a while, though, and you need to go back to work. Our table from hell isn't your only table."

"I told another server to cover for me while I took a break," he said. "So, yeah, I need to get back, but you can ask me something. Shoot."

"It's a parliamentarian question," I said. "When Aidan

broke up with me last night, he also told me to resign as vice president."

Sawyer was shaking his head.

I went on. "I told him no. He said he would go to Ms. Yates. I said I would go to you."

"Exactly." Sawyer sounded like his sarcastic self again. "There's nothing in the student council charter giving him that power. Ms. Yates knows that. After Friday's meeting, she also knows I understand the charter, and I'd make a stink. If they tried to take the position away from you, theoretically you could sue the school system for not following its own written rules. There's no way Principal Chen would let that happen."

"I shouldn't worry?" I asked. "I figured he was bluffing to see if he could make me resign."

"No," Sawyer said, "don't worry. The charter gives Aidan very little power. The only reason he has power around school is that he *says* he does, and other people believe him." He eyed me hard. By "other people" he meant me.

I would prove Sawyer wrong about this.

"Are you working tomorrow?" I asked.

"Yes."

"When?"

"All day."

I'd been afraid of this. "All night, too?"

"Yes."

"My parents are taking Barrett to the airport midafternoon. I'm going to make my escape, drive over here, explore some shops, and try to figure out where we might be able to hold the homecoming dance. Maybe I'll pop in to visit you."

"Do," he said. "I'll see you then." He didn't smile, exactly, but he looked a lot less tortured than he had when I'd come out here. I headed inside.

But as I looked back over my shoulder at him, he was staring out at the alleyway again. He ran his hand through his hair and gripped the back of his head like he wanted to pull his scalp off.

When I returned to the table, my parents were finishing their food. Barrett's plate was empty, and several of my shrimp had gone missing. Plopping down in my chair, I told my mother, "I hope you're happy. You scared the life out of Saw—"

I stopped as Sawyer himself appeared between my parents. He took my mother's plate, then Dad's. "How was everything?" he asked in his personable waiter voice.

"Delicious," Dad said. He ordered dessert.

My mother glared. Sawyer noticed and smiled at her. Oh, Sawyer.

As soon as he'd disappeared into the kitchen again, she told me, "I *meant* to scare the life out of him. I don't want that boy anywhere around you, after what I just found out about his father. Did you know—"

"Sylvia, don't," Dad said.

My mother spoke over him. "—his father grew up here in town and actually robbed a bank branch right down the road in Clearwater? That hits a little too close to home. Seth said it wasn't one of *my* branches, but—"

"Seth," I repeated. The only Seth I knew was Aidan's dad, who worked as an assistant district attorney for the county. "Did you *call Aidan's dad* right here from the restaurant so you could convince me how terrible Sawyer is? You made him look up that case on a Saturday night?"

"He didn't have to look it up," my mother said ominously. "He's the one who put that man in jail."

I could *not* believe this. Granted, Mr. De Luca sounded like a shadier and shadier character as my mother transformed his crimes from vague rumors into stark, brutal reality. But that only increased my growing respect for Sawyer.

I looked to Dad for help. He closed his eyes and took a deep breath through his nose like he was counting to ten. Barrett reached over to my plate and stole another of my shrimp. I was on my own.

I told my mother, "This is a logical fallacy, guilt by association. You damning Sawyer for what his dad did is like me damning you for what your—"

"Kaye," Dad said sternly.

My mother always sounded stern. Dad never did. His use of that tone was so surprising that I was shocked out of what I was going to say.

Which was exactly what he'd intended. And it was probably for the best. Because I'd been about to point out that my mother's brother had been murdered while selling heroin in the neighborhood where they grew up. She'd been sixteen years old.

As Sawyer set a slice of chocolate cake down in front of Dad, he looked cautiously around the table at our angry faces.

"I'm sure it's delicious," Dad told Sawyer, "but I've changed my mind. Could I get this boxed up to go?"

Eight

THE NEXT MORNING MY MOTHER COOKED A big breakfast, and Dad congratulated me on making it all the way through the meal without flouncing away. He must have talked my mother down. She didn't say another word about Sawyer or his jailbird father. And I was in a better mood because I had something to look forward to: seeing Sawyer again.

Right after my parents left to take Barrett to the airport, I drove downtown. The Crab Lab was my first stop. I hadn't counted on running straight into their two-for-one brunch special. Sawyer grinned brilliantly at me when I came in, but so many customers flagged him down that I stood by the door for five minutes before he even made it over to me. He said he couldn't talk just then, and I understood why. I would embark on my mission by myself.

I'd strolled the brick sidewalks of our historic downtown countless times, but I saw the buildings with new eyes now that

I was looking for something specific. The Crab Lab owned a restored warehouse for events. It stood to reason that, somewhere among these buildings, there was another space large enough to throw a homecoming dance. I just had to find it.

I spent hours walking into every storefront and asking the people behind the counter whether they owned such a space or knew of one. Most of them said no. Tia's sister Violet, who worked in an antiques shop, said she did have a space like that on the second floor, but we couldn't hold our dance there because it was full of dead bodies. Skeptical, I walked up the rickety stairs myself, straight into the store's antique taxidermy collection.

But Violet said the gay burlesque club might be an option. Their second story was an open dance floor practically *made* for homecoming. Dubious about my chances of convincing the owner to say yes, I walked in anyway—drawing arch looks from the men bellied up to the bar—and quickly told the bartender what I wanted.

"Well, *I'm* the owner," he said, "and of *course* you can use the second floor. In fact, I'll close down the whole place for the night so we don't have the barflies drinking among you tender innocents."

"You would do that for us?" It didn't seem real.

"I'm a graduate of your fine institution," he explained. "It's the least I can do for homecoming. Fight, Pelicans, fight!"

I drove home feeling lighter than I had since Friday. I rolled down the windows and enjoyed the hot wind scented with flowers. When I stopped at the intersection next to Aidan's house, I didn't even look to see whether he was home.

I should have stayed away from my own house a few more hours.

My parents had returned. My dad was probably upstairs on his porch, but my mother actually came out of her office to confront me.

I braced myself for another fight, but I was so, so weary.

She opened her arms.

I stiffened, resistant. Then, partly to prevent myself from crying in front of her, I walked into her embrace.

She hugged me tightly for a moment. Loosening her hold, she rubbed my back. She told me to sit down at the kitchen bar and served me two of Barrett's leftover cookies, even though they would probably spoil my dinner.

I should have known the other shoe would drop. Covering one of my hands with hers on the counter, she told me, "You can struggle, Kaye, and work, and go after your dreams. And one wrong move can ruin you forever."

I didn't retort as I had last night. I didn't have the heart. In her precisely made-up eyes, I saw real concern for me, bordering on panic. And I understood where she was coming from. She had braved terrible odds to get to college. By the time she graduated, everyone she'd loved back home was dead.

But she didn't need to worry about me. Not to this extent, anyway. My own world was nothing like hers had been. My future was not so fragile.

Was it?

"I wanted to apologize for flying off the handle a couple of times yesterday," she said.

Yep, Dad had definitely talked her down.

She said, "When I was growing up—"

And with that, she lost me. "I don't want to hear about it," I said quickly. "You grew up in a slum, surrounded by criminals and addicts. I'm sorry for what you went through, but my life is not like that."

She glowered at me for interrupting.

"Sorry," I grumbled.

"What I was going to say," she told me indignantly, "is that when I was growing up, people all around me made terrible mistakes. And those mistakes were often deadly. For that reason, it's hard for me to let people I love make mistakes. But you're right. You're not in the environment I was in. The mistakes you make won't kill you. I know that. I'll try to do better."

I shrugged, munching a cookie. For her, this was a pretty good apology, but she'd managed simultaneously to accuse me of failing at life.

"When I talked to Seth last night," she said, "he indicated that Aidan is really regretting asking you for a break."

"He did not ask," I said.

"Well. And I'm sure your feelings about this are still very raw. But Seth seemed to think the whole problem started because you made an error with the yearbook elections."

"Mr. O'Neill thinks so because that's what Aidan told him," I pointed out.

She nodded. "Aidan also told him you and Sawyer had been connected in some way in one of the polls. You and Sawyer have been spending more time together because of this cheerleading business, and now in student council. Aidan grew jealous and let his feelings get the better of him. He's going to ask you to take him back."

"I'm going to say no."

"And if you do," my mother said, "Seth and I won't interfere."

"Gee, thanks," I said.

She glowered at me again. This time I didn't say I was sorry.

Finally she went on. "But I want you to think about the three years you and Aidan dated. You told me time and time again you were going to marry him. Of course, that's a silly thing for a fourteen-year-old to say, but you were together so long that I began to think you'd found true love after all. You planned to go to Columbia together. Don't throw this away over one silly fight about a boy you're not going to date anyway."

We exchanged a long, unblinking look. She was making sure I'd gotten her message. I was thinking I wanted to try out Sawyer more than ever.

"When I was in high school," she said, "there was a boy I liked. He was *so fine*."

"Fine?" I asked skeptically.

"It was the eighties," she said. "Anyway, he was bad news. I knew he would take me down the wrong path, so I made a conscious decision to stay away from him."

My heart stopped. "And now you regret it," I said softly.

She side-eyed me. "No, he's in prison. If I'd done what he wanted, I would have ended up a single mother without a college degree, much less an MBA, working for minimum wage and struggling to make ends meet."

Oh, good Lord.

"What happened to letting me make my own mistakes?" I asked.

She shrugged. "You're right. I told you, it's hard for me to let go. I do want you to enjoy high school. But this year will fly by, and then your life will really start."

And with that she reached into the container for her own cookie.

I spent the rest of the night working on my pitch to Principal Chen for saving the dance. The student council had already put down deposits on the DJ and the caterer. If we canceled the dance altogether, we'd lose those student dues dollars with nothing to show for it. The best solution, both for fiscal responsibility and school morale, was simply to move the venue to the property of a local business owner and Pelican alumnus.

This speech made perfect sense. If Aidan somehow convinced Ms. Yates that I should be fired as student council vice president, Ms. Chen would never allow it, because I was obviously such a great school leader.

But as I rehearsed my speech in my head, I began to have misgivings about telling Ms. Chen we were moving the dance to a gay bar. If she didn't like this idea, she might not give me another chance.

And even if she did approve the move, the likelihood was high that someone's parents would complain. Our town was generally pretty accepting, but back in ninth grade, Angelica's mom had told Ms. Yates she shouldn't be teaching her impressionable child about evolution.

If we held homecoming at the gay burlesque club, there would be a stink.

The stink would lead to a petition.

Someone would post the petition online, where it would go viral.

Our school and our town would get a national reputation as closed-minded and backward.

It would be all my fault.

And my mother would look at me and say, *I told you so*.

Honestly, why didn't I leave well enough alone?

I lay on my bed, curled into a ball, staring out my window at the neighbor's yard, late into the night. When my mind was exhausted from weighing those options and mulling over the problem, it moved on to the conundrum of Sawyer. Maybe my mother was right. I was still furious with Aidan, but did I really want to throw our whole lives together away? We could take a break for a little longer and see if time healed our wounds.

But if I went out with Sawyer, or even acted like I wanted to, I could easily ruin everything with Aidan. I didn't buy Tia's argument that dating Sawyer would make Aidan jealous and bring him closer. Aidan's ego wouldn't survive that insult.

Besides, what proof did I have that Sawyer wanted to go out with *me*? He'd been sweet to me last night. He said he'd gotten flustered when he saw me. He'd acted like he wanted me to visit him today. But he hadn't asked me on a date. There were a lot of things I didn't understand about Sawyer, but this I knew: He went after what he wanted.

I got so little sleep that, in the morning, I put on clothes and makeup and stumbled downstairs in a haze. But I'd decided two things. I would tell the student council that Aidan had been right. I'd looked for a venue where we could hold the dance, and the only alternative I'd found wouldn't be acceptable to everyone. We should cancel after all.

And I would tell Sawyer it would be better that we didn't get together.

If he even asked.

"I hope your paper on *Crime and Punishment* turned out well," my mother said as I was walking out the door to my car.

My response was to gasp, which gave away to her that I'd completely forgotten about the paper.

"I thought that's what you were doing up in your room last night!" she shouted, anger flashing in her eyes. "You spent this entire weekend on everything *except* your paper?"

Dad had left early in the morning to drive to Miami for research on his new book. There was nobody left to say in a calming voice, "Sylvia," and stop my mother from freaking out.

"If you can't complete your basic assignments," she said, "we should definitely rethink this cheerleading mess."

I cried so hard on the drive to school that I thought several times about pulling off the road. Finally I parked, killed the engine, and searched the glove compartment for a tissue to clean up my mascara before I went inside.

I was blowing my nose in a fast-food napkin when I spotted Harper and Brody sitting on a bench near the school entrance, shaded by palms from the bright morning sun. He was talking close to her ear. Her hair was long and glossy, flowing over her shoulders, her dark eyes shining into the sunlight. A smile was frozen on her face because of something he'd said, but now she'd gotten distracted by a bird, a cloud, or the way the palm fronds waved in the breeze.

Farther away, walking across the parking lot toward school, Tia laughed loudly with Will. I could hear her even with my windows rolled up. She didn't look much different than she had in third grade: tall, disheveled, with her auburn hair pulled away from her face anyhow, laughing.

My favorite things about my friends, Tia loud and laughing and Harper daydreaming, were things my mother would have scolded me for doing. *Inside voice. Pay attention. Ivy League manners.*

I didn't even *have* a favorite thing about myself. I loved to dance. I loved to cheer. My mother made me feel like those activities were nonsense. All that was left of me was organizational skills and the ability to follow directions. My only two talents had had a fatal shoot-out in my brain overnight. Now I was an empty shell.

The bell rang to call everyone inside. My classmates who'd been moseying across the parking lot quickened their step. Tia and Will jumped the curb and high-fived Harper and Brody, who stood and stretched. They all disappeared beneath the parallel lines of palm trees leading into the school.

I had to go inside too, to face Mr. Frank with no paper and accept my first-ever zero. I knew this. But as I took one last breath of sticky air inside my car, I entertained a fantasy of turning the engine on again and driving in the opposite direction to play hooky at the beach. How much more trouble could I possibly get into this morning? Might as well enjoy myself, for once.

Two minutes later I was inside the crowded school hallway like a good girl, of course. I pulled my books for my first two periods out of my locker. Aidan leaned casually against the locker next to mine, just as he had countless times before, like we'd never broken up. When he saw my face, though, he straightened and asked, "What's wrong?"

"I forgot to write my paper for Mr. Frank," I said, hoarse from crying.

"Ha!" Aidan crowed. "That's one step closer to valedictorian for me."

I just looked at him with my mouth open. Aidan was competitive. He was callous. But until now I'd never known him to be cruel.

I slammed my locker as hard as I could and stomped down the hall.

"Hey!" I heard him calling after me. "I was *kidding*!"

I kept walking. The bell rang again, and the people remaining in the hallways slipped into classrooms. I was still moving. My history class was in the other direction, but I simply couldn't see myself sitting in a desk right now, facing the front, my stomach cramping with the knowledge that I'd just blown everything I'd worked for because of one crazy weekend.

Ahead of me, Sawyer stepped into the hallway and closed a door behind him. When he saw me, he froze with his hand on the doorknob, his face flushing bright pink.

I looked up at the nameplate on the door and saw why he felt caught. MS. MALONE, SCHOOL COUNSELOR.

But Sawyer was always quick to recover. The next second he didn't look self-conscious anymore. His hands were on my shoulders. "Wow, what's the matter?"

I flung myself into his arms.

Nine

AS SOON AS HIS ARMS ENCIRCLED ME, I WAS trying to pull away again. Nobody but us was in the hall right now. I could hear Ms. Chen's morning announcements echoing through an open door. But a teacher was likely to peek out at us any second, see us embracing, and send us straight to the principal's office. Plus, surveillance cameras frowned from the corners of the ceiling, keeping everyone safe from school shooters and public displays of affection.

Sawyer didn't let go of me. He held my head to his chest, saying, "Shhh. Tell me what's wrong, and we'll fix it."

I laughed and then coughed at the idea of Sawyer, with all his real problems, being able to solve any of my ridiculous ones. After a gargantuan sniffle, I said shakily, "I forgot to write my paper for Mr. Frank."

He held me at arm's length and looked into my eyes. "That's a major grade." Before I could cry again, he ordered me, "Stop. You mean you forgot to make your paper perfect, or you forgot to write it at all? How many words do you have?"

"None." I was about to lose it.

"Stop," he said again. "But you have your thesis statement and your notes and your outline, right? We did that in class."

I nodded.

"That's your blueprint. All you need to do is fill in the blanks. You have hours to get that done. We don't go to Mr. Frank's class until second-to-last period. You can write it on your computer and e-mail it to him while he's taking roll."

"But, Sawyer," I wailed, "I have class until then. I'm doing class during class."

"You've got study hall," he pointed out, "and lunch."

"I was going to talk to Ms. Chen about the homecoming dance during lunch," I said.

He shook me gently. "Kaye. Listen to me. You've got to let go of that shit and prioritize. Save your grade today. Do homecoming tomorrow." He released my arms and rubbed where he'd squeezed me. "There's lots of downtime during class, too. Even when teachers are talking, you can be working on your paper."

"What if one of them calls on me and I get in trouble?"

"To save your GPA, it's worth it," he declared. "And if things really get hairy, take your computer to the bathroom."

"This isn't going to work," I whispered.

He gave me an exasperated look. "Do you know how much homework I've done at the very last second in the bathroom?

You can do this, Kaye. You just have to believe it. Isn't your dad a famous writer?"

"He's not famous," I mumbled.

"But he works on deadline," Sawyer pointed out. "Just because you didn't obsess over this paper doesn't mean it won't be any good. Even if it does turn out to be shit, you'll get a fifty just for turning it in, which is way better for your average than a zero."

"Right." With a grade of fifty rather than a zero, I'd get a B for this grading period and lose hope of making valedictorian. But there was always salutatorian. That might be good enough for admission to Columbia, with my alumni parents backing me.

But nothing would save me in the eyes of my mother.

"Whatever you're thinking right now," Sawyer said, "snap out of it. Let me tell you what needs to go through your head for the next five hours, until you turn this paper in." He tapped one finger. "Dostoyevsky."

"Dostoyevsky," I repeated.

He tapped another finger. "Raskolnikov."

"Raskolnikov," I said.

"Alyona Ivanovna, Porfiry Petrovich, Sonia Marmeladov. Got that? Now, what's going through your head? Hint: The answer should be Dostoyevsky."

"I'm tardy for history," I sobbed, "and I don't have an excuse."

Sawyer gave me his crazy face with one eyebrow up,

clearly at the end of his patience. "I'll write you in on the one Ms. Malone gave me."

"That's forgery!"

Shaking his head, he grabbed my hand and knocked on Ms. Malone's door. When we heard "Come in," he pulled me inside.

"Back so soon?" Ms. Malone asked from behind her desk. She saw me and said, "Oh, hi there."

"Ms. Malone," Sawyer said, "this is Kaye Gordon."

Ms. Malone came around her desk to shake my hand. "We were just talking about you." Too late she realized this was not the right thing to say. Her eyes darted to Sawyer, who was blushing intensely all over again.

His flushed cheeks were the only clue Sawyer was mortified, and he continued smoothly, "Kaye would like to make an appointment to talk with you about stress management techniques."

"Yes, I see you're having a problem there," Ms. Malone agreed, scanning my tearstained and probably mascara-streaked face. "How about today?"

"Not today," Sawyer said quickly, "or anytime before homecoming, because that will just stress her out more. How about the Monday after homecoming?"

Ms. Malone stepped behind her desk again and flipped through her calendar. She looked up at me. "Is this period okay?"

I nodded dumbly.

She wrote my appointment time down on a card.

"And can she also have an excuse that says she was here talking to you?" Sawyer asked. "She's late for history."

Ms. Malone gave Sawyer the briefest look that let him know she saw right through his ploy.

But she paged through her book of preprinted excuses and filled one out for me. Handing it across her desk, she said, "All right, dear. You come see me sooner if you need to." She turned to Sawyer. "And you, here, tomorrow."

"Yes, ma'am." Sawyer put his arm around my shoulders and steered me out the door.

"Thank you," I breathed as we walked down the hall.

"You're welcome. I earned my shoulder rub."

"You did." I laughed and felt better, even though I had a horrible five hours in front of me, and my face was still wet with tears. "Did Ms. Malone help you? What did she say?"

"Don't think about that right now. Until one o'clock when you e-mail this paper to Mr. Frank, your only thoughts are Dostoyevsky, Raskolnikov—"

"Okay." I stopped in the hallway. He stopped too, in surprise. His eyes were full of concern.

I wanted to kiss him—not a show of lust, but of appreciation. I would get us both in hot water, though. I only kissed my finger and placed it on his lips.

He looked shocked for a moment. But as I pulled my hand away, he said solemnly, "I know. I feel that way too."

And we walked to history together.

* * *

The following Friday, I skipped out of calculus even earlier than I had the previous week for the student council meeting. I waited outside Ms. Yates's classroom. Sure enough, I'd beaten Sawyer by a hair. I watched him saunter up the hallway, walking more like the jaunty pelican than his usual cool self while he thought nobody was watching. His backpack hung heavy over one shoulder. It probably contained six different library books explaining *Robert's Rules of Order*. He wore the madras plaid shirt with the blue stripe that I loved so much. When he looked up at me, his blue eyes were arresting in the blank white hall. He broke into a wide grin.

He'd been kind to me Monday while I was writing my paper, checking on me between classes. During lunch I'd e-mailed him my mostly finished draft. He'd read over it on his phone while I was still typing the end, and he suggested places I could clarify my statements or add more detail. Best of all, he told me my paper wasn't crap. That kept me going. I didn't have time to eat lunch, but I typed my closing statement just as the bell rang to go to Mr. Frank's class, where Sawyer slipped me a candy bar underneath our desktops.

The way he'd treated me, and the way *Aidan* had acted when he found out I'd forgotten to write my paper, made me question my decision not to date Sawyer if he asked. The problem was, he didn't ask. All week we hung out during lunch and the classes we had together. People certainly saw *something* between us. Tia and Harper, wide-eyed, asked me for updates three times a day. The cheerleaders and my other friends who hadn't heard about everything that had passed between Sawyer and me demanded to know whether we were hooking up. Several of them told me they'd voted for Sawyer and me as Perfect Couple That Never Was, and they were disappointed when I was named Most Likely to Succeed with Aidan.

Me too. I hadn't felt that way when the Superlatives titles were first announced, but hindsight was 20/20.

Maybe I should have taken the plunge and asked *Sawyer* out. But he was holding back with me. That was unlike him. He must have some good reason. And I was enjoying being close to him so much that I was afraid of messing things up if I pushed too fast for a change.

"Hey," I said as he stopped beside me at Ms. Yates's door. "I wanted to catch you before the meeting. Were you planning to sit at Ms. Yates's desk again?"

"I don't have to," he said. "I only did that last week to make Aidan mad."

"Great minds think alike."

He didn't laugh. He watched me carefully, as if talking about Aidan was making him as uncomfortable as it was making me.

"I don't want to argue with him anymore," I said in a rush. "I'm just not interested. And I think it would help us get along with him if we let him have the desk. We're trying to get stuff done in student council, and we should pick our battles."

The bell rang. Sawyer and I stepped back into safety against the wall as Ms. Yates's freshmen streamed into the hall, followed by Ms. Yates, who hurried toward the teachers' lounge. She obviously couldn't deal with these meetings without a fresh cup of coffee. Considering the last meeting and Sawyer pulling out the rule book, I didn't blame her.

After the flood of freshmen had passed, I walked into the room and sat in a desk in the front row. Sawyer slid into the desk behind mine. Goose bumps rose on my skin as he whispered so close that I could feel his breath on my neck. "Will you marry me?"

"Yes," I said without hesitation, turning to smile at him. "I already told you."

He glanced up as the first reps walked in. Then he lowered his voice and asked, "Will you go to the prom with me?"

For the first time I really thought about our senior prom with Sawyer as my date. It could actually happen now. He would look dashing in a tux, a combination of handsome elegance and dangerous energy. I wanted to say yes.

Instead I said, "Prom is in April. A lot could happen before then. It's too soon to tell."

"Excuses, excuses," he said dismissively. "Nothing can happen before tonight, though. Will you sit in the van with me on the drive to the game?"

"I have to," I said, "because I owe you a shoulder rub."

He raised his eyebrows provocatively as if I'd said something very sexy. That's what I'd been counting on. Granted, he hadn't asked me out in the past week, or made anything that could be called a move on me. But we'd also seen each other only in public, usually fleetingly, like touching hands as we passed in the hall. Maybe we just needed some quality time together. We wouldn't be alone in the cheerleading van, but we'd definitely be stuck next to each other.

And I intended for something to happen.

When the classroom had filled with reps, Aidan swept in to take his proper place on the throne. As he sat down in Ms. Yates's chair, Sawyer sent him a message by noisily unzipping his backpack and thumping *Robert's Rules of Order* onto the corner of his desk where Aidan could see it.

Sawyer's threat worked. Aidan didn't deviate from the rules. He simply called on the committees to report about the student council's homecoming responsibilities. That is, he called on *me* to report on the various committees I headed.

I told the classroom that preparations for Monday's election of the homecoming court were going well. This meant I'd put some junior cheerleaders I trusted in charge. Preparations for the parade float build were also going well, because I'd delegated Will to handle them. He'd designed a gorgeous beach scene that he swore we could pull off with nothing but wood, chicken wire, and crepe paper, and he'd drafted Tia's contractor dad to take off work for once and supervise construction. Finally we got around to the dance.

"The dance preparations aren't progressing as I'd planned,"

I admitted. "I did find a potential place to hold it off campus." No need to bring up that the place was a gay bar. "But when I spoke with Principal Chen on Tuesday about moving the dance, she said we couldn't hold it off campus for liability reasons. If the dance is an official school function paid for with student dues, it needs to be held here on school grounds unless our lawyers okay a new location, and we don't have time to call them in."

"So it's dead?" Will called from the back of the room. "If we can't have it here, and we can't have it elsewhere, it's dead."

"It looks dead," I admitted. "I hoped one of you would have a brilliant idea. Throw me a Hail Mary pass here." I held up my hands, ready to catch the last-minute idea a rep would toss at me.

Nobody said anything. All eyes were on me, waiting for me to solve this problem myself.

"Well, y'all have my phone number," I concluded. "Text me over the weekend if you come up with something. If we don't have a solution by Monday, we won't have time to get the word out to students and parents, and the dance will definitely be dead."

The meeting progressed normally after that. Aidan didn't make a sarcastic comment about the dance or question why I'd pursued it in the first place. He didn't have to, because he'd already won.

But when he dismissed the meeting and the reps were filing out to the lunchroom, he walked over and put both hands on my desk, bending close, his face inches from mine. "Will you eat lunch with me today? We need to talk."

I eyed him. "About student council?"

"Of course," he said.

"About me resigning as vice president?" I asked. "I refuse to have that discussion again."

"I don't want you to resign as vice president," he said soothingly. "I was angry that night." This was as much of an apology as I ever got out of Aidan unless he also dropped his suave politician facade. This time he didn't.

"Will Ms. Yates be there?" I snapped. "I really enjoyed the last time I tried to eat lunch with you two."

"Just you and me," he said.

"All right. Let me do something first." I watched him return to Ms. Yates's desk to gather his papers. Then I faced Sawyer.

He was watching me, like he'd heard the whole conversation and expected an explanation.

"I'm eating lunch with Aidan," I said.

Sawyer nodded. He had no expression on his face, which was never a good sign.

But if he had nothing else to say, I wasn't going to hang around and try to draw him out. He *still* hadn't done anything to make me think he wanted us to get together. As far as I knew, the crush was all on my end.

I walked to the lunchroom with Aidan and a crowd of reps. Aidan went through the hot food line while I visited the salad bar—mainly because I was hoping for another word with Sawyer, not because I wanted salad. So much for not caring what Sawyer thought. I hadn't lasted five minutes. But I didn't see him anywhere.

Eventually I slid my salad onto a table across from Aidan, not in the teacher section but far away from our usual table too, in an unpopulated corner. As I sat down, he asked, "What'd you get on your *Crime and Punishment* paper?"

He uttered this like it was a casual question. It wasn't. He'd asked me all about my grades when we'd dated. But looking back on our time together, I realized my shoulders had tightened and my stomach had twisted with stress every time he'd grilled me. The constant competition with him over the years had been no fun. Being his girlfriend had made it worse.

I knew from experience, though, that not answering him would lead him to accuse me of getting a bad grade. That was something *my* ego couldn't withstand. I told him the happy truth: "A ninety-two." Not a grade up to my usual standards by any means, but way better than the zero I would have received if Sawyer hadn't stepped in to buoy me that day.

"Wow," he said between french fries, "you should get Sawyer to write your papers for you every time."

This was an insult meant to stab me in the heart. It didn't, because I knew I'd written my own paper. If he'd accused me of cheating two weeks ago, I would have been upset. His grip on me was slowly slipping.

And his mention of Sawyer turned me on. What if Sawyer *had* written my paper for me? Sure, that would be cheating. I would never do that. I didn't need to. But the idea suggested an intimacy between Sawyer and me that was more exciting than our tame reality.

So far.

"What did *you* get?" I asked Aidan.

"Are you scared?" he accused me. This meant he'd gotten lower than a ninety-two.

"All right, then," I said dismissively. "What's the student council business you wanted to discuss?" I took a bite of salad.

"It looks like you're not going to get your homecoming dance after all," he said.

I nodded without looking up.

"But if we do have one," he said, "I don't want you to go with Sawyer."

As he said this, I finally spotted Sawyer across the lunchroom. He stood behind a table where a lot of the cheerleaders sat, one hand on the back of Grace's chair and the other on the back of Cathy's, laughing with them. It wouldn't be long before I heard yet another rumor about his sexual exploits, as if my friendship with him was an addition to his life, not a change.

But I wasn't about to admit that to Aidan. I said, "You broke up with me. What I do now is none of your business."

"I didn't break up with you," he said, pointing at me with a french fry. "I said I wanted to take a *break*. I thought dating other people for a while would strengthen our relationship, but I didn't mean you could date *Sawyer*!"

I put my fork down. "You said you wanted to talk about

student council business. I wouldn't have agreed to eat lunch with you otherwise."

"This *is* student council business," Aidan said. "When you and I were dating, people knew we were on the same page, president and vice president. Now people are coming up to me constantly, asking whether you're dating Sawyer. I tell them, 'Yeah, she's obviously had an aneurysm or a small stroke, and suddenly she's decided she wants to date a loser.'"

"Why do you say he's a loser?" I demanded. "He's in the upper-level classes with us." I had no idea what sort of grades Sawyer got, but he must have tested well enough at *some* point to be placed in the college track. "He's the school mascot, a student council rep, and the parliamentarian. He doesn't sound like a loser to me."

Aidan's eyes were cold as ice as he said, "I don't like him, okay? I don't like the way he talks to you."

I had no idea what Aidan meant. Frowning, I asked, "How does he talk to me?"

"He stands very close to you," Aidan said, moving closer across the table himself. "He leads with his pelvis. And I don't understand what you see in him. Of course, there *are* ladies who marry men in prison."

"He's not in prison," I pointed out.

"He will be."

We stared each other down across our almost untouched food. I'd had plenty of conversations with Aidan in which he lobbed witty insults at me to make me feel bad. But he didn't usually *want* something from me. This time he was intense and certain. Whether or not I was a part of his life, he wanted Sawyer out of mine.

"Tell me something," I said, acting casual by picking up my fork again and stirring my salad. "Did your dad help prosecute Sawyer's dad when he went to jail?"

I wasn't looking at Aidan, but his hesitation told me I'd surprised him. After a few seconds, he said, "Yeah."

"And when Sawyer moved to town, your dad told you who he was. That's how everybody knew on Sawyer's very first day at school that his dad had been to jail. You made *sure* they knew."

"So?"

I looked up at Aidan. "Sawyer might be a different person today if you hadn't done that. He didn't know a soul in town except his dad. He hardly knew his dad, I imagine. And you ensured he was teased by the entire student body the second he stepped on campus. No wonder he's so defensive. Some school leader *you* are." I shouldered my book bag and picked up my salad. Ignoring Aidan when he called to me, I walked away.

I wasn't sure where to go, though, which put a damper on my dramatic exit. I'd almost forgotten that the last time I'd seen Sawyer, he was cozying up to Grace and Cathy. But he wasn't sitting with them now. After a quick scan of the room, I spied him at our usual table, working through an enormous salad and speaking an occasional word to Quinn next to him.

When I approached, he glanced up at me. He looked

down again without smiling, as if I wasn't welcome. He really *was* mad that I'd eaten lunch, however briefly, with Aidan. As I slid into the seat across from him with my salad in front of me, he concentrated on his own food. Then he asked flatly, "Did you finish with your student council business?"

"Yes."

"I've told you, I'm good at reading people. Don't tell me you were talking about student council."

Quinn looked at Sawyer, then at me, then wisely pretended to pay attention to a dirty joke Tia was messing up farther down the table.

I told Sawyer, "I don't know what you want me to say."

"Get back with him if you want to, Kaye." Sawyer sounded bitter. "I don't own you. That's your choice. But don't lie to me about it."

Now Noah beside me was eyeing us too, and Brody beyond him. I glared at Sawyer, letting him know I didn't find this public fight amusing.

He raised his eyebrows at me. He didn't care.

"Aidan and I were together for three years," I said. "We dated for a year before you even moved here. The way he broke up with me was ugly and open-ended. It's hard to pretend that didn't happen."

The angry expression in his eyes faded. He took another bite of salad, considering. Finally he said, "I get it. But don't expect me to be polite about it."

I almost laughed and told him that was fair enough. But

it *wasn't* fair. He was acting like a jealous boyfriend, except he wasn't my boyfriend, as far as I knew. I *wanted* us to be friends with bennies, but our bennies had gone missing.

I wasn't going to point this out with ten of our friends listening, though.

Instead, watching him reach the bottom of his salad plate, I asked, "Why did you become a vegan, anyway? Are the pelicans your brothers?"

He slammed his chair backward so suddenly that everyone at the table turned toward the screech. Rising, he said, "I'm tired of people telling me I'm a dumbass for going vegan. I know."

"I didn't say you were a dumbass!" I exclaimed.

"You didn't have to." He grabbed his backpack and his empty plate and stalked away.

As he went, I finally realized what he was telling me every time he got angry with me. People at school thought Sawyer had a thick skin, but he was sensitive after all. And he was upset that I'd found out.

Near the other end of the table, Tia caught my eye and jerked her thumb over her shoulder, asking if I wanted her to go after Sawyer and smooth things over.

I shook my head and returned to my salad with a sigh. I was beginning to think whatever was wrong between Sawyer and me was something that couldn't be fixed.

Ten

BY THAT EVENING, I WAS EAGER TO TRY AGAIN. I watched out the window of the cheerleading van for Sawyer's beat-up truck to appear, lumbering over curbs in the school parking lot. Just like last time he stopped right next to my car. That was no accident. He looked up at the window and saw me. I didn't turn away.

He climbed into the van wearing gym shorts and his Pelicans T-shirt, with his huge costume bag slung over his shoulder. He stood next to me in the aisle.

"Do you need to put your costume on before we make up?" I asked drily.

He glanced toward the rear of the van as if he was considering this.

"Go put it down," I said. "I owe you a shoulder rub, remember? Or is staying mad at me too important?"

"It's not *that* important," he admitted, already moving into the back to dump his bag.

He didn't make it all the way. He took two steps and chucked the bag over Ellen's head, making her squeal in fear. It landed on the back seat with a rustling of pompons.

He sank into the seat beside me. Before he could change his mind or feign anger again, I gripped both his shoulders and kneaded those tense muscles. He melted under my hands as if he'd never been touched before.

The ride home was even better. The cheerleaders were in a great mood after Brody led our team to yet another win. The highlights of the game had been Brody bulleting an impossibly long pass to our best tailback for the winning touchdown, and Sawyer directing the band. Usually when he wandered into the band's section of the stands, the band director, Ms. Nakamoto, made him leave, or DeMarcus, the drum major, wouldn't let him direct. This time everyone had been elated enough about our pending victory to forget all the times Sawyer had stolen flutes, disassembled them, and hidden them in the pelican's mouth. Ms. Nakamoto let Sawyer through. DeMarcus moved aside. The pelican directed a funny version of "Fight, Pelicans, Fight," speeding way up and then slowing way down and accelerating again. The cheerleaders, laughing, finally gave up trying to dance to it.

After the game, Sawyer disappeared into the locker room to take a shower. I carried his dead carcass of a costume back to the van, then retrieved his T-shirt and waited outside for him so he didn't have to look quite so buff and manly by walking across the parking lot bare chested. That's what I told him, anyway. Personally, I wouldn't have minded. When he was dressed, I extended my hand to him, and he took it. We held hands as we walked back to the van.

Ms. Howard already had the engine running. Sawyer and I were the last ones in. Before we'd even sat down, the van started moving, and the lights blinked out. This time he got into the seat first, taking the window. He propped his forehead against the glass, anticipating what I would do next, as I took his shoulders under my hands. The groan he let out caused Ellen and Grace to stand up from the seat behind us to see what was going on. Grace made a motion with her hand indicating I should jerk him off next. Grace. Sigh. If Sawyer had seen her do this, I would have died.

But she was right about one thing. I was giving Sawyer some pretty intense physical pleasure. And he was letting me know. I felt his groan in my crotch. I curled one thigh up and over his, letting my lower leg curve around his calf, as if this gave me better leverage.

"Oh God, Kaye," Sawyer said, guttural and appreciative.

"Ms. Howard!" Grace called. "I can't sleep because Kaye and Sawyer are having sex."

As a *wooooooo* echoed through the van, Sawyer straightened slowly so he wouldn't knock me onto the floor with a sudden movement. He pulled off his shirt and tossed it over the back of the seat at Grace.

"It's not a rock concert," Ellen said. "Geez." The shirt came sailing back to land on Sawyer's head.

"We want the shorts," Grace yawned.

Sawyer put his shirt back on—but not before I passed my hand down his bare back.

And he felt it. With the shirt over his head but not yet pulled down to cover his back, he looked over his shoulder at me. Our eyes met as the van passed under a light on the interstate. A shadow descended over his face when we drove away from that light and approached the next. Then his blue eyes lit up again.

I moved my hand down his arm and felt chill bumps.

He pulled his shirt the rest of the way on. "Your turn," he said, shifting in his seat.

"Here." I fished around in my bag and pulled out the pillow I brought on long trips. He propped it behind his back against the wall of the van. With one of his legs extended along the seat, he pulled me by the hips until I settled back against him.

His hands gripped my shoulders and massaged. Now I understood why he'd groaned under my touch. Aidan had never bothered to give me a sexy rub like this (and in his defense, I'd never given him one, either). Sawyer turned me to water under his fingers. I nearly groaned but stopped myself so Grace wouldn't holler any more orgasm jokes across the van. My groan came out as a squeak.

"And you said *I* was tense." Sawyer's voice was a low rumble in my ear. "What's this knot right here?" He kneaded a spot in my neck.

"Ah," I gasped.

"Put your head down," he said gently, his hands working their way up my neck, then down into the neckline of my cheerleading top. "I wish I could take this off."

"That could be arranged," I murmured as if I were Grace, or Tia.

My face flushed hot. He'd only made a joke. Maybe he hadn't even meant anything risqué, and I'd ruined the mood by going too far. I wondered if he could feel my neck and shoulders tensing up again.

He placed one kiss on the back of my neck, at the lowest dip of my neckline.

I shivered.

And then he passed one arm around my chest, drawing me even farther against him until I relaxed into him, and he eased back against the pillow.

The heat of his body soaked into me. He took one deep breath. My body rose and fell with his. He nestled his arm under my breasts, his hand resting protectively across my hip.

In the silence that came after, I didn't know what to say.

Finally I gave voice to what had been bothering me from lunchtime until he sat down with me in the van. I said quietly, "Aidan did tell me he wanted to talk about student council at lunch. You were there. You heard him."

"What did he really want to talk about?" Sawyer asked, his words vibrating through me.

"He wants to make sure I don't go out with you."

"Hm," Sawyer half laughed.

I waited for him to ask me out, or to tell me the idea of us going out was ridiculous, but he did neither. He only flattened his palm on my hip, then gripped me more firmly, which sent a jolt of electricity down my leg.

I said, "And he wanted to know what I got on my paper for Mr. Frank."

"Was he impressed?"

"He said you wrote it for me."

"He is an asshole," Sawyer said, "and he knows how to push your buttons. More importantly, was your mom impressed?" At some point during that horrible morning, I'd moaned to him about accidentally telling my mother what I'd done. Even if I pulled off a feat by scoring well on the paper, she'd still know I'd forgotten to write it until the last second—that is, failed.

And that's exactly how she'd reacted when I told her what my grade was. "No," I said, "she wasn't impressed. She's making me stay home tomorrow to write the next one."

"It's not due for two weeks."

"I know."

"We haven't even worked on the notes or the outline in class yet."

"Doesn't matter."

"How can you be in trouble when you're perfect?"

I nodded, careful not to bump his chin with the back of my head. "It's a question for the ages."

"*Most* importantly," he said, his breath tickling my earlobe and sending a fresh chill across my skin, "are you impressed with yourself?"

"No," I admitted, "and I know that's stupid. Ms. Malone will tell me this when I meet with her about handling stress. I've already heard it in self-esteem lectures, especially for girls only. I just can't shake it, though. When I don't accomplish something, I know it's my fault. When I do make good, I feel like I don't deserve it."

"I know that," he said, "but why do you feel that way?"

I shrugged automatically, then hoped I hadn't elbowed him. He put one hand up to rub my shoulders again, very gently.

I said, "People give me stuff because of what I've already done, or because of who my mother is."

"That's definitely not true," he said. "People don't want dipshits leading the student council. Well, scratch that. We elected Aidan president. But people definitely don't want an ugly, unpopular head cheerleader. When the school voted for you, nobody was thinking, 'Kaye's mom runs a bank.' They were thinking, 'Kaye has a firm ass.'"

This time I did elbow him softly in the ribs.

"Oof. Maybe that's just what *I* was thinking. But *nobody* was thinking about your mom. And you're in all the upper-level classes. That's no accident. You were in the Loser class way back when, right?" *The Loser class* was Sawyer's term for the gifted class. "If they put people in the Loser class based only on their hard-hitting parents, Tia wouldn't have been in it, because God knows whether her mom is dead or alive. Harper wouldn't have been in it. I love Ms. Davis, but she's not exactly playing with a full deck."

"She's an artist."

"That's one way to put it."

That's exactly what *I* thought of Harper's mom. I loved that Sawyer said he loved her. Everything I found out about him, every additional inch he pulled back the curtain on his life, made me like him more.

And every stroke of his skin across mine made me want him more. Yet if we followed our recent pattern, the closer we felt to each other, the sooner we'd have a dumb fight and push each other away again.

So I brought up the other thing that had been bothering me since lunch. "I didn't mean to offend you today when I asked if the pelicans were your brothers. I was just trying to snap you out of being mad about Aidan, and I picked the wrong thing to make a joke out of. I didn't know you were so serious about being a vegan."

"Why not?" he asked, dropping his sexy tone for the first time and sounding more like his normal self. "I have to eat, like, four gallons of salad to get any calories. Doesn't that seem serious to you?"

"You're never serious about anything."

"I'm serious a lot," he said.

"It looks exactly like kidding."

His sultry tone was back as he whispered, "Maybe you just don't know me that well."

"Maybe not." I pulled away from him and turned around in my seat.

"Don't go," he murmured.

I wasn't going anywhere. He was right. After two years, I felt like I hardly knew him at all. If he was as good at reading people as he claimed, he had me at a disadvantage. I wanted to look him in the eye when I posed my next question. I sat sideways, one knee bent and my foot up on the seat, open to him. "When did you go vegan?"

His eyebrows rose in surprise. "Last spring."

"Why?"

"I was about to try out for mascot. I was up against five other people, really funny characters—"

"Like who?"

"Chelsea."

"Oh, right! I'd forgotten she'd gone out for mascot." My friend Chelsea was a majorette in the marching band. Majorettes and cheerleaders tried out in front of the whole school, and students voted. These definitely were more popularity contests than any measure of talent—though I'd probably clinched the wow factor among cheerleaders with my ability to do ten back handsprings in a row. This boggled boys' minds.

Mascot selection was different. These candidates tried out in front of the principal, the football coach, and the cheerleading coach only. I guessed the faculty wanted to make damn sure the mascot would do a good job of representing the school. They weren't taking any chances on getting a lame pelican by letting students vote.

That meant the mascot selection had flown under my radar. I vaguely remembered the announcement that rising seniors could try out, and later, the shocking announcement that Sawyer had won. But this event had been as big a part of Sawyer's life as the cheerleader tryout had been for me.

Maybe bigger.

"They let us put the costume on for two minutes to see what it was like," Sawyer said, "and that was all. The next day we had to come back, get in the pelican suit, and convince them to give us the job. But my two minutes in the suit had taught me that a lot of the gags I'd been planning weren't going to work. You've got so much padding on that your movements have to be hugely exaggerated for the crowd to see what you're doing. I left wondering if I should even come back the next day."

"Really!" I exclaimed at the idea of Sawyer, discouraged. This was a new concept for me. Every time he identified a real emotion he'd had, I was shocked all over again.

"After school, before I went to work, I drove down to the marina and sat on the dock for a while, watching the pelicans, looking for inspiration." He moved one hand up, swooping like a seven-foot wingspan. "And—"

He stopped in midsentence, hand in midflight, lost in thought. In the dim van, his eyes were darkest blue, watching imaginary birds above us. I'd never seen him so unguarded before. I loved to look at him when he'd forgotten he was being watched.

He blinked and put his hand down. "Pelicans are dorks on land," he said, "little trolls waddling around. In the air they unfold their wings and grow huge, soaring and then diving for their dinner. It occurred to me that they're like a lot of students at this school. We're not so good at sitting in desks, staying still, and paying attention to a boring lecture."

He cut his eyes to me, and I knew the same thing was going through both our minds: *I* was good at that. But, granted, *he* wasn't.

"That doesn't mean we'll never be good at anything, though," he said. "There's almost no job out there where you sit at a desk and pay attention while someone else talks. I mean, I've already got a job I'm way better at than school."

True—Sawyer was a terrific waiter, as long as he wasn't mad at the customers.

"That's how I played the pelican," he said. "The other people trying out were just bopping around in this big padded suit, walking funny. I made the pelican into a character, a student at our school who gets no respect but who's a lot smarter than the teachers give him credit for. After I got the suit on, the first thing I did was walk behind the judges and try to look over their shoulders at everyone's scores."

I laughed. "That could have backfired." Principal Chen had her panties in a wad most of the time, and the football coach wasn't exactly open-minded, either.

"I knew that," Sawyer said, "but I figured I had to do *something*. I mean, all else being equal, would *you* pick me for *anything* over Chelsea?"

"No." But as soon as I said this, I felt the blood rush to my face, as it did so often when I was around Sawyer. I'd thought of several things I would pick Sawyer for over absolutely anybody, and all of them required sitting very close to him in the dark, just like this.

To cover up my embarrassment, I asked quickly, "How did this make you into a vegan?"

"Oh." He nodded. "It was when I was watching the pelicans. I felt like I was borrowing something from them. Like I was *one* with the pelicans, or something? I know that sounds stupid."

It didn't sound stupid, exactly, but it sounded like something Sawyer was making up to see if I would believe it, teasing me. I said carefully, so he couldn't tell whether I was buying it, "But people don't eat pelicans, do they?"

"Not unless they're desperate. I guess I was also thinking of a deer hunt I went on before I left Georgia. I've regretted it every day." He turned to look out the window at the interstate, lights and palm trees flashing past at even intervals. I could tell, though, that in his mind, he was lost in a dark Georgia forest.

I found his hand and covered it with mine. This was hard for me, making the first move. I'd never gone out of my way to touch Aidan like this. He hadn't ever tried to comfort *me*, either, which was probably why my three years with him seemed so sterile when I looked back at them now.

Sawyer turned away from the window. He took my hand in his and rubbed his thumb over my palm, watching me.

"What do you eat, as a vegan?" I asked. "Besides gallons of salad."

"Cereal, mostly."

"Dry? Vegans can't have milk or anything that comes from an animal, right?"

"Right."

I shook my head, disapproving. "Where do you get your calcium and vitamins and protein?"

"I guess I don't."

It occurred to me that, except for salad at lunch, I'd never actually seen Sawyer eat anything. "What did you eat before the 5K on Labor Day, when you nearly passed out?"

"Nothing."

I slid my hand out of his and poked him angrily in the leg. "You can't run three miles on nothing, Sawyer."

"Ow. I found that out, thanks."

"What did you eat the day you passed out at school?"

He shrugged. "I had a Bloody Mary for breakfast."

"With *vodka* in it?"

"And tomato juice, which is full of antioxidants." He cut his eyes sideways at me. "I know, I know. That's the day I realized I might have a problem."

Normally I would have interjected a sarcastic comment

here: *Oh,* that's *when you realized you had a problem?* Sawyer's problems had been obvious to me and everybody else the entire time he'd lived here. Some other guys in our class drank, but most of them didn't make alcohol their favorite hobby.

I amazed myself by not saying a word. It took a lot of self-control, but I simply moved my hand low on his back and slid my arm around his waist.

He set his head down on my shoulder.

We sat that way for a while. This was a serious step past holding hands. It would have attracted attention in the van if any of the cheerleaders had been awake to see. But they'd bedded down, propping pillows against each other and the walls of the van. The silence seemed heavy, like a question mark.

My skin burned underneath Sawyer's cheek, and my face felt flushed everywhere his soft hair brushed against it. I wondered if this truce signaled that we'd reached a different level of our relationship. I wondered if I wanted it to. I took a long breath through my nose, easily enough that he might not notice, and exhaled, trying to relax. I wanted to enjoy the sensation of him cuddling against me. I might not get it again.

I'd thought he'd fallen asleep, but he finally spoke. "You think being a vegan is stupid."

"I don't," I said. "I think you're not doing it right. Starvation, dry cereal, and alcohol do not equal a diet of any kind. My God, at least have some hummus."

He chuckled—a sound I loved.

"What made you decide to sober up?" I asked. "Being in the hospital?"

"Being in the hospital made me realize that nobody has my back." He sat up and leaned against the pillow again. We weren't touching each other anymore, for the first time since he'd come out of the locker room. He *looked* alone, the only boy in a van full of girls, his blond hair lit by the streetlights behind him like an ironic halo, his features dark and inscrutable.

"My dad was up in Panama City," he said. "Anybody else's dad or mom would have rushed home if their kid was hospitalized with heat exhaustion. Not mine. The nurse—DeMarcus's mom, actually—made me give her my dad's cell phone number. I told her it wouldn't do any good. She called him anyway, then came back in the room outraged that he wasn't coming home. Outraged at *me*."

"She wasn't outraged at you," I said.

"That's how it felt. Like, *What kind of family are you from?*" He took a long breath, still needing to calm himself down when he talked about this, even though it had happened a month ago. "My brother was in town, but he wouldn't take time off work to check me out of the hospital when they said I could go home. He needed the hours."

I nodded. *Needing the hours* was a foreign concept to me. My parents wanted Barrett and me to concentrate on school instead of getting jobs. Both of them had worked professionally since college. They hadn't been paid hourly in decades. My understanding of hourly work came solely from Tia talking about her dad. He'd worked at a factory until recently, *needing the hours* and missing her marching band performances. But he would never have stayed at work if she'd been hospitalized. Neither would her sisters, even though she didn't always get along with them.

The closer I got to Sawyer, the more isolated he seemed.

"Yeah," he said, "I realized while I was in the hospital that I had a short-term goal, to be a really good school mascot in ninety-degree heat, and I couldn't meet that goal without making some changes. But I also came to this new understanding of what could happen to me later. The biggest stoner in school is Jason Price, right?"

"I hope." Actually, I hadn't seen a lot of Jason lately. He'd gradually dropped out of the advanced-level classes. The last I'd heard, he was trolling business math and remedial English.

"Jason's parents are both doctors. If he ever gets arrested, they'll hire lawyers to have him released. Hell, they'll probably sue the police department for taking their baby in. If I get arrested, my family will leave me there to rot. Nothing will make you clean up your act like your parents abandoning you completely."

I didn't realize I'd tilted my head and lowered my shoulders in disbelief until Sawyer imitated me.

"Come on," I said. "Do you really think that?"

"You would hope my dad learned something during fifteen years of hard time," Sawyer said. "But he treats me like his family treated him. I try to understand where he's coming from. He didn't exactly have every advantage when he was growing up. But not everybody raised in adverse circumstances decides to make a better life for themselves and their kids, like your mom did. A lot of them are hell-bound to repeat the process for the next generation. Somebody has to put their foot down and say, 'I'm not playing that game.' That somebody is me.

"I've known that for a long time. I felt like an outsider up in Georgia, when my mom was dragging my brother and me around to mooch off one relative and then another. If you're on the outside looking in, it's easy to judge and to feel superior. It wasn't until I was lying in the hospital that I realized what I'd done. Instead of getting away from my relatives, I was becoming them. And if I got arrested at age twenty like my dad, my family would give me exactly as much help as his family gave him. I remember the exact moment it hit me."

I went very still, hoping that moment hadn't been some cruelty I'd paid him, one of those casual insults I'd lobbed at him before I knew the truth.

"You and everybody from school hadn't gotten to the hospital yet," Sawyer said. "It was just Will and me in the room. You know, he rode in the ambulance with me."

I nodded. Sawyer had passed out on the football field. Will had hefted him over one shoulder and carried him all the way up the stadium stairs, into the parking lot to meet the ambulance. I'd just stood there among the other cheerleaders with my hands pressed to my mouth, impressed and terrified. I hadn't known Will had this he-man superhero side. And up to that point, I'd never seen Sawyer vulnerable. Ever.

"I don't remember passing out," Sawyer said, "or throwing up in the parking lot, or being in the ambulance, even though Will says I was conscious for the whole ride. The first thing I remember is, Will's in the chair next to my hospital bed, making small talk. Whether the Buccaneers will suck less this year, what the Rays' chances are for a pennant, whether we can sneak past security to watch the Lightning practice. And I'm thinking what a shit I've been to this guy, and how little sense it makes for me to treat him that way. I mean, I want to *be* this guy. He has everything I want."

"Tia?" I breathed.

"No! A future." Sawyer frowned at me, only now understanding my question about Tia. His face softened.

"And then *you* walked into the hospital room," he said. "You looked beautiful in red."

"Ha," I said. "I came straight from cheerleading practice. I was wearing a Pelicans T-shirt."

"Yes, you were." He laid his arm along the back of the seat and put his hand in my hair.

I smiled at the sweet feel of his fingertips rubbing my nape. "You might have sworn off mind-altering substances that day, but it's not like you've changed personalities. You're still really mean to Kennedy," I pointed out.

His nostrils flared. "I strongly dislike Kennedy."

"And Aidan."

His hand stopped in midair, pulling one of my curls. "I hate Aidan." He let my curl go. It sprang back into place.

"You haven't changed as much as you think," I said. "You're incredibly smart and responsible about some things, like quitting drinking. On other things, like your diet, and getting along with certain people, you act like you're from another planet."

"Oh," he said, lifting his chin defiantly, "and *you're* not like that?"

"I'll bite," I said. "What am I smart about?"

"Almost everything," Sawyer declared. "Though, as you pointed out, you don't believe it. Is there anything you honestly think you're good at?"

"Being a cheerleader." I smoothed my hands over my short skirt, then lowered my voice to a whisper. "Not the part where I babysit Grace and Cathy and Ellen." In a normal tone I said, "The part where I actually cheer and dance. I love dancing. And of *course* this would be what I really enjoy, because my mother makes a comment every time I leave the house for practice. 'That's really going to help get you a job as a professional cheerleader.'"

"It could be a backup career if your corporate takeover falls through," Sawyer said.

"You laugh," I said. "But lately, every time I'm on the field during a game, I'm thinking, 'I don't want high school to end.' It's partly because I don't want to leave my friends. But I also don't look forward to spending the rest of my life sitting in a tiny room, ciphering. That's what my career is going to be like. That's what my college experience will be, too."

"Surely Columbia has cheerleaders," Sawyer said.

"I never really thought about it," I admitted. "But their football team sucks. Cheering them on wouldn't be much fun. The whole school seems focused on academics. They put classes ahead of sports in a way the entire state of Florida doesn't really comprehend."

"What about actually trying out as a professional cheerleader?" he asked. "You could do that while you're in school. I don't think it pays much at all. Those girls are trying to get discovered as models. But if you were just doing it for fun . . ."

"My mother would disown me." I enjoyed saying these words more than I expected. After picturing myself for half a second in a low-cut bra top and shorts the size of panties, I shook my head sadly. "I'll bet I can't try out until I'm twenty-one."

"I'll bet you're wrong," Sawyer said. "Men still make most of the rules in this country. Men aren't going to prevent an eighteen-year-old from being a professional cheerleader. It's her God-given right."

I stared at Sawyer, who watched me with his brows raised. The interstate lights caressed his face and released him, then slowly moved across his face again. I was so accustomed to Aidan talking me out of crazy schemes that I hardly ever came up with them anymore. This one was so nuts that I was having a flashback to eighth grade, before I started dating Aidan, when my friends laughed and called me a live wire. At some point along the way, the life had gone out of me.

And here was Sawyer, calmly encouraging me to do exactly what I wanted.

I fished in my bag for my phone, then looked up the Giants. "The Giants don't have cheerleaders." I typed the Jets into the search engine. "The Jets have a cheerleading squad called the Flight Crew. That's adorbs." I thumbed through to an information screen and enlarged the tiny print. "I can't do it. Tryouts are in March. My mother would never let me go up to New York for that. And I won't be eighteen by the deadline. But I could try out the next year, when I'm already at Columbia." I took a closer look at photos of the current squad. "They would make me relax my hair."

"You don't know that," Sawyer said, "but it makes an excellent excuse not to try."

I eyed him. "You're daring me."

"I'm definitely not. You'd be wearing next to nothing, and men would leer at you. I wouldn't encourage you to do it, except that you obviously want to. I think you understand the leering aspect and accept it, even want it. And that's okay."

"You wouldn't be jealous about the skimpy uniforms and the leering men?" My tone was teasing, but suddenly I wanted so badly for him to acknowledge that the thought made him crazy.

"Your body belongs to you," he said solemnly, "not any guy,

and not your mom. You really don't seem to understand that."

Across the aisle from me, Cathy shifted in her sleep and nearly fell off her seat. Instinctively I dodged away from her, cupping my hands over my phone screen.

"It's not a joint," Sawyer said.

"I feel awful even looking this up, like my mother is watching me and doing calculations about how much money I'm wasting if time is money."

"Anything making you feel that guilty is definitely worth doing."

I looked over at him, at his sharp nose and soft mouth coming in and out of focus as the van moved through the interstate lights. My lust for him had grown as the ride went on. I wondered if he meant we should indulge our own guilty pleasure. I'd reached the point that I wouldn't be able to sleep tonight, or ever, if I didn't find out.

I bent to slip my phone back into my bag. Then I moved toward him.

His eyes widened, but he didn't back away.

I cradled his chin in my hand, his blond stubble scratching across my fingertips.

His lips parted. He looked a little outraged, honestly, like this was unseemly behavior for a future valedictorian.

If I'd thought about the expression on his face, I would have backed away. But I was sick to death of thinking. I kissed him.

He opened his mouth for mine. I swept my tongue inside.

He didn't pull away, but he didn't reciprocate, either. I knew I could kiss. Aidan and I had had plenty of practice. But I felt as if I was initiating Sawyer in a decidedly unsexy way, like when DeMarcus had taught me to French kiss in front of an audience of our peers at his Halloween party in seventh grade, directly after Tia had taught DeMarcus.

I broke the kiss and pulled back until I could see Sawyer. His face was mostly in shadow. I wished yet again that I could gauge the look in his eyes. "I feel like I'm taking advantage of you, which is no fun at all. You don't want to kiss me?"

"I do." He swallowed, and he actually looked like he was in pain as he said, "I don't want to get hurt."

"This won't hurt." I slipped my hand into his hair and kissed him.

Again I felt that I was leading the dance. I was about to give up on him. That lasted about five seconds.

Then he was kissing me back. He pulled me closer, deepened the kiss, and explored my mouth. He bit my lip, almost hard enough to hurt. As I opened my mouth wider to protest, he gave me a taste of what other girls were talking about when they said Sawyer turned them on. In one minute he had controlled me completely.

He took his hand out of my hair and placed it on my breast. I broke the kiss to gasp at the intensity of tingles racing through me.

Just as suddenly as he'd started, he let go of me and backed away, his shoulders rising and falling rapidly as he panted. He said hoarsely, "We just can't. I want to, but I know this isn't going to work out."

I gaped at him. I could not *believe*, after everything we'd been through to get to this point, that he was dumping me when we'd hardly gotten started.

I'd heard so many reports of him having trysts like this with different girls. Strangely, those accounts included the beginning, and the good stuff, but never the ending of those relationships. Maybe that's because they all ended like this.

I jerked my pillow out from behind him, then grabbed my bag from the floor.

"Kaye." His hand circled my wrist.

I glowered at him. I wasn't sure he could see my face in the dark, but he knew what the sharp jerk of my head meant. He let me go and put his hand up, surrendering.

I stood and shuffled to the back of the van. Normally I was the one who told the other girls to treat their pompons right, leaving them in clean places rather than in pools of half-dried Coke on the concrete steps of the stadium. This time I was the one who unceremoniously knocked Sawyer's costume bag and a pile of pompons to the floor in a hiss of plastic streamers. I lay down with my pillow underneath my head and closed my eyes, listening for Sawyer over the drone of the van motor, and hating him.

What I heard was a grunt near the floor. After a few seconds I realized it wasn't a rogue bullfrog that had found its way onto the van but my phone vibrating in my bag and bouncing against the van's carpeted bottom. I snatched the phone out. I knew Sawyer was texting me.

Sawyer: I never had a chance to tell u what ur stupid abt.

I waited. I wasn't going to give him the satisfaction of prompting him: What's that, Sawyer? But he'd heard me take my phone out. He knew I was hanging on what he would say next.

Sawyer: Me.

I texted back so angrily that my thumbs pressed rogue characters and my message was full of)$&@. I had to take a deep breath. I wasn't going to send him an answer that was less than perfect. Finally I got it cleaned up and texted this:

Me: I'm not stupid about u. YOU lead me on and then shut me down. U have done that for the last time. 3 strikes and ur out.

I turned my phone off, threw it in my bag, and rolled over with my back to the van.

As soon as I'd done this, I regretted it. "3 strikes and ur out"? That was the kind of draconian statement my mother would make, setting limits and sticking to them no matter what, even if they had no meaning later and caused everyone misery.

But I wasn't wrong, was I? Showing Sawyer how much I liked him was hard for me. There were only so many times I could go out on a limb like that, only to have him cut off the limb at the trunk and watch me fall. I'd been worried at lunch that his problems were too serious for us to get over. Well, I was done. Now he could start worrying about *my* problems.

I pictured my life as I would start living it tomorrow: single. I wouldn't go after Sawyer. I wouldn't worry what Aidan was up to. I wouldn't try desperately to find a date for my nonexistent homecoming dance. I had great friends and lots to do my senior year—too much, according to my mother—and I could enjoy it all by myself.

I sat up and peered around the seat in front of me only once to see what Sawyer was doing. His worried face was lit clearly by the glow of his phone. He was still typing.

An hour later, the instant I arrived home and escaped to my room, I turned my phone back on and opened his texts.

Sawyer: 3 strikes makes it sound like ur playing a game w ME.

Sawyer: Kaye

Sawyer: We need to talk abt this. You can't just pretend I'm not here. I'm RIGHT HERE & if u don't answer I will do something inconceivably cruel to ur pompons.

Sawyer: Kaye

Sawyer: Kaye.

Eleven

THE NEXT NIGHT HARPER CALLED ME AFTER dinner. "What'cha doing?" she asked.

"My next paper for Mr. Frank."

"Oh, shit. On Saturday night? Have I missed something? I thought it wasn't due for another two weeks."

"It's not," I said. "My mother is making me write it early, because she doesn't trust me anymore. Like she ever did." I wished Harper hadn't asked. I hated the bitter sound of my voice. "What's up?"

"I was wondering if you would help me buy a car."

I waited for Harper to explain what the hell she was talking about. When she remained silent, I said, "What?"

"Remember my cheapskate granddad's birthday present for me?" she asked. "The *use* of his car? Well, he's taking it back. Now that he's dating, he's using his car more. *I* need it more too, because I'm getting photography jobs on weekends. I told him he couldn't take back my birthday present.

He gave me a thousand dollars basically to leave him alone."

"Nice!"

"Yeah. And I have a thousand of my own saved up, so I'm going to buy a car tonight. I have one picked out, and I looked up the blue book value. All I need is you."

"Why me?"

"Because your mom made you haggle for your own car."

"But you should haggle for *your* own car," I pointed out. "That's why my mother made me do it, so I'd have that adult experience under my belt and I wouldn't get taken to the cleaners later." At least, that's what she'd *said*. Actually, she'd made me do it because she'd brought me up in a comfortable suburban environment, and periodically she decided she needed to toughen me up by throwing me to the sharks.

"Why in the world would I do that when I have you?" Harper asked reasonably. "You're so much better at hanging tough than I am. You'll get me another two-fifty off."

"Harper." I sighed. "You're basically telling me I'm your bitch friend."

"Kaye, I would *never* tell you that."

I rolled my eyes so hard that Harper could probably hear it through the phone.

"Spin it however you want," she said, "but come pick me up."

Truthfully, I was glad to have an excuse to get out of the house. Dad was back from Miami, but he wrote a lot on weekends, so he wasn't available to save me from homework by inviting me to watch football with him or taking me out for ice cream. My Saturday had been full of nothing but my disapproving mother and research on Stephen Crane's *The Red Badge of Courage*. Mr. Frank had a thing for white male protagonists who whined and waffled.

Which made me angry all over again at Sawyer. Until the past week I would have said he was the *least* likely guy in the world to seem to want a girl, then back out.

He'd never had a problem like that with girls before. He had a problem only with me.

Fifteen minutes later I cruised into the parking lot behind the B and B. Stepping into my car, Harper flashed me her wad of hundreds, which I told her was very gangsta. We chatted about the football game last night and Brody's stellar performance. Finally I asked, "Why aren't you with Brody tonight?"

"He went out with some friends," she said, seemingly fascinated with the scene out her window, the parking lot of the movie theater.

I glanced where she was looking. "There's Chelsea's car. She must be at the movie with DeMarcus."

"With Tia," Harper corrected me.

"Really?" I asked. "I wonder why Tia isn't with Will. It must be another girls' night out."

"Must be," Harper said vaguely, as if she was thinking about something else.

"We'll probably be done with your car about the time Tia

and Chelsea get out of the movie. We should come back by and show them."

"Okay," Harper said absentmindedly.

Well, I had a question that would wake her up. "Do you think Tia and Will are doing it yet?"

Harper huffed out an embarrassed laugh. "Why don't you ask her?"

"Anytime I ask her about sex, she thinks I'm calling her a slut."

"That's because you *are* calling her a slut," Harper pointed out.

"I am *not*. I may have intimated in the past that she would get in trouble involving herself in such casual escapades with—" I stopped, realizing what I was about to say.

"Sawyer," Harper finished for me.

I felt all the blood rushing to my face.

To gloss over the uncomfortable moment, Harper hurried on. "I haven't asked Tia, but my sense is that she and Will haven't done it. They've done everything but. There's a lot of other stuff you can do if you're really into each other."

"It sounds like you speak from sexperience."

She laughed self-consciously. Bright pink spots appeared on her cheeks, noticeable on her porcelain skin. "I guess. I never expected dating someone I loved to be so . . ." She held up her hands. "Free. Dating Kennedy, I felt strapped down. Brody makes me feel good, and like there are more possibilities, bigger ones."

I envied her. But I supposed that's what she got when she and Brody were dating after a long, vague friendship, unlike the intense baggage that plagued Sawyer and me.

We reached the used car lot and peered into Harper's clunker of choice. The salesman didn't bother to come out of his little building to help two teenage girls. We obviously didn't have the money to buy anything. I understood now why my mother always dressed professionally in public. I should have gussied up tonight and made Harper do the same, but always doing everything the right way was too much hassle. I wanted to be seventeen sometimes, even if that meant doing things the hard way.

I hiked into the office with Harper behind me and told the salesman we wanted to go for a test drive, carefully listing the make and model rather than saying "that red car." I sat in the back while Harper drove and the salesman rode shotgun. It sounded like a car to me. I couldn't vouch for the engine, but at least the sale included a warranty. Around closing time Harper and I drove back toward downtown in separate cars.

We both pulled in to the movie theater parking lot just as Tia and Chelsea were walking out. They oohed over Harper's new ride *and* over how smart she'd been to ask me along. Despite myself, I beamed with pride. My mother might not think I had much sense, but *somebody* did.

"We're glad you came by." Chelsea grabbed my arm. "Aidan is in the movie," she said in a stage whisper, "with . . . guess who."

"Angelica!" I said.

"I have a theory about what old Angelica's up to," Tia said conspiratorially. "She dated DeMarcus last summer. Then Xavier. Now Aidan. She's systematically cycling through all the likely candidates for valedictorian. She even hedged her bet by going out with Will once, just in case he comes from behind and pulls off a long shot. So you know who's next!" She looked pointedly at me.

I said in my best redneck accent, "Shee-yut, I ain't wasting no time with that girl. I hear she don't put out."

"Is sex all you care about?" Tia shrieked, putting the back of her hand to her forehead and pretending to swoon, at the same time Chelsea said, "You are a shallow, sexist person." Harper snorted.

"Speaking of putting out," I said, "why are all of your menfolks missing at one time?"

"They're with *your* man," Chelsea said. "Didn't you know that?"

"What?" I asked, glancing from Chelsea to Tia, who was giving me shifty-eyes, to Harper, who looked downright alarmed. I prompted them, "DeMarcus and Will and Brody are all with Sawyer?"

"Well, you're obviously not supposed to find that out," Chelsea said self-righteously. She slapped the back of Tia's head. "Thanks for warning me before I blabbed."

"You already blabbed it to Aidan and Angelica," Tia said. "Could I have stopped you?"

I raised my brows at Tia, waiting for an explanation.

Exasperated, she said, "Sawyer is so in love with you."

Harper nodded vigorously at me. "He is."

Again I looked from one of them to the other. I'd been to this movie theater and stood in this parking lot a hundred times in my life, but suddenly the everyday scene seemed foreign because my heart was pounding and my life was shifting around me. I put one hand up to my face and repeated, "He's in love with me?"

"That's why he moved out of his dad's house in the first place," Tia said. "His dad said something about you that Sawyer didn't like."

I didn't ask what that something had been. I knew. For a white person insulting a black person, that something was always the same. The only part of this revelation making no sense to me was the timing. "Sawyer moved out before Aidan even broke up with me."

Tia and Harper nodded solemnly. And that meant Sawyer had been into me, intensely enough that his mean dad knew about it, before we'd even doubled down on toying with each other.

"Why doesn't he *act* like he's in love with me?" I cried. "I threw myself at him last night, and he dissed me. *Again!*"

I must have sounded hysterical. Harper put a hand on my shoulder. Tia said as gently as she could, "He's terrified, Kaye. He doesn't want to start something with you. He's certain it won't work out."

"Well, it's too late. He's already started it!" I exclaimed. "And why are y'all keeping me in the dark about this?"

"I promised him," Tia said solemnly.

"I promised him too," Harper chimed in.

"I had no knowledge of any of this shit," Chelsea said.

"Where are the boys?" I demanded, turning to Harper. "Are they at your granddad's beach?"

Harper looked at Tia hopelessly. They were at her granddad's beach, all right.

I headed around Harper's car to reach mine.

"Don't go to the beach," Tia pleaded.

"Why not?" I asked, opening my door. "Are they drinking?"

"Will's not." She was stalling. Will didn't drink.

"Is *Sawyer* drinking?" I clarified. "Because that would be a great way for me to get over him. Problem solved." I started my engine.

I already knew I wouldn't be catching him by surprise, though. Before I'd driven out of the parking lot, Tia was on her phone.

As I drove the few short blocks down the main road through town, my mind raced with everything that was happening behind my back. I could hardly comprehend it all. Sawyer was in love with me. He wanted to be with me. But he was afraid I would break his heart. All my best friends knew. He'd gone drinking down at the beach to find solace with his guy friends. And he was content to leave me at home, out of the loop, innocently obsessing over *The Red*

Badge of Courage. Was he even worth the trouble?

I pulled onto the sandy road that led to Harper's granddad's property, punched in the combination to open the gate, slowly drove through, and pulled the gate shut behind me. My car crept through the palm grove. No trucks were parked ahead of me. Possibly the boys had left when Tia sounded the alarm. More likely, especially if they were drinking, they'd walked here from their houses downtown.

I swung my car around to park exactly where Aidan and I had parked all three times we'd had sex. My headlights caught Sawyer waiting for me.

He stood on the threshold. The dark palm forest was in front of him, and behind him, the open beach, bright with moonlight. He wore his usual flip-flops and shorts, plus his blue polo shirt that matched his eyes exactly. This shirt didn't make an appearance as often as his madras one, presumably because it was so old that the collar was turning white at the edges.

His arms were folded across his chest. His blond hair played across his forehead in the ocean breeze. His eyes were on me, and he looked miserable.

Good.

I turned off the engine and the lights, got out, and slammed the door. His expression didn't change as I stomped toward him as best I could in slick flat sandals on mounds of sand. I stopped right in front of him and poked him on the forearm he was using to protect himself. "Why does everybody in the senior class know about this except me, huh? Am I just a big joke to you?"

He looked over his shoulder. The other guys—I recognized the three I'd known about, Will, Brody, and DeMarcus, plus Noah and Quinn—sat in a circle about halfway down the beach. The sound of the ocean must have muffled my voice, but they still heard me and turned. Will's dog thumped her tail in welcome.

Sawyer faced me again. "No!" Eyes wide, he sounded almost desperate. "It's just that I'm going to ruin your life, Kaye."

"Don't you think that should be my choice?" I shouted. "Do I get a say at all? In *anything*?"

He bit his lip, frustrated. "Come on," he said, grabbing my hand. He pulled me into motion down the beach.

We passed within a few yards of the other boys and the dog, but I was too mortified by this entire fiasco to say hi. I did notice a beer bottle next to Brody, and across the circle, the tiny orange glow of a cigarette or a joint. I called to Sawyer, "Are you stoned? Getting stoned because of me is not the way to win me over."

He stopped so suddenly that I smacked into him. He grabbed me by both arms to keep me from sliding down. "I told you, I quit all that," he said over the roar of the tide. "You don't believe anything I say."

"I *have* believed you," I snapped. "That's the whole problem. You've acted like you wanted us to get together. I bought it. I tried to follow through, and you decided on your own that you don't want me anymore."

"I *do* want—" He looked over my shoulder at the guys

behind us. "Come over the hill." He took my hand again and led me up and over a rise in the beach, where we were hidden. Now we could see the pier and the pavilion of the public park. It was closed for the night. We were alone.

He pulled me toward the ocean until the water lapped at my toes and made the bottoms of my sandals slimy.

"You're getting my sandals wet," I said.

Toeing off his flip-flops and kicking them up the beach, he said, "For once in your life, kick your shoes off." He made it sound like a challenge.

I rolled my eyes to show him that he didn't fool me. What I meant was, it was okay with me if he manipulated me, as long as he knew I knew he was doing it. I wiggled one shoe off the end of my toes, then the other, and stepped into the water with him. The warm tide raced around my ankles.

He walked forward into the ocean, tugging me after him. I thought we were just going for a wade. But he kept going until the warm water reached the middle of my calves and crept toward my knees.

"Sawyer," I called, digging my heels into the sand and pulling against his grip. "My skirt's getting wet."

He turned to me with an evil grin. "Take your skirt off for once."

Oh, as if he thought I was innocent, and Aidan and I had never done it? "I've taken my skirt off before," I said archly, before I gained complete understanding of how stupid that sounded.

"That's what I heard about you," he said.

I gaped at him. What had he heard? I was furious with Aidan now, and sorry I'd gone as far as I had with him. But I'd never suspected he'd given a third party the play-by-play—especially a third party who wouldn't keep that information in confidence, with the description eventually getting back to Sawyer.

"I'm joking," Sawyer said. "Take your skirt off anyway."

I might have if he'd given me any assurance that he wasn't setting me up again. I put my hands on my hips. "I thought you were afraid to get too close to me, and we were mad at each other. You wanted to talk it out."

"I *do* want to talk it out, but knowing us, we'd be mad at each other again in an hour. Maybe it would help if you took your skirt off."

"If you take your shorts off."

I made a mental note never to use Sawyer taking his clothes off as a countermeasure. Instantly he was wading closer to shore, where he could take off his shorts without getting them soaked. He unbuckled his belt and shoved his shorts down his hips, exposing his plaid boxers. Most girls would stare at him, straining to gauge the shape and size of him in the darkness. I got stuck on the fact that he was wearing a belt. He often wore a belt, in fact. It showed whenever his shirt rode up or he tucked it in. Knowing his personality, I would have thought he'd dress like a slob, but his casual clothes were neatly pressed. I felt like I was having another epiphany about the puzzle that was Sawyer, but really I was standing in the ocean, avoiding thinking about what was about to happen.

He snapped me out of it when he held out his hand for my skirt. "Hop to it, Gordon. We ain't getting any younger."

I waded after him, shimmied my skirt down my hips, and stepped out of it. Shining drops of ocean dashed dark stains across the fabric.

He bundled it with his shorts and tossed both to the shore, which was sandy and wet. So much for keeping my skirt dry.

He turned back to me. He looked me up and down, and his lips parted. "The bottom of your shirt's going to get wet. Why don't you take that off too, while we're at it."

My knee-jerk reaction was to be offended that he was using such a thin excuse to get my clothes off. But I loved that he wanted this. And I did feel a little silly standing in the ocean in my shirt and panties. A bra and panties were more like a bikini, at least.

Before I reached for my first button, I said, "You first."

Gamely he pulled his shirt off over his head, exposing his flat stomach, then his strong pecs, and finally his arms made of muscle. He balled up his shirt and nodded, prompting me.

I fumbled with the first button of my blouse, fingers shaking. Sawyer had seen me with less on than this. When I got undressed, I'd still be exposing exactly as much in my bra and panties as I did in a bikini. There was no reason for me to feel so nervous as I moved my fingers down to the next button, except for the way Sawyer watched me, jaw hard, eyes serious.

The breeze off the ocean toyed with the top sections of his hair, bright blond in the moonlight, and moved one lock back and forth across his forehead. He didn't brush it away.

He stared at my fingers until they reached the last button. As I pulled the shirt backward off my shoulders, his eyes rose to my face. Still looking at me, he held out his hand for my shirt. He wrapped his own shirt around it and tossed the bundle toward the shore, not looking to see where it went. Neither did I.

"Now we're seaworthy," he said, reaching out again, this time for my hand. Facing me, he backed deeper into the water, pulling me with him. I began to wonder if this was one of his practical jokes.

He stopped backing up but kept pulling me toward him until our bodies pressed against each other in the water. His lips found my neck, making me gasp and sending chills rushing across my skin. I felt my nipples tighten, straining against the lace of my bra.

"This is why we needed to come out here," he said in my ear, "where the guys couldn't hear or see us. I wanted to tell you how bad I am for you. I'm going to corrupt you. I wanted you to understand that and feel it for yourself." His hand slipped inside the front of my panties. His fingers found me and started circling.

"Ah." This was something Aidan had never done to me. In thirty seconds with Sawyer, I already understood why girls went crazy over him. Weak with pleasure, I collapsed into his shoulder, only caring about the position of my hips so he could still reach me.

With his other hand he lifted my chin from his chest and kissed me. The tentative boy from the van was gone. His mouth was hard on mine, his tongue exploring me. He slid his hand into my hair and tilted my head exactly where he wanted me.

Every minute this went on I got closer to climax—my first in front of anyone. I wasn't embarrassed. I had stopped thinking. My hands found his boxers on their own, and it was the shocking hardness of him, and the strange possessiveness I felt when I put my fingers around him, that finally sent me over the edge.

He kissed me harder, holding me up against him, knowing exactly what he was doing to me.

When it was over, I leaned against him, catching my breath, and finally pulled away to stand upright. Bare-chested, with the black ocean and the blue night behind him, his golden hair whipping in the wind, he looked like a god. A sarcastic one, smiling smugly at his accomplishment.

I took a deep, shaky breath. "Was that your way of getting rid of me once and for all? Because you have totally fucked that up."

"Good." He kissed my cheek. "It was just my one last, futile attempt to save us both." He kissed my neck. "I'm glad it didn't work." He kissed above my breast, his mouth lingering as if this was going to be his next thorough exploration.

A bright light shone in our eyes from the beach. "Police," said a man's voice through a megaphone. "Come out of the water."

Twelve

"STAY BEHIND ME UNTIL WE KNOW WHETHER they're really cops," Sawyer ordered me, leading me by the hand toward the beach.

He didn't have to convince me. I'd told myself before that wearing a bra and panties in the ocean was no worse than wearing a bikini. But now that men in addition to Sawyer were going to see me, I wondered how opaque the wet lace of my undies really was.

When we reached shore, the light was still too bright to discern much about the figures who'd found us, but they were big. Sawyer said, "Get your light out of my eyes, and show me your badges." His words were forceful, but his tone was reasonable enough that the light shifted to the police badges on their shirts. The names appliqued above their badges were, I swear to God, Sterns and Sorrow.

"Ma'am," Sorrow said to me, "will you step over here?"

"Don't make her do that." Sawyer sounded annoyed now,

which I didn't think was a good idea when talking to policemen. "We're obviously not hiding anything."

Sterns said, "We got a call because you're on park land."

"We're not," Sawyer said. "We're on Hiram Moreau's land, and we have permission to be here."

"You're on park land," Sterns insisted. "The line's right there." He shone the flashlight toward the palm trees. I had no idea exactly what he was pointing at or how he knew this. Maybe we'd walked far enough that we'd crossed the property line, but we shouldn't be arrested for trespassing when it had been an innocent mistake.

Well, maybe not an innocent one, considering what we'd been up to—but a genuine one.

"We were on Mr. Moreau's land," I insisted. "He's my best friend's grandfather. We were with—" I was about to name the other boys, hoping the police would recognize the name of one of them. Surely they'd heard of Brody. Articles about his football performances had filled the local paper lately.

"With her car," Sawyer interrupted me loudly. "You can check, and Kaye's car will be right up there."

I was still standing behind him, so I couldn't see his face. But he squeezed my hand. He was telling me he didn't want me to mention the guys. Some of them had been drinking underage, and I'd almost gotten them in trouble.

"Let her put her clothes on," Sawyer said.

The policemen allowed this. The catch was, they continued to grill Sawyer while I tripped along the beach in my undies in search of our clothing. I was able to shake the sand off my skirt and wiggle into it without much trouble, storing Sawyer's shorts under my elbow. But our shirts had hit the water. The tide had rolled them in and out and gotten them thoroughly soaked. I washed the sand out of them as best I could, squeezed out the salt water, and buttoned my shirt with my back to the policemen, wondering how in God's name I was going to explain this to my mother. I slipped on my sandals and snagged Sawyer's flip-flops. This was not how romantic trysts were supposed to end.

As I walked back to them, Sorrow was asking Sawyer, "Is she your girlfriend?"

"Of *course* she's my girlfriend. Look at her." Sawyer glanced over his shoulder at me and winked. I wasn't sure whether he was trying to reassure me because things were going to be okay, or comfort me because things were very, very bad.

"Do your parents know you're here?" Sterns asked. We both shook our heads. "Then give me your phone numbers. I'm going to let them know."

While he wrote on a pad, I recited Dad's number, not my mother's, because I wasn't insane. Sawyer said, "I can give you my dad's number, but he won't answer because he's drunk, and if you did reach him, he sure as hell wouldn't care I was making out with my girlfriend at the beach *legally*. But you're welcome to call Hiram Moreau, whose property *you're* trespassing on right now."

That was a lot of bravado for him to throw around while wearing wet underwear.

"Let's step up here to the patrol car while we figure this out." Sterns led the way over to the park while Sorrow fell in line behind us as if we were already jailbirds being marched from one cell to another.

Sterns put Sawyer in the back of the waiting patrol car. Sorrow led me to the opposite side and asked as I sat down, "What's the make and model of your car? Do you know the license plate number?" I gave him all that information. He closed the door with a frighteningly permanent-sounding *thunk*, shutting out the roar of the ocean.

"I hope the guys saw the flashlight and left," Sawyer told me quickly. "Quinn had a joint. I'm about to give them a little more time before the cop walks over there to look at your car, okay? Don't freak out."

"Okay," I breathed. I'd thought I couldn't be more horrified at what was happening. I was wrong.

"Hey!" Sawyer shouted at the cops. My ears rang.

Sorrow had taken two steps toward Harper's granddad's land. Sterns was on the phone. Both of them turned to look.

Sawyer held up his soaked shirt, which they'd thrown into the car with him. He wrung it out. Seawater streamed onto the floor of the car.

The policemen spoke to each other. Sterns put his other hand up to his ear to have a conversation with Dad. Sorrow stormed to Sawyer's side of the car. "Come here, bro," he said, yanking Sawyer out.

The door slammed. Sawyer's body slammed against it. His

bare chest pressed against the window. Sorrow moved up and down behind him, searching him, I supposed. Then Sorrow opened the door again and threw Sawyer in, handcuffed.

Sawyer was wearing that blank expression he got when he was beyond fury. He stared out the window as Sorrow trekked off in search of my car.

Shivering in my wet shirt, I said, "I hope Quinn appreciates what you did."

"It was my fault he was there in the first place," Sawyer muttered. "I asked him to come."

It wasn't Sawyer's fault Quinn was smoking pot, but I didn't argue that point. I said, "I'm afraid it's my fault we got caught in the first place."

Sawyer's face softened as he turned to me. "Not everything that goes wrong can be your fault, Kaye."

"Why would anybody call the cops on us?" I asked. "You had permission from Harper's granddad to be here. The park is closed, so nobody could have seen us from there. But Tia and Chelsea ran into Aidan at the movie. Chelsea mentioned you were here. Aidan had no idea *I* would be here. He just wanted to get *you* in trouble."

Sterns opened my door. I asked, "Officer, did you hear who called you down here? Sawyer has permission to be here, and the park is closed. I think my ex-boyfriend just wanted to get revenge on Sawyer. If you take us to jail, you'll be contributing to prison overcrowding, all for nothing."

Sterns shrugged. "All I know is, you are in serious trouble, young lady. I was talking to your dad at first, but then your mom got on the phone." He shut the door.

"Okay," Sawyer said soothingly, but I was already gasping for breath, trying not to cry and failing miserably. "Kaye," he called over my sobs. He was the one with his hands behind his back in cuffs, trying to make me feel better, and I was the one who was losing it because I'd gotten him into this.

"On a happier note," he said, "I think I've solved the prob lem of where to hold the homecoming dance."

Now I was crying and laughing at the same time, and hiccupping as a result. Wiping the tears from my cheeks, I said, "That is of absolutely no use to me in jail."

"You could hold the dance here," Sawyer said anyway. "People could leave their cars along the road and walk down here, and we could have it on the beach. Or maybe the city would let us leave our cars over there in the lot at the public park if we told them ahead of time. We could even hold it on the city's part of the beach. Just have everybody kick their shoes off, string some lights through the trees—"

"We can't have it off campus," I said. "Remember? Ms. Chen already shut that idea down. Too much liability."

"Then what if we made the football field look like the beach?" he suggested. "String some lights across the field, bring in some palms in pots, turn off the floodlights overhead—"

"I thought of that, too," I said. "I mean, I didn't think of making it look like the beach, but I already suggested having the dance in the stadium. The school doesn't want us standing on the grass and killing it. Grass is expensive and more important than our happiness." I sniffled.

"Then we hold it in the parking lot right outside the stadium," he said. "People don't even have to get back in their cars and drive after the game. It's on school property. There's plenty of room. We just cordon off a section—say, where the away team's buses will park, because they'll be gone by dance time—and string lights through the palm trees that are already there. It's not supposed to rain. No hurricanes in sight. If the school says no to that, they just don't want us to have a dance, and they should 'fess up."

I gasped. "Sawyer, that is a great idea."

"Some acknowledgment, please, that I came up with it while handcuffed in the back of a cop car, wrongly accused, in my boxers."

I patted his bare thigh, which was more solid than I'd imagined. "I'll give you all the acknowledgment you can handle if we ever get out of here."

He grinned mischievously at me.

"Our night together was so romantic, up to a point," I said. "We could recreate it for the dance."

"Would we ask the police to come and handcuff people?"

"Only if they're into that sort of kink. We could use it as a fund-raiser for the prom."

"Always thinking, aren't you, Gordon?" He glanced out the windshield. "Here they come. Now we're not trying to create a diversion. We only want to get out of trouble, so be humble and say nothing but 'Yes, sir,' and 'You're absolutely right.'"

Two minutes later we were hurrying back across the city beach and onto Harper's granddad's beach, hand in hand. Sterns had told my mother that I would drive straight home. I don't know what my mother had said to Sterns, but he'd seemed afraid for me.

"Listen," Sawyer said as we walked. "Whatever your parents tell you, you didn't do anything wrong. Don't let them make you feel like you did. They can punish you all they want, but don't let them convince you that you're a bad person, because you're not."

I nodded, hardly hearing him. I had a much more serious concern. "They're never going to let me see you again," I breathed.

"We'll see each other at school," he said gently. "And after we graduate in May, what they say won't matter."

I wasn't sure this was true. I'd planned to live with my parents until I left for Columbia in August. Even after that, conceivably they could continue to jerk me around by withholding my college tuition if I didn't do what they said.

Sawyer's words made me feel better anyway—because he considered how to get around unfair rules, which was totally foreign to my way of thinking. And because he assumed we'd still be together in May, no matter what.

At least, he talked the talk.

When he reached the passenger side of my car, he dropped

his flip-flops and slapped his wet clothes across the roof. "Give me a sec to put my clothes on," he said. "I've moved from Harper's house into the B and B."

"Oh, have you?"

"Yeah, and I don't want to frighten the elderly."

While he got dressed, I fished in my purse and checked my phone. "I have a message from DeMarcus, and one from Brody," I said as he got into the car. "They must be worried about us. One from Noah, one from Tia—"

"Don't think about that right now," Sawyer said.

"—two from Quinn, four from Harper, six from Will." None from Aidan. Either he hadn't heard he might have gotten me detained by the cops along with Sawyer, or he didn't care.

"I'll call them," Sawyer said. "You've got to get home. I'll say the cops accused us of trespassing and let us go. I'll leave out all the near-naked parts. Nobody at school will ever hear about that unless the cops blab."

"Or my parents," I muttered.

I started the engine and cruised under the palm trees. It was a very short drive to the B and B, so I didn't waste any time before telling him what was on mind. "If we're going to date, Sawyer—"

"If? Wait, what?"

"—I want to make sure that we're exclusive," I said. "That's the only way I want to do this."

He was very slowly massaging his wrists where the cop

had cuffed him, but he was looking at me. He glared at me so angrily across the car that my heart felt like it was failing.

"What?" he finally exclaimed again. "How long did you date Aidan?"

"Three years," I said.

"And in that three years, did you *ever* have a conversation with him in which you made sure you were both on the same page about dating exclusively?"

"No," I said meekly.

"Then why are you asking me?" he demanded.

"Sawyer!" I said, exasperated. "You have a reputation for getting around."

"When I wasn't dating *you*! Don't you think I would automatically stop going out with other girls if you and I were together? I said something like this to you before Aidan even broke up with you, because you said something like this to *me*. I mean, if you think so little of me, what do you want to date me for?"

I remembered, with a slow burn across my cheeks, the note I'd lost in Harper's house, in which Tia and I had discussed exactly this. I wondered again whether he'd found it.

I drove up to the gate and punched in the combination. But when it was open, I didn't pull out onto the road right away. I turned to Sawyer.

He had the same idea. "I'm sorry," he said. "We're both stressed out right now. I know that's not what you meant, and I didn't mean to—"

I leaned over and kissed him.

His arms wrapped around me and pulled me closer. He deepened the kiss, making it very, very sexy for a moment. Then he backed off and placed a series of light, sweet kisses on my lips. "You have to go," he whispered before kissing me again.

"I know."

His lips lingered on mine. "But I want to stay here forever with you"—kiss—"and get gawked at by passing motorists." A car zoomed by on the road.

"That is so romantic." I kissed him back, savoring what might be our last seconds together for a while. I truly wanted to stay there forever with him, too. Or, better yet, a hundred yards behind us, alone on the beach. The thought that finally made me leave was that if I stayed, I would make my punishment worse and, if I got grounded, my time away from Sawyer longer.

When I pulled in to my spot in the driveway, Dad was standing outside the garage in pajama pants and his ancient Columbia T-shirt. He said as I dragged my feet toward him, "I convinced your mother that she's too angry to speak with you tonight."

"Thanks." I sighed with relief.

"Are you okay?"

I nodded.

"You're wet."

I swallowed. "I didn't do anything wrong. I'm pretty sure Aidan called the police to get Sawyer in trouble for nothing."

"Whether you did something wrong is in the eye of the beholder," Dad said ominously. "In the morning, the beholder is going to be your mother."

Then he hugged me close and squeezed me. Immediately he let me go. "Ew, you're *really* wet." He took me by the shoulders and pressed his lips to my forehead for a long moment. "I'm glad you're safe."

But a conversation with my mother loomed in the morning. I didn't feel safe at all.

Thirteen

"GET. UP!"

Fight-or-flight adrenaline zipped through me. I sat straight up in bed. Morning light flooded my room. My mother, fully dressed, frowned at me with her fists on her hips. She was the definition of a rude awakening.

"Put some clothes on," she said, "and be in my car in two minutes." She stalked out.

In a minute and a half, I was at her Mercedes, but she was already waiting with the engine running like I was late and had a lot of nerve.

She didn't say anything for a long time as we drove through town. When we stopped at the intersection beside Aidan's house, I craned my neck and saw his car in the driveway. I'd never considered myself a violent person, but I would have loved to try a Molotov cocktail just then. A gasoline-soaked rag stuffed into a bottle, aimed to roll underneath and explode the car he'd screwed me in three times. I fire-bombed it with my eyes after we'd passed it, until I couldn't see it anymore.

"The police," my mother finally muttered as we cruised the interstate. "I get a call at eleven o'clock at night from the *police*, saying my seventeen-year-old daughter is half-naked on public property with the very boy I have told her to stay away from. This is not a poor grade we're talking about, Kaye, or a position at school. You are associating with a delinquent who has a bad reputation, and who is a bad influence on you."

"I agree he has a bad reputation." No arguing with that. "I don't agree that he's a bad influence. He's cleaned up his act lately. Anyway, you sound like you think I'm five, with no mind of my own."

"Because that's exactly how you're behaving, as if you can't see you're throwing your future away. Listen to me. I didn't go to school with anyone like Aidan."

"Oh, *Aidan,*" I exclaimed. "You still want me to get back with Aidan? Let me tell you what he—"

She interrupted me. "I went to school with *lots* of boys like Sawyer."

"You don't know what Sawyer's *like*," I said. "You hardly know him."

"I've heard plenty about him. In fact, I've heard half of it from *you*."

She had me there. I put my chin in my hand and stared out the window, cursing myself for repeating the cheerleaders' rumors about Sawyer over the years to my mother.

I was so angry, and my mind was spinning so fast, that I didn't even realize where we were headed. But when she turned onto the exit in the seediest section of Tampa, I knew. "Mom."

She didn't answer, just kept moving her land yacht smoothly down the ramp. I could see one muscle in her jaw working as she clenched her teeth. She sailed into the slum, deserted of cars except for one 1980s model far down the long, straight street, its axles up on cement blocks. But the neighborhood was busy with young men hanging out in the shadows of the run-down apartment buildings, and riding kids' dirt bikes in circles. Any sane person *not* looking to buy a dime bag would have recognized what she'd stumbled into and hightailed it out of there.

My mother was not sane. And it was getting worse. In the past she'd only slowed long enough to point out her old apartment building to Barrett and me. This time she actually pulled alongside the curb, put the car in park, and pushed the button to turn off the engine. She looked over at me and raised her eyebrows.

Instantly the car was surrounded. A guy on a bike hopped down the curb, into the street, and pedaled back and forth in front of the car. A boy in a baseball cap with a marijuana leaf on the front knocked on my mother's window. She didn't react.

Watching this in horror, I jumped, startled at a knock on my own window. I didn't turn, afraid of what I'd see, terrified that I was separated from these people by one pane of not-bulletproof glass.

My mother watched me smugly.

"Fine," I said. "You grew up in that corner apartment." I pointed to the second story across the lawn of brown grass and packed dirt, strewn with cigarette butts and trash. "Your brother died at sixteen on this very street, selling drugs. Your dad was robbed and killed coming home from work. At age forty-five your mom died of cancer, which could have been caught early and treated if she'd been able to afford health insurance."

My mother gave me a curt nod.

"You got good grades, participated in every academic competition available, and snagged a full scholarship to Columbia, so you and your new family could live to their full potential, and you would never have to face this crushing poverty again."

She raised her chin to nod again, but stopped when I said this:

"You got out of here. You ensured your children would never have to live here. And yet you have driven your daughter back here, and we're both about to get shot in the head, because you don't like my boyfriend!" I was shouting now.

Even if my mother didn't care, the drug dealers around the car did. The guy at my mother's window and the guy on the bike said something to each other and took off, jumping the curb and speeding around the far side of the apartment building. I felt rather than saw the shadow of the man at my window moving away.

Another knock sounded on my mother's side. I started again, and this time she jerked her head in that direction too. A policeman's tan uniform filled the window. I looked behind us and saw the cop car, blue lights flashing.

"Oh, and *I'm* the one who always gets arrested," I said.

"You shut your smart mouth." My mother pushed the button to start the car, pressed another button to roll down her window, and then turned the car off. "Yes, officer?"

"Ma'am, do you live around here?" I couldn't see his face above the roof of the car, but he sounded young.

"I live at the beach," my mother said icily.

"What are you doing in this part of town?" came his voice. "Did you know this neighborhood is full of drug activity?"

"I grew up in that apartment right there." She pointed to the corner. "I like to show it to my children now and again. That is not a crime, not yet, not even in Florida."

"Yes, ma'am," he said. "If you ask me, if I grew up here and got out of here, I wouldn't come back. I definitely wouldn't bring my daughter to this neighborhood."

"Young man," she seethed, "I did not ask you."

This could not be happening. I was going to sit in the back of a cop car for the second time in twelve hours, because I had a habit of hanging out with people who couldn't keep their attitudes in check and their big mouths shut.

But cops were more leery of my mother than they were of Sawyer, apparently. "Yes, ma'am," this one repeated. "Y'all have a safe afternoon." I watched his uniform pass the back seat window. He got into his patrol car, shut the door, and put his head down as if he was writing something. I suspected he was really waiting for us to leave. I wouldn't put it past my mother to outstay him just to spite him.

She pushed the button to start the car again with one elegantly manicured finger. Her hand was shaking, but she didn't say a word. She pressed the button to roll up the window, flicked on the blinker, looked behind her so as not to pull into oncoming traffic while a cop possibly had her on camera, and headed down the street.

"I learned a lot from that," I said.

"You are grounded," she said. "Your father is not going to talk me out of it this time. You may go to school and come home."

"You just made sure I won't get into Columbia, then. Nobody's going to write me a stellar recommendation letter if I shirk my responsibilities for student council. We're building the homecoming float every day after school next week—"

"You may build the homecoming float," she said stiffly.

"—and I've figured out a place to hold the homecoming dance. Actually, Sawyer figured it out. Do I get to go to my own homecoming dance?"

"Yes," she said carefully, "but not with that boy. Your father and I will volunteer as chaperones to make sure."

"Fantastic," I muttered. I'd gone to all the trouble of saving this dance for my friends. I was rewarded with a date with my parents.

When we got home, Dad was watching a pro football pregame show with his feet up on the coffee table. "Did you bring me a rock?"

"Shut up." My mother disappeared into her office.

"Hey, my Kaye," he said. "Get changed and meet me on my boat in five minutes."

"Really?" I whined. "I just went through this whole thing with one parent."

"Please," he said.

Obediently I changed into a bikini and a hat, smeared on sunscreen, and galloped across the yard and down the pier to the sailboat. I was still angry and not looking forward to whatever Dad had to say. But at least his run-up to a scolding was more enjoyable than my mother's. He'd made me a picnic basket full of breakfast, for one thing. The boat puttered through the lagoon on its impotent motor, but as soon as we hit the open Gulf, Dad unfurled the big sail. We sped through the sea breeze, past the harbor and Harper's granddad's beach and the public park that had caused all the trouble. I sat in the bow, enjoying the wind in my face. The late morning sun was warm and kind.

Finally I asked, "Well? When's the lecture? Let's get it over with."

"No lecture," Dad said. "I thought it would do you good to get out on the ocean."

Moving with uncharacteristic speed, he wound and unwound ropes until the sails dropped and the boat slowed to a crawl. He offered me his favorite fishing pole. I shook my head. He baited the hook for himself and skimmed it out over the sparkling water.

I shifted to sit close to him on a lawn chair in the stern. "Can I ask you something?"

He glanced at me like he was very afraid.

"You and Mom both majored in finance at Columbia."

"Yes."

"You both worked in Manhattan for a couple of years. Then she got an offer for a great position with the bank here. She grew up here, but you're from Boston. You didn't want to move to Florida. She bribed you by buying you this boat, and the house on a lagoon with access to the Gulf."

"Yes."

"Why did you give up?"

He gave me a look like that was crazy talk. "I didn't give up, exactly. Everyone seems to forget this, but I do have a job."

"I know. I didn't mean—"

"And in that job, I wrote a headlining article for *GQ* on how the hardest thing about being a writer and the secondary breadwinner and the primary caretaker is that your own kids think you're a loser."

I raised my voice, and it echoed back to me over the waves. "I don't think you're a loser. But you and Mom both had these power jobs in New York. She got her own bank. You became a writer. Something happened to you."

He reeled his line all the way in and flicked it out again

before he said, "Being a stockbroker is very stressful. I couldn't handle it."

"What do you mean, you couldn't handle it?"

"I just couldn't."

I tried to picture what he meant, and what this had looked like. "Did you go to a counselor?"

He laughed bitterly. "Of course not. Men don't do that."

That sounded familiar. I said, "That's dumb."

He shrugged, zigzagging the line across the water.

"So what did you do, when you couldn't handle it?"

"I quit. In the worst, most public way possible, sabotaging myself so I wouldn't be able to work in the finance industry in Manhattan again for a while."

I'd never heard this story before. I was dying to know more about his meltdown. But he seemed so traumatized describing it, even now, that I decided to press him for details another day. I only asked, "Did Mom lose her mind?"

"No." He sounded surprised. I couldn't tell whether he was surprised at my question, or surprised that my mother hadn't blown her top two decades ago. "She helped me brainstorm for another job I could get with this degree, a job that wouldn't drive me crazy. We figured out that I loved writing. I could write books and articles about finance, interpreting the stock market for lay people. And she said I might like living in Florida and slowing down. She promised that if I would let her have this bank, she would let me have this boat."

That didn't sound like my mother at all.

"You've been traveling a lot more lately," I said. "Are you trying to get away from Mom? Truthfully."

He gave me an expression of utter shock. "No!"

"Would you tell me if you were?" I kept on.

"I don't know, but that's not why. Your mom and I aren't having marital problems just because *you've* suddenly decided that I feel emasculated."

"You've been gone a lot, that's all," I muttered.

"I have a *job*."

"It's the same job you've always had, but you didn't travel like this before."

"I'm doing research for the new book and, at the moment, three different articles. I can accept more projects now that Barrett is gone and you're old enough to take care of yourself."

"Oh, it's all about Barrett," I sneered. "That makes sense."

"Don't go bitter on me. Barrett is a lot more fragile than you are. I worried about him. Still do. I've never worried about you. I thought you didn't need me around." He reeled his line all the way in, set the butt of his pole down on the deck, and turned to me. "Obviously I was wrong." Rummaging in his tackle box for a different lure, he commented, "Thanks to the book deal, I'm going to make more money than your mom this year."

"You *are*? That is a huge amount of money."

He nodded. "It doesn't make up for the last nineteen years, when she made more than me."

"You're not in a competition," I pointed out.

He straightened. "You're right. It feels that way, though. And I don't really care. I only care because society cares, and I'm supposed to." Satisfied with the new lure he'd found, he deftly slung the line out over the water again.

It was soothing to watch him skip the hook over the surface, reel it back in, throw it back out, thinking of nothing, rarely catching anything. Just enjoying the sun and the water and the day. A flock of pelicans, the more common brown ones rather than white, skimmed past us, close over the water. Their wingspans were impossibly wide. I watched until I lost them in the far-off color and movement of the harbor.

I mused, "I think I'm a lot more like you than I am like Mom."

"I think it's taken you a long time to figure that out."

He was silent for a while. The ocean was full of sound, though. Waves lapped against the boat. Seagulls cried. The fishing line buzzed over the water.

"But listen, my Kaye," he finally said. "You and your mom are at each other's throats right now, and I'm just trying to hang on. You're going through some growing pains. You are not easy to get along with at the present time. Your mom has never been easy to get along with, and never will be. She's got issues." He looked pointedly at me. "And I love her with all my heart. Don't forget that."

A few hours later, I hiked back to my room. I had an appointment with Stephen Crane, I supposed, but first I checked my phone for signs of Sawyer.

Sawyer: How much trouble? :(

Me: Much. I got taken to downtown Tampa to gawk at the drug deals.

Sawyer: That shit is dangerous. Way more dangerous than me. Don't let her do that again.

Me: Ha, "let."

Sawyer: Biz is slow & the CL gave me the p.m. off. Can you go out?

Me: They don't want me to go out w u anymore.

Immediately I started typing an explanation, but not fast enough. I hated that I'd sent that text by itself, accidentally making him wait for more. I wished I could take it back. Finally I sent this:

Me: I will work on them. We just need to wait a while if u will wait for me.

Sawyer: Duh

Almost instant gratification after I sent my vulnerable text. Sawyer was a lot better at this than I was.

Sawyer: What if we went out in the daylight when I am less likely to get u arrested?

Me: I don't know.

Sawyer: What if we did something innocent?

Me: You?

Sawyer: Girl, it takes two. I didn't do any of that stuff by myself.

I tried to type "Touché" but autocorrect kept changing it to "Touched," which sounded even dirtier than I'd intended in this context. I finally backspaced over it.

Me: What did u have in mind?

Sawyer: Tennis

Me: U know how to play tennis?

Sawyer: What do u mean, why can't I play tennis

Me: I just can't picture u playing tennis.

Sawyer: The YMCA in Georgia thought tennis would save the poor children. I have played a lot of tennis.

Me: How do u know I play tennis?

Sawyer: Princess Country Club knows how to play tennis.

He was right about that. When we were twelve, Ellen and I had won the Pinellas County junior girls' doubles championship.

Me: Let me ask.

First I peered into my parents' bedroom. Dad was a lot more likely to give me permission for anything, ever, than my mother. However, his playtime was over. The door onto his porch had a sign taped to it that said NO, which meant he was working. He never put out the sign during the week, only on the weekend when my mother was home. He'd definitely been my primary caregiver on weekdays when I was growing up, but on the weekends "NO" meant "I am finally getting my time to write; go find Mother."

I skipped down the staircase and through the kitchen, my steps slowing as I approached my mother's office. I knocked politely on the open door.

She was already wearing a frown as she turned from her desk.

I swallowed. "Sawyer—"

"No."

"—wanted to know—"

"No."

"—if we could go out during the wholesome daylight hours—"

"Katherine Beale Gordon, I said no."

"—to play tennis, because how can anybody possibly get arrested playing tennis?"

"That boy would find a way."

Angry all over again, I tromped upstairs and texted Sawyer the sad news. He sent me a hilarious answer. My mother would have been horrified to know that we texted back and forth for the rest of the day, into the night. I wasted hours with him and lost some sleep despite her, and fell for him that much harder.

On Monday the school elected Sawyer and me homecoming king and queen. Since cheerleading practice was on the football field with the band, DeMarcus held his phone and read the announcements Ms. Chen had e-mailed to him. As soon as he made this pronouncement, all the cheerleaders mobbed me, squealing and hugging, along with all the majorettes (except Angelica), and Tia, who'd abandoned her snare drum halfway across the field—despite Ms. Nakamoto calling through her megaphone, "Ms. Cruz? Let's keep it together until the end of practice, shall we?"

Sawyer had heard the announcement too, in football practice. A couple of guys who came to help with the homecoming float build after school told me the entire football team had ribbed Sawyer about what he and I were going to do to each other on homecoming night, which was kind of touching and kind of gross.

He called me from work. "What does this vote even mean?" he asked me. "We just sit on the float together?"

"And get crowned during halftime, yeah."

"Do we get a special prize at the dance?"

"Like my parents have a change of heart and let me go out with you? I seriously doubt it." I hated the way this sounded. I'd treasured every moment I'd stolen talking with him at school that day, but all I'd done while I was with him was complain bitterly about *not* being with him. If I kept this up, he wouldn't even *want* to date me for long, and my mother would have won.

"I'm wearing the costume, you know," he said. "Not at the dance, but of course at the game, and also on the float. The pelican has to make an appearance of some kind in the homecoming parade. Little kids might actually cry if he doesn't."

I planned to cheer during the game too. I wouldn't miss that to stand and grin at the crowd in a tiara for five minutes. During the parade, though, the cheerleaders just waved from the back of Grace's dad's farm truck. I might as well play queen in formal wear.

And I didn't need my mother to help me with that. I had

last year's prom gown. So I didn't even tell my parents about my achievement, which they wouldn't see as an achievement anyway. I just kept going to the homecoming float builds after school as if we weren't building it for me.

On Thursday night, Sawyer showed up at eight o'clock at the school's shop class, where we'd constructed the float. He said he'd gotten off work an hour early so he could help with last-minute preparations. By that time, though, the float was finished. Will's design of a blue crepe-paper wave rising behind the homecoming court had worked beautifully. I was one of the few students left in the shop, cleaning up stray scraps of paper on the floor. There was nothing for Sawyer to do.

"So let's go get a vegan dinner," he said, "on me. It has to be in downtown Tampa, though, where the vegans are."

I did a quick calculation in my head. The student council had spent some late nights on the float. My parents wouldn't expect me home until ten. I had time for sneaky vegan. "We need to go in separate cars, so they don't see mine abandoned here or catch me getting out of your truck."

"Okay."

"And I never want you to pay for mine. I get an allowance. You need your money."

"Don't worry about it." He grinned. "That night your family came to the Crab Lab, your dad tipped me a hundred bucks."

"You deserved every penny," I grumbled.

The restaurant he picked out had an Indian feel but an

international menu. "I'm surprised at all the choices," I admitted. "I wanted to come with you, but I'd pictured eating carrots dipped in ketchup."

"I'm surprised too," he said, turning the page. "I'm glad we came. I never even thought about eating half this stuff."

"It would be great if you could shift your attention to what you *can* eat," I said. "Until now, it seems like you've been totally focused on what you can't have."

He reached across the table for my hand. "Yeah, I have been."

I tilted my head and frowned at him. "Is this worth it if it makes us both miserable?"

He didn't answer. He slowly rubbed each of my fingers with his, then circled his fingertips in my palm, shooting delicious fiery sensations up my arm.

That was my answer. As long as he made me feel so good, this was worth it.

And I remembered what Tia had told me at the movie Saturday night, which had made it sound like Sawyer had a deep vested interest in me. "Tia said you left your dad's house because of something he said about me."

Sawyer's eyes widened. He let go of my hand and put his own in his lap. "I don't want to talk about it."

"Sawyer," I scolded him. "You think you're being chivalrous, but *my* mother doesn't like *you,* either. She dislikes you for a totally different reason, but still. And *I'm* not moving out."

Sawyer took a deep breath and sighed. "I could almost forgive him for what he said. Prison's supposed to rehabilitate people. Of course it only turns them into monsters if they weren't already. And the races don't mix there."

"I know that."

"It's not what he said. It's that he was stone-cold sober, and he insulted the one person he'd found out I care about. A couple of weeks ago when you came to the Crab Lab with Aidan, my brother saw that I was upset and figured out you were why. He told my dad about it. My dad went out of his way to make a comment, not to insult you, but to hurt me. People who love each other don't do that."

"So you're not going to live with someone who doesn't love you," I said slowly. "Maybe that's too much to expect. Maybe you move back in with him until May because you need a place to live and he's your father. As for the rest . . . maybe that comes with age."

He looked out the window onto the busy street, considering. Candlelight flickered across his face, glinting in the blond stubble on his chin. I wondered how old we would both grow before we got along with our parents and won the chance to date like everybody else.

"You need a roof over your head," I said, "and you need to eat. You can't do well at school or at work while you're worried about those basics. If you're determined to make a success of yourself, you need to start taking care of yourself first."

"That's exactly what Ms. Malone told me." He surprised me by standing, leaning across the table, and capturing my lips with his. As he sat back down, he promised me, "I'll think about it."

Fourteen

THE FOLLOWING AFTERNOON, JUST AS I WAS sitting my royal ass down on my crepe-paper throne in preparation for the parade, Sawyer came around the corner of the school dressed as the pelican. When he saw me, he jumped about two feet and threw up his wings in exaggerated surprise, then slapped his glove to his chest like he was having a heart attack.

I knew why. I'd changed my hair again.

The homecoming parade was a big deal in this town—because we didn't have that many big deals. So many people were in it that I was always surprised there was anyone left to watch it. And the school, which forced us to make up hurricane days, didn't mind letting half the student body out of last period to line up for marching band, suit up for dance troupes, and gussie up for waving at the crowd from elaborate constructions of wood and chicken wire.

That's why Chelsea, after she'd donned her majorette

leotard and pushed her tiara into place, had time to help me pick out my hair. I was going full Afro.

"And the final touch." She slid my official homecoming queen tiara into my round hair, making a dent. She squinted at me in the mirror. "Wow, I didn't know it would be so . . . big."

"Me neither," I admitted. In fact, I was having second thoughts about appearing in public like this, but there was no time for a redo. "What am I saying with this?"

"Well, for one thing, you're giving Aidan a big 'up yours' for making a comment about your hair a few weeks ago." She shot the mirror the bird.

"True." I hadn't said anything to Aidan about calling the cops on Sawyer. I had no proof, for one thing. And hardly anyone in the school seemed to have heard about the incident. I wanted to keep it that way. No need to provoke him.

But if he hadn't liked my big hair before, huge hair certainly let him know how much I cared about his opinion.

"You're also telling the school how you feel about having to struggle so hard just to hold a homecoming dance."

"I like it," I proclaimed, even though I didn't.

And so, a few minutes later when Sawyer fell on the ground and played dead in the sunshine, I knew why. I called, "Is it that bad?"

He leaped onto the float and took his head off—something he almost never did once he was in costume. Crepe paper crackled as he slid into place on the throne next to me. "I love it," he said, taking off a glove to slide his fingers into the back of my hair.

Of course he would love it. I felt myself glowing inside.

"It's fragile," I warned him, my voice trembling as he touched me. "It'll only stay this way for a short time."

"Like seaborgium," he suggested.

I laughed in an unregal way at this periodic table joke from nowhere. "It *does* look like a hairstyle that would have a radioactive half-life," I agreed. "It's for special occasions."

"This hair is a special occasion," he said. "It is its own holiday."

"With its own zip code," I agreed. "I'll disassemble it before tonight. It would never survive a back handspring."

"That's a shame." He moved toward me, his eyelids lowered sexily.

"Wait, lipstick, mmmm . . . ," I said as he kissed me.

I heard the familiar click of Harper's camera, and I broke the kiss in alarm.

"Sorry!" Harper called from the front of the float. She was wearing the cute clothes that had become her work uniform lately, cargo pants and a tight tank top, with the addition of her retro glasses. "I know I keep doing this to y'all, but I can't stand to miss a great shot. And your hair!"

"You won't put that in the yearbook, will you?" I pleaded. "You have to delete it. My mother can't see me kissing Sawyer."

"I'm not going to *delete* it!" she exclaimed, outraged. "But I'll put it in my 'Kaye's mom can't see this' file. Which is growing." Already spying another great shot, she wandered off without saying good-bye.

"Have you ever been felt up by a pelican?" Sawyer growled in my ear.

"I thought you said that's illegal in Florida."

"Hm," he said, leaning in to kiss me again. Technically this was grounds for suspension. School hours weren't officially over yet, and we were on campus. But the float had been dragged out of the shop building and parked behind the gym, at the very end of the floats and bands and horses and antique cars lined up for the parade. We were the pièce de résistance. Nobody was watching us steal this moment together.

Until Grace, who'd been elected homecoming senior maid, climbed up onto her own throne and called, "Principal Chen! Sawyer and Kaye are having sex on the homecoming float."

"My God, can't we get any privacy in this parking lot?" Sawyer complained. He put his foam head back on but wrapped his wing around me, sitting back casually and propping one big bird foot up on the opposite knee like he was sitting around a bonfire at the beach with his girl.

Just after school let out, the parade began to crawl through town—out of the school parking lot, down the avenue shaded with live oaks—to make a very difficult ninety-degree turn-on-a-dime into the historic downtown. The entire route was lined four people deep. I gave them a Queen Elizabeth wave. Some of them pointed at my hair. Everyone smiled.

Everyone, that is, except my mother. I still hadn't told her or my father that I'd been elected homecoming queen. It was too much to ask that she wouldn't find out. She stood on a corner in front of headquarters for her bank, surrounded by her best employees, wearing shades so I couldn't see her eyes. I imagined her calculating how much money I was wasting if time was money and I could have been spending mine on Stephen Crane.

I kept having to remind myself to enjoy the moment. I'd been elected *homecoming queen,* for God's sake. People might have voted for me for a variety of reasons, but one of them wasn't to get revenge on me because they didn't like me. I was popular, either because I got along with almost everybody or because I'd done a bang-up job on student council. Homecoming queen was an accomplishment few people could ever claim. Each time I came to this realization, I seized the moment like one of Harper's snapshots. Not many other students at my school would ever glimpse the beach from quite this angle, through the trees and six feet off the road, or look up and be able to touch the traffic lights framed with palm fronds overhead.

And the hour that the parade crept through town gave me time with Sawyer. Granted, we weren't really touching. We definitely weren't talking. He frequently jumped down from the float to high-five little kids, then pretended he was scrambling to catch up to us again with an exaggerated run. But there were also long interludes when he sat next to me on our throne, his feathery knees invading my personal space, his arm around me.

Even after I located my mother in the crowd, I wasn't self-conscious about touching Sawyer. I could say later that it was all part of his act. In truth, he gave me the warm fuzzies I'd always gotten when he treated me like his girlfriend while he was in costume. Sawyer and I might argue or break up or even come to hate each other because my mother was tearing us apart, but the pelican would always love me.

When the parade was over, I drove home. Carefully I took off my prom gown and hung it up, then flopped onto my bed in my underwear, exhausted. I couldn't rest now, though. I needed to get up and start the long process of reconstructing my hair.

But as soon as I lay down, my mind raced. The student council's responsibilities in the parade had gone off without a hitch. Boxes checked: tick, tick, tick. Everything was set up for the dance tonight to go smoothly, too. Since I would be cheering during the game, I'd delegated all the last-minute preparations to parents and teachers. Tick, tick, tick. I was about to suffer the indignity of being kept away from my boyfriend at the dance I'd personally constructed, but at least I would get to see him.

My heart raced along with my mind. I took long, deep breaths through my nose, trying very hard to slow everything down. I was amazed at how fast my heart beat anyway, like it knew something I didn't.

I was really looking forward to consulting with Ms. Malone on Monday.

My mother breezed into my room. I didn't need to open my eyes to know who was there. She was the parent who didn't knock. She paused at the foot of my bed. "Get your cheerleader uniform on," she sang like nothing was wrong. "You're not going to wear your hair like that to the game and the dance, are you? You've already squashed it. Let me help you."

Grudgingly I slipped on my top and skirt. I sat down in my bathroom while she worked my hair into twists, then pulled them out into curls of varying diameter, recreating how my hair had looked before. The feel of her hands in my hair was familiar, the motion of her arms in the mirror identical to a thousand repeats from my childhood. The difference was, we didn't speak.

A knock sounded on my bedroom door. "Come in," my mother called before I could. Dad peered at us, taking in the familiar act of sectioning and twisting hair, and our uneasy silence. Without a word, he left again.

Our football team had gotten so good that the games might have been boring with their guaranteed wins, except that we always seemed to get in trouble and come from behind at the last minute. And Brody always managed to get hurt. This time, in the second quarter, the opposing team's defense pushed through Noah and the other guard. Brody got sacked so hard that he flew several feet through the air before landing on his back with a two-hundred-pounder on top of him.

He did get up, very slowly. I glanced down the sideline

and felt terrible for Harper with her camera around her neck and her hands slapped to her mouth in horror.

I had my own scare a few minutes later. I'd never paid much attention to the local cops who patrolled the sidelines, keeping spectators off the field, but Sawyer had noticed they were Sterns and Sorrow. He followed them around for a few minutes. He imitated Sorrow's walk. He tapped Sterns's shoulder and jumped to the other side when Sterns turned around. I was afraid the whole stadium was about to find out how the police frisked a pelican.

He was saved by halftime. He loped over to wait with me and the rest of the homecoming court for our cue. Finally the announcer called our names one by one, the crowd cheered, and we walked slowly onto the field while the band endlessly played the alma mater.

Sawyer never missed an opportunity to incorporate a staid institution into his act. I'd thought the weirdest thing that would happen during my reign as homecoming queen would be that I was escorted onto the field by a six-foot-tall bird. I was wrong. Sawyer stole my glittery sash that said KAYE GORDON HOMECOMING QUEEN and put it on over his own head, upside down. He stole my roses and stored them in his beak. They didn't quite fit. The stems hung out. He tried to steal my tiara. I slapped him. The tiara fell off anyway when he dipped me and pretended to kiss me.

The crowd roared louder than it had when Brody threw a touchdown. This town loved Sawyer.

And, I was realizing, so did I.

* * *

Along with the other cheerleaders, I showered in the girls' locker room, changed into my cute outfit, and hurried across the parking lot to the dance. The night was clear and perfect, with real stars behind the imitation ones blinking in the palm trees. The air was nippy for the first time since March.

It had gotten around school that my mother wouldn't let me date Sawyer. Several girls in the locker room had told me what a shame it was that Sawyer and I had been elected homecoming king and queen together but couldn't be each other's date for homecoming. Ellen told me she thought it was romantic. I supposed it was, in a *Romeo and Juliet* sort of way, if you liked your romantic nights to *suck*.

Strangely, I wasn't a trembling, teary basket case as I walked with the other cheerleaders toward the oasis of light and movement in the corner of the parking lot nearest the stadium. My pulse hummed. I'd delegated most of the work of running the dance to adults, but as Aidan was fond of reminding me, ultimately the responsibility of making it successful rested with me. It was a burden I wouldn't shake until the event was over. And two hours of cheering and dancing almost nonstop had left me a shell of myself, running on air.

That's when I spied Sawyer in his regular clothes, standing at the entrance to the cordoned-off area of asphalt that served as the dance floor, waiting for me. Any blood that had been left in my brain seemed to leave it, and I actually felt dizzy as he closed the space between us.

"We can't talk long with my parents around," I whispered. As I said this, I glimpsed Dad trying to coax my mother into some kind of 1980s dance, even though the music blasting over the speakers was dubstep.

"We're going to have a slow dance together at homecoming," Sawyer promised me. "Keep your eyes peeled for an opportunity."

The dance was already going full blast—and amazingly, almost everyone was *dancing* at the dance. There were a few outliers like Aidan, who stubbornly stood at the periphery, looking on, making snide comments to Angelica, and anchoring her there in his misery. But the majority of students, even the boys, were getting down. Probably this had to do with the fact that Will and Chelsea were in the middle of a dance-off rematch, and they were a positive influence.

Sawyer passed very close to me while I was in the middle of the Wobble with the rest of the cheerleaders. In fact, he smacked right into me, just like he always did on the football field, except this time there was no padding between us.

"I beg your pardon!" he shouted, catching me and holding me to keep me from falling over, which wasn't really necessary. While I was still in his arms, he whispered, "Are you looking for our chance?"

"I haven't seen an opening yet." My parents had been watching me closely. Didn't they ever pee?

"Tenacious boogers, aren't they?" Sawyer commented.

"Yes, my parents are tenacious boogers," I called as he let

me go and disappeared back into the crowd. At least we could laugh about them while they made our lives miserable.

The next time I saw him, Will was trying to teach him to do the Dougie.

"I can't do it," Sawyer said.

With a glance at the edge of the crowd, I saw that my parents were talking to Ms. Chen. They would see us if they turned, but surely they didn't expect me to pretend Sawyer wasn't here at all. I said, "You do it in the pelican suit all the time."

"It's completely different in the suit," Sawyer said. "For you to do this without the suit"—he held his hands up slightly—"you'd have to do this in the suit." He held both hands straight up in the air. "Everything has to be exaggerated."

"That sounds a lot harder than I thought," Will said.

"It's exhausting." Sawyer *looked* exhausted, smiling with sleepy eyes. I wondered if he was skimming along his last wave of adrenaline, like me.

He turned to me. "Are they still watching?"

"Yes. Maybe later." I moved on before my parents got suspicious.

As I brushed past him, he touched my hand and whispered deliciously in my ear, "Later."

We had a few more encounters, but finally it was almost time for the dance to close down and we hadn't been alone together. I was grumbling about this to Harper as she snapped photos of the tired crowd. "Normally my parents would both be *all over* a catered buffet, but their daughter gets detained by the police just *one little time* and they're not hungry?"

Suddenly, from out of nowhere, Tia barreled into us. She swatted me with the end of one of her braids as she grabbed Harper in a tight hug. "My dad is totally hitting on your mom. Sis!"

Harper peered over Tia's shoulder at their parents. "Or, she's just trying to get a good price from him on redoing the exterior of the B and B," she said, sounding strangled.

Tia let Harper go and held her at arm's length. "And you don't get only me in the bargain. You get Violet, and Sophia, and Izzy, and all their children and shitty boyfriends. Think what fun Christmas will be for you from now on!"

Harper looked decidedly uneasy. "They're probably just talking." Then her eyes widened. "Oooh, Kaye, don't look, but they're laughing with your parents. None of them are watching the dance floor. Now's your chance."

I clutched at Tia. "Will you alert Sawyer for me? Send him behind the stadium."

She saluted me. "Ten-four," she said, which I was pretty sure was not what people were supposed to say when saluting. She vanished back into the crowd. I headed for the buffet as if I needed a word with the caterer. I kept going, behind the DJ's equipment and the caterer's van, into the darkness.

Sawyer stepped from behind one of the concrete pillars that held up the stadium. "Finally," he said.

I melted into his arms just as a slow dance started, the last song of the night. He made no move to kiss me. I didn't ask. After a long night of watching my friends touch their dates without a second thought, all I wanted was to tuck my head underneath Sawyer's chin and feel his arms around me. We swayed just like that until the final lyric.

"That's it." The DJ's amplified voice bounced around underneath the stadium. "Thanks, everyone, and have a good night! Fight, Pelicans, fight!"

Languidly, like waking up from the best dream, I pulled away from Sawyer and looked up into his eyes. "Happy homecoming."

He stroked a stray curl away from my face. "Everyone had a great time tonight. Against the odds, you did amazing work on all of this."

"I wouldn't have been able to do it without you."

He kissed me for one long, perfect moment.

And then he let me go, already receding into the shadows. "I'll walk this way. You go that way. We've fooled them all. Ha!"

I looked back at him making his way around the dark side of the stadium. At the same time, he was looking back at me.

We would see each other at school on Monday.

But at that moment, it felt like our romance was over, and I would never see him again.

As I stepped back into the cordoned-off area of the parking lot, I heard my mother call, "Kaye!" Most of the school was already moving toward their cars elsewhere in the vast lot. The crowd I'd intended to get lost in was gone. My mother must have seen me come out from behind the stadium, and she'd guessed what I'd done.

I wasn't going to drag my feet toward punishment one more time. Standing firm in my strappy sandals, shivering a little in my light sweater against the cool night, I let *her* cross the dance floor to *me*.

She stood eye to eye with me, silently assessing me, before she said, "You have done an excellent job with homecoming."

"Thanks," I said without enthusiasm, trying to disguise my relief that she hadn't seen me with Sawyer.

"Ms. Chen and Ms. Yates both sought me out to tell me how proud they are of you, and what strong leadership skills you have."

"Ms. Yates?" I'd thought she hated me. It was amazing how people threw their support behind something after it had been a success and they hadn't lifted a finger.

My mother glanced over at Dad, who was still talking with Tia's dad and Harper's mom. "Manuel says Tia's throwing an after-party at their house."

"She is," I said bitterly.

"Why didn't you ask me if you could go?"

"Because I'm grounded!" I hadn't even wanted to *think* about the party, much less tell *her* about it. All my best friends would go, and Sawyer would be there, while I stayed home. The pain was too much to bear.

My mother gazed at me like I was the biggest fool on this

earth. Didn't I know I was only grounded when I displeased her? She told me, "You can go."

I walked away. I hoped she didn't expect me to say thank you.

But secretly, my heart was beating a fast pattern that sounded like *Sawyer*.

I *almost* turned around and asked, "You *do* know Sawyer will be there, right?" But I would have said that out of anger, ruining any chance I had of seeing him again.

As it was, surely she suspected he would be at Tia's party, as close friends as he and Tia were. It almost seemed as if my mother was giving me just enough rope to hang myself with.

A few hours later, I would find out how right I'd been.

I stayed later than anyone but Ms. Chen to make sure the DJ got packed up, the caterer was paid, and the chairs we'd set out were folded and carted back to storage inside the school. But I texted Sawyer that I was coming.

When I finally arrived at the 1910 mansion that Tia and her dad were bringing back to life, half the party seemed to be waiting specifically for me. Cheerleaders greeted me in the grand doorway and parted as I made my way inside. I caught a glimpse of Aidan leaning on the staircase railing, drunk, which bore investigating. But the crowd closed in, and I lost sight of him. Then I wanted to peer into the mermaid fountain in the foyer, which was Tia's current restoration project. Instead, she took my hand, ignored my protests, and dragged me straight into the kitchen to say hi to her dad and Harper's mom, who were sipping coffee.

After a polite chat with Other People's Parents about the marvelous dance I'd put on, Tia shoved me out the back of the kitchen and closed the swinging door behind me. Harper waited for me in the darkness.

"Walk straight through," Harper whispered. "Sawyer's out back. My mom's here, so he'll take you over there to the B and B, and you can be alone. We'll cover for you."

Alarmed, I said, "I can't ask you to lie. I mean, I could ask a lot of people to lie, but not you."

"We're not lying," she said. "My mom and Tia's dad just saw you here and can verify your whereabouts, see?" Then she put her hand on my arm. "It's okay, really. I'm willing to lie if I have to, because your mom is wrong about this. Go. All of us will say you were here with us."

Fifteen

SAWYER UNLOCKED THE HEAVY FRONT DOOR of the B and B. "Take your shoes off, if you don't mind," he whispered over his shoulder.

"We're sneaking?" I joked. "You're not supposed to have girls in your room? There goes the neighborhood."

"No. Everybody in the B and B takes off their shoes late at night so we don't wake each other up." He carefully closed the towering door behind us, picked up his flip-flops and took my sandals, and led the way up the ancient staircase. Even in the darkness, his blond hair shone like a flashlight.

He closed and locked the door of his room behind us. "Can I get you something to drink?" he asked. "I have water, water, or water."

"I would love some water."

"Good choice." He disappeared into a bathroom.

My eyes wandered around the huge, high-ceilinged bedroom. Besides a massive four-poster bed, there was a carved dresser and a wardrobe with the door open a crack. Moving the door just a hair for minimal nosiness, I peered inside. Neatly pressed shirts hung there: his Crab Lab T-shirt, his Pelicans tee, a yellow polo, and the faded blue one. He was wearing the madras plaid, and that accounted for everything.

I snatched my hand away like I'd been burned as he walked back in with two plastic cups printed with the Crab Lab logo. "Something wrong?" he asked, handing me one.

"I guess I hadn't expected your room to be so neat."

"I cleaned up," he acknowledged.

"You knew I was coming over?"

"I hoped against hope that we would find a way." He sipped his water, looking uncomfortable. Now that I was here, he didn't know what to do with me. I suspected it was all the baggage we were carrying around with us now, floating behind me like I was towing it across the Gulf.

Trying to break the ice, I set my cup down on the table beside the bed. I hopped up on the high mattress and examined the blown glass figurines hanging in the window. Maybe they belonged to the room, but I thought I'd seen all Harper's mom's kooky art collections over the years. These belonged to Sawyer.

He slid onto the bed from the other side. "My dad learned to make those in prison. He used to send them to me on my birthday. This is my third birthday." He touched an orange fish. "This is my tenth." His finger swept around a red octopus, sending a shaft of red light swinging around the window casement. Mr. De Luca had definitely improved over the years.

"I don't keep them because of what he is to me now," Sawyer said. "I keep them because of how they made me feel when I was eight. Like there was somebody looking out for me."

"A guardian angel," I suggested.

"One in jail, yes. My mom always claimed she didn't have the money to take me to see him. Probably she didn't want to take a little kid into a state prison, which was an uncharacteristic stroke of brilliance on her part. I never met him until I moved here. Before that, it really was like he was dead." He didn't look at me as he sipped his water again.

I sat back on my heels, watching his pensive face brushed by faint light through the window. In the past few weeks Sawyer had seemed more like family to me than my own family. I wondered if he felt the same way about me. I almost asked.

I stopped with my lips barely parted. I must have expressed some tenderness like that to Aidan very early. I couldn't remember exactly, but I recognized the feeling of panic that washed over me when I was about to expose myself. I closed my mouth.

Sawyer turned to me, eyes hard, and deftly unbuttoned the first button of my blouse.

Something seemed missing here. The tenderness we'd shared last weekend at the beach had been beaten out of us by the police and my mother. But if I were to mention this, how did I expect him to respond? Wasn't this what I'd come here for? After his talk of us still being together next May, what we had in front of us was one night, like his many single nights with different girls. I'd known what I was getting into two Fridays ago when Tia convinced me to place his head in my lap.

I scooted down on the bed until I lay flat, and I reached up to unbuckle his belt.

An hour later, between soft kisses, he whispered, "Do you want to?"

"Yes."

He rolled out of bed. I clung to the sheets so they wouldn't slide off and expose me. He had no shame, though. He padded naked into the bathroom and came back with a condom, taking his time burrowing under the sheets and warming my body again. "Are you on something? In case this breaks, I don't want your dad to murder me."

"Oh, he won't murder you. My mother will have killed you already. But I have an IUD." In fact, my mother had suggested I get it when she saw that Aidan and I were growing more serious. I'd thought she was being silly at the time. Aidan and I hadn't done anything more than kiss. But the next summer, when he started to pressure me, I was very glad I had it.

As Sawyer opened the package and put the condom on, I tried to remember what I'd been thinking when I did this with Aidan. I couldn't believe I'd taken that step back then. I hadn't liked him nearly enough. I'd just *thought* I had, because I didn't have anyone to compare him with. And now that I did, sex with Aidan seemed like a real shame.

Sawyer looked over at me. "What's wrong? You seem sad, which is incorrect for this occasion. Maybe we should—"

I touched one finger to his lips to quiet him.

He nodded once, understanding. Then he rolled on top of me and settled his hips between mine, bracing himself above me on his forearms. His eyes roved across my face. "You look beautiful in nothing."

"So do you."

He smiled. "I never thought this day would come."

I didn't say "Me neither," because that would sound insulting. But I thought it. In the two years I'd known Sawyer, and watched him, and lobbed back the insults he served to me, I couldn't have predicted I would spend the darkest hours of homecoming night underneath him. Somewhere below me, past the foundation of this ancient building, under a layer of sandy soil and palm tree roots, past the ancient sea floor, deep within the earth's core, hell was freezing over.

A chill ran through me, starting on my bare arms and racing down my skin to my toes, despite the fact that we were draped with sheets and Sawyer's body covered mine.

He watched me, his blond hair tousled white across his forehead, his bright blue eyes just another tone of gray in the dusky room. He should ask me whether I was cold. But no, this was Sawyer, who knew exactly what made a girl shiver at a time like this. He should ask me if I was still sure I wanted to go through with this. But no, Sawyer wasn't one to ask again to be absolutely positive after he'd already gotten the answer he wanted—

"Oh," I heard myself exclaim as he moved into me. With a shuddering sigh, he set his forehead against mine and closed his eyes.

I didn't want to turn on the bathroom light, because that would break the spell. In the shadows of midnight I looked at myself in Sawyer's mirror and used my fingers to piece my curls back into place. The left side looked okay. The right was mangled, and there wasn't much I could do about it until I washed it and re-set it. And I couldn't see the back, but it felt flat. I'd have to tell my parents I'd driven around with my windows down. Not something I would have done a few weeks ago for fear of exactly this sort of hairtastrophe.

Something I definitely could see myself doing from now on.

Sawyer came in behind me and set his chin on top of my head. Normally I would have pushed him off me because this would cause more hair squashing, but his body felt too good behind mine.

"Do you have a second mirror, so I can see the back of my hair?" I asked.

"I seriously, *seriously* doubt I will ever be that sophisticated." He focused on my hair and fingered the curls. "Wow, you look like you just had sex."

"Do I?" I asked, heart sinking into my stomach.

"If it's any consolation, you look like you just had *excellent* sex."

Our eyes met in the mirror. His cocky grin faded, and we

were watching each other, dead serious. I was hyperaware of the warmth of his body behind me. Tingles raced across my chest, and the hair stood up on my arms.

I turned around to face him and caught a flash of his blond lashes as he bent down and his mouth took mine.

A few minutes later he finally broke the kiss to say "I love you." Hearing himself, he backed a few inches away and looked me in the eye.

"I love you, too." My voice cracked at the end.

"Will you marry me?"

This time his question wasn't as ridiculous as it had been every time before, so I wasn't as quick to say yes. I phrased my answer carefully and truthfully. "Ask me again when it's time."

He led me by the hand back to bed. I wanted to snag a T-shirt or a towel along the way to cover myself, but he wasn't entertaining ideas like that. Even when I tried to draw the sheets back over me, he tossed them away. I grabbed for them. He kicked them off the bed completely. I was exposed. The only cover was his hand smoothing across my skin.

"What's wrong?" he asked.

I took a deep breath, terrified to tell him. "If we get serious—"

"If!" he exclaimed, letting his head fall backward to the pillow. "What just happened? Maybe we need to do that again."

"*As* we get serious," I corrected myself, "have you thought about what happens in May? What are you doing after graduation?"

"Oh, you think I'm not good enough to go to college?" After all we'd been through, sarcastic Sawyer was back.

I *did* assume he wasn't going to college, honestly, but I didn't have to admit it. "No, why?"

"Because if you'd thought I was going to college, you would have asked 'Where are you going to college?' instead of 'What are you doing after graduation?'"

"Okay. Where are you going to college?"

"You're nuts. I'm not good enough for college."

I grabbed my empty Crab Lab cup from the table and held it over him. "I'm going to hit you with this."

"I'm going to culinary school," he said quickly.

"You are?"

"Yes."

"Where?"

"New York."

"Have you gotten in?" I asked.

"I haven't applied. I'm waiting to make sure you get in to Columbia."

"Are you sure you want to do that?" I'd been worried about this. The idea that he would simply move to New York too lifted a weight from my shoulders. But it couldn't be that simple. "What if we break up? You'd be stuck there."

"I'm never stuck anywhere," he assured me. "If I get into trouble, I haul myself back out. But I wouldn't want you to feel obligated to stay with me if you met somebody smarter at Columbia. You'll meet guys in college who've been to Paris.

Hell, guys who are *from* Paris. I'm just your high school boyfriend from back home. I don't want to be an albatross around your neck."

"Pelican."

"Right. If it makes you feel better, I've been incredibly jealous of you ever since I heard you wanted to go to college in New York. I've got to get out of here, and there's nowhere I'd rather go. New York is one of the world's best food cities."

He glanced sideways at me, seeming almost nervous. "If this seems stalkerish to you, I won't do it. I mean, New York is huge and we would never have to see each other. I started thinking about going because of you, but we don't have to date after high school. I don't want you to feel trapped." His words came out faster and faster. He was definitely nervous. *Sawyer De Luca was nervous.* "Oh God, what have I done? Say something."

I laughed, trying to put him at ease. "You just surprise me. Are you going to open your own restaurant?"

"I guess I'll have to, since I don't like people telling me what to do. This is when it's going to come in handy to have a finance major for a girlfriend. So I was wrong before. We can't break up."

"I don't know anymore about majoring in finance," I said slowly. "I'm rethinking everything." I squinted at him in the darkness. "This really surprises me. You've never talked about culinary school before." Maybe I just hadn't been listening, I thought guiltily.

"I can't afford it right now. I'll get a job in a high-end

restaurant and learn all I can. When I've lived in New York long enough to qualify for in-state tuition, I'll find a community college where I can get a business degree. Eventually I'll open my own restaurant."

"Vegan?" I guessed.

"Yes. That can't work just anywhere, but New York has enough weirdos like me to support it."

"That sounds like a good plan."

"At least it's a plan. I don't know if it's good. Luckily, one thing that separates me from other people is that I don't need my life planned out and structured. If this doesn't work, I'll do something else."

"I would believe that, except you sound so defensive."

He watched me, careful not to reveal anything he didn't want me to see. His face was devoid of expression, this time not out of anger, but from fear.

"Sawyer," I whispered. "It's okay to be scared." I kissed his cheek.

"*You* scare me."

"You scare the hell out of me, but it's a pleasant kind of scary, right?"

"So far, so good."

I smiled. "I don't want to be the one to make you question your culinary school plan. I don't know anything about that stuff. I just wonder if you're selling yourself short. Right now, though, you're not feeling good about yourself. You wouldn't believe anybody who told you that you're better than what you're aiming for. Not even me. You may need a year to figure that out for yourself."

He shrugged, looking away, but I could tell he was listening.

"I agree you need to get out of here. You've been through too much with your family. If you could start over someplace else, I'll bet you would be a completely different person. And I'd really like to meet that guy."

He grinned, looking perplexed. "Thanks, I think."

"How are your grades?" I asked.

"They're good," he said. "I'm no valedictorian, but I have a three-point-seven right now, and I'm trying to bring it up."

"My God, Sawyer."

"What?" he asked.

I didn't want to say what I was thinking, which was *Holy shit, that is a high GPA, and all this time I thought you were a slacker.* I skipped over that part and asked, "How are your entrance exam scores?"

"High."

"How high?"

He chuckled. "Higher than yours."

"Now, wait a minute." I didn't want to insult him, but he had to be kidding, because I'd knocked my entrance exams out of the park. "How do you know what I got?"

"I don't," he said, "but Ms. Malone told me my scores are the second highest in the school, right behind Tia's. I actually got higher than Tia on the verbal."

I stared at him in disbelief.

"What?" he asked again.

I tried to make his crazy face with one eyebrow up and the other down. I couldn't do it, so I lifted and lowered my brows with my fingertips.

"Don't do that to your face," he said.

"Sawyer," I said, exasperated, "you have grades and scores that high and you want to go to *culinary school*? And you don't see anything wrong with this picture?"

"Of course not," he said. "It's never wrong to pursue something you love." He twisted one of my curls around his finger.

"But you *don't* love cooking," I pointed out. "You don't bum around the Crab Lab kitchen after hours, inventing new recipes, do you? You happen to be a vegan, but just because you have special dietary preferences doesn't obligate you to open that kind of restaurant. There may not be a huge population of vegans in the Tampa Bay area, but there are plenty in the world, and they're not all going to culinary school and opening vegan restaurants. I think you've only come up with this idea because you work as a waiter, you know restaurants, and you're scared you'll fail at something else."

"Like what?"

"College. Just apply for college. Apply to Columbia."

He laughed. For once it was an ugly sound. "I would never get in to Columbia."

"How do you know if you don't try? It sounds to me like you'd have a good chance. You might get a need-based scholarship. On the essay part of the application, tell them a sob story about your dad and your situation."

"My *situation*?" He gave me the raised-eyebrow look.

"Yes. And by 'sob story,' I guess I mean you should tell them the truth."

He shook his head. His hair made the softest sound against the pillow. "I don't have the money for college applications."

"If your scores are that high, Ms. Malone will find you some money."

He stared thoughtfully at my face. His eyes traveled down to my breast. He touched me softly.

I shuddered.

He slid his phone from the table on his side of the bed and peered at it, probably checking the time. "We'd better go before we are discovered," he said in a voice from a cheesy movie. Then he laid his phone aside and rolled so that I was underneath him again.

"Katherine." He kissed my lips. "Beale Gordon."

"Yes?"

"This has been the best night of my life."

"Mine too," I said. "Sawyer . . ."

"Salvatore De Luca," he prompted me.

"Salvatore?"

"No," he laughed. "I'm kidding. My middle name is Charles."

"Charles?"

"Yeah. That's why I don't tell people my middle name."

"It's not as bad as Salvatore. Anyway, this has been—"

His phone vibrated on the table. "Hold on." He slid over and glanced at it.

The next second he leaped up to standing and was fumbling on the floor for his clothes.

"What's the matter?" I exclaimed.

"Harper texted me." His voice bounced as he jerked his shorts on. "Somebody at the party heard where we'd gone and told Angelica. Angelica told Aidan. Aidan called your parents. He's drunk and he just admitted it to everybody."

"No, no, no," I chanted, like that was going to help. "Where are you going?"

"Stay here. I don't want you to see your dad beat the fuck out of me."

"Sawyer, wait!" But he was already gone, not bothering to keep his shoes off to avoid waking the rest of the B and B. His flip-flops clattered down the stairs, and the front door slammed.

As I pulled my own clothes on, I tried to picture what was happening, and feared the worst. Dad was mild mannered, but he was huge. Sawyer was not huge, but he had a temper. There was no best-case scenario to this.

It wasn't either of their voices I heard yelling as I ran out the back door of the B and B to the parking lot, though. It was my mother's. She was yelling at Sawyer.

A cloud of white dust was still settling over the

gravel-and-shell driveway. As it cleared, I saw why. Both my mother's Mercedes *and* Dad's BMW were parked in the lot. Dad leaned against his car with his arms folded. Sawyer leaned against the Mercedes with his arms folded. They were like two captains of pirate ships in Tampa Bay, deciding whether to fire that first shot across the other's bow.

My mother was the one shooting from the hip, reciting to Sawyer a lot of his poor qualities that she'd listed for me in the past couple of weeks. "Hey," I said, which only drew some of the fire from him to me. I could see there was no way out of this now, though. I would never be able to go out with him again, if he even wanted to.

Help came from an unexpected place. Harper appeared from a trail through the trees, the same one Sawyer and I had followed to get here from Tia's house. "Hi, there!" she called as if my mother didn't sound murderous. "I beg your pardon. I'm so sorry. My mom's not here right now, but we have a rule at the B and B that we don't raise our voices because it might disturb the guests if they're sleeping." She nodded toward the second story of the Victorian towering over us. "Come on inside." She stepped away to unlock the front door of her own tiny house.

Nobody budged. Everyone glared at everyone else.

"Come on in," Harper repeated, daring to encircle my mother's waist with her arm and push her along toward the door. "Everyone's welcome inside, where you can continue to discipline your daughter and . . ." Harper was not the best at making small talk, which is why it had been a good idea for her to stop working at the B and B in the first place. ". . . castigate Sawyer," she finished.

Sawyer elbowed her.

"I said *castigate*," she told him.

"You see," my mother said straight to me as I followed Dad through the door, "this is what happens when you date trash. We all start acting like trash."

Sawyer dropped into one of the side chairs around the coffee table. He'd been ready to defend himself physically against Dad, but he was no match verbally for my mother.

"Gosh," Harper protested at the same time Dad started, "Sylvia—"

"No," I told my mother, "this is what happens when I finally stand up for something I want. You say you're training me to be a strong woman. But really, *you* want to be a strong woman with a weak daughter you can push around."

My mother stared at me in stunned silence.

"I refuse to be grounded anymore," I said. "I won't let you tell me who I can date. If you want to take away my car, fine. Kick me out of the house and I'll get a job and a place of my own. I'll take the bus to Tampa and try out as a professional cheerleader."

Harper raised her hand. "I don't think those jobs pay very much—"

"Listen," Dad said to me. "Your mother came here to give you a piece of her mind. Which she did." He turned to my mother. "I *followed* you here to tell this young man that as far as I'm concerned, he can ask Kaye out if he wants. He should consider me an ally, and I will work on you." He held out his hand to her. "Come on, I'll take you out for a drink."

She looked at him. Her expression was somewhere between a glare and a smile.

He wiggled his fingers. "Come on, I'm loaded. I just sold another article."

She took his hand, but she refused to look at anybody as he led her toward the door.

Dad patted Harper on the head as he passed her. "Sorry, honey."

"That's okay, Mr. Gordon," she said. "Glad to be of service."

He touched the tip of my nose. "Be home by two. And don't go looking for an apartment just yet." He opened the door for my mother and closed it behind them.

I collapsed into Harper's arms. "I am so sorry!"

"No, don't be sorry! It's all worked out!" She called over my shoulder, "Sawyer, it's all worked out. Are you okay?"

Sawyer was silent.

Frightened, I walked over to stand directly in front of his chair. He glared up at me. He wasn't expressionless, as when he was furious. He had a look even madder than that. His anger showed in every line on his face. I'd never seen this expression before, but I knew it when I saw it.

"He's not okay." I reached down and cupped his cheek in

my hand. "Baby, I don't blame you for feeling that way, but it doesn't matter now."

"It doesn't *matter*?" he exclaimed.

"Let's go back over to the party," Harper suggested brightly, "and forget all this."

"Let's do." I held out my hand to pull Sawyer up.

But I knew from the way he looked at me that it had not, in fact, all worked out.

Sixteen

HARPER WENT AHEAD, AND I HELD SAWYER'S hand, but the three of us didn't say much as we followed the path back to Tia's house. We were passing through several backyards after midnight, and every adult in Florida owned a gun.

When we arrived, though, Brody and Noah were playing a very slow, sore game of hoops in the driveway. Brody took one look at Sawyer and said, "Oh God, what's wrong? Don't let him go in there." But Sawyer had already broken away from me and disappeared inside.

"Why not?" Harper asked Brody.

"Aidan is plastered, and Will is in rare form."

That made Harper and me speed up. As we hustled inside, I could hear Tia talking with Angelica right beside the door. "Aidan dated Kaye for three years, Angelica. You can't expect him to forget that overnight— Oh." She'd seen me, and she stepped into my path. "Sawyer just came in. He looks awful. What happened?"

I just shook my head, but Harper right behind me said, "Everything we thought, and worse."

From the next room, I heard Will's voice rising. Along with Harper and several other people, I peered into one of about six living rooms or dens or libraries on the bottom floor of the vast house.

The first thing I saw was Sawyer, with the same scary look on his face, standing in the opposite doorway.

Second I focused on Will, who was standing over Aidan, pointing down at him. Aidan was *definitely* drunk. There wasn't any alcohol officially at this party. My class's usual way around that was to go drink in someone's parked car, then come back.

I'd known Aidan to imbibe that way. But not like this. His eyelids were heavy, and he seemed to be having a hard time keeping his head high as Will shouted down at him in his Minnesota accent. "How could you do that? So she's your ex-girlfriend. *You* broke up with *her*. You're trying to ruin her life, along with Sawyer's, and you don't care if you take some of the rest of us down too. We're just collateral damage. What kind of student council president *are* you?"

"Like Minnesota is the moral center of the universe!" Aidan roared.

Sawyer was gazing at Aidan with pure hatred. And Sawyer had been known to swing a punch in the heat of the moment. Quickly I crossed the room and pushed Sawyer into the next one, which wasn't as crowded. I whispered, "Do you need to leave? I don't want you to get in a fight with Aidan."

"I'm not angry with Aidan," he said, slowly turning to focus his furious gaze on me. "I don't have any room left for that, because I'm so angry with you."

"With me?" I breathed.

He pulled a folded sheet of paper from his pocket. Before he'd even opened it all the way, I knew what it was. I saw Tia's drawing of me lying like a dog.

"I lost that," I said carefully. "Did you find it stuffed down in the chair at Harper's?"

He stared at me silently, then shook the note at me. "I was your *experiment*? I asked you something like that the other day, and you lied to me. You said no."

"You don't understand," I said quickly. Lowering my voice to a whisper, I said, "This is just between you and me, but the Superlatives elections got messed up. A lot of the titles are wrong, including yours, and mine. We're actually the Perfect Couple That Never Was." In a normal tone—which was shaking now, because no matter what I told him, he didn't look any less angry—I said, "That's why I've been curious about you for a while, not just because Aidan broke up with me."

Sawyer gaped at me. "So I *was* your experiment," he repeated. "You thought it would be hilarious to fuck around with me, knowing that I've had a crush on you since I moved here."

It was my turn to stare at him with my mouth open until I covered it with my hand. "No, I had no idea about that."

"Tia told you," he prompted me.

"No," I said, "she didn't." But if she'd known, that explained why she'd been so keen on throwing me together with Sawyer.

"Harper told you," he said next.

I shook my head. "Harper keeps secrets." I wished she didn't. I really could have used this information a couple of weeks before.

He nodded. "Everything makes sense now. When I talked about following you to New York, you looked at me like I had three heads."

"Because I never thought about it before, Sawyer!"

"I've thought about it for two years," he said acidly. "And what do I get for my trouble? I've made Aidan so jealous that he'll want to take you back. You're welcome."

"No –" I had no intention of dating Aidan again, ever.

"What are you going to do once you graduate from high school," Sawyer sneered, "and from college, and there's no preplanned program for you to cycle through? There's no Most Likely to Succeed for the rest of your life to let you know you've succeeded. There's no office of student council vice president to let you know you're *almost* in charge, or head cheerleader to let you know you're the only popular girl anybody trusts to keep the rest of the cheerleaders out of trouble. How will you know how or when to be happy if nobody's telling you?"

Tears stung my eyes. "That's not fair."

He stepped very close to me. "You know what's not fair, Kaye? I risked everything for you. I could have been arrested.

Your mother could still have me evicted and fired from the B and B." He pointed in the general direction of that awful argument. "She just called me trash, all for the sake of your experiment."

Now he pointed at me. "I have been playing you straight this whole time. When I told you I loved you, that's what I meant. I never intended to be your experiment, or your walk on the wild side, or your favorite mistake." He blinked, appearing for a moment like he had tears in his eyes. "I can't even look at you."

That hurt worse than anything else he'd said. He'd loved to look at me even when it seemed nobody else did.

He stomped back through the doorway, bullied right through Will's lecture to Aidan, and parted the crowd around the front door. I tried to push through, but by the time I'd run down the front steps, the taillights of his clunker truck were disappearing down the street.

I turned slowly toward the house. Tia stood in the doorway. Our note with her dog drawing was crumpled in her hand. Sawyer must have shoved it at her on his way out.

"He'll be back for work in the morning," Harper said. "I promise. He never misses work."

She and Tia and I sat on the low wall of the mermaid fountain with the water flowing between our toes before it cascaded over exquisite antique mosaics. The party was winding down, and so were they, with their elbows on their knees and their chins in their hands.

I was past wound down. I'd cried so hard in the past fifteen minutes that I felt half dead. At least DeMarcus had driven Aidan home to get him away from the alcohol supply secreted in someone's car, and from Will, and from me.

I wished so hard that Sawyer would reappear in Aidan's place. To give me a comforting hug, or to drag our awful argument out. Anything, just to have him here with me a little longer.

But I knew he wasn't coming back.

"Why didn't you tell me Sawyer's had a crush on me for two years?" I finally whispered.

"I've only known for a couple of weeks," Harper said. She glanced at Tia for help.

Seeing the look on my face, Tia held up her hands. "He told me a month ago and swore me to secrecy."

Two years, and a thousand times that he'd called me a name or tried to sit in my lap. All that time he hadn't been bugging me for a laugh. He'd been flirting, and hoping I'd flirt back, when I was dating Aidan. It must have been torture for Sawyer.

"If it's any consolation," Tia said, "he hates me too now. Harper and I never should have tried to push you two together. But he was completely smitten with you, and it was making him miserable. Once I started looking, it seemed to me that you had a crush on him, too, whether you admitted it to yourself or not."

"I did," I sniffled.

"You'll get back together," Harper said soothingly. "You just need some time."

"I don't know," Tia said. "Kaye's lost a boyfriend, but Sawyer's lost a lot more than a girlfriend. He's lost himself. The first time he ever felt worthwhile was when he won the mascot position. The second time was when you went to find him at the beach, Kaye. Not that I think you can really understand what low self-esteem feels like, when you've grown up with everybody calling you princess."

Harper kicked water on Tia's bare leg. "That was the wrong thing to say."

"She meant it," I said, "or she'd be apologizing."

"Well," Tia muttered. "I'm not saying you should get back together with Sawyer just because you feel sorry for him. He would hate you when he found out, you would resent him, and that would make everything worse in the long run. But if you really love him, you can't let each other go just because you're both stubborn."

"He doesn't want me back," I assured her. "You didn't see the way he was looking at me."

"We *have* seen the way he looks at you," Harper interjected. "That's our whole point."

I took my feet out of the cold water and lay balanced along the wall. I listened to the burbling fountain, Harper and Tia's hushed conversation, music blaring from a few rooms away, an argument between Quinn and Noah, and laughter. And I thought:

What if Angelica hadn't intercepted a note from me to Harper about my crush on Aidan in Ms. Yates's ninth-grade science class? He would never have guessed I liked him. I'd hidden it well. And the next week, I would have moved on to someone else. At that age, my crushes had *seemed* crushing, but they weren't so bad that I couldn't get over them when another boy caught my eye at the movies on the weekend.

Aidan wouldn't have asked me out. When Sawyer moved to town two years ago, I would have been available. He would have asked me out instead.

I would have said no.

He would have worked on me.

I would have said yes.

I would have lost my virginity with him instead of Aidan.

"Wait a minute," Tia protested. "Then who would *I* have lost *my* virginity with?"

I hadn't realized I was talking out loud.

"I'm confident you would have found someone," I said.

If I'd dated Sawyer for the last two years—well, there was no way that would have happened. We would have fought and broken up and gotten back together and broken up again. My last two years would have been less like training camp and more like high school. Less like an accounting course and more like a life.

I fell asleep with that wistful dream in my head. I was only vaguely aware that Brody carried me to Harper's car, and they drove me home.

Seventeen

I SLEPT UNTIL NOON. AFTER THAT I STAYED IN bed for another hour, trying to go back to sleep just to avoid thinking about the night before. The bright sun wouldn't let me, and the deep blue sky flashed at me through the palm trees outside my window. If last night's cool front was any indication, today would be warm—not hot—and perfect for a jog. A jog would give me time to think, exactly what I couldn't stand. I rolled over for the millionth time.

A soft knock sounded at my door. I knew from the fact that the door opened without me giving permission that it was my mother. She sat on the edge of my bed and put her hand in my hair.

"Harper's mom called," she said. "We had a long talk. She's dating Tia's father!"

In answer I gave her a sigh.

"I guess I'm surprised enough for the two of us, then." She rubbed my shoulders vigorously, like trying to rub the life back into me. "Sit up and let's talk."

Slowly I dragged myself up against the pillows, because once she decided we were having a talk, she never went away until she was done.

"Oh, honey." She reached out to brush away the tears under my eyes. *Like you care,* I wanted to say, but that would just keep her here longer. I was all sassed out.

She smiled sympathetically at me. "Lynn actually called because she's worried about you. Harper told her what happened last night. Lynn wanted you—and me—to know that Sawyer moved out."

"Oh no!" I cried. "Where did he go?"

"Back to his father's house, though he'll still be working for Lynn in the mornings."

"Oh." I covered my mouth with my hand, relieved that he'd come back last night. And that he'd finally gone home.

My mother patted my leg under the covers. "You didn't tell me he's been having so much trouble."

"I didn't think that would help his case with you."

She nodded, gazing out my window at the blue sky. "Lynn loves him."

"A lot of people do."

"So does Harper's grandfather, which is saying a lot, because that man . . ." She didn't have to finish. Everybody knew Mr. Moreau was hard to get along with. If he loved Sawyer, Sawyer was special.

"Lynn says I've been too hard on him," my mother said, "and on you. After discussing it with your father, I think I was wrong to ground you, or to prevent you from dating him. But if you do have sex, you're using a condom in addition to your IUD every time, yes?"

"Mom," I said with both hands splayed in front of me, "we broke up."

"Oh." My mother sounded sad.

I was so angry with her that I couldn't even feel anymore. I flopped backward on the bed and closed my eyes.

"Tell me what happened," came my mother's voice.

"He stuck by me through a lot," I said woodenly, "but you have been awful. There was just so much even he could stand, I guess."

She shifted up the bed and twisted a lock of my hair to make a tighter curl when she fingered it out. "I'm confident you can solve that problem," she said. "You are smarter, and stronger, and more of a woman than I've given you credit for. I'm sorry."

I opened one eye, and then the other, to stare at her in disbelief. She concentrated on pulling out the twist and placing the curl across my temple, framing my face. Finally she met my gaze. She said again, "I'm sorry."

My voice sounded throaty with crying as I said, "I have an appointment Monday to see a counselor at school about stress management."

My mother raised her eyebrows. "That's a positive step."

"I think so too. It was Sawyer's idea. He set it up for me."

She nodded slowly. "Why don't you invite him over to go

out on the boat with you and your father tomorrow? He can stay for lunch."

"Because we are not spea-king," I enunciated. My mother didn't quite seem to get that Sawyer and I were broken up for good.

Then she said, "You need to eat breakfast, or lunch, or whatever you want to call it. I'll fix you anything you like. But right now, you need to hop downstairs, because Aidan is here."

"Oh. My. God." The last person on earth I wanted to deal with this afternoon. The thought of him made me feel like I weighed five hundred pounds and had sunk permanently into the bed. "I don't suppose you could tell him I'm asleep. Or dead?"

My mother shook her head, as I knew she would. She'd never in my life let me avoid a confrontation.

I rolled my eyes, put on a bra under my T-shirt, and slouched down the steps and onto the front porch. I never would have appeared like this in front of Aidan before, but I honestly didn't care what he thought of me anymore. My decision was reinforced when I saw he'd taken the swing with the comfortable cushion. I had to settle for the seat across from him. I didn't even bother to hold my head up, just collapsed across the wicker and waited for his bullshit.

"I came to apologize," he said.

Now I looked up at him, curious. This was one of those rare times he dropped his pompous tone and let me see the real boy he'd been hiding under all that bravado.

He really was sorry.

"I've been thinking hard about what I did to you last night," he said, "and what Will said to me afterward. I really regret it." He mumbled under his breath, "The hangover doesn't help."

I squinted my eyes to focus on him in the dappled shade. He *did* look a little green. I said, "I imagine not."

"The office of the president went to my head," Aidan said. "You've been telling me that, but I couldn't hear you. We've been drifting apart for a while. Probably ever since we started going out in the first place. I've been angry with you about that, which got rolled into my feelings about student council, and . . ." He heaved a sigh. "I hear you now."

"Good."

"The last time I was over here," he said, "I got that letter of recommendation from your mom. You were mad at me for waiting to break up with you until after. The truth is, I was thinking at that point that it would be cool if I got into Columbia and you didn't."

"Really." I swallowed. I'd understood he resented me. I hadn't realized how much.

"I should have known better than to ask you for a break rather than a breakup, and to try to hold on to you at the same time I was letting you go. I don't know where a lot of this negativity comes from. Maybe we just got together too young, and we were together too long."

I finally sat up. "It's not all your fault," I said. "Lately I've realized I was counting you as one of my accomplishments, something to put on college applications. You know, 'Dating the student council president, Most Likely to Succeed.' I thought that way in ninth grade. I guess I don't think that way anymore."

"Well, maybe we won't have to cross paths in college. I'm not sure I want to apply early admission to Columbia anymore. If we get in, we're locked in, and I'm not positive I want that to be my one and only choice."

"Me too," I said, seeing this for the first time. Flopping across the seat again, I asked, "Are you going to apologize to Angelica, too?"

He massaged his temple. "After last night, I think my relationship with Angelica is a lost cause. She's not a fan of drinking."

Or boyfriends who can't get over their old girlfriends, I thought. "Maybe there's still hope," I said cheerfully. "I overheard Tia talking with her. She was upset, which means she's into you. I've never seen Angelica express an emotion before, so that's huge."

He nodded slowly. "I heard you and Sawyer broke up. If I caused that, I'm sorry. If you actually wanted to be with him, I mean." He sounded doubtful.

"I did," I said.

A silence fell between us, long and dead, while Aidan squeaked back and forth on the swing.

"Well," I finally said, "we still have eight months of student council together. I'd like us to try to get along from now on.

We've broken up, but that doesn't mean the last three years didn't happen."

"Right." He leaned forward in the swing, put his hand on mine, and stroked his thumb over my palm. Maybe he was thinking about the fact that we'd been each other's first time.

As I gazed at him, I wished again that I'd waited. My attraction to him, and my dreams of spending the rest of my life with him, seemed to belong to another girl entirely. It was hard to believe I'd ever been young enough to love him.

I drew my hand away. "I'll see you at school Monday."

"Yeah." He stood, sending the swing into wild motion on its chains. "We need to start planning the student council haunted house."

"Oh boy. Maybe somebody else could head up the committee for this one. Will. Or Sawyer."

He coughed at my mention of Sawyer. But all he said was, "That will work. You deserve a break." He jogged down the steps, then turned around on the sidewalk. "By the way, Kaye, you did an awesome job on the elections, and the float, and especially the dance. I didn't want to admit it, but you were right and I was wrong."

"Thanks," I called.

I went back to bed.

But an hour later, I did get up and let my mother cook for me. I watched a little football with Dad. Then I spent a few hours doing something I rarely did at home: I blasted music in the backyard and worked out cheerleader choreography for a couple of new songs the marching band was playing.

My mother didn't say a word.

About four thirty, Harper surprised me by appearing in my driveway in my car. She had a key, but it was a real favor to bring my car over from Tia's without me asking. Brody was right behind her in her new (to her) car. He didn't get out to talk to me, though. He gave me a brief wave and disappeared into the back seat.

"What's up?" I asked Harper.

"Come with us to downtown Tampa, to the marching band's first competition of the year!" She announced this with the enthusiasm of a used-car salesman.

"Mmph. I don't feel like seeing anybody."

"I thought you hated being here with your mom nowadays."

I *had* complained to Harper about this in the last few weeks. But looking back at the house, I said, "I think we're over the worst of it."

"Well, you're the head cheerleader," she said. "You're the student council vice president. You have to support Will and Tia." She raised her eyebrows behind her glasses. "And I have things to give you, and things to tell you."

That did it for me. I'd almost forgotten that my time with mischievous Harper and crazy Tia was drawing to a close. I needed to enjoy every second.

As soon as we'd set off in her car, she handed me a little satin pouch. "This is for me?" I asked.

"Yes. From Sawyer's dad."

"Sawyer's *dad*. What in God's name. Is it dangerous?" I dumped the contents of the pouch out onto my lap, then wished I'd been more careful. It was a little glass pelican, carefully handmade, colored like Sawyer's costume with white feathers and a yellow beak and feet. This one had a tiny red heart on his chest. A red ribbon was looped through the back of the figure to turn it into a necklace.

"Sawyer brought it over," Harper said. "His dad made it out of the blue and wanted to tell you he's sorry about what he said, and sorry you found out."

I wasn't sure how I felt about that, but I put the ribbon over my head and touched the cold pendant. "Sounds like he and Sawyer had a heart-to-heart."

"They did."

My stomach was beginning to twist. That was all I wanted to hear about Sawyer. I changed the subject. "So, your mom and Tia's dad are officially dating?"

"Yes! Well, they're going out on a date tonight."

I asked carefully, "Is that okay with you?"

"I've always liked Mr. Cruz," she said. "I do not want four sisters. Maybe they'll just date for a while. And speaking of dating . . ." She glanced in the rearview mirror at Brody, who stretched across the back seat with his earbuds in, snoring softly.

"Poor thing," she said. "He got sacked so hard last night. Did you hear it?"

I shook my head. "I saw it, though. He was airborne. It looked painful."

"I heard it from the sidelines. It made me ill." Then she grinned at me and whispered, "We did it last night!"

"You *did*?" I squeaked.

"Shhh! Yes. After we took you home, he started to feel really bad. My mom was still hanging out with Tia's dad, so Brody and I went over to my house. We thought he might start to feel better if he could lie down for a while. We decided we'd better go ahead and have sex in case he died."

"That's . . ." I didn't have a word for it.

"A really great excuse to do it," she finished for me. "He couldn't move, so I was in control. I think that's been my problem all along."

"You seem happy about it," I said. Then I laughed at the understatement. She was blushing and glowing.

"I *am* happy. He's so great." She looked into the mirror again and smiled at the sleeping hulk of him. "For *not* being the perfect couple, I can't imagine it working out any more perfectly."

She must have suddenly remembered that Sawyer and I *were* the Perfect Couple That Never Was, in name only. She gave me a guilty look and put her eyes back on the road.

The parking lot at the stadium where the band contest was being held was littered with cars and buses. Harper cruised until she found our school buses, with our band hanging out the windows. She parked nearby.

While she was still helping Brody maneuver his damaged body out of her back seat, I popped out of the car and thought I recognized the car next to us. "Quinn and Noah are here," I mused, peering inside to see if it was really Quinn's. I was looking for the interchangeable components of his black leather Goth look. What I saw instead was Sawyer's madras button-down.

"Sawyer's here." Looking up, I recognized him before the words had escaped my mouth. In his mascot costume, he was bouncing along underneath the bus windows, high-fiving the marching band.

"Hey, pelican," I heard Tia call, "your girlfriend's looking for you."

Sawyer turned and saw me.

And least, I thought he did. I still wasn't sure which part of the bird head he saw from.

And then he was loping toward me with his wings open.

I crashed into him. His arms enveloped me. He squeezed me, picked me up, and twirled me in a circle. I never wanted to let him go. But the pelican was always kind to me. Sawyer was less likely to forgive.

When he finally put me down, I said, "Thank you for the necklace." I fingered it. "Or, thanks to your dad."

He nodded. Whereas this would have been a movement of an inch for anybody else, his beak moved up and down a foot.

"I'm sorry about last night."

He hugged me again.

"I don't want you to act like everything's okay between us in costume, when you're actually still mad."

He shrugged.

"Well, it matters to *me*," I said. "You have a hard time showing me how you feel when you're not in the costume. I have a hard time showing you how I feel at all. I'd really like us to try again. It took me a while, and a conversation with my dad, and another long while, to figure out that I love you with all my heart."

He put his hand over his own heart.

Then he reached up and tugged upward on his head. The thing was so big that it took a few seconds to pull off. Underneath, his hair was a riot of every shade of blond, and his eyes were bright blue. Looking deep into my eyes, he whispered, "Say that again, when I'm not in costume."

"I love you," I said, "with all my heart."

He put his free feathery glove into my hair and kissed me deeply.

"Woooooo," the band on the bus moaned appreciatively, which made us break the kiss. Damn band.

Investigating, Ms. Nakamoto hung from the pole inside the bus and leaned down the staircase, out the doorway. "Mr. De Luca, Ms. Gordon, this is a school function."

"Yes, ma'am," I called.

"We'll get back to this later tonight," Sawyer told me knowingly. He put his head on.

Swinging hands, we waited for Brody to limp over, followed by Harper, Noah, and Quinn. As we walked toward the stadium in the orange light of late afternoon, I wondered if we'd be allowed into a band competition with Sawyer dressed as a six-foot bird.

We would find a way.

ACKNOWLEDGMENTS

Heartfelt thanks to my amazing new editor, Sara Sargent; my brilliant literary agent, Laura Bradford; and my critique partner, Victoria Dahl. 2gether 4ever.

ABOUT THE AUTHOR

Jennifer Echols has written many romantic novels for teens and adults. She grew up in a small town on a beautiful lake in Alabama, where her high school senior class voted her Most Academic and Most Likely to Succeed. Please visit her at www.jennifer-echols.com.